BEG FOR ME

THE — MERCILESS WORLD COLLECTION

VOLUME I

W. WINTERS

THE
FRIEND

I didn't need anyone to tell me; I knew he was forbidden with a single glance.
He was a boy I should've been afraid of, and definitely a boy I should've never wanted.
No matter how much neither of those statements were true.

From the first time I saw him, Sebastian had a hard stare that pinned me in place. And years later, it hasn't softened.

We lived on the same street and went to the same school, although he was a year ahead.
Even so close, he was untouchable.
He was bad news and I was the sad girl who didn't belong.

One night changed everything.
We both had secrets. We both saw the pain in each other's eyes.
The gaze that gave me chills turned to a lust-filled haze that heated every inch of me.
But that didn't change who he was. A man who would take everything from me.

PROLOGUE

Chloe

THE KISS WAS BRUISING, JUST LIKE HIS PRESENCE ALWAYS WAS.

On the last Tuesday before school let out for the summer, and my ninth-grade year was over forever, Sebastian Black kissed me. No. He devoured me.

He destroyed everything I had in that moment. He took every bit and he made it his. *I* was his for that all-consuming kiss. My first kiss.

I still remember it so well. I couldn't breathe. I couldn't do anything but let the heat and electricity rip through my body as Sebastian pinned me against the wall. The rough brick scraped harshly against the small of my back, but I hadn't even noticed. I wouldn't notice until hours later, standing under the stream of water in a scalding shower. The sting I felt proved his kiss had left more than one mark on me.

His tongue was hot, his grip intense and his presence dominating as ever. When he followed me outside as I tried to hide around the corner behind the school, I didn't even see him coming. The chill in the air struck against my heated face as soon as the door swung open, and I could barely manage to feel anything but the cold sensation that flowed over my skin. I needed to hide. From the other kids, from the teachers who didn't care… from reality. I was always good at that.

I didn't expect anyone to follow me. No one had for the past few days. Each day proved harder than the last, although the nights were the worst.

I was still carelessly wiping away my tears—they were an unwanted nuisance just like how everyone else saw me—when I heard his hard steps behind me.

The sudden spike of fear I felt, paled in comparison to the effect Sebastian had on me. The sound of my startled gasp was dwarfed by the feel of my heart racing rapidly against his as he pinned me where he wanted me.

He always took what he wanted.

But I'd never once thought he wanted me.

His warm breath flowed over my face, and suddenly the iciness in the air was non-existent. Nothing existed but him. Not even the air that separated us.

If I hadn't been stunned, the confusion would have shown on my face. I'd always wondered what it would be like to be kissed by a boy like Sebastian. I'd assumed it would always be nothing more than a passing thought. But every time he walked by me, every time I caught him staring at me, I knew there was something between us. His piercing gaze seemed to capture me in place while also looking right through me.

I was no one, but I wanted it that way. Not being noticed was the best thing that could happen when you lived where I did. Unless you were Sebastian, and then everyone noticed you and everyone feared you just the same.

He pulled away from me before I could react to his lips on mine, both of us gasping for air.

I'll never forget that his eyes were closed, or how slowly he opened them to paralyze me with those steely blues of his. A mask of indifference slipped over his face, but I know my expression showed my awe, my shock… my lust that I had so painfully hidden since the first day I'd laid eyes on him.

"Stop crying," he said, and his command was harsh as if my tears were an insult to him. As if my pain had anything at all to do with him. His nostrils flared and the rage he was so well known for was evident on his handsome features.

But just as it had never affected me before, it didn't affect me then either. I knew he was forbidden. I knew I was supposed to be afraid of him. Maybe I was just stupid because I never felt anything but desire for him.

"Stop fucking crying," he gritted out between his clenched teeth, "and don't tell anyone I did this. Not a single fucking person," he threatened. He brought his lips even closer to mine in a gesture that should have been menacing, but I'd be damned if it didn't make me hot for him where I'd never felt heat before. His eyes searched mine.

"Or else I'll make you cry those tears harder than you can imagine." His words caused my gaze to move from his lips to his cold stare. He would never know how hard I had cried in the middle of the night. He didn't know what had really happened and how guilty I was.

I shook my head gently and replied, "You can't."

His grin was accompanied by a huff of masculine laughter like he thought it was a challenge, but before he could say whatever was on the tip of his tongue, I cut him off.

"You won't make me cry. I know you won't," I said and shook my head, meeting his gaze with every ounce of sincerity I could muster. "And I won't tell anyone." The last bit broke my heart in two, but I don't know why when there wasn't a single soul to tell anyway. There was no one I wanted to run to. No one but the boy who had lost control, kissed me, and obviously regretted it.

I watched as he swallowed, his throat tightening. The bit of stubble that ran up his neck tempted me to touch it. Whatever it was that had caused him to kiss me, whether it was only to silence my crying or something else, was gone. And I knew he'd never kiss me again.

Letting out a long breath, my lips still parted, I said nothing and let him walk away.

The masculine scent of a boy I should have feared and a boy I should have never wanted, was all that filled my lungs as I tried to steady myself. I sagged against the brick building and tried to make sense of what had just happened.

I stopped crying that day and didn't shed another tear. Not that week, and not at the funeral. Not when my uncle let me move in with him, so I would have a place to stay.

I never spoke of what happened and I started to question my sanity when he never spoke of it either.

A KISS
TO TELL

Nothing changed in the way he acted, or in the way he looked through me.
But I remember the way I touched my lips as he stalked away.
I remember how it felt and how it was everything I needed in that moment.

He could never have known what he'd done to me that day.
But neither of us would ever forget.

CHAPTER 1

Five years after the kiss

RANDOM STREETLIGHTS GOING OUT IS SOMETHING THAT USED TO TERRIFY ME. I hate the feeling that comes with the sudden flicker signifying what's about to happen. Then the light burns out, and all you're left with is darkness. Even just remembering how it's happened before makes me shudder.

One night two years ago, it took place in quick succession, the bright lights flickering briefly and then suddenly there was no light at all. It happened on my way home from old man Bailey's hardware store. I'd gone only an hour before sunset and spent longer than I thought I would. Some asshole had kicked in my front door the night before and there was no way I was going to leave the store without a new lock. I bought two just to be on the safe side.

And so, I was walking home alone in the dark when the lights went out, one after the other. I couldn't walk fast enough to get to the next light that hadn't burned out; I nearly ran to it.

I don't like to be outside at night, not unless I'm on my porch. But even then, I'd rather stay inside, where the idea of safety used to mean something.

Either way, I'd spent too long at the store and with the plastic bag dangling from my wrist, I quickened my pace when the first bulb died. I remember how I stared straight ahead at the next one, praying it would give me light long enough to get home. As if it was listening to my fears and wanted to mock me, the light vanished before my eyes.

Fear of darkness is reasonable. But the kind of inevitable dread that lingers when a light goes out while you're watching it used to follow me everywhere.

It haunted me during the day and never hesitated to steal my sleep at night.

I don't know when things changed, but as I make my way down Peck Avenue, the light flickers on my right and I don't miss a step, I don't even dare to look at it. In my periphery, I see shadow consume everything behind me. My fingers wrap a little tighter around the strap of my purse, but it's more instinctive than a conscious response.

My heart races and then steadies to the sound of my heels clicking rhythmically on the pavement.

One more block and I'll be home. In darkness or in light, it doesn't matter anymore. I've been through both.

I keep my eyes fixed straight ahead and think about the mundane task awaiting me at work tomorrow. I spent all day organizing Mr. Brown's new clients, and my back is killing me from leaning down to the filing cabinet and then looking at the computer, time and time again. A few more days and the new system will be in place. At least until he decides to change it again.

I used to think Marc Brown changed the system so frequently out of boredom, but after looking at his client list, I think the lawyer is a crook. Everyone in this city is, so it shouldn't have surprised me. I'd work for anyone else, doing anything else, but my options aren't exactly overflowing.

I have my high school diploma, but after trying for the last two years since graduation to get into any college at all and being rejected, a diploma is all I have and all I'll ever have. And that piece of paper is useless here.

My phone pings in my purse and I'm more than eager to pull it out.

I could use something to keep my mind from wandering back to the shit job I have. As I pull out my phone I see the old book I'd stowed in my purse earlier this week, ready to read the novel again. For the dozenth time.

A court-mandated shrink gave it to me five years ago. She loved to draw, although I remember thinking she wasn't really good at it. I used to have a picture from her of a duck she drew with a pencil. I don't know where it's gone, not that it matters much. I still have the books she gave me and, more importantly, a love of books. I wasn't so much into the drawing, but that shrink—I think her name was Rebecca—gave me a handful of fiction. She gave me a way to get lost in someone else's world. It wasn't long before I started writing as well, trying to create an escape from this life. I couldn't give two shits about her artwork, but I'll always be grateful to her for giving me a love of reading and writing.

Forgetting about the book and everything that happened back then, I focus on the text message.

You'll never guess what happened last night.

It's Angie, a friend from work. Well, I think she's my friend. She's new and doesn't do much but read magazines and chew gum while she tells off clients who want their paperwork faster than she can print it out, but she tells me all the details of her Tinder dates. I'm the only one she talks to at the office.

Mr. Brown exclusively hires girls in their twenties—and younger. Of the five of us, Angie likes to only talk to me. I get it, sort of. I don't care for the other women either. For the most part, they ignore me, which I'm used to, but they also stop their hushed whispers the moment I walk into the room. At first, I thought it was all in my head, but no, they like to talk about me. About the rumors of what happened years ago. *How sad it is.* They can go fuck themselves.

My family has history here, but it's no secret. Every person in this damn city comes from circumstances of shame. Luckily, I don't work with them much; it's usually Angie who I get paired with, and I should really be grateful to Marc for that.

What? I text her back, curious about the escapade of last night.

After dinner, I took him home and he was fucking amazing in bed. I think I'd use the word… enthusiastic.

My brow raises at the last word.

What does that mean? I ask her.

He did things to me I had no idea I even wanted.

I can feel my blood heat just thinking about what she may have done. I've never done anything with anyone. Having sex simply isn't on my to-do list. I'm not interested, not from anyone in this city. My phone pings again, and I look to see what else she's said.

He choked me.

I stop in my tracks for a moment, staring down at the glowing screen in my hand and rereading what she wrote.

And he told me he was going to take my ass and holy shit Chlo, anal is e v e r y t h i n g.

If anyone could see my face, they'd see the shock. I don't know how she can even surprise me anymore. My fingers reach up to my throat as I swallow, wondering why he'd want to do that to her and how she could enjoy it. The choking part. I watch my fair share of porn, but that's one I don't really understand.

I'll tell you more on Monday, but I had to tell SOMEONE. I read her text as if she'd spoken it to me, sprightly voice, and all.

Can't wait to hear all the deets. My reply can't convey my gratitude at being informed via text about the choking, so I can hide my naivety and shock from her at the realization she's into that.

You almost home? she asks, and a soft smile plays at my lips. A warmth I'm not used to courses through me and slowly I find my pace again.

One block to go, I answer her and wait for her to respond with the same thing she wrote a few nights ago. For me to tell her when I get in.

Last week I told her I live just outside of Fallbrook, and she kept pushing to know where exactly. When I told her I'm from Crescent Hills, the same city as Mr. Brown's office, her face paled. She's not from around here, but she knows the reputation of this place and what it's known for. Everyone does. If you want a taste of sin, Crescent Hills is where you'll find more than your fill.

I'm used to the embarrassment, but not from someone who chooses to work in this city. She doesn't have to be here any longer than a nine-to-five, and honestly, I don't know why she even chose to work in this run-down area when she lives in the big city. And that's exactly what I challenged her with when she told me I shouldn't be walking home.

I'm grown. I'm aware. I'm also broke and on my own since my uncle died two years ago, leaving me with bills, a mortgage, and no job to pay for any of it, so I told her she could take her high horse and shove it. But maybe not in those exact words, and maybe with a choked voice of shame.

The silence lasted only a minute or so, but it felt like an hour. She offered to walk me home and when I declined, as politely as I could, she snatched my phone from my desk. Before I could ask her what she was doing, she texted herself before handing it back, so we would have each other's number.

Text me when you're home, she told me, but I didn't answer her. When she texted again, apologizing, and asking if I'd made it home all right, I answered only because I thought she was genuinely worried. And things have been normal again ever since.

It's a small act of kindness, but it means more to me than it should. I'm smart enough to know that I shouldn't let it get to me like this. I can't rely on anyone or trust anyone.

Outsiders come and go here. Even Ang said she wasn't planning on staying at the law firm for long. I should know better than to think of her as a friend.

But when she sends texts like the one that just came through, I can't help but feel a little camaraderie. I smile as I reread the text. *See you Monday, prepare to be scandalized!*

My heels click on the asphalt, worn rough from years with no repairs. In the distance, I hear a siren, and farther down the block, a few kids are screaming at one another. It's nearly ten at night, but this is normal.

Just like the streetlights going out.

Back when I would have childish fears about the darkness swallowing me up, I also used to dream. I used to dream of leaving here. Of going anywhere but here and never returning. I wish I could forget those memories. But they cling to me like the filth that clings to the gutters on the side of the road.

I used to dream of running away. Mundane things like bills have a way of robbing you of your fantasies. At least I have my books and my writing. Even if I never escape this place, I can still escape into the worlds I build for myself in my stories.

Years ago, when I was still in school, I told my uncle that I'd leave here one day. I remember the sound of the porch swing as it swayed, how my fingers felt as they traced the rusted chain that held it in place. He told me this city didn't let anyone leave. It kept them rooted to this place.

I didn't know what he meant until he passed and there was no one here to pick up the pieces. No one but me.

My feet stumble and I come to a halt as I try desperately not to fall forward. The combination of rubble on the ground and the sight of someone's shadow laying across the very porch swing I'd just been thinking about are what almost cause me to trip.

My chest aches with a sudden pounding of anxiety. No one comes to visit me. It's one of the blessings I've been afforded by being the sad girl with her sob story. I keep my head down and I mind my own business. No one likes me, no one but Ang, and no one fucks with me either. Why would they? I have nothing.

But someone's there. I can't see their face, but the shadow is there and unmistakable.

The paint on the porch swing is weathered, and no one ever sits on it anymore, but I watch the empty seat move back and forth and then a man steps away from the shadows.

A man I see from time to time, but always in passing. Except for when I think of him late at night. Unfortunately, it happens more than I'll ever admit.

He's a man I used to want because he made me feel something I'd never felt before. A mixture of hope and desire. Like the silly dreams of getting away from this place, I used to want to be his. To be pinned down by his hands while his eyes held me in place.

I used to dream of him pressing his lips to mine and stealing my breath with a demanding kiss. I knew he could do it; I'd felt it once before.

His stubble-lined jaw looks sharper in the night with only the neighbor's porch light and the pale moonlight casting shadows down his face. My heart beats slower, yet faster all at once. Knowing Sebastian is on my porch waiting for me, I can hardly breathe, let alone move.

His steely blue eyes are next to come into view, and they immediately capture me. Staring straight at me, they pierce through me and see more of me than anyone else can. He must. I can feel it deep in the pit of my gut. He's always been able to do it. There was never a moment where Sebastian didn't have that power over me.

With clammy palms, I try to move my hands, but my fingers are as paralyzed as my body. It's not from fear, although I know that's what this man should elicit from me. That's the reaction he has on everyone else.

No, it's not fear. As a gust of wind blows, I sway gently in the breeze and it seems to free me from the spell his sharp blue eyes have placed on me. I refuse to look back into his gaze.

Instead, I stare at the chips in the old cement stairs that lead to my porch and feel my heart squeeze harder and tighter than it has in a very long time.

"What do you want?" I ask Sebastian in a hoarse voice, barely louder than a murmur.

His shadow shifts in my periphery, but I don't look up at him.

He's a man I would let do whatever he wanted to me. I would let him do completely as he pleased. There's no reasonable explanation for it. No justification. I'm fully aware that he'd chew me up and spit me out.

Maybe everyone has a person like that. That one person you know can destroy you, and you pine for it despite yourself. I crave what he's capable of. I want the bad things that come with the promise of being his. That confession alone is enough proof I belong in this shit city.

I can feel the danger, the dominance, the overwhelming presence that never leaves with Sebastian Black. I can even smell his masculine woodsy scent that sometimes filters into my dreams. With my lungs full of it, I close my eyes, letting it intoxicate me, but doing my best not to show it. I won't give him that satisfaction. Not when he chooses to give me nothing. Not when he pretends that I'm nothing to him. Although maybe I am. Why would I ever be more than nothing to a man like him?

"Why are you here?" I ask, hardening my voice, raising it, and daring to finally look at him. His shoulders fill the entrance to my front door. My *open* front door. It creaks and the sound echoes in the chilly night air as Sebastian looks me up and down, the hint of a smirk on his face until his gaze reaches mine again.

"I thought you were smarter than that, Chloe," he says and his deep voice rumbles. It's rough, and the way he says my name sounds dirty, even though he's only said it in the same manner as always. With a wanton heat building in my core and my breathing picking up, I stare into his eyes as he adds, "I'm here for a little chat… with you."

CHAPTER 2

Sebastian

CHLOE LOOKS SO DAMN TIRED. IT'S OBVIOUS THAT HER HAIR MUST HAVE BEEN up all day; I can still see the impression of where a band was wrapped around her wavy brunette locks. She swallows thickly, and I swear I can hear the faint sound even from where I am feet away from her. Even with the clamoring from the Higgins kids yelling down the block. With a heavy breath she looks up at me, and I can see she's biting her tongue in reaction to me telling her I came to chat. She's done it for years. The questions shine in her doe eyes though. They stare back at me with the well of emotion that runs deep between us.

The bags under her pale blue eyes only make her look that much more beautiful. I don't know how that's possible.

Every time she comes to mind, I tell myself I'm picturing her differently than she is. That whatever it is that attracts me to her, plays tricks on my memory and makes me think she's more gorgeous than she really is.

And every time I'm proven wrong when I see her.

"You going to let me in?" I ask her with a smirk on my lips. One that makes her eyes narrow.

"Seeing as how my door's already open," she starts off strong but has to take a heavy breath before she finishes, "why don't you be my guest?" She gestures and the purse on her shoulder slips down her arm. Although she struggles to grab on to it, she doesn't take her eyes off mine.

The tension between us is thick, but it's always been that way. From the second I saw her in tenth grade, until this very moment, there's something about her that draws me in like a moth to a flame. I know I get to her too, but only one of us can be the fire.

"After you." I push open her door a little wider and wait for her to pass me. She takes the stairs slowly and then quickly walks by me as if she's trying to get away from me as fast as she can. It's not the first time she's done that and the reaction it sparks in me is the same.

The desire to chase her.

The first time it happened, it didn't come over me until the school year was almost over, and I knew I wouldn't get my weekly dose of fantasizing about Chloe Rose from across the lunchroom anymore.

I gave in and went after her, and it only made the sweet, sad girl who stared back at me that much more desirable.

Kicking her front door shut and locking it, I keep my back to her until the light flicks on. I can hear her drop her purse and then continue walking to the back of the hall. She leaves me at the front door in silence, so I have to turn around and face her.

Her house is just like the rest in this area. All the townhouses here are original and were built by the same company that ran the steel mill. They were made for the workers employed by the mill.

Until it shut down, just like the coal mines did, leaving everyone in houses they couldn't afford, with jobs they didn't have anymore.

The slate floors have gouges in the corner; my guess is something heavy hit them, and then I remember what happened two years before. The tension I'm feeling evaporates and anger comes flooding back at the reminder. I take a quick look over my shoulder toward the door, but even through the somewhat recent coat of paint, I can see where the wood broke when it was kicked in. The main lock's been replaced, and there's an additional one above it.

I wonder if she thinks of that night every time she locks the door. I thought about telling her who did it. Marley was an addict who picked houses at random for items to fence to support his habit. Stealing anything and everything he could was his method. He got his last hit the night he stole from Chloe, leaving fear behind that didn't stray from her eyes for months.

He got his high and then fell to the bottom of the river where I dumped him.

Everyone in this city knows I have my limits. They didn't know Chloe was one of them until that night. I stayed away to keep the target off her back, but people don't forget in this city.

I may be young, and I may work for a man who doesn't venture into this territory, but I run these streets where she lives. No one owns Crescent Hills. If I wanted to take it though, there's not a single prick here who'd stand in my way.

But I don't want this city any more than it wanted me.

I want Chloe Rose. The thought catches me off guard. I've always known it's true, but I don't like to admit it. There's something about her that begs me to be something more for her.

That's the part that kills me though; there's nothing more to me than what she sees, what everyone sees. A ruthless man who's angry at life and makes his living by beating the piss out of pricks.

She's not like me. She's soft and kind and needs a gentler hand than I can give her. She deserves better.

"How'd you get in?" Chloe's voice is soft, although the edge of defiance is still there. Bringing my gaze back to her, I take her in again. From her long legs and skinny waist to those wide hips that beg me to bend her over and give her a punishing fuck, the sight of her makes even the misery of why I'm here vanish for a moment.

She crosses her arms as if she doesn't agree with what I'm thinking, but all that does is put a strain on the blouse she's wearing and push those gorgeous tits of hers together. They may be small, but all I need is a mouthful. My dick stirs, and I have to look away, heading to the living room and glancing around at her place as I go.

"I picked the lock," I tell her, although it's not true. I have a set of keys, got them the day she ordered them from the hardware store. It kept her waiting longer than she should've been there, but I had to do what I had to do. And that meant sneaking in later that night to make sure she was sleeping. Which she never did, but Chloe has a habit of missing sleep.

As do I.

So, she laid there quietly in bed and stiffened at the sound of me moving about, but she never turned around, she never dared to check. She has a habit of that too. Of thinking if she ignores the monsters she conjures in her head, they'll go away. The sad fact is sometimes those monsters in the dark aren't imaginary, but damn does she like to convince herself they are.

She huffs out a laugh that's flat and then brushes her hair back as she leans against the side table in the hall. "You making yourself at home?" she asks, daring me to keep walking and make my way to the living room. I don't answer her, still taking everything in and noting that it's all the same.

She hasn't changed a thing. Not one thing in this place for two years. For some fucked up reason, it sends a ripple of pain through my chest, more than the broken door did. The walls of the hallway still have the same framed photos her uncle had put up after she moved in with him.

Her uncle was more of a parent to her than her own mother was. Him taking her in after her mother's death was the best thing for her, but he was supposed to help her get out of this shit life, not have a heart attack and leave her here all alone.

"Come on over here and have a seat with me," I tell her as I sink into the large sofa that takes up half the room. The edges of the armrest are worn, but it smells like her. Exactly how I remember Chlo. A soft peach scent and some kind of flower. Nothing but sweet.

My fingers dig into the cushion as she stalks slowly to the opposite side of the sofa and seems to consider sitting down as she stands in place. She smooths out the back of her skirt as she stares at the seat and then kicks off her heels, letting the silence pass.

All I can do is stare at her, even as she refuses to look back at me. It makes me think about different possibilities. If we lived in a different city. If our lives were different. If any of that were the case, I never would have let her think she was anything but mine. There's something in my soul that recognizes her as belonging to me. She's mine to protect, to take in my bed, to give the world.

Brushing the rough pad of my thumb along my lip, I have to remind myself that's not the world we live in and she's not mine. Life is better for both of us that way.

I'm a threat to those who have control of the neighboring territories. And that little fact never leaves me. Especially after what happened last week.

I'm no good for Chloe.

She needs someone to take her away from here, and away from me.

Finally, she sinks back into the sofa, sighing and taking a peek at me. "Just tell me what you want, Sebastian."

Those eyes transfix me. It's like she sees through the bullshit, but she always has.

What I *want*. That word sends a wave of warmth and desire through my body. I want her. But that's not what I'm here for and she's something I'll never have.

"Have you been watching the news?" I lean forward as I ask her the question, resting my elbows on my knees. Her small body stiffens as she shakes her head. As if watching the news is a sin.

She's a horrible liar. The worst liar I've ever fucking met. Maybe that's why I feel so drawn to her. She can't hide from me. But I can't hide from her either. There's something so freeing about that simple fact. Something that makes being in her presence addictive.

Even if it's for a shit reason.

"Barry turned up yesterday, did you hear about that?" I ask her and immediately feel the waves of anxiety rolling off of her. Anything that triggers memories of her past causes her pain which is easily seen by anyone who would bother to look.

"I don't give two shits about Barry." Her voice turns harder as she pulls her knees into her chest. She stares straight ahead, and I follow her gaze to the peeling wallpaper.

"Do you know who did it?" At the question, her head whips in my direction with a bolt of anger flashing in her eyes.

"I don't know shit," she bites out and her defensiveness is exactly what the police will latch on to. "I'm going through a lot right now," she adds, but her voice wavers. Her gaze falls as she visibly swallows and tucks a lock of hair behind her ear before peeking back up to the wallpaper. "I don't want to think about any of it." Her voice lowers to a murmur as she says, "Sure as shit, not Barry."

As time slowly passes, her anger diminishes, and I watch as she returns to her typical quiet state. She's nestled in the sofa with the sad smile she always carries gracing her lips. Picking at the hem of her skirt, she glances at me thoughtfully. "Is that really what you wanted to know?"

"How are the nightmares?" I ask her, feeling my chest get tight as the smile vanishes and her eyes shift to a hollow expression I hate and know all too well. She's good at hiding. Hiding her pain behind a smile. Hiding her reality behind the thought that one day she'll get out of here. Well, she used to, anyway. She used to be good at all of that.

Time changes a lot of things.

She starts to answer me, but she can't hide the emotion in her voice. Before she can lie and tell me she's fine, her voice hitches and she turns her gaze toward the empty hallway.

"Why do you care?" Her words cut deep. Chloe's pain is clear, but does she really think I don't care about her?

She's smarter than this. It's the second time tonight I've had that thought. "You know I care," is all I give her. But for the first time since I stepped foot on her porch, I feel the mask slip from me, letting her see what's inside without putting up a wall for her to break through.

She can see it all anyway. If I stop trying to hide, maybe she will too.

She still hasn't answered my question though.

"So how are you handling them? The nightmares?"

"They're back. I've had them every night since Saturday," she tells me. Saturday. The day they caught her mother's killer. She's back to fidgeting with the hem of her skirt as her gaze flickers between me and the floor.

"How did you know?" she asks, peeking up at me and I almost allow myself to get lost in the pain reflected in her baby blues. I'd rather be lost in hers than mine.

"You look tired," I answer her honestly. She drops her gaze though, sighing deeply and pressing the palms of her hands against her eyes.

"Well if you wanted to know if I knew who killed Barry, I don't. So, you can go now, and I can get some sleep." She stands up and hugs her chest, although her posture is more aggressive than defensive.

For nearly a year, I could feel her watching me whenever I was near her. The pull to be at her side was stronger than anything else. Nothing could compete with her, but I resisted. I couldn't let her get caught up in this shit.

Now she's the one pushing me away. Fair enough, I suppose. It doesn't change the fact that this is a small world, and I know she still feels that draw, just like I do.

"I have something that can help you," I tell her as I stand with no intention of walking out just yet. She can pretend that she has the ability to tell me what to do. We both know that's not the case, but I respect her too much to rub it in her face. Besides, I can't let her push me away when I have something she needs.

"What is it?" She's wary but curious. That's the Chloe I know.

Reaching into my pocket, I pull out the vial I prepared before coming here and roll it between my fingers. "It's something to make you sleep."

"Drugs?" she scoffs and shakes her head at me, letting out a sarcastic laugh like I've gone mad.

"It's something you could get at any pharmacy," I offer her, letting a smile slip onto my lips.

That's not completely true. A friend gave it to me to see if there'd be any interest for it on the streets, but people in this city want harder drugs. Drugs to help them forget, to escape, even if just for a short time. I thought it could help Chloe though.

She's a good girl, but she needs this. The sweets will knock her out and give her the rest she so desperately needs. I would know.

"You're a bad liar," she says, and the irony doesn't escape me.

"I'll put a few drops in your tea," I tell her as I walk past her, brushing my arm against hers and feeling that familiar combination of heat and want seep into my blood. Her quick intake of air is all I need to keep moving forward, walking to her kitchen before I hear her take even a single step.

I go right to where I know she keeps her mugs and tea as I hear her walking toward the kitchen.

"I don't drink tea at night," she tells me, and I know she's lying again. Glancing at the box in my hands, I show her the label then pull out what I know is her favorite mug. She picked it up at a used bookstore last year. If she's not working or home, she's always at that bookstore.

"Decaffeinated tea then?" She only crosses her arms aggressively again and leans against the small table in the kitchen. "I'm getting tired of you lying to me tonight," I add with my back to her as I fill the mug with water and put it into the microwave.

When I turn to her, the hum of the microwave filling the room along with the tension between us, she meets my gaze with a hardened expression.

"How many years will go by this time? You know, before you barge into my life, then pretend I don't exist the next day?" She sounds bitter, but I know it's fake.

I cluck my tongue, keeping my eyes on her face instead of her chest. But with her arms crossed like that, she's not helping me. "Would you really want me to make this a habit?" I ask her, not realizing how much I actually care what her answer is until silence is all I'm given.

I already know the answer; I shouldn't have asked the question.

"What do you want from me, Sebastian? It wasn't to ask if I'd heard about some asshole getting mugged."

"It was." I wouldn't have come to see her if I didn't think I really had to be here. I don't like what she does to me. How she takes over every sense of reason and consumes my thoughts long after we've parted ways.

"The cops are going to question you about his death. I need you to tell them you don't want to talk about it. Because otherwise, you'll look guilty." The microwave goes off and I go back to making her tea when she starts to answer me.

"I didn't do it. I—"

"I know you didn't. But you look like you're lying when anyone brings up anything that has to do with your mother. Which is why it could be pinned on you."

With the bag of tea steeping, I stiffen at my own words. A sick feeling stirs in the pit of my stomach. I know what it's like when someone brings up shit you don't want to hear. How all of a sudden, you feel a coldness and pain all over like it's taken over everything inside of you.

I reach for the sugar on the counter and stir some into her tea. She doesn't object or ask how I knew she would want it. The spoon clinks gently against the ceramic and Chloe still hasn't responded, but when I turn to her, her eyes are glossy with unshed tears. I feel like a prick.

"This doesn't have anything to do with that," she says, although she barely gets out the words.

"That's not what the police think. Two bodies were found right after they caught the guy who killed your mom. You don't need to watch the news to know what the cops are thinking."

She starts to object, but I stop her and say, "Just tell me you won't talk to them." Grabbing the vial, I put three drops in her tea, making sure she's watching me, then set it next to the sugar.

"What could I possibly tell them?" Her tone is as tired as she looks, and she doesn't hide the pain that lingers beneath her words. "I don't know anything."

"They're looking for someone to blame. I don't want you to give them a reason to think that someone could be you." I know they tossed her name around as a possible suspect. She has motive, and emotions are raw for her. They want the case closed, and she's an easy target.

My throat feels tight although the words come out steady as I tell her, "If they come around, I need you to tell them you don't know anything, and you don't want to talk to them. That's it."

I hand her the mug I've prepared for her, my palm hot as I rotate it so she can grab it by the handle. "It doesn't matter how they'll push you for more or what they say. They want you to talk, and you're not going to. All you're going to tell them is that you don't know anything, and you don't have anything to say, right?" I ask her, and she nods obediently and with an understanding that supplants the sadness. The cops here are crooked and covering for whoever lines their pockets. Anyone can take the fall, and they'd be perfectly all right with that.

She takes the mug with both hands, letting her fingers brush against mine. The small bit of contact sends electric waves up my arms and shoulders, igniting every nerve ending and putting me on edge. So much so, that my body begs me to either step away or grab her wrist. But I do what I've always done. I resist. I let myself feel the discomfort of not having her but being so close that I could easily have her if I just gave in.

She's closer now, taking a half step toward me, her head at my chest and her gaze on the floor as she blows across the top of the hot cup of tea.

"I understand," she tells me, her lips close to the edge of the mug, but she doesn't drink it yet.

I reach over, one hand on either side of her head, and brush back her hair. She stares up at me with a longing I remember so well. A longing I've dreamed of for so many nights. The air is pulled from my lungs as I stare into her eyes. "Drink your tea and go to bed, Chloe." My words are rough, and it's hard to swallow. The moment her baby blues close with her nod, I get the fuck out of there before I do anything stupid. Anything that would put her in even more danger.

CHAPTER 3

Chloe

I'LL NEVER FORGET HER SCREAMS.

The second I hear the front door open as Sebastian leaves, it's all I can think about.

As I set down my tea on the kitchen table, not even Sebastian's lingering heat and scent can provide an adequate distraction. No, the moment he brought up my mother, I knew the memories would come back and they wouldn't leave.

Sebastian never stays for long. Never. No matter how much I wish he would.

Closing my eyes and gripping the edge of the chair, I take in a deep breath. I know I need to lock the door, but I'm desperately trying to calm and steady myself.

At war with the memories of that night my mother died are the thoughts of Sebastian having been in my house just now.

He was here for business. But whatever the reason, he doesn't want me to say anything, and so I won't. I don't have anything to say to the cops regardless, but I am emotional, and I could see myself spewing all sorts of hate for the dead man whose murder could easily be pinned on me.

Whatever Sebastian is involved with, and whatever his intention is behind telling me to keep my mouth shut, I'm grateful for it.

This addition to my tea, however, I don't know what to think about that. I don't know what it is, and I don't believe him when he said it's something I could get at the drugstore. I may be attracted to him for some unknown reason, but I'm not fucking stupid. The thought resonates with me as I turn the locks on the front door.

It was the nightmares that led him to me the first time. Or my reaction to the nightmares really. The constant crying.

It was five years ago when I was in ninth grade and he was in tenth. I turn around as a chill flows up my arm, traveling to the back of my neck and causing every hair in its path to stand on end. I'd sag against the hard door if my body wasn't frozen at the memories.

Her scream. *Screams.* The shrill sound still wakes me up at night, tears streaming down my face as I try to keep my heart from leaping out of my chest.

When it happened, I was cross-legged on the floor of our townhouse one block down from where I am now, and my friend Andrea was on the sofa.

Justice Street. Ironic isn't the right word for the name of the street I grew up on. It's pathetic and riddled with agony that the word is allowed to exist in this city. I know now that she was nearly two blocks away, in the alley right across from both the park and the bars she had frequented.

The fact her screams carried that far, is evidence enough of how desperate she was for someone to help her.

The first scream came at 11:14 p.m. I remember how the red lines of the digital display shone brightly on the microwave's clock.

"What the fuck are you doing?" Andrea asked me with wide, disbelieving eyes as she slapped the phone from my hand. It fucking hurt. The memory brings the sting back, making my left hand move on top of my right. Absently I rub soothing circles over it, staring straight ahead although I don't see the hall to my uncle's home. Technically, it's mine now, but I don't want to feel any sense of ownership for a damn thing in this city.

She coughed on the hit she took from her blunt and I remember the sound so clearly.

All I see is Andrea's angry expression, but fear was also evident as she locked her eyes with mine. My heart beat faster back then, knowing I needed to call someone to help whoever it was that was screaming. But now it beats slow at the memory as if my body wishes I could stop time. As if it's doing everything it can to try to make that happen, to go back.

I heard another faint cry for help and Andrea followed my gaze to the open window. The smoke billowed toward it. I sat there numbly as she quickly ran to the window and closed it.

"We have to call—" I tried to plead with her, knowing deep in the marrow of my bones that whoever was screaming was in agonizing pain.

"No, we don't," Andrea pushed back, waving the smoke from her face. "The cops can't come here," she argued with me. "Someone else will call… if whoever that was even needs help," she told me, but both of our eyes strayed back to the window at the muffled sound of another shrill scream.

I didn't move to my phone.

Instead, I took a shower. Of all the things I could have done, I stepped into a stream of hot water, listening to the white noise of the shower, praying for the water to wash the feelings away. The guilt, the disgust, all of it.

But that's not something water can do.

When I stepped out of the shower, I swear I heard it again, but it sounded exactly the same. Andrea said I was crazy and that it was all in my head. That it was only the one time anyone had screamed at all, which she corrected to two when I stared back at her.

The last faint cry I heard was well after midnight. Andrea convinced me it was just a couple fighting; the Ruhills were good for that on the weekends as they were both angry drunks who spent their paychecks at the bar, but now I know that's not true.

Over an hour had passed. And no one went to help her. Not me, not a single person in this city.

It was nearly 9 a.m. when the police banged on the door and I answered. I thought my mother had lost her keys and locked herself out. It wouldn't have been the first time. When I opened the door, it still hadn't dawned on me that the screams had belonged to her.

She was the one I didn't help save.

No one did.

Not a single person for blocks around helped her.

Andrea wasn't the only one to close the window and tell the cops that's all they'd done. Screams in this place are a constant. Cries for help come often. And everyone assumed someone else would call the cops or offer street justice. But it didn't happen that way.

That fucker, Barry, the one who turned up dead in the news today, I'll never forget how he laughed at the bar as he bragged to anyone who would listen about how he'd turned up his television because she wouldn't stop screaming. He'd shut the window and turned up the volume until he couldn't hear her cries anymore. He'd heard her, he'd known she was begging for help, and yet he did nothing and dared to be arrogant about it.

It was easier to hate him than it was to hate myself for knowing I could have helped her. I could have tried to help her. I could have done something, anything—rather than listen to Andrea.

I never spoke to her again. Not that she cared much. With my mother gone, there'd be no one to fill my medicine cabinet with what Andrea referred to as the good shit.

The terrors that came with my mother's death are justified. I deserve so much worse. I would do anything to go back. *Anything.*

My numb body finally moves to prevent what's coming next. The memories of who my mother truly was, an abusive alcoholic who never wanted me. They're joined by the fears I had back when I was a kid, that she was coming to punish me. That I deserved so badly to be punished.

"She's long gone," I whisper as two kids yelling up the street remind me that I'm here, in my uncle's house, only a block away from my childhood home. And even farther away from where my mother was raped and murdered. More importantly, it's years later.

As my tired eyes yearn for sleep, I walk slowly down the hall back to the kitchen. The chill of the memories follows me. It took all this time to find her killer, a fifty-year-old man who'd once been a high school teacher. They found him dead in his house three cities over. They only know it was him because he was being prosecuted for the rape of some other young woman and the DNA matched. He killed himself rather than being taken in last Saturday.

That wasn't even a week ago, and then Amber Talbott died a few days later. She saw and heard everything, yet she did nothing but record part of the attack and send it to her friend. It wasn't enough to solve my mother's murder.

Shot from behind, it only captured the back of the man who'd done it as he viciously punched my mother, shoving her deeper into the alley. Amber had claimed she sent it to her friend because she was scared, but the texts between them implied otherwise. I know the video; I can see it clearly now. It's only half a minute long and was taken from Amber's window across the street.

My mother saw her in those final moments, or at the very least she saw the phone. Up until the moment I saw the video, I thought the worst thing you could see before being murdered would have to be your killer's eyes. But that's wrong. It has to be. Because how horrible would it be if the last thing you ever saw was someone hearing your cries, knowing you were in pain, but choosing to do nothing? Or simply walking away, shutting their window, or worse, filming it for their own amusement.

Amber said she thought the guy had just mugged my mother and then moved along. She told me to my face that she was sorry, and she wished she could have done something else. I didn't believe her.

She could have done something if she'd really wanted to. She was older than me. She was closer, too. She could have sent that video to the cops. Five years later, just days ago, someone mugged her and left her for dead in an alley next to the hair salon where she worked.

No one did anything to help her, either.

And now Barry's dead. Two people who I hated so much for so long, both killed within days of each other and after my mother's killer was found dead.

Barry was an old man who couldn't be bothered unless you wanted to talk about the winning lottery numbers or placing bets. Horses and the tracks were his favorite. I used to like him because he'd show me pictures of the races. But when I heard how cavalier he was when it came to my mother's murder, I couldn't stand the sound of his name, let alone the sight of his face.

I'm glad he's dead. And if I'm being honest, I'm glad Amber's dead too, but it doesn't change the root of my pain.

Nothing can change the past. Nothing can take away the guilt.

I feel empty and hollowed out as I walk back to the kitchen table. The chills refuse to leave me.

Just as the nightmares don't. But I had those even before my mother died. They were my constant companion, just like the bruises back then.

The night terrors got worse after she was gone, but the bruises eventually faded.

Staring at the cup of tea, I reflect on Sebastian. I remember how being around him, being *kissed* by him, took so much of the pain away. Even just thinking about him helped.

But I'll never be okay. It's only a pipe dream. Sebastian may pull me away, pull me closer to him and into his world, but it's only temporary. He's proven that too many times for me to put much faith in him at all.

I grab the cup and dump it in the sink, watching as the dark liquid swirls down the drain.

I don't want to sleep. My mother waits for me there.

CHAPTER 4

Sebastian

I CAN STILL FEEL HER FINGERS AGAINST MINE. HER TOUCH HASN'T LEFT ME SINCE last night. My mind wanders to what she would have said if I'd told her I wanted to stay.

The rumble from the engine turns to white noise as I think about all the ways I could take the pain away from her. I imagine lying in bed beside her and taking her how I've dreamed of for as long as I can remember. My grip tightens on the steering wheel and the breeze from the rolled-down window pauses as I slow to a stop at a red light.

The radio station being changed to something else grabs my attention and I have to clear my throat and adjust in my seat to play off what was going through my mind. Carter changes the station again, but he's not going to find what he needs by picking a different song. There's nothing in this world that's going to help take his mind off of the pain.

"You staying with me tonight?" I ask him. His dad kicked him out of the house again. Not that the kid did a damn thing wrong. He's sixteen and involved with the wrong crowd, namely me, but he never does anything wrong. Not since his mom got sick last year.

He flicks the radio off, choosing silence over the commercial on the last station.

"I don't know," he tells me solemnly and then falls back against the passenger seat, staring listlessly out the window. Chewing on his thumbnail, he avoids looking back at me.

Which is fine, because the fucker behind us yells at me to get going while honking his horn. The red light's turned green. One look in the rearview, catching the driver's gaze silences him. He sees who I am, and suddenly the pissed off expression on his face vanishes. I wait for a beat, then another as the assholes settles into his seat and averts his eyes, waiting for me to do whatever the fuck I want to do.

I'm careful as I step on the gas, and more careful with what I say next. "How's your mom doing?"

Even that simple question gets him worked up. Carter shakes his head but doesn't say anything. He tries but he's too choked up.

Carter's mom keeps asking for him to help instead of his dad. It ranges from changing her position in bed and helping her go to the bathroom, to just being by her side to talk. His father doesn't like that though. He's a drunk and a deadbeat.

With five boys and her health deteriorating, I can only guess his mother is hoping that Carter will take care of the others when she's gone. He's the oldest. Hell knows his father won't.

"Let's talk about something else," he suggests as I turn down Peck Avenue. "Like where we're going?"

My lips kick up in a half smile at his response. He texted me earlier, asking me to pick him up, but didn't question where I was taking him. He asks so often now, almost every day. I guess he doesn't care where we go so long as he has somewhere to get away. He always goes home though. For his mother. For his brothers too.

"I want to check on someone," I tell him as I round the corner, passing over a speed bump and slowing down at the weathered stop sign that marks that we're close to our destination.

Carter's brow furrows. I don't know if I've ever told him I want to check on someone before, but when I turn down Dixon Street and slow in front of Chloe's house, he gives me a shit-eating grin. As if I just told him his favorite joke.

"Like old times," he says with a rough laugh. Carter's my only friend and that's because I know who he is to his core. He's six years younger than me, but he's like family, the only family I have.

All he has are his brothers; he's told me that so many times. But it's always followed up with a pat on my back as he tells me I'm one of them. I have to admit, it's nice to feel wanted, and even nicer to feel like you're part of a family. Even if you know deep down that's not really true.

I was eighteen and he was twelve when we met. He got caught shoplifting bread of all things. Dumb fuck couldn't even pick something that fit under his jacket.

Grabbing him by his collar, I yanked him away from the clerk hellbent on beating the shit out of him. If you let one person get away with stealing your shit, everyone will come running with duffle bags.

So you have to send a message, loud and clear. I was in charge of keeping that shop out of harm's way; it was one of my first jobs from Romano.

I looked the clerk in the eye and told him the kid was going to pay for what he'd done. I had a reputation and the clerk was happy enough to let me handle it, knowing he could tell his story about how I'd kicked the kid's ass for trying to steal from his store.

Carter was a scrawny thing and still is, although he's starting to fill out. I picked him up like he was nothing and he didn't try to fight it.

The look of fear in his eyes wasn't there, only a look of disappointment, even as I dragged him around back. I remember how I felt something I hadn't in so long. Something like regret, maybe?

He wasn't like the others, the ones looking for a fight.

Carter already had enough to fight for and to fight against, so to him I was just one more thing he had to endure. I could see the weary resignation in his eyes.

I didn't kick his ass. Instead, I told him to go home. I made the decision to let him go because he wasn't like the others. And also, because the idea of beating up on a lanky twelve-year-old made me sick to my stomach.

That was when I saw his anger and his fight. His passion.

"I'm not going home without it," he told me with determination, even though his voice shook. His hands balled into fists, but he didn't raise them.

"Get home, kid," I told him, walking over to where I'd thrown him and towering over him.

He stared me in the eyes as he shook his head. "I'm not leaving without it."

"For a fucking loaf of bread, you're willing to get your ass beat?" The kid was stupid. I still tell him he's stupid and it's true half the time.

"I have to make sandwiches, my mom told me—" He started to say something else, but I cut him off.

"Well your mom can make it herself," I spat back at him, with a pent-up rage he didn't deserve. He was only a kid, and some of the kids didn't know. My mother was a whore. A bitch. I don't have a single nice thing to say about her. Even with her dead in the ground after spending the last minutes of her life with her favorite needle, I can't bring myself to say one good thing about her. I never had a family aside from my grandmother, bless her soul. And I never would. It's as simple as that. It was as deeply ingrained in me as whatever possessed Carter that night.

"She can't!" he yelled at me. I took one step closer to him, and he stiffened. My spine was stiff, my shoulders straight and the aggression and threats evident just from my stare at him.

His bottom lip quivered as he took in a quick breath, but he didn't give up. "I have to feed them tonight and we don't have anything… but I can make sandwiches." He gritted out the last words with tears in his eyes. "I just need bread."

"And what are you going to put on the bread? You going to steal something else too?" I berated him, even though I believed him.

"There's peanut butter already."

"You can eat it with a spoon," I said dismissively, turning my back to him and ready to get the hell away from him. Something about the way he looked and acted bothered me to my core. He wasn't frightened, and he wasn't angry. *He was desperate.*

"She said to make sandwiches for my brothers-"

I lost it again with the kid, thinking about my own mother and how she'd forced me to fend for myself. She never told me to make dinner, I just had to. No one else would. "And why didn't she do it then? Huh? She can dish out orders, but-"

"She's in the hospital. She told me on the phone to make sandwiches and I just need bread." He stumbled over his words, but he never took his eyes from me. "I told him, the clerk," he gestured to the shop, "we'd pay him, but I don't have the money right now." He visibly swallowed and continued, "My mom will pay him when she's back. And it's going to be real soon. She'll be okay real soon." He started rambling on and on and I could feel his sob story getting to me. I could feel myself getting played like I'd played everyone else as I grew up on the streets.

"So, you're stealing bread to make sandwiches for your brothers?" I lowered my head to his. "Here's a hint, kid. When you're told to do something, you don't have to follow it to a T." I licked my lower lip, slipping my hands into my pockets and expecting him to give up and go home already. To leave the corner store alone and my reputation intact and go eat the fucking peanut butter out of the jar like a normal asshole would.

But he didn't get what I was saying.

"Are you dumb?" I asked him as he stood up, faced me and held his ground.

"She said to make them sandwiches. I'm not leaving until I get the bread."

I searched his eyes for the longest time before going in and grabbing the bread for him. But I followed him home, telling him I wasn't going to give it to him until I saw that he was telling the truth. I knew he was one of the kids who lived on the edge of the city. I remembered seeing a bunch of them out that way. I make it a habit to know everyone and for them to know me.

If he was lying to me, he'd learn real quick to never do it again.

I didn't know that he had four brothers, or that their place was a mess because they'd just moved in. I heard they were on the run from where they came from, but I didn't know that their mother was in the hospital because of their grandfather. Apparently, he's who they were running from and he'd found out where they ran off to. Which is how his mom wound up in the ER and why their father in jail as a result of it all, paying Carter's grandfather back for what he'd done to his mother. Leaving five kids alone in a new place without a damn thing to eat.

I didn't know, and I didn't care, not until I saw how happy they were just to eat. Even something as simple as peanut butter sandwiches. I asked him how long it'd been since she went to the hospital.

It had been four days. And they were starving, but he'd promised his mom he would feed them, and he did.

Twelve years old, and he was the oldest of five. She stayed in the hospital for another three days before the doctors would let her come home. Now she's back in the hospital, but not with bruises and broken ribs. Two years ago, she was diagnosed with cancer. She's been fighting it all this time, but Carter's still taking care of his brothers, and now her too.

That was the first time I met Carter, four years ago. I took him under my wing at first, but now he's a friend. A friend who's been through some shit and is still in it. He has a family though and a reason to fight. I've only ever fought to stay alive or to rule with fear. That difference is something I'm not sure he'll ever understand.

"Is she home?" he asks me, and it brings me back to the present. To being on the other side of the city, close to my place and in front of Chloe's.

Letting out a sigh and running a hand through my hair, I shrug like I don't know.

"You like her," he tells me like it's a fucking joke. He doesn't know what's going on. Not entirely, but even if he suspects it, he won't ask. He doesn't like to look for the darkness, not when he's surrounded by it already.

"She doesn't need me asking her out," I mutter under my breath and ignore Carter's eyes pinned on me.

It takes a second and then another for him to start putting the puzzle pieces together.

"You going to tell me why we're here?" he asks me with a brow cocked. He's feigning lightheartedness; concern is clearly etched on his face.

I've told him more than once that he doesn't pay attention enough. That life is shit, it always will be, and either you accept it for what it is and protect yourself, or you fall victim to whatever fate chooses to inflict on us. But given the weight of what I'm hiding, I don't tell him. I don't want it to be real.

I lie to him and say, "I just wanted to see if anyone was snooping around here."

"Cops? Or Romano's people?" Carter asks and the gravity of either of the two options sends a chill down my spine. I can handle the cops, Chloe can't. But neither of us could handle Romano if he decided to go after her. He runs the territory up north and I work for him on occasion. I may be his muscle, but I'm not sure even I know the extent of the shit Romano's involved with.

As I'm thinking about the last fucked up thing Romano had me do, Carter asks something I wish he hadn't, because it's too close to being true. "Is this about that thing Marcus gave you?" His voice is even, but his expression's fallen.

Pushing back in my seat and hiding my anxiety, I tell him, "I told you not to mention that."

He only nods and seems to shrug it off, like it doesn't matter if Marcus is the reason we're here. Both of us know that's bullshit though. Even saying his name is something no one likes to do around here. Romano may run the territory up north from us, he may even make an appearance down here on occasion when he needs something, but you always see him coming and he's only dangerous because of the men he controls.

Marcus is a different sort of threat. By the time you see him coming, you're already dead. He doesn't have a territory, he doesn't have men. When he makes demands, they're always about death. They called him the Grim Reaper when I was younger. He doesn't want money, he doesn't bargain. What Marcus decides is final and there's no room to negotiate. He's only one man, but he's killed every man who's crossed him and even more men simply because they were on his list.

A minute passes before Carter reaches for the radio again and lets the music ease the tension.

"It's fine." My words come out casually as I watch Chloe's house. Not a thing looks out of place. It's not fine though. This shit is exactly why I could never be with her. One day you're on top, the next you're in a ditch. That's how this lifestyle is, and I'll never bring anyone into this shit life if I can help it. That especially goes for Chloe Rose.

"When are you going to ask her out?" he asks with a wide smile. He still has happiness in his soul. Enough to bring a bit of light to every dark situation. One day it'll go out. It always does for men like us. But I'll do my damnedest to keep it from happening.

"I know you want her," he chides again.

He doesn't know the half of it. I've known Chloe for a long time. And I made sure she never knew how I watched over her when her mother died. She wasn't okay. Everyone knew it. Just like they knew I wasn't okay when my mother died.

No one gives a shit though. People die, and somehow you keep going.

Then more people die and one day it's you.

One time I walked up to her porch and peeked in her window after she'd moved into her uncle's. The TV was on and I thought maybe she was watching it. That she'd be okay. It had been weeks. Weeks of nothing but her crying, constantly crying and hating herself. And I despised it. I fucking loathed it. The whole street could hear her uncle yelling at her to stop crying. That he'd lost his sister too and that she needed to stop.

When I looked in, she was still crying, but her eyes were wide open, her cheeks tearstained, and she saw me.

I know she did, not that it changed anything. I knew at that moment when she didn't do anything or say anything, that I was just as dead to her as her mother was. It hurt me like nothing else in this world had to know that just then, I meant nothing to her. I couldn't take her pain away. I was nobody special.

I'd never been more sure of anything in my life. I was nothing that night.

But the next day, I proved her wrong. When she kissed me back, I proved her wrong.

CHAPTER 5

HE COMES BY EVERY DAY. FRIDAY NIGHT HE STOOD IN MY KITCHEN. SATURDAY, he drove by with Carter Cross, Sunday he came alone and now it's Monday night and he's outside again.

I act like I don't see him. I've always done that. Everyone leaves you alone if you act like you don't exist.

The thing about Sebastian though, is that he doesn't leave until he knows I know he's watching me. Or maybe that's just what I think because I feel his gaze on me every time and I have no desire not to look back at him.

I pull back my curtain when the car outside idles and idles. A book is open in my hand, its pages unread. I let it shut as I peek outside to see who it is. The large text closes with a dull thud that matches the single pound in my chest when I see him out there.

I try to swallow but my throat's dry.

Angie said it's an intimidation tactic. I shouldn't have told her anything about Sebastian coming by like this. She concocted about a dozen theories of what's going on with the murders and Sebastian and why he's checking on me and instructing me on what to tell the cops. She was animated, to say the least, but I was more interested in hearing about what she did on Sunday with her new boy toy than anything that has to do with this shit city.

My eyes drift down, meeting Sebastian's and instead of glancing away, I hold his gaze for a moment.

I would feel it, wouldn't I? If his intention was to intimidate me, I'd feel fear, or a chill maybe? I'd feel something other than the quiet stillness that settles deep in my bones, the smoldering heat that simmers in my blood. Just looking at him, my body relaxes.

I swear I even see his lips tug into an asymmetric smile when I don't look away.

My heart does that thud again, and I have to loosen my grip on the thin curtain and let my head fall back against the headboard.

He'll only ever be at arm's length, so this power he has over me, this innate emotion he controls inside of me, can't be good.

The idling stops, fading into the sounds of the night and that warmth and soothing feeling disappear with it. It's sickening that something so small could garner so much emotion from me. As I reach for my book, I see my phone out of the corner of my eye.

I don't have a fucking clue where I left off. My fingers run along the edges of the pages as if my memory can lead me to the right page, but all I can focus on is the phone.

Shoving the book off my lap, I reach for it.

The cops didn't come to question me. I text the number I know is Sebastian's. He's never explicitly said it was him and usually he texts me, but I know it's his number. I want to tell him he can resume pretending I don't exist.

When he doesn't reply, I skim through the previous messages.

The first one reads: *You did good today.* He sent it a few nights after the infamous kiss. The night I first slept peacefully in this house after my uncle took me in.

Who is this? I asked, but he never answered.

When I first moved in, my uncle didn't have a spare room ready for me. We'd had to clear out the cluttered room he sometimes used as an office. Almost all of my mother's things had to be thrown away in the move. Same thing with some of my possessions, not that I had much. This townhouse was already full, and I wasn't even sure if I was staying here for long. No one told me anything. No one but Sebastian in a nameless text.

The phone pinging in my hand scares the shit out of me, spiking my adrenaline and forcing my heart to race up my throat. I nearly slam my head back against the headboard, but somehow manage to calm myself down.

The memories of the week my mother died have always haunted me. That week brought awful nightmares, ones that have come back in full force now that the past is being dredged up.

It's only Sebastian, I tell myself and breathe in deeply, calming every bit of me, although the task feels even more impossible than staying awake long enough to see what he's written.

How are you sleeping?

It's fitting he would ask that just as I rub my eyes with the palm of my hand and feel the sting of the burning need to sleep.

I chew on my lip, my fingers hovering over the screen. I don't want to lie to him here, not on the phone; I don't want to taint these messages that mean so much. After a moment I tell him the truth and see exactly what I expect in return.

Not well.

Have you been drinking your tea?

The vial is on my nightstand, staring at me as if I'm to blame for this shit. I nearly took it last night, but I don't do drugs. Not any sort. I've seen what addiction can do. Although I've also seen what desperation can do. And I'm desperate for one night where I close my eyes and I'm not haunted by memories of the past. I was doing so well for years. Her murderer being found is what set everything off. And the nightmares have come back with a vengeance.

Take it. His message sends a chill down my spine. It's as if he can hear my thoughts.

It takes me longer than I thought it would to write him back. Mostly because I don't know what his answer will be, but I know what I want to read.

If I take it, will you leave me alone? I text him and then grab the vial. I don't have a cup of tea handy, but I have a glass of water. Without even thinking, I put one drop, then another, then the third.

I watch the liquid swirl as I wait for his message. The other night I thought it was clear, since in the tea I couldn't see its color.

But it's pink, a pale, pale pink that quickly disappears in the water.

Before I take a sip, I check my phone only to see he hasn't responded. The lip of the glass feels cold as I bring it up and take the first gulp, wondering what it will taste like.

It tastes like nothing at all. Maybe a tinge of sugar. Just a faint hint.

I'm still considering the taste when the phone goes off on my lap. *You need to sleep.* How typical of Sebastian to respond without answering my question.

He has no fucking idea how badly I need to sleep. I'm delirious.

I chug the rest of the glass and intend on telling him that I drank the stuff he gave me, or maybe telling him something just so he'll stay with me on the phone until I've fallen asleep.

That doesn't happen though. Instead, I stare at the empty glass, feeling lightheaded and drowsy all at once. My sense of time begins to warp, feeling like it passes slowly but quickly just the same.

I barely get the glass on the nightstand before the darkness takes over. I'm able to slip under the covers, feeling the weight of sleep pulling at me. And I give in to it, so easily.

⸻◆⸻

"You're late." Tamra's voice is clear as can be. She always had a slight rasp in the last word of every sentence and she kept her lips in the shape of that word for what seemed like an odd amount of time.

Where am I? I can feel my brow pinch; this room is familiar, but not so much that I know where I am. The carpet's thin and worn out in front of the television where the car seats are. There are three of them, although they're empty now. No one's here but me, sitting on the sofa that's just as worn as the carpet and Tamra, who's standing in front of the open door.

"He made me stay overtime." My mother's voice drifts in through the tense air. She's agitated and suddenly anxiety runs through me.

"Well, then, this is overtime for me. I can't watch these brats for free."

I'm not a brat. I swear I was good. I was good. I want to tell my mother, but I know to be quiet. With my hands in my lap, I wait stiffly. I'll only move when I'm told, I'll only speak when I'm spoken to. With my throat tight and dry, I wring my fingers around one another and glance at my bookbag at the end of the sofa. It's already packed, and I didn't forget anything. I never forget. If I do, I don't tell my mom and I hope she doesn't find out.

"Of course, you're gonna fucking charge me," my mother spits out her anger at Tamra. Anger which I know will be directed at me on Monday when she watches me again unless she tells my mom she's not going to watch me anymore without being paid early. Which she's done before. In that case, I stay in my room all day and don't answer the door. But Mom got in trouble for doing that once.

"Let's go, Chloe." My mom barges into the living room as Tamra stays where she is, keeping the front door open. It's late and I still have homework to do, but I don't know how to

do it. I don't know how to read the words and I need someone to tell me, but Tamra won't and Mom's mad so I know better than to bother her.

I can tell from the way she stomps across the room it would be a mistake for me to do anything or say anything. I get up quickly. But I have to be quicker. If I move fast enough it won't burn when she grabs my arm.

"I'm coming," I tell her as fast as I can, snatching my bookbag and scurrying to her side even though fear is racing through me and begging me to run.

I'll be quiet; I'll go to sleep. Miss Parker will help me. It's only second grade, she keeps telling me I have time to do it at school if I get there early, but that I have to learn to read. I'm trying. I promise her I am.

"You see how no one helped me?" I hear a voice from outside this moment, a voice that sounds so close, so real. So full of rage and vengeance. My mother. Fear runs down my skin and up the back of my neck, freezing me where I am as I swear I feel her hot breath at the shell of my ear.

She didn't say that in the memory. She's telling me now.

I look back at Miss Tamra, still trying to keep up with my mother, even though her grip tightens so hard it's going to bruise. My blood runs cold and a scream is caught in my throat at the sight of Tamra leaning against the back wall, her left hand on the sofa. Blood coats her hair where a bullet wound mars her skull and it leaks down to her cheek, dripping onto her collarbone. I blink and suddenly she's standing there, yelling at my mother that she's an ungrateful bitch.

The chill doesn't go away, the sight from just before still stealing my breath and sanity.

The hand around my arm twists, burning my skin where my mother is touching me. It hurts. Mom, it hurts! I scream out, but the words don't come. I'm no longer there. It's dark and the bruising hold changes to something else, feeling like the kiss of a spider climbing up my arm in the darkness. I try to jump back, but I'm trapped, with nowhere to go and I can't see a damn thing.

She's here. My heart races and dread ignites inside of me, but I can't run. I can't see her. I can only hear her so close to me.

"No one ever helped me," she tells me. "They're going to pay for that."

<hr>

It felt so real last night, the sensation of my mother being so close to me.

An uncontrollable shudder runs through me as I slowly walk down the stairs. My heart won't stop racing and I can't clear my throat. I feel like I'm suffocating.

It was only a dream.

It's only a dream.

My chest tightens and the fear rips through me anew as I swear I hear something upstairs, something in the bedroom.

"Knock it off," I grit between my teeth.

The floor behind me creaks, loud and heavy. It almost sounds like someone's walking down behind me quickly and not hiding their weight, making me scream and I nearly fall down the last four steps. My back pressed against the wall and my chest frantically rising and falling, I stare behind me. No one's there. No one's here.

"It's only a dream," I remind myself and ignore the flow of ice that rolls over my body and how every hair on my body stands on end as I remember my mother's words. *They're going to pay for that.*

I'm not crazy, but I feel like I am. Crossing my arms over my chest, I feel my blunt nails dig in and remind myself that I'm alive.

The night after my mom died, I had the same type of dreams. The ones where she felt so real, following me even when I woke up.

"Please, go away," I beg her as I fall to the floor, sitting on the steps and wishing the wave of coldness that keeps coming over me would go away. Go away forever.

I told you, I hear my mother's voice, but I know it's just a memory.

She's not real. This isn't real.

The dead don't stay away for long. And they'll pay. Every single one of them will pay.

CHAPTER 6

Sebastian

IT'S BEEN THREE YEARS SINCE ROMANO GAVE ME THIS JOB. THE KNIFE SLAMS DOWN on the cutting board as the thought hits me. I grab the carved meat and put it in the tub with the rest of the chunks.

I'm the butcher of a shop that rides the line of his territory. When Romano hired me to work here at Paul's Butcher Shop, I thought it meant something different. I thought it meant he was hiring me to be a part of his crew.

Now I know better; he just wanted to watch me. Train me, or maybe mentor me if he ever needed someone like me. The line of customers coming in for their packages distracts me and I glance up for a moment. Eddie, Paul's son, rings them up one by one. I stay in the back with a few other guys, processing all the orders and occasionally we have to stay here later, after closing hours.

Like when Romano has a special order.

Picking up the butcher knife, I slam it down with my teeth gritting together. This isn't his turf, but I'm not ready to start a war or gather an army against him. There's no one here to recruit, just the addicts who camp out behind the line of the highway that separates his area from Crescent Hills.

Most of the meat here is shipped off to God knows where. This place sees plenty of money come in and go out, but the numbers don't actually add up. We're just doing his bidding.

Still, I cut the fucking carcass up like I'm told, and stay on the right side of a would-be enemy while I have to.

I vaguely wonder how long that'll be. And when the time comes, which side I'll be on.

The bells hanging over the front door bells, two cheap bells that ding and then ding again as the door is open and closed quickly.

My gaze rises and goes back down, only to rise again with an unsettled feeling flashing through me, to take another look.

Chloe's not dressed to be out in public. She's in pajama pants and a baggy t-shirt with sneakers that aren't even laced like she couldn't get out of the house fast enough. Her hair's down and windblown.

"What the fuck is she doing here?" I mutter beneath my breath and drop the knife on the cutting board. Before I can even wipe my hands off, she's brushing past Eddie, ignoring him completely. She doesn't hesitate to go around the counter and make her way back here. "Sebastian," she gasps my name with a mix of relief and desperation.

My heart pounds harder as every man and woman in this place watches us. I can feel all their eyes on me as I keep my shoulders straight and head to the sink to wash my hands. I'm trying not to let her or anyone else see what I'm feeling deep down in my gut. This isn't a good look.

"I need you," Chloe speaks before the swinging door that separates the kitchen from the front of this small shop even closes.

The adrenaline pumps harder in my veins.

"Aren't you supposed to be at work?" I ask her although my gaze is focused on Eddie. I try to swallow but can't, so instead, I watch the water run down the drain before turning off the faucet and drying off my hands. She doesn't answer me, but she steps closer to me at the sink.

"What are you doing here?" I ask her in a harsh tone with no room for her to question how I feel about this shit. No one comes here. No one who knows any better. *She* should know better.

Her baby blues flash with something—shock, or anger—I'm not sure which. Her loose t-shirt nearly slips down her shoulder as she takes a step back. The place is silent save the exhaust fans as she takes a moment to look me up and down.

"I need you," she tells me honestly, with a sincerity that everyone could hear, even if only spoken in a whisper. She brushes her wavy hair behind her ear and moves her gaze to the vinyl floor of the kitchen, blinking away the emotions ravaging her. The muscles of her throat tighten as she wraps her arms around herself. "Do you have a minute?" she asks as if she didn't just run back here and disrupt everything while having no consideration for what she's doing. The type of danger she's putting herself into.

With a deep crease in the center of her forehead and a pained expression in her eyes, she tells me again, "I need you." It's the third time she's said it since she got here, but she's never said those words to me until today. Fuck, I can't describe what it does to me. Her left foot kicks the floor as she slowly seems to notice everyone else as if they didn't even exist before.

I watch her gaze as it moves to Eddie, who's looking at me curiously and I give him an icy stare until he looks away.

I know he tells Romano everything that happens and having her come in making a scene like this is something that would get his attention. Talking to me about something as if I can save her… that would get his attention too. Romano needs to know everything, or so he tells us. But I don't plan on telling him shit.

Especially because it's her. And the way she's going about this is going to cause problems.

That anxiety comes rushing back, not just from what everyone else is wondering, but also from what Chloe has to say.

"Aren't you supposed to be at work?" I ask her again and toss the hand towel onto the steel counter.

"Angie keeps asking me that too," she mutters beneath her breath. Swallowing thickly, she looks over her shoulder before gripping my forearm and whispering, "I need to talk to you."

Her pale blue eyes plead with me, sinking deep inside of me like she always does. And for the first time in so long, I wish she wouldn't.

"Did something happen?" I ask her innocently, every hair on the back of my neck standing on end. I can hear people moving again, going back to their business, but they're quiet and slow to move. They're listening to everything.

"Did you see the news?" she asks me, and I stare back at her straight-faced as I shake my head no. I already know what's coming before she keeps going. It's only now that I regret going to see her; I invited her to think she could rely on me. She doesn't know what she's doing though, and all the shit I'm in right now.

"Tamra Stetson is dead," she tells me in the barest of whispers as if she's speaking a sin in the holiest of churches.

She has no idea what she's doing. She doesn't know how everyone is watching her. Watching *us*.

This city will talk, and word spreads like wildfire. That could be dangerous, but I already knew I was fucked. I just can't risk her going down for this.

"Why don't we go out back?" The question is really a demand as I grab her elbow. Her gasp is short-lived as she walks quickly beside me and my grip on her tightens. Using my forearm, I shove open the back door and pull her out back. The heat and the sun are blinding for a split second.

There may be no one out here, but there are plenty of people watching. Listening. It'd be naive of me to think that Eddie is the only person keeping tabs on me for Romano. Waiting to hear something they can use against anyone who has anything they could want.

Like her.

Chloe hisses between her teeth as the door closes with a loud clack. "Did you have to be such a dick?" she asks me with a fierceness I fucking love.

She rips her arm away and the action makes her shirt slip off her shoulder, showing me more of her soft skin and the dip in her collar.

The second she sees me looking there, she pulls it back into place.

"You should know better than to come here," I warn her, keeping my voice low, making sure she hears the threat. She's reckless, beautifully so, but it's dangerous. Right now, I can't have it.

"I need you, and—"

"It can wait," I cut her off, feeling my heart slam harder. Every time she says those words it does something to me. It rips me apart knowing how badly I want those words to be true and how wrong she is.

"But Tamra—"

"No one gives a fuck about Tamra." My answer is brutal, and I bite it out quickly, defensively even. Enough that I notice the change in my tone, but she doesn't.

"You don't understand, I wrote this list." She barely gets the words out before shoving half a sheet of paper against my chest. It's ragged like it was ripped from a spiral notebook and crumpled up before being smoothed out. It looks old as fuck and takes me a moment to recognize what it is.

Seeing the column of names on that piece of paper sends ice through my blood.

"Each in order," she says, and I hear her swallow before she looks back up at me. "It's every name in order."

Amber
Barry
Tamra
Mr. Adler
Dave
Andrea

"I didn't put last names, but look at them, look at the list." She doesn't have to explain it for me to know. "It's happening right in order," she continues and struggles to breathe as if every word is suffocating her.

All the recent deaths have taken place according to this list. First Amber, then Barry, and now Tamra. Everyone knows about Jeff Adler. He'd been with Chloe's mother that night in the bar bathroom. He told the cops he'd heard her screaming but didn't feel like dealing with her. He's a piece of shit, always has been.

"Why would you even write this?" I can feel my anger and the tension in my body. The heat that's running in my blood, but the sight of her changes it as her hands wrap around my hand holding the note.

"Tell me it's a coincidence," she begs me with a choked voice. The tears in her eyes linger and she only stares at the paper, rather than returning my gaze that I know she can feel. She struggles to breathe again and then covers her mouth.

When she lifts her eyes to mine, everything in her begs me to answer her with what she wants to hear. "Tell me this is all a coincidence, please. I keep dreaming about them. My mother and…" She trails off, but her regret and remorse are palpable. She shakes her head when I don't answer, as I stand there stunned by the raw emotion and innocence.

"I'm just going crazy, aren't I?" she asks me, and I let the tension between us wane. I give her a moment to calm down as she lets out a hard breath of air. "I'm just having these nightmares and—"

"Was there another name?" I ask her, cutting her off, and rub my thumb against where I can feel the indentations from a pencil. Where it's obvious she put her own name down before erasing it. I know it was there, just beneath Andrea. I know it.

She chooses to go the route she always does with me, she lies, shaking her head and sending her hair swishing around her shoulders.

She grabs the piece of paper, trying to calm herself down and collect her composure.

"I wrote down the names of all the people who I thought deserved to die. I wanted them to die when they said they did nothing to help my mother when they admitted it with no remorse. I wrote it years ago, but just remembered it this morning when I turned on the TV. I was getting breakfast… and…. and suddenly I remembered. And when I saw it…"

The sound of a car backfiring in the distance makes her jump, but then her eyes close as she shakes her head as if admonishing herself. Her eyes open slowly and the pale blues stare at nothing.

"What if someone found this?" she asks although I don't know if she actually wants me to answer.

"It's in your hands," I tell her with strained frustration.

The huff she lets out is short and full of bitterness. Shoving the paper into her purse, she keeps going, keeps letting her emotions get the better of her.

"I've literally gone crazy." She wipes at her eyes although she doesn't dare cry. "I just don't understand. It's three in a row, like a fucking checklist." The anger comes out before she breathes in deep and says softly, "That's not a coincidence."

Spearing her fingers in her hair, she grips onto the roots at her temple. Her shoulders are hunched, and she looks worse now than she did years ago. "It's not a coincidence," she says quietly and her voice is shaky.

It looks bad. It looks really fucking bad. I can see why she'd be freaked out, but this isn't the way she should have handled it.

I can hear her breathe in sharply as I lay a hand on her shoulder, but I make sure to keep my touch gentle, and she slowly melts. Every bit of her is breaking down.

She licks her lower lip and struggles to look me in the eye as she tells me, "Ever since they found him…" She trails off and rolls her eyes although sadness and guilt even, mar her expression.

"Calm down," I tell her as she takes in a breath. "You're all right." I try to pull her in close to me, to be close to her like I was a few nights ago, but she pulls away enough that my hands fall from her.

She looks me in the eyes as she confesses, "Ever since that night, I've had these nightmares… My mom…" She takes in a shaky breath.

"You need to sleep and eat and let it all go, Chloe." I hold her gaze as I take a step closer to her, willing her to let it go. "People die."

"They're being killed," she replies forcefully, although her bottom lip wobbles. Her eyes dart from me to the door as she takes a half step back. "I dreamed of her last night," she whispers darkly. "With Tamra. And the others before."

Letting out a breath, I straighten my back and run a hand through my hair. Behind the butcher's is a mechanic shop and I stare at a patch of rust on an old beat-up hood as a wind gust blows by and the heat lets up for a moment.

"You didn't do this," I tell her without looking at her.

"I feel like I'm going crazy," she says in a sad voice that forces me to look at her. Her doe eyes reach mine. "Truly crazy, Sebastian."

"You're scared and searching for meaning where there is none," I tell her, hoping she'll just drop it already.

"I don't know what to think, but it's not—"

"A coincidence?" I cut her off, staring into her eyes and forcing her to let it go. "It is. That's all this is."

Her head wavers with the smallest of shakes and she looks at me bewildered. "But even you said the cops would think—"

"Jesus," I cut her off again and run a hand down my face. "Is that what got to you?" I ask her, tilting my head and staring at her like she should know better. I can feel my brow furrow as she struggles to come up with an answer.

"Chloe, you can't be doing this. You need to sleep-"

"I did!" she protests.

"More than one night," I add. "And you need to eat. You need to take care of yourself and stop worrying about those assholes."

She lifts her hand up to her shoulder and lets her thumb drag along the collar of her shirt as she looks out onto the mechanic's shop. "It's just a coincidence?" she asks me, although it sounds more like a hopeful statement. I wait until her eyes are on me to tell her, "Yeah, you're just tired, Chlo."

She holds my gaze for a second and I swear if it had been a second longer, I would have had to look away.

"I'm sorry," she says with another shake of her head. Biting down on her bottom lip she looks away from me and says, "I didn't mean to come here and…"

"You definitely shouldn't have come here," I tell her with a seriousness that makes her flinch.

"I…" she starts to respond and then corrects herself, "I said I was sorry." The instant the words slip from her, I can feel her walls start to go up. For a moment I had her, but I'll be damned, I don't want to lose it. Not again.

"Come have lunch with me." I don't offer her an out or a chance to turn me down. Feeling the heat get to me from the direct sun, I wipe my hand down the back of my neck. "You need to eat anyway."

"I don't know that I should," she tells me although her words come out as if she's asking a question.

A huff of disbelief leaves me. "So, you think it's okay to come here and talk to me about people being murdered?" I wait for her eyes to meet mine before I continue. "But going out to lunch is where you draw the line?" I let my expression show a bit of disappointment, even a little sadness. She's always been a sucker for that.

"I'm sorry." Her expression shifts to one of sympathy as she says, "I didn't mean—"

"I know what you meant," I tell her and splay my hand on the small of her back, giving the shop one more look before guiding Chloe around the building to the front parking lot. "You need to eat."

CHAPTER 7

Chloe

THIS DINER ISN'T REMARKABLE, BUT THE FOOD IS. I THINK IT'S ALL THE SALT they put on everything. They even put it on the pizza.

Even though it's my favorite place to eat, I'm surprised I was able to eat anything at all.

The fear and paranoia are embarrassing. I'm fucking embarrassed I got so worked up this morning. It's just… finding that list and the nightmares really got to me. I felt like I was drowning in a childish fear that still has its claws rooted deep in my thoughts.

The fear faded to uneasiness when Sebastian talked me down. Just being around him makes me feel safe and protected. If I could be with him always, I would. Because he settles something deep down inside of me. He makes me crave more. More from life, but also more from him.

A different kind of nervousness took over the moment I got into his car. The soft leather was something I didn't expect. The hum of the air conditioner and the occasional clearing of Sebastian's throat were the only noises the entire ride.

This morning, I had to tell someone and he's my only someone, even if that's a pathetic truth. I didn't think twice. He didn't answer his phone, so I went to where I knew he'd be. It made every bit of sense to me at the time.

Until I slipped into his car and was engulfed in his scent. Until I peeked at him as he drove his car with an air of dominance and authority.

In a room with other people, or even in a room I'm used to being in, Sebastian is still the boy who kissed me. But alone, in his car, something changed. And suddenly I lost my voice along with every thought I ever had, except for the dirty ones that crept up late at night about Sebastian doing more than just kissing me.

Today has been nothing but a series of fucked up thoughts running wild in my head.

"What's on your mind, Chloe Rose?" His deep, rough voice breaks into my thoughts and I take my time reaching for another fry, carefully taking a bite before answering him.

"Just wondering about how much can change in a single day."

I can feel the heat rise up my chest and to my cheeks, all the way to my hairline as he leans forward, his broad shoulders stretching out the t-shirt as he tells me, "I would swear you were thinking about something else."

His steely blue eyes seize all my attention and hold me accountable. I can barely breathe, but he doesn't need the confirmation. He's plenty full of himself already, so I simply eat the rest of the fry and shrug. I ignore the butterflies and the desire to push him for more of that teasing side of him. This is the part of his personality I've craved, but I don't want to appear desperate or say something stupid. I don't want to ruin it. I can barely believe I'm here with him. I don't even want to think about it for too long; I'm afraid if I do, it'll all go away.

His cocky half smirk is what makes me look anywhere but at him as I try to remember how I ended up here with him.

Thoughts that I wish I hadn't tried to return to.

Remembering when my mother died, how I felt the same way. Afraid and paranoid. I felt like no one understood why I was so completely distraught. The mix of emotions never felt right, and I never had any control over them. They hit me relentlessly, like the constant blow of boughs as I was forced to run through trees in a forest. Swiping at me, scratching me, taking me by surprise. I was only a girl, but old enough to remember, old enough to know I could have done something.

"I thought I was done with all this," I tell him absently.

"How's that?" Sebastian asks me with his brow furrowed and a look in his eyes that's compassionate and curious. This is how I imagined he'd look when I read those texts all that time ago. It was only an image conjured in my head because I'd never seen anything of him other than the hard, dangerous boy he wanted everyone to see.

"Do you really want to know?" I question him, the uneasiness returning. He nods his head once and I figure, why not? I have no one to talk to and after this, I'm not sure he'll even talk to me again. So why not let it all out?

"I thought I was over feeling like this…" Before I can finish, the air conditioner blows across my skin from above me just then, and a flow of goosebumps trails down my arm and shoulders making me wish I hadn't picked this seat.

"You want to switch spots?" Sebastian asks and again, I'm surprised he would ask me that.

I gently shake my head and try to recall what I was thinking only seconds ago. Before Sebastian destroyed my thoughts again with a mere five words. He's good at that.

Clearing my throat, I stare down at the half-eaten pile of fries and remember the gut-wrenching feeling and sickness of what's to come. The living in fear and agony part. Oh yes, that's what he took my mind from.

"I thought I'd gotten over this feeling of being in constant state of fear and guilt." I don't look at him as I speak this time. If I do, I'm not certain that my mind will stay on course. "Even after you…" I don't mention what he did, and my gaze almost darts up to meet his eyes, but instead, they fall on his lips. "Even after school let out that year," I say, choosing to settle on the time rather than the action we both know I'm referring to. "Even then, at night there was this feeling, but it drifted away. And then when my uncle died, I was just angry." My voice raises at the thought, my breathing coming in faster.

Sitting back into my seat, I look at him and feel as if I should feel ashamed, but I'm not.

"Angry?" he questions.

"Yeah. I was angry. It wasn't fair that I was stuck here." Emotions threaten to come up at my admission. I loved my uncle and he'd passed only two years ago, right before I graduated high school. I was old enough to take the shit debt he left behind. "I know it's not his fault; he wanted better for me…"

I don't finish that line of thinking. "The point is, I thought I was done with all of this. For the first time in so long, I was fine."

"You were relying on yourself. So, of course, you were fine." Sebastian sounds confident in his response, but he doesn't get it. Parts of me are so thoroughly broken that even the idea I have to rely on myself is horrifying. Rebecca used to say it was understandable after the trauma I'd been through. What she called trauma, I just called my childhood. No wonder I turned to books and writing to help me cope. Getting lost in my stories was a lot more enjoyable than facing reality.

"Everyone needs someone," I answer him, holding his gaze and praying he can feel what I mean. That he can know how deeply settled I am in that decision.

"You didn't have a someone, and you were fine."

I almost answer him with, I didn't say everyone *deserves* someone. Almost. But I decide to swallow it down. I sure as hell don't want his pity.

The ping of my phone distracts me from the conversation. Sebastian's here with me, so it must be Angie. Pulling it out, I see I'm right.

Where the hell are you? Stop being a bitch and answer me!

Angie certainly has a way with words.

I'm not coming in. I send her the response and then think better of it and add, *I'm sorry. I'm just not feeling all that well today.*

Before she can reply, I silence my phone and slip it back into my purse. She wouldn't understand. She'd think I'm crazy. Shit, I think I'm crazy. My heart beats a little faster at remembering the pure fear that ran through me when I saw Tamra died. My name was on the bottom of that list. If someone else made a list like mine, would my name be on theirs too?

The chill from the air conditioner comes back and I let my head fall back with my eyes closed, suppressing the urge to feel anything at all. I'd rather be numb to it all. Goosebumps prick along my skin once again, slowly this time. It's just the chill, I tell myself. It's definitely from the air conditioner.

"Who's that?"

Sebastian's question distracts me from my thoughts and I open my eyes slowly to tell him, "Nobody."

"So, nobody texted you?" Sebastian asks with what feels like a touch of jealousy. I'm ashamed by the way my body reacts. I feel a heat that swells from the pit of my stomach, rising up but also moving lower. Forcing a small smile to my lips, I answer him, "Just a friend."

When his expression doesn't change, I roll my eyes at him and say, "I finally got one of those." My answer is pitiful, but I own it. I don't care that I'm a loner who prefers books and writing and hiding away in my stories. Books are cheap, and the people in them are better than the ones I have left here.

He looks like he's going to say something else, but he doesn't. He finishes his drink and then reaches for his wallet.

"I can buy lunch," I offer. "After all, I kind of ruined your day." He cocks a brow and doesn't answer me. Instead he puts some cash down on the table, more than enough to pay for both of us.

"I said I can get this one," I tell him and reach for the cash to shove it back to him, but he snatches my wrist. Electricity shoots through me, the desire returning with a blazing force.

He releases me slowly and I bring my wrist back to me, staring at it as if it's been singed. I'm reeling in the shivers that flow through my body.

"I pay," is all he says, with a forcefulness that spikes desire through me. I can't break his gaze, I can't speak.

"I want to," he adds in a gentler tone.

"How do you do this to me?" I ask him, but then I think of a different question. "Why are you doing this?"

"Because I want to." He uses the same intensity as before, but somehow his words come out softer, almost comforting. The tension is thick between us and I wonder if he feels the same pull I do. "Why did you come to see me?" he asks me, and the question breaks the spell, my eyes falling to the table and the realization that the lunch is over. That this moment is only temporary, just like Sebastian's presence in my life.

"Because I wanted to," I offer him a similar response, shrugging and then pulling up the baggy sleeves to my t-shirt. How is it that hours have passed, and I've only just now realized I'm in my pajamas? I didn't even bother to put on mascara. I always put on mascara, I look so much younger without it.

"Are you going to tell me why you're doing this?" I ask him again, feeling irritated by everything, especially my reaction to the series of events that happened today.

"I just wanted to have a nice meal with you." Hearing those words from him makes me smile and let out a short laugh. My mirth doesn't wane when he looks at me with confusion, instead, it only makes me grin harder. Maybe I truly am crazy.

"What'd I say?" he asks, and I just shake my head, taking a peek at him while lowering my lips to have a sip of Coke from the straw.

I let the bubbling fizz relax me and then straighten myself to tell him, "Just the thought of you having a nice lunch and then heading off to your nine-to-five job."

The charming grin grows on his face, revealing his perfect white teeth. "Don't you know I'm a hardworking, blue-collar type of man?"

I hold his gaze and keep my smile in place as I tell him, "I know who you are, Sebastian Black."

My taunting doesn't get me the reaction I'm after. Instead, he slips his mask back into place, hiding from me.

My next breath is accompanied by a long stretch and then I take another drink. A coldness sets in between us. I can feel it coming. It used to come so often when we were forced to be together. The moment he knew he'd let me in, he'd shut it down.

I should have known better than to think it would last. Maybe I didn't think it would, but I sure as fuck want it to.

"Something is truly wrong with me," I speak the thought without conscious consent.

"You're a product of your environment," Sebastian answers me. He sinks back against the booth and stares at me long and hard. The fake, thin leather protests as he watches the front door.

"I should get home," I tell him, so we can end whatever this moment has been. "I'm sorry I came and…. decided to be crazy and vent to you."

"I'm not." He answers me the same way he did with paying for lunch. No nonsense, no bullshit. And the same response flows through my body. For years, in school and up till the day my uncle died, I wanted him to be like this with me. To just talk to me.

"Be careful what you say at the shop though," he tells me and then adds, "people listen." The tone in which he says it brings an uneasy feeling over me and with a tightness in my throat, I start to tell him I'm sorry, but he cuts me off.

"Just so you know for next time." The softness to him, it does something to me I can't explain. *Next time.* As if I could have this moment again with him.

"You're different," I marvel at the revelation out loud.

"I'm not the one who's different."

"What do you mean?" I search his eyes for answers, wanting to know how he meant me to take that statement. *Needing* to know.

"Does it matter?"

"I don't know what matters anymore."

"What do you know, Chloe Rose?"

The way he asks it, or maybe it's just my own thoughts, but it feels like the way he asks it is so much dirtier than what he actually asked.

"I know I should go to work or go home." Neither of those options sounds appealing, but both are true.

"It'll already be two by the time you get to work," he says and shakes his head, "don't bother."

"Home it is then," I say, easily conceding, and reaching for my purse as I scoot out of the booth to stand. "Thank you for lunch," I tell him and then add, "I can walk since it's—"

"Let me take you home." He doesn't look me in the eyes when he gives the command, he doesn't even look at me. It's clearly non-negotiable, so I don't bother objecting.

The drive back to my place is even worse than the drive to the diner. Thankfully, it only takes about four minutes. And two of those were spent at a red light.

"I really could have walked," I tell him as I slip out of his car. He opened his door first, intent on getting out rather than just dropping me off, so I walk a little quicker, eager to get to my front door first and cut him off there. I just want to be alone for a while. I want to hide away if I can. I need to process everything, but Sebastian has a way of bringing me out of my hiding place and showing me more of this world that makes me want to risk living.

"Should I come in and look around?" he asks as his car keys dangle from his hand. He stands in front of me expectantly, but I can't give him that.

"I'd prefer it if you didn't." The moment I unlock the door and turn around, I block the doorway and put a hand on the doorknob. It's only open wide enough for me to stand in the gap comfortably. "I think I need to decompress; today's been a lot to handle."

He cocks a brow at me in that way I like. "You wouldn't lock me out, would you?"

The way he asks makes me smirk, which slowly shifts into a genuine smile as I consider him. He's so tall, so much taller than how he is in my thoughts. And his shoulders, so wide. He could protect me from anything. That pull to him is so strong it's scary. But Sebastian himself doesn't scare me, not in the least. He never has. It's the power he has over me that's terrifying. "I would… but if you asked to come in, I'd let you."

My answer puts a smile on his face that matches mine. "See? I told you, you're different."

I huff a laugh, shaking my head. I'm not so sure that I'm different. It's more like I'm letting him see more of me. That's not the same thing.

He leans in close as I fail to summon a response, so close that I know exactly what he would want if I didn't lock him out tonight. I'm in over my head with him, hot and bothered and wanting the same thing he does.

I need to get away from this city more than ever.

"Get some sleep then," he says softly, in a deep, rugged tone when my eyes meet his. The carnal need that burns in his gaze sets my body on fire. I'm still standing there, watching him walk away when I can finally breathe again.

What is he doing to me?

The feeling deep in my gut, the one that used to be constantly present, still lingers as I walk up the stairs. Something is telling me it's not all right, it's not a coincidence. But that something is quieted by the thoughts of Sebastian and the idea that if it's not all right, I can run to him. It brings out a strength in me I desperately need. He does that to me. And I find it hard not to be drawn to him even more because of it, my stupid heart especially. He's been good at hurting it in the past, but it still wants more of him.

CHAPTER 8

Sebastian

THE SECOND HER DOOR CLOSED, I FELT EYES ON THE BACK OF MY HEAD. I COULD feel someone watching. But when I turned around, there wasn't a single soul in sight. No neighbors on their porch, no kids playing in the street.

Fuck, I'm just as paranoid as she is. The sound of my boots slapping on the cement stairs pounds as hard as my pulse does in my ears.

When I get in my car, I lock the doors but don't turn the key in the ignition. Not just yet. The light in her bedroom isn't on and I wait, staring at the curtains until the soft yellow glow floods the window. Even though dusk hasn't hinted at its arrival, I can still see she's turned on the light.

I'm tired as fuck. I couldn't sleep last night, and I don't have a clue when I'll finally be able to rest easy again. The image of Chloe in my bed soothes the beast inside me. The caged animal that needs to be released. If she was next to me, in my arms and in my bed, I'd sleep then.

I pick up my phone and call Carter, needing some relief tonight and wondering if he'd drive by and keep a lookout for me. I don't like the way she's thinking and worse, the way she's acting. I can't risk her doing anything stupid, like telling anyone else about that list.

The phone rings. And rings. An unsettling feeling in my gut churns until he picks up. I'm reminded that his mom's doing worse and worse. One day he'll answer and tell me she's gone. I fucking dread that day. The cancer's been eating at her for two years now; she doesn't look like herself anymore with all the weight she's lost. She can't go anywhere without getting winded. It's only a matter of time at this point.

"Hey man, I'm having a rough time. I was just about to call you."

"What's going on?" I ask him, feeling guilty that I forgot the shit he's going through.

There's silence for a long time before he tells me, "It's just getting harder."

"You all right?"

I can hear him swallow before he replies, "As all right as I can be." I forget what it's like to have a family, let alone what it would be like to watch someone you love to slowly die in front of you. "You need me to do anything?" I ask him.

Again, there's only silence.

"Nah," he says, "What is it you needed?"

With his question, comes a beep signaling I've received a text and instantly I think it's Chloe. Looking up and watching as the light goes off and the window loses its light, I answer him, "It was just a passing thought, it doesn't matter."

"You sure?"

"Yeah," I answer him. "But if you need anything, let me know. I got you."

I don't rush getting off the phone with Carter, but he does, ending the call right then with the sound of his father yelling in the background. My heart goes out to the kid.

More than a time or two I've thought about showing his dad what it's like to have someone take out their anger and fear on a man, but I don't know if Carter would forgive me for stepping in. Or whether it would just make things worse on him. His family is his. It's what he told me when I suggested it once. I never want to get between him and his family. Never. No matter how fucked up they are.

The second the line goes dead, I check my text messages, but the message isn't from her.

Are you going back on your word?

I read the text from the unknown number with a mix of anger and fear coloring my consciousness as I stare at the words.

I turn the key in the ignition, although I know I'll be back tonight once the sun has set. I'm dead set on staying right here tonight. Right in front of her house until the early morning's passed. I don't need to sleep. I can sleep when I'm dead.

I answer, *No, I understand what I have to do. She's staying out of it. She doesn't know.*

The unknown number replies, *Good. I'd hate for you to find out what would happen if you go back on your word.*

CHAPTER 9

Chloe

"YOU DIDN'T COME VISIT ME ON MY BIRTHDAY."

I hear my mom's voice in the pitch black of my dream. The darkness spreads all around me. I can't see.

"I missed you," she says but her voice sounds closer this time and it echoes all around me. The only other sounds are my chaotic breathing and the pounding of my heart as fear filters into my blood. Every pulse feels harder and forces the desperation to get out of here to climb high into my throat.

Run.

I try to run; I try to scream. But I can't.

Open your eyes. Wake up!

I wish I could obey my own pleas.

Slowly my eyes open, but I'm not in my bed. I'm in the alley on Park Street. I swear I feel tears on my face. My throat is raw from hours of screaming. My nails are broken and there's blood everywhere. The metallic scent of it, the feel of it dried but still sticky and wet in other places over my skin, it's all I can smell and feel.

My body is so heavy.

"Why didn't you come visit me?" My mother's voice taunts me as I try to lift my head. My body's heavy, lying on the ground. My cheek is flat against the cold, hard asphalt.

"I wanted to sing you a lullaby, baby girl. I miss being your mama." I feel fresh tears start.

"Please don't," I whimper where I am. The pain flows as freely as the fear of seeing her again. I wish I could run.

"So, did I, baby girl," my mother responds to my unspoken thoughts. "Or for someone to help me," she adds.

I hear footsteps behind me and my heart pounds harder and faster. The adrenaline in my body is useless.

On instinct, I scream for help, but my voice is so quiet.

"No one can hear you, baby girl." She's closer. My body trembles and I try so hard to move, but not a single limb obeys. I try my fingers. One by one, please. Please move, but nothing moves. I'm cemented where I am.

"Well, maybe they can, but they don't listen."

The chill from the night air gets colder as a darker shadow covers my body. She's behind me now. I try to swallow, so I can clear my throat and beg her, but it's pointless.

"It's time for your lullaby," she threatens.

"I promise I'll sleep." My words come out as a strangled plea. I remember the way the heavy base of the glass vodka bottle landed against my temple. She didn't sing it like this, so calmly. It started out this way though. And once she started, she never stopped. Not until I was unconscious. She knew when I was pretending. She always knew.

"Go to sleep," she sings to me in a gravelly voice, dry and slurred from drinking, "go to sleep, lit-tle Chlo-e."

Tears stream down my cheeks.

"Close your eyes, rest your head."

Remembering how she beat me furiously with the bottle.

She drags her finger across my skin, trailing along the curve where my neck meets my shoulders. Her nail is jagged and slick with fresh blood. Pulling my hair behind my neck so she can whisper in my ear, she finishes the lullaby, "It's time for bed."

CHAPTER 10

Sebastian

I DEBATE ON SENDING THE TEXT. I'M STARING AT THE PHONE IN MY HAND LIKE I'M back in high school.

You didn't go to work today either?

The words stay right where they are, waiting for me to send them. I know she's all right; no one's approached her, no one's messaged her. Although, she hasn't left the house since I walked her to her door. Not two nights ago, not last night and she called out from work again this morning.

I know she's in there. I've been watching every inch of that place.

"Mr. Black." A man's deep voice disrupts me from my thoughts. Sitting at the lone desk in the back room of the shop, I can see him through the open door. He's standing in the front of the butcher shop, peeking behind the counter, and trying to get a look into the kitchen.

"Officer Harold," I answer him in a monotone and slip the phone into my pocket. I just got in and didn't see his car in the lot. But I didn't check for it either. I didn't do anything except worry about leaving Chloe Rose alone in that house. She's getting to me even worse than she did back in high school.

All I can do is think about her, and that's a mistake. For both of us.

"What can I do for you?" I ask him as I walk out of the back and head straight toward him. As I cross my arms, I make a mental note of who all's in here. Eddie's behind the front counter and watching everything, although he's pretending to go through the weekly invoices. I don't know why he bothers putting up a front. Officer Harold is in Romano's back pocket and Eddie knows that. As does everyone else who's working in the back.

So that means Romano sent him, or this is a test.

Either way, I don't care for it. Other than Eddie, I don't think anyone else is here yet. Which could be bad news for Eddie if this goes south.

"Have you heard about the recent killing spree?" he asks me and gestures to one of the two small tables in this place. They're circular with peeling, flaking vinyl on the top and thin metal legs that match the rickety chairs. They're dated and not meant to keep people wanting to stay. Most of the people who come in here pick up their packages and leave. Those who decide they want to hang around often change their minds as quickly as they can sit their asses down in these spindly seats.

"Killings?" I question him like I haven't thought much about it. The sound of the metal feet of the chair dragging across the floor makes Eddie cringe as he peeks up from scratching his pencil on the notepad. "I know Tamra Stetson was shot and killed, I heard about that the other day."

"Tamra and before her, Barry Jones, a few days before him a girl named Amber Talbott was found dead." Officer Harold doesn't sit like I do. Instead, he remains standing. Fucking prick.

I push back the chair and spread my legs wide as I sit back and shrug. "I only know what you know," I offer him, and he gives me a smug smirk.

"And what is it that you think I know?" he taunts me, sucking his teeth and keeping his back to Eddie. Eddie doesn't hide the fact he's watching.

Again, I shrug and say, "Whatever's in the paper and on the news."

It's quiet for a moment. Not a sound from anything. Not the air conditioner, not the cars outside. Nothing as he watches me, looking over my expression. I keep it easy and relaxed. It's something I worked hard to accomplish. You never let them see a damn thing from you. Carter said his dad taught him that once. That you don't give anyone anything. It's the one thing Carter taught me that's helped me survive longer than I would have otherwise.

"And what about your girl, Chloe?" Officer Harold asks me, and Eddie stops jotting on his pad. The scratching of the pencil halts and my heart pounds heaviy. I can feel my lips twitching on my face to pull down into a scowl and the need for my forehead to show a sharp crease.

I want to rip out his throat for even mentioning her name. I wish I could see her right now. That I could see she's safe and ensure they'll leave her out of this. Adrenaline pumps hard in my blood knowing she's involved now, but she did that to herself when she came here. Fuck, I wish I could take it back.

I can protect her though. I *will* protect her; I'll make this right.

"Chloe Rose?" I say her name and force my face to soften, to stay casual wondering how the best way to play this would be. I rub the stubble on my chin and look past him. "What about her?"

"Why did you go to see her?" he asks me. Anxiety races through me. She's always flown under the radar. Gorgeous and tempting, but no one's paid her any mind. No one wants to deal with the sad girl who's stuck here with no one and nothing. Now she's a person of interest, all because of me.

"She came to see me," I correct him.

"That's not what I heard." My pulse pounds at my temples. And again, I struggle to keep my composure. I feel my throat get tight as I swallow.

Letting out a low sigh, I exaggerate. "A few nights ago, she was walking home." I meet his eyes to add, "Alone. And the streetlight went out. Spooked her some."

His eyes stay hard as I sniff and shrug my shoulders. "She wanted some company. I checked out her place. I don't know if you know this, officer, but someone broke into her house a while back."

His eyes narrow; I know damn well that he knows what I did. I had to tell Romano, who tells Officer Harold when he doesn't have to go searching for a killer. Problem is, Romano doesn't know who's doing these killings. Romano should know if I had something to do with it, I'd tell him. The fact that Officer Harold is here is telling. The uneasiness flows through me the more I think about it.

I shrug. "I guess she liked that I was willing to give her some company." I tilt my hips up some, implying a little more happened. "I liked it too."

"So, this has nothing to do with Tamra Stetson or the killing spree?" he asks me and sucks his teeth again, but his demeanor has changed. No longer on the attack, instead he's desperate for a lead.

"It's freaking Chloe out some, being alone and watching these girls turning up dead… which is only helping me get laid. But I don't know shit that could help you."

"Just to clarify." The good officer puts both hands on the table and leans forward, getting so close I can see where he nicked his chin when he was shaving. "For everyone," he adds, although the heavy implication is that Romano will hear about whatever I say. I already know that though. This little visit was obviously triggered by Chloe running in here the other day. I know damn well that Romano doesn't know shit, and neither does this prick.

"Whatever you want to know," I say and stare him dead in his eyes, feeling the tension rise.

"You don't know anything?" His eyes search mine as I answer him, "Not a damn thing."

My heart beats chaotically and I swear if he could hear, he'd know I'm lying.

Sniffing and standing straight, Harold fixes his shirt, tucking it back in. "If you hear anything…" he says even though he's already walking out. With his back to me, he doesn't bother to give any parting words. Only the sound of the bells bids him farewell.

"What's up his ass?" I ask Eddie even though my eyes are on the glass door as it closes behind him.

After a moment with no response, I look over at Eddie, but he's already gone. The notepad remains on the counter, the top piece ripped off.

There are enemies everywhere. Every step of the way.

The deeper I get with Romano, the less likely it is I'll ever have a chance to leave.

CHAPTER 11

Chloe

THEY FEEL SO REAL. THAT'S WHY I CAN'T SHAKE THEM.

The nightmares are something I was used to when I hadn't come to terms with the reality.

My mother's gone.

She died years ago.

I remind myself once again and blow across the top of the full cup of tea in my hands, but it's no longer hot, it's barely lukewarm. I've only just now realized I must have been holding it for a while without even taking a single sip. I'm slow to set the cup down on the end table and then reach for the blanket. My fingers grip on to the soft woven fabric like it can save me. Just as I used to think when I was a child.

My mother's gone.

She died years ago.

It was hard to say the words back then, but I have to keep saying them now.

Not because I don't believe them, but because every time I fall asleep now, she's there, haunting me and saying things that scare me. Things she knows would put true fear into my heart. She's reminding me of memories I've long buried.

She's angry and wants revenge for what happened. I can feel it. Her killer joining her six feet in the dirt isn't enough justice. She's starved for more. A taste of his blood wasn't enough.

When I wake up breathless and terrified by how realistic the dreams are, I can feel the weight of her hand gripping my arm, but no sane person would believe me. I would just sound crazy.

I'm going crazy. I know that's what they'd say and as I pull my knees into my chest on the sofa, I struggle to deny it. I'm fucking insane.

All I can think, is that whatever Sebastian gave me is fucking with my head. I can't sleep without seeing her, without *feeling* her. I swear the scratch on the back of my neck is from her.

I don't want to go to sleep. I only took the sweets, as Sebastian calls it, that one time, but I've been so fucked up since then. Although, so much more has happened since then too.

My fingers press into my tired eyes, feeling the burning need to sleep and I remember how I woke up last night, sweating, crying, my throat raw as if I'd been screaming.

I prayed like I'd never prayed before and when I whispered for someone to help me, I felt the coldness of her presence. As the chill traveled up my spine, I swear I heard my mother whisper, "I am."

A sudden knock at the door has my heart galloping in my chest. Two days of not sleeping but also not knowing what to do has left me jolting at every sudden sound.

"Chlo," I hear Sebastian's voice call out through the front door and he knocks again as he says, "Open up."

Just hearing his voice is calming, and I easily swing my legs down and listen to my bare feet pad across the floor as I go to unlock the door and let him in.

I swing open the door without even looking in the small mirror in the hall to see if I look presentable. I'm sure I look like hell, and I wouldn't keep him waiting, so it doesn't matter anyway.

With his hand still raised to knock again, we both stand there for a moment, waiting for the other to say something. I swallow thickly, feeling the nervousness rise up again. He's never taken so long to say anything before.

"You look like you're ready for me to drag you to bed," he finally tells me and then steps inside, not waiting for me to invite him in.

"If you're lucky, I'd let you." I try to make it sound like a joke, but at this point, I would. "I feel like I'm going to fall over," I tell him groggily and turn my back on him to saunter back to the living room, but he grabs my wrist as he kicks the door shut behind him.

It closes with a click.

"What?" I ask him, staring pointedly where his fingers are wrapped possessively around my wrist. "I wasn't serious. You aren't dragging me anywhere."

Keeping my face deadpan, he cracks a smile and then I mirror his, a small simper of a smile, but it doesn't reflect anything that I feel.

"You okay?" he asks me.

Blowing a lock of hair away from my face and straightening the strap of the tank top on my shoulder I nod and ask, "What's going on?" No matter how much I want to tell someone about my nightmares, I refuse to speak the words out loud. It would only make me sound unhinged.

"The cops wanted to know why I came to see you."

Cops. That was the last thing I wanted to hear. My stomach drops, as does my gaze and I pick under my nails to distract myself.

"How would they even know?" I ask him without thinking, but if I'd just let it sink in for one second, I'd know better. *Everyone here is crooked, everyone knows everything.* It was the only good advice my mother ever gave me. *If you keep that in mind, you'll be all right.*

"Ignore me," I tell him absently and rub the tiredness from my eyes as I walk to the sofa. I plunk back down into my cozy seat and pull the throw blanket around me again.

When I peek up at Sebastian, he's eyeing me with a look I can't place. "What did you tell them?" I ask him to get the attention away from me.

"Well, I had to tell a white lie."

"What did you say?" I whisper and fight off the yawn that threatens.

"I told them you meant something to me and I was just checking in on you."

It's quiet for a moment as I take in his words. I have to remind myself of what he said. Me meaning anything to him is a white lie. The thought makes my fingers ball into a fist under the blanket.

"Okay," is all I give him as I sit there, with my neck craned so I can stare up at him as he stands in front of me.

"And now they think we may be a thing." His eyes assess me, and if I wasn't so tired, I would blush, practically ignite like I've done before. But right now, all I can think is how he said it was a white lie.

I almost ask him what a white lie means, so he can tell me to my face in blunt terms that I don't mean anything to him. Instead, I just ignore it all and focus on a pounding ache that grows in my temple.

"What's in that stuff you gave me?" I ask him a question that's been nagging at the back of my head.

"Nothing serious." His forehead creases as he answers me. "Why?"

"It feels serious to me," I tell him. although my heart beats rapidly, begging me not to push him away with my insanity.

The moment passes, and with the silence, the tension grows.

"What happened?" he asks me. "Are you sick?" The concern in his voice is so genuine that I nearly tell him to be careful, that everyone will see that I mean something to him. But the spite and jabs from his white lie comment mean nothing to me right now.

He's here. He's listening to me. Whether he realizes it or not, I know I mean something to him. So, I couldn't care less if that's what the cops think. I couldn't care less about people running their mouths or any of that right now.

There's only one thing haunting me at this moment.

"I'm just…" I trail off and swallow thickly, burying the words in my throat.

"When's the last time you took it?" he pushes for more information as he takes the seat next to me, making the old sofa groan with his weight. He sits closer to me than I sat to him last time. He's so close, I can still feel that heat that lingers on his shirt from the summer sun.

"I only took it the one night." I look up into his steely blue eyes and watch the grey flecks mesmerize me as I add, "The night I texted you."

"You're supposed to take it every night, Chlo. It doesn't stay in your system for long."

"Are you sure?" I ask him quickly. "Because it feels like it's still in my system."

The sofa protests as I readjust in my seat to face him more and he asks, "Have you been sleeping?"

I only nod with a small frown gracing my lips as my chest tightens with worry. "I don't want to though," I whisper the confession.

"Chlo," he scolds me, immediately running the middle finger and thumb of his right hand down his temples. His large hand covers his eyes as he does it.

"Don't do that," I bite back, not hiding the sadness and disappointment at his reaction. "I'm not a child and I'm not okay." Although my voice wavers, I say the words as strongly as I can.

He lets out a heavy breath as his hand drops to his side and my eyes plead with him to understand.

"I'm afraid. I'm dreaming these things…" I gulp down the confession and settle on a simple truth as I conclude, "and it's not okay. I think it's what you gave me."

"You think the sweets has something to do with what you're dreaming about?" he asks me, and I can only nod with a tension in my stomach that threatens to make me sick. "Tell me," he says, and his command is soft and comforting. As if confiding in him will make it all go away. "Tell me what's got you worked up like this."

"It's my mother," I tell him and struggle to confess to him that every time I drift to sleep, I relive the hell that existed before she died. Every memory I've shut away and buried with her is back. "I feel crazy because the nightmares are so real." I can feel myself breaking down and the moment Sebastian notices, both of his hands are on me. One on my thigh, rubbing back and forth and the other on my shoulder. I'm in a sleep shirt that comes down to my knees, my legs covered by the blanket. His right hand though is touching my bare skin. The rough pad of his thumb rubs soothing circles against my collarbone and I lean into it. I've never felt the need to be touched so gently before. The need to be held.

If I had even a hint that he'd still respect me after, I'd climb into his lap right now.

"It's all right." His voice is strong, but also frustrated and it reminds me of that day back in high school. He's barely keeping it together as he takes me in.

"I'm sorry." I don't know what else to do other than apologize. "I don't want to be this way," I plead with him to understand. "I think when I drank the—"

"It's not the sweets. It's what's going on around us. This shit is bringing up old memories. The drug is just a knockoff pharmaceutical. Most people don't even know about it. It's like any other sleep med, Chlo. A friend gave it to me to sell, but no one buys sleep meds off the street."

"You don't understand," I tell him.

"Make me understand."

I think long and hard about exactly how to explain it. It's not an old memory. These terrors are so real and lifelike, they don't leave me when I wake up. "I'm scared," is all I can say, and the confession comes out as a whisper.

"I want you to come spend the night with me," Sebastian speaks like it's a request, but it's not. I can hear it in his voice and along with the shock is something else.

Desperation.

I can't move, thinking I've misheard him. All I can do is stare into his eyes and listen to every single beat of my heart.

"It's in my best interest to keep an eye on you," he tells me slowly and then licks his lower lip. It's slow and sensual but there's something else there like he can't quite figure something out. "You look like you could use some company. It'll do us both good."

He gives me five minutes to gather a few things. It hardly takes me that long as I toss my toiletries on top of a stack of folded clean clothes and grab my purse. That's it. I don't bother with anything else.

We're not driving far, but even so, the car ride is quiet in a way that absorbs my every thought. Sebastian Black… and me. Maybe one day I'll wake up and all of this will be a dream. Or maybe one day, he'll come with me and we can run away from this nightmare.

"Haven't you ever thought about leaving?" I let the internal thought wander to my lips as I rest my cheek against the car window. The hum of the engine and the gentle vibrations threaten to lure me to sleep, but I fight it.

"You don't think I want to leave too?" he asks me, taking his eyes from the road to look at me. I don't answer, I just take him in, right here at this moment. The strength that is Sebastian Black, veiled with the secret that he'd rather run away. My heart hurts for him in this instant; I always thought he ran this city and that he thrived because of it. How foolish I was. I realize that now as he tells me, "When you figure out where you're going to run to, let me know."

CHAPTER 12

Sebastian

I DIDN'T EVEN THINK TO BE EMBARRASSED OR ASHAMED UNTIL CHLOE STOPPED IN the foyer. All I was thinking was that I was done leaving her alone. I don't have a good feeling about any of this shit and I just want to keep her close. I never considered what she'd think of my place though. Or what she'd think of me.

"Welcome home," I tell her as I toss my keys onto the skinny kitchen counter next to the pile of unopened mail I got yesterday.

There's a sofa, a coffee table, and a TV. Nothing else in this room. It's never looked bare before, until now. It's never felt like it was lacking in any way until I see Chloe not moving from where she is.

The sofa came with throw pillows I didn't like, so I tossed them out, but there's a standard bed pillow and an old blanket in a heap on the far end of the sofa. That's where Carter sleeps when he needs a place to crash.

This house is small, with only one bedroom and the kitchen is the size of a freaking dime, directly across from the living room. But I paid with cash and I own it. That's the only thing I was looking for when I knew I needed to leave my ma's old place. There was too much shit there. Too much of the past cluttering and smothering my every thought.

"Not what you expected?" I ask her dully and keep walking to the sofa to take off my shoes.

I have a nice car and nice threads for when I need them. All my cash is hidden in the floorboard under my cabinet sink. I don't spend anything I don't have to. You never know when you may need to run, and I'll have the cash for that, make no mistake about it.

"You're such a man. You could at least grab a candle at the corner store or something. Maybe hang a picture?" she suggests, and her lips pull up into a teasing smile.

She finally walks into the room, kicking off her shoes next to mine and slipping into the side of the sofa Carter usually takes. She goes to grab his blanket, but I stop her. It's weird seeing her gravitate to his things. And to want his things.

"You can have the bed," I offer her and then add, "That's Carter's stuff."

"Oh." A shyness spreads through her expression as she gently pushes it away. "Sorry," she adds and then clears her throat. "Do you have a throw for out here?" she asks.

"You like being under the covers, don't you?" I ask teasingly, and it makes her smile.

as she nods. I like that. I like how I can make her smile. I like that even when she's worked up and upset. When her mind is wandering to disturbing things, I can make her smile and give her something to take away the pain.

"Let me grab you the other blanket," I say as I stand up. There's a small linen closet outside of the bathroom, and I have my old blanket in there.

"I don't know that the Cross boys like me much," she tells me from the living room even though I can barely hear her in here.

I just washed the blanket the other night and I can still smell the laundry detergent as I bring it out to her. "Why would you think that?" I ask her and play dumb even though I know why she would.

"My mom was kind of into their dad once, and couldn't take a hint," she says softly, but cheers up when she sees my blanket. "Ninja Turtles?"

A huff of comforting humor leaves me as I nod.

"You aren't your mom. They know that," I say to try to ease her worries.

"Yeah, but…" she starts to say, but I shake my head and she trails off, waiting patiently to hear what I'm going to tell her. She brushes a lock of hair behind her ear and snuggles into the sofa, resting her head on the back cushion.

"I know Carter, and he likes you just fine. More than he likes most people." I focus on Carter, not his family. It wouldn't be fair to blame Chloe for her mother's mistakes. That'd be like her judging Carter for his father's actions.

"I think he's all right, too," she says softly with her eyes closed, nestling deeper into the sofa.

"I said you could sleep in the bed, Chlo," I remind her and watch as her eyes slowly open, giving me more of that soft blue mix of pale hues that look through me.

"I don't want to sleep," she tells me just above a murmur.

A sickness spreads through my chest and down to my gut, settling into a heavy pit there. "You need to sleep."

Even though my words are hard and non-negotiable, she gives me a sad smile. "No shit. I can't stay awake forever, but it feels like I'm trying."

"You don't like the sweets?" I ask her, remembering what she said about it fucking with her and making her remember shit she didn't want to. "It's just supposed to relax you. I think everything that's going on is messing with your head."

"I don't want it to happen again." Sadness slowly seeps into her eyes, but she doesn't elaborate.

"Don't want what exactly?" I ask her, and her expression falls completely as she searches my gaze.

"They're just nightmares," she whispers, and I don't know if it's more to convince herself or me.

"They come and go; you can't stop them by running yourself into the ground like this," I tell her and run my hand over the back of my head. As I do, I feel the weight of my own exhaustion taking over.

"I have Benadryl. I could go get Nyquil?" I give her some options, just hoping she'll take something. The person who gave me the sweets made it sound like it was the best thing to take to relax and sleep easy. That's the only reason I gave it to her. It worked for me and I thought it might help her. "You gotta sleep, Chlo."

"I know I do," she tells me and then readjusts her head on the cushion until she's more comfortable, but still looking at me. The look of exhaustion drives a primal need inside me to help her sleep however I can. Even if that means fucking her into my bed. The thought is only a flash in my vision of her legs wrapped around my hips, her heels digging into my ass as I pound into her. A split second of that thought has me rock hard instantly.

I want to kiss her again, but that would just complicate everything. It feels good to have someone needing you like this though. Wanting you and letting you get close.

Word is already going around. As long as I do what I'm supposed to, maybe I can have her...

"Let's go to bed," I suggest, readjusting and trying to ignore the aching need that's pressing against the zipper of my jeans. I've wanted her for so fucking long. With a quick glance at her curves hidden beneath the covers, I start wondering if she'd let me. If she needs me like I need her.

"Sebastian, tell me you didn't bring me here just so you could fuck me." Her voice is breathy, but there's a tinge of fear there. She hasn't moved from where she's sitting, but she's still as she waits for my answer.

"Why do I keep finding myself telling you that you should know better?" I expect her to flinch at my tone, or to drop the subject altogether. I don't expect her to press me, which is exactly what she does.

"So, you don't want to sleep with me?" she asks, and I don't hesitate to tell her, "I want to fuck you more than I want to breathe right now."

Chloe Rose's eyes widen and her breath hitches as my blood heats.

"But it's not why I brought you here, and you know it," I add.

I can hear her swallow as she glances at my throbbing cock. "We can just go to sleep. I'm tired too," I offer her.

I hadn't realized I was holding my breath until she nods her head. "Okay," she says, already pushing off the sofa and standing up with a yawn. "Should I bring this one too?" she asks, holding up the corner of my blanket.

"Leave it there," I answer her and start walking down the hall. I walk slowly so she knows to follow, and she does. Her footsteps are soft and hesitant.

Pulling back the sheets for her, I look over my shoulder and then nod to the left side of the bed, the farthest from the doorway where she's still standing.

She has one hand on each side of it, and in her sleep shirt, her legs are on full display. Smooth and lush. She rubs one calf against the other as she nervously waits in the doorway. "No funny business?" she asks.

"Not unless you want," I tell her, feeling the disappointment overwhelm me. I've thought about having her here for years. Literally, years. I have to stare at my nightstand as I strip out of my shirt. When I unzip my pants, I see her walk around the bed, but more importantly, I feel her eyes on me. Her lust-filled gaze doesn't see mine on hers as she nearly walks into the bed in her rush to get under the sheets. She doesn't notice how I watch her lick the seam of her lips as her gaze travels down my body.

And I'll never forget how her eyes widen and her bottom lip drops slightly for her to take a deep inhale when I kick off my pants and she sees what I have for her.

Every fucking inch of it will slide into that tight cunt of hers.

Maybe not tonight, but knowing how much she wants me, how much she's desperate for what she sees, brings a cocky smirk to my face that I can't hide.

When the sheets stop rustling and Chloe's nestled under the comforter, I ask her, "You want to be the big spoon or little spoon?"

And I'm rewarded with the sweet, sarcastic laugh I knew she'd give me.

"No spooning," she answers with the smile still firmly on her face.

"You sure?" I ask as I slip into bed beside her. "It can get a little cold, you may find yourself wanting some warmth." I cock a brow, but she's not having it. "I'm practically a heater myself. My body temperature is just a little hotter than normal."

When she laughs this time, I smile wider and set my head down on the other pillow in the bed. She rubs her eyes and then rolls over to lie on her side, facing me with both of her hands tucked under her pillow.

"You're the different one," she whispers, reminding me of the night I dropped her off at her house when she said I was different and I said it right back to her. "This wouldn't be so easy if you were still the way you were before."

I have to lick my lower lip to keep from saying anything. She has no idea. "I guess we're both a little different, but can I tell you a secret?"

She only nods, her hair ruffling against the pillow as she does. "I've always wanted you."

With her teeth sinking into her bottom lip, she tries to stifle her smile, but she can't.

"Aw, aren't you cute when you blush?" I tease her, and I'm rewarded with a little more of a smile.

"What if we did do something?" she asks after a moment. Her breathing picks up and I can feel her nervousness.

I nearly groan from my cock leaking precum at the thought of doing *something* with her.

"What kind of something?" I ask her, doing my best to tread lightly. I get the feeling that she'd run from me and put those walls back up if I made a single misstep. I'm so eager to be inside of her, I could stumble and fall my way down a flight of stairs into fucking this up.

She shrugs and waits for me to say something.

"Is there anything you wouldn't do?" I ask her out of pure curiosity. With her hips, the image of her face down on my bed with her ass up is everything I want right now. My cock stiffens again at the thought and this time I let out a small groan.

Her eyes travel away from my gaze and downward.

"I'm sure there's a lot I wouldn't do… or maybe not," she says absently. "My friend said she liked being choked." The mention of choking catches me off guard. Of all the things for my innocent Chloe Rose to say, that wasn't one I couldn't have guessed.

"You want me to choke you?" I ask her, not hiding my surprise.

"No!" Pushing her hand against my chest, she backpedals real quick. "You were just asking what I wouldn't want to do but I don't know what that list would be." She nestles back down as I try to think of what she needs to hear next.

I know what I want to say. I want to go through my list of all the dirty shit I want to do to her and then have her tell me where her limits are. But I'm pretty sure that'll have her jumping out of bed faster than I can finish my laundry list of how to make Chloe Rose cum harder than she ever has before.

Confusion mars my face; I can feel it in the deep crease on my forehead. "I'm getting some mixed signals here, and I don't want to fuck this up." It's such a simple thing to admit that, but as I swallow, I feel more vulnerable than I have in a long time. Probably since the day she ran from me in school, when she ran out the door and I followed her.

"I don't want to fuck it up either," she whispers and then leans in closer, pressing a small, quick kiss to my lips. Before I can deepen it, she's already pulling away. My hand was already half up, ready to spear through her hair and keep her pressed to me, but I'm too slow, too shocked that she'd make the first move.

"If we did do something, it would only be because I think I would sleep really well after," she tells me softly, watching my expression and judging my reaction.

"You love lying to me, don't you?" I ask her with a cocked brow as I stretch out, putting one arm behind her head. She lets out a small laugh but also inches closer and rests her cheek on my arm.

With her thumbnail between her teeth, she keeps her arm up between us and I don't miss how the bottom half of her body is still farther away from me.

I glance at the clock and see how late it is before taking a look back at her, nestled in my arm with her eyes closed.

"What if tonight you take from me, whatever you want?" I offer her and then say the second half of my suggestion when her eyes flutter open. "And tomorrow night, I take from you. Whatever I want." My blood pressure rises instantly at the thought of her agreeing. I'm hot and wound up and ready to make a deal with her. "Whatever you want," I add.

Her lips part and there's a sudden movement of the bed along with the comforter. "You have to squeeze your thighs together like that?" I tease her even though the very thought of her scissoring her legs right now is killing me.

"We can do that," she agrees in a single breath. Again, she inches closer, so close, but her ass is still pointed the wrong way.

"How do you want me?" I ask her and then add, "Tomorrow night when you're ready, that's how I want you to ask me too." I'm so damn hard at the thought of her asking me that I nearly lose it when she nods her head in agreement.

"So, how do I want you?" she asks, her wide doe eyes shining with a desire that must reflect my own.

With my body coursing with adrenaline at the thought of fucking her tonight, I nod my head and say, "Tell me what you want."

She turns away from me, and for a split second I think she's going to say she doesn't want to do anything, but then she brings her ass closer to mine and all that desire rises inside of me again.

She peeks over her shoulder and grabs my hand, kissing the tip of my fingers one by one as my heart beats faster and faster. "I want your hand here," she whispers and pulls down her panties while telling me, "I've never been fingered; I want you to get me off with your hand."

I don't believe her for one second, but I don't argue. I don't even consider arguing.

All I can focus on is that she's in my bed, taking off her panties and telling me she wants me to finger fuck her. I'm content getting to third base from Chloe tonight because tomorrow night I'm getting everything I want.

Planting a small kiss on her jawline, I let her move my fingers between her legs. She's hot and already slick with arousal. Fuck, I don't know how I don't immediately cum just from grazing my fingers across her clit.

"You're so fucking wet," I tell her the second my fingertips touch her hot entrance. I force back a groan as I push my fingers inside of her. "And so tight," I comment out loud, but the next thought is whether or not I can even fit my cock inside of her. I have to work my fingers in slowly, pressing against her front wall and holding her body down as she bucks out of instinct.

Her hips tilt up and I press my thumb against her clit. Slowly she adjusts, letting me push my fingers in deeper and deeper and stroking her front wall to get those sweet sounds to spill from her lips in a strangled moan.

Her cry of pleasure is accompanied with her pushing her head back into my shoulder as her neck arches and her body begs to do the same.

I'm barely inside of her and she's already so responsive. So easy to pleasure. As her hand moves to the back of my head, her fingernails scratching as they go down my scalp, I lean forward to kiss her neck. I'm teasing and slow with each calculated kiss, nipping and biting from the sensitive part just below her ear down to the crook of her neck.

My eyes stay open the entire time as I push my fingers deeper and deeper inside of her, working her and desperate to warm her up so she can take me.

"Fuck," she moans a muted sigh of the word. My fingers press against her front wall, rubbing hard and forcing her pleasure from her, all while keeping my thumb pressed to her clit.

Her body writhes against me as she tries to turn over, to move away, but I wrap one leg around hers and move my arm around her chest, pinning her body to mine and holding her in place. Strangled moans are all she gives me as I pump my fingers in and out of her cunt.

My touch turns ruthless as her heels slam into the bed and she frantically grabs at the sheets. She's so fucking close. "Give it to me," I command her through clenched teeth. I can't even breathe, knowing how close she is.

"Bastian," she's moaning my name as her body trembles with my relentless touch.

I've never heard anything sound so fucking perfect as Chloe Rose moaning my name.

"Say it again," I command her, and she gasps while yelling it at the same time, "Bastian, Bastian!"

I can't help rocking my hips against her, loving how she does the same, grinding her ass against me.

"I want you," I beg her, pressing my cock against her, the only shield being the thin fabric of my boxers.

I've never wanted a girl this much. I've never felt the need to be inside of a woman like this before. I need her. I need to feel her pussy wrapped this tight around my dick. My heart races with hers as she gets closer.

"I want you," I moan again against the shell of her ear as I press my dick against her ass, searching for relief. Instantly her pussy clamps down on my fingers, tightening and spasming as she cums.

I cum violently with her. If she wasn't so preoccupied with her own climax, I'd be embarrassed that I just came in my boxers, dry humping her.

I take my hand away from her slowly, letting her sag on her side as she tries to catch her breath. I have to hide that I'm doing the same as I flip my fingers in my mouth and make sure she's watching as I suck.

"You taste sweet too," I tell her and smile wide when she blushes that much harder.

"How did that feel, Chloe Rose?" I breathe against the shell of her ear before nipping her lobe. Pride and the heat of my own orgasm roll through my chest.

"Bastian," she whispers my name as sleep finally claims her. Her body's still trembling next to mine.

"Answer the question," I say before getting up to wash my hands and get her a washcloth, but she shakes her head slightly before I leave the room, ignoring my question as she passes out in my bed.

CHAPTER 13

Chloe

I T'S AMAZING WHAT A GOOD NIGHT OF SLEEP CAN DO TO A PERSON. AND A GOOD fuck for that matter.

Sebastian was right, I was just tired and needed to sleep. It all feels so stupid now, even though the uneasiness still lingers whenever I hear whispers about the recent murders.

I can still feel Sebastian inside of me. Even as Marc, my boss, gave me a ridiculous lecture about how many sick days I have left, all I could think about was how Sebastian touched me last night.

Not just touched me. There isn't a suitable word for what he did to me. How he dragged the pleasure from me in a way I didn't know could exist.

And that was just foreplay.

The memory of how his lips felt, how his hard body felt, how his hard cock felt…

My nipples harden as a shudder rolls through my body at the thought of tonight. Sebastian is handsome, classically so with a darkness that hints at danger, but last night, everything about him resembled a sex god. The way the dim light caressed his stubble, the way his lips seemed to pout and then glisten when he licked them. And his eyes swirled with a desire I imagine could never be tamed. It's more than just lust though. The more I'm around Sebastian, the more I let myself believe there's something *more* between us.

The click of the air conditioner in the office brings my gaze up to it and then to Angie, sitting in the desk chair cross-legged and on her phone. While I'm on the floor with six piles of paper as I try to organize these documents alphabetically by last name.

"Oh, my God," Ang drags out the last word as she throws her head back and stares at the ceiling in exasperation. "Can it just be five already?" She drops her gaze to me and I have to crack a smile.

"Hard day?" I taunt her, knowing she didn't do shit. We had four clients come in today. So, she checked in four people. And that's all she's done. For eight hours.

I sit upright, stretching my back. "We could switch on Monday?" I offer her, and she tilts her head.

"I don't know why you even agreed to that shit," she tells me while making a circle with her pointer finger to encompass the papers on the floor, right before going back to her phone.

Agreed? It's my job. I bite my inner cheek to keep from responding. I need my paycheck. I need to add it to my meager savings.

The thought of why I'm so desperate to save up makes my heart squeeze in my chest.

It's so I can leave and get out of here. But things have changed. That would mean leaving Sebastian and whatever it is that we have going on now.

It's odd to feel so much, so quickly. To feel that raw loss at the thought of one day getting out of here. I'm so used to feeling lonely that it didn't take much for me to feel some sort of attachment to him. Although that feeling has come and gone for years and yet every time, I know there's something between us I'd never have with anyone else.

It only took that single kiss years ago to know that.

"I say we just get out of here," Angie suggests, interrupting my thoughts.

I shrug at her suggestion. "Marc won't notice, that's for sure."

I'm not leaving this city any time soon. And whatever I have with Sebastian will more than likely be short-lived. I'm still shocked it's happening at all.

I'll be counting the days until it ends.

Even knowing that, so confidently certain it will end, I'm still going to give myself to him tonight. I didn't question it for a moment.

I was always his to take. And that's exactly what I want. For him to be my first.

My breathing comes out shaky as I realize the clock is ticking down to that moment and I still haven't decided if I'm going to tell him or not.

"Okay, let's just get out of here." Angie hops down from her seat, letting it roll backward and carelessly slam into her desk as she slips her ridiculously high heels back on.

"Why do you even work here?" I feel the sarcastic question slip out before I can stop myself. I feel like half a bitch, but with the nerves of what I'm going to do tonight, I'm not as careful with my words as I should be.

Angie pauses for a second and then laughs, loud and unrestrained. She shrugs, slipping on the first heel and then the second. "The perv wanted to hire me," she says and looks up at me as she continues, "and I had to pay my rent."

One point for honesty, I suppose. "Fair enough." I can't argue with that. Pushing on my thighs, I force myself to stand up and stack the piles, so I can get back to filing tomorrow and not lose my place. As I'm setting a generic glass paperweight on the stack, Angie asks me if I want a ride.

My heart does a somersault, the weirdest movement as the jitters set through me. It's been like this on and off all day.

I'm going to go to Sebastian.

Sebastian Black is going to fuck me tonight. All the anxiety and nerves mix in the pit of my stomach. Maybe if I keep telling myself it's just sex, my heart will start believing it.

"I'm good; I'm going to walk." I think I do a good job at keeping the nerves out of my voice, but I have to stare at the stack instead of looking at her.

I can feel her eyes on me though, and when I peek up, looking as innocently as I can at the only woman I've ever met who owns her sexuality like she does, she asks, "You sure?"

That little place between her eyebrows is scrunched and I'm sure she can tell something's off, but I'm not telling her shit. Not. One. Word. I don't want advice; I don't want to hear stories. Worse, I don't want her to tell me the list of women he's screwed. She has a habit of doing that whenever a man's name comes up. She's a walking encyclopedia of all things sexual and provocative.

"Yeah, I'm good," I tell her nonchalantly, and her expression tells me that she isn't buying any of it, but she doesn't ask again. She grips the doorway once, looking between the pile of papers I refuse to take my eyes from and then back up to my face.

"See you tomorrow then?" she asks and then adds, "You're not going to take another mini vacay, right?"

The smile she gets from me is genuine. "Your concern is adorable," I tell her and roll my eyes before adding, "but no, I'll see you tomorrow."

"All right, sweet cheeks," she says while tapping the doorway, "See you in the morning."

"Have a good night, Buttercup," I tell her and then scrunch my nose at Buttercup. I could have come up with something better, but the more I let it sit, the more I like it.

I listen to her heels as she walks out and then immediately grab my bag and head out the back, rather than the front. The stairwell is all concrete steps down the back, which is why no one ever leaves this way, but it heads to the north part of the city, where the butcher shop is.

My fingers feel sweaty as I pull my purse onto my shoulder, the nerves kicking into high gear.

Every step I get closer to him, I get more nervous about each detail.

I don't have sexy lingerie, but I can wait for him naked.

I didn't pack all of my makeup yesterday when he brought me back to his place, only my mascara, so that's all I have to work with.

I have to clear my throat to get the knot out of it as I get closer. I know he's working, and he told me to come to him when I was done, so I am.

Part of me recognizes how… docile I'm being. The only thing that keeps me moving forward and only mildly second-guessing all of this, is how easy Bastian is making it for me. He's not giving me hard glares until I look away. He isn't pretending I don't exist. He isn't ignoring me.

Something changed and I don't know what, but he still makes me feel safe. He always has. I may be crazy in other ways. But I know what I've felt for Sebastian for years has merit. There's something real between us, and that's not a white lie. And I wish one of us would have the courage to say it out loud because deep down I know that neither of us can deny it.

⸻

I don't know if they'll let me stay here now that my uncle's dead. He died last week and right before my eighteenth birthday. The lawyer said he willed everything to me, but with the debt he left behind, they may have to take the house from me to put into the estate.

And then I'll have no one and nowhere to go.

Those are the thoughts that keep me up tonight even though I know school will come tomorrow. I can't keep skipping class, so I need to sleep, but I can't.

I'm so fucking angry. That's what I feel most guilty about. I had one person who barely even spoke to me, but he let me stay here, and occasionally it felt like we were family. Uncle Travis was a good man, a trucker his whole life, but he didn't much like other people. A lot of the time, I wondered if that meant me too. Being alone for so long will do that to you.

He came home two weeks ago, and we talked about what was coming after high school. Tears flood my eyes again at the thought and I angrily brush them away.

Even if he wasn't physically here for me, or even if he never showed me much of anything other than a place to stay, I knew without a doubt last week that he loved me.

And now he's gone. It's not fair.

I take in a staggered breath and try to calm down as I cling to my pillow. I've never felt as selfish as I do now, being filled with anger when I should be mourning him.

What's wrong with me?

Just as I think the question, I hear the floorboards creak behind me, toward the open door to the hall.

A shiver runs down my spine as my eyes open wider and then narrow. Swallowing thickly, I know it wasn't just the chill in the air that made the old boards bend in the night. I can hear whoever it is walking closer.

It better be him, I think bitterly as I reach slowly into the nightstand. My uncle left everything to me, and that means his gun too.

"You don't need it," the deep voice calls out from the doorway just as my fingertips brush the cold metal. Slowly shutting the drawer, I let my eyes close and try to calm the adrenaline racing through my body.

"Why are you here?" I ask him without turning to face him. My chest aches with a pain I can't describe. Sebastian used to come all the time at night when I first moved in here.

"It's been a while," I tell him and hate the nostalgia in my tone.

He's quiet; he always is.

He kissed me, he followed me, and then he left me alone.

"I'm fine," I tell him and then turn in bed, slowly bringing myself up to sit cross-legged under the covers. "As fine as I can be." Years ago, when he'd come, he wouldn't leave until he believed me when I said those words.

And I loved him for it. Truly and deeply, I loved him for it. If it had been anyone else, I'd have been terrified, angry and a mix of everything hateful, but it's not just anyone. It's Sebastian.

Tears cloud my vision of his dark shadowy frame in the doorway.

"You don't look fine."

"Well gee," I say sarcastically, bitterly even as I wipe my eyes. "So kind of you to point out the obvious." It's been years since he's visited me and I'm not the same person I was back then. I've stopped praying for him to come and wishing he'd slip into bed with me and hold me.

I don't want to be held by anyone anymore. Even as I think it, I know it's not true.

"Just go," I tell him and then lie down, turning my back to him and pulling the covers up closer to my face so I can use the soft bedding to wipe at my eyes. "You're good at leaving," I add and hate myself for even bothering to speak with him when he merely chuckles. It's a deep low rumble that fills the bedroom and sends a shiver of want across my skin, igniting something I thought was long forgotten. It seems the hate I have for him leaving me, ignoring me day in and day out isn't enough to drown out the desire to be held by him after all.

"Someone told me you might be leaving."

"Who said that?" I barely speak the question. My heart does a stupid pitter-patter at the

thought of leaving him. My heart is stupid. I listen as he walks into the bedroom. He stops somewhere far from the bed, but I don't know where and I don't turn to look at him.

"Are you leaving?" he asks me.

"I hope not," I answer him, and the truth of that answer makes me close my eyes tightly. I couldn't wait to get out of here, but I need a place to stay. Everyone needs a home, somewhere they can run to.

"Is it money? Or are you moving somewhere else to be with other family?" he asks me.

"There is no other family," I admit, feeling lonelier by the second.

"So, it's money?"

Time ticks by slowly until I answer him, "Yeah."

He's quiet and doesn't say anything for a long time. So long, I think maybe he's left me until he says, "It'll be okay. Go to sleep, Chloe Rose."

I remember thinking how much I wish I didn't want him to be here as I drifted to sleep, feeling his eyes on me. But I did. I had no one. And of everyone in this place, he was the only one I wanted. So, if that was the way I could have him, I'd take it.

I don't know if he heard me later that night when I woke up and started to cry out of nowhere. I confessed how much I missed him and how lonely I was as I wiped the tears away, still huddled in my spot, gripping the pillow. Or maybe that part was a dream. It's hard to know anymore.

CHAPTER 14

Sebastian

"WELL, YOU ONLY HAVE ONE MORE YEAR," I TELL CARTER.

"I don't have time for it," he answers me as he bounces the old tennis ball against the worn brick of the building.

"You don't have time for school?" I ask him in a tone that's as filled with disbelief as my expression is. "Remind me again, where is it that you make your money?"

Carter's being a dipshit. "You don't need to start working for Romano. You need to graduate, and you can make that extra cash from the schoolyard."

He's a dealer at Crescent Hills High, only pot but he makes some good cash since he's the only one with good shit in this area. The only other dealers are past Walnut Street and the highway that runs behind it, but those are claimed territories, one of them being Romano's.

"Romano's never going to hire you anyway since you're Irish."

I feel like a prick reminding him that he'll never be trusted, but it's for his own damn good. He should be focused on finishing school and then he can figure out a way to go down south and make some good cash at the fishery on the docks or some other shit. Something better than this.

"You don't get it." His voice is tight and his teeth are clenched. "We have bills."

He throws the ball harder at the wall and catches it after it ricochets with a force that sounds like it hurt. "You forget there's more than one person I have to look after."

It fucking hurts every time he brings it up. To me, he's my kid brother. To him, he's the older brother taking care of his family. A family I'm not a part of.

"It's good money," I remind him. "Both the fishery and the pot. Romano's not going to pay you shit."

I'm still shaking my head when he looks back at me. "Because I'm fucking Irish?"

"Because he doesn't have a need for you." I'm blunt and harsh and my stomach twists. There's no room for him in Romano's territory, but even if there was, I'd lie. He doesn't have the stomach for this shit. He should be better than me. He *is* better than me. I get paid to fuck up people who owe money to the wrong guys, assholes who think they can steal from establishments who pay for protection. I get paid to be a villain, a thug, and a version of myself I hate. It used to help with the anger; it made me feel like there was a purpose to it.

all. But that's bullshit. I fucking hate who I am, and I don't want this life for him. I don't want it for anyone.

It's quiet other than the thud of the ball hitting the brick as he considers everything.

"It's just one more year, Carter."

"A lot can change in a year." His voice is muted, low and defeated. I know he wants a change because of his mom, but I can't help him there. I can't keep her from dying. The rubble beneath my feet kicks up as I walk to the cement steps and face the parking lot.

"Is that Chloe?" Carter asks me, and I have to get up to look down the street.

Just the sight of her pulls my lips up into an asymmetric grin. "Yeah, that's her."

"So much for picking her up," he tells me with a glint in his eyes. I check my watch and see she's early, then peek back up at her.

With her jeans hugging her curves, I watch as she walks up the street, not taking my eyes off her.

"Real quick," Carter tries to get my attention, so I give him a short hum of an answer to let him know I heard him, but I refuse to look away from her as she walks to me.

"Can you come with me to give my dad that money?" His question is enough to break the stare I have on her. He adds, "Tomorrow night?"

"Yeah, of course," I answer him with a shrug like it's no big deal. His mom's bills are adding up, so I'm loaning him some cash to keep them afloat. But the last time I did that, Carter's dad laid into him, thinking he stole it and wanting to know from where.

It's not really a loan, as I never want to be paid back, but Carter insists I call it that. For only being sixteen with not much to be proud of, he's a proud kid.

"How is she doing with everything?" Carter asks to change the subject. I know that's why he did it. "Is she still freaking out?"

My gaze is brought back to her as he asks. Nice timing on his part, as she's just walking up the parking lot.

"She slept at my place last night," I tell him. She slept easily and deep like she hadn't slept in years, waking up with a yawn and a stretch that was so relaxed and at ease. Although the second she saw me, she blushed violently and tried to hide under the covers. "Good morning," were the first words she greeted me with as she covered her mouth and hid under the sheets.

Carter's chuckle cuts off any thoughts of sharing particulars. "So that's how you deal with it," he says and nods his head in approval with a wide grin.

If I had that ball in my hands, I'd throw it at him. But damn if the pride in my chest won't go away at him thinking I fucked her worries away.

"Hey." Chloe gives a hello while she's still a good ten feet away, walking through the parking lot and to the back behind the shop where we're standing.

Thump, Carter tosses the ball at the wall, but I don't break my gaze from her. She's already blushing. Her skin is so beautiful like that, with that rosy tinge creeping up her cheeks and growing hotter every second I keep my eyes on her.

"I don't get a hello?" Carter asks jokingly, and for the first time since she's walked up here, her attention goes to him.

"What makes you think I wasn't waiting for you to say hello first?" she asks him, quipping back without missing a beat and with the trace of a friendly smile on her lips. I can see she's a little tense; it's the way she is around people. Tense at first, quiet too, but if she wants, Chloe opens up easily and what's inside is raw and beautiful.

Carter grins back at her as he says, "Hello." He pronounces the word carefully, enunciating each syllable and it makes her laugh although that shyness is still there.

"Are you working here too?" she asks him and the hair raise on the back of my neck. Everyone here works for Romano, but Carter needs something better than this. I keep my thoughts to myself and wait for him to reply.

"Still in school," he answers and she's quick to add, "I always forget you're younger than us."

It's odd how she says it. Like she knows him or maybe she's just paired us together like other people have.

"Were your ears burning?" Carter asks her with his brow raised. "We were just talking about you."

Chloe hums a small laugh with her lips closed tight although she can't hide her smile. "I hope good things," she adds after a moment of the two of us staring at her and waiting for her reply.

"Mostly," Carter jokes with her, but I can tell he makes her nervous by the way her smile slips.

"Yeah," she says honestly. "I kind of figured you might be…" her voice trails off and she offers me a small smile although I can see how nervous she is. She picks at the hem of her shirt while she talks. "I might have been talking about you too," she tells me, biting down on her lip after and looking me up and down.

"Is that right?" I ask her and she's quick to shake her head. "No, I'm just playing."

Carter barks out a laugh while I stand there looking like an asshole.

"I didn't give you anything good to talk about?" I joke with her, but she just clears her throat, slowly letting those walls come back up.

She didn't talk about me because she has no one to talk to. I feel like a prick when the realization hits me.

"I'll make that up to you tonight then," I add before she has to say anything. Her cheeks must be on fire to be that red.

I let my hand travel to the small of her back to lead her away and I nod a goodbye to Carter. He's waiting for the bus to go to the hospital, but it'll be here in minutes. It's almost 5:15.

"See you later, Carter," Chloe says sweetly, giving him a small wave as I walk her to my car.

I open the door for her, but before she can slip in, I wrap my hand around her hip and bring her closer to me. I have one hand on the door, with the other on her hip and her stance mirrors mine. It's as if she's waiting for what my next move will be, so she can determine hers.

Her lips are parted and her eyes dart between my gaze and where Carter's standing behind me.

All I wanted was to give her a small kiss. So, I do, just a short one on her lips. Pressing my mouth to hers and making sure to run the tip of my nose over hers. The cops already know; people are already talking. Might as well give them a show.

That shy smile I love plays on her lips and she can barely look me in the eyes.

"You nervous?" I whisper against her cheek before pulling away. Her wide eyes stay on mine as she settles into the seat and answers honestly in a single breath, "Yeah."

CHAPTER 15

Chloe

My heart's being stupid. It keeps fluttering and flipping all sorts of ways like it's trying to escape or run away. I try to swallow again, but I can't. Instead, I snuggle closer to Sebastian on the sofa, although every inch of his side is covered with mine right now.

It's just sex.

I keep reminding myself. Every time the nerves work their way up from my heart to my brain, I have to remind myself. It's just sex.

Not just that, but every part of me feels like it was supposed to be this way. Like Sebastian was meant to have me. Even the little bits of me hidden away in the pages of my books, all the way down to the marrow in my bones; it was supposed to happen like this.

I haven't told him, although I almost did earlier. We were sitting on the sofa, but not cuddling like this, sitting cross-legged, and eating Chinese food from the cartons. He's been good at keeping the conversation going and giving me those cocky smiles. I think he's drawing it out on purpose.

First dinner and now a movie, although it's almost over.

And thus, my heart is doing that stupid thing knowing the movie will be over soon. I swallow it all down as best I can and nestle my head into Sebastian's chest.

"You comfortable?" he asks me although it sounds like he's picking on me. I only hum a response.

"You can't go to sleep," he tells me, and instantly my eyelids fall shut just to fuck with him. He shrugs his shoulder and I give him a look.

"Stop moving," I complain in as flirtatious of a voice as I can and feel pride rise when he rewards me with that charming smile of his that drives me wild.

He smells like fresh woods, the kind you want to get lost in; his body is hard and dominating. Every piece of him chiseled like Adonis. I splay my hand on his chest and revel in the fact that he's letting me.

Back in school, I thought that he was avoiding me because he was older. At least at first. Then when I realized who he was and why everyone else avoided him, I wondered how a boy like him could be interested in a girl like me. The more he avoided me, the stupider I felt.

When the only piece of reality you crave is revealed to be all in your head, it does something awful to you.

"I like you coming to me after work, but I could have picked you up." Sebastian starts up a conversation as the credits to the comedy scroll on the screen. If someone asked me to repeat a line from what we just watched, I'd come up with nothing. All I'm thinking about is how Sebastian is going to fuck me.

I've masturbated but I don't know if I have a hymen or not. I've used a few toys I've read about in books although I don't often feel the need to do that. Not unless I read a steamier romance. Or one where the hero reminds me of Sebastian.

"I wanted to leave work early. It was a short walk." I answer him with a shrug and try to keep my train of thought on the fact that he hasn't made a move yet. He hasn't done anything other than to put his arm around my shoulder and pull me to close to him under the covers on the sofa.

"You sure like to walk everywhere," he remarks like he doesn't like it.

"I don't mind it." It's one of the things that took me a long time to do alone. I don't know if it's because I was old enough to understand what happened to my mother, or if I was always afraid of walking alone, but learning to accept the fear and proving it wrong is one way to cope. "Sometimes it's nice," I add, swallowing down the memories that beg to ruin this moment.

Sebastian shifts on the sofa and it dips, making me fall slightly.

"You ready for bed?" he asks me, pulling me back up by my waist and shifting me into his lap. His warm breath tickles my shoulder as he kisses me for the first time since we came back to his place. Right on the crook of my neck, sending shivers down my body and hardening my nipples.

My body feels alive with need. Every nerve ending is waiting to go off and sitting on an edge that feels so close.

With both of my eyes closed, I hum a response. "I was wondering what was taking you so long," I tell him as he stands, leaving me with the chill of his immediate absence and forcing me to open my eyes.

He offers me a hand and I take it to stand but he only smirks at me, not giving me any words in the least.

Cue my stupid heart.

It's just sex.

That ball of nerves threatens to suffocate me as I walk in time with Sebastian to the bedroom. He doesn't waste any time stripping down to nothing. So, I follow suit. First my shirt and then my pants, but by the time I'm left in my bra and underwear, he's already naked and stroking his erection.

Oh, my God.

My pussy heats and clenches around nothing. Fire blazes inside of me. I can't take my stare away from him as he strokes himself.

He's cocky as he asks me, "Need a hand?"

A voice inside of me begs me to tell him I haven't done this before, but instead, I meet his gaze steadily and unhook my bra, letting it fall carelessly to the floor. Then I easily step out of my thong, even though I know he's let his own gaze wander to my body.

He doesn't say anything. No comment on my body at all as I walk to the bed and get under the covers. It's dark in his bedroom, but there's enough light enough to see. There's hardly any light from the windows with the curtains drawn even though there are streetlights close by. And he left the hall light on, which he didn't do yesterday, so that had to be on purpose. So, he could see.

Adrenaline races through my veins as the bed groans with his weight and dips.

Still, I feel like he can see everything. Even as I'm hiding under the covers.

"No covers," he says with a playfulness I wasn't expecting. "I get to have you my way tonight, Chloe Rose," he teases me.

"I'm cold." The excuse slips easily from my lips as my heart pounds furiously in my chest.

His lips find mine in a slow, languid kiss. His hot tongue dips into my mouth as he pulls back the covers.

Suddenly, I actually am cold. In every place, he isn't touching me, and I feel like I'll freeze to death if his hands don't find every inch of my body right this second.

He breaks the kiss, towering over me and climbing on top of me to tell me, "I'll warm you up." I expect another kiss, but his lips fall to the dip below my collar. One kiss there, then one an inch below. I can't breathe.

Goosebumps flow down my arms and the heat burrows itself in the pit of my stomach.

"I'm hot," I moan out into the air and then my eyes open wide, realizing what I said. Sebastian could tease me, taunt me for being hot and cold, but all he does is kiss lower and lower, fueling the fire that licks over my body.

By the time his stubble is tickling my inner thighs, my hands are on his shoulders, my blunt nails digging into his skin. I'm at war with myself, not knowing if I want to push him down that last inch or push him away for fear of being inadequate.

A single languid lick from my entrance to my clit has my back bowing.

Sebastian chuckles and the vibrations nearly send me over. My cheeks are hot with embarrassment, but the threat of pushing me over so soon is looming larger and more aggressively than anything else I could feel.

His tongue flicks my clit and again I buck my hips, but his hands are already there, pushing me down and keeping me in place. Panting, I struggle to breathe and to know where to put my hands. So, I grab the sheets and fist them as he sucks my clit and massages it with his tongue.

My toes curl and a strangled sound is forced from me. With my eyes closed, I don't see him, but I feel all of him. He shoves his fingers inside of me and a pool of desire ignites in my core when he does it, forcing my back to arch and sending waves of heat through my body that feel uncontained.

With his mouth on my clit and his fingers inside me, I scream out his name from the pleasure that rolls through me. I push myself into his face shamelessly.

He finger fucks me brutally and doesn't let up on either ministration until I'm biting down on my lip hard enough to hurt and cumming on his hand.

The paralyzing pleasure rolls through me in waves like a vengeful tide, taking from me ruthlessly. I can't breathe or even move as he leaves kisses along my curves and guides the head of his dick to my entrance.

The battering ram in my chest is at it again and I force my head to turn, to look him in the eyes and nearly tell him.

But his eyes are filled with shades of blue so bright, so filled with the frenzy of passion, that even if I could stop him at this moment, I wouldn't. I won't take this from him. He was meant to have me. And this is how he wanted me.

"I want to feel you," he says, and his plea is a deep rumble of desire. He nudges the tip of his nose against mine. "No condom?" he asks.

No words come to me, so I simply nod my head and kiss him, eager to feel him too.

His large body is hot against mine and I shut my eyes as I'm inundated with emotion as he hovers over me, but without my eyes on him, he growls. It sounds like a growl. Deep and low in his chest, primal and threatening.

My eyes whip back to him and he crashes his lips to mine. With a gasp, I open for him and he uses that moment to spread my legs wider, nestling his hips between my legs and pushing himself inside of me just slightly.

I'm overwhelmed. Unable to come back from the high of my pleasure, from the high of knowing Sebastian wants me, and from the all-consuming kiss that he devours me with, I'm completely at his mercy.

I brace myself, ready for him to shove himself inside of me in one swift stroke. For him to tear through me and take me how I've always wanted him to, but as his heart slams against his chest and in tandem with mine, he pulls away from our kiss and nudges the tip of his nose against mine once again. My lashes flutter open and I stare into his gaze as he slowly pushes himself into me.

His lips are parted, and they widen just slightly as he lets out a deep breath and moves deeper inside of me.

I can't help that my lips part as well, that they form an O as he stretches me and the sharp pain of it mixes with the sweet, lingering pleasure. As he rocks out of me and then back in, he mutters with his eyes closed, "You're so tight," and I don't know what to say.

I should tell him, but I don't. I don't want to change anything.

"Take me," I beg him in a whispered plea and reach up to grab his shoulders while wrapping my legs around his hips.

I wasn't prepared for him to slam inside of me. For him to lower his lips to the crook of my neck as he fills me completely and stretches me beyond what I can handle. He groans a deep masculine sound of satisfaction as he tears through me, breathing me in and taking my virginity in a single movement. The pain makes me close my eyes tightly, it makes me tense and dig my heels into his ass. I feel hot and full, and it's too much. It hurts. Fuck, it hurts. It's more than I can handle.

But with my teeth clenched and no words spoken, Sebastian moves out of me slowly, giving me slight relief. It only lasts for a split second before he savagely slams back into me. My eyes close tight and I bite down on my lip to keep from screaming.

Again, and again, he thrusts, each time picking up his pace and each time the pain mixes with pleasure.

Each time I think it's too much, but every time he pulls away, no matter how briefly, it feels like a loss. I want this, I want him. I want more.

The bliss that thrills every nerve ending is caught in a vise. I can't control how my body begs for more, but it simultaneously wants to push him away.

It hurts.

It fucking hurts.

But it feels so good, it feels like everything I've ever wanted.

As he picks up his pace, my head thrashes, but Sebastian's hands stay on my hips, pushing me down and keeping me right where he wants me. His lips roam my body, sending kisses down my neck and shoulder, over my collarbone and everywhere. It feels like he's everywhere. And it's almost too much—almost, but it's not. I know it's not because my body wants to focus on how viciously he's fucking me.

My body focuses on the intense pain and equally intense pleasure.

Tears leak from the corner of my eyes, and I struggle to breathe, but somehow, I cry out his name. "Bastian." It's a single strangled breath. It's not from the pain, not all of it anyway. It's from everything. I'm losing myself to him and it's everything. I wish I could stop the well of emotion pouring up from me, but with every thrust, every sound, every touch from him… I can't stop it.

My nails rake down his back as he shoves himself deep inside of me, past the brink of pain and toward something blinding, numbing yet igniting. My head falls back limply as the pleasure rips through me, tearing every bit of me apart into a million pieces.

And then he stops, and the world is motionless with the orgasm still racing through me.

"Chlo?" Sebastian's voice is full of worry as the rough pad of his thumb wipes at the tears still falling down my face.

"Don't stop," I beg him but even my voice sounds pained, and he pulls himself out of me.

"Fuck, are you okay?" he asks me and reaches across me to the nightstand, turning on the bright light. I can only close my eyes as the pleasure still rages through me. The dull pain turns to a vibrant ache as I try to close my legs and involuntarily let out a pained moan as I curl over on my side.

"No, fuck," Sebastian's voice, full of worry and regret sends embarrassment and shame through me, and the tears come on harder and I can't stop them. My body is confused and the emotions inside of me are welling up and I can't stop them.

"I'm fine," I barely manage to say as I wipe at the embarrassing tears.

"Don't lie to me, what did I do?" He sounds angry as he tries to push my legs apart. "Fuck," is the last word he says before climbing off the bed and running to the bathroom. As my eyes adjust to the light, I peer down my body to see bright red staining the sheets. Both of my hands cover my face with the regret, and dread overwhelms me to the point where I wish I could disappear.

"I'm sorry." I hear Sebastian before I see him, but even as I register his words, he's already on the bed. He rubs a damp, warm washcloth soothingly on my inner thigh to clean me up.

The shock from the concern on his expression and how carefully he's cleaning me without worrying about the sheets keeps me from being able to speak.

He kisses my outer thigh with his eyes still open, gives me another kiss and gets closer. "I'm sorry," he whispers against my skin. "I knew you were tight, but fuck… I didn't mean to hurt you." I can't stand the look in his eyes like this was his fault. Like he has anything to be sorry for at all.

"I'm a virgin." The words leave an awful feeling in my throat as they come up like I'm suffocating. "I was… before… I should have told you," I whisper with my eyes closed.

And there's nothing but silence. He doesn't move or speak for what feels like forever. But finally, he asks, "Does it hurt?" I shake my head no as quickly as I can, refusing to cry anymore.

"You're crying, Chlo, please don't lie to me. I'll never forgive myself."

"Please, just pretend I'm not," I try to plead with him, my eyes still closed tightly and my hands reaching up to cover my face.

"Fuck that," he tells me, grabbing my hands and pulling them away. "Tell me the truth," his sternly spoken words force my eyes open. Through the haze of tears, I stare into his demanding gaze. "Did I hurt you?"

I shake my head, searching for the words to explain. "It's a mix, but the more you…" I have to pause and swallow before continuing, "the more you're inside of me, the better…" I struggle to calm myself and my racing heart, which doesn't seem so stupid now for wanting to escape earlier. If I could vanish now, I would.

His hand cups my jaw, his thumb running along my bottom lip before he asks me, "Would you tell me to stop if it was too much?" Before he can even finish his question, I'm shaking my head.

"I need you to," he demands. His voice is laced with concern plus a plea I don't expect. "I need you to tell me." His eyes search mine, glancing over my face as he brushes the tears away. With him maneuvering himself back to where he was, my body calms and the heat lingers in my core.

"I want you," I beg him. "Please, I need this to be—"

"I want you too." His words calm every bit of anxiety and I reach up to kiss him, but it's shortened as he pulls away.

"You can have me," he whispers before giving me a chaste kiss I try to deepen, "but you need to tell me if it hurts too much." He says the last part with his eyes closed and then opens them, piercing me with his gaze. "Don't do that again," he warns me. "Don't let me hurt you."

His words are so full of certainty and a darkness I can't deny, so I speak immediately. "I won't. "I'm sorry," I quickly add and feel the weight of regret bury the embarrassment.

"I'm afraid if you never tell me, I'll never know." His confession makes me repeat myself, "I'm sorry."

"Look at me, Chlo," he says then grabs my chin between his thumb and forefinger. Without hesitating he kisses me once, then again and a third time, silencing the doubt and regret. A kiss from Sebastian Black soothes everything. He is the healing balm to my soul. As long as he kisses me, as long as he wants my lips to brush against his, I'm safe and cherished in a way I can't describe. Even if it's all in my head, it's all I need.

With his eyes closed, his forehead resting against mine, he whispers between us, "If you don't tell me, I will hurt you. I know I will. I know it. And I don't want to."

I nudge him with my nose to get him to look at me. "It hurt, but it was going too regardless," I tell him and try to make him understand. "I thought I could hide the pain and when I couldn't, it didn't matter anyway because it felt… like everything." I cling to his shoulders and make him look me in the eyes. "I promise you, I want this." I breathe once, just once, waiting for him to say anything. "I want you and I want you to have me how you want."

"We have time for me to… to," he swallows thickly, "Chlo, I wanted to fucking destroy you." His words make me blush furiously. I watch the way he swallows, mesmerized by his confession as he adds, "I wanted to make sure you still felt me tomorrow, so whoever had gotten to you before me, didn't stand a chance at being remembered as a good lay."

"It's okay," I say but can barely get the words out. The idea of still feeling him inside of me tomorrow and what his intentions were does nothing but fill me with lust and make me wish I hadn't cried. I wish I could have hidden the pain like I've read about before. "You can have me, however—"

"Knock it off, Chlo," Sebastian reprimands, but he says it with a smile that calms my nerves. "I want you to remember this for other reasons. Now that I know…"

I'm hot all over and still trying to gain control of my body and my emotions when he tells me, "Don't hide this shit from me, Chloe Rose. I'll find out." His command comes out more teasing than anything else as he nudges his nose against mine. He reaches between his legs, his arm brushing my clit as he does, and it makes my head fall back against the pillow.

"I'll tell you everything," I promise him with the sweet feeling of pleasure building. He's stroking himself and moving back to where he was, but every small movement brushes against me too, burning hotter than before.

"Then tell me you want me."

The rhythm of my heart skips a beat. "I want you, Sebastian."

It races as he tells me, "Spread your legs for me." I obey him instantly. With him guiding himself back inside of me, I try to hide the wince from the lingering, stinging pain, but he sees. "I'll make it feel good." His words are soothing as he pushes himself inside of me and captures my scream with his kiss.

He rocks his hips steadily, each time brushing his pubic bone to my clit and he never takes his lips from mine. So long as I can kiss him back, he keeps his pace and massages his tongue along mine in swift strokes. A warmth floods through me as the pain morphs into divine pleasure.

I gasp for breath the second he parts his lips from mine, but then immediately he seeks them again. My eyes are closed and every touch of is his gentle, save the ruthless way he fucks me.

"Harder," I beg him while gasping for air, but instead of harder, he moves his hand between us and pushes his thumb to my clit.

Fireworks go off along my skin and deep in the pit of my stomach and lower.

With every thrust from him, I gasp. The sounds of our breathing, of him fucking me and the bed protesting, only fuel me to want more. I don't dare rip my eyes from his gaze as I cum, feeling him cum with me. I can feel everything, the way he pulses and puts more pressure against my walls, the way he fills me.

And then when he pulls away, I feel everything. Every sensation and tingling need to curl onto my side and recover from what he's done to me. My body's trembling, literally shaking.

I hear him go to the bathroom, but I can't open my eyes to see him. It feels like he's still there. I'm swollen and the ache is still raw.

But so is this feeling that takes over every inch of me. The rolling tide of pleasure that refuses to leave.

When he comes back to the bed, I want to ask him if it's always like that, but I don't.

Instead, I ask him if he wants me to take off the sheets, in a voice still breathless, but he shushes me, getting in behind me and scooting me to the other side of the bed. Even with fatigue weighing me down and the overwhelming sensation of pleasure still racing through me, I want to do something for him, anything.

There's a crushing need to make things right with him, to show him that it's okay and even better than okay. And that I'm sorry. I feel so fucking sorry.

But he hushes me again and plants a kiss on the side of my jaw, wrapping his heavy arm around me and pulling me close.

"Thank you," I whisper although I feel foolish doing it. Sebastian doesn't say anything; he just holds me tighter. I don't know if I've ruined everything and part of me starts to wonder if I have. It was intense and emotional and I'm still riding the high, but the nagging feeling that I'm alone, and that I destroyed whatever we had creeps into my thoughts.

"How did that feel, Chloe Rose?" The deep rumble of his chest accompanies his question.

It felt like he owned me. Body and soul.

"You can do that to me whenever you want," I answer him with sweet sorrow mixing in my chest. I don't know what tomorrow will bring, but tonight, I'll have forever.

He arranges me so I'm nestled perfectly against his chest on my side, his hand splayed on my belly as he kisses my hair and then my shoulder. Nothing but warmth and comfort flow through me. I've never felt so loved. Never in my life have I felt like this. So wholly wanted and cherished. It's the way he's brutal, but gentle just the same. I want to believe it's because of me, because of us. That it isn't like this with other girls. That he isn't treating me differently because he found out I'm a virgin. And although the doubt and worry are there, tonight it feels real.

I swear I hear him whisper, "I love you, Chloe Rose," as my eyes become heavier. He whispered it at the back of my neck. But as quickly as I thought I heard the words, I start to think I imagined it. It's something I've always wanted to hear from him, and I need to hear it now. I desperately need to hear it.

I don't know if it's a dream, maybe one I once had long ago and wish to remember, or if it's real. But as I feel sleep pull me under, I hold on to those words. Deep down inside of my soul, I know they'll keep me safe.

I only wish I had the strength to say them to him.

CHAPTER 16

Hour could I not have known?

I can't get the nagging thought to go the fuck away. I was so eager to have Chloe, to ruin her, to make sure she'd remember me forever, that I didn't stop to consider the possibility I'd be her first.

If I had known, I would have done it differently. She'd have a better memory of her first time.

I should have fucking known.

Drew dated her for a month when I was away, up north with Romano. He told me he was lying about the rumors of her sucking him off behind the school, but at the time, I wasn't sure if he was telling me the truth or not because I was slamming his face into the cement. I thought he took her first. The day I heard what he was telling other people, I thought he'd taken her V-card.

Her only other boyfriend was Jared Santack.

They went to semi formals together and I saw him kiss her. I know they went home together that night. It was the night I came home from my first stint in jail. I remember thinking for a split second how she deserved someone like Jared, then I planned how I'd fuck up his car the next day, just because he needed to have something of his broken too.

"What the hell is wrong with you?" Carter asks me from across the dining room.

My gaze shifts to him and I try to fix the pissed off look I know is on my face, but I can't. Last night fucked me up in a way I can't explain. I run my hand down my face and try to shrug it all off. The chair legs scratch on the floor as I get up from the table and go to the window. Carter's family's house is on the outskirts of the city and backs up to the woods. It's dark and there's not much to look at out there, but I stare outside anyway, trying to get my shit together.

My knuckles rap on the worn-out buffet table in front of the window as he asks me, "She getting to you?"

Is Chloe Rose getting to me?

She's *always* gotten to me.

I don't answer him, instead, I try to make up a lie, but it doesn't occur to me that the lie is a truth until the words are spoken. "Being here just reminds me of family," I tell him. My spine stiffens and a chill runs through me.

"Shit, man," Carter tells me, "I'm sorry." As if it's his fault. As if he has anything at all to be sorry about.

I shake it off, hating that tonight of all nights I'm making this about me. That I can't focus and be there for my only friend.

"How did the treatment go?" I ask him. And the look on his face instantly changes. The sympathy morphs into anguish.

He doesn't say anything, although he tries. Instead, he looks me in the eyes and shakes his head.

My heart drops down to the pit of my stomach. "Fuck." It's all I can give him and then we're both looking out the window.

"Tell me something good."

His request catches me off guard and I consider him for a moment.

Something good. It takes me longer than it should to think of something. All thoughts lead back to Chloe Rose.

"I fucked Chlo last night," I tell him. "I was her first."

"Shit, really?" he asks. "She's twenty?" I nod, waiting for him to say something else. For him to understand what it meant to me. But I don't think he will. No one will. They don't get it. I don't even understand it.

Ever since I laid eyes on her, she was mine. It didn't matter that I didn't want anyone, because I didn't have a choice. She was mine. Fate picked her for me, and vice versa. Last night was meant to happen. I know it.

The sound of the door opening distracts us both, drawing our attention to the front door we can't see.

Carter grabs the edge of the buffet tighter at the sound of his dad calling out for him. "Back here," he replies and steels himself, staring straight ahead and trying to relax his posture.

I fucking hate it. I hate how he's scared of his own father. He tells me it's the way it is and that it's no different from how his father was raised, but that doesn't make it right.

I expect his father to be drunk and angry, like the last few times I've seen him. He pissed himself the one night he was so hammered, we had to drag him home.

His steps get louder and then the old man is right in front of us, his hands slipping into his pockets as he leans against the doorway. "You two eat already?" he asks us and gives me a short nod before pulling out a smoke.

He lights up as we answer him. I can feel the aggression rolling off of me, my expression getting tighter, but I know that's no good for Carter. He doesn't want a war, he just wants to do what's right by his mom.

Mr. Cross walks to the dining room table, sifting through the bills and puffing on his cigarette.

"How is she?" Carter asks him, and I glance between the two of them. His father's expression falters for a split second before he changes it to something else, something stronger than the weak man who's withering away just as his wife is.

He nods at Carter and tells him, "She had a good day." With his lips pressed in a thin line, he tells us he's going to bed. Carter told me the days he doesn't drink are different, but

I haven't seen him like this in a long time. A long damn time. It's been two years of hell, with my hate growing for this man, but seeing him sober is different.

Carter nudges me as his father starts to walk away and I reach in my back pocket for the cash. "Mr. Cross," I call out to him and take the three steps forward to pass him the bundle. "I just wanted to help out if you'll take it," I offer. "I won it on a bet and I don't need it."

"I wish I had the decency not to," he answers me. "This isn't charity."

"Call it a loan then," I answer him quickly as he tries to give it back. Taking a step away from him, I tell him, "I don't care either way." He nods his head in agreement, but the old man's eyes turn paler and glossy.

It's quiet for a long time as I watch the man do his best not to break down in front of me, tapping the wad of cash against his palm.

"I don't know how to tell your brothers." He talks to Carter without looking at me, staring down at the cash before slapping it down on the dining room table. The strength he had diminishes, and his face crumples with hopelessness.

"She's not going to be here for much longer," he starts to cry and it fucking hurts watching a grown man lose it. "I can't lose your mother." He covers his face with one hand, his other bracing him on the table to keep himself upright.

"They know, Dad," Carter tells him, although he doesn't go to his dad, he doesn't try to comfort him. He stands strong and his father only seems to respect the decision as he rights himself, brushing away the tears and sniffling hard to be done with it.

"They don't know," he says in a single breath, his face going stony. "They can't know until it happens. Nothing can prepare you for it."

Carter looks down and stares at his mud-covered boots; I know he wants to object.

His father's right though. Even knowing the end is coming can't help. Nothing can prepare you for the type of destruction death brings.

"We'll be all right," his father sniffs and grabs Carter's shoulder, squeezing it and waiting for Carter to look him in the eye. "All boys," his father says and huffs a humorless laugh although a faint smile is on his lips. He looks at me as he asks, "Can you believe that?"

I offer him a weak laugh, feeling awkward and out of place.

"Their mother wanted a little girl and instead I gave her five sons. All Irish; the Irish boys have to be tough." He nods his head as he talks to neither of us in particular. "The men have to be tough," he repeats and then gives his son's shoulder one more squeeze.

"Carter will do good," he says and then sniffles again, giving me a glance before walking toward the worn doorway. "Carter will take care of them," he says softly.

"You're talking like you're already dead," Carter comments. "You're still here." The tension between them changes to something else, and for the first time, I see why Carter doesn't blame his father. He would never go against his father. It's the fear of losing him that keeps him loyal. Between the alcohol and his hopelessness, he's already close to losing him.

"I won't live much longer after she goes. That's how it works." His father doesn't say anything else in the awkward silence that follows and neither does Carter.

It's only when the stairs creak with the weight of his father going to bed, that Carter says anything.

"He's a different man when he isn't drinking. You see it, right?" Carter asks me, his voice more hopeful than I thought it'd be. "He's not all bad."

I can only nod, not wanting to fight with Carter. Carter's told me his father treats him differently from Daniel, who's the second oldest. He's told me some days he doesn't even know if his father loves him. I can't forgive a man for treating his son like that. I won't.

"Thanks for the loan, man," he tells me, even though I'm aware he doesn't like that he had to take it.

"Yeah, no problem. It's nothing," I say and try to brush it off like it doesn't matter. "I have to go home to Chlo."

"Look at you," Carter jokes and I can feel the tension leave him, grateful to move on to a different subject. "Don't fuck it up."

I almost joke back and tell him that I know I'm going to ruin it somehow. But it's too close to the truth and I don't want to speak life into the words.

It wasn't supposed to be this way in my head, not like this.

"She has no one," I tell Carter, just wanting him to understand her the way I do. "The worst thing I can imagine is having no one." It's only when the words are spoken that I realize how alone I've really been. I wait for Carter to say something, but his mind is elsewhere.

Maybe there is something worse though. Like having someone, but knowing you're bound to lose them.

CHAPTER 17

Chloe

I T'S WEIRD BEING ALONE IN THIS PLACE WITHOUT SEBASTIAN. I'M SURPRISED HE let me stay here at all. I'd planned on sneaking out in the morning and being weird on my own rather than weird with him.

The biggest fucking lie I've ever told myself is that this is just sex. Last night was more than sex for me.

I woke up a few hours after I'd passed out, and I couldn't get back to sleep. I was wide awake and so very aware of everything that happened. With his arm still around me, I wanted so badly to stay in that moment. The moment where it felt like he still wanted me.

I knew it would hurt down there, and at 4 a.m. every tiny shift in my body seemed to be connected to the ache between my legs. It still hurts now in the evening after. I knew it would. But I didn't expect the emotional change, the emotional pain that comes with it.

Not able to sleep, and knowing I'd made a fool of myself, I thought I'd sneak out, leave him a note, and let him decide if he still wanted me. If I was worth still being around or with, or whatever it is that we have going on. I wanted to make it easy for him because I knew what I was doing, and it wasn't fair to him not to tell him.

That was the conclusion I came to at four in the morning as I breathed in his masculine scent one last time and felt the warmth of his hard chest at my back. I closed my eyes and savored that moment, memorizing it, just in case it would be the only moment I had like that with him. Of all the things that have happened between us, that's the one I wanted to hold on to.

Where he took from me what he needed, and I took from him what I needed.

With a deep and slow breath, I carefully crawled out of bed, taking my time and being as quiet and gentle as I could so I wouldn't wake him. It wasn't until my first foot hit the floor that I winced and seethed. It hurt more than I realized.

He woke up instantly, reaching behind him to turn on the lamp. He's so fucking beautiful. It's an odd word for a man, but it's true. With sleep still in his eyes and his stubble longer than usual, he looked groggy but sexy as fuck. Maybe it's the way the light hit him, or maybe it's the hormones and lack of sleep, but I've never been more attracted to a man before. I don't think I ever will be either.

"You all right?" His voice was laced with sleep and accompanied by the bed groaning as he sat up.

"Lie back down, I'm fine," I whispered as if he was being ridiculous, although my heart pounded knowing I was trying to sneak out and failed.

I thought it through right then. He'd turn out the light and lie down, I'd go to the bathroom to clean up. After a while, when I thought he'd fallen asleep again, I'd sneak out and let him text me. I didn't want to risk taking the time to leave a note and making it more awkward than it already was if he caught me.

I could walk to my house from here and at this time of day, no one would be up. There would be no one to bother me on the short walk home.

"You aren't sneaking out, right?" Bastian questioned. "'Cause I want to wake up with you in the morning." He said it so definitively, so sincerely.

If there was ever a moment where I knew I was his completely, it was then.

And that was over twelve hours ago.

Now I'm alone in his house wondering what to do with myself, other than snoop through his shit. Which has been a rather disappointing endeavor.

My phone pings as I close the last drawer in his dresser, finding nothing but a pair of his pajama pants. They're flannel and smell like him, so I slip them on and with my baggy t-shirt, I couldn't be more comfortable.

Sprawled out on his bed, I check my texts and bust out laughing. I'd texted Angie, *Sex is better than masturbation.*

And she finally responded. *Tell me who, you whore!*

I feel the blush rise to my cheeks, but the butterflies in my chest and belly are more prominent.

I consider telling her, but I'm not ready to share him, so instead, I tell her it has to wait till Monday. I assume the slew of texts afterward are from her, but I lie on the bed, staring up at his ceiling and wondering about how Bastian got to be the way that he is rather than answering them.

Every thought that comes only makes my heart hurt more for him.

The texts don't stop coming and as I remember every detail I know about Bastian and the way he was in high school, they annoy me more and more.

Grabbing my phone off the bed where I tossed it, I'm ready to silence it until I see the most recent text.

Did you hear about Mr. Adler? They found him dead.

My blood runs cold and I swear I feel it all drain from my face. Angie's still messaging me and threatening to do all sorts of stupid shit if I don't confide in her right this second. But I couldn't give two shits about her right now. Mr. Adler was next on the list. I feel fucking sick.

The message is from an unknown number. My fingers shake as I text the person back with the obvious question. *Who is this?*

Breathe, just breathe. I have to keep myself calm even as I start to shake from the adrenaline coursing through me. The fourth person on the list. Right in a row. One. Two. Three. Four. All found dead.

My phone pings and I look down to see a new text from the unknown number. All it reads is: *That doesn't answer my question.*

I can't stop trembling as I stare down at my phone.

Who else would text me? No one. No one else. The only other person who has my number is Marc because I had to give it to him.

I didn't mean to frighten you.

Another message comes through and my heart beats faster. The front door is locked, I know it is, but still, I climb out of bed and check it. It's hard to even swallow with my heart in my fucking throat.

Who is this? I text back and then add, *I'm not frightened. It's fine, I just hadn't heard that Mr. Adler had died.*

I almost write more. All lies though. Lies meant to deceive. Something to make it feel casual, normal even. Something that would prove I'm not terrified. But all that's running through my mind is that the person on the other end is a killer. The killer the cops have been looking for and failing to find.

I repeat over and over that I'm not crazy, I'm not paranoid. I remind myself what Sebastian said, that I'm scared and looking for answers. Which I am. Four in a row. It's a fucking hit list.

"Fuck," I grip my hair and clench my teeth before calling Sebastian. My throat's tight as I stand in the middle of the living room, vaguely aware that I'm on the brink of a panic attack.

I'm not crazy. I'm not crazy.

I don't know what to think. Other than someone has a copy of that list, or made the same list, but how?

Voicemail. It goes to voicemail. An hour ago, I felt untouchable here; now I feel like I'm in a cage, unable to go anywhere and so easily seen by anyone who could be watching.

Please call me. I text Sebastian as another text comes through.

I shouldn't have texted you.

Who is this? I ask again, but no reply comes. Not then and not thirty minutes later when I'm huddled in a ball on the sofa, wondering if calling the cops is even an option. There's no news at all that Jeff Adler was found dead. Not on the news online and not a hint of it on any social media.

Is he even dead? And if he is, and the person who texted me knew, but no one else…

The number is still silent an hour later when I leave a voicemail on Sebastian's phone. I wish it wasn't real. I wish I could blink and the messages would be gone. I would rather know I truly am crazy than to be living this nightmare. I don't mention any of it in the voicemail to Sebastian, I just beg him to please come back or return my call. The second I hang up, I lose it.

It's a slow spiral of a breakdown, and maybe that's what the person wanted.

I text the unknown number again and beg them to tell me who they are. And I get nothing. For hours, I have nothing but my own fear and a random text that was designed to inflict it.

Someone wanted to hurt me.

There's only one person I think of over and over again who could be behind this and it proves I'm insane.

It can't be my mother, but when I dig through my purse and find the list, a list no one else knows about, I can't think of anything other than her and the nightmares.

My mother is dead. *It's not her*, I tell myself over and over, resting my cheek against the flannel fabric on my knees and rocking back and forth. It takes everything in me to calm myself down, telling myself that I'm safe here with Sebastian. Whoever it was is an asshole. Someone who overheard me at the butcher shop maybe. Someone playing a cruel trick on me.

Whoever it is can go fuck themselves.

The anger and hopeful explanation are all that keeps me together. Just barely. I'm holding on by a thread and watching the clock tick by, wondering where Sebastian is and why he hasn't messaged me back.

For hours.

CHAPTER 18

Sebastian

"WHERE WERE YOU?" CHLO ASKS BEFORE THE FRONT DOOR IS EVEN CLOSED. Her voice is filled with accusations that make my body freeze.

Her eyes are bloodshot as she peeks up at me above her knees on the sofa. It's not too late yet. Past dinnertime, but it's not so late that she should be coming at me like this. Unless she knew something.

What the fuck happened? It's all I can think. My movements are slow as I toss the keys on the table and kick off my boots, taking her in as she watches me. My heart's hammering and I'm fucking confused. This isn't my Chloe.

"I was with Carter, they don't get good reception out there," I tell her and hope she accepts it as the truth. "What's wrong?" She can't be mad that I left her alone all day. There's no fucking way that's it when I know for a fact she was going to leave me last night.

"Someone texted me," she says in a quick breath and then closes her eyes to swallow. "I'm being stupid," she says while shaking her head, her eyes closed tightly.

"What'd they say?" I ask her, trying to hide the adrenaline and rage that mixes in a deadly concoction. I walk carefully to her, watching as she rubs her eyes. Sitting close to her and pulling her into me, I try to calm her down so she'll just talk to me. And she lets me, which is already a relief. "Just tell me what happened," I say, and the words come out even and calm. Deadly calm.

"I feel like… Bastian." Her words are choked as she buries her head in her knees, pulling away from me.

The only thing I focus on is keeping my hands on her. She's here with me. My Chloe Rose is right here, and I've got her.

"Whoever it was just wanted to freak me out, but I don't know how they know about the list unless they overheard at the butcher shop. But I didn't say the names out loud, did I?" Her words come one after the other, stumbling over each other, but the second she's done, she breathes in deep and rubs her eyes. "I know I didn't." She answers her own question before I can say anything. My blood is hot with rage, wanting to know exactly who messaged her and why the fuck they'd get in my way.

Still not looking at me, she apologizes. "I'm sorry."

Frozen and struggling to push the command through clenched teeth, I repeat my question, "Who texted you?" If they're fucking with her, they're fucking with me.

"They said Jeff Adler's dead. I don't know who it is. I don't…" She doesn't finish. Instead, she shakes out her hands and grabs onto her knees, burying her head so she doesn't have to look at me.

My blood runs cold. He's next on the list. She knows it. I know it. Only two left.

With a deep exhalation, she finally looks up at me and she apologizes again. "I'm sorry," she says, and her voice is soft. "I feel like I'm being crazy, but I'm scared."

She has no idea how ridiculous those words are coming from her mouth.

"I saw," I tell her, knowing she needs to be told enough so she thinks it's okay. That everything is okay. "On my way back from Carter's, there's a bunch of people around the site. Looks like a car hit him." Her mouth drops slowly as I give her the partial truth.

"What? No." Her first reaction is denial and she reaches for her phone, but I take it from her, hellbent on finding the number and who it belongs to. "I looked, no one was saying anything."

I don't respond to her and she stays stiff at my side as I look up the number and put it in my own phone. Nothing. Reading the texts, I know who sent it. I just don't know why and every thought that comes up makes my knuckles turn white as I try not to break the fucking phone in my hand.

Anger is a deadly thing.

"He's dead." Her voice shakes with fear and it's that sound that pulls me back to her.

"It was an accident." I'm firm with her, pulling her in closer to me. "Word gets around." I start coming up with an explanation. "I think people know you're freaked is all, Chlo." I feel her eyes on me, but I can't look down at her. If she looks into my eyes, she'll know I'm lying.

I have to stand up and start walking to the bedroom, stripping down and making it look like I'm anything but on the brink of tearing this place apart.

"People know what?" she calls out and I hear her get off the sofa to come after me, her footsteps echoing down the hall.

I need to calm the fuck down. If for no other reason than to calm her down, so she stops thinking about it all. She can't do anything to fuck this up.

With my jaw hard and my back stiff, I turn to her slowly, seeing her prettily framed in the doorway. I force a small smile to my lips. "It's no one, Chlo, but it's okay. I'd be freaked out too. Whoever it was, wasn't thinking."

I have to hide my shock at how well I just lied. How easy it came out. Desperation is an ugly thing.

Her distraught expression slowly fades, replaced with hesitant relief. Her lips stay parted as she lets my words sink in, slowly believing the little lies I'm feeding her.

And it fucking kills me. What I'm doing to her destroys everything in me.

"Come here," I tell her as I tear my shirt off over my head and toss it carelessly on the floor. My three steps take up the entire space of the room as I go to her, wrapping her in my arms and kissing her temple. Her fingers wrap around my forearm and she looks up at me, eyes wide and wanting so badly to believe what I'm telling her.

"I'm sorry you got spooked, but it's nothing. An accident."

"Another coincidence?" she questions me, but her tone isn't a question. My heart thrums and a chill spread over my body.

"It was an accident," I repeat, making my tone a little harder and staring into her eyes until she believes me.

"I don't know… that text and—"

I huff, cutting her off and staring past her. She squirms in my periphery and I'm a fucking asshole. I'm an asshole for making her think this is all in her head.

"This isn't how I wanted tonight to go," I say softly, thinking about last night and how easy it was to get lost in her. If I could live in that moment, I would.

"I'm sorry," she mumbles and her warm breath flows over my skin.

Glancing down at her, I feel like the prick I am. "It's not your fault," I whisper in her hair and then plant a small kiss on her crown. She's so warm in my arms, so small and fragile in so many ways. "I get it, Chlo, but I promise you it's nothing."

She stares deeply into my eyes for what feels like forever and I whisper against her lips, "It's all right, just have faith in me."

She kisses me tenderly, softly, and slowly, even though the pain and worry are still etched in her eyes.

"Come on, let me tell you a story." My hand splays on her back as I lean out into the hallway to turn off the light and then take her to bed.

She crawls in slowly, climbing on top of the sheets before pulling them back and sitting cross-legged where she slept last night.

"My grandmom used to do this thing late at night when she'd come home from work." I latch onto the first story I can think of, so I can occupy her thoughts with something else.

She leans forward slightly, waiting for more and eager to hear what I have to tell her. The way she looks at me with her beautiful blue eyes does something to me and I have to look away.

"Back when I was real little," I say and swallow the lump growing in my throat, "I still remember it."

I settle into the sheets next to her, kicking off my jeans first and flicking on the lamp to cast some light onto her face. When I get into bed, I slip off my watch and it clinks as I set it on the nightstand.

"I never met her," Chloe Rose whispers as she lies down like I'm doing, getting closer to me, and letting me put my arm around her so she can rest her cheek on my chest. Just knowing I have her like this, knowing I can ease her fears and she trusts me… it's everything.

"She worked real late, at least it was late for me."

"Where'd she work?" Chlo asks as I remember how I used to wait up every night for her, but sometimes I couldn't do it.

"At the diner past Walnut. She was a waitress up till the day she died."

Chloe nods and her hair tickles against my chest when she does, but I love it. It brings a comfort that rolls through my chest and I reach up to let my fingers slip through her hair.

"So, I'd wait up every night I could and if I did, she always had something for me. She always had a little gift." My words make Chloe perk up to look at me.

"Like what kind of gift?" She seems far too interested in that detail and it makes me smirk down at her with a huff of humor slipping through my lips.

That bright blush I love to see colors her expression and she finally looks like she might be getting over the text messages, thank fuck. "Sorry, I was just thinking you know how I'd like to get you something for being so nice to me," she confesses and then lets her finger trace up my chest. "I don't know what you like though."

My chest rises as I shrug and say, "You don't have to get me anything."

"I'm fully aware that I don't have to. That doesn't change the fact I *want* to get you something." She gives me a soft smile as she adds, "Thank you, by the way."

"For what?"

"For this," she tells me with that sadness and fear returning to her eyes. I can't respond, knowing what I'm doing, but I don't have to. She kisses my jaw and tells me, "Ignore me, keep going. I like hearing stories. Especially if they're about you."

"You sure you're not going to interrupt as soon as I get going again?" I tease her and instantly feel her smile against my chest. That makes it all right. It makes it all right because she's smiling now and that's what matters.

"Time will tell," is all she says, and I love it. I love all of her.

"So, my grandmom, she'd come home and put her purse down, and I'd get all excited." I glance down at Chlo and get back to running my hand in her hair as I remember what it used to feel like. "I never slept in my room, always the living room so I could hear her when she got in.

"Every time she'd smile down at me, like me waiting up for her made her the happiest person in the world. And I really believed it too. She'd set everything down and come sit in the recliner, letting me sit on her lap and tell her everything that happened that day at school."

It fucking hurts remembering the small pieces of it that come to me. Things I didn't even know I remembered.

"She'd always have a candy for me. Always. Sometimes there'd be a toy too, something small. Like things you'd get in a piñata."

Chloe hums a small acknowledgment and lifts her leg to lay over mine as she peeks up at me. I pull her in closer, loving that she's letting me tell her this.

"I always thought that she would go get something for me before coming home, you know?" I clear my throat, remembering how some nights if I wasn't able to stay up, I actually felt bad. She'd gone through that trouble of getting me something, and I couldn't even stay up for her. I remember wondering if that was why mom left. Because I didn't stay up for her.

"I was six, I think when she died. And after the funeral, everyone came back to the house." The depth of emotions that play in the soft blues of Chloe's eyes force me to look at the ceiling rather than at her.

"And I didn't know any of the people. I hardly recognized my own mother, because she'd been gone for years, but this one guy, an older guy with glasses, sat down in my grandmom's recliner. And when he did, he pulled up a Zip-loc bag, and it had all the treats in it."

I can feel Chloe's eyes on me, but I can't look down at her. It's so stupid, but I can feel tears pricking my eyes.

"Grandmom had a stash I didn't know about. She didn't pick one out every night. It was right there all along." I clear my throat and tell her, "I kicked him, Chlo. I kicked him hard and grabbed the bag from him. I grabbed it so hard that it tore, and the candy and little toys fell everywhere. They weren't his though. They were Grandmom's. It was her stash to give to me."

I feel the tears on my chest at the same time as I hear Chloe sniffle.

"I'm sorry," she whispers, and I hold her closer to me.

"It's all right, Chlo. Just a story I remembered." I don't tell her the rest. How my mom beat my ass in front of everyone and made me throw away all the candy. She struck me so hard I fell to the floor. I don't tell her how I cried uncontrollably and my mother, who I hadn't seen in years, held my face up for everyone to see that she was punishing her brat of a child who didn't deserve any candy. And that was why she left. That's what she told them. That she was cursed with a bad kid.

She was so proud that everyone got to see her being the mother she never was. And the only thing I had to hold on to, was that those tears weren't for her. They were never for her.

"Your grandmother sounds like a wonderful person."

"She was," I tell her and we're both quiet for a long time.

"Hey, if you could up and leave, where would you go?" I ask her even though I can see sleep taking her already. She's going to pass out soon and then I need to take care of some shit. I'll be careful; I won't wake her up.

"Anywhere that would take me," she says playfully.

"I'm serious. What would you do?" I ask her, wondering if she's really thought about it. If she'd really run away one day. She props herself up on her elbow, still lying on her stomach and considers me.

"I think I could be a writer. Not like a reporter… but like my books. Fiction."

"If you could do anything at all, you'd write?" It takes me a minute to visualize it. Her bundled up on a sofa, with a mug of tea beside her, jotting down notes or typing away. I could see it. She'd be good at it.

"I feel like that's where I belong, you know? I can kind of be a little weird in person, but when I read or write, it's so freeing."

"I get that," I tell her, feeling a knot growing in my throat. "You could do it, Chlo. You know?" I ask her even though everything in me is telling me not to put those thoughts in her head. I don't want her to run away, I don't want her to leave me.

She gives me a weak smile that mixes with her shyness as she tucks a lock of hair behind her ear before settling back down and yawning.

"And what would you do?" she asks as she nudges me, peeking up at me to add, "If you could do anything."

I think about her question for a long time, long after I shrug and tell her to go to bed. Long after she nuzzles up next to me and falls asleep in my arms. The only answer I can think of is if I could do anything in the world, I'd run away with her.

The only place I want to be is with her.

"Chlo," I whisper her name not long after sleep's taken her from me. Her brow is pinched and the sweet expression on her beautiful face has been replaced by something else. Something that lingers in the place between fear and worry. A small whimper is all I get from her as her nails dig into my arm, holding on to me for dear life. Whatever's got her mind now isn't what I want her thinking about.

The only thing on her mind should be thoughts of us together. It would only be fair since she's the only thing I can think about anymore.

With one hand on her shoulder, I give her a gentle shake to wake her, hard enough to know I'll snap her out of her sleep. "Chloe Rose." I keep my voice gentle and soothing as her wide doe eyes peer up at me, the traces of fear still dancing in her gaze.

Her chest rises and falls with a slow and steadying breath as she looks past me, at the room and then back to my gaze. "You're with me, Chloe Rose." My words are meant to be soothing, but the reaction I get from her is more powerful than I could ever imagine. She pulls herself closer to me, molding every inch of her soft body to mine, kissing my neck, my collar, my chest. Her hands roam down my stomach and then she slips her hand up my chest, letting her fingers play with the small smattering of hair that trails down to my lower half.

The next time I say her name, it's merely a stifled groan. "Chlo." My dick is harder than it's ever been before.

She wants me. She fucking wants me.

"Sebastian," she whispers my name with desperation, brushing her lips against my neck again and letting her kisses trail everywhere they can.

She's in need and so am I.

I roll her over onto her back, and she lets out a small squeal of surprise. It's short-lived as I climb on top of her, kicking off my pants while her fingers spear through my hair and her lips hungrily find mine.

Her tongue brushes against the seam of my lips as I push my fingers inside of her. I have to pull away from the kiss, groaning deep and low in my chest from how hot and wet she is for me already.

"I need you," she whispers and rocks her cunt against my dick.

I don't make her wait, I push myself inside of her, getting harder from the sweet, tortured sounds she gives me in return. She's still so tight, so fucking hot and wet too. It takes me far too long to be buried deep inside of her and when I finally am, giving her a moment to acclimate to my size, her heels dig into my ass, her nails at my back and she begs, fucking begs me, to take her hard.

I give her everything she wants. With one slam of my hips, she screams out my name. Another thrust and she's biting her lip and muffling her cries, but her gaze stays on mine. Those beautiful hues of baby blue swirling with desire, and something else. Something deeper. Something that stirs the beast inside of me to do anything for her, give her anything she ever needs. And to make her mine.

All mine.

Rutting between her legs, I piston my hips, feeling the cold sweat spread along my skin as I hold back my need to cum.

"Bastian," she moans my name as her pussy tightens and her back bows under me.

"Cum for me," I command her in a voice I don't recognize. One desperate and breathless. One that's just for her.

And she does. She obeys me, instantly spasming on my cock. Her head falls back and her lips part as her orgasm rocks through her.

I don't stop. The second her gaze is off mine, I fuck her harder, ruthlessly, riding through her orgasm and prolonging every bit of it that I can. Dragging it out of her.

She writhes under me and her head thrashes.

My heart beats hard against my chest, feeling hers in time with me.

She's mine. All of her is mine. For always.

Fuck Romano; fuck this city.

I pound into her harder, wanting her to feel every emotion that's raging through me. I'm staying with her.

Her gasp is followed with a strangled moan that fuels me to grip her hips harder, giving her every bit of me.

Nothing's going to keep me from her.

Nothing.

CHAPTER 19

Chloe

Sebastian's phone keeps going off. I thought it was in my dream at first. My mother was hissing something. I still hear her words as my eyes flutter open. She said, *He's lying to you.* Her voice keeps me frozen under the warm sheets as the bed dips and Sebastian sits up to grab his phone.

I'm motionless as he moves. She was right here. I can still feel her. She was here.

His voice is groggy as I try to breathe and shake off the eerie feeling that my mother still haunts me in my sleep, even if I can't remember what the dream was.

He's lying to you.

"Yeah, what is it?" Sebastian's voice sounds off. The worry that lingers in his tone grabs my full attention, leaving the thoughts of my mother and whatever had come to me in my sleep where it belongs, in the past. In my unconscious.

"No, no…" He rubs his brow and turns away from me as whoever it is who's called him talks loud enough that I can almost hear the replies on the other end. "I'm sorry," he says with a pained voice, "Yeah, yeah. Are you okay?"

The dread grows as I watch him, how he looks so hurt sitting on the edge of the bed and listening to whoever it is on the other line.

He swallows thickly before saying goodbye and tossing the phone on his nightstand. With his head hung low, I can hear him swallow.

"Who was it?" I dare to ask in a whisper as if speaking too loudly would cause the pain he's feeling to cut even deeper.

I scoot closer to him, but slowly as he lifts his head to answer, "Carter."

My stomach twists into a knot, just like the one in my heart as Bastian adds, "His mom died."

My throat is tight as the swell of sadness rises. I didn't know her at all, but I knew the end had to be closer after she was moved into their house for hospice.

It's devastating to lose your mother, whether you know it's coming or not.

"So much death." The words escape me slowly as I tally up the number of gravestones.

"I care more about him than any of those assholes." Bastian's tone is harsh and unforgiving. I peek over at him as he rubs the sleep from his eyes angrily, his feet on the floor while he still sits on the bed. I've never seen him look so tired, so ragged from everything.

and the pain of it all forces me to move closer to him, pushing the sheets and covers away to just hold him. I rest my cheek to his back and wrap my arms around him from behind.

"I'm sorry," I whisper against his back and then lift myself up, so I can plant a small kiss on his neck. "I'm so sorry," I tell him again.

I don't know how close he was with Carter's mom, but it doesn't matter. He's hurting. Lacing his fingers through mine, he kisses my inner wrist. "Are you okay?" he asks me, turning his head so he can look me in the eyes. Of all the things to ask, he wants to know if I'm all right.

His eyes are red with lack of sleep, his stubble is too long, and there are dark bags under his eyes as well. I have to slip my hand from his to cup his cheek and sit up to kiss him on his lips. A chaste, sweet kiss. My heart flutters every time I kiss him. It's an odd feeling, like a magnetic pull to him.

I brush his lips with the pad of my thumb and whisper to him, "It's not always about me, Bastian." With his name on my lips, I look him in the eyes and say, "I'll be okay."

"You're wrong," he tells me, shifting to sit so he's facing me. "It is always about you."

His answer steals my breath, numbing me as he kisses my wrist again.

"You shouldn't say things like that." I can't help but tell him as the words come to me.

His steely blue eyes catch me off guard; they pierce into me and hold me hostage as he asks, "And why is that?"

"You make me feel like I'm more to you than I am." The words come unbidden, his simple question enough to draw the raw truth from me. I lick my lips as I blink away the haze of the spell he casts over me. Bringing my knees into my chest, I scoot away from him and wish I could take those words back.

"You're wrong again," he tells me, and I feel foolish.

"I know I'm an easy lay," I tell him dully, feeling my heart squeeze in my chest. I would let him have me whenever he wanted.

"I didn't say you were. I don't do this; I don't sleep around. I don't have girls stay over, so we're even there. So, whatever you're thinking right now, stop it."

Guilt rises inside of me and makes me feel sick to my stomach. This is not the time, nor the place. I can feel his gaze on me, I know he's waiting for me to simply agree and so I swallow the spiked knot and nod, but I can't look him in the eyes.

"You know you mean more to me than that. You're more than that." His conviction is unmistakable, but I don't know that. I only know what he's told me, which is nothing.

He never tells me anything and I let him into my life because that's where I want him. It's as simple as that.

Taking a steadying breath, I turn to him.

"Tell me you know that," he commands me, and my eyes are drawn to his throat as he swallows. "Tell me you know you're more than just a lay for me."

"I do," I tell him. Things have always been *more* between us, but why? I don't know. And tomorrow holds no promises for me.

"I want to have someone, Bastian," I confess to him. "Even if I may lose them one day. I don't want to be alone anymore." I don't know where the words come from. Maybe it's the fatigue that still lingers. The sadness from hearing of Carter's mom passing. Or maybe it's because I feel a crack in Sebastian's armor, he's giving me a way in to tell him exactly how I feel.

It's too quiet as I stare straight ahead at nothing in particular, rather than at Sebastian.

He cups the side of my face and forces me to look at him. His touch is hot and his gaze even hotter as he tells me, "Then let me be that someone."

My heart beats in slow motion.

"What am I to you?" I whisper. Because deep in my soul, I already know Sebastian is that person for me. What I don't know is whether or not I'm that person for him.

"You were just the sad girl who looked at me like you couldn't wait to run from me. So, I refused to chase you, Chloe. Now that I have you, I'm begging you, don't run from me."

I love you is on the tip of my tongue, but the strength to let the words be heard is nowhere to be found.

"People know you're with me now, anyway," he tells me when I don't say anything. "There's nowhere to run."

"I want to run away from here. I don't know that I can stay here, Bastian." I don't know why that's what comes out of me, but it's all I can say.

His answer is simple and unexpected. "When you figure out where, tell me."

His hand falls from my cheek and he gets off the bed, making my body sway where it is. My gaze drifts to him, watching him stand at the dresser and open a drawer, and then to the faint light of early morning filtering in through the window.

"Where are you going?" I ask him and then add, "To Carter's?" He only nods solemnly. Of course, he'd want to be with him. I'm sure Carter needs him there too.

"Do you want me to go with you?" I offer. I'd do anything for him.

"You keep looking for a way to run from me, Chloe Rose," he says and although he isn't facing me as he slips on a white cotton t-shirt, I can hear the smile that must be gracing his lips, "but I need you this time. You're not allowed to leave now."

"So, that's a yes?" I push him for more, feeling a warmth spread through my body and cloaking the sadness still buried within.

"It's a, 'you should have known you're coming with me.'"

CHAPTER 20

Sebastian

I KNEW IT WAS COMING. WE ALL DID. BUT WE'RE DYING EVERY DAY, COMING CLOSER to the end of our time here on earth, and it's never easy to accept.

It's been four days since she passed. And four days of Carter not calling. I keep texting him, but he just gives me one-word answers. His dad was right, nothing can prepare you; I didn't think Carter would push me away though, not when he needs someone there for him. Even if it's just to sit around and do nothing, I don't care what, I just want to be there for him.

But he has his brothers.

Let me know when I can come over, I text him. And it takes a few minutes with only the sound of the paper bags rustling from Chlo getting the Chinese food out before Carter replies that he will.

I think he's lying though. I don't think he's going to ask for help or for anyone to come around. He's not okay.

"You should go to him," Chloe speaks up, dishing out the lo mein on both of the paper plates with the white plastic forks they threw in the bag. "I think he'd like that," she adds. She's on her knees in front of the coffee table in nothing but a shirt of mine.

Tossing my phone on the sofa, I get down on the floor with her. It's awkward and I have to push the coffee table away a foot, so I can fit between it and the sofa.

The sound of her small laugh soothes a piece of me that's hurting for Carter. I peer up at her with a smirk on my lips. "Not everyone's a tiny little thing like you," I tell her and watch that soft blush creep up in her cheeks.

"I love making you smile," I say and it only makes her blush harder. She bites down on her lip, reaching for another carton. She dishes out the General Tso's quietly until both plates have more than enough on them.

"I love it when you make me smile too," she says sheepishly, sitting back on her heels. "But seriously," she tells me, "I think he'd be happy if you stopped by."

"Yeah," I agree with her, remembering how she was at Carter's house and then at the funeral. She was quiet and polite, but the moment someone was ready to break down, she was right there. For Carter, but for Daniel too, his younger brother. All she wanted to do was be there to take away the pain as much as she could.

I love her for it.

I love her for being her.

She peeks up at me as the thought occurs to me, but she quickly looks away and repositions herself. She's barely eating, just pushing the food around on her plate.

"What's wrong?" I ask her, a nagging feeling inside of me that what we have is going to go away. It's all going to slip through my fingers and I'm going to lose her.

She clears her throat and glances at me, her gaze shifting between the untouched plate and then back to me. I have to put my fork down and push the plate away to face her. "Tell me what's wrong."

"I think I love you." Her answer is immediate, although each word feels hesitant like it was afraid to be spoken. "I think I'm weird and needy… and that I have problems," she says then swallows thickly, and the blush that was on her face turns a darker shade of red before she looks up at me again with those blue eyes shining with vulnerability. "But I think I love you, and I don't know if… if it's okay that I tell you." She bites down on her bottom lip and then nods once like she's said her piece. "But I wanted to tell you," she adds quickly before I can answer her.

She'll never know how she breaks something inside of me with her confession. With how genuine and sincere those words come out. I know she means it. She feels that she loves me, and she loves the part of me she knows. It shatters something deep down inside of me. The part of me that's hiding from her sight, the part of me I hate, that part of me falls to my knees for her, praying I could atone for all my sins and be worthy of that love.

"Lie down, Chloe Rose," I give her the command, feeling my heart slamming against my chest, begging me to tell her how I feel. I'm not ready though. I love seeing her squirm, and a part of me thinks if she knew how much she meant to me, she'd run.

She glances at me warily before setting her fork down and scooting out from between the coffee table and the sofa to lie down on her side only to ask, "On my back?"

Letting out a single huff of a laugh, I grin at her and say, "Yeah."

With her heels on the floor and her knees bent, she lies on her back, the t-shirt riding up and she lets it, so I can see her underwear.

"Take them off," I tell her from where I'm sitting, feeling my cock get harder for her. Pulling her hair behind her first, she obeys me. Shimmying out of her underwear and setting it next to her, she daintily readjusts so her legs are flat and I can't see her cunt.

"Like you were before, Chloe Rose. I want to see you."

Slowly, she picks up each of her heels, her pussy on full display, her center a dark, bright pink and glistening from arousal.

"Tell me you love me again."

She brings her gaze to meet mine and licks her lips. "I love you," she tells me like it's obvious. Like it doesn't change anything at all.

I have to practically crawl to her from where I'm sitting, but I don't give a fuck.

I don't need food; I don't need sleep. I don't need a damn thing, so long as she loves me.

With a single finger, I push on her inner knees and she instantly moves her legs farther apart for me. I trace her pussy, sending shivers through her body.

"So, does that mean you're my girlfriend?" I ask her the question I wanted to so many years ago. If I hadn't already been involved with Romano, heading down a path I knew she was too good for, I'd have asked her then. Shit, I'd have begged her to be mine.

The corners of her lips turn up as she smiles wide and beautifully. "Yeah," she answers me in a single breath and I reward her by brushing the rough pad of my thumb over her swollen clit. Her sweet, soft moan makes precum leak from the slit of my cock and I can't take it anymore.

She watches as I undress fast and recklessly, kicking the coffee table and almost spilling the food, but it doesn't matter. None of that shit matters.

She spreads her legs farther as I climb on top of her, bracing my forearms on either side of her head and kissing her softly, gently and giving her every ounce of goodness, I have, even if it is so little.

"You still sore, Chlo?" I ask her as I push into her slick folds just enough to feel her tight cunt gripping my cock before pulling out.

With her neck arched back, her lips parted, and her eyes closed, she whimpers, "No."

"Good," I tell her, "'Cause tomorrow you're going to be." I slam into her all the way to the hilt in a swift, merciless stroke. Her sweet gasps fuel me to fuck her on the thin carpet until she doesn't have a scream left in her.

CHAPTER 21

Chloe

"**I** LOVED COMING HERE." MY MOTHER'S VOICE IS CALM AND SOBER, WHICH IS AT odds with the noise of the bottles clinking and everyone talking in the bar. It sounds like everyone's talking at once and over each other. The billiard balls collide on the break and the sound of a new game starting draws my attention briefly. The television's on with a football game and some of the guys cheer a player on, but he the whole bar voices its dismay as he's quickly tackled.

I recognize a few faces, one of them Carter's dad as he orders a drink.

"That man's going soon." My mother's voice catches my attention. Goosebumps flow over my skin; she's so close to me. A thin, sickly smile is on her lips. She nods, not taking her gaze away from the far end of the bar as we sit on two stools next to each other.

I look back to the man I recognize and ask, "Mr. Cross?"

"No, no, baby girl," my mother tsks me, "the bartender."

Dave.

Ice flows over my skin as my mom laughs at my reaction. Fifth on the list.

The billiard balls clack noisily, and the bar carries on like nothing's happening. Like they can't even see us.

Sharp nails dig into my shoulder as my mom comes closer to me, whispering in my ear and making my body stiffen.

"I used to fuck him at the end of the night," she tells me with her smile growing. "He'd clear my tab in return, although sometimes he just wanted me to suck him off like a whore."

My words fail me and I struggle to breathe or to know what to say. It's only a dream.

"Yeah, yeah, baby girl. But that doesn't make it any less true," my mom tells me before letting go and sitting upright in her seat.

I swallow the tight knot in my throat and peek up at her.

"Just because you're dreaming doesn't mean shit." The smile fades and she stares at the bartender as he pours a glass of some clear liquor for Mr. Cross.

The music seems to die down, everything except my mother's voice turning to white noise.

"At one point, I thought he loved me," my mom tells me, staring down at the drink on the bar.

It takes me a moment to realize the smudge on the glass is blood. My gaze darts to her

My heart pounds, the anxiety and fear rising as her voice hardens and she picks up the drink. "Men don't love, Chloe." She sets the glass against her lips, but she doesn't drink. Instead, she stares at the man behind the bar. She stares down the bartender who doesn't see either of us. "Don't you ever believe that shit."

I grip the barstool tighter, feeling the blood draining from me as she looks me in the eyes, her own pale and lifeless. "Don't believe him, Chloe Rose."

I wake up drenched in sweat and alone. Trembling, I can hear the faint sounds of someone outside. I can't help getting out of bed, my heart still racing as I check to see who it is.

Peeking through the blinds, it's just two guys walking down the street. Guys I've seen before on the porch of a house down the street. They look like they're on their way back from the liquor store, carrying bags full of large glass bottles. That would explain the noises I heard in my sleep.

I'm still shaking as I turn from the window and slowly walk back to the bed, my mind racing with the memory of the dream. Of the bar. Of Dave.

I reach out to Bastian's side of the bed, but the sheets are cold.

Blinking the sleep from my eyes, I walk to the bathroom, my bare feet padding against the cold floor. The door's partially open and it's dark inside, but still, I push it open wide and flick on the light.

The brightness makes me wince, and I find it empty.

"Bastian?" I call out for him even though I know he's not here. His place is empty.

Where the hell is he? The clock on the stove reads 3:46. "Where the fuck is he?" I mutter, still breathless from the fear that woke me. I'd rather focus on Bastian than on the night terror, but when I get to my phone that I'd left on the coffee table, my blood runs cold.

Dave now too. They're going one by one.

I stare at the text message, reading it over and over.

Dave is dead.

I dreamed of it. And he's dead. I'm so cold. I can't feel anything but the horror I felt from the nightmare.

I don't know how I'm still standing. The scream of fear is silent in my throat, but it's there.

Tears prick my eyes and I can't control the shaking. Adrenaline and the need to run kick in before I can do anything. It all happens so slowly, each level of despair falling on its own. Like dominoes. And between each blow, I reread the text.

Dave now too. They're going one by one.

My knees collapse, and I drop the phone, pressing my hands together and begging them to stop shaking.

It was a dream. She's not real.

It's not real. Tell me the text isn't real. It's not true.

It's just some asshole fucking with me. There's no truth to it.

I swallow each of the thoughts, pushing my head into the carpet and trying to steady my head from spinning with the fear racing through me.

But how can it be a coincidence? It can't. It can't be.

It's not real.

"Bastian," I cry out for him like the crutch he is. The panic is slow to set in.

I know he'll make it better. He's a balm each and every time. He can make it go away.

But he can't explain this. Nothing can explain this.

I reach for my phone and miss it, but then I grab it again, my nails digging into the carpet as I drag it closer to me. "Pull your shit together," I mutter under my breath. I lift my gaze to the front door as I scroll for Sebastian's number.

My body is hot, and tense and the fear threatens to consume me.

It's locked. The door is locked.

Ring, ring, ring.

No answer.

I stare at the screen as if it's lying to me. I don't know how long I sit there on my knees, my ass on my heels as I stare at the fucking phone, hating it and hating this place and freezing. I'm so cold. I'm so fucking cold.

It was a nightmare, it's not real.

I try again and get the same result, voicemail.

Swallowing thickly, I brave looking at the text message again.

I could ask who it is, but they won't tell me.

I could ask for proof, but I don't want to see.

Instead, I try Sebastian again because he's all I have. And still, I get nothing. My heart races and the anxiety grows inside me, burning me from the inside out and nearly shoving me over the brink of insanity.

It's okay, I tell myself as I rock on the floor. *It's okay.*

It's just a nightmare. Just a text.

Just another coincidence.

"Bastian," I cry out for him and feel so unworthy. So unhinged.

Where is he?

He has to be with Carter, out on the edge of the city where there's no reception. It's my fault. I told him to go there. It's my fault, I repeat to myself.

Finally, my body moves. I need to get dressed and go to him. I can't stay here. I won't do it. I need to tell him; I need to tell someone. I'm breaking down and I don't know what to do. I don't know what's real.

I'm not crazy.

A scream tears through me as the phone rings in my hand. I drop it, the vibrations feeling like fire against my skin.

It rings again, and I see it's Sebastian.

My fingers shake as I answer it and wait for his voice.

"Chlo?" he asks, and I struggle to put what's going on into words.

"I need you," is all I manage. I can barely breathe.

"Chloe, it's okay." I hear the tone of his voice morph from curious to concerned. "What's wrong?" he asks me.

"I had a nightmare," I cover my mouth with my wrist, remembering my mom and her words.

"Chlo, it's just a dream," he tells me as tears prick my eyes.

"I dreamed about Dave and then I got a text," I push the words out and take in a deep breath. Shaking out my other hand, and staring straight ahead at the stark white wall, I wait for him to say something that makes sense, something that will make me feel better.

"I'll be there soon," he tells me, and I nod my head, my throat raw with emotion.

"I'm not okay," I tell him in strangled words.

"It'll be all right," is his only answer before the line goes dead. But it's not all right. It's not going to be all right. I wanted them all to die for having done nothing while my mother cried out for help. I wanted them to feel the pain and regret that I felt every damn day for years when I cried myself to sleep. They felt nothing, and it wasn't fair. That was years ago though and I don't want this. I would never ask for this now.

I'm living in my own hell.

CHAPTER 22

I HANG UP THE CALL AND STARE AT THE DIRT AND BLOOD ON MY HAND THAT'S holding the phone.

"I need to shower at your place before I go home," I call out to Carter who's still leaning against his father's beat-up truck.

My hands are numb and yet they still burn from the blisters that'll come tomorrow. I don't know what I'll tell Chlo if she notices them. The shovel did a number on me and it all proved for shit.

"You hear me?" I ask him, my voice barely carrying into the early morning darkness.

"Yeah." Carter's answer is weak. He looks like shit. He looks like he just lost it and that makes sense. 'Cause that's exactly what happened.

The river babbles in the night along with the sound of the crickets. It's all I can hear as the sun starts to peek over the horizon.

Another night with no sleep and another night with Chloe falling apart. She knows too much.

"You ready?" he asks me before pounding his fist so hard into the truck I swear he's going to dent it. He's losing it. He can't hold himself together.

The dew on the grass soaks into my jeans as I walk through the tall grass to the truck.

I grab his shoulder, shaking him. "It's over with; it's done." I'm firm with him even though my heart is pounding recklessly.

Carter nods his head but immediately throws up. He vomits off the side of the truck with both hands on his upper thighs. The smell is rancid, and I can't stand to be around it.

I feel fucking sick to my stomach too. I hate this. I hate this life.

I lay a hand on his back, patting him hard once before walking away from him and climbing into the driver's side. The truck rocks as I do, and I can't shake the eerie feeling that I'm being fucked over.

He texted her again. I'm blocking that fucking number. He crossed a line doing that shit, and I don't give a fuck who he is. I won't let him get to her. My Chloe is off-limits. There's no exception to that.

It wasn't supposed to happen this way, but it doesn't matter. He knows. I know he knows.

Laying my head back against the leather headrest, I wait for Carter, looking over my shoulder and watching him wipe his mouth with the sleeve of his shirt. He takes it off, leaving on his t-shirt underneath and throws it into the back of the truck before getting in.

The rusty door closes with a protest, right before slamming shut with finality.

"I'm sorry," he tells me as he looks out the window. I feel bad for him; more than anything, I feel fucking awful for the kid. I can handle Chloe. I'll figure it out for her, but this fucked him up.

"You're all right," I tell him and then swallow the rest of the thought. "It's fine."

It's this place. How many times have I said that recently? Crescent Hills is a living—waking—nightmare for everyone in it. Only the devil himself could live here and feel at peace.

"I have to tell Marcus he's here, but I won't tell anyone else, all right?" The truck rumbles as I start it up. Carter looks like he's going to lose his shit again; he's still shaking.

"It's just the adrenaline," I tell him, to try to calm him down.

He peeks up at me, the early morning light making his worn expression look that much more ragged. "I killed him," he tells me again. I can't count how many times he's told me that tonight.

Nodding at him, I look in the rearview at the river where I ditched Dave's body before putting the truck into drive.

"He was going to die anyway," I tell Carter although I stare straight ahead at the dirt road rather than looking at him again. "His name was on the list."

CHAPTER 23

I F Dave is dead, Andrea is next.

And then me.

There are no coincidences like this, and I can't just wait around to be a sitting duck. I can't ignore it any longer. I can't pretend to be okay and walk through this life as if I'm only a ghost. It's what I've done for as long as I can remember, and maybe weeks ago, I would have prayed for the end to come quickly and peacefully.

But I'm not ready to go. I don't want to die.

I want to run away from all of this.

I want to be free of it all.

I want more than this shit life.

More than anything, I want Sebastian to come with me.

The front door to his house opens, and I don't wait for him to speak. "There's something wrong with me," I tell him, feeling every inch of my throat go dry and the pit in my stomach growing heavier and heavier. I heave the words up my throat. "Someone is killing them and if you don't believe me, that's fine." The last word cracks as I feel myself unraveling.

Sebastian stays by the door, completely still and watching me, watching as I transform into a lunatic in front of him. I don't know what he thinks of all this, of how often I'm nothing but an emotional mess. The nightmares, the list. I can't imagine what he thinks, he always brushes it aside, but I can't do it any longer.

"I can't pretend it's a coincidence."

He finally speaks, low and with a note of apprehension, "What brought this on? The text?"

My body is ice cold as I sit on the sofa, pulling my knees into my chest and refusing to look him in the eyes. "I don't think it's someone messing with me." I dare to peek up at him, willing him to feel the very real fear that keeps me on the edge of sanity.

"I wish I could kill him. Whoever it is that's fucking with you."

It shreds me inside to hear the pain in his voice. "I'm not crazy," I beg him to understand.

"I wrote that list, Bastian. I wrote it." The confession is so close, it's begging to come out and be brought to life. With each word scarring its way through my chest, I give in to the weight of it. "And my name was on that list. I wanted them dead and I wanted to die," I tell him as the tears prick at the back of my eyes and I hold myself closer.

Tears leak down my cheek as I rest my heated face against my knee. "I don't want to die," I repeat the one thing I know to be true right now, even if that hasn't always been the case.

"Shh," Bastian shushes me, coming closer and sitting next to me on his sofa. I'll never know how he so easily comforts me, how he doesn't hesitate to wipe my tears away and pull me into his arms. When I'm like this, on the brink of insanity.

"I'm not crazy," I whisper and wonder if it's true.

He rocks me as I gasp for air and try to force the crying to stop. "It's my fault they died," I whisper the harsh truth and his rocking stops, but then continues. My heart races, needing him to tell me something. Anything. To tell me I'm not crazy and that he'd run away with me. That's what I want more than anything.

"Please," I beg him, but I don't have the strength to voice the only thing I've ever wanted.

"There's nothing on the news about Dave," he tells me after a long moment. My head shakes, wanting him to listen to me and believe me. I don't care what's on the news; I know what I feel in my gut.

"I need you to believe me." I try to convince him as I say, "I can feel it. I know it. Whoever it is, they aren't lying."

I'm holding him so tightly; my knuckles turn white. "I can't go to the cops, and I can't run from whoever it is. I feel helpless, Bastian." I've felt helpless for so long and there's only so much a person can take before it turns to hopelessness. "I don't know what to do." The last words are barely spoken. All that lives inside of me now is true fear.

"You need to relax," he tells me softly, but his steely eyes aren't cold. They hold so much sympathy that it nearly makes me break. As if there was any piece of me still whole.

"I can't explain this without sounding crazy," I tell him, although I can't look him in the eyes when I say it. I wipe at my face, hating how weak I am. I would give anything to be strong. "I could wait for the night to come. I have my gun—"

"Chlo, stop it," he warns me, his tone threatening.

"I could try to—"

"Stop it!" he yells at me, so loudly, it shakes me. My body's trembling as I try to get a grip. I have no one and no idea when it's coming. There's one more person before me if Dave is really dead. That's all I know.

"I don't want to live here anymore."

"Then what do you want to do?" he asks me with a hard look that would force me to be silent if it were on anyone else's face.

"I want to run away… for good." My body is numb as I hold my breath, waiting for him to say anything at all, but my chest squeezes with a new kind of pain when he says nothing.

"Please say something," I beg him.

"You have no idea what lengths I would go for you. But you need to stop this, please. Don't do this. Please, Chlo, for me." His words are a plea that rubs salt in the sharpest and deepest wounds I have.

"You don't understand." I take in a quick breath and then another, feeling lightheaded as I confess, "I heard my mom screaming for help and did nothing. I did nothing." I search his eyes for understanding, but also for the hate I felt for myself so long ago. "Whoever is killing them… if it has to do with her… they're going to come for me."

"Chloe, please," he tries to silence me, to brush it off again and I push his arm away instead of accepting the comfort that comes with his touch.

"I don't feel safe here," I tell him while backing away. "I won't stay here any longer." The words themselves are both freeing and suffocating.

I've never belonged here; I've always wanted a way out.

But I've always belonged to Sebastian. In every way. And the idea of running, to never see him again, is the most painful thing I could ever feel.

"Please," I beg him, not just to understand but to come with me.

"If you can't come with me," I try to be strong, to force the words out, but instead I turn into a blubbering fool. Covering my heated face with both of my hands, I feel the tears burn into my flesh.

"I'll never let you leave me," he tells me, and it only makes me cry harder. Because I don't want him to let me go, I want him to come with me. I need him to come with me. "I don't want to leave you." I gasp for air and give him a singular truth in a despite whisper, "I can't leave you."

He pulls me in close to him, even though I'm no help at all, covering my face and ashamed of what I've become.

"I just need time," he answers me and my head shakes of its own accord.

"I can't… I can't stay here anymore." The last words come out strangled as tears prick my eyes. I can't stay, but I can't leave without him either.

I swear I could be a better person. I could be happy and sane. But not here. All I am here is a name on a list. Waiting for my death.

"I love you, Chloe. I love you." Sebastian's voice is soothing as he wraps both of his arms around me. I crave his touch so much that I bury my head into his chest. He whispers, "I can take you away. We can leave tomorrow."

My body stills, my heart beating far too loud to be sure of what I heard. *Please, let me have heard right.* I can barely manage to swallow as I look into his steely blue eyes, praying he's telling me the truth and not just saying what he knows I want to hear.

He kisses my hair and then brushes it away from my face as he repeats himself, "I can run away with you."

"I love you, Bastian. I love you." The words tumble from my lips. "Please tell me you're telling the truth." I interlock my fingers with his, needing to feel him and know that he means it. "I want to run away with you."

"I love you," he tells me, his gaze never straying from mine, "we can't stay here. I can't stay here anymore."

CHAPTER 24

I DID THIS TO HER.

But I wouldn't take it back.

I wouldn't take it back because I have her now. I'll run away with her, as far as she wants. I'll hold her every night and watch her fall asleep in my arms.

Always.

She'll never be without me again.

"Is there anyone you still want to talk to?" I ask her as I figure out every detail. Every single thing that has to be done before we leave. She's nestled in the crook of my arm in my bed, her small frame curved around my side. Her hair brushes my arm while she shakes her head. "No," she whispers. Clearing her throat, she adds, "I just want to leave."

I know she does. She's always wanted to leave. Ever since the first day I met her, I knew I'd run away with her if I could.

"I want you to leave your phone," I tell her, and she asks quickly, "Because of the person who texted about Dave?"

"Partly," I tell her honestly, feeling the anxiety spike inside of me. I don't want her to know the truth. I'll never tell her all of the truth. Never. "I don't know who it is. And I don't like that." I play the possessive card, although I'm sure she can see right through it. "If there's no one you want to call, I'd rather you just leave it behind."

She's quiet for a moment, but instead of asking questions, she concedes. "I can leave it behind. I can leave everything behind." I release a breath I didn't know I was holding and stroke her hair.

"There are a few things I have to do tomorrow. I'll run into work, come back, pack and then we leave." Adrenaline is coursing through me, knowing this is a decision I can't go back on. Once I leave, that's it. There's no coming back and I have no idea where we'll run to.

"Just like that?" she asks with slight disbelief, peeking up at me through her lashes.

"Just like that," I tell her and bend down to kiss her, listening to the bed groan in time with a faint siren from outside. No more streetlights drifting through the window, no more yelling down the street. No more of this city and the people in it. Wherever we go, I want it to be quiet and far, far away from here. I need somewhere we can escape to where no one will find us and where it'll feel like home.

"It's all going to be okay," I whisper against her hair before planting a small kiss on her forehead. She holds me tightly, like she'll never let me go. "It's all going to be all right."

"Promise me you'll run with me?" she asks me again like I'll back out of it.

"Tomorrow we pack up everything in one car," I tell her firmly, "and we leave." I'll do it. I'll leave it all behind to be with her and keep her safe.

"And we leave forever, promise me?" her voice begs me, and I swear I'd give her anything I could. Anything and everything I ever have will be hers.

She's tense at my side, waiting for my answer. I know there's no going back, but I choose her. It's always been her.

"As long as you love me forever," I give her my one condition, feeling the tension in my heart, needing her to agree and say she's mine forever.

"I can make that promise," she breathes, "I'll love you forever."

"I've always loved you," I whisper against her cheek. And it's true. There have never been truer words spoken.

I turn nine tomorrow. I think, anyway. I want to ask the guy behind the counter, so I'll know for sure. I don't know why I care; I just want to know, I guess.

Peeking over my shoulder, I make sure Jim and my mom are occupied so I can go ask what day it is.

We just moved here. Mom took me with her, although part of me wishes she'd left me at Grandmom's, even if there's no one there anymore. At least I have the memories there. This city is different, everyone's always watching me. Looking at me like I'm going to do something so they can pick a fight.

They say I'm a bad kid. They say I'm angry.

I used to think they were wrong, but I don't anymore.

Boys like me are trouble. Too tall for my age, too smart for my own good. I'm not worth the air I breathe. That's Jim's new saying. He likes to remind me every chance he gets, even though he's the one giving my mom that shit that makes her go numb. He's the one who isn't worth the air he breathes but saying that only gets me punched in the face until I go numb too and black out.

I pull out the candy from my pocket. I only have two pieces left and as I pull out my hand, both of them drop to the floor and one rolls faster than I can catch it.

The candy stops rolling when it hits the edge of the counter and bounces off, only to stop in front of a small pair of shoes. They're white but scuffed up and I slowly lift my gaze to the owner of the shoes. To the short girl who's bending down to pick up my candy.

She can't have it!

My jaw's hard, and I clench my teeth even though the bruise there makes it hurt. My hands turn to fists. All I have left of my grandmom are these two pieces.

She can't have it!

She picks it up so delicately and carefully, then smooths out her dress. It's then that I notice how dirty it is like she's been sitting on the ground all day. It's wrinkled too. When she stands up her big doe eyes are filled with worry and she turns to look at a woman by the fridge doors.

The woman's skinny, skinny like my mom. That's what I think as the bottles she's picking up clink together.

The girl looks like she wants to say something, but she's scared, so she says nothing. Her gaze drops to the ground, then she lifts her head back up to look around.

She's looking for me; I know she is.

The instant she sees me, the worry goes away and she smiles. A genuine smile that's just for me.

"Is this yours?" she offers in a soft voice that makes the anger go away. Only for a second though, because the moment she asks me, she peeks over at the woman and looks nervous to even be talking to me.

Because I'm a bad kid. That's why. Everyone knows it. Even her.

Her knees nearly buckle as she stands there, holding the candy out to me even though I'm feet away from her.

She's afraid to move. "My mom told me to stay here," she explains.

I nod and swallow the lump in my throat. She looks sad like me until she smiles at me, then it changes everything.

She's strange. Like she doesn't want to be here.

I may not belong here, but she doesn't either.

"Thanks," I tell her as I walk to her and she nervously looks between me and the woman again, her mom.

She's shy as she talks to me. "I haven't met you before." And then she smiles again, even sweeter this time. She smiles at me like her happiness was meant to belong to me. Like I could take that happiness from her. Like I could be happy too. "I'm Chloe Rose."

CHAPTER 25

MAYBE IF I LEAVE, THE NIGHTMARES WILL GO AWAY.

Places hold memories. They can't help it. The image of a dented brass doorknob comes to mind. I'll never forget the memory of what put that dent into the hard metal. The sound of a click against a window, the window he crept through late at night. It can't help but exist, yet it carries so much heaviness with it. So much more than just an object, so much more than just a place.

I'm done crying; I'm done remembering.

I think I've been ready to leave for a long time. Longer than the time that first light went out on the street and I had the urge to run in such a primitive way. I think I was ready to run the first time Bastian's lips pressed against mine. My heart knew it, but it would only beat if he came with me.

There's a method to the way I place each item in the old duffle bag. I was given the bag in gym class one year in high school. It was a promotion for some sports drink and I think it could carry at least two weeks' worth of clothes. That's all I need.

Each piece fits in easily. My books I can put in a cardboard box and place in the back. I'll always need my books.

Other than my clothes, I don't know what I'll take. Toiletries, obviously. But these photographs aren't mine and the ones I have, I don't want.

The light catches the glass of a photo on the far right of the wall. A photo of my mother when she was young, and I was in her arms. I don't remember that far back, but my uncle said she loved me deeply. That she bundled me up in that picture because it was so cold out and she was worried about taking me outside for the photos.

She loved me once.

But she loved the alcohol more.

I'm okay with it. I'm okay with it all. Because I survived, and I still know how to love. A piece of me will always love her. I'll love the woman in this photo because she's not the woman in my nightmares.

My fingertips brush along the edges of the frame as my throat tightens and I wish I could go back to that time to tell her. I wish I could go back to so much.

You can only move forward, a voice tells me, and I close my eyes, letting the last tears fall. They linger on my lashes as I open my eyes again and say goodbye to her, leaving the photo where it is.

I carelessly brush them away, gazing at the full duffle bag as my phone pings. It's only one of two people. I already know that.

Please tell me you're okay. I read the text message from Angie and my heart sinks. I think I would have been good friends with her. Even though neither of us ever belonged here. I'm grateful to leave, but I don't know how much this place will take from her before she walks away, if she can even walk away.

I don't know why she'd stay here any longer than she has to. But it's her choice, and she knows what she's doing. Maybe me leaving will push her to run; I try to justify leaving her in the dark with the thought of her being warned to stay away with my disappearance. I can only hope that's what she does.

There's not a damn thing good that lives in Crescent Hills.

Answer me, she texts me, but I don't text her back. The next time it pings, I turn off the phone without looking.

Bastian said it's better to just disappear and for no one to know where we've gone. He's right, and I don't want anyone to come looking for me. If I could disappear and be lost in the wind with Bastian forever, I would. Tonight, I'm going to try to do just that.

I leave the phone on the bed, on the sheets that never belonged to me. It can stay there and when the men come and take everything inside because the bills go unpaid, they can have it.

They can have every piece of what's here.

It never belonged to me and I'm done belonging to it.

CHAPTER 26

Sebastian

I can't stop staring at the note on the counter. It's only a Post-it with the words, "Leaving for the weekend—Seb" written on the yellow square. Eddie will get it on Monday, or maybe this weekend if anyone comes in. The shop is supposed to be empty, with most of the guys going down to the docks for Romano this weekend. There's a large order of coke coming in. And the butcher shop isn't needed for that.

I'll leave a note and I'll ghost. He can try to find me all he wants, but I'm done with Romano and this place. Just as the thought hits me, I hear the bells chime at the front door and a chill seeps into my veins.

"Eddie," I greet him with a grin, hiding the fact that I didn't want anyone to know I was leaving until I was gone. I didn't want anyone to ask questions. "What are you doing here?" I ask and casually lean against the counter. The spool of butcher's cord is right below me. All of us who work in the shop are familiar with it; we use it to secure packages and orders.

I don't reach for it yet, but with the pounding of my blood, I know it's going to end like this. The desire to get it over with forces a numbness through my fingers and I shake it off, smiling as he answers me.

"What am I doing? How about, what the fuck are you doing here?" He shoots me a twisted grin as if he's being friendly, but the look in his eyes is filled with the psychotic glee he's known for. "I heard Romano wants to talk to you," he adds as he walks to the counter, the sound of his boots slapping against the floor in time with the pounding of my heart. He tosses the keys to the shop down on the counter and leans closer to me just as I reach for the cord.

I wind it over my fingers under the counter. The dumb fuck is so hellbent on letting me know my days are numbered in the darkened butcher shop that he doesn't realize his own imminent demise is only a moment away.

"Seems he thinks you have something to do with those assholes coming up dead," he tells me, eyeing me and then glancing out the window as the headlights of a passing car shine through the glass.

Dread rips through me, thinking it's someone else and I won't have time to finish Eddie off, but it's not. The lights flash and keep on going, heading down to the mechanic shop behind us.

"Why would he think that?" I ask him, wrapping the rope around once more and then starting on the other hand. I leave less than a foot of cord between the two. Enough to get the thin rope over his head, but not so much that it'll be too loose when I choke him out.

"Someone said Marcus came looking for information and was directed to you."

My lungs halt and a harsh thud slams in my chest. I ask him quietly, knowing the smirk on my face is dimming and finding it hard to swallow, "And who would that be?"

"Yours truly," he gives me the answer with his grin widening. "It was kind of a test," he tells me as I take in a single deep breath and grip the rope tightly with both hands, my thumbs running along the rough bundles that are fastened around both my hands. "And you failed, Sebastian." For the first time, his smile fades and he shrugs. "I'm sure there's a reason though," he says, feigning sympathy.

I nod once, making it look like I'm full of regret. And I am. I regret not killing this fucker sooner.

In one swift moment, my arms are up and around his head. He tries to turn and get out of my reach, but all that does is spin him around, so his back is to my chest as I get the rope right where I want it.

His feet come back first, trying to kick me as his hands reach up and try to grab the rope before it tightens. He gets the tip of two fingers in the loop, but I don't give a fuck. I'm squeezing so tight I can't breathe, I can't move. My muscles are on fire and my teeth grind together as I grunt out the pain. His large body slams into me, shoving me against the back wall. I grit my teeth as his boots squeak against the floor as he throws his head back into my shoulder.

He throws his body to the left, knocking us both into the tables and I almost lose my grip as I fall hard, smacking the side of my head against the edge of one chair as we tumble to the floor, but I hold on with everything I have, feeling the thin rope dig in deeper.

I watch his face closely, seeing how red his eyes are getting and how pale his face is.

His cheeks puff out as his strength wanes. Another kick, but this one's weaker. A few more seconds and his head lolls. I still can't breathe, and I pull back harder, feeling the rope nearly cut into his fingers, giving it more slack as the bones break. I hold on tight for another moment, and he doesn't react. He's limp and heavy, his dead eyes bloodshot and staring ahead at nothing.

When I finally release him, I have to slowly unwind the rope and bring the circulation back to my numb fingers. It's still dark as I pick up the chairs and tables, grabbing Eddie's corpse by the ankles to move him out of the way. There's no blood, no sign of a struggle. I check the wall we crashed into, feeling the burn and sting of my muscles. I'll bruise, but there's no dents or any sign of what happened. And that's what matters.

My shoulders burn as I drag his heavy ass to the back, kicking the swinging door open and pulling him through the kitchen to get to where the freezers are. He isn't the first and he won't be the last dead body to be stored here.

I shut the door hard, giving it the last of my anger and locking it with a loud click that resonates through every inch of me. My body is still on fire, my pulse hammering in my ears.

Shipments come on Mondays. I'll be long gone by then. I lock the freezer and look down at my hands. They're red and the skin is ripped from the rough rope digging into them. Swallowing thickly and breathing in deeply to calm the adrenaline still racing through me, I let a moment pass.

Sitting in the car, I'm still making sure I've thought through every bit of this.

Romano will send people to watch out for me to return, and he'll send people out looking for me, I know he will. He'll never find us though and I'm never coming back. I already know that.

Marcus will let me go, so long as everything happens the way it's supposed to tomorrow.

Carter though. I can't stop thinking about leaving him behind. Ever since we got in the car, I haven't let go of Chloe Rose's hand. She gives me the strength I've never had, but nothing can help me with this. With saying goodbye to him.

The keys jingle as I turn off the ignition after pulling up in front of Carter's house.

"Stay in the car," I tell her, turning off the headlights and passing the keys to her hand. Her fingers against mine still ignite something primitive and deep inside of me.

It stirs a warmth in my heart I never thought existed.

Her baby blue eyes plead with me not to stop, to just keep going and never look back. I lean forward, spearing my fingers in her hair and resting my forehead against hers. "I won't be long, I promise," I whisper against her lips.

She's quick to take a kiss, pressing her lips against mine and then pulling away to nuzzle the tip of her nose against mine.

"Kiss me first," she demands softly, with her eyes closed and her hands on my thigh. Her fingers lay across my jeans and when she tries to scoot closer to me, the sound of her nails against the denim is all I can hear along with my heart beating faster.

It beats fast and steady for her.

"I can tell that you love me when you kiss me," she whispers, her eyes looking deep into mine as the moonlight caresses her face. "Part of me can. Even if my mind can't keep up," she adds.

"Your mind can't keep up?" I ask her with a hint of a smile on my lip as I cup her chin. My gaze leaves her as I see a shadow on the sidewalk. Carter's outside and waiting for me.

Chloe shrugs, although it's a sad movement. "There's just something about the way you kiss me," she tells me.

"I love you, Chloe Rose," I tell her and as she parts her lips to tell me the same, I press my own against hers, slipping my tongue through the seam she gives me. She deepens the kiss, but for only a moment. My heart races and my blood heats.

She was always meant to be mine.

The second our lips part, both of us breathing heavier, she whispers, "I love you too."

I know she does, and with the parting thought, I open my door and close it as quietly as I can, so I can go to Carter.

My best friend. Only friend. And the only family I ever had.

"I was wondering if you'd come tonight," Carter says while I'm still a few feet away.

"Is that right?" I ask him as I walk up. Out here is more in the sticks than Dixon Street. All I can hear are grasshoppers and some kids playing ball in the street a block down.

Carter only nods in response and I can't fucking stand what I'm about to do.

"I have something to ask you," I start out and then backtrack. "How's it going? You guys doing all right?"

Carter gives me a weak smile and a half-assed laugh before kicking the ground. "Get on with it, man." His eyes reflect the way I feel. Like he already knows it's coming.

"Maybe we should settle the other thing first," I tell him, more willing to put an end to that shit than I am to say my final goodbye to him.

"Is it done?" Carter asks me the second I hesitate to speak. Standing outside of his house on the cracked sidewalk, he shoves both of his hands in his leather jacket pockets. He looks anxious as his eyes dart between the car and me. "I've got this feeling," he starts to tell me and then swallows visibly, before shaking his head.

I grip both of his shoulders and look him in the eyes. "It's done," I tell him with a strength that's undeniable. "Marcus left the cash yesterday."

"Cash?"

"I didn't know either. I thought it was, do what he said or die. I didn't expect the money."

Peeking over my shoulder, I take a look back at Chloe, my sweet innocent girl who will never know any of this shit. I'll protect her from it and from the man I was before her until my last breath. With the stack of cash in my pocket, I reach for it as I watch Chloe stare straight ahead at the dead-end street we'll never drive down again.

"Here it is," I say and hand it over to Carter, opening up his jacket and shoving it in before he can tell me he doesn't want it.

I'm the one who was told to kill them, all the names on the photocopy of the list that Marcus gave me. Marcus told me in the alley behind the butcher shop that he wanted information.

He gave me a list, and I was to get information for him and not say shit to Romano. I wasn't supposed to ask questions. There are whispers of Marcus, but no one ever sees him. He stays in shadows and they say if you ever see him, you're dead.

I was scared shitless that he chose me, and I was ready to do whatever he said to stay off his radar.

But her name was there.

It was right fucking there at the bottom of the list. I had to tell him whatever he wanted with this list, it couldn't be her. I had to beg for her life. He wanted them all dead. Every one of them.

Not her was all I could tell him.

However, he got a hold of Chloe's list, for whatever reason, she hadn't erased her name yet. The photocopy had her name there, written clearly at the bottom. And he'd added the last names in his own handwriting. At the time, I thought it was odd that two people had each written half of the names, but I never guessed it was her that wrote the list, I would never have known.

She'd made a list of who she blamed, or hated, I don't know which is more true. But Marcus decided it would be a hit list and now was the time for all of them to die.

I've never known fear like I did when I told Marcus it couldn't be her. I told him she couldn't die. Anyone but her.

He said he would spare her, but that he didn't want information anymore. He wanted them all dead in the span of three weeks and he didn't care how.

I bartered for her life, and then I killed them all. Each and every one. I set their deaths in motion. I paid off a thug with a pack of heroin to take care of Amber. Tamra was a bullet in her head. I can still hear the ringing in my ears. I'm a murderer.

But I did it to spare Chlo. I had to do it. I'd do it again if kept her safe. I don't care what kind of man that makes me, so long as she's still breathing.

Tomorrow is day twenty, leaving a single day to spare of his morbid deadline.

"Andrea picks up her package tomorrow. Can you just make sure she gets it?" I ask Carter. Andrea gets an eightball of coke on the regular. I knew that's how she needed to go when she came to the shop two weeks ago, but Marcus wanted them done in order. So, she had to wait until tomorrow.

Now I wonder if he requested that on purpose. If somehow, he knew it'd freak Chlo out and that's why he texted her the way he did.

He's a sick fuck, but I lived up to my end of the bargain.

"She's done, and it's done," I tell him. It's laced with so much shit, it'll be quick and easy. Marcus won't come looking for us. It'll all be over with.

We'll run away, and this nightmare will be over.

Dave was an accident, Carter's accident. He didn't know he was on the list, but Dave had it coming to him regardless, for what he did to Carter and his family. I could never blame Carter for what he did. It's his story to tell, even if it did fuck him up more than it should have. The fucker was going to die anyway. I told him that.

Carter's not a killer; he's not meant for this life.

"The money's yours. I can at least give you that," I tell him, knowing that money won't go far with the debt they have. But it's better than nothing.

"Take it back," Carter tells me angrily. "I don't want it."

"Maybe not, but you need it," I tell him, putting my hands up to refuse the money and then looking back to make sure Chloe can't see.

She can never know.

"I know you're leaving." Carter's voice breaks. I don't know how he knew. Word spreads fast, but if that's going around, Romano is going to hear it before long and that means I need to get the fuck out of here as fast as I can. I don't need him looking for me, or worse, finding the body I left in his shop before the weekly deliveries on Monday.

"Who told you?" I ask him, my pulse beating harder in my temples. My jaw stiffens with the fear of a fight coming.

"No one," he answers, "but I know when goodbyes are coming."

Time passes slowly, and I feel myself breaking down. My first reaction is to go to Chloe Rose. I forget it all with her. I forget who I am and all the pain that comes with it. With her, I'm not alone.

"You need it. You can't run far without cash." He gives me a look of complete sincerity as he pushes it back into my hand. "It's not for me, and I don't want it." His voice is clear like he knew I'd give it to him.

"I have enough cash," I tell him. "Take it for your brothers then." My heart squeezes harder in my chest knowing how fucked they all are. It's two grand, and two grand more than he'll get selling dope on the street corner like he thinks he can do. I worked for Romano, but Carter doesn't. And it's not safe.

Carter gives me a weak smile and shakes his head. "We'll be all right. I'm heading up to the north side. I'll take care of us." I know that means he's dealing something. Although what and for who, I don't know.

His eyes are so serious. He seems so much older to me now.

"You can come with me," I tell him. "I don't want to leave you here. Come with us."

The weak smile is pulled into a smirk, one cloaked with sadness. Goodbyes are never easy, but they shouldn't hurt this much. "Don't stay here," I beg him. "I want more for you than this."

"I can't leave my brothers," he tells me and then licks his lips before handing the money back to me. "Take it." The bills brush against my knuckles and I'm reluctant to take it, but I do. "Find a better place than here." The money weighs heavy in my hand as he pulls his away. I won't take it. If anything, I'll leave it in the mailbox and pray one of them finds it.

"It's good you're skipping out," Carter tells me in a tone that lets me know something's up.

"What's going on?" I ask him, feeling my nerves ramp up.

"I heard Eddie say Romano wants to talk to you on Monday. I think they know you're involved and they're pissed they didn't know."

"Good thing I won't be around Monday." I start thinking about all the possible outcomes of that meeting and I don't like a single one of them. I could never rat Marcus out, he'd kill me. And even if I did, Romano would kill me for following someone else's orders. I have protection from no one and enemies everywhere.

"Did you tell her?" Carter changes the subject abruptly. "Does she know you killed them?"

I shake my head, wishing all of this was a nightmare I could wake from. All of it but Chloe. "I had to lie to her, but it's never felt like that," I tell him, confiding in my best friend one last time.

"Felt like what?" he asks me.

"Felt like I was hurting her by lying to her. I've never wanted so much from someone and to give her so much in return."

He smiles a genuine but sad smile that reaches his dark eyes. "I knew you loved her," he says lightheartedly. Brushing his thumb against his nose, he peeks behind him. It's darker now than it was before, not a single star in the sky to cast light down on us.

"I think it is love," I tell him and kick the rubble on the broken concrete.

"It's all right to say it," he jokes, "I won't make fun of you."

"I only just got her. I can't lose her, Carter," I confess to him. If it wasn't for her need to run away from here, I'd stay for him.

"Go ahead, I'll be all right," he tells me, and I want to believe him. "Hey, do you have that stuff though? Before you go?"

It takes me a minute to realize he's talking about the sweets. I have the last vial in my pocket and I know Chlo is never going to want to take it again, so I hand it over to him.

He's quick to slip the vial into his pocket. "Thanks, man. It's been rough sleeping."

Giving him a nod of understanding, I wonder if I should tell him that Chlo thinks some of her paranoia is from the drug, but I think she's wrong. She was right the entire time. Call it fear and intuition maybe.

"I hope it helps you sleep," I tell him and then glance back at the car.

"Get out of here, man. Get out while you still can," Carter tells me and it fucking hurts that I'm leaving him, but I have to. I have to get the hell out of here and take Chloe far away.

I have to reach out and hug him, pulling him hard into my chest. And he's quick to give me a hard pat on the back, followed by a grip I'll never forget.

There's no way I'd have made it out alive without him. I know that much.

Before the tears can show, I pull away from him, the only family I've ever had. "She can't stay here," I tell him as if I'm begging him to understand, but he already knows.

She's never belonged here.

"Come with us," I plead with him one last time even though I already know his answer.

"I have to stay." His voice is calm this time like he's resigned to his fate.

EPILOGUE

Two weeks later

Chloe

THE COOL WIND FLOWS THROUGH MY FINGERS AS I REST MY HAND AGAINST THE window. We've been off the highway for a little while now, still venturing into the unknown.

It's odd how the unfamiliar can offer so much comfort. How easy it is to leave everything behind and start a new life.

Countless times I've felt the fear of what could be waiting for us if we ever went back. And almost as if Bastian can read my mind, he asks me every time we stop somewhere new, "How about this place?"

"I can be a butcher anywhere. Or anything. We can be anything," he keeps telling me. "Just don't leave me." He says that a lot. As if I'd ever want to. One day, I think he'll know in every way that I'll never do that.

In every beat of my heart, I know I was supposed to run away with him. And he was supposed to run away with me.

We should have left when we were only children. We shouldn't have stayed in that place as long as we did. When the lights around you flicker and dim, it's a sign to run. To run far away and toward light and hope. It's an innate feeling I knew deep in my gut, but I swallowed it down and nearly let the darkness choke out what little life I had left in me.

It's only taken days of being away with Bastian at my side, holding my hand as we drive farther and farther away to know that's true.

I can smell the salty ocean air as the sun kisses my skin through the window. We're close to the ocean.

A line springs to mind and I jot it down in my notebook. It's half-full already, with ideas for a book so close to what I've been through. Some changes here and there because it's hard to write about the truth. It's hard to imagine what people would think of me if I told them my story. It's even harder for me to write it all down and to be okay with everything that happened. Because of what happened in my life, the things that were done to me and the things I did... well, it will never be okay but maybe it would make a memorable tale.

"Do you want to stop here?" Bastian asks, pointing to the left at a sign for a burger place.

My shoulders lift easily in a contented shrug. With my cheek resting against the head-rest, I ask him for the tenth time since we left, "Where do you think we're going?" I need answers to what we'll become. I know I love him and I only want to be with him, but the stirring in my stomach that this is too good to be true hasn't let up.

Bastian's large hand wraps around mine as he pulls my knuckles to his lips to kiss them one by one. The car idles at the stop sign and he looks me deep in my eyes.

"We're going where we're supposed to go. Together." His words are a balm to my broken soul. It's the only word that matters. It's the only word that's ever mattered. *Together.*

With tears pricking my eyes, the tears I wish would go away, even if they are from a happiness I never thought I'd feel, I whisper, "I love you."

He braces his hands on either side of my head, stealing a ravenous kiss from me, taking my pain away like he did so many years ago. But the pain now is minuscule and it's because of him. He's taken it all away. And I'll spend my life making sure I do the same for him.

With a bruising kiss, I can hardly breathe until he pulls away from me, letting the tip of his nose brush against mine. His eyes are still closed, his hands still tangled in my hair as he tells me, "I've always loved you. And I'll never stop loving you. I'll always choose you."

⸻ ⬩ ⸻

Sebastian
Years later

About two weeks after we got in the car and sped away as fast as we could, I got a call from Carter's brother, Daniel. I didn't let her see as I broke down against the bathroom door of the motel we'd stayed in for the night. We'd move from one place to the next, constantly on the go until we found a spot on the West Coast, far away from Crescent Hills. A local bed and breakfast was looking to hire a butcher for their farm and also in need of a book-keeper for the inn. Fate gave us our opportunity to stay, to find a new home, and we did. We grabbed it with both hands and didn't let go.

That night in the motel though, it almost didn't happen. The first few days we were on the road, everything changed with a single phone call. I almost got into the car and drove back to that hellhole when Daniel told me what happened. I would never have brought Chloe, but she wouldn't have let me leave her behind either.

The Talvery crew almost beat him to death the night we left. Carter nearly died for selling on the wrong turf. Daniel told me not to come back, that my name had been marked now, and I knew what that meant. If I went back, I was dead.

When I talked to Carter, I knew I'd made a mistake letting him stay. He had no one anymore, and everyone to provide for.

If I could go back, I would.

I'd never leave him behind.

It took over a decade before I dared show my face in that city again. Years of the phone calls coming less and less often. Years of building a life with the girl I always loved, while the memories of my past faded to bad dreams.

Life is a compromise. I left behind a friend, destined to stay, and be held captive to a city that had no mercy.

It would force him to become a brutal man I didn't recognize.

The Carter I abandoned in Crescent Hills, died that night I ran, and I'll never forgive myself for it.

NEVER BEFORE SEEN SCENE

Chloe

Five years ago and two days after the kiss

DON'T THINK ABOUT IT. THAT'S WHAT I WAS THINKING ABOUT WHEN THE SPILL happened. I was thinking not to think about the funeral. My neighbor says it's like the white elephant. If you tell yourself not to think about it, it's all you'll think about. Yet, I find myself thinking about my mother's funeral regardless. If I'm consciously telling myself not to think about it or trying to focus on my English homework… all I can see is the field and the mound of fresh dirt. It's all I can smell. That dirt.

With my books gripped tight to my chest, three of them, the three classes I just finished and the three books I planned to stow away in my locker, I realized I shouldn't remember the smell of dirt. It should have been of cheap perfume and cologne and cigars and cigarettes and whiskey even. Because that's what the men and women my mother grew up with and the men she called friends always smelled like.

But they weren't there.

Don't think about it. I told myself and then tripped over my own two feet. *Clumsy girl.*

Rubbing my left arm where a pink groove rests from the aftermath of the books hurling from my arm, I sit there on the ground, noting how my right knee hurts more than anything and staring at the back of my history text book as the black letters blur.

Don't cry.

It's just a fall. It's just books.

Everyone around me keeps walking, talking moving on with their life and I should be grateful for that. Don't notice me. Please. No one notice that I'm still falling apart. All I have to do is make it till Friday. Till the last day and then I can hide away.

One book lifts with shaky hands and my exhale is unsteady.

Don't you dare cry. Don't you cry over a trip in the hallway.

With a quick sniff I manage to get onto my knees but I drop the first book.

Don't cry. Don't smell the dirt. Don't think about the fact that no one was there who should have been. There should have been more people there. They didn't help her. They could have at least come.

Maybe it's the shame—

"Hey," the sudden masculine voice disrupts my thoughts. *Sebastian.*

He smells like the woods and fresh water, like a creek in the middle of a summer forest. Fresh but alluring. I wish he'd been there. I wish I could smell him all the time, and not the dirt that makes me think of the burial and loneliness.

Maybe I imagined his tone. I thought it was careful, gentle, kind even, but a look of annoyance stares back at me on his handsome face as the pile of books clunk together. There's a deep groove in the center of his forehead and I can't look at it, so my gaze travels down the simple white tee and worn jeans he's wearing as the heat rises in my cheeks.

At least I don't want to cry anymore.

"It's just books," he says and again, there's a kindness there, something he can't deny. No matter how much his dark gaze tries to lock with mine. It's intimidating. He's intimidating, the intensity that crackles inside of me, burning to look back at him nearly smothers me.

"I know," I whisper and have to clear my throat. He stands straight before I can, but I follow suit and finally look him in the eye.

"I just tripped." The statement is bland as I hold out my arms, wanting to take the books from him and thank him. The words are stuck though, every word is held captive as our surroundings blur and everything turns to white noise.

He licks his lower lip and seems to want to say something, but nothing comes. Just the two of us, standing two feet apart in a crowded hallway.

Don't think about the kiss. Don't think about his lips or the way he tastes or how I swear my pillow smells a little like him when I can't fall asleep.

Most importantly, don't think about how just one more kiss would make so much pain disappear.

The bell rings, loud and annoyingly. It won't be ignored and the moment is lost as is the racing of my heart. It turns sore, falling back to where it is supposed to be.

"You're okay," Sebastian tells me; he doesn't ask but still I answer, "Yeah. I'm okay."

Don't think about the kiss.

THE
BROTHER

POSSESSIVE

Some men are born with a black heart and a tainted soul.

It's in my blood and in my bones. In every impure thought and desire.

I tried to walk away from my past.

But then she came back into my life.

Stumbling toward me and looking up at me as if I was the one she'd been looking for all this time.

As if I could be her savior and take her pain away.

If only she knew.

She brings out what I hate most about myself.

Selfish, ruthless, *possessive.*

I tried to be a good man. To be cold and distant and warn her away.

She should have taken the hint and run.

She didn't …

And now she's *mine.*

PREFACE

Addison

I
T'S EASY TO SMILE AROUND TYLER.

It's how he got me. We were in calculus, and he made some stupid joke about angles. I don't even remember what it was. Something about never discussing infinity with a mathematician because you'll never hear the end of it. He's a cute dork with his jokes. He knows some dirty ones too.

A year later and he still makes me laugh. Even when we're fighting. He says he just wants to see me smile. How can I leave when he says things like that? I believe him with everything in me.

My friend's grandmother told me once to fall in love with someone who loves you back just a little more.

Even as my shoulders shake with a small laugh and he leans forward to nip my neck, I know that I'll never really love Tyler the way he loves me.

And it makes me ashamed. Truly.

I'm still laughing when his bedroom door creaks open. Tyler plants a small kiss on my shoulder. It's not an open-mouth kiss, but still it leaves a trace on my skin and sends a warmth through my body. It's fleeting though.

The cool air passes between the two of us as Tyler leans back and smiles broadly at his brother.

I may be seated on my boyfriend's lap, but the way Daniel looks at me makes me feel like I'm alone. His eyes pierce through me with a sharpness that makes me afraid to move. Afraid to even breathe.

I don't know why he does this to me.

He makes me hot and cold at the same time. It's like I've disappointed him simply by being here. As if he doesn't like me. Yet there's something else.

Something that's forbidden.

It creeps up on me whenever I hear Daniel's rough voice; whenever I catch him watching Tyler and me. It's like I've been caught cheating, which makes no sense at all. I don't belong to Daniel, no matter how much that idea haunts my dreams.

He's twenty-one now and I'm only seventeen. But more importantly, he's Tyler's brother.

It's all in my head. I tell myself over and over again that the electricity between us is *something I've made up. That my body doesn't burn for Daniel. That my soul doesn't ache for him to rip me away and punish me for daring to let his brother touch me.*

It's only when Tyler speaks to him that Daniel looks away from me, tossing something down beside us.

Tyler's oblivious to everything happening. And suddenly I can breathe again.

My eyelids flutter open, my body hot under the stifling blankets. I don't react to the memory in my dreams anymore. Not at first, anyway. It sinks in slowly. The recognition of what that day would lead to growing heavier in my heart with each second that passes. Like a wave crashing on the shore, but taking its time. Threatening to engulf me as it approaches.

It was years ago, but the memory remains.

The feeling of betrayal, for fantasizing about Tyler's older brother.

The heartache from knowing what happened only three weeks after that night.

The desire and desperation to go back to that point and beg Tyler to never come looking for me.

All of those emotions swirl into a deadly concoction in the pit of my stomach. It's been years since I've been tormented by the remembrance of Tyler and what we had. And by the memories of Daniel and what never was.

Years have passed.

But it all comes back to me after seeing Daniel last night.

CHAPTER 1

Addison

The night before

I LOVE THIS BAR. IRON HEART BREWERY. IT'S NESTLED IN THE CENTER OF THE CITY and located at the corner of this street. The town itself has history. Hints of the old cobblestone streets peek through the torn asphalt and all the signs here are worn and faded, decorated with weathered paint. I can't help but to be drawn here.

And with the varied memorabilia lining the walls, from signed knickknacks to old glass bottles of liquor, this place is flooded with a welcoming warmth. It's a quiet bar with all local and draft beers a few blocks away from the chaos of campus. So it's just right for me.

"Make up your mind?"

My body jolts at the sudden question. It only gets me a rough laugh from the tall man on my left, the bartender who spooked me. A grey shirt with the brewery logo on it fits the man well, forming to his muscular shoulders. With a bit of stubble and a charming smirk, he's not bad looking. And at that thought, my cheeks heat with a blush.

I could see us making out behind the bar; I can even hear the bottles clinking as we crash against the wall in a moment of passion. But that's where it would end for me. No hot and dirty sex on the hard floor. No taking him back to my barely furnished apartment.

I roll my eyes at the thought and blow a strand of hair away from my face as I meet his gaze.

I'm sure he flirts with everyone. But it doesn't make it any less fun for the moment.

"Whatever your favorite is," I tell him sheepishly. "I'm not picky." I have to press my lips together and hold back my smile when he widens his and nods.

"You new to town?" he asks me.

I shrug and have to slide the strap to my tank top back up onto my shoulder. Before I can answer, the door to the brewery and bar swings open, bringing in the sounds of the nightlife with it. It closes after two more customers leave. Looking over my shoulder through the large glass door at the front, I can see them heading out. The woman is leaning heavily against a strong man who's obviously her significant other.

Giving the bartender my attention again, I'm very much aware that there are only six of us here now. Two older men at the high top bar, talking in hushed voices and occasionally laughing so loud that I have to take a peek at them.

And one other couple who are seated at a table in the corner of the bar. The couple who just left had been sitting with them. All four are older than I am. I'd guess married with children and having a night out on the town.

And then there's the bartender and me.

"I'm not really from here, no."

"Just passing through?" he asks me as he walks toward the bar. I'm a table away, but he keeps his eyes on me as he reaches for a glass and hits the tap to fill it with something dark and decadent.

"I'm thinking about going to the university actually. To study business. I came to check it out." I don't tell him that I'm putting down some temporary roots regardless of whether or not I like the school here. Every year or so I move somewhere new … searching for what could feel like home.

His eyebrow raises and he looks me up and down, making me feel naked. "Your ID isn't fake, right?" he asks and then tilts the tall glass in his hand to let the foam slide down the side.

"It isn't fake, I swear," I say with a smile and hold up my hands in defense. "I chose to travel instead of going to college. I've got a little business, but I thought finally learning more about the technicalities of it all would be a step in the right direction." I pause, thinking about how a degree feels more like a distraction than anything else. It's a reason to settle down and stop moving from place to place. It could be the change I need. Something needs to change.

His expression turns curious and I can practically hear all the questions on his lips. *Where did you go? What did you do? Why did you leave your home so young and naïve?* I've heard them all before and I have a prepared list of answers in my head for such questions.

But they're all lies. Pretty little lies.

He cleans off the glass before walking back over and pulling out the seat across from me.

Just as the legs of the chair scrape across the floor, the door behind me opens again, interrupting our conversation and the soft strums of the acoustic guitar playing in the background.

The motion brings a cold breeze with it that sends goosebumps down my shoulder and spine. A chill I can't ignore.

The bartender's ass doesn't even touch the chair. Whoever it is has his full attention.

As I lean down to reach for the cardigan laying on top of my purse, he puts up a finger and mouths, "One second."

The smile on my face is for him, but it falters when I hear the voice behind me.

Everything goes quiet as the door shuts and I listen to them talking. My body tenses and my breath leaves me. Frozen in place, I can't even slip on the cardigan as my blood runs cold.

My heart skips one beat and then another as a rough laugh rises above the background noise of the small bar.

"Yeah, I'll take an ale, something local," I hear Daniel say before he slips into view. I know it's him. That voice haunted me for years. His strides are confident and strong, just like I remember them. And as he passes me to take a seat by the bar, I can't take my eyes off of him.

He's taller and he looks older, but the slight resemblance to Tyler is still there. As my heart learns its rhythm again, I notice his sharp cheekbones and my gaze drifts to his hard jaw, covered with a five o'clock shadow. I'd always thought of him as tall and handsome, albeit in a dark and brooding way. And that's still true.

He could fool you with his charm, but there's a darkness that never leaves his eyes.

His fingers spear through his hair as he checks out the beer options written in chalk on the board behind the bar. His hair's longer on top than it is on the sides, and I can't help but to imagine what it would feel like to grab on to it. It's a fantasy I've always had.

The timbre in his voice makes my body shudder.

And then heat.

I watch his throat as he talks, I notice the little movements as he pulls out a chair in the corner of the bar across from me. If only he would look my way, he'd see me.

Breathe. Just breathe.

My tongue darts out to lick my lips and I try to avert my eyes, but I can't.

I can't do a damn thing but wait for him to notice me.

I almost whisper the command, *look at me.* I think it so loud I'm sure it can be heard by every soul in this bar.

And finally, as if hearing the silent plea, he looks my way. His knuckles rap the table as he waits for his beer, but they stop mid-motion when his gaze reaches mine.

There's a heat, a spark of recognition. So intense and so raw that my body lights, every nerve ending alive with awareness.

And then it vanishes. Replaced with a bitter chill as he turns away. Casually. As if there was nothing there. As if he doesn't even recognize me.

I used to think it was all in my mind back then. Five years ago when we'd share a glance and that same feeling would ignite within me.

But this just happened. I know it did.

And I know he knows who I am.

With anger beginning to rise, my lips part to say his name, but it's caught in my throat. It smothers the sadness that's rising just as quickly. Slowly my fingers curl, forming a fist until my nails dig into my skin.

I don't stop staring at him, willing him to look at me and at least give me the courtesy of acknowledging me.

I know he can feel my eyes on him. He's stopped rapping his knuckles on the table and the smile on his face has faded.

Maybe the crushing feeling in my chest is shared by both of us.

Maybe I'm only a reminder to him. A reminder he ran away from too.

I don't know what I expected. I've dreamed of running into Daniel so many nights. Brushing shoulders on the way into a coffee shop. Meeting each other again through new friends. Every time I wound up back home, if you can even call it that, I always checked out every person passing me by, secretly wishing one would be him. Just so I'd have a reason to say his name.

Winding up at the same bar on a lonely Tuesday night hours away from the town we grew up in … that was one of those daydreams too. But it didn't go like this in my head.

"Daniel." I say his name before I can stop myself. It comes out like a croak and he reluctantly turns his head as the bartender sets down the beer on the wooden table.

I swear it's so quiet, I can hear the foam fizzing as it settles in the glass.

His lips part just slightly, as if he's about to speak. And then he visibly inhales. It's a sharp breath and matches the gaze he gives me. First it's one of confusion, then anger … and then nothing.

I have to remind my lungs to do their job as I clear my throat to correct myself, but both efforts are in vain.

He looks past me as if it wasn't me who was trying to get his attention.

"Jake," he speaks up, licking his lips and stretching his back. "I actually can't stay," he bellows from his spot to where the bartender, apparently named Jake, is chucking ice into a large glass. The music seems to get louder as the crushing weight of being so obviously dismissed and rejected settles in me.

I'm struck by how cold he is as he gets up. I can't stand to look at him as he readies to leave, but his name leaves me again. This time with bite.

His back stiffens as he shrugs his thin jacket around his shoulders and slowly turns to look at me.

I can feel his eyes on me, commanding me to look back at him and I do. I dare to look him in the eyes and say, "It's good to see you." It's surprising how even the words come out. How I can appear to be so calm when inside I'm burning with both anger and … something else I don't care to admit. What a lie those words are.

I hate how he gets to me. How I never had a choice.

With a hint of a nod, Daniel barely acknowledges me. His smile is tight, practically nonexistent, and then he's gone.

CHAPTER 2

MY FATHER TAUGHT ME AN IMPORTANT LESSON I'LL NEVER FORGET.

Never let a soul know what you really feel.

Never express it.

Only show them what you want them to see.

I hear his voice as I slip my hands in my jacket pockets and keep walking down Lincoln Street with my heart pounding in my chest and anxiety coursing in my blood. Two more blocks and I'll wait there. The alley is the perfect place to wait and collect myself.

Until then, my blood will pound in my ears, my veins will turn cold and my muscles will stay coiled. But I won't let anyone see that. Never.

I remember how my father gripped my shoulder when he looked me in the eyes and gave me that advice.

His dark stare was something no one ever forgot. It was impassive and cold. I lived many days wondering if my father loved me. I know my mother did. We were family and his blood, but he would never show any emotion and after that night, neither would I.

I was fourteen years old. And standing only a few feet away from the body of someone I once knew. I don't even remember his name. A friend of my father's. He worked in the business and gave the wrong person the wrong impression.

When you reveal that fear, that anger, that emotion, you give someone a hint of how to get to you. And that's what my father's friend had done. When someone gets to you, you end up dead.

My shoes slap on the concrete sidewalk as I slow down at the intersection, as if I'm merely waiting for the cars to stop at the red light so I can cross. It's not a busy night, so only a few people are walking down the street. A man to my right lights up a cigarette and leans against the brick wall to a liquor store.

I make my way around the block, replaying what happened in my head. It was supposed to be a simple, easy night. Another night of waiting for Marcus to show for the drop-off or waiting to hear word about what's going on with the deal between my brother and the cartel.

She caught me off guard.

Addison Fawn.

She's always been able to do that. She gets to me in a way I despise.

She makes me remember.

She makes me weak.

Another step and I see her face. Her high cheekbones and piercing green eyes. I love the way her hair falls in front of her face. There's always something effortless about it, like she doesn't put an ounce of work into looking as fuckable as she does.

The cool night air whips past me as I round the corner. The next alley will take me where I want to go. Directly across from the lot where her car must be. It's the only parking lot on this street for three blocks.

I swallow thickly, checking my phone again. It's been three minutes since I've left.

Three minutes is more than enough time for her to pay the tab and walk off.

I don't know if she will though.

It's been years since I've felt like I've known who she is.

Years since I've heard her say my name.

The corners of my lips turn up in a smirk as I hear the hesitancy in her voice replay in my memory and I let it. Like she was scared to say my name out loud.

It echoes in my head as I lean against the wall of the dark alley and gives me a thrill I haven't felt in a long time. *Too long.*

The alley is narrow, the type of passageway built decades and decades ago before the world knew better. Before humanity realized they were inviting sins in the night with small spaces like these.

My phone vibrates in my pocket, and I take a quick look around me before pulling it out.

There are four cars parked in the dirt lot. The streetlight on the right side illuminates the area easily, as do the headlights of a passing car.

My eyes flicker to the text on my phone and the amusement from only moments ago leaves me instantly.

Who's the girl? Jake texted and I'm reminded that I upped and left as if she mattered. As if her existence would cause an issue.

And of course it does. More than anyone could know.

My shoulders rise as I draw in a deep breath and let it out slowly, releasing the anger from letting her get to me and I focus on regaining control. Control is everything.

No one, I write him back but think better of it. It's obvious she's someone to me and Jake needs to be reassured. *My brother's ex,* I add.

My body tenses as I wait for him to respond. I keep my posture relaxed, although I'm anything but.

Off limits? Jake must have a fucking death wish.

I can't help the way my teeth grind as I text a response and then delete it before finally firing off a quick message.

For now. If Marcus comes tonight, tell him I'll be back late. I'm smoldering with rage as I realize how stupid it was to risk missing the meet with Marcus all over a quick emotion I couldn't suppress. Shock, anger ... fear even. She's only a girl. Inwardly, I can hear myself seething.

Alright, Jake messages me, making the phone vibrate in my hand. I almost ask him if Addison is still there. My fingertips itch to push for information.

But it's not needed.

Even as Jake continues to text me about the drop-off, I watch the skirt sway around Addison's hips. It's the color of cream and loose on her, not giving me any hints of how her ass looks right now. But her legs are on full display.

I've always thought of Addison the same way, even after everything that went down. From the first day I met her until this very second. She's a sad, but beautiful girl. You can see her pain in every bit of her features when she doesn't know someone's looking. Like I often did. From the way her full lips pout delicately, to the way her eyes seem to stare off in the distance, even when she's looking right at you it's as if she can see through you.

Those eyes have haunted me. The beautiful shades of green and brown are like the sunset over a forest. Like flecks of light peeking through and enhancing the darkness that's soon to come.

She runs her hand over her soft porcelain skin and through the modest waves in her thick dark hair. Even those slight movements and the swing of her hips as she walks carry a sadness with them. It never leaves her. It defines her. But it suits her well.

More than sad, and more than beautiful, Addison is memorable. *Unforgettable.*

Her car beeps as she unlocks it, a shiny new black Honda from the looks of it, and the sound echoes in the alley. She's parked in the third spot in the row of cars lined up under the streetlight. She looks to the left and right, cursing as she drops her keys in the gravel.

My dick stirs in my pants, straining against the fabric and I let out a low groan at the sight of her bent over. Her hair is swept to one side and the strap of her top is falling off her shoulder, giving me a view of that soft spot in the crook of her neck.

I adjust my dick and memorize the curves of her hips and waist until she opens up her car door and slips inside.

Every second my breaths come in heavier. The air around me feels as if it wants to suffocate me. Her tires kick up the gravel in the lot and I have to take a step back into the alley to avoid her headlights as she turns out onto the street.

I tell myself it's only out of instinct that I take a picture of her license plate as she drives off.

Well I try to, but I'm a poor liar.

When she's gone from view, I step back out onto the concrete sidewalk, staring down the desolate street and letting the brisk night air cool my hot skin.

Addison is back.

The only question on my mind is what I'm going to do with her.

CHAPTER 3

Addison

I'VE HATED DANIEL FOR A LOT OF THINGS. I'VE NEVER REALLY TALLIED THEM UP before.

The silent drive back to this tiny apartment provided plenty of time to recount each and every moment that bastard has made me feel inadequate, embarrassed … undeserving.

I take in a deep, calming breath then toss the keys onto the small kitchenette table and head right for the wine.

This day was going so well.

The thought settles me as I open the fridge and quickly grab a half-full bottle of red blend. I use my teeth to pull out the cork and pour the wine into a bright yellow coffee mug with sunflowers engraved on it. It's the closest thing to me and all my glasses are still packed in boxes.

It'll do fine to hold the wine, I think as I take a small sip. And then a large one.

I don't have a buzz yet, but in fifteen minutes I'm sure I will.

As I lick the sweet wine off my lips, I stare aimlessly at the glass bottle. I have to be careful not to fall into old patterns. It's been a long time since I've needed wine to sleep. But I can see myself relying on that bad habit tonight. *That's what some memories will do to you.*

I take a good, hard look at the bottle. It's more than halfway empty as it is. I'll be fine.

Leaning against the counter, I let the past flicker in front of me and trace the outline of the flowers on the mug.

Each memory is accompanied by another gulp of wine, each one tasting more and more bitter.

So many times Daniel's left me feeling less than. And it's my fault.

Even the first time was my fault.

The sudden memory of Tyler both warms my heart and makes my vision blur as my eyes gloss over with tears. I can't think of him for long without feeling a deep pain in my chest.

He was my first. My first everything.

Just like his brother Daniel and just like the rest of the men in their family, Tyler Cross was stubborn. And he didn't let up until I finally caved and said yes to being his girlfriend.

I told myself he was nice and that it felt good to be wanted. And my God, it did. When you're an orphan, you learn rather quickly people don't want you.

It's a hard thing to unlearn.

And at sixteen years old and in my fourth foster home, I didn't believe Tyler wanted anything more than a kiss, or to cop a feel. To get into my pants. Just like the previous foster dad wanted from me. He was a rotten bastard.

I run the tip of my finger along the edge of the mug, remembering how Tyler didn't give up on making me feel wanted. I only stayed with the Brauns, my fourth foster home in three years, because of how Tyler made me feel.

I didn't want to move to another school district.

I finally wanted to stay somewhere.

The Brauns would get their check and I would be a good kid, I'd be quiet. I'd put up with whatever it was I had to do in order for them not to send me back.

All because Tyler genuinely made me feel wanted. Even if it was obvious the Brauns, like the other foster parents, only wanted to get paid. Having to watch over a teenager with hormones and homework wasn't on their wish list.

Looking back on it now though, I don't much mind Jenny and Mitch Braun. They were okay people. Maybe if I hadn't run away when everything happened, I'd have a relationship with them. Or a semblance of one.

They didn't like Tyler though. They were probably the only people on the face of the earth who didn't like that boy. I can't blame them, since he did in fact want to get into my pants when they eventually met him.

I cover my mouth with my hand as I let out a small laugh at the memory.

He had to meet my guardians before I'd go anywhere near his house.

I have to give Tyler credit, he put up a good showing.

And then I had to face his family.

There was one big difference though. One massive separation between what he had to do and what I had to do in our little agreement.

Tyler had a real family.

That was so obvious to me. Actual relatives. Like I had once. It's an odd feeling standing in a room with people who belong together. Especially when you don't, but you want to. You desperately want to.

It was wrong of me. Every reason I had for staying with Tyler was selfish.

I was young back then. Young and stupid and incredibly selfish.

I know that now and it only makes the shame that much worse.

I remember how I could hardly look at anyone as Tyler wrapped his arm around my shoulders. Like he was proud of me and I belonged to him.

His mother had died years before, something Tyler and I had in common. His father was in the leather recliner in the living room, seated in front of the television although I'm certain he was sleeping.

Tyler told me his father worked late nights, but I could read between the lines. I knew the type of family the Crosses were. I knew by the way people spoke in hushed voices around them with traces of both fear and intrigue. And I heard the whispers.

There were little clues too. Tyler and his brother Jase were always being handed money under the cafeteria table and making quick exchanges. Certain people avoided them, certain red-eyed and scrawny potheads, to be exact.

It didn't matter to me.

In fact, I liked that their family was doing some type of business that meant his father would be asleep when I was forced to meet them all. Five boys in the family and Tyler was the youngest.

One less male to have to endure was fine by me. Declan, the middle boy, gave the impression of being disinterested in life in general. Let alone his brother's girlfriend. He was the first of Tyler's brothers I met, and even he seemed to be kind, if nothing else.

And that continued as I met his other brothers. They all welcomed me. There was no hidden agenda, no sneers or snide comments about where I was from or what the Brauns did at the local tavern two weeks ago.

That's one thing people liked to gossip about at school when I first got there. Foster parents aren't supposed to be drunks. Funny how that type of talk died when Tyler staked his claim on me.

Yet another reason I stayed and gave more and more of myself to a boy who could never have all of me.

It was so obvious that he never would. Especially that first day he brought me home.

The moment I thought I could relax, I met the last brother.

Daniel.

Tyler knocked on the door to his room, tapping out song lyrics and telling him to open up.

I remember exactly the way my polish had chipped on my thumbnail. I'm a nervous picker and I was busy chipping away at it when the door opened.

"What?" The word came out hard and my body stilled. I could feel the anger coming off of him from being interrupted.

He gripped the doorframe, which made his shoulders and height seem that much more intimidating. It was his toned muscles and the dark stubble lining his upper throat and jaw that let me know he was older.

And the heat in his stare as he let his gaze wander to where I stood that let me know I wasn't welcome.

That was the first time Daniel made me feel the same way I do now.

And the first time I knew I'd never love Tyler the way he deserved.

But I stayed with him. Deep inside I know it's because a very large part of me wanted Daniel to want me back. I wanted Daniel to want me the way that I instantly wanted him.

CHAPTER 4

Daniel

THE BACK DOOR TO IRON HEART BREWERY IS PROPPED OPEN A COUPLE INCHES with a brick. There's a small stack of them next to the dumpster and I've seen a few of them used for a number of things.

The door creaks open slowly as I take a look to my left and right. It's pitch black out now and deserted. It's been four hours since I left. Enough time to pass for me to get my shit together and figure out what it is that I want and how I'm going to handle this.

The entire town is quiet now that everything on Lincoln Street is closed.

I sneak in the back, hearing the clinking of glass around the corner and past the stockroom. The fresh scent of hoppy beer in this place never gets old.

I've only been here a couple months and I thought I'd get bored fast. So far there's not much action or competition. For a college town, it's surprising. But feeling out this area and waiting on information about future deals for my brother hasn't been the pain in the ass it usually is.

Other than Jake. He's not good for a damn thing other than asking for a beer or who comes around here when I'm away. He knows this place is used for drops, but that's as far as our relationship goes.

Jake's got his earbuds in, he's not paying attention in the least. My shoulder leans against the wall closest to the far end of the bar, and just enough so I can see the table where Addison sat earlier today.

I let the memory linger for a moment before speaking loud enough for Jake to hear over the music blaring in his ears.

"Marcus show up?" I call out and Jake startles, hitting his lower back against the counter and dropping a glass to the ground.

It breaks, cracking into a few large pieces rather than shattering.

Pushing off the wall, I take a few steps closer to him.

"Shit, dude," he tells me as he slowly lowers himself to the floor, catching his breath, and starts picking up the shards. "You scared the shit out of me." He starts to ask, "How did you get—" before stopping and looking past me to answer the question himself.

"Sorry," I offer him and crouch down to pick up the single piece of broken glass that's left. It's a solid piece a couple inches long with a sharp tip. I slide my finger along the blunt, slick side of it, toying with it as I talk to him. "Didn't mean to startle you." It's hard to keep the grin off my face, but it's easier if Jake is somewhat relaxed. He needs to know to fear me, but only so much that he doesn't do anything stupid. So long as he's easygoing, so is everything else that goes down here. He can keep looking the other way and I can keep everything moving as it should.

"No worries, man," he says as he stands up and deposits the chunks in his hand into a bin under the counter. He's still shaking and instead of reaching out for the piece I'm holding, he takes out the rectangular basin and offers it to me.

I hold his gaze as I toss it in to join the rest of them.

"What's going on?" he asks as he sets it back into place and pretends that he's not scared. That he doesn't look like he's going to piss himself.

"How long was the girl here?" I ask him and take a look around the counter. This section of the bar is small and narrow. There's a lone window on the other side and it's cracked open, letting in a small breeze.

"Addison?" he asks, saying her name out loud and I don't trust myself to speak as the anger swells inside of me, so I wait for him to look at me and give a short nod.

"Not long," he answers and gets back to wiping down a few of the glasses still lined up on the far side of the sink. "She left right after you."

"What was she here for?" I ask him and pray it wasn't for a meet. They're all done here. It's the perfect place, in the perfect town. Any necessary conversations can happen right here. And any arguments can be settled in the back … with those bricks. But this city may be more useful and profitable. Time will tell.

"Just coming in for a drink."

I nod my head and remember how I've found a few guys I know sitting at the bar, completely oblivious to what was going on around them. Like Dean. He had no idea; he was too wrapped up in his own story to realize what was happening here.

"Who is she?" Jake asks, interrupting my recollection.

"A girl," I answer and then go back to being the one asking the questions. "She come in with anyone?"

"Nope, she's single. She didn't say she knew anyone or that she was looking for anyone." He replies with the information I was hoping for. It was just a coincidence that she was here. But the way he answers it doesn't quite sit right with me.

He's a funny kid and a good guy in some ways, but he's the type who looks the other way and likes to pretend everything's friendly and fine and nothing fucked up is going on.

I don't have any problems with him. *Yet.*

"Is that so?"

"Yeah, she's looking at going to the university. New to town. You know, that kind of thing."

"Hey Jake," I start and wait for him to look up at me. "How do you know her name?" My body's tense and tight, even though I don't think he has a clue how badly I'll fuck him up if he hit on her. He's a flirt, young and carefree. He gets plenty of action from girls coming in here to get a drink and drown out their problems with alcohol.

The fucker looks up at me like it's a given and says, "From her credit card."

I don't like his tone, or the ease with which he talks about her. But my body's relaxed, and the smile on my face grows as I tell him, "Of course. Sorry, she's got me a little wound up."

"I could tell." My back stiffens at his confession. "I mean I get it, she's hot," he says, completely oblivious to how my hand reflexively forms a fist. He shrugs and dries off the last glass. "You want me to keep tabs on her?"

The correct answer is no. But it's not the word that slips from my tongue. "Yes," I reply and it comes out harder than it should, with a desperate need clinging to the single syllable.

Jake pauses and takes in my appearance.

"I have a soft spot for her," I tell him and inwardly I hate myself. Both for the lie and for the hint at the truth. He nods his head and hangs up the dish towel in his hands.

"So she's going to the university?" I ask him and he returns to his normal easy self.

"I didn't get much information from her. She'd just gotten here and Mickey was at the bar."

"Well, don't worry about it. But if she comes in here again, text me."

"No problem. You need anything else?" he asks and I remind him of my earlier question.

"Did Marcus come?" I already know the answer. He hasn't shown up yet. Carter, my brother, messaged me to let me know not to waste my time in the bar tonight. But I know Marcus is a lot like me. He likes to know people's habits and if I tell him I'll meet him, I want him to know I'll be there.

This isn't my first run-in with him. Last time it took weeks before he finally showed.

There aren't a lot of men I'd wait on, but Carter says this is important and Marcus and I have history.

"He didn't. I don't know why he—"

"Looks like you're almost done," I cut him off with a trace of a smile on my lips. "Sorry to keep you."

"Not a problem," he says to my back as I turn and leave the bar.

The bright light of the Iron Heart sign casts a shadow beneath my feet as I walk toward the barren parking lot with only one thing on my mind—how to find little miss Addison Fawn.

CHAPTER 5

Addison

D ANIEL'S A PRICK.

Why is it that the assholes stay in your head, rankling and festering their way into your thoughts while the nice guys are passed over?

I went shopping on the strip downtown to distract myself. I spent a pretty penny on décor for this apartment and on the softest comforter I've felt in my life.

One tweed rug, two woven baskets and a dozen rustic wood picture frames later and my living room is acceptable. Snapshot after snapshot I post the different angles on Instagram, where I have my largest following and where I sell most of my photos.

But it's all done absentmindedly. And it's not like these are for sale, just pictures that serve as an update to let my followers know I've found a new place.

I don't have an ounce of interest flowing through me.

I came here to settle down. To finally give myself a reason to stay and possibly take formal classes to breathe new life into my business.

And instead I've been pushed back to when I was only seventeen.

No home.

No life.

No reason to do anything at all.

My throat tightens and my eyes prick, but I refuse to let a single tear fall.

It's all because I'm still not worthy enough for Daniel fucking Cross.

My phone pings and I go into the messenger app on Facebook to see who it is.

Another person wanting me to photograph their wedding.

I don't do functions.

I politely message back that I don't do shoots. I only photograph the things around me and tell my own story. Not other people's. In other words, I'm not for hire. Photography is my business, but also my therapy. I photograph what I want and nothing else. It's the only way I've survived and I won't compromise that.

That's how I've made a living for the past few years. Little sales here and there. Enough to keep my head above water and to keep moving from place to place.

Searching for Something is what I eventually called my business.

Not that it started as a business. I was just taking pictures of every little thing that reminded me of Tyler.

All I had was my camera, the only present my last foster mother had ever given me. Tyler told her she should get it for me for Christmas. He said if she wouldn't, he would. He would've given me anything.

And so it started with me wanting to take a photograph of the snow around his old Chevy truck that couldn't run anymore. The rusted-out hood. The flat back left tire.

I started taking pictures of everything, obsessively. It was something Tyler and I had done together and it made sense to do at the time.

I needed something and although I didn't know what that something would be, I took photos of everything on my way to find what I was looking for.

Something to take the guilt away. Something to make me smile the way a boy who loved me in a way I didn't deserve had.

Searching for Something.

What it turned out to be was profitable.

A myriad of photos all priced ridiculously high. In my opinion, at least. But that's what everyone else was doing. The competition's pictures sold for hundreds. And mine looked like a steal simply because of the price tag.

I adopted the "fake it till you make it" strategy. And it's been working. But I don't know shit about running a business.

The random person on Facebook shoots back an apology and I don't bother to respond. My customer service isn't the best either.

Some days are better than others.

Some days are filled with reminders of the past. And those days are the worst for me personally, but the best for the things I see and can capture with a lens. And they sell well. Not just well, like serious money.

The shots I've taken today don't tell my story. It should be a part of my journey, but the pretty images of wooden frames and white tweed with pale blue accents are what I wanted before last night. Before I went to Iron Heart and ran into that asshole.

This is a décor shoot for a new life with new roots. It'll look pretty on Instagram with a soft filter, but that's about all it is. Just a series of pretty pictures.

My phone pings and pings with updates and I put it on vibrate before heading to the kitchen, where I place it on the table.

Next week is the kitchen makeover.

For now, it's all black and white with pops of cherry. A red teapot sits untouched on the stove as I shove my sunflower mug into the microwave to heat up water for tea.

I doubt I'll ever use that teapot.

My phone vibrates yet again, rattling the table just as the microwave beeps. A heavy sigh of irritation leaves me, but I know it's not the messages, nor the headache from stress and exhaustion.

It's because of Daniel. Just like years ago, I'm losing sleep over the asshole. Back then I never said a word. I let him treat me how he wanted, and I cowered away.

I'm older now and last night I should have said something. I should have gotten up and slapped him for being such a dismissive prick. Well, maybe that's taking things a little too far. But he deserves to know how much it hurt me. How I still struggle with what happened and how him treating me like that only makes the pain that much worse.

As the tea bag sinks into the steaming water, an idea hits me to search for Daniel on Instagram.

If not Instagram, then Facebook. Everyone is somewhere online now.

With my feet up on the chic glass table and the mug in my right hand, I search both on my cell phone.

And when both of those prove useless I try Twitter.

The steady, rhythmic ticking of the simple clock across from me and above the little kitchenette gets my attention when my search proves to be futile. I stare at the second hand that's marching along, willing it to give me an answer.

But time's a fickle bitch and she's never helped me with anything.

I take another sip of the now lukewarm tea before getting up for another cup.

As I wait for it to heat, I decide to search Iron Heart Brewery on Church and Lincoln Street.

Slowly a grin forms on my lips. Jake Holsteder stares back at me from a black and white photo where he's holding up a beer in cheers. The bartender from last night is apparently the owner. Jake has links to his social media accounts.

And more importantly, Daniel knows Jake.

It's a stretch, but I send a message to Jake on Facebook and then prepare my second cup of tea.

Nice to meet you last night. Sorry I left early.

It's a simple message and if he doesn't respond, I can always go back to the bar. I'm vaguely aware that I'm chasing after Daniel. After the man whose very existence brings back the ghosts of my past. But I don't care. I live off instinct and everything is telling me that I need to find Daniel. If for no other reason than to tell him he knows damn well who I am.

I add more sugar to the cup this time than last and the spoon clinks against the ceramic edge of the mug as my phone vibrates.

No worries. You leave for any reason in particular?

I chew on the inside of my cheek at his message.

Just had to go. But I wanted to come back and try that beer. I don't even remember what the hell the beer was called, but then I add, *I'd love to take pictures of the place too if that's okay?*

I purse my lips and tap my thumb against my phone before finally sending the message.

Pictures? That's all he answers.

I send him a link to my Instagram and then text, *Your place gives me so much inspiration.*

NICE!

Even if he's only being polite, I appreciate it. *Thanks!*

He writes, *Seriously, these are beautiful. You should try selling them.*

I do. It's what I do for a living and I'd love to take some pics in your bar. The whole place gives me a ton of inspiration. Maybe we can chat too?

He takes a moment and then another to respond. Each second makes my heart beat a little faster and I find myself picking at my nails. *You come by looking for him?*

Him? I play coy.

I thought maybe you knew Daniel? he asks me although it's a statement.

I did, but I haven't seen him in years. I send the message without checking it. Maybe I gave away too much.

You should stay away, Jake warns me and although I know he's right, it pisses me off. All the kids at school told me that about Tyler too—well, more about his family than him specifically, and he was the only good thing I've ever had in my life. And I really don't like people telling me what to do.

I didn't go to your bar looking for an old friend. I pause before adding, *I'm here to make new ones.*

It feels like a hand's squeezing my heart in my chest as an anxious feeling comes over me. The only sense I can gather from it all is that I know I'm only doing this to piss Daniel off. And that's something I shouldn't do; I've done it once before and the memory makes me feel weak.

You can come by anytime. What's your number? he asks me and although it's forward, I send it over. Jake knows Daniel. So maybe I can get some intel at the very least.

Daniel was always the possessive type. Even if he hated me, he hated anyone who showed me any attention more. So maybe finding out Jake has my number will piss him off. I can only hope.

I feel petty as I walk away from the phone, listening to it vibrate in time with the ticking of the clock.

As I peek out of the sheer white curtains and down onto the street below me, an eerie feeling washes through me. It slowly pricks along my skin until the hairs on the back of my neck stand up.

It's a feeling like someone's watching me. I'm slow as I turn so I'm facing my living room. There's no one else here in my studio apartment. Not a soul.

My hand wraps around the hot mug and I pull the curtains shut. It's only the memory of Tyler that's brought this back.

I couldn't go anywhere without feeling him there. Watching me. A shudder runs down my spine as I remember each day. Each photo I took as I whipped around, expecting to find someone lurking in the shadows. There was never anyone there. It was only my shame that followed me.

I hate Daniel even more in this moment.

It took me years to get to where I was days ago. And with one look, I've gone back to being the girl I was trying to leave behind.

CHAPTER 6

Daniel

"IT'S BEEN LONG ENOUGH, HASN'T IT?" MY BROTHER'S VOICE ASKS ON THE OTHER end of the phone.

My eyes close as I try to push down the irritation. Madison Street is busy today in the quiet town. Cars pass and I can hear the hums and rumbles with the windows opened in the diner as I lean back in the booth. The vinyl coverings protest as I lean forward and wave the waitress away before she can offer me another cup of coffee.

"We go through this every few months, Carter." I close my eyes again as I continue, "Do you really want to have the same conversation again?"

Across the street is a coffee shop. And inside it, Addison. She's hunched over in the corner with her laptop on a small circular table as she sits cross-legged in a chair. Some things never change.

I watch her from a distance in the safety of the diner. I'm within view; she could see me if she wanted to. But that's the thing about Addison. She never wanted to see me.

"How long are you going to keep this up?" Carter asks me. He's older than me by a year, almost on the dot. Irish twins, so to speak. I don't bother answering him and instead I remember the details of her address that Marcus gave me.

Funny how he can't show up to deliver the package from the Romanos. But one encrypted message from me to him with Addison's license plate number sparks enough interest for him to respond.

I suppose he hasn't forgotten. Marcus has a good memory.

"Whatever, I just need the package." Carter sighs on the other end of the phone. "I need to know what we're getting into before we decide…"

He doesn't continue, but I know what he's getting at. It's best not to speak those things where others can hear.

"He'll show. You know how he is."

"He's a pain in my ass."

The corner of my lip kicks up at his comment. "So many things are a pain in your ass, Carter. It's hard to believe you can sit down without wincing," I joke as I watch Addison take a large drink from her coffee cup. It's the tallest size the shop has and it looks like she's almost done.

"You're fucking hilarious, you know that?" I laugh at Carter's comment even though he says it with disdain. He runs the family business now. What started as a way for my father to make extra cash became an empire formed from ruthless and cutthroat tactics. Carter's the head, but I do his bidding more from a vague obligation that we're blood than anything else.

"Are you coming home after this? As soon as this package arrives? There's no reason for you to stay away and we need you here."

Her name is on the tip of my tongue. *Addison.* I may deal in addiction, but she's the only addiction I've ever had and the only one I desire.

"Well?" he presses.

"I'm curious about something," I answer my brother.

"What's that?"

"Something of personal interest," I mutter and the words come out lower than I intend them to. He's quiet for a long moment. And my focus is momentarily distracted. A man in a thin leather jacket walks past the coffee shop slowly, but his gaze is on Addison.

My eyes narrow as he stops in his tracks and glances inside the place. I shake off the possessive feelings. I'm only projecting.

Carter's voice brings my attention back to him. "With that shit your friend Dean pulled, there's too much heat around you." He ignores my earlier comment and I decide it's for the best. There's no need for anyone to know what I'm doing.

I'm quick to answer him. "Which is exactly why I need to stay. Leaving would raise suspicion."

A line of cars pass on the street in front of me, temporarily blocking Addison from my view. At their movement, she peeks up through the large glass windows of the shop.

Her hair brushes her shoulder and falls down her back as she takes a break to look out onto the street. Her pouty lips are turned down. They always are. There's a sadness that's always followed Addison. It's only a matter of whether or not she's trying to hide it, but it's always there.

Her green eyes are deep and even from this distance they seem to darken. Her hand moves to the back of her neck, massaging away a dull ache from sitting there for hours now. With each breath, her chest rises and falls and I'm mesmerized by her. By all of her.

More so by what she does to me.

The hate and anger I felt toward her years ago has numbed into something else each minute I sit here.

Curiosity maybe.

"Just get the package from Marcus. You've been gone long enough and we could use you here."

"I don't know if I want to come back," I tell him honestly and flatly.

"It's not a matter of want," he replies but his words come out hollow and with no authority although he wishes he had it. "We're your blood." He plays the only card he has that can get me to do his bidding.

"You never fail to remind me."

My phone vibrates with a message and I'm more than happy to end this call.

"I've got to go." My phone vibrates again. "I'll update you when I can." I don't wait for him to acknowledge what I've said, let alone tell me goodbye. I've never been close to my brothers. Not like they are toward each other. I'm the black sheep, I suppose.

I crack my neck as my phone vibrates for a third time. Before checking it I glance back at Addison only to see she's gone, although her laptop is still there. My heart stills and my body tenses until I see her by the counter, ordering something else.

Annoyance rises in me as I realize how much pull she has over me in this moment. I've turned back into what I hate. My teeth grit as I pull up my texts and that annoyance grows to an agitation that makes me grip the edge of the table to keep me from doing something stupid.

Three messages, each from Jake.

Marcus isn't coming tonight. He said there are complications.

I have your girl's number though if you want it.

And I think she's coming here tonight.

Jake wants to die. That's the only explanation. He literally wants me to kill his ass.

My glare moves from the cell phone in my hand back to the coffee shop across the street. Addison's cardigan dangles loosely around her as she moves back to her spot. Her jeans are tight and I can just imagine how they'd feel against my hands as I ripped them off of her. It'd be difficult, but I would fucking love it.

"Do you …" I hear a small, hesitant voice next to me and I have to school my expression before I can look back at the waitress.

She's an older woman, with soft lines around her eyes. A stray lock of dark hair with a line of silver running through it falls from her bun and into her face as she offers me a smile and holds up a pot of coffee. "You're all out this time," she says, like it's a reason to have another.

"Sure," I say and smile politely as she fills the cup.

The hot coffee steams and I stare at it as she leaves me be.

So Addison is giving her number out.

I wonder if she would have given it to me. I replay that scene in my head and instead of leaving, I slip in beside her.

I don't deserve Addison. That's a given.

But I'll be damned if I let some asshole like Jake get his hands on her.

CHAPTER 7

Addison

IT TOOK THREE DAYS TO ACTUALLY GO THROUGH WITH IT AND GO BACK TO IRON Heart Brewery.

Three days and this feeling in my gut that won't leave.

Three days of fiddling with images in Photoshop and hating each and every one because I can't focus.

And worst of all, three nights of not sleeping.

Every night I keep dreaming of the bar and every time the scene ends differently. It starts out how I'd have liked for it to have gone. With him giving me the time of day. With him offering to get me a drink. But then it turns dark and wicked. Daniel grabs me. Or worse. I hear Tyler tell me to stay away.

And I wake up shaken.

I feel just like I did that winter I ran away.

And I hate it. I hate Daniel even more for making it all come back. And if I can find that asshole I'm going to tell him exactly how he makes me feel. Not just the way he made me feel the other night, but also the way I felt all those years ago.

Part of me wants to run. But I already did that. I can't keep running forever.

I open the heavy glass door to the bar with the buzz of the late traffic behind me. This is an old town, but on weekends everyone is out and about.

I'm immediately hit with the aroma of pale ale lingering in the air and the chatter of everyone in here. The air outside was crisp, but only two steps in and the warmth lets me slip off my cardigan.

"Addison," Jake says my name from his place behind the bar. It carries over the hubbub and a man seated on a stool by him turns to look back at me.

Jake's smile is broad and welcoming as he gestures to an open seat at the bar.

For a small moment I forget the churning in my gut. I think that's what really happened these past couple of years. I slowly forgot. And if that isn't a tragedy, I don't know what is.

"You alright?" Jake asks with his forehead creased and a frown on his lips.

"Sorry," I tell him and shake my head as I fold the cardigan over the barstool and then slip on top of it, resting my elbows on the bar. "Been a long few days."

"What's bothering you?" he asks while passing a beer down the bar to an old man with salt and pepper hair and bushy eyebrows that are colored just the same.

The man waves him a thanks without breaking his conversation. Something about a football game coming up.

Letting out an easy sigh, I pull the hair away from my face and into a small ponytail although I don't have a band, so it falls down my back as I talk. "Oh, you know. Just moving and getting settled." I smile easily as I lie to him. "So, how's it been going for you?"

Even as I ask him I'm almost painfully aware of how I couldn't care less. I'm eager for information and that's all I want. I rest my chin in my hand and lean forward, pretending to give him my full attention even though my mind's on all the questions on the tip of my tongue.

How often does Daniel come here?

Do you think he'll be here tonight?

Do you know where I can find him if he doesn't come?

Instead I smile and laugh politely when I'm supposed to; all the while Jake chitchats about the bar and points to the pictures on the wall. Occasionally he answers his phone and texts or gets someone a beer.

Although it's crowded and I'm having a real conversation for the first time since three nights ago, I've never felt more alone.

"So we go around from place to place, collecting all of them we can find," Jake wraps up something he said that I was only half listening to and then takes a seat on his side of the bar.

"What's really bothering you?" he asks and it catches me off guard. My simper slips, and my heart skips a beat.

"What do you mean?" I ask him as if I haven't got a clue and then quickly follow up with, "I'm just tired." It sounds phony to my own ears, so I'm sure I sound like a bad liar to him too.

"You seemed a little shaken the other night," Jake says softly, leaning forward. Someone calls out his name and he barely acknowledges them, holding up his hand to tell them to wait. "Maybe you came in looking for something?" he asks me with his eyes narrowed.

The playfulness is gone, as is the sound of all conversation in the busy bar. In its place is the rapid thumping of my heart.

"Or someone?" he says as somebody else calls out his name again, breaking me from the moment. I turn to the man with the bushy eyebrows as Jake tells him, "One minute!" in not the most patient of tones.

"So what is it?" he says and waits for me.

"I didn't come in here looking for anything or anyone." I tell him the truth. My voice is small, pleading even.

"But you found something," he prompts.

I only nod my head and he pushes off of the bar, standing up and making his way back to the draft beers to satisfy the old man's order.

"If you don't want to see him again, you should leave now," Jake speaks without looking at me and then smiles and jokes with the man at the end of the bar.

"Why's that?" I call after him, my voice raised so he can hear me and the bar top digging into my stomach as I lean over it to get a good view of him.

Just as Jake opens his mouth to answer me, the door to the bar opens and I can feel the atmosphere change.

No one else stops talking. No one else turns to look over their shoulder.

But I do. I'm drawn to him and always have been. It's like my body knows his. Like my soul was waiting for his.

Daniel's always had an intensity about him. There's a dominance that lingers in the way he carries himself. A threat just barely contained. The rough stubble over his hard jaw begs me to run my hand against it. The black leather of his jacket is stretched over his shoulders.

Thump … thump … my heart ticks along and then stops.

Daniel's dark eyes meet mine instantly. They swirl with an emotion I can't place as they narrow, and I can't breathe until he takes a step. We both hang there for what feels like forever. He must know I've come here for him.

I watch as he moves, or rather stalks toward me. Each movement is careful, barely contained. Like it's taking everything in him just to be near me. I know he wants to appear relaxed, but he's faking it.

And with another step toward me, I can finally tear my gaze away.

I look forward, my back straight and my eyes on the beer in front of me as he walks behind me. I can hear each step and the scratch of the barstool on the floor directly to my left as he pulls it out.

I remind myself I came here for him. No, not *for* him. To see him. To clear the air.

I came here to this small town for me because I finally had my life together.

And he ruined it. The memory of his cold reception and dismissal hurts more and more with each passing second. I'm not a little girl for him to shove aside anymore and treat like I'm some annoyance.

The thought strengthens my resolve and I turn sharply to the left just as he takes his seat. He's so close my breasts nearly brush his bicep and it forces the words to a grinding halt as I pull back.

I'd forgotten what he smells like, a woody scent with a freshness to it. Like trees on the far edge of a forest by the water. I'd forgotten what it feels like to be this close to him.

To be too close to what can ruin you is a disconcerting feeling.

"Addison," he says and although his voice is deep and masculine, in that smooth cadence my name sounds positively sinful. The irritation in his tone that was constant in my memory is absent.

"Daniel." I barely manage to get his name out and I clear my throat, slowly sitting back in my seat to grab the beer in front of me. "I was wondering if I'd find you here," I admit and then peek up at him.

A genuine grin grows slowly on his handsome face. I swear his teeth are perfectly white. It's a crime for a man to look this good.

"You came here looking for me?" he asks me with a cockiness that reminds me of a boy I once knew and again, for the second time, my confidence is shaken. As I lick my lower lip to respond, I fail to find the words.

"Do I intimidate you, Addison?" he asks in a teasing voice and I roll my eyes and then lift the beer to my lips. I assume he'll say something else as I drink, but he doesn't.

As I set the glass down, I look him in the eyes. "You know you do and I hate it." There's a heat between us that ignites in an instant. As if a drop of truth could set fire to us both. I can barely breathe looking into his dark eyes.

"Do you now?" he asks again in that same playful tone. "So you came here looking for me because you hate me?"

"Yes," I answer him without hesitation, although it's not quite truthful. That's not why, but I'm fine with him thinking that.

His brow raises slightly and he tilts his head as if he wasn't expecting that answer. Slowly he corrects it, and I can feel his guard slowly climb up. It's this thing he always did. It's odd how I remember it so well. For only moments, only glimpses, I swear he let me in. But just like that it was gone, and a distance grew between us, even if we hadn't moved an inch.

"Don't do that," I tell him as soon as I sense it and his eyes narrow at me. "I don't hate you. I hate that you were rude to me."

"I wasn't rude."

"You were a dick." My words come out with an edge that can't be denied and I wish I could swallow them back down.

"I'm sorry," he tells me and he looks apprehensive. It's weird hearing him say those words. I can't think of him ever speaking them to anyone before. "You came looking for an apology?"

"No, not really," I tell him and shrug, wanting to take a step back from the tense air, but my ass is firmly planted on this stool. He turns to his left and I look back at the glass while I continue, just wanting to get it out of me before he's gone again.

"I just wanted to talk." The words finally come out, although they're not quite right. I want to spill every word that's inside of me. From the last night I saw him all those years ago, to everything that's happened up until this moment. There aren't a lot of people who can relate to what we've gone through.

He still hasn't said a word. His gaze is focused on me as if he's trying to read me, but can't make out what's written. If only he'd ask, I'd tell him. I don't have time for games or secrets, and our history makes up too much of who I am to disrespect it with falsehoods.

"Are you going to run off again?" I ask as he only stares back at me.

"Do you want me to?" he asks me in return.

"No," I answer instantly and a little too loud. As if what he'd said was a threat. I'm quieter as I add, "I don't want you to go." The desperation in my voice is markedly apparent.

"Well what do you want then?" he asks me and I know the answer. *I want him.* I take in a breath slowly, knowing the truth but also knowing I'd never confess it.

"I haven't been able to sleep since the other night," I confess and my gaze flickers from the glass to his eyes. My nail taps on the glass again and again and the small tinkling persuades me to continue. "I had a rough time for a while, but I was doing really well until I saw you." I don't glance up to see how he reacts; I'm merely grateful the words are finally coming to me. "When you didn't even bother to look at me, much less talk to me …" I swallow thickly and then throw back more of the beer.

"It was a shock to see you." Daniel says the words as if he's testing them on his tongue. Like they aren't the truth, although I'm sure they are. I look into his eyes as he says, "I didn't mean to upset you."

"What did you mean then?" I ask him without wasting a second.

He hesitates again, careful to say just what he wants. "I didn't know what to say, so I left."

"That seems reasonable." Or at least that seems like the version of Daniel I remember. I take another sip of beer before I say, "It hurt though."

"I already said I was sorry." His words are short, harsh even, but they don't faze me.

"I wasn't looking for an apology. I only wanted you to know how you make me feel."

He responds quickly this time, still looking over my expression as if he's not sure what to make of it. "And how do I make you feel now?"

I swear his breathing comes in heavier, and it makes mine do the same. "Like I have someone to talk to."

That gets a huff of a laugh from him. A disbelieving one. "I'm sure you have better options for that."

I shake my head and answer before taking another sip, "You'd be wrong then."

It's never felt pathetic before. The fact is I don't talk to many people and the one friend I have is thousands of miles away. But admitting that to him and seeing the trace of the grin fall on his lips makes it feel slightly pitiful.

I muster a small smile although it's weak, and time grows between us. The seconds tick by and I know I'm losing him, but I can't voice any of the things I'm feeling.

"It's been a while," he says and I nod my head as I answer, "Since the funeral."

I don't think I've ever said it out loud and it's the first mention of Tyler between us. The air turns tense but not in a way that's uncomfortable. At least not for me. I even have the courage to look back at him. I can see hints of Tyler in Daniel. But Tyler was so young and he looked it. Still, there are small things.

"You remind me of him, you know?" All while I speak, Daniel stares at my lips. He doesn't hide the fact in the least. I think he wants me to know. I swallow and his gaze moves to my throat, then he leans in just slightly before correcting himself. The hot air is tense and as he finally looks me in the eyes again, the noise of the bar disappears from the pure intensity of his stare.

"You do the same for me, I think."

"You think?" I ask him to clarify.

"You bring back certain things," he says icily, so cold it sends a chill down my spine.

My shoulders are tight as I straighten myself in the seat, again looking into the glass of beer that's nearly gone as if it can save me. Or as if I can drown in it.

It's only the sound of him standing up that makes me look back toward him. "Are you leaving?" I ask him like an idiot and then feel like it.

He only nods and I'm sure he's going to walk off, but instead he steps closer to me. He shoves a piece of paper in front of me onto the bar and then grips the barstool I'm sitting on with both of his hands.

He's so close I can feel his heat as he whispers to me, "I'll see you soon, Addison."

CHAPTER 8

Daniel

Five years ago

THE WIND HOWLS AS IT WHIPS PAST US. WE'RE ALL DRESSED IN BLACK SUITS, BUT *the shoes we spent all last night shining are buried beneath the pure white snow. The ice melts and seeps between the seams, letting the freezing cold sink into what was once warm. It's fitting as we stare at the upturned dirt in front of us.*

We're the last ones here. We stopped on our way back from the dinner since the sun has yet to set, and there's still a bit of light left.

The sky beyond us is blurred and the air brutally cold, the kind that makes my lungs hurt each time I try to breathe.

One of my brothers cries. It's a whimper at first but I don't move to see who's the weakest of us. My muscles coil at the thought, hating how I've judged. Hating how I view strength. I'm pathetic. I'm the weak one.

Jase, the farthest from me, sniffles as his shoulders crumple and then he covers his face.

He was the closest to Tyler but now he's the baby, taking Tyler's place. The air turns cruel, biting at the back of my neck with a harsh chill as his cries come to a halt. My throat's tight as I try to swallow. It makes me bitter to be standing here, knowing I need to leave and can't stay here. That I'm the one who gets to continue breathing. That fate chose to take one of the good ones, and leave the ruthless and depraved behind.

Five brothers are now only four.

Four of us stand over Tyler's body. Six feet in the ground.

All of us will mourn him. The world is at a loss for not knowing him. I finally get the expression about how it's better to have loved and lost than never to have loved at all.

Tyler was good through and through. He would have lived his days making the world a better place. He'd try to start a conversation with anyone; just to get to know them, just to make them laugh if he could.

All four of us lined up and saying our final goodbyes will never be the same after losing our youngest brother.

But only one of us knows the truth.

Only one of us is guilty.

The worst part is when I leave. I'm the last of us to finally part from Tyler's grave, but when I leave, my gaze stays rooted to where her car was. Where Addison had parked. My memories aren't of my father crying helplessly against the brick wall of the church, refusing to go in when he couldn't hide his pain. The images that flash before my eyes as my shoes crunch against the icy snow aren't of all his friends and teachers and family who have come from states away to tell us how sorry they are and how much Tyler will be missed.

All I can think about is Addison. How she stood so quietly on the fringes of the crowd, her fingers intertwined, her eyes glossy. How even as the wind ripped her scarf from her shoulders, carrying it into the distance and leaving her shoulders bare, she didn't move. She didn't even shudder. She was already numb.

The picture of her standing there motionless, staring at the casket is what I think about as I leave my brother.

I didn't know then how dangerous that was. Or maybe I did and I didn't want to believe it. But Addison would haunt me long after that night, as do so many other things.

She's only a girl. One small, weak girl.

Her red cheeks and nose and windblown hair made her look that much more tempting. Everything about her is ruined. At least she appeared to be that night. But I knew she had more left in her. More life and spirit. More emotion to give.

I may be cruel and unforgiving, but I'm right. I'm always right.

CHAPTER 9

Addison

Tʜᴇ ɴɪɢʜᴛ Tʏʟᴇʀ ᴅɪᴇᴅ, I ѕᴀᴡ ɪᴛ ᴀʟʟ ʜᴀᴘᴘᴇɴ.

I was there and I heard the tires squeal.

At the memory, I can practically feel the cold raindrops from that night pelting my skin. I turn on the faucet to the hottest it can go and wait until steam fills the room. I step into the shower, ignoring how the sounds of water falling are so similar to the rain that night as I stood outside the corner store. He called my name. My eyes close and my throat feels tight as I hear Tyler's voice.

The last thing he said was my name as he stepped into the street.

It takes a lot to leave someone because you fell in love with somebody else. Somebody who would never love you back.

It takes even more of your heart to witness the death of someone who truly deserved to live. More than I'll ever deserve it.

And to know that they died because they were looking for you …

God and fate are not kind or just. They take without reason. And the world is at a loss for Tyler being taken from us.

I thought I was doing the right thing by leaving Tyler. I didn't know he'd come looking for me. If I could take it back, I would.

The water hits my face and I pretend like the tears aren't there. It's easier to cry in the shower.

I was fine until I saw Daniel again. It took me years to feel just okay. That's the part I can't get over. Maybe this is what a relapse is? One moment and I've lost all the strength I've gained over the years. All of the acceptance that I can't change what happened and that it'll be okay. It's all gone in an instant.

I lean my back against the cold tile wall and sink to the floor. The smooth granite feels hard against my back as I sit there, letting the water crash down on me as I remember that night over and over. Just a few moments in particular. The moment Tyler saw me, then the moment he spoke my name and moved toward me.

The moment I screamed at the sight of him stepping into the road.

The car was right there. There was no time.

It didn't matter how I threw myself forward, racing toward him even as the car struck him.

I swear I acted as fast as I could. But it wasn't good enough.

My head rests on my knees as my shoulders shake.

Life wasn't supposed to be so cruel. Not to him.

"Deep breaths," I tell myself. "One at a time," I say, brushing at my eyes even though the water is still splashing down.

Standing up makes me feel weak. The water's colder, but the air is still hot.

Just breathe.

As I open up the shower door to inhale some cool air, I hear something. My heart stops and my body freezes. The water's still on but my eyes stare at the bathroom door.

The mirrors are fogged even though I left the door open slightly. A second passes and then another.

My body refuses to move even after I will myself to reach for the towel. My knuckles turn white and keep me where I am. I know I heard something. Something fell. Or something was pushed. Something beyond the door. *Something.* I don't know what, but I heard something.

I force myself to take one step onto the bath mat, and then another onto the tile floor.

I keep moving. I take the towel in both hands and then wrap it around myself although I can't take my eyes off the door.

Water drips down my back, but I don't bother with drying my hair. I make myself open the door and it groans in protest as I do.

The second it's open wide, I feel foolish.

It's only a picture I'd put up with hanging tape strips. It's fallen and the paint on the wall where it was hung, a Tiffany blue, is marred.

I should have used nails or screws to hang it.

Even as I pick up the picture and roll my eyes, my body is still tense; my heart still races. The frame is cracked and broken. When I place it onto the dresser, I catch a glimpse of the piece of paper Daniel gave me. It's a ripped portion of something—maybe a bill, I'm not sure. But on it is his number. The number I texted so he would have mine and to ask when we could meet. The number that didn't answer, even though the message was marked as read.

I leave the paper there with the broken frame and head back to the bathroom to finally turn off the water. But I stop just shy of entering.

Peeking at the door to my bedroom, a chill travels down my spine.

I don't remember leaving it open.

CHAPTER 10

Daniel

I WOULD SAY I DON'T HAVE TIME FOR THIS SHIT, BUT I DO. I REALLY DO.

I would make time for it if I didn't already have it in spades.

I'm cradling my chin while I drum the fingers of my other hand in a rhythmic pattern on the sleek mahogany tabletop. The soft sound doesn't even reach my ears, mixing with the chatter and hum of small talk and the clinking of silverware in the restaurant.

The Madison Grille has gotten a facelift recently. It's obvious. From the new wood beams that make the place smell like cedar, to the industrial lighting with exposed bulbs. I deliberately chose a place that wasn't too expensive or elegant so this wouldn't seem like a date. But it's better than a bar. There's privacy here that I'm eager to take advantage of. I waited to message her until only hours ago. Last night took a lot out of me, but once I decided, there was no turning back.

"Would you like anything while you wait?" The waiter already has his pad out and pen ready to go. There are a lot of things I'd like right now. Addison bent over the table, for one. Simply for inviting me back into her life. She may not know how much she taunted me, but she's smart enough to know the attraction was there and still she teased me.

"A whiskey sour and two waters," I tell him and he waits for more, but a tight smile sends him away.

Again my fingers drum as I think about each and every curve of the woman I'm waiting for.

Addison is all grown up.

And that look in her eyes is one I recognize. Desire. My blood feels hotter with every second I sit here thinking about what I wanted to do last night. And what I plan to do tonight.

I can imagine those pouty lips of hers wrapping around my cock and the sounds she'd make as I shoved my dick down her throat.

If nothing else, I can finally get a piece of what I wanted when I first laid eyes on her. Just the thought makes my dick harden and I stifle back a groan as the zipper of my jeans digs into me.

It took everything in me not to take her last night.

When she looked at me like she could see right through me.

When she told me to stop, as if she could command me.

When she spilled her little heart out as if I was the one meant for those words.

I'll be damn sure to make the time for Addison. Finally having her is worth all the fucking time in the world.

Sheets of rain batter against the large front window of this place and crash noisily on the tin roof.

I hate the rain. I hate what it does to me. The memories it brings back.

Addison is out there in the rain right now. Feeling it beat against her skin. Listening to the familiar sound.

And the unwanted memories that come with it.

I should feel a good number of things with the memory of Tyler besetting me right now as I wait for Addison. Shame, maybe even disgust. Swallowing thickly, I replay the memories, but this time focus on *her*. How she looked at me and shied away. How she couldn't talk to me while looking me in the eyes. How she blushed every time she caught me staring. Her reaction to me and only me was everything.

It was never about Tyler and I stayed away back then for him. It was always about Addison.

My thoughts are interrupted by the drinks I ordered being set on the table in front of me.

"Will you be dining tonight?" the waiter asks and I shake my head no and reply, "Just drinks."

"Let me know if I can get you anything else." With that he's gone and I'm left sitting alone at the table in the back. Staring at the entrance and waiting.

The soft lighting is reflected in my watch face as I turn my wrist over, showing the time is nearly ten minutes past the hour. She's late.

My eyes narrow as I look back toward the entrance, willing her to walk through the doors. There's a mix of worry and fear that I'm vaguely aware of. Fate's been a cruel bitch to me and I wouldn't put it past her to take the one thing I've always wanted. The one person I'm so close to getting.

Before I can let the unwanted emotions get the best of me, the door opens and Addison steps inside, huddled under an umbrella that she's quick to shake out over the mat and close. The hostess greets her as I sit paralyzed, watching Addison.

It's still surreal to see her here. I don't know how to react to her.

My fingers long to help her slip out of her jacket, but instead they grip onto the table.

I frown at the sweet smile she gives the hostess for helping her with her things. Addison hasn't given me one. In fact, it falls as she's directed toward me.

The happiness so evident only a second ago is gone as she walks over.

It makes my blood heat to a simmer but I stand anyway, pulling out the chair across from me for her to sit.

"Hi," she offers politely and the scent of her shampoo wafts toward me.

I don't trust myself to say anything, so I only offer her an inkling of a smile. I'm better than this. I know better too. "Thank you," she says softly as I retake my seat.

"I didn't know what you'd like to drink," I tell her even though I know she'll order a red wine. On the sweeter side.

"Oh, I'm fine with anything," she says agreeably and just like that, the bits of irritation slowly ebb and start to fade. She offers me a hesitant smile as she adds, "I'm glad you texted me."

Her smile broadens and she takes a sip of water before the waiter comes by again. And she orders cabernet. She's a creature of habit, little Addison.

"You wanted to talk?" I sit back easier in my seat now that she's here.

"I do, but I don't know how."

A genuine smile creeps onto my face. Little things like her innocent nature have always intrigued me. "Just say whatever you want, Addison."

"Do you hate me?" she asks me quietly. The seriousness is unexpected and catches me off guard.

"No, I don't hate you." I hated that I couldn't have her. But that was then.

"I feel like you should," she tells me although she's staring at her glass. She does that a lot. She looks down when she talks to me. I don't like it. My chest feels tighter and the easiness of tonight and what I want from it tangle into a knot in my stomach. I reach for my drink, letting it burn on the way down.

The words to ease her are somewhere. I know they exist, but they fail me now because the truth that begs to come out is all I can focus on.

I'm saved by her glass of cabernet that she accepts from the waiter graciously.

"Tyler did mean a lot to me, you know?" she asks me as if my acceptance means everything. As if I couldn't see it in her eyes back then. Every fucking time I saw them together it was obvious. He was all she had and I think she hated that fact, but loved him for simply being there for her.

"That was never a question," I tell her with a chill in my voice. One that I can't control.

"I just feel like," she pauses and swallows, then takes a sip of wine. With her nervous fidgeting, she's clearly uncomfortable and it's pissing me off. "I'm just afraid of what you and your brothers think. Your dad, too."

"My father died two years ago," I tell her and ignore the twinge of guilt running through me plus the pain of the memory. The knot seems to tie tighter.

I went home for the first time in years only to watch him being put in the ground next to my mother, just twenty plots down from Tyler's grave. And I haven't been back since. It's funny how guilt spreads like that. How it only gets worse, not better.

"Oh my God," Addison gasps and reaches her small hand out on the table for mine. "I'm so sorry." One thing I've always admired about Addison is how easy it is to read her. How genuine she is. How honest. Even if the things she was thinking were less than appealing.

"My father liked you, so he told Tyler that you would come back." I don't know why I tell her that. The memory doesn't sit well with me and the conversation isn't going where I'd like it to. Uncomfortable is an emotion I don't often experience. I suppose it makes sense that I am now though. Yet again … that's Addison's doing. But I allow it. It would be easy to get up and leave, to not have to deal with this conversation. But having Addison tonight is worth it.

Barely catching a glimpse of the starched white shirt of the waiter, I hold up my hand just in time to stop him.

"Yes?" he asks and I order two rounds of black rose shots, which are a mix of vodka and tequila and the restaurant's drink of choice. Plus another whiskey sour. I greatly underestimated this conversation and the need for alcohol to go along with it.

"Anything else?" the waiter asks and Addison pipes up. With her hands folded in her lap, she orders the bruschetta.

It's only once the waiter's left that she leans forward, tucking her hair behind her ear and says, "I didn't eat much today."

"Get whatever you'd like," I tell her easily and keep my gaze from wandering straight down her blouse. It's only a peek. Only a hint at what's under the thin cotton, but I can see the lace of her bra and it begs me to look.

"I have to get this off my chest." Her words distract me and looking at the serious expression in her eyes I'm irritated again, but I keep my lips shut tight. It will be worth it when it's over with. It better be.

"I just … even that day when I left, I didn't want you to think that I didn't appreciate everything."

She has no fucking idea. How is it even possible that she could be so blind?

She lived under our roof. It was off and on for nearly a year while the two of them dated. Tyler insisted. And the nights she didn't stay felt off toward the end. Each and every time she left I thought it was my doing.

But she always came back.

Tyler wasn't one to make demands, but he wanted her there with him. He wanted her protected and cared for. And when he told us why, when he told us what she'd been through, my father agreed.

It wasn't just that she had a tragic backstory. That she'd lost her parents and had no one.

It was the story of her previous foster father that changed my father's mind.

You could see it in the way Addison shied away from everything and everyone. And how she didn't want to go back to a stranger's house and hope nothing like that ever happened again.

She was safe with us. Even if she felt like she was intruding, every one of us wanted her there.

Even more so after we paid that sick fuck a visit.

It wasn't in Tyler's nature to want to hurt someone. Addison had a good way of bringing out a different part of him. She's good at that, at bringing out facets of your personality that were dormant before.

Carter was the one who decided when and how we'd take care of the asshole who'd touched her the year before. He was forty years old with a fifteen-year-old girl under his care.

Carter decided all five of us would go together while Addison was at class. The drive was only three hours away. Too long to do it at night, because she'd have noticed. But we had plenty of time during the day.

Carter always has a plan, and I was supposed to go around the back. Which is right where the asshole was raking up leaves.

I'd never killed anyone with gardening equipment before. I still wonder what it would have been like had I used the sharp tines of the metal but the damn thing broke in half. The spike of the splintered wooden handle worked well enough.

He got out one scream, if you can even call it that. More of a pathetic cry.

My family may have sheltered her.

I killed for her.

Tyler should have told her back then, and I have a mind to tell her now. But I don't break promises, not even to the dead.

So I keep that little bit of our history to myself.

The memory gives me the strength to look her in the eyes as I tell her, "You care a lot about what other people think. You'd be happier if you didn't."

"I'm not sure I would be," she answers softly with the corners of her lips turned down.

Again, the alcohol saves the conversation. The shots hit the table one by one.

"I think you need a drink."

I sure as fuck do. I didn't have her come here for a heart to heart. This isn't going how I'd planned. Wine and dine and fuck her is what I wanted. The first two I could take or leave, but the last I've needed for so long.

"I could use one … or six," she jokes and pulls her hair over her shoulder, twirling the dark locks around her finger.

Addison's entire demeanor changes as she watches the dark purple shot swirl in the glass.

"Thank you," she says as she smiles up at the waiter.

"Cheers." I tilt my shot toward her in jest and down it before she can say otherwise. No salutes to the dead, or to anything else for that matter.

When my glass hits the table, Addison's is just reaching her lips.

Everything about the way she drinks it turns me on. From the way her slender fingers hold the glass, to the way her throat moves as she swallows.

A million images of how she'd look as she sucks my cock are going through my head until she speaks again.

"You make me feel …" she trails off and hesitates to continue.

"Scared?" I offer her. I'm used to making certain people feel that way. Only when I need them to remember what I'm capable of.

"No … unworthy." I'm struck by her candor.

"If you think that, it's because you've come to that conclusion on your own."

"You've always made me think that. Even back when I was with Tyler." My spine stiffens hearing her bring him up so casually this time. Like it's easy to use his name in conversation.

"Your bruschetta," the waiter says, setting the plate down in the center of the table. I've never wanted to kill a waiter for delivering an appetizer before. Not until this moment.

He starts to speak again and I cut him off. "We're good here, thank you." My words are rushed and hard and I pray for his sake he takes the fucking hint.

My gaze moves from him to Addison, and her expression makes me regret it.

"You made me think that when I got here." Addison looks as if she's debating on eating. I guess the topic has ruined her appetite. It takes me a second to remember what she even said … *unworthy*.

"You were late."

"I got here as soon as I could," she protests weakly. As if she's truly apologetic and the part that pisses me off the most is that I know she is.

"If you don't want me to be angry, then don't make me wait." I'm wound tighter and tighter by the second. It's amazing how a girl like Addison can tempt my self-control.

"You didn't have to wait. You can go," she retorts, saying each word while staring straight into my eyes. Daring me.

I smile. "I don't want to leave."

The anger in her features softens at my response. "I just hit traffic."

A heavy breath comes and goes as I settle back in my seat, watching for her reaction. This tit for tat is different for me. "It's fine," I tell her, hoping to end it. And move back to the plan.

"Why do you look at me like that?" she asks me and I still.

"How is it that I look at you?" I ask her to clarify. It's usually so easy to manipulate others into seeing me how I need them to. But Addison is observant beyond measure. She always has been. And she's always been different.

"Like you don't trust me. Or maybe you don't know what to expect from me."

I shrug. "I don't trust anyone. Don't take it personal."

She laughs and her shoulders shake slightly. "Maybe that's because of the people you hang out with?" she suggests and quirks a brow at me.

"I don't hang out with anyone." I answer her simply, with no emotion. Merely stating a truth.

She hums a response and reaches out for a piece of the toasted bread. As she bites into it, the bread crunches loudly and diced tomatoes fall into her hand. She actually blushes, and after she swallows she says defensively, "You should eat some, it's weird with you just watching me."

I let a rough chuckle vibrate up my chest. "I'm not hungry."

"I hate being rude and eating it all myself, but the alcohol is already hitting me."

Good. I don't say the thought out loud.

As she wipes her hands on her napkin, I ask her, "What is it that you want from me, Addison?" My hands clench under the table as I wait. I know exactly what I want from her. To fuck her out of my system. To be done with an obsession from long ago.

She shoots me a sweet, genuine smile and the blush grows hotter on her face. "I think it's the alcohol talking."

Her smile is addictive and I feel my own lips twitch up into a lopsided grin. "Why's that?"

"Because I want to tell you I've always wondered what it would be like to kiss you."

I feel myself swallow. I feel everything in this moment. Watching her blush and smile at me like that, I want more of it. I don't know if it's the vodka, the tequila or the wine. Maybe a combination of the three. But whatever's making her blush, she needs more of it.

My heart beats rapidly and my cock hardens to the point where it's nearly unbearable.

As she covers her face with her hands, the waiter walks by casually and I reach out, fisting his shirt and stopping him in his tracks.

The look on his face is a mix of shock and fear. But I'm quick to loosen my grip and tell him, "More shots."

CHAPTER 11

Addison

WHEN I'M DRUNK, I HAVE SOME ODD THOUGHTS. SOME DO MAKE SENSE. FOR instance, how many shots did we have? That one seems like a logical thought, and I'm not sure of the exact answer, but at least three. Which is probably three too many but with how tense and awkward I was at the start of dinner, maybe three was just the right number.

Also, what happened to my car? I should be concerned about that. But I'm drunk, so walking seems smart. I keep my feet moving, one after the other even though I sway slightly. Only slightly though.

The thought that matters the most and the one I keep coming back to is whether or not Daniel can see how my hands keep trembling.

I'm sure the heat in my cheeks is obvious. And the butterflies in my stomach aren't staying where they ought to. They fly up and mess with my heart. Fluttering wildly and with an anxiousness that makes it feel like they're caged and trying to escape.

Maybe it's normal for what I'm doing.

When you want to kiss someone who's obviously a dick, it makes sense that your body would feel anxious and like you should run, right? Not to mention I'm sure he's still dealing. When your family's business is crime, you don't exactly walk away from that life. This heated nervousness won't leave me. I can't stop fidgeting with my hands and I'm sure it's ridiculous, but what else could be expected of me?

And then there's the fact that he's my ex's brother. An ex who's gone. And in many ways, it's because of me. It should make me feel worse than I do. But in a lot of ways, it feels the same way as running has. Only this time, I'm running to Daniel. A man I've dreamed for so long would comfort me and tell me these feelings were alright.

Obviously, that never happened. And I'm not sure it ever will.

There's a part of my mind that won't stop picking at that fact. A part that wonders how Daniel can even stand to be around me. A part that wonders if he's only toying with me. Like he's waiting to get his revenge and tell me how he truly feels.

And that's the part that scares me when I look up at him. I don't care how many times he'll tell me that no one blames me. How could they not?

I don't know what's happening, but I'm too afraid to stop, because I really want to find out. I'm too eager to finally know what it feels like to be wanted by him.

"You're so nervous," he says as if he's amused.

"Aren't you?"

His smile dims and he runs his hand through his hair, looking to his left at the stop sign. "Let's go to my place."

We're standing on the corner of Church and Fifth and I know I just need to go six blocks and I'll be two streets over from my apartment building … I think. There are bus stops everywhere in this college town. So even if I get lost, I could find my way back home by just hopping on a bus.

"Your place?" I question him while squinting at the signs. I'm more than a little tipsy. But everything feels so good.

"Let's go," he answers and then takes my hand in his, pulling me across the street even though the sign at the crosswalk is still red.

"Still a rule breaker," I tease and I think that one is from the alcohol. I must find it funnier than he does though, because once we're on the other side, I'm the one smiling at my little joke while he stands there. Staring at me like he's not sure what to do with me.

"So you aren't nervous?" I ask him, daring to broach the subject again. I don't mind what he does to me. I crave it. And I'll be damned if he tells me he doesn't want me. I can see it in his eyes.

But what exactly he wants me for? That I have yet to know for sure.

A good fuck seems to be first on the list though. And I can't argue with that.

"I don't get nervous."

"Everyone gets nervous." The words slip out of my mouth and I tell him about a study my friend Rae told me about. She's a psychology major and she told me about public speakers and how even professional public speakers' adrenaline levels spike when they get on the stage. Everyone gets nervous. "There's no denying it."

"If you say so, Addison." That's all I get from him as the night air seems to get colder and I shiver. That's when I notice he's still holding my hand.

"This doesn't make you nervous? It doesn't make you question if … if we should be doing this?" I lift up our clasped hands and he lets me, but he doesn't stop walking.

"Why shouldn't we?" he responds, but I hear the hard edge in his voice. *He knows.*

"There are so many reasons," I tell him and look straight ahead.

"Can I tell you a secret?" he whispers and the way he does it makes me giggle. A silly little girl giggle that would embarrass me if I wasn't on the left side of tipsy.

"Anything," I breathe.

"I was jealous that Tyler got to have you."

I nearly stumble and my smile slips. That erratic beating in my chest makes me want to reach up and pound on my heart to knock it off.

He continues once I get my footing back. "You were too young and Tyler got to you first."

I walk with my lips parted, but not knowing what to say or do.

Daniel's arm moves to my waist as his steps slow and I look up to see a row of houses. Cute little houses a few blocks from the university campus. They're the type of houses that come equipped with white picket fences and for the second time in fifteen minutes, I nearly trip.

"How drunk are you?" Daniel questions with a serious tone.

"Sorry, not that drunk," I answer him as we walk up the paved drive to the front door of a cute house with blue shutters. My heart won't knock it off, but I ignore it and change the subject. "This is your place?"

"Just renting."

I nod my head and as much as that makes sense, it's also one less thing to question. And now I find myself on the front steps of Daniel's place, with his hand on mine. Drunk after I've confessed to him how I feel.

Not the smartest thing I've ever done, and not the best decision I've made in my life.

But maybe I'll wake up in five minutes, and this will just be another one of my dreams.

My breathing comes in pants as Daniel lets his hand travel lower down my back and I instantly heat everywhere for him. My heart pounds and my blood pressure rises. I'm almost afraid of how my body is reacting so intensely. He has to see it, but if he does, he doesn't let on.

I don't need Rae or a shrink or anyone to tell me I'm going to regret this. I know that already.

Maybe I can blame it on the alcohol.

Or the sudden flood of memories.

Sleep deprivation, that's a good excuse too.

I don't care what I blame it on. So long as it happens. I wanted him for so long, even if it was from a distance. An unrequited and forbidden lust, not love. I refuse to believe it was love.

I lost the chance long ago to have what I always wanted. There's no way I won't push for it now.

I watch as Daniel reaches for the doorknob but stops, dropping his hand and directing his gaze to me.

"What are you thinking?" Daniel asks me and instinctively I look up at him, swallowing hard and licking my lips. I love how his eyes flicker to them and I hesitantly reach up, spearing my fingers through his hair.

And he lets me.

He lowers his lips and gently brushes them against mine although he doesn't kiss me yet. The lingering scents of whiskey and vodka mingle with my lust and love of bad decisions, giving me a heady feeling.

"I always knew you were bad for me," I whisper against his lips as he bends down to kiss me. To actually press his hot lips against mine this time. His tongue demands entrance, licking against the seam of my lips and I grant him his wish. The heated kiss is short-lived and I'm left breathless.

I can feel his smile as he pulls away, taking the key from his pocket and licking his lower lip. I love how he does it like that. Slow and sensual and like he's hiding a secret that thrills him to no end.

"Bad for you doesn't even begin to cover it, Addison."

CHAPTER 12

Daniel

BARELY CONTAINED.

Everything about me is barely contained. All I can think about is ripping off Addison's clothes and finally getting inside her tight cunt. I know she wants me. She's sighing softly every time I let my skin touch hers, filling the night air with her little pants of need.

Tiny touches. It started out as a way to tease her as we walked back to the house I'm renting. Little caresses that made me smile at her desperation.

She's so responsive. So needy.

I can't fucking stand it.

I've always known I was selfish. It's something my father said I inherited from him. He looked at me with pride when he said it too.

Tonight I'm going to take advantage of that particular trait of mine.

The front door swings open and it's pitch black inside. I don't waste my time stumbling for a light in the foyer.

I'm fucking her in my bed. I've already decided that.

"Daniel—" Addison gasps my name as I pick her up with one arm, forcing her legs to wrap around my hips. The door slams shut and I lock it as I crush my lips against hers.

My name. She's gasping my name. She'll scream it too. Hearing that hauntingly sweet voice say my name as if it's the only word meant to fall from her lips is everything I've ever wanted. Fucking music to my ears.

She moans into my mouth and then pulls away to breathe, her neck arching as I press my stiff erection against her heat, pushing her into the door and nipping at her neck.

"Upstairs," I groan against her hot skin although she doesn't have a choice in the matter. I've only said it to remind myself that I'm not fucking her here.

Not just yet. Only seconds away. Only seconds.

I take the stairs two at a time, making her cling to me. My heart feels as though it's losing control, beating chaotically. All the blood in my body must be in my dick. Her lips crash against my neck over and over and her nails dig into my shoulders through my shirt.

"Daniel," she moans and my name on her lips is a sin. I kick the bedroom door open and moonlight is shining through the blinds, giving me everything I need to see all of this.

I want to remember every detail. I can barely breathe and the alcohol is coursing through my blood, but I will remember every fucking detail of this night.

The bed groans with her surprised gasp as I toss her onto it and pull my shirt over my shoulders. She's still trying to get her balance as I kick off my pants and crawl on the bed to get to her. My breaths are coming in short and frantic. I'd be embarrassed, but Addison is just the same. She's just as eager and there isn't a thing in this world that could make me feel more desire than the way she stares back at me with nothing but lust.

Something tears as I pull at her dress, ripping it off her shoulders and down her body. Before I take her panties off her to join the puddle of clothes by the bed, I cup her hot pussy as I kiss her again. And this time it's me that moans into her mouth.

My dick is already impossibly hard, and precum is leaking from me at the feel of the silken fabric beneath my fingers, hot and damp with her arousal.

I don't bother to take them off gently. But I never thought I would either. Shredding them with my hands, I ignore her gasp of surprise and quickly lower my mouth to her cunt.

She falls back onto the mattress, spearing her fingers through my hair as I lick her from her entrance to her clit.

So fucking sweet. Sweeter than the shots. Sweeter than the trace of wine on her lips as she kissed me.

There's not enough time in a single night for everything I want to do to her. I barely pull myself off her clit to shove two fingers inside of her. I'm not gentle as I finger fuck her, thrusting as deep as I can go.

Her back arches, threatening to pull her pussy away from me, but I pin her hip down and curl my fingers up to stroke against her front wall. The sweet, strangled moans are everything I need and everything I've ever wanted.

I pause for only a second to watch her reaction. How her eyes are half-lidded but she's staring at me. Her dark green eyes meet mine and I press my thumb to her swollen nub to see her throw her head back in pleasure. Her pussy clenches around my fingers with need.

"So tight," I say with reverence.

"It's been a while," she breathes out while writhing.

I almost ask how long. *Almost.*

There's a small voice in the back of my head that keeps hissing that she doesn't belong to me and when she utters those words, I'm acutely aware of how my brother had her first.

He might have been her first, but I'll ruin her.

I'll make her mine and make her forget about any other man who's touched her.

My dick throbs with a nearly unbearable pain from the desire to be inside her. To thrust into her and take her exactly how I've been picturing since I saw her four nights ago.

My fingers wrap around her throat, and at the same time I palm my dick.

"I want you to look at me," I tell her although I'm breathing heavily. I feel her swallow against my grip and then she nods. Lining up my dick, I press the head between her folds and she shudders beneath me.

Her soft moan vibrates against my hand and then I slam all of me inside of her. Every bit of me, and I watch her eyes widen and her mouth drop open with a sharp gasp.

Fuck! She feels too good and she immediately spasms around my dick. I can't move or breathe. If I do, I'll cum with her without a second thought.

It takes every ounce of control I have to keep my eyes on hers. To watch her so I can remember this forever.

Her body trembles as she tries to bow her back, but I'm holding her down, making her take it all. Her hands reach up to her neck. Her nails are digging into my fingers as I thrust again and again, tightening my grip but still letting her breathe. *Yes!* I love how she lets me own her body. *Mine. All mine.*

Her cunt tightens around my cock to the point where it's fucking strangling me the way I am her. The room is filled with the noises of me fucking her relentlessly.

I loosen my grip as I pound into her and she sucks in a deep breath. Feeling her pant and struggle against me, my lips slam against hers. With her chest pressed against me, I can feel her heart beating just as hard against mine.

Her nails rake down my arms and I can tell she isn't sure if she wants to cling to me for dear life or shove me away. I lift my lips from hers to breathe and she screams out my name with reverence. Her reaction only makes me fuck her harder, with every ounce of energy in me. *Mine.*

My fingers dig into her hips as I keep up my ruthless pace, each stroke taking me higher and higher to a pleasure that nearly makes me cum. My toes curl and I struggle to breathe, but I put every bit of energy into looking into her eyes.

As she screams out my name, her teeth clench and her heels dig into my ass. Her nails break the skin at my lower back as she cums violently on my dick.

My body begs me to give in and bury my head in the crook of her neck as I cum inside of her, but I can't. Not yet.

Mine. The word slips from my lips as she screams out my name again. Her back arches while she struggles beneath me, shoving against my chest.

"Look at me," I command her as I shove myself deep within her, all the way to the hilt, pausing for the first time since I've entered her. My dick slams against the back of her warmth, stretching her and forcing her lips to make a perfect "O."

Her eyes meet mine, dilated with a wildness to them I've never seen. I brush my pubic hair against her clit, angling just slightly and rocking. Just to see how much she can take.

"Daniel," she whimpers my name as she thrashes her head from side to side, cumming again even though I've stilled inside of her. Her pussy clenches and tries to milk my cock. And I groan from deep in my chest at the sensation. "Fuck," I mutter then hold my breath and tense my body.

Not yet. I can't cum yet.

It's only once her release has passed and her body is still that I move again.

One more. One more is all I can take.

My forehead rests on the mattress above her shoulder and I gently kiss her soft skin although she flinches from the sensation. Even that's too much for her. She's already cumming again.

I ride through her orgasm, pounding into her heat and with each thrust the word mine escapes between my clenched teeth.

Even as I cum deep inside of her, not breathing, not moving with the only exception being the pulsing of my dick. Even in that moment I whisper the word against the shell of her ear. *Mine.*

I've never been able to sleep well.

Some people aren't meant to be heavy sleepers.

So instead of trying to sleep, I watch Addison in the dark. My eyes adjust easily and with the moonlight shining through the slats of the blinds, I can see every feature of hers clearly. I can see the gentle rise and fall of her chest with her steady breathing and the little dip in her collar that begs me to kiss it.

I'd forgotten how badly I wanted her all those years ago. The thrill of having her near and the desire to hold on to her outweighed the memories. But seeing her beauty so close and the beast inside me sated, there's no denying the attraction.

No one has ever held my attention like Addison. No one makes me forget like she does. Nothing else matters when she's near me. Only the need to make sure she knows that I see her, that I feel her, that I want her.

And now I have her.

A deep rumble of satisfaction leaves my chest. Addison mirrors me in her sleep, a sweet moan slipping through her lips as she nuzzles closer to me. But then she stiffens.

My body tenses at her reaction.

I watch her lashes flutter and the realization show in her expression. Shock is evident on her face as she slowly lifts up her body, bracing herself on one palm. Covering her chest with the sheet, her lips part and her forehead pinches. She clenches her thighs and I've never been so proud in my fucking life.

There's a warmth in my body, knowing how I took her as if her body was mine alone to ruin.

It's been hours, hours of me simply watching her so close to me and memorizing the curves of her body. And she can still feel me inside of her.

With the ghost of a whimper on her lips, she slowly slips off the mattress, ignoring how it dips and could wake me. As if she wouldn't mind me waking.

My heart stutters and the hint of happiness in my expression falls. She's leaving? The fuck she is.

"What are you doing?" My voice is sharp in the still night air and it startles her. But only enough that she turns to face me. With one hand splayed across her chest and the other covering her bare pussy, she looks from me to the pile of her clothes on the floor.

Seeing her naked, and even better, trying to hide that nakedness from me makes my spent dick hard in an instant. I'm already eager for more of her. The slit of my cock is wet with precum and my thick shaft twitches at the thought of taking her again. I can keep her here. She'll stay. I fucking know she will.

"I have to go," she speaks softly, her words a murmur.

"You don't have to do anything but get back in my bed," I command her and then let my eyes roam down her body, making sure she knows exactly what I want. "Lie down."

She hesitates, but only for a moment. And then she lowers herself slowly, first leaning on her elbow and then nestling into the covers. That warmth comes back as soon as she's back where she belongs. The trace of the fear of losing her and the sickening feeling that she's leaving are both still present, but muted.

As soon as she's settled, staring up at me in the darkness with the moonlight highlighting her face, I lean down and kiss her on the lips. Not a gentle kiss, and not a goodnight kiss either.

She's breathless when I pull back and my own chest heaves for air, but I speak calmly, with the control I've come to expect.

"Spread your legs for me," I tell her and before her back is even settled, she does as she's told. Her thighs part so easily as a blush covers her skin and her eyes shine with the same hunger I remember from so long ago.

I take her by surprise, shoving my hand between her thighs and thrusting my fingers into her cunt. Slamming my lips down on hers, I silence her screams. Her back bows and she squirms under me, trying to get away from the intensity.

Pinning her hip down, I keep her where I want her and finger fuck her until she's screaming into my mouth. My teeth sink into her lip and then nip along her jaw, all while I'm enjoying her cries of pleasure and how tight her pussy gets when it spasms around my thick fingers. With my thumb on her clit, I don't stop until she's breathless and can no longer make a sound as she cums on my hand. Her body's still trembling when I finally thrust myself deep inside of her.

And it's my name on her lips.

My dick wrapped in her warmth.

My bed she sleeps in.

All mine.

CHAPTER 13

Addison

Five years ago

I KNOW I SHOULD STOP THIS. MY BELLY ACHES WITH THIS DISGUST. I HATE MYSELF *for it.*

For using Tyler as a distraction.

We go out every day, taking pictures of all sorts of things. The project is over, but he keeps asking if I want to go. And I never tell him no.

It's better than going back to the Brauns' place.

"Let's go over there," Tyler says and points toward a run-down path in the woods behind the park. We're at the far end of the park and I know this area. In front of us is the creek and if we go left and walk half a mile or so, we'll end up at the highway line and can follow that back to the parking lot. There are running trails along the way too. Although I don't like to run. I just walk and take pictures. I like doing that with Tyler.

One step to follow him. Two steps and he reaches for my hand.

I slip mine inside of his and he squeezes tight when he holds it. It's a little thing, but he really holds my hand like he means it. And that sick feeling in my stomach feels like nothing compared to the bittersweet sensation in my heart. I'm not sure if it's really pain or what it is.

I want more of it though.

A part of me knows it's selfish. That part's quiet as fallen branches crack beneath our weight and we stop at a clearing on the edge of the creek.

"It's beautiful," I whisper, staring out at the bubbling brook. It's the softest shade of blue although it gets darker where it's deeper.

"Like you," he says and gives me a charming smile. When he lets go of my hand to take his jacket off and lays it on the ground, those feelings mix, and the resulting brew is something I don't know how to handle.

But Tyler knows my secrets, and he's seen me in those moments I wish I didn't have. The ones where I cry and sometimes it's hard to know what's caused the outburst.

I swear I used to be happy. I used to be normal. But I'll never be normal again.

Although Tyler's jacket is laid flat, he sits next to it in the dirt and beckons me, patting the fabric and looking up at me with big puppy dog eyes. He doesn't ask much of me, but I can't help feeling like today may be different.

My shoulders hunch in a little as I sit down and tuck my hair behind my ear.

It takes everything in me to look at him. To look at Tyler and try to gauge his intention.

"Do you want to sleep with me?" I ask him bluntly.

He lets out a bark of a laugh and rests his forearms on his knees as he looks out onto the creek. Looking back at me he answers, "I read once, I think in a biology book, that teenage guys are horny as fuck."

I can't help the smile that cracks on my face at his joke. That's the way Tyler handled anything serious. He'd just make a joke and deflect.

"Seriously though," I say then wipe the palms of my hands on my knees instead of looking at him as I continue, "I don't get why you keep coming out with me."

He shrugs. "I like spending time with you," he tells me.

"So you don't want to get into my pants."

"I definitely want to fuck you."

I'm shocked by his candor. Tyler's … careful around me. I feel like he considers each word carefully before speaking to me. Like if he says the wrong thing, I'd run. And that's not too far from the truth.

"You haven't tried anything … though."

"Don't confuse my patience for a lack of interest." The second the words slip from him, Tyler lets out a genuine laugh. "Of all the dirty things I could say, that's what gets you to blush?"

It's only then that I feel the heat in my cheeks. It matches other places too.

Minutes pass with both of us taking small glances at each other, watching the sunset descend behind the forest with shades of orange and red in the clear blue sky. He even tosses a few twigs and rocks into the creek. He tries to skip them, but he's not very good at it.

"I think you'd like it if I kissed you here." He almost mumbles his words when he catches me staring at him. They're spoken so low and nearly absently.

His lips brush along my neck and desire sweeps through my body unexpectedly. Both of my hands move up to his chest and I push away from his overwhelming touch with my lips parted, my breath stolen.

He blinks away the lust in his gaze and slowly a smile forms on his face. "I knew you'd like it."

As I bite my lip, he leans forward cautiously, judging my reaction and then he does it again. His lips kiss over every part of my neck and up to the soft spot behind my ear.

And that's why I slept with Tyler. He said and did everything that made sleeping with him feel like it was right and meant to be.

As soon as we started walking back to his truck, that sick feeling returned. And I began to think that tomorrow he'd be different. That he'd gotten what he wanted, so he wouldn't want to be with me anymore.

But I was wrong again. He held me tighter. Talked to me sweeter. And loved me harder than before.

Tyler was patient. He didn't look at me as if I was broken, but he treated me like breaking me would be the worst sin in the world.

I could never tell him no.
Even if I still thought of his brother in ways I shouldn't have.

You shouldn't compare lovers.

Certainly not brothers.

It was a fantasy come alive to feel Daniel's skin against mine. To finally know what it's like to writhe under him.

But that's all he can ever be. A fantasy.

One that I'm prolonging by letting the days blend together in a whirlwind of alcohol and sex. He messages me where to meet and I go. We drink. We fuck. There are no more awkward conversations of our past, but the reminder stays deep in the pit of my stomach.

I'm not stupid. Daniel's no good. And this thing between us is merely two people giving in to a pipe dream we had long ago.

It's all-consuming and I wouldn't have it any other way.

But the moment this cloud of lust and bliss dissipates, I'll be left with the sobering truth.

I've given myself to a man who's only ever seen me as a plaything.

I've slept with someone who should truly hate me for being the reason his brother is dead.

And the events I've allowed to occur are something that should shame me for a lifetime.

There's no getting around those hard facts. But it's nice to ignore them for a while and in the moments when Daniel's with me, it feels different. It feels like nothing else exists.

And when your world is made of nothing but painful memories you're constantly trying to outrun, it's a relief for nothing else to exist.

Well, nothing but this flutter in my chest and this ache between my thighs. I love it. I love feeling this way even if nervousness and tiny bits of fear creep in.

It was better than I ever could have imagined. Even when I woke up alone in the morning. Even as I took the bus home with my hair a mess and still in the clothes from the night before.

A walk of shame had never felt so fucking good.

I bite down on my lip to keep the smile on my face from being too smug.

It was something I know I'll regret, but right now all I'm going to do is love this horrible mistake.

Over and over again.

The spoon clangs against the ceramic mug as I stir in the sugar for my tea. I need caffeine badly. I've slept soundly for the past three days, two of them in Daniel's bed, only to be woken up on occasion and fucked into the mattress. It feels good to be back at my apartment though, where I can rest undisturbed. He had a meet last night so I slept alone, which is a good thing. I'm too sore for any more of Daniel right now.

A smile graces my face as I lift the mug to my lips.

I blow across the top of the mug, breathing in the calming smell of the black tea and avoiding the hot steam. With my eyes closed I feel like I could go back to bed right now.

My little moment is interrupted by the sound of my phone going off. It's a distinct noise and I know exactly who it is by the tone. It's from an app that allows you to text people overseas for cheap. Which means it's Rae.

The mug hits the counter a little more aggressively than I'd like, sloshing a touch of tea on the counter as I reach for my phone.

"Shit," I mumble under my breath, but I don't bother with it. I need to talk to Rae.

How are you love? Miss you.

She always calls me *love*. She says things like *cheeky* and *cow* too. I love the diction of the United Kingdom and their accents. A very big part of me misses her and the small farm town she lives in. But it will never be home for me.

I message her back, *Miss you to pieces. How's your mom?*

I wait with my eyes on the screen and my lips pursed. She doesn't write back quickly so I busy myself with cleaning up the spill and having another sip of tea. Rae's mom is going through some health issues. I know it's been a pain in the ass for both of them. Or *arse* if it's Rae talking about it.

Mum's fine. Happy for now and enjoying the time off work. How have you been?

I start to text her everything from the very beginning, but then delete it. And then I try once more, but the words don't come out quite right. Before I can even message her anything, she texts again.

I'm thinking of going back to that bar in Leeds and having another go at the boy bands there. Made me think of you.

The reminder makes me smile and spreads a sense of warmth and ease through me. Enough that I reply simply, *I think I'm seeing someone. But I'm not sure if it's good or bad.*

"Seeing someone" might be a stretch. It's just fucking. I'm smart enough to know that.

She writes back quickly this time. *Spill it.*

You already know him. Well, of him. It's Daniel.

I feel a momentary pang of guilt, like I've betrayed him. As if saying what's between us out loud will ruin it. Because no one else will understand.

Tyler's brother?

I stare at her response and feel that spike of chagrin and shame I should have known was coming.

Yes.

It's all I can write back. The mug trembles slightly in my hands, but I ignore it, taking a drink although now the heat feels different on my lips. Less soothing and less comforting. Even if it isn't lukewarm yet.

Seeing him? she questions.

I put the mug back down and gather up the courage to try to make her understand. She knows everything. Including how I left Tyler because of what I felt for Daniel. What I thought was one-sided and an indication of how awful a person I was. All I had to do was love Tyler back. Instead I ruined what we were over dirty thoughts I couldn't stop.

We ran into each other. And I told him how I felt about him.

A moment passes, and then another. And that feeling in my gut and heart keeps at it. Twisting and squeezing until I feel wrung out. I wish I could say I don't care what she thinks about this. But she's the only person I have left. I'm careful not to get too close to anyone. Everyone I love dies. So it's best I don't let people in. Rae is the only exception.

How do you feel about it?

I let out a single chuckle, like a breath of a laugh at her response. I text back, *You sound like a shrink.*

You sound like you might need one.

Her response makes the small bit of relief wash away. *Maybe I do.*

I just worry about you, she texts me and then adds, *I know it has to bring back memories and other unpleasant things.*

It does. But it also feels like a relief in a way. And so much more than that.

Are you dating? she asks.

I roll my eyes at that question. She knows better. *I don't date.*

She sends back an emoji rolling its eyes and a genuine snicker leaves me.

Just take care of yourself, will you?

She's a good friend and I know better than to think she'd be anything other than concerned.

You burst my bubble, I tell her and I really mean it.

⋅—◦◦⋅◦◦—⋅

Five years ago

Tyler's lips slip down to the crook of my neck. He knows just the spot that makes me wet for him.

My palms push against his chest and the motion makes my body sink deeper into the mattress beneath him.

"Spread your legs." He gives the command against my skin, making me hotter … needier. But my eyes dart to the door and then back to him.

"But your brothers," I whisper as if my words are a secret.

Tyler pulls away, breathless and panting with need. He always makes love to me wildly. Like it's all he needs. Each time is quick, but he takes care of me first. I bite down on my bottom lip as he hovers over me and then looks over his shoulder at the door.

"They don't care," he tells me and I can only swallow the lump in my throat.

One brother cares. I know he does. He looks at me like I'm a whore whenever I stay over here. And I haven't even slept with Tyler under the Cross roof yet.

"I don't want them to think I'm staying over just so we can have sex."

"They don't think that." Tyler smiles and brushes the hair from my face as I pull the covers up closer around me. I still have my nightgown on; Tyler's just pulled the fabric up around my waist.

"What if they think I'm using you so I don't have to go back home? Like I'm spreading my legs just so I can have a place to stay." I heard a girl say that at school a week ago and the thought hasn't left me. It's true I don't want to go back. But I'm not a whore either.

"I have to fucking beg you to stay here, Addie. They can hear that. They know that. And we've been dating for how long now?"

Almost six months to the day he first tapped on my shoulder in science class.

The uneasiness still doesn't leave me and I stare at the door until Tyler's hand cups my chin.

"We can be quiet," he whispers and lowers his lips to mine.

My eyes close and I let myself feel his warmth and comfort.

"Just kiss me," he tells me as he slips his hand between my legs, parting my thighs for him.

I keep my eyes shut and try to be quiet. My muffled moans carried through the walls though and so did the unmistakable sounds and steady rhythm of Tyler fucking me.

I know because of the way Daniel looked at me late that night when I snuck into the hall to use the bathroom.

My hand was on the doorknob when he opened his bedroom door. Caught in his heated gaze, I couldn't move; I couldn't breathe. He let his stare trail down my nightgown before looking back into my eyes.

I'll never forget the way my body heated for him and how my heart pounded. I thought he was going to punish me, to pin me against the wall and make me scream. That's the way he would have fucked me. The kind of sex where you can't keep quiet.

Instead of doing or saying anything, Daniel turned around, going straight back into his room.

I sat in the bathroom for the longest time, feeling like the worst thing in the world. Like a whore and a fraud and an ungrateful bitch.

I snuck out in my nightgown, with my clothes clenched into a ball in my hand and drove home as quickly as I could.

I didn't go back to the Cross house for weeks. And the next time I let Tyler fuck me in his bed, I wasn't quiet about anything.

CHAPTER 14

I T'S CUTE HOW SHE KEEPS LOOKING AT ME LIKE SHE'S WAITING FOR ME TO WALK away. Like how yesterday she was surprised that I told her to come over. I'll never forget the shy look on her face. How her eyes scanned mine and she was hesitant to come back in.

So long as I'm in this small town, she needs to be in my bed. Every second I can have her. Our one-night stand turned into one week … turned into two.

I've waited for so long to have her. Did she think I'd have my fill of her so quickly?

As she stretches on my bed, the sheet slips and reveals more of her back, along with the curve of her waist.

I could get used to this. Waking up with her in my bed, going to sleep alongside her.

If I could keep her here forever, I would.

"That was nice," she whispers as she rolls back over and lays her hand on my bare chest. Her finger traces up to the dip below my throat then moves lower, and lower still. Stirring my already spent dick back to life.

"Be careful what you ask for," I warn her in a rough timbre as I hold back a groan.

I can feel her smile against my shoulder and then she laughs sweetly.

"I think I need a shower first," she says.

"You'll need another when I'm done with you." I don't miss the way her legs scissor under the sheets at my comment.

"Shower first," she says as if she's decided. Had I slept well at all last night, I'd slip my tongue between her thighs and convince her otherwise. But the meeting location changed yesterday and then again. It seems the message I've been waiting on Marcus to deliver has changed as well and Carter's on edge with what's coming our way.

The unwanted thought is what motivates me to get up. I've been in a daze with Addison. She's a distraction.

I crack my neck and stretch my arms before getting out of bed with a twisted feeling in my gut.

With my back to Addison, she traces the small scar on the bottom of my shoulder. A scar I've long since forgotten. There are a few really, but they're faint. Only one is easily seen.

"How'd you get that?" she asks me and I clench my jaw as I stand up.

She always liked my father. He was a good man … to her at least. And maybe the family business wouldn't have survived if he hadn't been so hard on Carter and me.

"I popped off to my father," I explain, keeping it short and simple as I get off the bed and grab a pair of boxer briefs from the dresser. My voice sounds strained even to my own ears.

My dick's already hard and wanting more of her, but the unpleasant reminder of my childhood makes me want to bury myself in work. I have an encrypted file I should look over with details for a big shipment coming in next week. It includes a list of new hires and Carter always gets wary when it comes to new people unloading stock.

"You popped off?" she asks and I turn around to the sound of her saddened voice. My stomach twists when I see her expression. Like she can't believe my father would have ever struck me.

She has no idea.

"I should have known better." My words don't do a thing to change the look in her eyes and when they move from the thin scattering of silver scars on my back to my own gaze, all I see is sympathy. And I don't fucking want it. Not from anyone, and sure as fuck not from her.

"Leave it alone, Addison." I move back to the dresser for pants and a shirt, opening one drawer and slamming it shut before moving to the next.

"What did you say?" I hear her ask softly as I shut a third drawer, still not finding what I'm looking for. The fourth drawer slams shut harder than I intended.

"It doesn't matter." My response doesn't faze her.

"I wouldn't have thought he'd ever-"

"He saved that side of himself for Carter and me," I say, cutting her off sharply before I can stop myself. Apparently the anger is stronger than I thought. Up until now I assumed the animosity was buried with him when he died.

"I'm sorry," she says softly and it only amplifies my agitation.

The air is tense in the bedroom as I slip on a t-shirt and pajama pants, an old plaid flannel pair.

"Pass me one?" Addison asks, apparently ready to move on from the revelation that my father wasn't the saint Tyler made him out to be.

I almost toss the black cotton Henley toward the bed, but instead I walk it to her. Letting her take it from me and when she does, her slender fingers brush against mine.

There's nothing sexier than watching her pad around this place in nothing but my t-shirt. Her occupation means she can work anywhere, which means her ass is staying right here with me. *For now.*

Gripping her hand as she takes the shirt, I pull her closer to me and steal a quick kiss. And then another as I release her.

She props herself up on the bed, getting onto her knees and deepening the small kiss. As she bites gently on my bottom lip, she tangles both of her hands in my hair. I let myself fall forward, bracing my impact with one arm on either side of her.

She doesn't open her eyes until she gives me a sweet peck right where she bit me. Her green eyes stare back at me for only a moment before she closes them again and brushes the tip of her nose against mine.

My fucking heart is a bastard for wanting to believe the kiss has anything to do with the conversation we just had. But it flips in my chest as if that little nudge and the fact that her eyes were closed meant everything in the world.

I've always had a bastard heart when it comes to her.

"I have to work," I tell her and quickly bend down to plant a quick kiss on her temple. I'd better leave before I wind up doing nothing but staying in bed.

"So you don't want to come with me to check out the campus?"

"I'm not sure there's a polite way to say this, but fuck no." It amazes me how easy it is to be candid with Addison. Maybe it's because just like now, she isn't offended or taken aback. She simply takes what I have to give and smiles.

"So you think I shouldn't go here?" she asks and from her tone I know it's a loaded question.

"Why would you?" I offer in rebuttal.

She breaks eye contact and shrugs, picking at a thread on the comforter. "It seems like a business degree would make sense."

"You already have your business set up and it's successful, isn't it?"

"I'm doing well. How'd you know? You look me up?" she asks playfully, but I ignore her and the twinge in my chest.

"Then why bother?"

She peeks up at me over her shoulder with a defensive look on her face. "Well, why do you bother?"

Leaning forward, I lower my voice to answer her. "I don't. I'm not staying."

"You're going home?" she asks and the very idea of home doesn't quite sit right with me, but neither does the expression on her face. The hurt one that she can't hide although I'm not sure she would bother even if she was aware of how transparent her emotions are.

"I'm working and that might lead me back to where we grew up."

As I lower myself back onto the bed slowly, I question being so honest with her. The coy and curious nature I've come to enjoy from her turns timid. Like she's walking into dangerous territory.

"Should I ask?" Her voice is quiet and she doesn't look me in the eye.

"That depends on what you want to know." She hasn't asked a single question since we've started hooking up. She's smart enough to know. Maybe smart enough to know not to ask too.

Finally, her gorgeous green eyes look back at me and she presses, "Would you tell me the truth if I did? Tyler never did."

"Tyler wasn't ever involved in anything serious." I ignore how everything in me turns cold at the mention of his name. Being with Addison … knowing he was her first. It hurts to swallow as she keeps talking. Especially after the memory of my father. *I don't like to remember.*

She answers me, "Your version of serious and mine are different, I think."

The time passes as I fail to come up with a response. She doesn't need to know about any of this shit. It would be better if she didn't.

Another second. Another thought.

"Is that why you left him?" I ask her and although it hurts deep down in my core, I need to know if her idea of what he did for work is what made her leave him. I don't say his name though.

"I don't want to talk about that night." Her answer comes out sharper than I expect. With a bite and a threat not to question her. It only makes me that much more curious.

"The night you broke things off?" I ask her to clarify. That night isn't the one that haunts me. That's not the night that's unspeakable to me.

Addison stands on shaky legs with her back to me. Finding her packed bag and unzipping it as she speaks.

"I just don't like thinking about how the last couple of times I saw him I was turning him away," she says with a tinge of emotion I don't like to hear. The kind of emotion that's indicative of love.

A love I know for certain he had for her.

"You weren't the first seventeen-year-old girl to end a high school relationship," I remind her and also me. It was puppy love. That's all it ever was.

"Yeah well, I didn't know what it would lead to," she says and her voice trembles as she slips on a pair of underwear and sweatpants.

I'm not sure I want to know the answer, but I have to ask. "So if you could go back?"

Addison's quiet at my question and I walk toward her although her back is still to me. "If you could go back, you'd still be with him?" Her hesitation makes my muscles tighten. My fist clenches as a tic in my jaw spasms.

I've been kidding myself to think otherwise. Of course she'd be with him and not me. My breathing comes in ragged as she answers.

"If he were here now—" she starts to say, but I cut her off.

"He's not, and he never will be." The anger simmers. Everything that's been pushed down for so long rises up quickly. All the years of control and denial.

The hate that my brother was taken from me. And the pain of knowing it was my fault and that I've never told a soul. I could tell her now. But I never would. It's too late to confess.

Addison turns to face me with wide eyes. "Don't say that."

Maybe it's the denial, the guilt that plagues me. But I sneer at her, "You think it's easy for me? You got over his death far easier than I did."

I don't see the slap coming until the sting greets my cheek. My hand instinctively moves to where she's struck me. I flex my jaw and feel the burn radiate down the side of my face.

Her beautiful countenance is bright red with anger and her eyes are narrowed. I've never seen her this full of rage. Never.

Her hands tremble as she yells at me.

"You don't know how many nights his death haunted me!"

I do.

Her voice wavers and I know she's on the verge of tears. The kind that paralyze you because they're so overwhelming. But instead of giving in to grief, she screams at me.

"You don't know how I blamed myself to the point where I begged God to just kill me and let me take his place." She takes each breath in heavily.

I do.

Adrenaline rushes through my blood. The hate, the shame, and the unrelenting guilt surge within me. And I can't say anything back. I can't have this conversation with her.

When I don't say anything, when I feel myself shutting down, she snaps. "Fuck you," she tries to yell at me but her voice cracks as she grabs her bag and storms out of the room.

She doesn't have her shoes on and she's not wearing a bra under my shirt.

"You're not leaving?" It's meant to be a statement but the question is there in the undertone. All because I said she got over his death easier than I did? It's a fact. I fucking know it is.

"Yes, I am," she snaps as she turns around just as I walk up behind her. I have to halt my pace and take half a step back as she cranes her neck to bite out, "How dare you tell me that it was easy for me."

"You don't know-" I try to tell her that she has no idea how well I relate to her pain, but she doesn't let me finish.

"Leave me alone."

She angrily brushes under her eyes as she quickly descends the stairs with me right behind her. The front door is right there and she makes a beeline for it.

She's out of her fucking mind if she thinks I'm letting her leave here like this. "Addison. Wait a fucking minute."

"Don't tell me what to do," she yells back and tries to whip open the door. My palm hits it first, slamming it back shut.

"You're not leaving like this," I warn her. My muscles are coiled, but it's the fear making me wound so tight. She's leaving. And she's not coming back.

I can feel it in every inch of me.

"Yes, I am," she replies, though with shaken confidence.

"The fuck you are." My words are pushed through clenched teeth.

"If you respect me in any sense of the word, you will let me leave. Right now."

"Addison, don't do that."

"I mean it, Daniel. I need to be alone right now."

"I want to be there for you." I don't know how true the words are until I've said them. And oh, how fucking ironic they are.

"Well, you can't." She shuts me down.

Her green eyes stare up at me and all I can see is the same look she'd give Tyler when he was being clingy. The look that so obviously said she needed time and that she was overwhelmed. I get it now why he always hovered.

I'm afraid if I let her go now, she's never coming back. I can't lose her. Not again.

"I'm coming by tonight." I give her the only compromise I'm capable of.

I lower my arm but she doesn't respond. With a swift tug she pulls the door open and walks out, bare feet and all.

I stand in the doorway and watch her reach in her bag for flip-flops then put them on at the corner of the street.

She keeps looking over her shoulder, maybe to see if I'm coming for her.

And I am. She knows better than to think otherwise.

But I'll let her get a head start.

⸺•❖•⸺

Five years ago

He hovers. Constantly hovering.

We all know why. It's so fucking obvious every time he brings her around.

She's waiting to run.

She's cute and sweet, but there's something about her that makes it almost painfully apparent that a kid like Tyler could never hold on to her. It would take a man to keep that cute little ass.

Just thinking that as I stand in the kitchen, watching the two of them in the dining room makes me feel like a pervert. She's only sixteen, although her curves make her look like more of a woman and less of a girl.

He gives her little touches as they sit next to each other watching something on his laptop. Her laugh makes him smile.

He's foolish to think she'll stay with him. Girls like that don't stay with men like us. He can keep pretending if he wants to. He can keep bringing her home and cuddling up with her because he doesn't know how easy it is for people to shove you away.

She'll shove, she'll push, she'll leave. And I can't blame her.

Her shoulders shake as she laughs and leans into him. His broad smile grows and like the kid he is, he wraps his arm around her shoulders.

The smile dies when Addison leans forward and away.

He doesn't know she needs space.

It's not his fault though. Tyler has a lot to learn. Hard life lessons.

Like the ones I've had to endure.

Cancer took our mother and left us a bitter father who likes the belt a little too much. Not to mention a pile of bills that a single person couldn't possibly afford. It's taken years to turn my father's small-time dealing into a thriving business. Years of destroying what little life I had left.

"Let's not," I hear Addison say and when I look up her eyes are on me. Caught in her gaze, I hold her there, but it doesn't last long. Tyler's always there to reclaim her attention.

A sense of loss runs through me, followed by disgust.

I haven't been a good person in so long, maybe I've forgotten how. Or maybe I never was a good person to begin with.

*"You and Carter going out tonight?" my father asks as he interrupts the view I have of Tyler and **his** girlfriend.*

It's only ever Carter and me. Never my other brothers. We're the oldest, after all. The ones who need to pick up my father's slack. The ones who pay these bills and make the business what it is.

We're the ones who have to shoulder the burden. And really it's Carter's hard work and brutal business tactics that make any of this possible. It sure as fuck isn't my father. He's good at hiding his pain. But every time he remembers my mother, I know he copes with a different addiction. One that makes using that belt easier.

Only ever for Carter and me though.

"Yeah," I tell him and wait for him to hint that he wants us to bring some of the supply back for his personal use. Friday marks four years since our mother's been gone and I know a relapse is coming. He'll disappear for days, maybe even weeks. It was worse when she first passed. I guess I should be grateful that he's better now than he was then.

"Be careful coming home. I heard there's a patrol on the east side so maybe come up the back way after you get the shipment."

A second passes and then another before I nod.

Some days I wonder if he cares for me anymore. He was always a hard man. But when Mom passed, he was nothing but angry. The years have maybe changed him to be less full of hate. But it doesn't mean he has anything in him to take its place.

I give him another nod and look past him as the sound of Tyler and Addison getting up from the table catches my attention.

My father glances over his shoulder in the direction I'm staring and then turns back to me. He only shakes his head and makes to leave, but I hear him mutter, "She isn't yours."

I hate him even more in this moment. Because he's right.

The sad, pretty girl doesn't belong to me.

No matter how much I think she'd take my pain away.

CHAPTER 15

I WONDER WHAT THE GIRL I USED TO BE WOULD THINK OF ME.
The girl who still had both her parents and a life worth living for.
I think she'd make up excuses for my poor behavior. She'd say I was sad, but she has no idea how pathetic I am.

Grief isn't static. It's not a point on a chart where you can say, "Here, at this time, I grieved." Because grief doesn't know time. It comes and goes as it pleases, then small things taunt it back into your life. The memories haunt you forever and carry the grief with them. Yes, grief is carried. That's a good way to put it.

I pull a pillow on the sofa into my lap and stare at the television screen although my eyes are puffy and sore and I don't even know what's on.

Playing with the small zipper on the side of the pillow absently, I think about what happened. How it all unraveled.

I think it started with his scar, the past being brought up. But just like scars, some of our past will never leave us. The old wounds were showing. That's what it was really about.

I always knew Daniel was broken in ways Tyler wasn't. But I didn't know about his father. I didn't know any of that. I don't even know if Tyler knew.

But what happened between Daniel and me, that … I don't even have a word for it. It was like a light switch being turned off. Everything was fine, better than fine. Then darkness was abrupt and sudden, with no way to escape.

My eyes dart to the screen as a commercial appears and its volume is louder than whatever show or movie was playing. I sniffle as I flick the TV off and look at my phone again.

I'm sorry. Daniel messaged me earlier and I do believe he is, but I don't know if that will be enough. My happy little bubble of lust has been popped and the self-awareness isn't pretty.

I'm sorry too. It's all I can say back to him and he reads it. But there's nothing left for either of us to say now. I wonder if this will be the end of us.

We can't have a conversation about the bad things that have happened. That's the simple truth. It's awkward, tense. And we can't escape the moments coming up in conversation. There's no way getting around that.

It's easy to blame it on my past. On things I had no control over and things I can't change.

It's a lot like what I did when I left Dixon Falls. But really I was running, just like I had been since the day my parents died. Tyler was a distraction, a pleasant one that made me feel something other than the agonizing loneliness that had turned me bitter.

And then there was Daniel. He left me breathless and wanting, and that's a hard temptation to run away from.

I'm woman enough to admit that.

So sure, I can blame it on our past.

It's easy to blame it on grief, but it's still a lie. It's because neither of us can talk about what happened.

I startle at the vibration of the phone on the coffee table.

My heart beats hard with each passing second; all the while a long-lost voice in the back of my head begs me to answer a simple question. *What am I doing?*

Or maybe the right question is, *What did I expect?*

My gaze drifts across each photo on the far wall of the living room and it stops on three. Each of the photos meant something more when I took them. There are a little more than a dozen in total. Each photographed in a moment of time when I knew I was changing.

I keep them hung up because they look pretty from a distance; the pictures themselves are pleasant and invoke warm feelings.

More than that, the photos are a timeline of moments I never want to forget. I refuse to let myself forget.

But the three I keep staring at are so relevant to how I feel in this moment.

The first photo was taken at my parents' grave. Just a simple picture really, small forget-me-nots that had sprouted in the early spring. There was a thin layer of snow on the ground, but they'd already pushed through the hard dirt and bloomed. Maybe they knew I was coming and wanted to make sure I saw them.

In the photo you can't even tell they've bloomed on graves. The photo is cropped short and close. But I'll always remember that the flowers were on my parents' grave.

Tyler was with me when I took it. It wasn't the first, second or even the third time we'd gone out. But it was the first time I'd cried in such a long time and the one friend I'd met and trusted was there to witness it. I thought I was being sly asking him to drive to a cemetery hours away. Back to where I'd grown up. I hadn't been there in so long, but on that day when Tyler said we could go anywhere, I told him about the angel statue at the front of a cemetery I'd once seen that would be perfect for the photography project.

I didn't tell him that my parents were buried there, but he found out shortly after we arrived.

Part of me will forever be his for how he handled that day. For letting me cry and holding me. For not forcing me to talk, but being there when I was ready to.

Like I said, I never deserved him.

The second is a picture of the first place I'd rented after I ran away from Dixon Falls. I went from place to place, spending every cent I'd gathered over the years and not staying anywhere any longer than I had to. Until I found this farm cottage in the UK and met Rae.

She's such the opposite of me in every way. And she reminded me of Tyler. The happiness and kindness, the fact that she never stopped smiling and joking. Some people just do that to you … and because of it, I stayed. For a long time.

She's the one who took me to the bar in Leeds where I kissed another boy for the first time after Tyler's death.

She's the one who showed me how to really market my photography and introduced me to a gallery owner. She made me want to stay in that little cottage I'd rented for much longer than I'd planned. But feeling so happy and having everything be too easy felt wrong. It was wrong that I could move on and it made me feel like what had happened in the past was right, when I knew without a doubt that it wasn't.

It would never be right and that realization made me see Tyler everywhere all over again. I needed to leave. It was okay to remember, but it wasn't okay to forget. And I did leave. Each place I stopped at was closer and closer to Dixon Falls. At first I didn't realize it. But when I picked this university, I was keenly aware that I'd only be hours away.

The third picture is only a silhouette I took in Paris.

I don't know the people.

It's the shadows of four men standing outside of a church with a deep sunset behind them.

From a distance, all I could see were the Cross boys. And I took picture after picture, snapping away as quickly as I could. As if they'd vanish if I stopped. I wanted them back badly. I wanted them to forgive me and tell me it was alright. After all, they were the only family I had for a long time and just like my parents, I lost them.

That picture hurts the most. Because there should be five people in the shot. And because when the men did leave the hilltop behind the church and come closer, they weren't the Cross boys and I knew in that moment I'd never see them again. Daniel was never going to show up for me to stare at from a distance. It would never be them, no matter how much I prayed for it to happen.

Three pretty pictures, mixed in with the others. All hues of indigo, my favorite color, and all seemingly serene and beautiful. But each a memory of something that's made me the person I am.

My phone vibrates with the reminder of the most recent message. It's Daniel, of course. *Come over.*

I need to work, I text him and snort at his immediate response. *No you don't.*

I do, in fact, need to work. I could easily work at his place. That's what I've been doing and I actually enjoy it. I love it when he kisses my shoulder and tells me what he thinks of the photo I'm working on. He makes me feel less alone and he understands how I see the pictures and why they mean so much to me.

I want to apologize.

You did and I get it, I tell him even though it makes the ache in my chest that much deeper.

Please, just give me another chance.

Please is another word I'm not used to hearing from Daniel and as much as I want to give in, I need a little time.

I really do have to work. We can meet up next week. As I press send, I realize I'm caving in. Simply prolonging what is sure to end. But then I remember the men by the church. If

I could go back in time and make them stand there forever so I'd never have to face the fact that they weren't the Crosses, I would.

It hurts deep in my chest. Denial is a damning thing.

And that's what this is, isn't it? Just a futile attempt to deny that we could ever exist without our past tearing us apart.

The phone sits there silent, indicating no new message from him although I know he sees my response. Picking up a tissue from the coffee table, I dry my nose and pick myself up off the sofa.

Life doesn't wait for you. That's something I've learned well.

Before I can take a step toward the kitchen to toss the tissue, a message from Daniel comes in. *I promise I will make it up to you.*

I don't know what to write back. There's no way to make this right.

So instead I focus on the work that's waiting for me and choose not to respond.

I've barely been active online for a week now. Instead I've been taking pictures. Lots of them. Some of Daniel in abstract ways. Others of little things that remind me of him from when we were younger. I haven't posted those yet though. I'm not sure I will either. No matter how beautiful I think they are.

I haven't answered messages or sent out any packages. I don't even know how my sales are going. When you run a business all by yourself, you can't afford to take time off. For years I've buried myself in my passion and work, although really I'd just been running from reality. From my past.

Staring at the message from Daniel, the black and white text that's so easy to read, I can't answer the one question that matters.

What am I doing?

Six years ago

"Hey ... hey ..."

I hear a persistent voice but I ignore it. No one in this school has said a word to me. At least not to my face.

With a tug on my shirt, I'm forced to turn around and face a boy. A boy who's nearly a man. He doesn't have a baby face, and I can tell he shaves, but there's a kindness about him that makes him appear young. And likable. Which is something I haven't felt in the last two years.

"What are you doing?" he asks me and my forehead pinches.

I lift the pencil in the air and point to the chalkboard in science class as I say, "It's called taking notes."

The handsome guy laughs, a rough chuckle that forces me to smile. Some people's happiness is simply contagious.

"No, I mean tonight."

I don't bother to respond other than to shrug. I do the same thing every night. Nothing. My life is nothing.

"My brothers and I are having a little party."

"I don't really do parties," I answer him and nearly turn back around in my seat, but his smile doesn't falter and that in itself keeps my attention.

Shrugging, he says, "We can do something else."

"I don't really do much," I tell him honestly. I don't really feel like doing anything. Each day is only a date on a calendar. That's all they've been for a long time now.

"What about the assignment for art class? We could take some pictures for the photography project?" It takes me a moment to place him, but now that he's mentioned it, I think I did see him in the back row yesterday in art class.

"It's not my day for the camera." The budget for the art department is small, so we have to take turns checking out the equipment.

"I've got one we can use—well, it's my brother's."

"Your brother?"

"Yeah, his name's Daniel." It all clicks when he says his brother's name. I've seen him. It must be him. I've watched as this boy I'm talking to waits outside at the entrance to the school and another boy picks him up. Except he's not a boy. There's no question about that. Daniel is a man and it only took one glimpse of him to cause me to search him out each and every time the bell rings and I'm waiting in line for the bus.

"Now I know your brother's name, but I don't know yours."

"It's Tyler." I repeat his name softly and when I look at him, I see traces of his older brother. But where Daniel has an edge to him, Tyler is warm and inviting.

"I'm Addison."

"So what do you think, Addison?"

"I think that sounds like fun. I wasn't doing anything anyway."

Maybe fate knew I wasn't going to be able to keep Tyler. It was going to take him from me. So it gave me Daniel to keep me from loving Tyler too much.

I don't know for sure and there's no point in speculating.

All I know for certain is that Daniel will consume me, chew me up and spit me back out.

I need to end this before I get hurt ... well, before it gets worse than it already is.

CHAPTER 16

Daniel

I'M LOSING IT.

I can feel myself slipping backward into a dark abyss.

Addison and I are alike in more ways than she knows. In ways I'd never dare to whisper out loud. She's lying to herself when she says she needs space.

She doesn't.

She needs me, just like I need her. She's the only thing that takes the pain away and I do that for her too. I know I do. I can feel it. I can see it in her.

The light from the computer screen is the only thing that saves the living room from being in complete darkness. I've been staring at it, waiting for him to see I've been logged in for hours.

I'm trying to stay away from Addison. I'm trying to do what's best.

It's been a long time, Marcus finally responds. It's not his name or his alias in this chat. But I know it's him.

Three years now, I answer, leaning back into my seat with my laptop on my thighs and trying to ignore the shame that rings in my blood. It's been three years since I've logged into this black market chat and sought him out. Three years since I've felt the urge to watch over Addison every second of every day. Three years since I've had a hit of my sweet addiction.

What brings you back? he asks me and I swallow thickly.

She came back into my life. But you already know that.

She, as in Addison? he asks me to keep up this charade.

The keys beneath my fingertips click faintly as I type. It's odd how I find it comforting, the soft sounds tempting me to confess my sins.

I wasn't stalking her or trying to find her. The first time was a coincidence.

How many times have there been? he asks me.

A lot, I admit but then add, *but she's been with me this time. It's not me hiding in the shadows. She sought me out.*

Do you think that makes it healthier? The text stares back at me on the brightly lit screen and I want to answer yes. Of course it is. This time isn't anything like what happened years ago. He doesn't wait for me to answer before he poses another question.

Obsession may be the wrong word. I think possessive is better. She's mine. My reason to move on from what happened before. My desire for more. My only way to cope.

It's different this time. This time she wanted me there.

Wanted? he presses, and the shame of why I'm even here in this anonymous chat makes my chest feel tight. *As in past tense?*

She asked me for time apart and I'm having difficulties. I'm slipping back into old habits.

It's called stalking, Daniel.

I'm aware of that, Marcus.

I use his name, just like he uses mine. No one else knows it's him, but I do. Because years ago, when I watched Addison finally sleep without crying, when she could say Tyler's name with a sad smile instead of barely restrained agony, he was there for me. All those years ago when she moved on and I was still struggling to cope with the guilt of Tyler's death, Marcus is the one who stopped me from pulling the trigger with a gun pressed to my head.

It took nearly two years before it came to that point. A year and a half of following her, of watching her and living out my pain vicariously through hers. And months of slowly losing myself and any reason not to end it.

She kept me sane in a way she'll never know as I watched her grieve with the same pain I had.

But as the months went by, she started to smile again.

It made me feel worse than the day Tyler took his last breath.

She got better, when I didn't. Every laugh, every bit of happiness made zero sense to me.

I could only cope through her sadness. I understood it; I needed it.

Does she know about the past? he asks me.

She'll never understand, I type into the chat box, but I don't send it.

I shake my head, remembering how I followed her everywhere after Tyler's death. How I watched her run and that alone was enough to take my pain away. She loved him after all and felt responsible like I did. And if she could move on, so could I. But I could never move on from Addison.

⸺ ⋅ ⸺

Five years ago

I tell myself the only reason I'm on this train is to speak to her.

To tell her it's not her fault and I'm the one to blame.

That's the reason I've followed her, stalking her in the shadows and silently watching her as she struggles with what to do.

I tell myself that, but I don't move. I'm struggling too.

The train comes to another stop and my grip tightens on the rail as I wait to see what she does. Where she goes, I'll go.

I need to make sure she's okay, that she doesn't have the same thoughts I do. I'll protect her.

Her hoodie is up, hiding her face as she leans against the wall of the train. Unmoving.

My body tightens, wanting to go to her. To hold her, to check on her and make sure she's still breathing. She saw him die like I did. That changes you. There's no way to deny it or to recover.

It will forever be with us.

CHAPTER 17

Addison

I**T'S FUNNY HOW TIME MOVES.**

It crawled along for years before and after Tyler came into my life. Each day's only purpose was to be a box on a calendar I could cross off with a deep red marker. If I bothered to even count.

But the days with Tyler, when I was really with him? They flew by. Because time is quite like fate, it's a bitch.

And the same thing happened with Daniel. The days were whirlwinds of moments that made me feel like everything was alright. Like it was okay to simply live in his bed and sleep in his arms. Like the selfishness of ignoring everything else was how life is supposed to go.

But the past few days without him … it's been worse than the slowest pain. There's a coldness that feels like it's just below the surface of my skin. As if my blood refuses to heat. And the nights are filled with memories designed to play on my weakest moments.

Knock. Knock. Knock.

My focus is shifted to the front door of my apartment as I sit cross-legged on my sofa with my laptop cradled on me. The screen's gone black and I don't know how long it's been like that.

He knocks again. There's only one person it could be. *Daniel.*

Every day and night since we last talked I've thought about him. And about what I need to do. Each text he sends is met with a short response that makes the pain in my chest grow.

I'm no longer in denial. It's time to move on. That means moving on from everything, including Daniel. And that hurts. But it's supposed to.

My neck is killing me from bending over the computer for hours. I have a standing desk; I should really use it, but I don't. I spend hours a day sitting on the sofa with my computer in my lap while I Photoshop my pictures. There are at least three dozen more I want to edit and post before going out and searching for my next muse. Although I don't know if I'll find it here. Maybe it's time to move on already.

My sore body aches all over when I stand, but that pain is temporary, so I don't mind it.

Each step to the front door makes me feel like I'm running in the opposite direction from where I was going days ago. I've come to the only logical decision there is and I've never liked breaking up with anyone. The way Daniel made me feel is unlike anything I've ever felt. Wild and crazy, I suppose. Thanks to the late night sex and not caring about anything, not even our next breath so long as our skin was touching and our desires seeking out refuge in each other.

Pausing with my hand on the doorknob, I let out a deep breath. He'll understand. He's probably here to do the same. This thing between us could never last.

I feel like I'm being stabbed in the heart, but the moment the door is opened, the pain dims and that other feeling, that fluttering sickness I have trouble describing takes its place. The kind of pain that I want more of, but it scares me.

"Daniel." I whisper his name as his dark eyes meet mine and then soften. His leather jacket creases as he puts his hand on the doorframe and leans in slightly.

"You still mad at me?" he asks with a deep timbre to his voice that speaks to vulnerability and I answer him honestly, shaking my head.

"I'm not mad at you." Forgiving others is easy. It's forgiving myself that's hard.

Daniel lets out a breath and starts to come in, but I can't do this. It's better to stop it now and not do the easier thing. Which would be to fall back into bed with him and numb the pain with his touch.

It's not healthy.

My palm hits his chest and his expression turns to confusion, but he stops just outside the threshold.

"I've been thinking," I start to tell Daniel and he tilts his head, his eyes narrowing.

"This sounds like the *we have to talk* conversation." There's a trace of a threat in his voice.

"It kind of is," I say softly and the pain in my heart grows. "I've just been thinking about every way this is going to end."

"End?" he asks incredulously, moving forward and closing the distance between us. He's standing on the threshold now.

It's hard to speak, but I have to be honest with myself and him. I have to protect myself.

"I'm not sure we should do this at all."

Stunned is how I'd describe the look on Daniel's face, and it surprises me. "It doesn't make sense for us to continue this-"

"You don't want me?" Daniel asks, cutting me off in a voice devoid of anything but sadness. I've never heard the sound from his lips before. The tone pains my heart in a way nothing else ever will. I know it for a fact. Some things simply break a piece of you that can never be mended.

"That's not what I meant. Not at all. I didn't anticipate this happening," I try to explain. What I thought would be a simple conversation ending with Daniel leaving me behind escalates to something I hadn't anticipated. "I didn't think you would care." My words come out rushed.

"You thought I wouldn't care that you're done with me?"

"I'm not done … I could never be done with you. But this," I gesture between us, "this is something I know is going to hurt me. And both of us know will never last."

"I'm not Tyler. That's why?" Daniel's words should be cutting. They should hurt me. But I only hurt for him. How could he think that?

I have to swallow hard before I can tell him, "I want you." I almost say Tyler's name.

I almost tell him how I wanted the love Tyler gave me and how I wanted to love Tyler back but never did. But I can't. I can't bring him into this. "It's not that at all, Daniel. I've wanted you for the longest time and I hated myself for it. We can't even have a simple conversation about anything before…" I swallow hard, the lump in my throat refusing to let any more words pass.

"You hate yourself for wanting me?" The sadness is gone and anger quickly takes its place. Suddenly I'm suffocating, finding myself taking a step back and then another although he stays in the doorway, radiating a dominance barely self-contained.

"You're scaring me," I whisper and Daniel flinches. The emotions cycle through him one by one. The anger, the shock, the frustration from not knowing what to do.

And I've felt them all, I've also suffered the torture of not knowing what to do for so long. Every day that I felt loved by Tyler but knew I loved Daniel more. I know his pain as if it was my own. But there's no way to make this right. And the sooner this is over, the better.

"I want you Daniel, but it's wrong."

"It's not wrong," he says and his words come out strangled, his breathing heavier. He almost takes a step forward and then stops himself, gripping the edge of the door-frame and lowering his head, hanging it in shame. I'm reminded of the day I first met him and that makes the agony that much worse. "I don't know how to …" he trails off and swallows thickly.

"There's no way this is going to be more than … than what we were doing."

His head whips up and his dark eyes pin me in place. Daniel's always been intense, always been dangerous. For others, I'm sure it's similar. But they'll never feel *this*. Not the way I feel for Daniel.

"Why does it need to be *more* right now? Why can't we hold on to what we have?"

"It's not good for either of us, Daniel," I whisper and wrap my arms around my chest. I don't know how else to explain it and how he could fail to understand that.

The silence grows. All I can hear is my own breath as Daniel stands there stiffly, staring at the faded carpet beneath his feet. Finally, he looks me in the eye again and the intensity and pain there shatter me to the very center of my soul.

"I know that you belonged to Tyler first, as much as I hate to admit that. I hate to say his name. I don't want to imagine what used to …"

"Daniel, please don't," I say and reach for him, my heart hurting for his and I hate myself in this moment. Why did I have to do this?

"We can't change the past, Addison. I wish I could. But it's over now. And right now I want you."

There was never a point in my life where I thought I'd hear those words from Daniel. And the shock, the sadness, and the conflict of not knowing how to protect myself and what I should do keep the words I'm desperate to say trapped in my throat.

I want to believe what he's saying. But he's already said the words I need to hold on to the conviction of leaving him. *There will never be more.*

"You know where to find me if you want to see me." Daniel's last words are flat, with a defeated tone.

I can't form a coherent thought as he turns his back to me and walks off. This isn't what I wanted or how I'd planned for it to go. "I didn't mean for this to happen," I say, but my choked words are barely audible to me, let alone Daniel as he disappears in the distance.

I worry my bottom lip and a storm brews inside of me. A storm that feels as though it's never left, like it was only waiting in the darkness. Preparing for when it could come out and destroy the little piece of me that remains.

It's not until Daniel's gone that I close the door, lean my back against it and fall to the floor on my ass.

I've made a mistake. More than one. But I can't keep going on like this, making mistake after mistake and running from them.

Helplessness overwhelms me and I've never felt weaker. Why is it all so complicated? Why can't love and lust be one, and right and wrong easier to decipher?

CHAPTER 18

EVERY SMALL MOVEMENT MAKES THE PAIN SPREAD DEEPER. I shouldn't have called him a drunk. I shouldn't have yelled back when my father yelled at me. I know better. I brought this on myself.

I let out a deep breath, but even breathing hurts. Carter will cover for me. He always does. I swallow thickly as I hear heavy footsteps coming to my door and my heart pounds for a moment, thinking it's him. Thinking I fucked something up.

Like I did last night, losing thousands of dollars. Thousands and thousands of money and merchandise are gone. Stolen off the truck. And it's my fault. I'm the one who opened it, getting the fucking CD Addison left in there and not remembering to lock it back up.

This is all because of her.

There's only a slight bit of relief when I hear Tyler yell out my name as he bangs on the door.

I struggle to put my shirt back on, but do it through clenched teeth while wincing. It was only a belt, I grit out with the part of me that thinks I'm pathetic. That I deserve all of this and more.

I open the door without thinking of the cuts on my back and the pain sears through me.

"Why do you have to be such an asshole all the time?"

Tyler's question is met with nothing from me. Not a single emotion that I can give him.

"You don't have to make her feel like she's not welcome."

Anger makes me swallow hard. I still don't respond.

I'll never tell him how I feel about her, but at least now I know how she feels about me.

"Are you going to say anything?"

My lips part and I want to give him something, anything. But the fact that I went out of my way for her last night … maybe that's why. Maybe she knows I want her. The idea hits and steals my words from me.

"She's a good person," Tyler tells me as if that's why I stay away from her.

"I love you, Tyler. God knows it. But you're a fucking idiot."

I should have kept my mouth shut, but everyone has their limits.

"She loves me and she's not going anywhere," he tells me with a confidence I've never seen in my baby brother.

My baby brother who's oblivious to what we really are and what goes on here.

My baby brother who's never been struck once by my father.

My perfect baby brother who wants to make everyone around him smile because he's never known pain like I have.

"She only loves you because she has no one else who loves her." My gaze pins him where he is as I say the words. "Remember that."

Loneliness is a bitter pill to swallow. I know I've brought it on myself, but still. A sarcastic, humorless huff leaves me as I grab the bottle of whiskey and take a swig.

It must be karma.

I left Addison to her loneliness so I could survive.

Now she's leaving me to mine to ruin me.

Touché, little love.

The whiskey burns as I take another heavy drink. And with it every possibility of where I lost her flashes in my mind. The times from back when we were younger and I held back so much, to only moments ago when I didn't hold back a damn thing.

I lick my lower lip and then pick the bottle back up, but a timid knock stops me from chugging back more of the amber liquid.

"Daniel," I hear Addison's voice from beyond the door. Hope flickers deep inside of me, flirting with a darkness that's nearly consumed me.

My heart pauses. So do my lungs. It's only when I hear her again that they both decide to function again. She's here. *She came to me.*

My blood buzzes as I stand up and make my way to the front door. All while I stride to the door the alcohol sets in, and I hear her call out again. "Please open the door, Daniel."

She's mid-motion of knocking again with her mouth parted and more to say when I pull the door open. She looks shocked and even flinches slightly.

"Daniel," she says my name with a hint of surprise, but quickly her expression and tone change. "I wanted to explain."

And that right there is why I didn't let that hope grow. The coldness in my chest puts out the small flame. It's hard to school my expression. It's hard to hide it from her. But a part of me is screaming not to. To let her see what she's doing to me. To make sure she knows she's destroying me bit by bit.

"Explain?" The question comes out with a bit of anger and I have to readjust my grip on the door and look away from her for a moment.

"You don't owe me anything, Addison," I tell her and turn to walk down the hall, but I leave the door open. I let her come to me willingly.

When I hear the door shut and her following me inside, a smile slowly forms on my face. It's only a trace of genuine happiness. But at least I know she can't let me go as easily as she thinks she can.

"Daniel, please," she says as she catches up to me in the living room, gripping my shirt and making me turn to face her.

"What is it you want to explain?" I ask her and almost call her little love. Almost.

"I didn't think that you wanted anything but a good fuck." God, she does something to me when she talks like that. When foul and dirty words come out of that pretty little mouth of hers.

My own indecent thoughts keep me from responding quickly enough. So she storms over to the leather chair in the corner of the room and sits down angrily, crossing her legs and then her arms.

Of course that's what she thought. It's what this started out as. But she's fooling herself if she thinks what we have could ever be anything so shallow. Even I can admit it. "I'm not leaving until you talk to me," she demands and it's cute. She's so fucking adorable thinking she can make demands like that. My bare feet sink into the rug as I make my way to the chair opposite hers.

With the blinds closed, the only light in the room is that of the tall lamp in the corner.

"Say something, please. I feel awful. I didn't expect you to react the way you did." She leans forward and grips the armrests of the chair. "The last thing I wanted to do was hurt you," she confesses and I know she's telling the truth. Addison isn't a liar.

And that gives me hope.

"I don't know what I want, other than you." My voice comes out rough as I lean forward and put my elbows on my knees so I can sink down to her eye level.

"What does that mean?" she asks breathlessly. Her chest rises and falls as if my answer is everything she's ever needed. The only thing she's ever desired.

Licking my lower lip, I stare into her eyes but the words don't come. I don't know how else to say it. I want her.

I want her to be mine. It's all I've ever wanted.

Not just in my bed. I want her touches, her kisses, her intentions. Moving forward, I want each piece of her. Every little piece. I want them all.

More than that, I want her to give them to me.

Her words spin chaotically, as do her emotions. "I need something to hold on to, Daniel, and this, this is intense and overwhelming and emotional-"

"But do you want it?" I cut her off, asking the simple question.

"Why did you come get me in that bar? Don't lie to me. You knew I'd be there, didn't you?" she asks me and I don't know if she knows more than she should, or if she's just that damn good at knowing who I am.

I lean back in my seat and decide to be careful with my words as I slowly say, "I wanted you for so long."

"So that's all this is? You wanted to fuck me, so you finally did?

"You already know that's a lie." My words come out like a vicious sting and she drops the act. "I know you feel this too." I finally speak the words that feel as if they'll break me. But they're true. "There's always been something between us."

Addison's expression is pained.

"I know you feel guilty admitting it, Addison. I do too. I'm just as much to blame." She doesn't know how true those words are.

Time wears on and more than a moment passes. Addison pulls her knees into her chest and all I want to do is grab her ass and pull her into my lap. But my fingers dig into the leather, pinning me where I am until I have the only answer I need from her.

"Do you want me?" I ask her.

"It's not that easy," she whimpers. Torn between the desire she feels and the guilt she won't let go of.

My body tenses and the rage from knowing the past may forever darken my future takes over as I lean forward. "The fuck it isn't."

I have to close my eyes and focus on what I want, what she needs to hear. I speak so low I'm not sure she can hear me, but I pray she can. "I can't tell you what will happen a week from now, but I know I'll still want you." I open my eyes to find her watching me intently as I continue, "I've always wanted you. It's not going to stop, and I don't care about anything that happened yesterday as long as I get you tomorrow."

"When did you turn into this man?" Addison's question is quiet, but full of sincerity. "I don't remember any of this from you."

The answer is right there. So obvious to me.

Because she wasn't mine and couldn't be.

"You were young, and belonged to someone else." I can't bring myself to speak Tyler's name. The alcohol and thought of losing her if he comes up again is too much.

Before she can respond to the omission I ask her the only thing that matters, "Do you want me?"

Her green eyes shine with sincerity as she barely whispers the word, "Yes." She bites down on her lip as I rise from my seat and make my way to her. Slowly and carefully, with each step knowing I'm so close to keeping her.

"If you stay here Addison, I swear I won't let you leave." I swallow thickly and clear my throat when she searches my eyes and knows I'm speaking the truth. "This is your last chance to run from me." I owe her that at least. One last chance to run.

"I've never wanted to run from you." Her words are laced with raw emotion and she reaches up to cup my face. "We're doing this?"

"You can't leave me, Addison. You have to promise me, no matter what happens," I say and hope she can't hear the desperation in my voice. "No matter if we fight." I start to say more, but I choke on the obvious. *No matter if Tyler comes up again.*

I can barely breathe as she strokes the stubble of my jaw with her thumb and whispers, "I promise."

She falls into my lap so easily. Her warmth and soft touches light every nerve ending in me on fire. But so much more than that too. The pounding in my chest. The need to be close to her. To be skin to skin and show her she's mine again.

I'm dying inside, needing to take her, but I move so achingly slowly. Cherishing every second of something I almost lost. Every second of *her*.

"Daniel?" Her voice is hesitant, but raw. As if the question itself will break her as I kiss the crook of her neck and let my fingers barely graze her skin, just a whisper of a touch.

"Addison?" I answer her with a playful air and smile against her skin when she breathes easily.

"I'm scared," she whispers into the air and when I pull away from her, her face is toward the ceiling with her eyes closed tight. Her fingers dig into my shoulders as I nudge her chin with my nose to get her attention.

"I won't hurt you," I whisper when she doesn't respond. My heart races, though not in a steady rhythm. But when she lowers her gaze, her green eyes finding mine, it steadies and slows. It's lost without her.

Addison nods, a small nod of recognition, but the hesitancy is still there. Her slender fingers pull at my shirt and I help her, leaning back and pulling it off. Then I remove hers, and move lower. We strip each other slowly, each movement met with the sound of our breathing. Kisses in between each garment being tossed to the floor, each turning more desperate, more breathy. *More.*

And when I finally slip my fingers between her folds, she's soaking wet with need and rocks her hot pussy into my hand. Her eyes are still closed as she rides my palm and my thumb presses against her clit. Groaning against her throat, I grab my dick and push myself inside of her until I can let go and grab her hips as I fill her tight cunt.

Sucking in a breath, her fingers move to my shoulders, her blunt nails digging into my flesh.

Her wide eyes meet mine and I'm entranced.

Every thrust up, I dig my fingers deeper into her shoulder. My abs burn as I fuck her like this over and over, as deep as I can while I stare into her eyes.

The need to kiss her is all-consuming. But I can't break her gaze either.

Her lips part just slightly as her pussy flutters and then spasms on my dick. My name slips from her lips as a strangled moan. And it's only when she shudders and an orgasm rips through her that she breaks my gaze. She falls forward in my arms as I keep up my pace, riding through her climax.

I kiss her shoulder, her neck, her hair, every bit of her ravenously, worshipping her as she grips on to me for dear life.

My release comes in a wave so strong, I'm not ready. I'm not at all ready for this to end. But I swear I hear her whisper against my skin, her hot breath sending a chill down my spine as the intense pleasure rocks through me. I swear I hear her whisper as her lips graze my neck.

I love you.

My arms wrap around her and I don't move; I don't let her move either. I can't say the words back. And I don't know if she'll say them again. But I swear I heard them.

I swear I heard her say those words to me.

To me.

CHAPTER 19

Addison

DANIEL CROSS IS MY BOYFRIEND.
How high school. But still …

That's all I sent to Rae this week. I'm used to giving her long descriptions of where I'm going next. It's all I've ever considered and she loves to hear stories of what new places are like. But this town brought me Daniel and I don't want to share a ton of details. He's mine.

A snicker makes me lean back from the laptop as I read Rae's response to my email. *How big is his dick?* is her opening line. Leave it to Rae to relieve the tension.

I've been worried about what she's going to say. And knowing that she isn't judging me makes everything so much easier to accept. She even said, *As long as you're happy, I'm happy.*

That's all I wanted. As I click out of the email, ready to close the laptop, I see my subject line again. *Daniel Cross is my boyfriend.*

I cover my smile with my hand as I pull my heels up onto the sofa. With my pillow snuggled up close to me, I'm in for a night of binge-watching housewives and reality television.

But I couldn't really care less about any of that. I can't get into a show to save my life—or work, for that matter. All I keep thinking is that Daniel wants to be … *mine.*

It's been over a week and that's still the case. Nights of hanging out, watching TV or looking over photographs I've taken. It's almost normal.

Those stupid butterflies in my stomach won't quit and it makes me feel childish and giddy. But even in the eye of the storm that surrounds us, I want him and he wants me.

That should be all that matters, right?

As I reach for my glass of wine sitting on the coffee table, I can't help but feel like the bottom is going to fall out from under us. Like there's something waiting on the edge of all this. I can feel it with everything in me.

Life doesn't work like this. You don't get what you want simply by asking for it.

I swallow a sip of the wine and the sweetness I was feeling only a moment ago tastes bitter with the last thought.

Daniel feels like everything. Like there was nothing before him even though I'm fully aware there was. There's no way with our history that there will be more between us, no matter what he says and how well we play house together. There won't be any family dinners with his brothers or any sense of normalcy in that respect.

No matter how much I wish that were the case.

Every day I'm waiting for Daniel to tell me he was wrong and it's over. Or that he's ready to go home and that I'm not welcome there. I like to think that my guard is up and that it won't hurt when he does it. But each day that passes is another crack in that armor.

He fucks me like he owns me. He holds me at night so tight; like if he lets go, he'll lose me forever.

And he kisses me like he's dying for the air I breathe.

We don't talk about the one thing that plagues me. About how we're supposed to just ignore our past. He thinks we've said enough, but if that were the case, I would be able to sleep without the memories haunting me.

It's hard to explain how I feel. I want to be happy and grateful. But it's obvious I'm being naïve. This is too good and I know good things always come to an end.

"You want anything while I'm out?" Daniel asks, interrupting my thoughts as he steps out of the hall to the bedroom and strides toward me. It's odd seeing him in my apartment still. I'm more used to his place, but tonight he'll be gone for a while and I need the space.

The fresh smell of his body wash follows him into the room and I find myself humming in agreement although I didn't quite hear him. He's too distracting when he's dressed like this. Black jeans and a crisp white button-up with one sleeve already rolled up while he works on rolling the other. Freshly shaven with his high cheekbones and strong jaw on display, it almost makes me wish he was always cleanly shaven. But that stubble …

Either way, he looks like a fucking sex god. He fucks like one too. *My* sex god.

"I might be out for a while, but I can bring back something for breakfast if it's too late."

I watch the muscles in his forearm as he rolls up his sleeve and as I do, the desire is slightly muted by his comment.

That's another thing we don't talk about. We don't talk about what he does late at night. I was quiet whenever Tyler would leave to go do something early in the mornings or skip school because he had to do something for "work."

But we aren't children anymore, and what Daniel's involved with isn't a high school game.

"Is this stuff for … back home?" I'm careful with my words as he grabs his keys off the kitchen counter. The jangling is the only sound in the room.

Well, and the ever-present clicking of the clock.

"Back home? As in, the family business?"

My gaze is on the tile in the kitchen. Soft gray with dark gray grout. It's nothing special, but I can't bring myself to look at Daniel and meet his gaze that's obviously on me, so I keep my eyes right where they are.

He works for his brother Carter. Dealing drugs and God knows what else.

He'll leave one day. Soon. He keeps mentioning it. The one question I ask myself every time he leaves is simple. Do I stay? Or do I go with him?

"Yeah, that's what I was asking."

"You know better than that, Addison," Daniel reprimands me and that's what gets me to look at him.

"Better than to be careful about who and what I involve myself with?" My tone dares him to question that logic.

"You already made your choice, didn't you?" The way he speaks to me simultaneously strikes a bit of fear in my heart and heats my blood with lust.

"There are lots of choices, Daniel." I know in my mind he's right. I've already decided I'd go with him. I don't want to be alone again and I crave the feeling of family and acceptance I once had with the Cross brothers. But that was then, and this is now. I don't know what it would be like to face them knowing I'm now with Daniel. It feels like a betrayal of the worst kind.

"Only one when it comes to me. Don't forget that you're the one who started this. You're the one who came back to the bar. You're the one who came to my house after you ended it. I don't like being played with."

"Funny, because you sure do like being the one doing the playing."

My comment rewards me with a charming smirk on his lips.

"With you?" he questions as he stalks toward me and grips my chin between his fingers. "Always."

My eyes close as he plants a kiss on my lips. Mine mold to his and my body melts. It's over too soon and I find myself sitting up a little taller to prolong it just slightly.

Daniel keeps his grip on me and a crease forms on his forehead as he looks down at me with a question in his eyes.

"Are you thinking of leaving me?" he finally asks and I reach up to take his hand in mine.

"No," I tell him, practically rolling my eyes and getting more comfortable in the corner of my sofa.

"Good," he says although he still eyes me curiously.

"If I hadn't come to your place, would you have let me leave you?" I don't know why I feel so compelled to ask in this moment. Maybe I already know the truth and I just want to see if he'll tell me or not.

His dark eyes seem to get darker, although his voice stays even as he answers me, "I would have tried."

I chew the inside of my cheek and look away at his response.

"Why does that disappoint you?"

"Can't you feel it?" I barely whisper the words. He makes me feel weak and foolish. But admitting there's something undeniable that pulls you to someone like it does no one else isn't weak at all. It takes every bit of strength in me.

Daniel's eyes leave mine for a moment and I begin to doubt myself. I can barely swallow until he says, "I said I would try. I didn't say I was capable."

My eyes close and I wish I could will all of this overwhelming emotion away. But that's what Daniel's always done to me. Overwhelmed me.

"I'll keep you safe. Always."

My heart soars and plummets with his words. That's how it feels and the relief on my lips falls with it.

"I just know … your job … is dangerous." I hate how my throat feels tight as I speak. "I knew what I was getting into. It's different when you wait at home alone wondering …"

"But I'm a dangerous man, Addison. I know what I'm doing."

I search his dark eyes for reassurance and it's there, but still I can't help adding, "Don't die. Everyone I love dies."

"What if it's more like anyone who loves you dies?" he questions and it doesn't help me feel any better at all. He shrugs and points out, "Then I'm dying anyway, so you might as well love me back."

Although I realize the words were spoken in a lighthearted way, the acknowledgement is there. That there's something more between us and we both feel it. We both recognize it for what it is. I don't dare to speak it again. I'm too caught up in those flutters in my chest. The ones that hurt in the best of ways. My eyes start to gloss over and I shove all the emotion away.

"Just be safe, my dangerous sex god." My voice is playful and nonchalant as I reach for the remote, ending the conversation. It's too much, too soon. But it feels like everything that's always been missing. It feels right. It feels like home. And I'm so afraid to lose it.

Daniel chuckles and leans down to cup my cheek and plant a soft kiss in my hair. "I'll be back as soon as I can," he whispers and it tickles me enough to make me pull away and snatch a kiss from his lips myself.

It's only been weeks, but this is everything I've ever wished for.

As the door clicks shut, leaving me alone in my apartment, I remember a certain saying.

Be careful what you wish for.

CHAPTER 20

Daniel

ago

I KNEW SOMETHING WAS OFF WHEN I WALKED IN AT 4 A.M. AND THE DINING ROOM light was on. *The yellow glow carries into the kitchen and I follow it to see Tyler at the end of the large table, head in his hand staring at the screen to his laptop.*

I expect to hear something, maybe see him watching a video. But the screen has gone black and that's when I see his expression. Defeated and exhausted.

"You still up?" I ask him, which is a stupid question. It gets his attention though, although his exhaustion makes him blink several times before he can answer me. It's then that I see his eyes are puffy, not with sleep, but with something else.

"Yeah, couldn't sleep," he answers and then visibly swallows as he closes the laptop.

My jacket rustles as I slip it off and hang it over the chair in front of me. I still feel like an asshole for snapping at him the other day. Of everyone living under this roof, Tyler's the last person who needs my shit. "Everything alright?"

He sits back and lets out a heavy breath, but instead of answering verbally, he only shakes his head no.

"You want to talk about it?" I ask as I grip the back of the chair and prepare myself for the answer I know is coming. Addison isn't here and Tyler can't sleep. She left him.

"You were right," Tyler says and then turns away from me.

"I was an asshole who was trying to be an asshole. I'm never right. You know that?"

He lets out a huff of a laugh and wipes under his eyes.

"What happened?" I ask him.

"She said it's too much for her. That she needs space."

I nod my head in understanding. "Nothing wrong with a little space," I say and try to make it sound like it's not a big deal.

"I know her, Daniel. I know it's her way of putting distance between us so I'll be the one to leave."

The legs of the chair scratch along the floor as I pull it out and take a seat. A heavy breath leaves me as I put my elbows on the table and lean closer to him. "Girls are hormonal," I say to try to make him crack a smile. He's the one who's good at this, not me.

"I think she's done with me, but I don't know why."

"She loves you," I tell Tyler although it makes a spike of pain go through my heart. She does love him. I know it by the way she kisses him. It's obvious she does.

"I don't know," he says in a whisper, shaking his head.

"Just give her a day or two, cut class if you have to. Give her time to miss you." I hate that I'm giving him this advice. But I hate to see him like this more.

"What did Mom used to say, huh? If you give someone love, they'll love you back. Right?"

He nods his head, although he still doesn't speak. It's been a while since I brought up Mom. And it still doesn't feel right, but Tyler was her baby boy. He may have been younger when she got sick, but it hit him hard. He didn't understand.

"I promise you," I tell him as I pat his back. "Come with me for the next two days. I have to make a trip to Philly for a shipment. Come up with me and let her miss you."

He's reluctant for a moment but then he nods. "I could use the distraction, I guess."

"Perfect." I stand up quickly and leave him be as fast as I can. "Get some sleep," I say over my shoulder and I don't stop walking or respond when he tells me thanks.

As I climb the stairs to go pass out, loneliness settles in my chest.

The idea of Addison never coming back hits me hard. The possibility of never seeing her again.

It's very obvious to me in this moment that I don't like it.

More than I don't like how she's younger than me.

More than I don't like how she looks at me the way I look at her when I know she's not looking.

More than I don't like that she's Tyler's.

⸺•⸺

Every day there's a memory I've forgotten. Haunting me. Showing me how I could have stopped the inevitable. Or at least changed our fates.

Late at night, holding Addison as she sleeps, I wonder if Tyler would still be alive if I had done something different. Or if I'd be the one buried in the ground now.

Fall has arrived and each step I take down Rodney Street is accompanied with the crunch of dead and withered leaves. My steps are heavy tonight because I know Marcus is going to be here.

He's finally come with whatever it is Carter's been waiting for. I know Marcus' patterns. He spends weeks scouting out a place and making sure you go to one location he has constant eyes on. And when he's found where he's comfortable, he delivers.

He's found that place at the park on the corner of Rodney and Seventh.

After tonight I have no reason to stay here. Addison will either come with me, or leave me. It's too good right now to think she'll refuse me, but she's run before and it's entirely possible she'll do it again.

I glance down the side street to see what block I'm on and my heart freezes.

The man in the black leather jacket, the one who stopped to look at Addison. That first day I watched her in the coffee shop and saw him staring at her. It's him. I swear I saw him melt into the shadows down the street.

"Hey!" I call out, more to see if he'll move than to actually get a reaction. But there's only silence. I barely glance to my right to check for cars as I run across the street. The cool air does nothing to calm my heated skin or the anxiety rushing through my blood.

I'm ready for a fight when I get there, but the shadowy corner is only a dead end. And no one's there.

A chill flows over my skin and I look all around me. It's no one. There's no one here.

It's hard to swallow as I walk back across the street. *It's just paranoia*, I tell myself. It's nothing. But still, all of my thoughts lead back to Addison. To her being alone.

She's messing with my head.

I think about every way she's consumed me with each step I take.

I can't see anything other than her when she's around me.

Every breath she takes depletes the air from my lungs.

I hated her for it back then, back when she was with Tyler. When she smiled at him instead of me. She tempted me, and I couldn't do a damn thing about it.

But time changes everything.

Every step she takes closer to me makes my fingers itch to grab on to her and never let go.

Fate simply waits for men like me. So it can fuck us over until we fall to our knees and admit there isn't a damn good thing about us.

Addison has no idea what she does to me.

She'll be the death of all that's good in me. I would lose focus of everything just to have a miniscule piece of her attention. I'd steal for her. I'd kill for her. I already have.

Goosebumps still cover my body as I get to the empty park. It's in the back of a small church that's surrounded by woods. I guess for Sunday school.

My gaze scans the perimeter of the park, but there's no one there. It's empty.

Marcus is never late. I check my watch and make sure I'm on time.

A minute passes as I walk toward the church and then back. It's not a good look to loiter and I don't need anyone getting suspicious.

Another minute and my anger and anxiety start to get the best of me.

A flash of white catches my eye as the breeze goes by; the squeaks of the swing's rusty chains make me turn toward them.

A note. I walk toward it without hesitation. Marcus and his fucking games.

There's a message on the swing.

Another address.

Tomorrow night. Check the mailbox. That's all you'll need.

Gritting my teeth, I hold back the urge to scream out toward the forest in anger. I know that fucker's in there watching. Making sure I got the memo.

The paper crumples in my hand as I stare out into the forest and wonder why he didn't meet in person.

Marcus always meets me in person. I've heard tales of him not showing and only leaving notes. Everything is fucked after. Marcus doesn't like to meet with you if he knows you're about to be fucked over.

A chill runs down my spine.

The only guess I have is that it has something to do with Addison. She's the only thing that's changed.

He knows everything. He knows about what happened the night Tyler died. He knows about my obsession. And he knows she's back.

My eyes flicker to the woods, searching him out but coming up with nothing. Every small sound of a branch breaking or the wind rustling the leaves reminds me of that night, the images flashing in front of me.

The night that Tyler died.

I'd just finished a meet with Marcus. It was an easy transaction for a hit we needed. He seems to like those better than being a messenger. He responds faster.

He knows that on my way home, I saw Addison in the diner.

I saw him across the street watching me after I'd sent the message to Tyler. She was in pain and I knew Tyler could take it away.

Marcus followed me as I followed Addison. I couldn't leave her, knowing Marcus saw me watching her. I didn't trust him. So I followed her from place to place. The diner, the bookstore and finally the corner store. And Marcus was there, every step of the way. I told myself it was only to satisfy his sick curiosity.

And worse than anything, Marcus was there; he was the closest when Tyler died right in front of us.

Marcus knows everything and he's not coming to see me in person. That leaves a bad taste in my mouth.

Deep breaths come and go.

This doesn't have anything to do with her. It's about Carter. It has to be about Carter and not about the shit Marcus knows about Addison.

Part of me questions if I should confess to her and tell her the truth before someone else does. She blamed herself for so long and I know she did. But I'm the one who sent Tyler after her.

He knew where she was because of me.

He went to see her because I told him he should.

It's all my fault. It was never hers.

CHAPTER 21

Addison

I T'S BEEN STRANGE.

My fingers hover over the keys and I delete my last words. I don't know how to tell Rae what's going on. I shift on my sofa, feeling uneasy. This whole day has felt different. Daniel hasn't touched me since yesterday morning. And things have been off since he got back from his meeting. It's also when the word "love" was said. Maybe he didn't realize he'd said it until after he left.

I've gotten short kisses, but nothing else. It feels different.

It's a way that makes me feel uneasy.

It's a way that makes me feel like the end is here and I was right all along.

All the flutters stop and the butterflies fall into a deep pit in my stomach.

That's the way he's making me feel.

The hall light flicks on and Daniel's large frame takes up the opening of the narrow passage. He doesn't look at me as he strides to the kitchen, walking right behind the sofa. He's not talking to me, but he doesn't want to leave either.

I can't take this. I prepare myself to type up the email telling Rae what I'd like to say to Daniel. Before I can even type a word I get fed up and slam it shut, turning sideways to face him. All of my frustration and nervous feelings snowball together into nothing but anger.

This time he's looking right at me.

"Something's wrong." That's all I can say and instead of answering me, Daniel reaches for a mug from the cabinet.

"Could you give me something?" I ask him with all this pent-up frustration and shove the laptop onto the coffee table. "You've barely looked at me, spoken to me, or touched me. Something happened or something's wrong, and if it's us I need to know."

Silence. I get silence in return. "If it's just work, you can tell me." My voice cracks and I hate that I'm so emotional while he gives me nothing.

It would be easy for him to simply say it has nothing to do with us. I can accept that. But he doesn't and that's when the sick feeling that's been twisting my gut all day travels to my heart.

I'm already halfway to him, determined to get some answers when he finally says something.

"I have to leave tomorrow night."

My bare feet stop on the cold tile floor in front of him. "That quick?"

"Either then or the next morning at the latest."

I swallow down my heart and breathe out somewhat in relief, but it's short-lived as I cross my arms over my chest. "You have to leave?" I ask him that question because the other one is too scared to leave me.

What happens to us?

He answers the unspoken question. "I want you to come home with me."

"Home?" I say the word with a humorless huff and pull out one of the chairs at the kitchen island. I don't know where home is. Taking a seat, I tell him, "Are you sure they'll even want me there?"

It's hard to swallow when I look at him. I can say goodbye to the idea of college, or at least this college, easily. But facing his brothers? That's something else entirely.

"They'll be happy to see you again." He says the words with compassion, but there's something there, something else that he's holding back.

"When did you find out you need to leave?" I ask, prying for more answers.

"Last night." He clears his throat and adds, "It's not my brothers that I'm worried about. It's you ... deciding to leave me again."

"Stop it," I snap at him and then correct myself. "Why would you even say something like that?"

"I've done some things," he says and then leaves the empty mug on the counter. It's quiet and all I can hear is the sound of my heart beating as he takes a seat on the sofa in the living room. Although I know something bad is coming, I follow him, taking the cue to sit next to him.

"You're scaring me again," I whisper to him with a pleading voice and wait for him to look at me.

With his elbows on his knees, his head is just a smidge lower than mine as he turns to look at me and says, "It's because I'm a bad man. That's what bad men do. They scare people."

"I told you to stop it," I tell him as I reach up to put a hand on his broad shoulders. His shirt is stretched tight, making him seem caged beneath it. "You're a good person inside. I know you are."

"You think I'm good?" he says with an air of disbelief and then he turns to look straight ahead. When he speaks again, it's as if the words aren't directed at me. "I'm sure you think you can see the good in everyone."

"I don't like you talking like this. Seriously. You need to stop." I find myself struggling to speak. "I don't know what's making you say these things, but you have to stop."

"I think I should tell you something." Daniel speaks as he runs his finger around the lip of the coffee table in front of him. He focuses on it as the silence stretches out and I wait.

"Whatever it is, you can tell me." My heart flickers, the light going out for a moment. Maybe from fear, or maybe from knowing it's a lie I've spoken. There are so many things Daniel could say that would destroy me. But he knows that already.

"You're so breakable, Addison."

I huff a laugh, although it's drowned out by relief. "Is that the big news? Because I knew that already."

His dark eyes lift to meet mine and the intensity swirling within is something I haven't felt for a long time.

"No, that's not the news, but it's why I don't want to tell you."

My shoulders rise with a heavy breath. "If you have something to tell me, then I want to hear it."

Daniel relaxes his posture, sitting back and sinking into the cushion of the sofa as he stares at me. His hands are folded in his lap and I can tell he's deciding. Judging. And I allow it.

Because he's right. I am breakable. And the last person I want to break me is him.

He clears his throat, bringing his fist to his mouth and then looks at the decorative pillow that's next to him. I suppose it's just so he doesn't have to look at me. He runs his thumbnail over the fabric of the sofa as he talks, busying his hands. "When Tyler died, you left and didn't say goodbye."

I nod my head and ready myself to answer, leaning forward and even scooting slightly closer. He has to know how ashamed and riddled with guilt I was. I could barely speak to anyone.

I wanted to tell them all goodbye, but I couldn't even look them in the eye.

My words are halted when Daniel continues, not waiting for a response from me at all.

"And when I went to your house," he pauses and licks his lips before moving his gaze to mine. "I could lie to you here, and say you were already gone."

My heart beats hard and my breathing halts from the danger that flashes in his stare.

"But you hadn't left yet and so I watched you pack. I wanted to pack too. I didn't want to stay where Tyler had just walked, just sat. Where I'd just listened to him tell me about that beat-up truck he wanted to fix but never would." Daniel runs his thumb along his lower lip as his eyes gloss over. "I wanted to run like you wanted to, but I didn't think I would be capable until I saw you do it."

"You watched me leave?" I ask him, not knowing where this is going, but fearing what he has to say because of his tone and bearing. Because of how the air thickens and threatens to strangle me. As if even it would rather I be dead than for Daniel to destroy me with the history between us.

"I wish it were as easy as that," he says with a smile that doesn't reach his eyes. "I watched you board the train with that heavy suitcase, and I got on too. I watched you check in to a motel four cities over. And I requested a room next to yours."

Every word he says makes my heart feel tighter.

"I watched you for days before finally breaking myself away from you to call Carter and tell him I wasn't coming back. I'd decided to spend my time doing one thing." The heat in his eyes intensifies at the memory and his gaze feels like fire against my skin. "Watching you."

"You stalked me?" I ask him although the words stumble over each other and barely come out as a croak. I can't deny the fear that begs my body to run, but I'm frozen where I am, waiting for his confession to release me.

"I watched you because I needed to. You blamed yourself and your pain was so raw and genuine. So full of everything that I didn't have. Of course I hated every bit of who I was because Tyler had to die, while God chose to let me live. I wanted to cry and mourn like you did. A very large part of me wanted you to cry harder as you hugged your pillow to your chest in the dark. Some nights you couldn't even stand long enough to make it to the bed."

He cocks his head as he looks me in the eye and asks, "Do you remember how you'd sleep on the floor even when the bed was so close?" His last words come out as a whisper and I can't answer. I can hardly breathe as tears leak from my eyes.

"I thought about picking you up and putting you in the comfort of your sheets-"

"You came in?" I cut him off and suck in a deep breath. "You broke in to my room?"

"Addison, I couldn't be away from you." His admission elicits a very real fear that makes my body tremble as I shy away from him. Scooting farther away on the sofa, but not quite able to run.

"Not until you started getting better," he adds and then stands up. I cling to the cushion, cowering under him and backing away when he tries to touch me.

The tears fall freely as the extent of my fears from so long ago is realized. I swear I heard things. I heard someone walking in my room in the darkness. I swear I felt eyes on me. "I thought it was him," I cry out and cover my burning face. I thought Tyler was with me for so long. And it took me years to think that it wasn't because he wished me harm. I thought he hated me and wanted me to be scared. And then I loathed myself that much more for thinking so poorly of such a good soul.

"I needed to watch you, Addison. I'm sorry."

I stand up quickly, and I'm close to him. So close I nearly smack the top of my head against his chin as I stand. "I need to get away from you," I sputter, crossing my arms over my chest and walking around the sofa although I have no idea how I can even breathe, let alone speak and move.

I can barely see where I'm going, but I know where the door is.

Gripping the handle, I swing it open and face him. My legs are weak and I feel like I'm going to throw up. He made me crazy. It was him all along.

"I never did anything to hurt you, Addison, and I didn't want to." Daniel speaks calmly, the other side of him starting to emerge. The side that's okay with Daniel dropping his defenses. The vulnerable side that wants me to understand and isn't pushing me away. But that's exactly what I need to do right now. I need to shove him far away.

"I want you to leave," I tell him and sniffle, swiping under my eyes aggressively, willing the tears to stop. I'm shaking. Physically shaking.

"You need to go," I tell him because it's the only truth I know. My mind is a chaotic storm and everything I'd been keeping at bay, all the fear and sorrow are screaming at me until I can't hear anything. I can't make out anything. The exception being the man standing right in front of me who's the cause of my pain.

"Who did you think I was, Addison?" he asks me as if this is my fault.

And maybe part of it is.

"You knew I wasn't a good man back then, and you know that now."

"Get out." They're the only words I can say.

"It was years ago."

"I said get out!" I scream at him, but he only gets closer to me until I shove him away. He can't hold me and make this right.

"You stalked me." I can barely get the words out. I'm in disbelief and terrified, although I'm not sure which reaction is winning.

"You had hope," he says back hard as if it justifies everything. "You had happiness.

You had everything I wanted. You were everything I wanted. You can hate me for it, but you can't deny that. It's the truth."

"I want you to leave."

"Please don't make me leave," he tells me as if it's only just now getting through to him. He looks at the open doorway and then back at me. The hall is empty and cold and a draft comes in, making me shudder.

"Get. Out." I can't look at him as he stares at me, waiting for me to say something else.

"Addison-"

"Out!" I yell as loud as I can. So hard my throat screams with pain and my heart hurts. Even over my rushing blood I hear each of his footsteps as he walks away from me.

"You said you wouldn't leave me," Daniel grits between his teeth as he stands on the threshold of my door.

The words leave me as I slam the door shut in his face. "I lied."

CHAPTER 22

Daniel

THE HEAVY PIT IN MY STOMACH IS WHY I DON'T GIVE PEOPLE A DAMN PIECE OF myself. That sick feeling that I swear is never going to go away is why I play it close to the vest.

I thought she was different.

I close my eyes, swallowing although my throat is tight and listening to the busy traffic on Lincoln Street. I'm close to the address Marcus gave me. Close to being done with this town and having no reason to stay.

It's only when the street quiets that I open my eyes and force myself to move forward. Going through with the motions.

She *is* different. She does know better. She knows who and what I am.

She just doesn't want to accept it.

And how can I really blame her? I don't want to accept it either. I didn't even get to tell her all of the truth. I didn't get to take her pain away from thinking she's to blame.

And that makes everything that much harder to swallow.

Passing a corner liquor store, I make sure I track the movements of the few people scattered around me. I keep to myself, heading south down the street. It's late and only the moon and streetlights illuminate the road ahead of me. But dark is good when you don't want to be seen.

I try to focus, but with the quiet of the night, I can't help but to think of Addison. She's always comforted me in the darkness.

I finally had her. Really had her. I felt what I always knew there could be between us. And I let her get away. I lost her by confessing.

Maybe that's why it hurts this fucking bad. She loved who I am, but hates what I've done. And there's no way I can take it back.

She saw the truth of what I was, but I could have sworn she knew it all along.

Maybe I should have just hinted at it. And let her ask if she wanted to know more.

You can't change the past. If anyone knows that fact all too well, it's me.

Give her time. I close my eyes, remembering the advice I gave Tyler once. If only it was that easy.

The chill in the autumn air is just what I need as I steady my pace with my hands in my jacket pockets. The metal of the gun feels cold against my hand as I glance from house number to house number.

55 West Planes. In the mailbox.

That's what Marcus said. Simple instructions. But an easy setup if he's planning one.

They say he's a man with no trace, no past, and nothing to use against him. A ghost. A man who doesn't exist.

He knows everything and only tells you what he wants when he wants to deliver it. But he's a safe in-between for people like us to use. Because if Marcus tells you something, it's because he wants you to know it.

And that's a good thing, unless he wants you dead.

I brush my hair back as I glance from right to left. There's a group of guys on the steps of an old brick house across the street and on its mailbox is 147.

I cross the street after passing them, so I'm on the odd-numbered side. The block before this was numbered in the two hundreds. So one more block.

The adrenaline pumps in my blood and I finger the gun inside my jacket pocket.

I have to will away the thoughts of Addison, no matter how much they cling to me and plague me every waking second.

My father taught us all to pay attention. Distractions are what get you killed.

A huff of a laugh leaves me at the memory of his lesson.

I guess when you don't care if you live or die, the severity of his words don't send pricks down your skin like they did when you were a child.

Tyler wasn't with me that day. I wonder if my father ever bothered to give Tyler that advice. Addison was as big of a distraction to him as she was to me.

With the tragic memories threatening to destroy me, I halt in my tracks, realizing I wasn't even looking at the numbers.

And I happened to stop right at 55. The mailbox is only two steps away.

The cold metal door of the mailbox opens with a creak. The sound travels in the tense air and the inside appears dark and empty. I dare to reach inside and pull out only an unmarked envelope. Nothing else.

My forehead pinches as I consider it. It's thin and looks as if it's not even carrying anything. But it's sealed and this is the right address.

All of this for one little envelope.

Slamming the door to the mailbox shut, I walk a few blocks, gripping the envelope in my hand and looking for a bus stop.

I text my brother even though I don't want to. I don't want him to know it's done. That I have what he's been waiting for. *It's just an envelope.*

It's marked as read almost immediately and he responds just as quickly.

Good. Come back home.

Staring at his text, that pit in my stomach grows. I'm frozen to the cement sidewalk, knowing I have to leave and hating that fact.

I know I need to move and not stay here, lingering when Marcus will be watching. But with the phone staring back at me with no new messages or missed calls, the compulsive habit of calling Addison takes over.

The phone rings and rings and goes to her voicemail.

I haven't stopped trying and I don't intend to.

I stayed as long as I could outside her door. I listened to her cry until she had nothing left. I don't know if I should have tried to talk to her and made her aware that I was still there wanting to comfort her, or if it would have only made her angrier.

A heavy burden weighs on my chest as I slip the envelope into my jacket, careful to fold it down the center and keep moving in the night.

I have no choice but to take this back to Carter. There's no way I can stay.

For the first time in a long time, I feel trapped. Suffocated by what's coming.

I can't leave her again.

I can't watch her walk away, and I can't leave her either.

But it was never my choice.

It's always been hers.

CHAPTER 23

Addison

I can't count the number of times I swore I was haunted. Not the hotels I stayed in or the places I moved. But me. A Romani woman in New Orleans once told me that it's not places, it's people who are haunted.

And since the day Tyler died, I swore up and down that he decided he would haunt me as I ran from place to place, never finding sanctuary.

From the creaks in the floorboards, to small things being misplaced. Every time I tried to find meaning in those moments. Each time I thought it was something Tyler wanted me to know and see.

There were so many nights when I cried out loud, begging him to forgive me. Even when I couldn't forgive myself.

I wonder if Daniel heard my pleas.

My phone pings on the coffee table and out of a need to know what he has to say this time, I reach for it. I haven't answered a single call or message from him. I don't know what to tell him.

It's fucked up. He's fucked up.

He hurt me beyond recognition.

I should tell him how I couldn't move for days on end. But the bastard knows that already.

I truly loved him, but a lie from years ago makes me question everything. He could have helped me heal. He could have shouldered the burden of my pain and I would have done the same for him. But just like when Tyler was alive, he was silent. He gave me nothing.

I'm surprised by the hurt that ripples through me when I see it's Rae and not Daniel.

It's a shocking feeling. And it takes me a moment to realize what I really want. I want him to beg me to forgive him. I want him to know my pain.

I let the idea resonate with me as I ignore Rae and click over to Daniel's texts. Six of them in a row.

I'm sorry.

I was wrong.

I couldn't help myself.

If I wasn't with you and watching you it was too much for me to take.

I wish you would understand.

I would never hurt you. I never will.

I read his texts and the anger boils as I text back. *You'll never know how much it hurt to go through that alone. And you made it worse for me. You sat in silence while I was in pain. How could you ever think I'd forgive you?*

I realize I'm more disturbed that he didn't try to help me than the fact that he stalked me. I guess that's not so different from what he did when I was with Tyler.

I press send without thinking twice. And then I click over to Rae, who wants to know how it's going. *Fucking priceless*, I think bitterly.

I roll my eyes, letting a shudder run through my body and tears roll down my cheeks. Instead of answering her, I move to the kitchen for a bottle of wine.

I still haven't unpacked my wine glasses and I know it's because part of me was already envisioning leaving with Daniel. I knew he wasn't staying long and I'd go anywhere with him. I would have done anything he wanted to be by his side.

My phone pings again as I bend down and grab a bottle of merlot by the neck from the bottom shelf of my wine rack. I pretend I'm going to let the phone sit there, but I'm too eager to see what he has to say. I'm a slave to his response.

He writes back, *Because I was in pain too. And I'm sorry. It wasn't to hurt you. It was only to distract me from the guilt I felt.*

Pain and guilt and agony and death make people do awful things. But it's no excuse.

I write back instantly, *You used me.*

I did.

I hate you for it. I stare at the text message and with the pain in my heart, I already know it's not hate. It just hurts so much that he watched and did nothing.

Can you love me and hate me at the same time?

I'll never forgive you.

He types some and then the bubbles that indicate he's writing stop. And then they continue, but suddenly stop again. All the while I grip my phone tightly.

Instead of waiting, I write more. My hands shake and the anger in me confuses itself for sorrow.

I needed someone and I had no one. I wanted you, you had to know. I blamed myself for everything when there was no reason to think otherwise. You could have helped me, but you only watched. You made my pain so much worse than it needed to be.

I send it to him and although it's marked as read, nothing comes. Minutes pass and the ticking of the clock serves as a constant reminder of every second going by with nothing to fill the gaping hole in my heart.

The moment I set the phone down on the counter and reach for the corkscrew, the phone beeps. I have to read it twice and then reread the message I'd sent him before the sob escapes me.

That's the way I felt every time you kissed him.

My shoulders shake so hard that I fall to the ground, my phone falling as well, although the screen doesn't shatter. I cover my face as I cry, hating myself even more and not knowing how to make anything better.

My phone pings again, but I can't answer it for the longest time. Even though it feels pathetic, I cry so hard it hurts every piece of my heart. The piece I gave Tyler when I gave myself to him. The piece I thought I'd left behind when I walked away from him. The piece that left me when he was laid to rest, and the piece I gave Daniel. There are many pieces. Pieces from years ago, from only days ago and the very big piece he just took.

I want him back instantly. I want him to hold me. There's a part of me that knows it's weak and pathetic to feel this desperate need for someone else. But deep inside I know I'd live my life happily being weak and pathetic for him. Isn't he weak for me just the same?

Sniffling and wiping at my face, I somehow get up, bracing myself against the counter and reaching for the faucet. My face is hot and I can still hardly breathe.

I don't think you ever get over the death of someone who's taken up space in your soul. It isn't possible. There are only moments when you remember that you're a pale imitation of what you could be if they were still with you. And those moments hurt more than anything else in this world.

As I turn off the faucet, I swear I hear something behind me and I whip around, a chill flowing over my skin and leaving goosebumps in its wake.

It takes every ounce of strength in me to lower myself to the ground, although my eyes stay on the skinny hallway where the noise came from.

It's silent as I pick up the phone, barely breathing, and quickly message Daniel. *Are you here now?*

It was a long time ago. I promise you. I wasn't well. I'm sorry.

I stare at his answer, feeling a chill flow over my skin and the hairs on the back of my neck raise.

So it's not you? I will myself to keep my eyes on the hallway, my back to the counter as I type. I can barely breathe.

Someone there?

I don't answer him and a series of texts come through. Ping. Ping. Ping. Each another sound that echoes down the hall.

Without looking at the messages I text, *I'm fine.*

His answer comes through before I look back to the hall. *I'm coming over.*

At his response I push forward, forcing myself to walk down the hall and to the loft bedroom. There's only one door and I push it open, telling myself it's nothing as the phone pings in my hand again.

It pings again as I take in the bedroom, cautiously stepping forward until I see a picture has fallen from the collage on the far side of the room.

My phone pings a third time and I can finally breathe. It's only a photo that's fallen.

I read his latest text and roll my eyes. *Answer me.*

My heart nearly jumps out of my chest as the phone rings and I drop it on the floor. It takes the entire time it's ringing for me to catch my breath and when I do I pick up the phone to text him. *It was only a picture falling.*

I'm on my way.

Don't come here, I text back while I'm still on the floor and I hope he can feel the anger that's still there. I add, *I don't want you here.*

It hurts me to tell him that. Partly because it's a lie. It hasn't even been twenty-four hours and I can already see myself forgiving him.

Addison please. Don't shut me out.

It took us long enough to admit what we needed.

I miss you. I need you.

If you're scared I need to be there.

With the fear and regret and everything else that's tortured me today, I just want to give in to him after reading his rapid-fire texts. But I won't.

I just need sleep, I reply and then add, *Don't come.*

Please forgive me, he finally texts and I can't respond right now, so I shut the phone off and fall onto the bed. I don't know how long I stare at the wall or at what point I decide I have enough energy to clean up the fallen picture, but I know it's longer than I'd like.

The command tape is stuck to the wall this time. I swear I'll never use it again.

Just like I'll never let myself give in to Daniel again.

Some people you're meant to miss.

They're just no good for you.

I think the words, but I don't know if I really feel them.

With that thought in mind I move to where the picture frame lays facedown on the ground and lift it carefully. Luckily there's no broken glass.

I almost feel okay as I turn it over to inspect the frame.

But then I see the picture that fell. One I took myself, five years ago.

A still life of Tyler's rusty old truck.

And that's when I lose it all over again. I'm forced to come to terms with the fact that some wounds never heal. And they aren't meant to be forgotten.

CHAPTER 24

Daniel

THE PHONE RINGS AND RINGS AS I THROW A ZIPPED UP BAG INTO THE CORNER with the rest of the luggage. I've packed light for years, but it's never bothered me before.

Looking at the small pile that comprises everything I own, I've never felt so worthless. Or so tired. I didn't sleep at all.

The phone goes silent and instead of calling Addison again, I scroll to Carter's number and call him. I could easily text him to let him know I'm on my way, but I don't want to. I want him to hear the defeat in my voice. And I need to talk to someone. Someone real. I'm losing everything, slowly feeling it drain from me.

I need someone. Desperately. I stayed awake outside Addison's apartment all night. I had to make sure she was okay. But time doesn't wait, and I had to pack … and now I have to leave.

It only rings twice before he picks up, greeting me with my name although it comes out as a question. And I know why he'd be confused to see I'm calling him.

I don't call anyone ever. I don't care to talk to him or any of my brothers, and they're the only ones alive I love. *My brothers and Addison.*

"Do you miss him?" I ask Carter without prefacing my question. "Not like Mom and Dad, where we knew it was coming and it made sense." Carter tries to talk on the other end of the line, but I keep going, pinching the bridge of my nose and sitting on the end of the bed. It protests with my weight. "The kind of missing someone where it feels better to pretend they're coming back? The kind of missing where you talk to them like they can hear you and it makes you feel better?" I know why I don't go home. It's because he's there in my head. I know what home is, and he's there. I refuse to accept otherwise. I can't.

I tell him I'm sorry every time I'm reminded of him. I hate going south, too many old trucks. I could never tell the difference, but they were Tyler's thing. He was an old soul like that.

"Every day," Carter says as I sit there quietly.

"I did something," I start to confess to Carter but stop myself. I'm too ashamed, so I settle on something else. "I ran into Addison." Her name leaves me in a rush, taking all the air in my lungs with it.

"Tyler's Addison? That's what brought this up?" he questions me and I nod my head like an ass, as if he can see.

"Yeah," I almost repeat, *Tyler's Addison*. But she never belonged to him. As much as I love him, she was always mine. Maybe he was meant to be her first, but I'll be her last. My throat tightens and my heart hammers in my chest. She's not his anymore. She's mine. And telling Carter feels like a betrayal of the worst kind. It feels like I'm telling Tyler. And as much as I thought it would be easy to admit it, I don't want them to hate me. They have to understand.

"And?" Carter presses and I'm not sure where to begin.

"When I left … after Tyler died five years ago … when I left you and the family, I followed her." The words spill from me. "Watching her cry made me feel normal. She gave me hope that I wasn't broken, because she felt the same way. But she stopped crying, Carter. She moved on without me."

"Daniel," Carter warns and I hate him for it.

"You'll listen to me," I seethe with barely concealed anger. He will listen and accept it. There are no other options. I can't have it end any other way. "I have no one."

"You chose no one. You left us."

"You know why." They gave Tyler's phone to Carter after the dust settled. Carter saw. He never spoke it out loud. But I was there and I know he saw that I was the one texting him.

I'm the one who led Tyler to his death.

"You didn't have to go." His voice is sincere, but soft and full of sympathy.

"Well I'm coming back now," I tell him.

"Does she know?" he asks me and I answer him with, "I shouldn't have told her."

"She knows you followed her? Is she going to press charges?" he asks and I huff a humorless laugh and then stare at the ceiling fan that's perfectly still.

"I don't think so," I say and it's only then that question becomes a possibility. I've only been thinking about what I can do to make her forgive me.

"She has to forgive me," I tell him with words stronger than I feel.

"She doesn't have to do anything," Carter answers me and the silence stretches as my disdain for him grows.

"What did she say?" he asks me just as I'm ready to hang up.

"That she hates me." It doesn't hurt me to say the words today like they hurt me yesterday. There's hope, only a small piece, but it's there. "She didn't mean it," I tell him.

"Did you do anything else?" Carter asks me with a tone that's cautious, like he already knows.

"I've done lots of things, brother."

"With her. With Addison." My gaze wanders to my shoes by the bed and I bend down to put them on and lace them while I tell him, "I tried to stay away from her, but she sought me out … before she knew."

"Did she fuck you?" he asks me and it strikes me as if he's said it backward.

"I fucked her, yes." The irritation gives me strength and I stare at the pile of shit next to the door that I'll take with me back home and nearly leave it behind. It's all meaningless.

"Is she …" Carter hesitates to ask.

"She's mine." The words leave me quickly, whipping out as if they're meant to lash him, hating how he questions it. *She's always been mine.*

I almost tell him that she'll forgive me, but the doubt in me stops the words on the tip of my tongue.

"I'm coming home. I've been running away for a long time."

"If you bring her, tell me so I can tell the others."

"Why tell them?" Although I don't give a shit what they think, I know Addison will.

"She was like a sister to us, Daniel. She didn't just leave Tyler, she left all of us."

She didn't just leave us once. She left us twice.

When I heard her break up with Tyler in the kitchen, I could hear every word. I stood by the window, watching her leave.

I can't let her leave a third time. I can't let her go.

Before I can stop myself, I speak into the phone, "I'll let you know."

Staring at the closed door to this rented house, I can see Addison so clearly all those years ago. Driving away and I never bothered to stop her or tell her how she wasn't allowed to leave.

She could never leave.

She was meant to be there.

Not with Tyler, but with me.

Maybe if I had bothered to tell either of them that, Tyler would still be here and none of this would have happened.

CHAPTER 25

Addison

THIS COLDNESS WON'T GO AWAY.

It follows me everywhere. Even burying myself under the blankets doesn't take the chill away.

I can't sleep. I can only wait for updates from Daniel. He texted me all night. He's really leaving.

It all feels so final and I have no time to process anything. There's a heaviness in my chest and a soreness in my lungs that I'm so painfully aware of. They won't leave me alone.

Another message, another plea from him.

Please meet me, he begs. *I can't lose you again.*

Looking at his message stirs up so much emotion. I don't want to lose him. That's the worst part of all of this. It's the fact that I don't want to be alone and without him again.

But how can you forgive someone for watching you suffer when they knew they could save you?

I'll wait outside. I'm on my way and I'll wait for you, but I can't wait long. Please Addison.

The seconds tick by as I stare at his message.

Tick-tock. Tick-tock.

It's early in the morning; the sun is still rising. A new day.

I can tell him goodbye. Just one last kiss. A kiss for the love we had. The love we shared for another too. A final goodbye that I should have had years ago.

I can pretend that's what this will be, but I already feel myself clinging to him.

Some people you're meant to say goodbye to, and others you aren't.

I don't text him back. Instead I head to the bathroom. I look exactly how I feel, which is fucking awful. I half question getting myself somewhat put together to see him.

But I don't want him to remember me like this if it really is the last time I'll see him.

I take a few minutes, each one seeming longer and longer even though hardly any time has passed. And when I look up, I see a pretty version of me, with mascara and concealer to hide the exhaustion. I can't hide the pain though.

I'll try to let him go and move on.

Because that's what I'm supposed to do. Isn't it? It's what a sane, strong woman would do.

The zipper seems so loud as I close the makeup bag, as does the click of the light switch. There's hardly any light from the early morning sunrise as I make my way out and down the stairs to the side entrance of the apartment.

Each step feels heavier than the last and my heart won't stop breaking.

It's a slow break, straight down the center. My heart hates me, but yet again, it's something that seems so fitting.

There's a large window on the side entrance door and I'm staring out of it, looking for Daniel's car when I push it open. He isn't here yet. Not that I can see.

I want more time before I have to say goodbye and it makes it painfully obvious that I don't want to speak the words. But I can't be weak and I don't know that I can forgive him.

The cool air hits my face as the wind whips by and I walk slowly down the stairs. I take my time, not wanting this to end but knowing it's so close and there's nothing I can do to stop it.

The second I hit the bottom step and see Daniel's car pull up to the curb, a large hand covers my face at the same time that I'm pulled back into a heavy wall—no, a man's chest.

A man. Someone's grabbed me. The realization hits me in a wave. I didn't see him coming. I still can't see him.

A scream rips up my throat as I try to swing back and hit him. Daniel! I try to scream, but I can't. The man whirls around and my vision is blurred as I hit a brick wall, my arm scraping against it.

I don't stop screaming; I don't stop fighting with everything I have. My knee thumps against the brick wall as the man sneers at me to be quiet, the black leather glove on his hand making my face feel hot. I kick off the wall with the fear, the anger, and the knowledge that if I don't scream for Daniel, he won't know. He won't be able to save me.

My knee burns with pain as I shove my weight into the man and push at the same time, falling to the asphalt and breaking free for only a split second.

I scream out for Daniel, although I don't know if he heard me. I can't breathe as a man in a black hoodie with bloodshot eyes shoves his hand down on my face so hard that I think he broke my nose for a moment. The pain radiates and tears stream from my eyes.

I always thought the worst thing you could see when you die was the face of someone who loved you, but couldn't help you.

Staring into the black eyes of this man, I question that.

But relief comes quickly.

Through my blurred vision, I see a boot slam into his head, knocking him off of me although I struggle to get myself free and scramble away.

Bang! Bang!

I hear gunshots and I scream out again out of instinct, falling onto my side and huddling into a ball. *Bang!*

One last shot.

One heartbeat.

Another.

Silence.

And then I look up to see the man lying still, but Daniel clutching at his chest. He breathes heavily and then stumbles.

"No!" I cry out as blood soaks through his white cotton t-shirt and into the open button-up layered over it.

"Daniel," I cry out with fear gripping my heart.

He screams at me, even though the strength is gone. "Get inside!"

My body refuses to obey as he pulls his hand away from his chest. There's blood. So much blood.

Daniel's expression only changes from worried for me to angered as he stares at his hand. His focus moves to the man lying motionless on the asphalt and he points the gun at his head, firing.

Bang! Bang! Bang! Each shot makes my body tremble. The man's body doesn't react. His face is one I don't recognize as he stares lifelessly at nothing.

My gaze shifts from his dead eyes back to Daniel as he hunches over and grips his chest, falling to his knees on the ground.

That's the moment I can finally move again. And I run to him as fast as I can with one thought running through my mind.

Everyone I love dies.

Every.

Single.

One.

CHAPTER 26

Daniel

FUCK. Hot blood pours from my wound and soaks into my shirt as I lean against the brick wall, feeling sharp, shooting pains run up and down my spine. I apply pressure to the gunshot to try to stop the flow.

I can barely breathe through my clenched teeth at the pain.

"Go inside," I try to yell at Addison as she hovers over me. "Now," I grit out and my words come out weak.

"Daniel, get up. Get up!" she yells at me. And it actually makes me smile.

As I try to stand, with her pulling on me and attempting to aid me, I look back down at my hand. It's bright red, not black. That's the first good sign. But when I look down to my chest and see how much it's still bleeding, the lightheadedness nearly makes me collapse.

"Come with me," she begs. "We have to go to the hospital."

"No, no hospital. No cops." I'm still okay enough to know better than that. "You can't stay here; the cops will be coming. You have to go."

"I'm not leaving you," she yells at me with disbelief. "Just stay with me. Hide in my apartment. Let me help you, please," she begs me and that's the only reason I let her wrap an arm around me and guide me back to her apartment.

Thank fuck it's so early in the morning and everything went down in the back alley.

Dark alley.

A man who knew where to be and when.

Someone with information.

Not Marcus … but it's someone who must know Marcus. My gaze moves to Addison's pale face as she opens the door to her apartment. Someone who wanted her. Someone who wanted to hurt me. And Marcus had to have told them. He's the only one who knew I was with her and what she meant to me.

"Come on." She tries to push me into her apartment and for a moment I hesitate, but if Marcus or someone else is after Addison, I have to be beside her.

It's too late for me to say goodbye.

I feel breathless as my gaze darts from the door behind us to the counter, then to the window. I have to tell Carter. At the thought a pain shoots up my back and down my shoulder, making me grit my teeth.

Fuck! Holding my breath, I put more pressure on the wound.

My steps are wide as I walk in and head for the kitchen. To the tile floor where it will be easy to clean up.

"Was there blood in the alley?" I ask Addison in a pained voice that I can't control and look behind me as I walk. Nothing's spilling onto the floor. Not a drop. My shirt is soaked with blood, but hopefully there's nothing that will lead the cops up to Addison.

"A lot of it," she answers me as she rips open the cabinet door and pulls out a roll of paper towels.

"Did it lead up the stairs?" I ask her breathlessly and then wince from the pain. *Fuck! Make it stop. Please.*

She looks at me wide-eyed before realizing I was talking about my blood. Not the asshole who dared to put his hands on her. She visibly swallows while shaking her head frantically. "No, nothing." She winds the paper towels around her hand before giving me the bundle of them. Her hands are still trembling. My poor Addison.

I take a quick look, as quickly as I can. Looks like the bullet exited cleanly. The wound isn't the problem. It'll bleed, but it'll heal. It's the infection that'll kill me if I don't have one of the guys take a look at it.

"Come sit," she tells me while also reaching for my shirt. "Sit down," she commands again. Her hands are shaking and her voice trembles, but she's trying to be strong.

I reach out and grab her hand to stop her. My blood smears on her soft skin. "I'm fine," I say to try to comfort her.

Addison shakes her head with tears in her eyes. "Sit down and let me take care of you." She swallows her tears back and adds, "If you won't go to the hospital, it's the least you can do."

A breath leaves me and makes me feel weak.

Another and my hand releases hers, but she doesn't look at it. She doesn't even wipe the blood away; she's still searching my eyes for approval.

Nodding, I take a step back and push the chair at the kitchen island far back enough to sit.

I watch her face the entire time she helps me pull my shirt off. She cares about me still. I know she does. *She'll forgive me.*

"Didn't you say you'd hate me forever?" I ask her. Maybe I'm delirious. I don't know why I push her.

"I said I'd never forgive you," she tells me flatly and doesn't look me in the eyes. Instead she pulls the wad of paper towels away, which are mostly soaked with blood and she quickly balls up more and presses against the wound.

"But you came down to see me," I say without thinking. "It had to mean something." The hope in my chest falters with her silence.

And when she does speak, its light dims.

"It means I was ready to say goodbye."

"I don't believe you," I tell her without hesitation and she looks up at me teary eyed.

"Don't cry," I command weakly. "I didn't want to upset you."

She sucks in a breath and blinks the tears away, but pain is clearly written on her face.

"I'm sorry," I whisper as she wipes the tears from her eyes. "I didn't mean for this-"

"Oh, shut up. You couldn't have known that this ..." her voice breaks before she can finish and she closes her eyes and struggles to calm her breathing.

"It's fine, Addison," I try to reassure her, reaching out even though it sends a lance of pain through my chest. I run my hand down her arm and then pull her in closer, positioning her between my legs.

"It's okay," I whisper into her hair and then plant a small kiss on her temple as I hear sirens outside. She opens her eyes and looks to the far side of her living room, where the alley is just below.

"They may knock, but you don't have to answer," I tell her softly, and she only nods once, her eyes never moving.

"I'm sorry. I can't say goodbye to you," I tell her as I wish I hadn't ever come back to the bar. I wish I hadn't brought this on her. She doesn't know. I'm sure she thinks it was a random mugging or attempted rape. She has no idea. But I know there's no way it's a coincidence.

"I wish I could say goodbye to you again. I wish I could tell you I'll let you go, because it really is what a good man would do."

"Here you go with words about good and bad men when you don't even know the difference." Addison's tone is flat but there's the hint of a smile waiting for me. I can feel it.

"Thank you for taking care of me," I speak as she pulls the wad of paper towels away and there's less blood. I try to take a deep breath, but it hurts and I wince.

"Let me clean and bandage you," she says although I'm not sure she really wants a response. I swallow thickly and let her work. She can do whatever she wants to me, since I'm just grateful that she's here for me.

I don't deserve her. I know I don't. And that's all I can think about as she tapes the sterile gauze in place. Even as she poured rubbing alcohol over my wound I barely felt a thing.

"I need you to go lie down." Addison speaks with authority although she looks like a beautiful mess herself.

The desperate need for sleep begs me to listen to her, although Carter is expecting me. He knows I'm coming.

As if reading my mind Addison says, "It can wait. You can't drive right now anyway."

"Will you lie down with me?" I would give anything to feel her soft body next to mine and hold her right now. The thought sends a warmth through me, but it vanishes when I look up.

Her sad eyes meet mine with something they haven't before. Regret, maybe? Or denial? I'm not sure, but I'm certain she's going to tell me no.

"Please," I add and my voice trembles. "Even if it's only a little while?"

She's reluctant to nod, but she does and my throat closes with a pain that's sure to haunt me forever.

At least I have one more night. But I know in my heart, it's only one more night.

CHAPTER 27

Addison

I DON'T WANT TO WAKE UP. I DON'T WANT TO MOVE.

Because right now I have a man I desperately want, and it doesn't make me weak to be with him. But when this moment is over, that's what I'll be. It's not about forgiving him anymore; it's accepting who I am if I'm with him.

I'm not sure how long we've been in bed, but the knocks at the door from the cops came and went. And at least hours have passed, because my eyes don't feel so heavy, only sore.

"You're awake." Daniel's deep rumble makes his chest vibrate. And it's only then that I realize how close to him I am, how I'm curled around him and his arm is behind my back, holding me to him.

I roll over slightly, only enough so my head is on the pillow and not his chest. There are so many things to say. And so little time.

You can want a person but know they're bad for you. That's the person Daniel's been for me since I've met him. And it's not going to change.

Daniel lifts the sheet and checks his gunshot wound. I can only see a faint circle of blood and I try to gauge his reaction, but he doesn't say anything.

"Are you going to be okay?" I ask him and try to swallow down my worry.

"Are you going to leave me if I say I'll be fine?" he asks, turning his face toward me and his lips are only inches from mine.

I huff a small laugh and a trace of a smile is there for a moment, but the pain of the unknown is quick to take it away. The smile on my lips quivers and I have to take in a deep breath.

"I don't know where we go from here." It's hard to tell him the truth.

I hear him swallow and then he looks up at the ceiling, rather than at me.

"I still want you," he says in a whisper although I'm not sure he meant for it to come out that way. "I can't let go of you," he says and puts his gaze back on me, assessing my reaction.

I can't explain how it feels to hear him say the only words I want to hear. I want to beg him not to let go of me because I'm so afraid to lose myself with him, but I don't ever want to be apart.

A second passes, and then another. And I don't know what to do or think or say. I only know time is running out.

"I'll never stop watching you, Addison. My heart thinks you belong to me and it always has. Whether I want it, whether you want it. It doesn't matter—I'll always feel this need to watch over you."

"It's not the watching part," I try to tell him and then shake my head. My hair slides against the pillow and I struggle to speak, but somehow I do. "It just hurts."

"I'm sorry." He says the same words as before, but the pain is so much more real now as he turns over slightly and puts his hand on mine.

"Do you want me?" he asks me and then adds, "Do you want to come home with me? I'll make it better. I swear I will."

He squeezes my hand and I don't know what to say. I just want everything to feel better and to not hate myself for running back to him.

"I don't want you to come with me because you're lost or lonely or scared. If you want me, I want you. I can't help it and I can't stop it. I tried and when I finally let go of you, there was nothing left of me."

My heart aches for him and for me. I know exactly how he feels. Tears prick my eyes and I can hardly breathe.

I can't answer him, so instead I tell him what I'd planned on saying when I was ready to say goodbye.

My words come out in shuddered breaths. "If you'd come to me back then, I would have let you in. Instead of watching me in pain, I would have loved you for being there for me and I would have been there for you too."

"You're blind to how you were back then. You may have had feelings for me. But you loved him."

"I loved you too though." My voice cracks as I protest and I heave in a breath.

"You wouldn't if you knew the truth. It was my fault-"

I cut him off, pressing my finger to his lips to silence him. "I'm done with the past, Daniel. I don't need to know every horrible thing you once did. I only wanted you to know that I would have let you in." I almost add, *just like I am now.* I can feel myself falling back to him after nearly losing him. After almost seeing him die. There's no way I can let him go again.

Something lifts in my chest. A lightness that gives me more room to breathe. It's the truth, and knowing that makes me feel anything but weak.

He pauses, considering what I've said and looks past me at the window to the bedroom before speaking again. "You think you would have, but I couldn't take the chance that you'd turn me away. I never had a chance, Addison. Even after he was gone you still loved him, and I hated myself for even thinking about taking his place in your heart. I don't care anymore. I already hate myself, but at least I can have you. I can love you better than anyone else."

He swallows thickly and adds, "I can promise you that."

"Love is a strong word." I'm still afraid to tell him I love him. I don't want him to die. More than anything else, I can't lose him. I know deep down inside, I love Daniel Cross and always have.

"It's the right word for what we have, but we can pretend to go slow?" he questions as if I've already forgiven him. As if I've agreed to go back home with him.

"So you think I'm yours again?" I ask him as I wipe under my eyes and sniffle. "Just like that?"

He holds my gaze as he tells me, "You've always been mine."

And I don't have any words for him in return.

It's true.

Daniel says that he's the one who never had a chance back then.

But the truth is Tyler never did.

I was always Daniel's and I don't think I had it in me to say that out loud. Because I don't know if Tyler could have ever forgiven me if he knew.

Daniel leans closer to me with the intent to kiss me. But just before he can cup the back of my head, he winces in pain.

"Shit," the word leaves my lips quickly and I hover over him. "For the love of God, lie down and rest." I pull up the sheets to check on the wound, but it looks the same.

"No, I need to kiss you," he says softly and when my eyes meet his, he smiles weakly and pleadingly.

"I need to kiss you too," I whisper and tears prick my eyes.

I lean down to press my lips to his. I mean it to be soft and sweet, but it deepens instantly and naturally. One of his hands cradles the back of my head, his fingers spearing through my hair. The other grips onto my hip, holding me there as his tongue sweeps over mine and his hot breath mingles with mine.

My body heats, feeling completely at home in his embrace.

"I need you," he whispers against my lips with his eyes closed. My pussy clenches at his words and it's then that I feel his erection against my thigh. The agony breaks and I wipe under my eyes.

"You're hurt," I tell him as I weakly shake my head and cup his strong jaw in my hand.

"Doesn't matter, I'll always need you. Always want you."

My heart pounds and pounds again. Recognizing how true it is, because it's the same for me.

"I love you," I say the words in a whisper even though they frighten me. "I can't lose you."

"I love you more," he tells me and I lean down to kiss him again and shut him up before he makes that pain in my heart grow even more.

CHAPTER 28

Tyler

Five years ago

I FEEL SO FUCKING STUPID.

I don't know how I didn't see it before.

It took him texting me where she is for me to realize it.

Daniel's in love with Addison.

And she's in love with him.

It all makes sense now.

I check the map on my phone to make sure I'm going the right way, although every step makes my heart hurt more.

He doesn't know that I know. Neither does she, but I can do them both a favor and tell them.

I want to kiss her one last time though.

I know it's wrong. But it's just a goodbye kiss. Something to remember her by. Something to let her know that it's okay. That I'm okay with her loving him. I just want her to be happy. She needs it more than anyone. I can see it in her eyes.

My throat feels tight as I walk past Fourth Street. The rain starts coming down harder and it feels fitting.

I pull up my hoodie around my head and listen to my sneakers squeak on the sidewalk as I make my way closer to heartbreak.

I thought her telling me that she couldn't be with me anymore was the worst thing I'd ever feel.

But knowing she loves my brother and wants him more than she wants me? Fuck, it hurts. It hurts so fucking much.

My phone vibrates and I look down to see a text from Daniel. She's gone into the corner store now and Daniel said it looks like she's been crying. She's been doing it at school too. But she won't let me near her this time. She won't let me comfort her when she needs it so badly.

This isn't the first time she's dumped me. My brothers don't know because I'm too ashamed to tell them.

But each time she did, I'd find her crying somewhere and she'd let me hold her to make it feel better.

I just loved her, hoping she loved me back. And I know some part of her does. But I never thought she didn't love me fully because there was someone else.

I thought it was just the way she is. That she just pushes people away and that I would have to handle her more gently. I should have known by the way she avoided Daniel and the way he asked about her.

How was I so fucking stupid?

Do you want me to go to her? Daniel texts me and I stop one block over from where she is. Where both of them are. So close, I can see the window of the store. The light is dim in the sheets of rain. So close, but so far away.

I should tell him yes. I should let him go to her. I bet she'd let him comfort her.

But I just want one last kiss. Just one more time before I let her go.

It's all I want. Just one last kiss before I let her go.

CHAPTER 29

Addison

"I DON'T THINK I CAN BREATHE."

"I'm not inside you right now, so you should be fine," Daniel quips as the car door shuts behind us. He leaves his black Mercedes in the paved horseshoe driveway as we step up to the Cross estate. The stubborn asshole wouldn't let me drive. The painkillers definitely helped him. But I'm looking forward to someone taking a look at him. Someone who knows what they're doing.

"It's different from the other house," I state, ignoring Daniel's joke and how easy this is for him. It's not just different. It's massive. They used to live in a small house off the back-roads. This is … something else.

"Home looks different when you're different," he tells me and walks forward, leaving me standing in the shadow of the large white stone house. Is it even a house? It looks like a mansion.

"Who lives here?" I ask Daniel and he wraps his arm around my waist. "It's for all of us."

I haven't seen any of his brother's since the funeral and on that day, I couldn't look any of them in the eye. I could barely speak to them. I could barely do anything because the guilt was so strong. My pulse quickens as he pushes me forward.

"I don't know …"

"I know you can. And you'll feel better when you do. Both of us will feel better when we go in there." His eyes plead with me—not just to go in for him, but to be *with* him.

He holds out his hand for me, leaving it in the air until I finally grip on to him.

"Don't leave me," I whisper and stare into his eyes.

A tight smile is the response I get, followed by him leaning down to kiss me once on the lips.

His hot breath tickles my skin in the crisp fall air as he lowers his mouth to the shell of my ear. "I know this isn't …" He trails off and I can hear him lick his lips. "This isn't a fairytale. But there's nothing for me in there if it isn't also for you," he finally says and then pulls back.

My heart clenches with a pain that I think I love. A pain of a shared past, but of knowing we can have a future together.

Standing in front of the estate, with his thin black cotton shirt stretched tight across his shoulders, a shade of black that almost matches the darkness in his eyes, how could I deny him?

"They know you're coming. They know you're mine." He speaks with a conviction I feel in my soul.

It's not the first part of what he said that comforts me. It's everything in the second part.

I want to be his, and they know that I am.

I swallow thickly and ignore the churning in the pit of my stomach as we walk up the stairs to the entryway.

It's safe. Everything is alright. I'm with Daniel.

The thoughts are comforting enough to give me the strength to breathe as he opens the large front door and leads me inside.

Each step is harder to take and I feel myself pulling away from him. I don't want to face his brothers. I'm too afraid of what they'll think. I'm afraid of their judgment and hate. Because I've only ever had love for them. Not the kind of love I had for Tyler, and not what I have for Daniel. But love nonetheless. They gave me a home when I had none. They were my family.

And right now … I can't bear for them to send me away.

"It's okay," Daniel says and holds me in the quiet foyer. "It's going to be hard at first. The memories are the hardest part, I think, and there are a lot between us all."

"I don't know if I can do this," I admit to him, wiping under my eyes to see a blurry vision of mascara smeared on my fingertips. I sniffle and then wish I hadn't come.

"We'll have good days and bad days, like everything else. And if it gets to be too much, we'll leave for a while, however long we need. We can go wherever you want to go. We don't have to stay here. I'm fine as long as we stay together. All that matters is that you stay with me." His eyes search mine as we hold each other.

I'll stay with him. Daniel is where my home is. "I'm not going anywhere."

"I've wanted you for far too long to not have you forever now."

"I'm yours," I promise him.

"You've always been mine."

The sound of footsteps is drowned out by a voice that echoes down into the open space. It's grand to say the least, but I can't take it in. I can only watch two men walk into the foyer.

"Addison," one of them says, catching me by surprise. It takes me a long time to realize it's Jase. I almost cry when I do. He looks so much more like Tyler than Daniel does. They always looked alike. Daniel tightens his grip on me as my voice cracks. "Jase."

I clear my throat as Jase stands tall in front of me.

"You look so different," Jase tells me.

"You don't," I say quickly but then take it back. "I mean you do, but you don't."

He smirks down at me and runs his forefinger and thumb over his chin. "Funny, I don't remember you being this shy."

I can only shrug; I don't trust myself to speak and I can hardly keep eye contact as I remember all the memories together. Jase and Tyler were close. The closest. And unless Tyler wanted privacy, Jase was there. Like an annoying brother.

Part of me is still aware that I'm holding on to Daniel with a white-knuckled grip. And that part of me wants to let go, so I can hug Jase.

"It's good to have you home. Everyone else thinks so too, trust me."

"Do you-" I falter and pick worriedly at the pocket of my jeans with the hand not being held firmly by Daniel. The questions I have are all begging to come out at once.

Do you hate me for leaving him?

Do you blame me for what happened?

Do you forgive me? That's the one that lingers. That's the only one that matters. "I'm sorry-" I start to say, but the words are tainted with a small cry.

"Addison." A voice to my right startles me before I can gather the strength to chance the apology. "So how'd you get him back here?" a deep voice asks me and I know immediately it's Declan.

Daniel pulls me in closer, planting a small kiss on my temple in front of both of them as we stand in the foyer. It's all too much, but none of them seem taken aback. Neither of the brothers is looking at me as if anything is off.

As if I'm not a reminder of what they've lost. Not an outsider. Not an enemy.

My lips part and I'm not sure what to say, but I'm grateful. I'm so grateful that I'm welcome. And that I get to see them again.

I never thought I would.

"Where's Carter?" Daniel asks Declan, wrapping his arm around my waist and pulling me in more just slightly, but still easy and casually. His thumb hooks into my jeans and gently caresses my hip as he talks to both brothers.

I try not to make it awkward.

It takes everything in me not to cry upon seeing both of them.

I'm surprised when Daniel loosens his grip on me and whatever they were talking about comes to a halt.

I'm even more surprised when Jase leans in close.

"It's good to see you, Addie," Jase says and hugs me hard, so hard that Daniel has to take a step back. Finally letting my hand go as Jase pulls me to him. It's been a long time since someone's called me Addie. They all did back then. All of them but Daniel. I was always Addison to him.

The hug is short-lived and I'm still numb from it along with the shock of everything when Daniel asks for a minute. As soon as his brothers turn away, I press my palms to my eyes and try to calm myself down. It's emotionally taxing to see those you've mourned because you thought you'd lost them forever.

"I'm okay," I tell Daniel weakly as he rubs my back.

"I promise I'll love you forever." Daniel whispers words that frighten me. Words that threaten to take him from me one day. I hesitate to say it back and he adds, "Just stay with me."

It's a plea from the lips of a man who could destroy me.

Sometimes when you walk into a darkness, a place filled with both what terrifies you from the past and what will forever haunt you in the future, you get a sick feeling that washes over you.

Like you know bad things are coming.

"I love you too," I whisper to Daniel and let him take my hand.

He squeezes lightly as I step further into the Cross estate.

It's brightly lit, but it doesn't fool me. The darkness is here.

There's a certain feeling in the pit of your stomach. I felt it when Tyler brought me to his home all those years ago.

It's a feeling that tells you you're doing something wrong. Something you know you shouldn't, but it tempts you and whispers all the right things; it promises you that you're meant to be here.

Not unlike what I've felt since the moment I met Daniel. This force of needing to be with him. Of knowing I was supposed to be his all along.

Even if the very thought of being his was enough to send a chill over me each time he dared to breathe near me.

That feeling is supposed to warn you, to keep you safe.

Daniel kisses the underside of my wrist as I let the feeling settle through me.

Sometimes that feeling is terrifying.

Sometimes that feeling is home.

CHAPTER 30

Carter

I'M NOT USED TO THE ANXIOUSNESS RINGING IN MY BLOOD.

But times have changed and until this shit is settled, I'm going to be on edge.

I need all the help I can get.

And judging by the way Daniel can't take his eyes off of Addison, he's not in the right mindset.

But the important thing is that he's back.

Daniel cranes his neck to look up at me from where he's seated with her in the den.

Addison Fawn. I never thought I'd see her again. I thought I'd lost her when I lost my brother.

"Do you have a minute?" I ask him, getting their attention. Addison glances between Daniel and me, and I give her an easy smile. I've barely spoken to her, but it's only because of everything else. The war that's starting. That's what has my attention. That, and whoever decided to fuck with us.

Whoever decided to touch Addison and fuck with Daniel.

It's only a matter of time before we know who. Although the thought of Marcus being involved sends a chill through my blood.

Daniel winces as he stands, reminding me of the gunshot and rekindling that anger inside of me. He bends at the waist to kiss Addison. My eyes stay on her, noting how she pulls back slightly, but his hand on the back of her neck keeps her there. Her doe eyes look back into his and he brushes the tip of his nose against hers. And then she reaches up to kiss him this time.

I don't know what she did to my brother, but it's been a long damn time since I've seen him care about anything other than himself.

It's a good look for him.

"I was wondering when you were going to come for me," Daniel says as we walk back to the office. I keep him in sight even as he looks over his shoulder to check on her.

"You think she's going to run off?" I ask him jokingly, but it only makes his expression harden. Maybe he's still blind to it. But it's obvious she loves him. It was obvious five years ago too.

Silence escorts us until I close the door to the office with a loud click.

Daniel takes a seat in front of the large desk and rather than sitting at the head of it, I take the seat across from him, feeling the worn brown leather beneath my hands.

"I need that package," I tell him and wait for whatever the hell it is. He's already been here for hours, but Addison needed him for a little while. I could afford them that.

With a nod, Daniel slips the envelope from his back pocket. My teeth grind against one another. Hundreds of thousands of dollars in trades and a war between drug lords are on the line over whatever the fuck the Romanos are offering us.

And it's only a thin envelope, folded and creased down the center.

Our fingers brush as he hands it to me, but he doesn't let it go.

With my arm outstretched I look back at my brother, waiting for what he has to say, but nothing comes. A second ticks by and he releases it, sitting back in his chair but still not saying a word.

"What's gotten into you?" I ask him. Ever since Tyler died, Daniel's been a shell of who he once was. Until recently. Until she came back and brought him with her.

"She reminds you of Tyler?" he asks me.

"She reminds me of what you were like when he died," I answer him without thinking. And it's true. "You were on the edge of going one way or the other back then, but it looks like you've come back around."

"What do you mean?"

"I thought you were going to take care of her back then." I bite my tongue, wondering if I should tell him what Jase told me when Addison broke up with Tyler. When she said her goodbyes, she could hardly even look at Tyler. Instead she kept looking upstairs toward Daniel's room.

Everyone knew how Daniel felt about her. She was only seventeen and we had bigger and better shit to concern ourselves with. But that day it was more than obvious why she was leaving.

It was only the three of them who were blind to it.

Daniel shakes his head as if what I'm saying is ridiculous. Even after all these years he can't admit it.

"It doesn't matter. You're back, and she's with you. I don't care about anything else and neither does anyone else."

It's quiet for a long moment and Daniel runs his hand down his face, letting his head fall back and looking at the ceiling before he breathes in deep.

"Do you think he'd ever forgive me?" he asks me.

"Tyler forgave everyone," I answer him and it's true. He was the only good one of us. Of course he's the one who died young. "And Tyler wanted her to have a home. To have a family."

He nods his head, although it takes him a long moment before he looks back at me.

"It feels too good to be true," he says softly and I know why.

"Did you tell her the truth?"

"The truth?" he asks as if I don't know.

It only takes me glancing at his side where he was shot for him to understand my question.

"She has no idea. She thinks it was random. A coincidence."

"Is it Marcus?" I have a bad feeling in my gut, but he's the only person that this leads to.

"Yeah." His answer is quick and met with a simmering anger that I recognize from him. There's the brother I know and love. "I told him about her. I needed his help."

"You told Marcus. Who else?"

"He's the only one I told. It had to be him or someone he told."

"Why did you tell him anything?"

"I had her license plate and nothing else."

My thumb rubs in circular motions over my pointer finger as I take it all in.

He adds, "I couldn't lose her again." I know he could have told Jase. Jase could have looked up her information. But I don't remind him of that. He holds on to guilt too much.

I have nothing but silence as I think of any reason that Marcus would come for us. He's not a man I want as an enemy, but I'm also not certain it's him.

"It wasn't supposed to happen like that. It will never happen again." He strengthens his resolve and leans forward, daring me to object. And I do.

"And what if she leaves you again?" I ask him and he stares back at me, his chest rising and falling with determination. "What if she finds out something she shouldn't?"

He doesn't say what I expect him to, that she won't. Instead he merely answers, "Then I'll follow her."

My breath leaves me slowly, words failing me.

"She's mine," he says as if nothing else matters. And maybe it doesn't.

I nod my head once.

The hands of the clock in the office are all I can hear as I run my thumbnail under the flap of the envelope and stare back at my brother. "She's changed you."

"How's that?" he asks me. Again he's on the defensive, and it makes me smile. I like to see him showing something that's real.

"It's hard to pretend when you'd do anything for someone you love."

His gaze flickers to the envelope in my hand and he stares at it as he says, "I didn't come here for a heart to heart, Carter."

"You didn't open it?" Although the words come out with disbelief, the corners of my lips kick up with amusement. He's so consumed with Addison he didn't give a fuck about the one thing I've been losing sleep over.

"Marcus said it was a message of what's to come," he tells me as I finally open it. The paper tears easily and inside I'm surprised to find only a one-by-one-inch square photo. It falls into my palm facedown and I toss the crumpled envelope onto the desk, then flip the small piece of photo paper over.

"I went through all that shit for that?" Daniel asks, but I ignore him, too drawn to the picture.

I trace the curve of her porcelain face. I let the rough pad of my thumb run along the edge of the photo as I note her beautiful smile and the way her dark hair is lit with the sunshine in the image.

My heart pounds hard and I can't hear what Daniel's saying. I can't hear anything but the conversation I had with Tony Romano in the basement cellar months ago. The man who I've been avoiding, and the man who reached out to Marcus to deliver the message rather than tell me himself.

The dimly lit, cold and dark room was as unforgiving and unmoving as I was when he made his case and I turned him down.

Then he started bartering with things that didn't belong to him.

With women the Talverys were shipping off. His enemies. He wanted me to help him in a war against the Talverys and he was offering their property as payment. There was no way I'd ever accept.

"What it is?" Daniel presses, barely interrupting my memory.

"The gift from the Romanos." I don't know how the words come out strong as I gently place the photo onto the desk. "They want us on their side of this war they're starting."

I remember the way the heavy knife felt in my hand as I picked it up from his desk and stabbed it down onto the splintered wood in front of him. The sharp tip struck the paper in front of him.

The photo of the enemy family.

"If you give me any woman to start a war, it better be this one," I sneered in his face. I remember the stale stench of whiskey and cigars as I turned my back on him, leaving the knife where it was. With the tip of it stabbing the shoulder of the enemy's daughter. The shoulder her father's large hand was clenched around tightly.

His pride and joy, and one and only heir.

I didn't think he'd ever have the balls to take her and offer her to me.

"A gift?" Daniel questions with his brows raised and then picks up the photo.

"Yes," I answer him impatiently, quick to hide my depravity.

The photo of the one thing I asked for—Aria Talvery.

"In exchange for a war … she's mine."

The End.

THE
BEAST

MERCILESS

PREFACE

Carter

"**I** SHOULD HAVE FUCKED YOU SO MUCH SOONER."

I remember that first day, how she screamed and cried for me to let her go, back when I hated her and she hated me.

Even with my tight grip on her throat, with my touch sending sparks through her body , she forces her head to shake, not taking her eyes off of mine.

"No," she whispers and my dick hardens even more, begging me to punish her for daring to defy me. But then she adds, "This is how it was supposed to be."

Her breathing is heavy as she closes her eyes, her body bowed on my lap. She's completely at my mercy and her pouty lips are there for the taking.

All of her. Every piece of her is mine and she knows it.

Mine.

CHAPTER 1

Carter

WAR IS COMING.

It's something I've known for over two years.

Tick-tock. Tick-tock.

A tic in my jaw clenches in time with the rhythm of the clock, while the skin over my knuckles turns white as my fist squeezes tighter. Tension rises in my stiff shoulders and I have to remind myself to breathe in deeply and let the strain of it all go away.

Tick-tock. It's the only sound echoing off the walls of my office and with each pass of the pendulum, the anger grows.

It's always like this before I go to a meet. This one, in particular, sends a thrill through my blood, the adrenaline pumping harder with each passing minute.

My gaze drifts from the grandfather clock in my office to the shelves next to it, then beneath them to the box made of mahogany and steel. It's only three feet deep and three feet tall by six feet long. It blends into the wall of my office, surrounded by old books.

I paid more than I should have simply to put on a display. All any of this is merely a façade. People's perceptions are their reality. And so I paint the picture they need to see so I can use them as I see fit. The expensive books and artworks, polished furniture carved from rare wood… All of it is bullshit.

Except for the box. The story that came with it will stay with me forever. In all the years, it's one of the few memories I can pinpoint as a defining moment. The box never leaves me.

The words from the man who gave it to me are still so fresh, as is the image of his pale green eyes, glossed over as he told me his story.

About how it kept him safe when he was a child. He told me how his mother had shoved him in it to protect him.

I swallow thickly, feeling my throat tighten and the cords in my neck strain at the recollection. He set the scene so well.

He told me how he clung to his mother, seeing how panicked she was. But he did as he was told. He stayed quiet in the safe box and could only listen while the men murdered his mother.

He offered to barter for his life with the box. And the story he gave me reminded me of my own mother telling me goodbye before she passed.

Yes, his story was touching, but I put a gun to his head and pulled the trigger regardless.

He tried to steal from me and then pay me with a box as if the money he embezzled was a debt or a loan. William was good at thieving, at telling stories, but the fucker was a dumb prick.

I didn't get to where I am by playing nicely and being weak. On that day, I took the box that saved him as a reminder of who I was. Who I needed to be.

I made sure that box has been within my sight for every meeting I've had in this office. It's a powerful reminder I can stare at as I make deal after deal with criminal after criminal and collect wealth and power in this godforsaken room.

It cost me a fortune to get this office exactly how I wanted it. But if it were to burn down, I could easily afford to replace everything.

Everything except for that box.

"You really think they're going through with it?" I hear my brother, Daniel, before I see him. The remembrance fades in an instant.

It takes a second for me to be conscious of my facial expression, to relax my jaw and let go of the anger before I can raise my gaze to his.

"With the war and the deal? You think he'll go through with it and take her tonight?" he clarifies.

A small huff leaves me, accompanied by a smirk as I answer, "He wants this more than anything else. He said they set her up and it's already happening. Only hours until they're done."

Daniel stalks into the room slowly, the heavy door to my office closing with a soft kick of his heel before he comes to stand across from me.

"And you're sure you want to be right in the middle of it?"

I lick my lower lip and stand, stretching as I do and turning my gaze to the window in my office. I can hear Daniel walking around the desk as I lean against it and cross my arms.

I tell him, "We won't be in the middle of it. It'll be the two of them, and our territory is close, but we can stay back."

"Bullshit. He wants you to fight with him. He's going to start this war tonight and you know it."

I nod slowly, the memory of the smell of Romano's cigars filling my lungs at the thought of him.

"There's still time to call it off," Daniel says, and it makes my brow pinch and forehead crease. He can't be that naïve.

It's the first time I've really looked at him since he's been back. He spent years away. And every fucking day I fought for what we have. He's gone soft. Or maybe it's Addison who's turned him into the man standing here now.

"This war has to happen." My words are final, and the tone is one not to be questioned. I may have grown this business on fear and anger, each step forward followed by the hollow sound of a body dropping behind me, but that's not how it started. You can't build an empire with bloodstained hands and not expect death to follow you.

His dark eyes narrow as he moves closer to the window, his gaze flickering between me and the meticulously maintained garden several stories below us.

"Are you sure you want to do this?" His voice is low, and I barely hear it. He doesn't look back at me and a chill flows across the back of my neck and down my arms as I take in his solemn expression.

It takes me back to years ago. Back to when we had a choice and chose wrong.

When whether or not we wanted to go through with any of this still meant something.

"There are men to the left of us," I tell him as I step forward and close the distance between us. "There are men to the right. There is no possible outcome where we don't pick a side."

He nods once and slides his thumb across the stubble on his chin before looking back at me. "And the girl?" he asks, his piercing eyes reminding me that both of us fought, both of us survived, and we each had a tragic path that led us to where we are today.

"Aria?" I dare to speak her name and the sound of my smooth voice seems to linger in the space between us. I don't wait for him to acknowledge me—or her, rather.

"She has no choice." My voice tightens as I say the words.

Clearing my throat, I brace my palms against the window, feeling the frigid fall beneath my hands and lean forward to see Addison beneath us. "What do you think they would have done to Addison if they'd succeeded in taking her?"

His jaw clenches, but he doesn't answer my question. Instead he replies, "We don't know who tried to take her from me."

I shrug as if it's semantics and not at all relevant. "Still. Women aren't meant to be touched, but they went for Addison first."

"That doesn't make it right," Daniel says with indignation in his tone.

"Isn't it better she come to us?" My head tilts as I pose the question and this time he takes a moment to respond.

"She's not one of us. Not like Addison, and you know what Romano expects you to do with her."

"Yes, the daughter of the enemy…" My heart beats hard in my chest, and the steady rhythm reminds me of the ticking of the clock. "I know exactly what he wants me to do with her."

CHAPTER 2

Aria

THERE ARE A FEW THINGS YOU SHOULD KNOW ABOUT ME.

I like to wake up with a hot cup of coffee every morning. Preferably with enough creamer and sugar to drown out the taste of the bitter caffeine addiction.

I love red wine at night. I can't have white; it gives me a headache and a hangover that will leave me miserable when I wake up.

Well, those aren't things that really matter. They're the superficial details you give people when you don't want to tell them the truth.

What do you really need to know?

My name is Aria Talvery and I'm the daughter of the most violent crime family in Fallbrook.

The reason I like to have wine at night is because I desperately need it so I can get a few hours of sleep.

My mother was murdered in front of me when I was only eight years old and I've never been okay since then, although I've learned to be good at pretending I am.

My father's a crook, but he kept me safe and tolerated me even though every day he reminded me how much it hurt him to look at my face and see nothing but my mother.

It's because of my eyes. I know it is.

They're a hazel-green concoction, just like hers were. Like the soft mix of colors you'd see in a deep neck of the woods when looking up at the canopy of leaves in late summer, early fall. That's how my mother used to describe it. She was poetic that way. And maybe some of that rubbed off on me.

Fact number… whatever we're on: I love to draw. I hate the life I live and hide away in the sketches and smeared ink. Away from the madness and danger my existence inherently brings.

And that love of art, the one thing I have that still connects me to my mother, is why I ended up at this bar, tracking down the asshole who stole my sketchbook from me. The prick who thinks he's funny and that I'm some stupid joke or a toy he can play with because I'm a woman living in a man's world, a dangerous one at that.

But I inherited my temper from my father. And that's why I ended up at the Iron

Heart Brewery on Church Street. Yes, a bar on a street called "church." What's more ironic is how much sin has seeped into these walls.

And so I went willingly, after my precious notebook that was stolen and walked right into the enemy's arms.

It was a setup, but my mother would have called it kismet. You should know I'm smiling now, but it's a sarcastic smile as a huff of feigned laughter leaves me. Maybe all of this is her fault to begin with. After all, that notebook was irreplaceable to me because the only picture I had of her was tucked into the spine.

The last thing you should know, and the most important of them all, is that I refuse to break. I don't give in and I don't back down. Not for anyone, and especially not for Carter Cross. The bastard who took me from my family. Locked me in a room and told me in simple words that my life was over, and I belonged to him.

It won't be his cutting words from his sharp tongue. Or his broad shoulders and muscular arms that pin me down and trap me. It won't be his charming smile that utters filthy words that makes me cave. And it won't be that spark in his eyes, the flames licking and flickering brighter and hotter every time he looks at me.

No, I refuse to give in. Even if that same heat echoes in my chest and travels lower.

But there's this thing about breaking; the more you harden yourself and try to fight it, the easier and sharper the snap is when you inevitably break.

And I know this all too well.

The day my life changed forever...

There's a constant ringing in my ears. My fists are clenched so tight that my knuckles have turned white. Every time I have to face these assholes my father works with, this is how it feels.

Like I'm on edge.

My heart thuds, thuds, thuds as I pass the all-glass front door to Iron Heart Brewery and keep walking like I'm not going in. The front exterior is all windows, so they can easily see who's coming and going; bulletproof, too. Because of the clientele. Word is my father fronted that bill, but that seems overly generous for a man like him.

Cold. Selfish. Greedy. That's how I'd describe my father, and I hate myself for it.

I should be grateful; I should love him. But I'm loyal at least, and loyalty is all that matters. When you grow up in this life, you learn that little tidbit quickly.

Resting my shoulder against the dark red brick just past the windows, I take a look at the parking lot across the street. They aren't here yet.

A frustrated breath leaves a trail of fog in the tense fall air as I cross my arms.

This is where my father's men go on a night off and I know Mika is going to be here.

I hate being here alone, but I can't wait for someone to save me. I hope Nikolai will come with them too. He's a childhood friend, although now a soldier of my father's, and my saving grace. Really, he's my only friend and he's put that bastard Mika in his place more than once when my father wasn't there for me.

Even knowing that to be true, that if Nikolai comes there won't be any problems in the least, I hate that I have to be here at all. My thumb runs along the tips of my cold fingers, remembering how I held the notebook only moments before Mika came into the room. The photograph was tucked safely inside. Waiting for me to be inspired by it.

A notebook is only a notebook, but that photograph is the only one I have of my mother and me the year she died.

My father didn't have time for my "meaningless shit," as he called it, and the vise around my heart tightened at his response.

A shiver runs down my shoulders and I let out another heavy breath. I can feel the chill on my nose and cheeks. My thin jacket isn't doing a damn thing to help me. I hadn't realized fall had come with intentions of revenge on the smoldering summer.

Peeking up through my lashes, I read the chalkboard sign above the bar through the windows. They're all locals, all drafts. I guess I could have one drink while I wait.

The smooth music hits my ears as I walk into the bar, my heart beating faster as I take in a few of the men seated on the stools. It's funny how a bar being mostly empty sends greater fear through me than one that's packed. One where I can blend in.

Right here, right now? I don't belong, and every soul here knows it.

Maybe this is why Mika thought he could get away with it, I think bitterly as I try to ignore the scared little girl inside of me. He thinks he can steal from me because my father won't stop him and I'm too spineless to even come out of my room unless called upon.

I force myself to straighten my back as I move closer to the bar and set down my clutch. I have a plan and I go over it as I try to swallow, form a smile, and order a drink.

"Vodka and Sprite," I order easily as I slip onto the barstool and meet the bartender's eyes. With a nod he moves seamlessly to the glasses, making them clink and then filling one with ice.

I'll wait for the guys. Even if they scare me because I know what they're capable of. I'll look Mika in the eyes and tell him to give my sketchbook back to me by tomorrow. And then I'll walk away. No threats. It's a simple request. He wants to play around and tease me and I won't give him the time to do so. That's the only reason he took it.

He gets a thrill from goading me.

The wind batters against the glass windows to my right and it startles me. None of the men lining the room seem to have noticed it.

I'm too busy watching the hanging sign for the brewery banging against the window that I don't see the bartender come up to me.

The sound of the glass hitting the hard maple bar top sends a spike of fear through me and I jump in surprise.

The sudden stillness and immediate silence that accompanies all of their eyes on me force me to tense. I can barely form a smile as I stare straight ahead and thank the bartender.

First, I feel a rush of embarrassment, followed by fear that they know I'm weak. Then that all-consuming anxiety that everything is going to go wrong washes over me. Very wrong.

It makes me want to throw up, but instead, I lift the cold glass to my lips. One sip of the sweet cocktail does nothing. Two, and my throat still feels dry.

I'm a foolish girl. I lick a bit of soda from my bottom lip and set the glass down on the counter as I stare at all the colorful labels of liquor bottles lining the shelves.

There's no one who will stand up for me and I can't even bring myself to think about confrontation without getting jumpy. Trying to swallow proves useless and so I push myself off the stool with both hands clinging to the cold bar.

My palms are clammy, and I nearly tell the bartender I'm just going to the restroom as if he'd care. As if anyone cares.

That feeling of complete insignificance follows me with each step to the left of the bar as I head down a skinny hallway. It's the only way to go, so the restrooms must be there. I only make it a few steps before I think I hear a shot. My body tenses and my heart goes still. It knows that if it were to beat, I wouldn't be able to hear a single thing else.

There's no scream. There's nothing but the sound of the music. I must have only thought I heard one. It's all in my head.

My eyes close as I will myself to breathe. But then they bolt open at a familiar noise.

It's not the harsh sound of a gun going off. It's the whiz of a gun with a silencer, followed by the thud of a body hitting the floor.

Bang, bang! Two of them back to back, and this time everything sounds closer. Another shot. My body clings to the wall as if it can hide me.

I force myself to move, to head to the back and find a way out or place to hide. I might be a scared little girl, barely surviving in my father's world, but I'm not a fucking idiot.

I quicken my pace as I round the corner, motivated by the sheer will to live. But every bit of strength I have, even if it is minuscule, is for nothing.

The scream that's torn from my throat is barely heard as a thick bag covers my head.

My clutch falls to the floor, hitting my thigh as I kick out and miss the man in front of me. My heels go with it, each kick accompanied by the rough laughter of several men.

I try to fight, but it's no use.

It's more than one man, I know that. Their hands are strong and their bodies like bricks.

I don't stop and won't, but nothing I do is helping. I punch and yell and kick as terror flows through me, begging me to push them away and run. I can't see, and my arms scream in pain as they're pinned behind me.

I only know we're outside because of the wind slicing through my thin jacket. I only know I'm in a trunk because of the telltale sound of it opening before I'm tossed in, my small body crashing against the back of it as it's quickly shut.

Silence.

Darkness.

My breathing is ragged, and it makes me lightheaded.

When my screaming stops, my voice is hoarse, and my throat burns with harsh pain every time I try to swallow. When my banging ends, my wrists are rubbed raw and cut from the cuffs and my muscles are aching with the type of pain that's scorching hot and forces me to tremble.

Another feeling takes over. It's not quite panic. It's something else.

It's not a sense of hopelessness. Not that either.

When you're alone and you know nothing is okay and nothing's going to be okay, there's this feeling that's overwhelming and inescapable.

My heart keeps ticking along despite everything. But it's going too fast. Everything is going too fast and it hurts. And I can't stop it. I can't stop any of it.

When you've done everything you can, and you're left with nothing but fear of both the unknown and the known, there's only one way to describe it.

That feeling is true terror.

CHAPTER 3

Carter

"You're going to keep her here?" It's not much of a question from my brother; more of a statement as he looks around the cell. Jase was the middle child of five boys and never learned how to start a conversation without being direct and blunt. I suppose I can't blame him. The thought reminds me of Tyler. The fifth brother who died years ago. His memory numbs the reality of the present, but only for a moment.

Jase leans against the far wall with his arms loosely crossed and waits for me to answer.

We leave in only an hour. Each small tick of the Rolex on my wrist reminds me that I'm so close to having her. Only time separates us now.

Glancing from the thin mattress lying on the floor to the metal toilet on the other side of the cell, I tell him, "I think I'll add a chair."

His quizzical expression only changes slightly. He may not even realize it, but I see it on his face. The disappointment. The disgust. I can hear the unspoken question that lingers on the tip of his tongue as he shifts his gaze from me to the steel door behind us. *When did you become this fucked up?* He has no idea.

"I'll need a place to sit." I keep my voice even, almost playful as if this is a joke. It's Jase though, and he knows me better than anyone. Much better than either Daniel or Declan. The three of them and I make the four Cross brothers. But out of all of us, Jase and I are the closest.

As much as I can hide the anxiousness of getting my hands on Aria from everyone else, he can see it. I can tell by how careful he's been around me since I told him.

"How long?" he asks me.

"How long what?"

"Will you keep her here?"

"As long as it takes." *For what?* The question is there in his eyes, but he doesn't ask it and I have no intention of telling him regardless. I could lie and tell him as long as it takes for the war to end. As long as it takes to see if she'll be useful in negotiations if Talvery wins. The lies could pour from me, but the truth is simple. As long as it takes for me to decide what I want from her.

"There's no shower," he remarks.

"There's a faucet by the side of the toilet and a drain. She'll figure it out while she's in here."

Time passes and a chill settles in the already cold air. I know this is something I've never done, and it crosses more than one line. But in times of war, there is no right and wrong.

"I could give her other things. Little by little." Although I'm answering his question, I'm merely thinking out loud.

"Last time I was here, I was getting some very useful intel," Jase comments as he moves to the corner of the room. I know he's looking at the rim of the drain, inspecting it for any remnants of the blood.

The cell has only been used for one thing prior to this. It's what Jase excels at.

"Are you planning on getting information from her?" Jase asks with genuine curiosity and before I can answer he quickly adds, "I don't think Talvery is known for speaking business openly."

I would commend Jase for prying, but this isn't a matter I want him or anyone else involved in. She's mine and mine alone in this deal. And I'll do whatever I want with her. My brothers and everyone else can go fuck themselves where she's concerned.

"No, I don't think she knows anything."

Jase walks casually around the small room. Ten feet by ten feet. That's more than enough space. His boot brushes against the mattress and then he kicks it. There are no springs or coils in the thing. There's nothing in here she could use as a weapon.

I made sure of that.

"Just a mattress and a chair?" he asks, still skirting around the questions he wants answered. After years of me leading us and making the decisions, he knows better than to question me, but this is fucking killing him. It's eating him alive that he doesn't know what I want to do with her or why I want her. And the knowledge that it's killing him only thrills me.

"For now. I imagine she's going to want to fight and the fewer things in here, the better."

"And you think this is a sign that we can trust the Romanos? He gives you the girl, risking everything to get her, and you trust him to go to war? If he really has her and is willing to hand her over to you?" He's reaching, prying still.

"We can't trust anyone." I make sure he holds my gaze as I add, "That truth will never change." We only have each other. That's how we survived, and that's the only way we'll continue to live.

He's smarter than that. I imagine Jase will realize why all of this is happening before anyone else. That's his job, to gather any and all information necessary. By any means.

"Then this is a test?" he questions. His forehead is creased, a deep line evident. He's lucky he's my brother and that I still feel guilty for bringing him into this. For bringing all of them deeper and deeper into my hell I've created.

"The Romanos want the Talverys dead and vice versa. All over a decade-old feud for territory. The Romanos need allies and the upper hand. It was only a matter of time before I agreed to war; she just happened to be the first casualty. I wanted something, and Romano is going to give it to me, so we back him and not the Talverys."

"Casualty?" he asks to clarify if I really am going to kill her.

"You and I both know if she stays with her father, she'll die at his side… or worse," I say easily as I leave the cell. Jase's footsteps echo behind me.

"Why save her?" Jase's question echoes in my veins. Agreeing to take her is a risk I shouldn't have taken.

"It was an impulsive decision."

"It's unlike you," Jase pushes, and I have to steady my breathing to keep from telling him to fuck off. He has no idea that Aria once saved me. No one does, not even her. Whether I hate her for it, or something else, I have yet to decide.

"After this is over, what do we do with her?" Jase asks me.

Closing the steel door, I shut it tightly and pull the edge of the painting back over the barely visible slit of the frame. The door is designed to be concealed. If you didn't know how to maneuver the painting just so to unlock the hidden seal, you'd never see a door at all.

It's a soundproof cell no one would ever find. Impenetrable and fitted with an electronic cloak so any type of tracking is silenced. It's Aria's new home.

His question resonates with me as I turn my back to the cell. *What am I going to do with her afterward?*

"I haven't thought that far ahead," I reply, and the tone of my answer puts an end to his questioning.

CHAPTER 4

Y HEART WILL KILL ME BEFORE THESE MEN DO. THAT'S ALL I CAN THINK AS it races in my chest. I've never felt fear like this.

Maybe it's a lie that I've never felt it before. But it's been so long, and I don't remember my heart pounding like it is now.

My hot breath makes me feel faint as I try to breathe steadily. My eyes open even though all I can see is darkness with the bag still wrapped around my head.

I have to be smart. As much as I'd love to fight, I have to be smart or I'll die.

It's impossible to be smart when you're terrified though.

The dry lump in my throat feels scratchy as I swallow, opening my eyes to see nothing but the scant light that seeps through the burlap. I can't make out anything but I can hear everything. My erratic heartbeat blasting in my ears, the sound of several men in the room, and the scraping of chairs across the floor. One of them is named Romano and I'm fully aware that he's a man who hates my father. *I'm in the hands of the enemy.* I know I'm on a plastic tarp. I can feel the slickness beneath my fingers. It almost feels like a trash bag beneath me.

That's what scares me the most. I've never seen my father kill anyone, but I know they line the floor before they go through with it. It makes it easier for cleaning up.

I try to swallow again, gently lifting my head because I feel like I'm going to suffocate if I don't breathe.

"Bitch is up." My breathing hitches at the gruff voice coming from somewhere in front of me.

I tried and failed, not to let them on to the fact that I'm awake. Even when the cigar smoke woke me, and I thought I was in a fire, I was still. A few minutes have passed at most; I haven't learned shit that's going to help me though, other than that I'm lying on a floor and helpless.

Someone else responds, "Just in time." And then rough laughter erupts in the room.

My aching body stiffens, my hands clenching and making the cuffs dig deeper into my broken skin. I'm so terrified, I don't react to the pain shooting up my arms.

Every second that passes is agonizing. They speak calmly, softly, and in Italian. A language of which I know very few words.

I know *baldracca* though. It's the word for whore and hearing that makes my shoulders hunch in a useless and pathetic effort to hide myself as a new sense of fear overwhelms me.

There's no doubt in my mind that I'm being held captive by one of my father's enemies. Romano, and he's one of many. I would give them anything to be able to run back home and stay there forever.

"Please," I can't help the attempt to bargain that slips from me. "My father will pay you whatever you want." The tears come without notice and my voice cracks on every other word. The warmth of my breath makes my heated face feel even hotter.

I've never thought of myself as such a weak person. But tied up and knowing my fate includes death or being a whore, the desperation outweighs anything else.

"There is no saving you Talvery trash," a man sneers as he walks closer to me with deliberate steps. His heavy footfalls get louder and quicker. Instinctively I try to back away, despite being on my side with my ankles and wrists cuffed behind my back. The struggle is useless. With my back against a wall and nowhere to go, all I can do is hunch my body inward as the heavy boot kicks brutally into my gut.

The air leaves me in a harrowing instant. Pain bursts inside of me, radiating outward but coiling in my stomach. It sinks deep inside of me, making me want to throw up to get rid of the agonizing pain.

I sputter and heave, trying my best to remain quiet. Bastard tears leak from my eyes and I can't stop them. I can't do anything.

This is a hell I've been terrified of for so damn long. A nightmare that I knew could be a reality. Helpless takes on a new meaning.

My body trembles and the fear is overwhelming. But then I remind myself, be quiet. Be smart. There is always hope. Always. I'm smart enough to find a way. The idea is soothing for a moment until I hear the boot rise again and my instinct to cower is greeted with laughter in the room.

I pray that maybe I'll wake up. Although I know it's not a possibility I'm asleep, because pain doesn't follow you to your dreams. Not this kind.

But the thought gives me a heady comfort that allows me to stay quiet as the men talk and laugh, their banter mocking me and my helplessness.

My father will come for me. That last thought I nearly whisper to myself. My lips mouth the words and I stay in the fetal position with my eyes closed.

He will save me.

It's his pride at risk. If for no other reason, stealing me is a sign of weakness for him. He won't allow it. My breathing slows at the thought, the adrenaline in my blood seemingly ebbing away from me. He has to save me.

"Do you think we should torture her first? Get any information out of her?" The two questions are asked by another man farther away from me and on my left. One with a casual and lighthearted way about the fucked up questions which leads to the room being filled with Italian comments and some amused chuckle from my right.

Sweat covers my skin. Turning hot and cold as the air smothers me.

The laughter is silenced with the sound of the door opening and greetings are exchanged. Only three men speak, and I can't make out the words until the door is shut again.

Something's changed. The air in the room is different. I can feel it.

"Is that her?" a deep, rough voice asks. The velvet cadence of the man who interrupted the jovial laughter makes everything still. Goosebumps flow over every inch of my skin.

There's no answer for a moment, but I imagine someone may have nodded.

Again, my heart beats and I wish it would stop. I need to hear. All I can think is that I'm going to be slaughtered.

I can't be. Not like this. Please, God, not like this.

My adrenaline spikes and I can't help that my head turns to hear better. Everything in the room is still and so quiet that I can hear the puff of a cigar. It's so clear I can imagine his lips as he exhales, the deep breath overshadowing everything else.

"I didn't think you'd do it," the new man's voice says calmly and in control. The others had an accent to them, but this one is from here. American descent, born and raised. Still, his voice commands fear. There's something about it, the intonation that feels like power in and of itself. He says, "It's very rare that I'm proven wrong."

Fear and hope flow through me. The fear I expected, but hope doesn't make sense. It's alive in me though. Some part of me urges to beg the smooth-voiced man to save me as if it knows he's my savior.

"Aria Talvery." He says my name with reverence, but even so, as he steps closer to me, the tread of his shoes on the floor not nearly as heavy and foreboding as the man who kicked me, I instinctively move away.

I don't even notice how calm my heart is until he says the words that create utter chaos.

"The deal wasn't meant to be taken literally." A slew of Italian fills the room. Not everyone's yelling, I know that, but several are and their anger ricochets through the room.

"You said you'd do it; you'd side with me in the war in exchange for her. Are you going back on your word?" One voice is louder than the rest. Deeper and raspier. It sends a sickening chill through my bones.

"I didn't, actually. And terms need to be negotiated."

The man with the raspy voice responds quickly and doesn't hide his irritation as he retorts, "You've known about this for three days. Three fucking days!" He yells the last three words and they make me jump as much as I can in this position.

Speaking with nothing but control, the man who sent for me answers him, "Like I said, I didn't think you'd do it."

"*Bastardo*," a new voice spits and it's followed by the crunching sound of a punch.

"Fuck!" another man yell, but I don't recognize his voice, and the sound of guns being cocked fills the room.

"Jase, no need."

My eyes are wide open as I lie helpless on the ground. My fingertips search for something, anything to help me but the only progress I'm making is pulling at the plastic beneath me.

Without any warning, three heavy steps come closer and the burlap bag is ripped off my head, taking a bit of my hair with it and forcing a scream from me. The bright light blinds me as I'm pulled up by the nape of my neck, clear off the ground and then hurled down to the floor.

I have no hands free to catch myself, they're still cuffed behind me and so my shoulder hits the ground first, then my face. The hint of blood fills my mouth, and pain shoots up my shoulder.

Fuck, it hurts. Everything hurts.

I rock onto my back as I cry out.

Please, make it stop. Please. I wish I could take myself away from here. I wish it were only a dream. But as my arm twists and scrapes on the cement in an effort to right myself, I know this is real. I can't escape this. I whimper and give into the pain. There is no nightmare to wake from. This is my reality.

"You said you'd back me if I gave her to you!" A violent scream tears through the small room. My neck cranes to see the man who spoke over a table. A rough and splintered, unfinished wood table. The man's dress shirt looks damp with sweat and his face glistens with it too. Dark, black eyes stare across the room toward me, but not looking at me. The anger on his face is undeniable and I can't look anywhere else as he screams words that make my body shudder with fear. "I won't let you go back on this!" My eyes close tight.

I've heard the whispers of war for years from man after man. It's been so long since I've actually feared the hint of it. Maybe that's where I made my first mistake. I forgot that I should be terrified and that the dangers are always lurking and waiting to strike.

Please take me far away from here. I can imagine this going wrong so quickly. I could be shot and never even given the chance to escape. My heart races wildly and the terror makes my body tremble.

"And now you've damaged her," the man, the one with control, says quietly and calmly but with an uncontained anger that's brimming with threats. The deadliness of his simple sentence silences the room once again. It's only then that I dare to open my eyes, slowly peeking up through my lashes.

Dark eyes stare deep into mine as a tall man crouches down in front of me. Not black like the other man's, not so darkened. But a mixture of browns and amber, like a piece of burned wood from a raging fire.

There's no heat there though. His eyes are so cold they make my blood freeze and instantly the air turns to ice. There's a hint of something in his gaze that speaks of inexplicable things. My body tenses, my lungs fear to move and I stay still like prey caught in the beautiful hunter's gaze.

Time passes slowly as he considers me. And I find myself hoping and praying that he'll save me. How ridiculous that I would, but there's something about his eyes. I can't refuse the pull, the electricity surrounding him that seems to bend the air between us, making me feel closer to him. So close that he could save me.

His intentions aren't any better than these men. But there's only one of him and he's a man of control. I prefer that to the chaos I'm currently in.

I know it. He can save me.

Even if it's only by killing me right now in this moment and ending the pain. And I'm acutely aware he could do it. There's not a thing about him that could hide the fact that he's a ruthless, cold-hearted killer.

His fingers brush along his stubble as he tilts his head, considering me. The sole light overhead, a bright light in the middle of the room casts a shadow down his face that somehow makes his chiseled and hard jaw look even sharper.

His presence alone speaks of a power that steals the air from me. I'm nothing beneath him as he towers over me. My eyes close slowly as he reaches out and gently brushes the hair from my face. His hot touch melts everything inside of me. It's tender but deliberate. The soothing caress makes me weaker as his fingers travel down my chin and to my throat.

His masculinity is undeniable, the fear of his power only adding to the forbidden desire that rages through me. The man is everything I've been taught to fear, although the sensation is mixed with something else entirely. Something I'd never admit.

And that's when he grips me, his fingers wrapping around my throat and forcing me to open my eyes, staring back into the dark abyss of his gaze.

CHAPTER 5

"I ASKED FOR HER, YES," I FINALLY ANSWER ROMANO ALTHOUGH I'M STILL STARING at Aria's face, those lips of hers parted and swollen from the fall as I tighten my grip just slightly. Anger ripples through me at the sight of the fresh wounds. That fucker put his hands on her. They hurt her. They hurt what's mine. The tic in my jaw spasms again as the rage intensifies. They should know better than to touch what's mine.

I force the boiling rage down to a simmer; I'm not a fool. There are six men in this room and only one is on my side. I'm not just outnumbered. I'm not prepared to fight. And I don't intend to either.

I want to take my gift and leave this prick to his war. I want that feeling back, humming in my veins. The sheer power of having her at my mercy, feeling her breath cut short and her blood rushing beneath my grasp. She's mine. Finally.

"But not for a beaten and broken version of her," I grit the words through my teeth and they come out lower than I expected. I'm barely contained as I loosen my grip, allowing her to break eye contact and suck in a deep breath.

If I hear another plea or whimper from her in reaction to this fucker, I know I'll shoot Romano without a second thought. And that can't happen. Not yet. The second I get my hands on Aria, her father will be after me. I need Romano to distract him just as much as Romano needs me.

Romano doesn't answer, and I imagine it's because my back is to him as I look over Aria. But he'll have to fucking deal with that. So long as she's here, she'll be looking at me and no one else.

I scan every inch of her and each time I see an injury, my teeth clench, and my muscles coil. The cut on her swollen lip. The scratches and scrapes around her wrists. There's a bruise on her arm and I'm sure there are more I can't see.

"We just got her two hours ago. She's not broken. You better not fuck me over." Romano's words are rushed and desperate as I stand tall, leaving the girl where she is.

My heart races, but I don't let on. To them, she's only a girl I randomly chose. A girl who was harder to kidnap. Just a challenge for them and nothing more.

"This isn't a fight or debate," I tell Romano with my back still to him. I want him to know in his truest of hearts that I'm the one helping him, and it's only out of my desire to do so. He's fucked over more than one of his allies in the past. I'm going to make him think twice before he decides I can be used as a pawn.

Even knowing how much is at stake in this very moment, I can hardly think.

I can't pry my eyes from Aria. Her chest rises and falls steadily as she rolls onto her side. Her lips are a gorgeous hue of red. Her hair tousled and flowing over her bare shoulder. But what's better is how she keeps looking at me with a mixture of both fear and hope swirling in those striking hazel eyes. I didn't imagine she'd look like this. The sight is addictive.

"Plea-" she starts to say—to me—but Romano cuts her off. His sickening and desperate voice hushes the soft sounds of her speaking to me. My fists clench, nearly splitting the tight skin across my tense knuckles and instantly my suit feels like it's suffocating me. His ignorance will be the death of him.

"We had a deal and it will benefit both of us, Cross."

As I loosen my collar, walking closer to him in the filthy room, he continues, "You don't have to do anything but give me that territory, Carter." He raises his hands in defense when I stare daggers at him. "Only for a little while, just so we can strike first. You're closer to Talvery. You don't want your men to do the work, so what other choice do I have than to take it over?"

My gaze sweeps over a pile of crates in the corner of the room. There are three of them on top of empty pallets. The wooden table is etched and weathered. I can only imagine the blood and sweat and drugs that have seeped into the wood. Even over the smell of smoke, the stench is revolting.

Each man in the room is dressed similarly, except myself and Jase. I always wear a suit; it's better to overdress than under. Romano's attempt at an ill-fitting suit didn't last long. His wrinkled jacket is a puddle of cheap fabric laying across the back of his chair. The others wear nondescript hoodies and shirts with faded baggy jeans. Each of the thugs looks at me as I survey them, and each one of their questioning gazes falls without a word uttered from their insignificant lips.

And then I look back to her. Back to the soft curves of her waist, the messy halo of dark hair around her pale skin. Her slender throat that's so exposed as she writhes quietly and hopelessly on the ground. This beautiful, broken creature. She's all mine.

"Your men are positioned between Fourth and Weston, give that territory to me so I can take his men down." Romano starts to speak terms. "We'll take them all down at the same time on every edge of his territory. Any man who stands against us after that will die. It's simple. They back us, or they die like the rest of them."

"I've heard this all before," I mutter. He says he'll kill them all. Erase any trace of Talvery from our existence. It's related to unfinished business started a decade before me. All in the name of greed.

"Just give me access to that territory and the suppliers for the guns." He reeks of desperation as he adds, "That's what you agreed to!"

I expected a lot of things when I came here. But this amount of irritation is something I never accounted for. As the seconds pass, I imagine how I could kill each and every one of the men in this room. How long it would take. How many shots they'd get off. Jase is behind me and I know he could hold his own.

I have to will away the temptation and eagerness to get Aria alone. Leaving the image of her beautiful figure crumpled at my feet, I focus on the business at hand.

"You want me to back down, clear the path for your men?" I ask him.

"They'll never see it coming if we take them from both your side and mine. We take over on the edge of your territory—" I cut the fucker off before he can finish.

"He'll think it's me killing them off. When his men around the edge of my territory start dying, he'll come after me without a second thought." My words come out deadly. "This isn't me starting a war, it's you."

"I'm giving her to you for a reason." He rushes his words with sincere bewilderment.

"No deal," I say and turn to leave, but Aria's whimper pierces through the air. Even without a word spoken, I can hear her plea not to leave her at their mercy. It does things to me that it shouldn't. Just the knowledge that the threat of my absence can create a reaction from her is everything to me in this moment.

"Wait!" Romano's hands smack on the wooden table in the center of the room. "What if," he swallows visibly as he pushes off the table and then lets out a heavy breath. I peek at Jase for the first time since we've been in here. In a slim-fitting suit and his arms hanging loosely in front of him, he could be the usher at a fucking wedding right now. Well, if it weren't for the glare on his face that can only be read one way, for anyone looking at him to fuck off.

"What if…" he pauses and clears his throat before looking me in the eye. "Once I take over Talvery's territory, we could split it." He earns himself a small reaction from me, the tilt of my head for him to continue. "I want to start flooding the product at the top, closest to just outside of the tri-state area, to keep the cops away from our bases."

"And?" I question him. "None of this is relevant to splitting a damn thing."

"I only need his territory in the Upper West Side. I don't even have enough men to cover the rest," he says in a lighter, nearly comical tone as if the problem's already been solved.

"I'm not interested in more territory," I state, and my barely spoken words cause the hopeful expression on his face to fade. "But I'd happily take a percentage of the profits to cover my losses," I offer. "Fifteen percent every quarter until my losses are paid."

"Deal." Romano is so quick to oblige, even his own men stare at him rather than at me. They can't be that stupid. An even-numbered war is never a good thing. They need men and territory and backing. I'll give them the minimum, and pray they still kill each other off.

I nod my head once. "Deal," I say and while forcing a semblance of a smile to my lips, I offer him an outstretched hand.

I have to keep the grin from spreading as I turn my attention back to the wide-eyed girl, still tied up on the floor. "Jase." I speak to my brother although I keep my gaze on her, "Put her in the trunk."

CHAPTER 6

I T's ODD, THE THINGS THAT YOU THINK WHEN YOU'RE ALONE FOR HOURS IN A ROOM filled with nothing but hopelessness and anger. Some thoughts make sense of course. Thoughts of Mika and how he should have been there. He should have been at the bar, and I find myself wondering if he knew. If he took my notebook because he knew how much I loved my art and I'd know he had it and come after him. I find it hard to believe he wouldn't expect me to go after it. Or else why do it? I've spent hours trying to determine the intentions of a psychotic asshole.

But the truth is that I wouldn't have gone after him for any other reason. I wouldn't have left the safety of home… if that picture hadn't been tucked safely inside.

The thoughts of Mika and how bleak my reality is seem reasonable.

Other thoughts though… other thoughts don't make sense.

Like the flashbacks of my mother.

I've been haunted by so many images of what happened the day she died for years now. But none of those keep me company as I rock on the cement floor in the corner of the cell.

It's the sweeter things I remember that are driving me mad.

My thumb brushes against the cut on my lip, sending a sharp pain through me that reminds me this isn't a dream.

"Aria," I hear my mother call out for me in the memory. I was hiding in the closet, so proud that I'd hidden so well. "Ria?" Her voice changed to fear and desperation, and my smile vanished. "Ria, please!" she begged as her hushed cry from the hallway beckoned me to show myself. My fingers gripped the door of the closet just as she forced the guest room door open. I remember how her light blue dress swung around her knees. How her perfectly pinned hair didn't come undone. Yet her voice and her bearing were nothing but distraught.

I wish I could go back to that moment. Where she was running toward me and so close. Where she'd inevitably be in reach.

"Don't hide from me." Her words were ragged as she pulled me into her chest. She rocked me too fast, she held me too hard before gripping my arms and making me look her in the eyes. I'll never forget how hers watered over. "You can't hide like that." Her words were so pained, they came out as only a whisper.

"I'm sorry, Momma," I tried to speak the words, so she knew I meant them. "I was only playing."

Tears leaked from the corners of her eyes as she pulled me back into her arms and rocked me.

She whispered many things, but the one that's stayed with me is that we don't live in a world where we can play.

I should have known better than to run after Mika.

Every possible situation of a setup runs through my head as I bite my thumbnail and rock against the cement wall. I can't sit. My legs beg me to run, but with nowhere to go, I simply stand and lean on the far wall across from the door. Waiting for it to open.

I was only playing myself, thinking that I could prove myself to be anything when I went to hunt down Mika. I was childish and foolish. I can hear my mother saying it now. How foolish she was, she said it all the time before she died. And foolish is what I've become.

I keep whispering that I'm sorry, and I know the man is watching me. Carter. That's what the men called him.

Carter Cross. I know he can hear my whispers of despair.

I'm not saying it to him though; it's an apology to my mother. I should have known better than to chase after the memory of her in that picture. The words are spoken as I focus on the metal drain in the corner of the room.

Between the toilet, mattress, and drain, I know this room is meant for prisoners, but also for torture and murder. One and then the other.

I've searched every inch; the sides of my hands are bruised from pounding against the tall steel door. There's simply no escape. One way in, and one way out.

I should have fought harder when Jase Cross, Carter's brother from what I overheard, held the rag to my mouth.

Stolen, drugged, and reassigned to a prison: that's what my life has become.

The faint sounds of the camera moving drag my attention back to it. It's the one thing in the room I wish I could destroy. There's only one from what I can tell, and it's in the far right corner of the room.

But the camera is encased in cement and untouchable, if throwing the metal chair was any indication. As I stare at the mattress, I wrap my arms around myself. I won't sleep on it; there's no way my back will ever touch it.

I suck in a deep breath, reliving the feeling of those dark eyes pinning me in place.

I know what he wants from me, but he'll have to fight me to get it. I'll kick him, bite him, scratch him until my nails break and bleed.

I'll make him regret this if it's the last thing I do.

My fingers lift slowly up to my jaw and then trail down my throat. Remembering how his gentle comfort so easily became a threat.

My heart thumps hard, once then twice as I hear the fucking camera move again.

"What are you moving it for?" I scream out like a madwoman, as loud as I can. My throat is hoarse from the screaming before, my body screaming along with me in a shuddered breath.

"I'm not fucking going anywhere!" I scream again and then wrap my arms tighter around myself as I fall to the floor on my ass and then my side. Just the way I was when that monster first found me.

The cuts on the sides of my wrists touch the dirty cement floor. I should lie on the mattress. I know I should, even as my tearstained cheeks rest on the unforgiving floor.

If, for no other reason than to have the energy to fight another day. He's waiting me out, I think. And that's something I can't fight. Hours and hours have passed.

I don't know how much time has elapsed exactly, but I know I have to sleep. I can't stay awake forever, waiting for whatever's next.

I'm powerless and completely at Carter's mercy. And he's not even here. He had me stolen from my home, then nearly left me in the kidnapper's arms. And now that he has me, he's left me to go crazy on my own.

That's exactly how I feel as my heavy eyes stare at the steel door and sleep threatens to take over. When you don't know what's waiting for you, what you'll have to fight, it can do that to you. It can make you feel crazy.

Another hour passes, or more. So much time escapes and all my fight has gone. In its place, only fear and exhaustion remain.

"Why are you doing this to me?" I whisper as I stare at the camera, imagining all the answers it could give me. And not a single one of them offers me comfort.

I find it hard to believe that when I first heard his voice, I was so desperate for him to take me away. The blame lays on my survival instincts. The fear of what those men would have done to me made me desperate for Carter to steal me away. My mind drifts back to that moment, and I wish I'd looked harder for a different escape.

He's going to come back. And I need to be able to fight him. But how can I, when I don't know when he's coming, and I have to sleep? Eventually, I have to sleep.

I doze off once, at least once that I know of, and startle awake only to find myself aching on the floor. Forcing myself up, I try to open the door once again and then cry on the floor beneath it. I imagine him opening it in that moment, and that alone scares me to move to the farthest corner in the room.

How heartbreaking it is, that the only bit of comfort I have is knowing that when the monster comes back, I'll be as far away from him as I can possibly be. Even if it is only ten feet.

But it's what I needed to finally give in to sleep.

Of all the things to dream about, I dream of my mother.

And once again, I should have known better than to let my mind wander to the memory of her death.

CHAPTER 7

Carter

SHE FELL ASLEEP AFTER FOURTEEN HOURS OF LOOKING FOR AN ESCAPE, SLAMMING the chair into the door, screaming profanities, rocking against the wall, and whispering all her regrets.

And I watched every minute of it well into the early morning. Obsessed with what she'd do and watching the fight leave her as every hour passed.

After she'd realized her efforts were hopeless, she hummed softly. So low, that I thought it was only a buzz from the camera until I turned up the volume. She hummed for hours. I don't even know if she noticed.

She'd finally fallen asleep, the hum of a lullaby still soft on her lips. The thrill of victory sang in my blood.

It was only then that I left my office and the monitors, reminding myself to be patient. I wouldn't be surprised if the carpet beneath my desk is worn from the pacing of my shoes against it.

My last thought as I left the office and checked the monitor on my phone, was that as much as she was fighting now, she'd cave. She'd give in and obey. She has no choice. And time is on my side. Not hers.

An hour into going through orders and updates on each of the deliveries, I heard her screaming again. But instead of it bringing the buzz of a challenge, her screams curdled my blood.

The sweat is still hot on my skin by the time I finally get to the cell and kick the door open with the gun cocked in my hand. My heart pounds in my chest. Aria's screams are violent and shrill.

I don't know what the fuck happened, who the hell got to her or how they got in here. But someone has their hands on her.

My heart hammers and the anger of her defiance is dulled by something primal, a raw fear that sends a prickle of unease through my body in an instant. I can hear the terror in her voice as she cries out into the dark room for someone to help her.

Someone's in there. Someone's hurting her. It's undeniable in her screams. I can't fucking breathe. I finally have her in my grasp. *Mine.*

My breathing is barely controlled with the gun raised in the air above her place on the floor. Whoever it is will die a painful death for taking what's mine. "Please!" she cries out, her eyes shut tight as her body stiffens and her back arches on the mattress. She screams again, trembling, and helpless. Her small body is cradled into itself.

"Carter!" I hear Jase call out to me, the door to the cell still open. I can hear him running down the hall.

Now that the cell is open, anyone and everyone in here can hear her screams.

My gun lowers slowly as Jase enters the room behind me. His breathing is ragged as he closes the distance and stands next to me. Our shadows tower over her small frame, lying destitute in the bed. She doesn't stop crying out, and although she doesn't sob, the sounds are there.

She's captive to her dreams.

"Night terror," Jase says with a heavy breath. The metal of his gun rubs against his jeans as he slips it back into place and then looks at me. "I thought someone got in here." Tiredness is etched onto his face, but also the raw look of fear. He takes a moment to compose himself before starting to tell me, "I thought…"

As he starts to speak, she screams out again and the sharpness of the pain sends spikes over my skin that scrape their way down my body.

It's a desperate cry that sounds foreign to my ears, although I'm so used to hearing something similar. Pleas for mercy, which I never show.

"What do you want to do about it?" Jase asks me. He's still catching his breath, just like I am. I can feel him staring at me, wanting to know what to do next. I can't tear my eyes from her as she curls on her side.

Jase turns to the door as the sounds of someone else coming down the hall makes their presence known.

"I'll put her on the mattress," I tell him absently. "Take care of whoever that is and shut the door behind you," I order him, and my words come out flat. I try to keep the emotion away, but a sense of despair is evident. This wasn't a part of my plans. My fingers dip into my pocket, fingering the clicker that will open the door to the cell while I'm on the inside.

"You think they did something to her? Romano? Or maybe it's what she thinks is coming?" Jase asks and finally I turn to look at him.

"How the fuck would I know?" My words come out harsh. The anger at him suggesting her terror is caused by thoughts of what I'll do to her is unexpected and more than that, unwanted. Of all the things I expected from her, I didn't anticipate this.

It cuts me in a way I can't explain. I want to consume her every waking thought. I want her to live and breathe for me and my desires. And maybe this is the cost of it all. That I can have her during her days, but her nights will destroy her.

"Just a nightmare then," Jase says as if it's a casual observation. The whimpers still slipping through her parted lips are accompanied with a strangled sound of pain.

"You aren't supposed to wake them, you know?" Jase breathes out. "When they have night terrors, you're not supposed to wake them up."

The light from the door is blocked and the shadow of someone else covers Aria's slender neck and bared shoulders. I don't turn to look, but I don't have to. It's Declan, asking what's wrong. He knew she was here, but he doesn't want any part of this.

"It's fine," Jase tells him and then continues, "I don't think you can do anything really."

"Just go," I tell them both and stand as still as I can as they leave the room, taking with them the light from the hall as the door shuts. The creak of the steel is met with a thud and then the click of the lock. It takes a moment for my eyes to adjust. Another moment of her small cries and then a scream. A terrified scream.

"What did I do that earned me this?" I question her although I know she can't hear. I haven't touched her; we haven't even started. I almost touch the cuts on her wrists, but I pull back. I'll give her ointment and bandages in the morning. She'll have to do it herself until she earns my touch.

"Please don't," she begs in her sleep. Her words are whispered so softly, and I wonder if they came out that way in her dream. "Please," she begs.

"You don't know what you're asking, songbird," I tell her softly and consider my own sanity in this moment. "You never had a choice. The moment your father left me alive, your fate was sealed," I confess to her. Something I've never said aloud to anyone.

He should have killed me. It's Nicholas Talvery's fault I'm allowed to live another day.

His fault... and someone else's. The moment the thought comes to me, I see her tremble. Beautifully weak on the cold, unforgiving ground, the sleep taking more and more of her as her words become quieter.

She worries her bottom lip between her teeth, and it's the only part of her that moves. "*Please.*" Her lips mouth the word.

Kneeling before her, I'm slow and deliberate as I pick her up. Conscious of where my gun is tucked away in case she's playing me. She's light and fits easily into my arms. I thought she may fight me. That she'd react in fear to my touch. But instead, she molds her body to me and her slender fingers grip onto my shirt. Holding me tighter to her.

Her lips brush against the crook of my neck as I carry her the few feet to the mattress. Her pleas are still whispered, and the gentle warmth of her breath sends a tingle down my spine. I barely contain a groan of desire as I move her to the mattress. She clings to me still, holding tightly and begging me. This time she begs me not to leave her.

"Don't go. Stay with me... please," I barely hear her words. Her face is still pained, but there's gentleness in her cries as I shift her onto the mattress.

Her hand fits in mine as I pull her fingers from me and place them on her chest. Her chest rises and falls as she calms herself, slowly drifting to a different place.

Time passes quickly. Too quickly as I sit on the mattress, making it dip with my weight and staring down at her. Her heavy sighs emphasize her breasts, the bit of lace from her black bra peeking from her shirt. It almost tempts me as much as the dip of her waist.

My gaze caresses each curve of her body as I remember the first time I heard her name.

The day my life changed forever.

Her bed groans in protest as Aria turns in her sleep, settling into the mattress and my body stiffens. I shouldn't be here right now. That's not how I gain the control I want. I can't breathe until she's still and her own breathing evens out. But as I move to stand, shifting my weight ever so slightly, the mattress slumps and her hand falls, her soft fingers brushing mine, the tips touching.

My hand stays still beneath hers, but it begs me to explore. To thread my fingers between hers. Closing my eyes and inhaling deeply, I remind myself that there is time.

Time will change everything.

My eyes open at the reminder. Just like that day did years ago.

The day my father dropped me off at the corner of West and Eighth by the liquor store to sell that last bit of his pain pills. I was more approachable, according to him and we needed to pay the bills. It didn't matter what I said or how much I didn't want to do it. I was the oldest of five, my mother was dead, and I had nothing left in me. Nothing but pain.

My father dropped me off on Talvery's territory unknowingly. And it wasn't long before I learned what it meant to sell drugs on his ground.

I was only a child before that day.

But one day changes everything.

CHAPTER 8

WAKING UP WITH MY HEART BEATING OUT OF MY CHEST, THE HOPE THAT IT was all a nightmare crumbles into dust when all I can see is cement and cinder block walls.

I have to close my eyes and cover my face to keep from losing it. "This can't be happening." The trembling words leave my lips unbidden. Wrapping my arms around my knees, I try to tell myself that it's all a dream. I rock back and forth, and as I do, the sounds of the mattress creaking beneath me and the feel of my heels digging into the comforter makes my body freeze.

I try to remember last night, and I know full well I slept on the ground only a few feet away. I know I did.

My hands fly over my body. As if they could check to see if I was touched.

I feel the sharp edges of a scratchy throat but swallow thickly, trying to suppress the terror of what he could have done to me.

I must have crept into the bed and not remember it. I know I haven't been touched. I would know, wouldn't I? "I would," I say the words aloud as if I was speaking to someone else. Maybe I just needed the reassurance. I don't remember a thing after falling asleep. I wish I could have just stayed awake.

The whispered words echo in the hollow room as I glance up at the door. And then to the camera as it moves. Carter Cross, I almost speak his name aloud. I've heard his name before, always spoken with anger. I know he's one of a number of brothers and the head of a drug cartel. That's where the information ends. My father never liked me knowing anything and the only bits I learned were slivers of the truth from Nikolai. And he only told me what I needed to know. They said it was to protect me, but I would give anything to know what I'm up against.

I'd give anything to know what Cross is capable of.

Is he just going to leave me here to die? My throat pains in a way I didn't think was possible.

"Let me out," my raspy voice begs and the words themselves are like knives raking up my throat. I haven't eaten or had a drink of water since I've been here, and I don't even know how long that's been.

I stand a little too quickly, and nearly fall as I try to make my way to the door. I'm dizzy, lightheaded, and I think I may throw up.

Still, I head straight for the door, pulling at the doorknob and desperately trying to open it. My fist slams against it, over and over.

There's no use, stupid girl.

Again, I slam my fist and scream out, "Let me go!" but I'm only met with an unmovable door in an empty room, with no way out and no idea of what will happen to me.

The pain from the next slam of my fist makes me wince and cradle my hand to my chest. My back presses against the door as I fall down slowly onto my ass, resting my head against the door.

So many slow moments pass. Moments where I just try to breathe. Moments where my fingers brush along the cuts at my wrists. Moments where I stand and stretch and pretend like it's not odd to stretch when you're caged like an animal. What's the point if there's no escape?

It takes me longer than it should to see the foam tray with a grilled cheese sandwich and the cup of water next to it.

And a bucket of water with a sponge behind it. I spent so much time staring at the door, I didn't see it.

He came in here.

He was here.

My chest heaves and again my fingers travel to my thighs. He didn't. I would know. I can barely contain the fear of knowing he came in here while I slept. It's hard to swallow and I stay far away from the tray of food.

Time slips by again. And then more time. There is no change in my predicament, save my sanity.

Although my stomach grumbles and the delicious scents of butter and cheese are all I can smell, I leave the tray where it sits.

I don't eat, and I don't undress to bathe myself. Not with him watching. The anger boils and rises to such an extreme that I almost slam the bucket across the room, straight at the camera.

I'm not his pet or his test subject. He can take that foam tray and go fuck himself with it. At least that's what I think when I first move closer to see it; the thought even gives me joy. Hours pass and then more. How much time, I don't know. There's nothing in this room and loneliness and boredom are only two of the emotions I'm not sure I'll be able to handle if this is how my new life will proceed.

My mind starts playing tricks on me and I find myself etching small things into the cinder blocks with a button on my shirt. The shirt's already ripped so it doesn't matter. The top two buttons have been pulled off, the first one long lost and the second now a writing tool. A small and poor one, but there's nothing else to do but pace and let my mind wander.

And that leads me to awful places.

I'm busy carving a pattern, a useless, meaningless pattern of birds and vines into a block that's not even deep enough to be seen clearly when the door opens behind me.

My heart lurches and I swing my body around so violently that the back of my head collides with the wall, the button slips from my hand and the sound of it pinging to a stop on the ground fills the room.

The flood of light is lost quickly as Cross steps inside my cell and closes the door behind him. His figure is like a shadow of darkness as he walks toward me.

"What do you want?" I ask instinctually, barely able to breathe, let alone swallow the pathetic words before I can speak them. I'm glad I didn't eat because if I had I would have lost it all in this moment. Panic rages inside of me.

He's quiet as he takes one step forward and then another. He only takes his eyes from me once, and that's to look at the chair in the corner of the room.

"My father will come for me," I tell him as he walks toward the chair and positions it so he can sit and face me. "He's going to kill you," I add, and my words are strangled, but audible.

All I'm rewarded with is a soft smile on his lips. The stubble on his jaw is more noticeable and his eyes seem darker, but maybe it's just the light. Everything else about him is more foreboding than I remember. His height and broad shoulders, the lean build of his body with the rippled accents of his muscles. God made him to do deadly, sinful things. One look and that's obvious.

As if reading my mind, he grins at me, forcing me to take a step back, which only widens the grin to a charming and perfect smile. I feel like I'm caught in a cage. A little mouse to a lion. And he's only toying with me.

"You're sick," I spit at him, clenching my hands into fists.

"I'm well aware of that little fact, Aria. Tell me, what else do you know about me?" His voice is smooth velvet, and it echoes in a deep way from wall to wall in the room. The kind of echo you feel deep in your gut, one that haunts you so much later in the night.

"I know my father will gut you," I answer him with sickening contempt.

"He isn't going to do anything. He doesn't even know I'm the one who has you." His head tilts slightly as he examines my every reaction.

"Yes, he does," I breathe as if it will be true if only I say it is. His look turns to pity, but only for a moment. It passes so quickly I wonder if I even saw it, or maybe it was only the dim light in the room playing tricks on me.

"He doesn't and even if he did, he's useless." Menace lingers on the heels of his words, falling hard and crashing to the ground around me.

He adds, "He couldn't even defend your mother's honor."

"Fuck you," I dare to sneer at him. Anger rises quickly inside of me and my breathing quickens.

"You fight now, but you'll submit later," Cross says easily, completely unaffected by my words.

"Submit?" the fear is evident in my voice.

"You'll do as I say. Every command. Kneel at my feet, undress, lie in my bed… Spread your legs for me." The depth of conviction in his voice is frightening.

"I'll die before I submit to you." My throat dries and tightens. I can barely breathe as he stands.

He's not quick, not hurried in the least to stalk toward me. I can run. I know I can, but the room is small; there's nothing to hide behind and he's so tall, it wouldn't take much beyond a lunge for him to catch me.

My knees weaken, and I nearly fall to the ground, but I don't. I stay as tall as I can although I have to crane my neck to look Cross in the eyes. My heart pounds chaotically as if it's trying to escape. For every step he takes forward, I take one back until I've hit the wall.

"How did you sleep?" he asks me in an eerily calm voice.

"Like a baby," I say, and my answer is nothing but defiant. I surprise myself with the immediate answer. Fuck him. Fuck Carter Cross.

A crooked smile twitches onto his lips. "Do you always have nightmares?" he asks and the strength inside of me wavers. My gaze flickers from him to the floor.

"It seemed like a terrible dream," he adds, his eyes blazing with a threat.

I get the sense that he was here, that he knows I had a nightmare because he was here, not from the camera. As much as I'd like to hide the sickening sense of defeat from my expression, I can't. He sees my weakness, and I can't hide from him.

"Answer me." His command comes out tense and deep.

I almost tell him, no, but then decide on silence, pretending to ignore how the fear that's growing inside of me makes my limbs feel numb. I expect anger from him, but all I can see is the twinkle of humor in his eyes.

"You will give me everything that I want," Cross says and then reaches out to me. My eyes close tightly as his fingers brush the hair from my face. He tucks the lock behind my ear and I think about biting him, about fighting him when I remember the first time he touched me so comfortingly, only to then grip my throat and hold me like his prized possession.

With another step forward, he bathes me in darkness, blocking the light and forcing me to push myself against the wall and stare up at him with genuine fear I wish I could deny.

"You're going to love doing it too," he whispers in the small space, heating the air between us and my body betrays me at the thought.

It makes no sense at all. Save the scent of his presence. He smells like the woods. Inhaling the deep scent reminds me of the way my mother used to describe our eyes. Like the canopy of the forest after a long day of rain. Maybe I could blame it on instinct.

Or maybe I'm just meant to be the whore to a monster.

I don't admit my response to him. There's no way in hell I ever would.

"Let me go," I whimper the plea and hate myself for it. I can pretend to be strong. He can't see what's deep inside of me. I can pretend to be stronger than he knows.

His only response is to chuckle, a deep and rough masculine sound that rumbles his chest and the anger I feel from it overwhelms me.

I'm barely holding on to my composure. I know if I strike him, he'll respond, and I will lose. I'm not stupid. *This is what he wants.* The realization makes my eyes widen. He's playing with his shiny new toy.

"Just kill me." My muscles scream as I stiffen them, refusing to lash out. Although my body heats and adrenaline pumps faster at the thought of him doing it, I still tell him to just get it over with. I don't want to be played with. "I'll never give you anything."

"Now what would that accomplish for me, songbird?"

I don't want to cry and give him the satisfaction. I refuse to. My eyes are already burning from being so fucking weak. I won't be weak. I won't let him win.

Be smart. A million possibilities run through my head at what the smart choice would be in this moment, but the only situation I allow to rule my actions is to not give in. I'll wait. I'll survive day by day until my father comes. He will come. I know he will.

"I'll fight you until the day I die," I sneer at him with every ounce of conviction I can gather.

It only makes him smile. A wicked grin that sends a chill through my blood. "You'll find comfort in thinking that… for a little while." With a growing smile of triumph, he leaves me where I am. His shoes smack on the ground, and the sound grows quieter as he confidently strides to the door and turns the knob with ease.

How? He's simply walking away, and the door opens for him. I don't have time to consider anything. All I know at this moment is that the door is open. And whether or not he's there, I need to try to run. He opens the door just enough to get through. But I still run to it. I do my damnedest to make it to the door before it shuts and like the merciless prick he is, he leaves it open.

My bare heels bash against the cement as I sprint toward the light, but just as I make it, my hopes are so easily dashed. Just as the hope that I'll actually get out of here so easily burns into my chest, his tall broad frame fills the doorway, standing with a foreboding presence and taking a large step toward me.

A step so powerful and undeniably in control that I stagger backward, my foot scraping against the cement and throwing me off balance.

My ass hits the floor first and my head would have smacked against the concrete as well if Cross's hand wasn't wrapped firmly around my forearm. His fingers dig in and I let out a squeal of both surprise and pain.

"You're smarter than this," he hisses. The rage in his eyes swirls with darkness, but with it are golden flecks of intrigue and delight. "You won't leave this room until I say so."

I'm paralyzed by the certainty in his voice. The strength of his grip. The desire that drips from each of his words.

"You. Are. Mine. Aria." He says each word lower and lower until I can barely hear him over the pounding of my heart. The concept of being owned by this man is a deadly concoction that sends a ripple of both fear and desire straight to my core.

Without warning, he releases me, and I fall to the ground, still shaken but staring up at him. "I'm not an object to own. No one owns me!" I scream at him even though I don't believe my own words in this moment.

He merely smiles at me. As if it's all a joke to him.

"Let me go," I try to scream at him as if it's a demand, but the words are a pitiful plea even to my own ears.

Still, I try to stand, to get back up as he smiles and closes the door, leaving me right where he wants me.

I swear I hear him answer me before the steel door closes with finality. I would swear on my life I heard him say, "Never."

CHAPTER 9

Carter

DANIEL IS MY ONLY BROTHER WHO DOESN'T KNOCK. HE NEVER HAS. I know he isn't going to this time either. His steps are hurried, angered and I have to suppress a sigh of irritation. I'm fucking tired and I don't have time for his bullshit.

"This war between Talvery and the Romanos doesn't have anything to do with us."

Daniel's always had a knack for speaking as he enters the room, regardless of whether or not my gaze is down on my desk, focused on a spreadsheet of product and how much is selling. Having high demand is good, but some of this doesn't make sense. And it's only on the border of our territory that touches the Romanos' territory.

Pinching the bridge of my nose, I ignore him.

"Did you go to the club with Jase?" I ask Daniel as I continue down the order of supplies.

"Did you hear me?" Daniel questions me, kicking the office door shut and making his way across the office to sit in the chair opposite me.

"I did. You didn't tell me anything I don't already know." Shutting the laptop computer, I finally give him my attention and for a moment I'm caught off guard.

"You look like shit," I say, and I don't hide the surprise in my voice.

My brother's eyes spark with a hint of humor as he smirks at me and replies, "And you look like a fucking Ken doll. Drug dealer Barbie style."

A huff of a laugh escapes me as he runs his hand along the scruff on his jaw. "Addison isn't sleeping. She's having a hard time with this."

"With what?" I ask him, feeling a chill in my blood.

"With the shit that's going on. The war, not knowing who tried to take her or what they were planning."

"She doesn't need to know about a damn thing," I say beneath my breath with every bit of humor long gone. "You shouldn't have told her anything. We stay on lockdown. We wait for the Talverys and Romanos to trim their own numbers. If you have to tell her anything, that's all she should know."

Daniel's head tilts back slightly and he runs a hand down his face, his body slumped in the chair. "She's not allowed in the north wing and I don't want her leaving without me or someone else with her… and I'm not supposed to tell her anything?" he questions me, letting his chin drop and daring to look me in the eyes.

"The women should stay out of this." He fucking knows better.

"Says the man who started a war over a piece of ass."

"Careful." He cocks a brow at my response, but I stay firm.

Leaning forward, he puts both palms on the desk and asks quietly, like it's a secret, "What's going on with you?"

I steady my back against the leather chair, letting one hand fall to the armrest, my fingers tracing along the steel nail heads.

"I wish I knew," I tell him in a breath. "We have to move forward with this and there are some things that will benefit us, but it's a careful walk from here until the end."

Daniel nods his head, his eyes never leaving mine. "And when are we getting revenge on Marcus? The man who tried to take what's mine?"

"We don't know that it was Marcus who tried to take her."

"Who else would have done it?" Daniel asks but even as the last words slip out, his conviction wanes. Our enemies are surrounding us. The only saving grace is that they fear us, and they have other wars to fight.

"He has yet to answer any of our messages and no one's confirmed he had anything to do with it." Daniel's nostrils flare as he slams himself back into his seat, making the front legs of the chair nearly come off the floor while he looks past me and out the window.

"So, I'm supposed to do nothing and keep Addison in the dark?" Daniel asks with contempt. "I need to do *something*. I can't let him or whoever the fuck it was get away with it." His frustration is getting the better of him. And I understand. I do. But we have to be smart and know how best to move forward before we act.

"We don't know who did it. There will be nothing done until we do." My answer is absolute, with no room for negotiation, and the air tenses as Daniel considers me. A moment passes, and I can't breathe. My brothers are everything to me. All I have. And they've never questioned me. Not until this past week.

I'm losing my grip; I can feel it. And that's never a good thing.

Finally, he nods once and relaxes his posture, moving one ankle to rest on his knee.

"Can I ask you something else?" he asks, and I rest my elbow on the desk and then my chin in my hand, nodding as I do. He's going to ask me regardless.

"What are you doing with her?"

"It's personal." That short answer already reveals more than I've told anyone else, but Daniel shakes his head, a look of disappointment clearly written on his face.

"You aren't the brother I remember." He'll never know the pain that comment causes me.

"Tell me what you remember, Daniel? You never saw anything past Addison." I practically hiss her name.

"What the fuck does that mean?" His anger is evident, and his jaw tightens.

"You had her and I had no one." My voice cracks at the revelation. Time marches on as we stare at each other. He has no idea how she saved him. Having someone to love, even if it is from a distance can give you hope. And hope is everything.

"We had each other," he finally tells me. I know he's thinking about the same shit I am.

All the shit we went through. There were five of us, five brothers, but Daniel and I were the oldest and the two our father paid more attention to. If you can call what he did *attention*.

I let the anger and every other emotion fade, opening up the laptop to cue that this meeting is over. The truth slips by me unintentionally as I point out, "It's not the same."

"I just want to know you're not hurting her." He won't let it go. My grip tightens on the laptop as I try to remain calm.

"You have to trust me. Everything is about to change and if that girl had stayed where she was, she would have died." He waits for more. Proof, maybe. I don't know what he wants, but the less he knows, the better. "There's so much you don't know."

"You could tell me." There's a hint of sadness in his voice, or maybe I imagined it.

"Soon," I promise him. "Soon."

He doesn't say goodbye as he walks away. But as he makes it to the door, gripping the handle and swinging it open, I remember what he said about Addison. "Daniel. Give her this," I call out to him as I open the drawer. I have a few vials of S2L inside the small safe and toss one to him. He nods once and says something about Jase, but I don't hear, and he's already gone before I can question him.

Staring at the closed door, I think about how my brothers are the only constant I've had. Only them and no one else.

But admitting the truth out loud… I can't trust myself to do it.

The last time I admitted something of this weight, my world changed. I sparked the depraved monster inside of me to life and it changed everything.

The day Talvery left me to rot where he found me. I'll never forget the feeling as I heard my father's truck come to a stop. The old thing sputtered, and the sound was so comforting until his door shut and the anger in his voice was clear.

"What the fuck are you doing out in the open? Do you want someone to call the cops?" he yelled at me and when he tugged on my arm, the burns and cuts shot a horrible pain through my arm that made me scream in the dark alley. Bloodied and bruised, my father still tossed me around like I was nothing.

Couldn't he see what they'd done to me? I could hardly open my eyes.

"We'll get whoever did this, but come the fuck on before someone sees," he hissed between his teeth.

"They wanted to know who I worked for," I barely spoke as I hobbled to the car. Every bit of me hurt just to breathe. I slumped into the seat as he rounded the truck. And I know they saw. They had to have been watching me. Waiting to see who would come.

Country music played out as my father shut his door and took off down the street toward the dirt roads. I wanted to roll down my window so badly. I remember thinking I was dying, so I wanted to feel the wind on my face one last time. I'd coughed up so much blood, there was no way I'd be okay. My father ignored me as I asked him to do it, and instead, he turned down the music so only the sounds of the rumbling truck and his questions could be heard.

"Who's 'they?'" my father asked as he raced over a speed bump and my body jolted forward. I cried out like a bitch and he screamed the question again at me. It was fear in his voice though, not anger.

I know it now. Fear is what dictated his actions. Not strength like the man who'd done this to me.

"Talvery," I answered in a single painful breath. As I said his name, I remembered the look of Nicholas Talvery's freshly cleaned face only an inch from mine. I would never forget the way he looked at me like I was nothing and how much joy it brought him to know he could do whatever he wanted with me.

"What did you tell him?" he asked, and I looked at my father. I made sure to really look at him as I told him he was safe.

"I said I was just selling my dead mother's cancer meds. I said I was no one. And they believed me."

My heart has never hurt as much as it did at that moment when my father nodded his head and seemed to calm down. He was good at taking care of himself. He was good at living in fear.

That was the last day he looked at me as if I was a pawn in his game. My wounds were still fresh when I started hitting him back. And I never stopped. I wouldn't do the stupid shit he wanted me to. I would make money, a fuckton of it. But I never set foot on Talvery's turf again. I wasn't a dumb fuck like my father. And the next time he pushed me into the truck and screamed in my face so loud it shook my veins and the spittle hit my skin, I let my anger come forward, slamming my fist into his jaw.

I let the fear rule me in that moment. But it's the fear I saw in my father's eyes that defined the change between us.

Each time I went out, leading a life I didn't choose, I thought it would be my last. I wanted to die, and it wasn't the first time in my life that I wished for sweet death to end it all.

But without fear of death, I learned what power really was.

And none of my brothers understand that.

Not a single fucking one of them.

CHAPTER 10

Aria

HIS EYES WON'T LEAVE MINE.
He won't leave the room.
He won't give me any space.

I don't know how many days I've been here, but I do know that today is different by the look in Cross's eyes.

It's hard to count the days. My eyes flicker to the carving of stripes on the wall just beyond Carter Cross's never-changing stern expression. Sitting on the metal chair a few feet from me puts him at the perfect height to block the etched stripes. One for each of the days I've been here. But I stopped a while ago.

My sleep is fucked and there aren't any windows in the room. I've noticed that when I lie down and curl up to sleep, the lights go off. Which means two things, as far as I can tell.

He wants me to sleep. And he doesn't want me to know how much time has passed. It could be midnight a week from when I was taken. Or it could be noon with even more days between now and my last day of freedom.

There are four stripes on the wall. One scrawled after each time I slept. But on the fifth day, I slept on and off with terrors of my childhood that woke me up constantly.

The first two days I got three meals, always delivered the same way. A small slot in the door opened, the food was shoved inside on a small foam tray and then the slot quickly shut with a deafening slam. I waited for hours by it on the third day, praying I could catch it, snatch the hand… I don't know what. All I knew was that on the other side was freedom. But I quickly found that the slot only opened when I was in the corner of the room farthest from the door. Otherwise, no food would come.

I can barely eat as it is, but hunger won a few times. And instantly, I slept afterward. I don't know if he drugged me or not, but the fear of sleeping is at war with the need to eat.

Either way, the food I'm given doesn't aid me in knowing what time of day it is. There doesn't seem to be a rhyme or reason as to what's on the tray.

There haven't been any breakfast foods at all. The last thing I ate was a biscuit and a chunk of ham. It was glazed with honey and my stomach was grateful. I devoured every scrap and then immediately regretted not eating whatever it was he'd given me before. If I don't eat what's given, he simply takes it away when I sleep. And somehow he knows when

I'm faking sleep. I tried that, too. I don't know how many times I laid in the darkness waiting for him to open the door, only to fool myself into sleeping and waking to the tray being gone.

So much wasted time.

Maybe losing the time is the first sign of victory for him.

But I want it back.

"What day is it?" I ask him and it's the first thing I've said in the time he's been in here.

He comes in every so often, merely watching me. Scooting his chair closer and waiting for something. I don't know what.

"It's Sunday."

Sunday… It was Thursday when I left to go to the bar. I know it was Thursday. "So, that means it's only been three days?" I ask him although inwardly my gut churns. It's not possible.

A devilish smile plays across his face.

"You slept a lot, songbird. It's been ten days."

His words steal the bit of courage from me and I turn to face the door rather than him, pulling my legs into my chest and sucking in a deep, calming breath. Ten days of screaming and crying in this room. Of not knowing when help is coming, or if it ever will. Of barely eating and only bathing from a bucket of water while hiding under my dirty clothes.

"If you would only kneel for me when I come in, I would give you so much more than this."

"Why are you doing this to me?" My question is a whispered breath. No tears come from my dry eyes and the pain in my chest is dull. There's only so much a person can take before they break. I don't need sleep or food even. I need answers.

"You ask that often," is his only response, as he straightens himself in the chair. Squaring his shoulders toward me and making the pressed dress shirt stretch tight across his shoulders.

His handsome features look like nothing but sin as he stares at me. I have to rip my eyes away from him. I can't look at him. He's a monster and that's the only thing I need to know about Carter Cross. A beautiful monster who enjoys depriving me and watching me fade into nothing.

"How about we play a game?" he asks me, and a chaotic laugh erupts from my lips.

"Come now, I promise you'll enjoy it," he says, and his voice is a promising caress.

"And what's the game, Cross?" I say his name out loud, staring defiantly into his eyes. I imagined his aggravation, maybe even anger at my response, but instead, he only grins at me. A crooked grin on a charming face. I wish I could smack it off.

"An answer for an answer," he says and that's when it hits me.

"You think I know a thing about my father's business? You're wasting your time," I say but my voice betrays me as I speak. It cracks on my last words.

So, this is his plan? Steal me, lock me in a room with nothing for days until I'm desperate for change so he can get information from me? I know it's merely because I'm a woman. That's why they haven't tortured me. But it will come eventually, and I have nothing to give them.

My eyes burn with the need to cry, but I don't let it happen. "I swear to you," I barely get out and then stare into Cross's dark eyes, willing him to believe me, "I don't know anything."

"I know you don't." It takes a moment for me to register what he's said.

"Is this a trick?" I ask him, feeling as if I must be going crazy. The hope in my chest is fluttering so strongly. "I don't want to die," I whisper the confession.

"I'm not going to kill you." He answers simply, devoid of emotion, giving me nothing to hold on to other than the matter-of-fact words. "The Romanos would have killed you. You would have died or been captured and given a much crueler fate if I hadn't taken you first." I'm silent as I listen to him talk about me as if I'm merely a pawn to sacrifice. "Your best chance at surviving what's to come is with me."

Tears threaten to leak down my cheeks at the thought of men infiltrating my father's estate. At Nikolai being shot as he sits at the kitchen table where he always sits on the early weekend mornings. At my father being killed in the same room where my mother's life ended.

"Do you want to play the game?"

"I've never done well with games," I answer breathily, watching every inch of his expression for a hint at what's to come.

"The blanket is yours for playing," he says and nods toward a pile of fabric he'd tossed at my feet when he came in. And inwardly, I'm grateful. "Why don't you eat?" he asks me, and I know the game has started. An answer for an answer and he holds the first question.

Staring down at myself, I answer him with half honesty. "I'm not hungry." Ten days… I try to remember how many times I've eaten. Maybe six meals. At the realization, my stomach roils.

A moment passes before he shifts in the chair, leaning back but keeping his hands on his thighs. "If you lie, then I can lie," he says and the way he says the word "lie" forces me to stare into his eyes. It's like the devil himself discussing deceit. "That's the way this game works."

"I don't trust that you aren't going to drug me or poison me. Or something." The truth so easily pours from my lips.

My eyes drop to the ground at the reminder of all the horrific ideas that have flitted through my head since I've been here.

"It's only food and you need to eat." Again, there's no emotion, only a statement of fact. I watch him intently as he leans forward, resting his elbows on his knees and clasping his hands in front of him. "Your turn."

"What are you going to do with me?" I ask him without thinking twice.

"Feed you and keep you in here with nothing but what you have until you submit to me." He readjusts in the chair and adds, "You're a social creature and lonely. I can see how lonely you are." As he speaks to me, my gaze wanders and the hollow ache in my chest rises.

"I'm used to being lonely."

"I hear your prayers in the dark, songbird. I hear your wishes for someone to save you. Your father. Nikolai… Who is Nikolai?"

"A friend," I answer him, feeling the pain and agony sweep over my body. And feeling like a liar. The word friend sounds false even to my own ears, but it's been so long since Nikolai was anything else. And a friend is what he needed to be. Nothing more. Or else my father would have found out.

"Wrong answer. He is no one anymore. They're all gone, and no one is coming to save you."

"Gone?" The word comes out like a question, but the monster in front of me doesn't answer. My eyes close as I inhale deeply, thinking he's lying. They're coming. They'll come for me.

"You're bored, alone, and starving yourself into nothing. You will submit to me, or you will stay like this forever."

My lips kick up into a small smile I can't contain, and I don't know why. I must be going crazy.

"You think that's funny?" A hint of anger greets his words and it only makes my smile grow, but it's accompanied with tears leaking from the corner of my eyes. And I don't even know when I started crying.

Shaking my head, I brush away the tears from just under my eyes. "It's not funny, no. And now it's your turn." He's going to keep me here like this? He could keep me here forever.

Even as I think the statement, the overwhelming loneliness consumes me. I have nothing and this prison is eating my sanity alive. Hours pass where I simply stare at the wall, praying it will offer me something different than the day before.

He watches me as I sway from side to side slightly.

"What does submit mean?" I talk over him just as he starts to speak. My words are harsher than I thought they'd be and he cocks his brow, not answering me and then asks his question.

Rules of the game, I suppose.

"What is your favorite food?"

Dizziness overwhelms me for a moment and I rest my head against the wall. He's going to win this game. And all the others. He's cheating and I'm deteriorating.

"Bacon, I guess. Everyone loves bacon," I answer halfheartedly, partly because I'm tired of this game already and partly because I need a little humor in this situation. "There's this sandwich from the corner store by my house. My mother used to take me there." I stare at the ceiling while I talk, not really to him, but just to talk and think about something other than this. Although it's nice to have someone around. I feel an empty hollowness inside of me. I'd rather that than the sickening feeling of defeat.

Licking my lower lip, I continue. "She took me there every weekend. Coffee and pastries for her, but they had this sandwich I loved, and they still have it. It's turkey and bacon with ranch dressing on a pretzel roll." My head lolls to the side and I glance at Cross, whose usual stern expression has been replaced by a look of curiosity. "I think that may be my favorite."

The memory of my mother makes me smile and I almost tell him more. I almost tell him about the day she died and how we went there first. But she didn't get her usual pastries or coffee, and we didn't stay long. I was so upset that she didn't get me my sandwich, but she promised we'd get it tomorrow.

If I hadn't been so young and foolish, I would have known what was happening. How my mother was running from someone she'd spotted. How she ran home for protection, only to find the monster was already there.

God, I miss her. I miss anyone and everyone. I hadn't realized how lonely I'd become.

"Would you like to go home when this is over?" Cross's question distracts me from the thoughts of the past.

"When it's over?" I ask for clarification and I only receive a nod from him.

A deal with the devil. It's all I can think. The war doesn't matter, even if that's what he's hinting at. He'll keep me however long he wants, regardless of what he tells me now.

"You already know the answer to that." They're the only words I give him. It's my turn once more, so I ask him again, "What do I have to do to leave?"

"There is no leaving unless I want you to leave."

"Then why I am here?" The desperation is evident.

"I've already told you. I want you to submit to me. To desire my touch and earn it by kneeling and waiting to obey me. To be mine, in every way."

"You know that would never happen," I say absently. "I'll stay in this room forever or wait for something else to happen. I have nothing but time."

"I'm going to make a change to your routine," Cross says as if it's a threat.

Again, my head falls to the side to look at him, my energy waning. "Is that so?" I ask him, and he quirks a devious grin.

"You'll only eat when I feed you. Bite by bite." His eyes flicker with a heat that should scare me, but it does other things to me that I choose to ignore. "You should have eaten before, songbird. Your defiance is only hurting you."

The thought of him feeding me is something that will haunt me for hours once he's gone, I already know it. It's not just the loneliness that attracts me to Cross. I felt it the moment I saw him.

"I wasn't going to eat anyway," I tell him in a single breath rather than allowing my imagination to get the best of me. I've heard death by starvation is a horrible way to die and I know I'll have to figure out another way. I know I'll cave, just like I already have. As if reading my mind or maybe knowing better, Cross smirks at me, but it's different from the previous ones. There's something almost melancholy about this one.

"You'll eat," he tells me and then stands up without another word. As he turns the doorknob, I close my eyes knowing the bright light is coming. Even with my eyes closed, I can see it. And then it's gone, and once again I'm alone and trapped in the room.

I should feel a touch of ease, knowing he's given me some information I can hold on to. But all I can think about is my mother and the last day I saw her.

She wanted to leave and run away. She begged me to understand. And I cried when she told me, "*Ria, please.*"

I'll never forget the wretched way my name fell from her lips that day. The fatal flaw of any mother is how much her love for her children will blind her. It's my fault. Fresh tears leak down my face and I don't even bother wiping them away as I crawl to the mattress.

It takes a bit longer than usual for him to do it, but with the blanket wrapped tightly around me, the lights in the room go off. Loneliness is my only companion unless I give in to the memories. And I hadn't realized how harmful they can be. My own past is becoming my enemy.

I find myself filled with nothing but regret as sleep takes over.

If only I could go back and not fight her.

If only I could go back and tell her, we can't go home.

CHAPTER 11

It's different when I'm in the cell with her. When there's nothing but an isolated war between the two of us. I know she'll break, and she'll love it when she does.

When I'm in there with her, staring her down and watching every small, calculated movement from her, all I feel is the need to bring her to that edge and watch her fall.

I can picture her beautiful hair a tangled mess as I fist it in my hand, taking my pleasure from her even if she'd give it freely. She'll be on her knees, desiring the same things that I do.

It consumes me when the four walls of the cell surround me, but the moment the steel door closes behind me with a finality that another day has passed where I don't have control of her, the desire changes to desperation.

She *has* to submit. To kneel when I walk into her cell and to wait eagerly for my command.

And soon.

I have other plans and I want her to be a part of them. She needs to give in. It starts with a simple kneel.

I'm still reeling from seeing her sweet defiance when the door shuts tight. Slipping the painting back into place, I get a glimpse of my brother as he walks toward me in the hall.

"You're waiting for me?" I ask him, and he matches my pace as we head toward my office.

"I think I know why it's hitting heavier on the edge of the south side, closer to the Romanos." He doesn't waste a second to start talking business.

"The supply?" I ask him for clarification. The drug market is predictable. That's the best part about an addiction. It's steady, rampant, and easily maintained. When demand increases in only one area, there's a reason for it. And I need to know why this shift is so unexpected.

"Romanos have their hands on it. They have to be producing it by the amount they're selling." My blood chills in response to Jase's revelation. My jaw tenses as we make our way down the stairs. Each step only emphasizes the hollow pounding in my ears.

He wanted an ally.

He wanted to do business together.

He's nothing but a liar, a thief, and a spineless prick.

But none of that is news to me.

"He's selling S2L?" I ask him. "Are you sure?" The drug is ours. Ours alone. It was only a matter of time before everyone else wanted it, but instead of getting the details, Romano stole it. The stupid fuck.

"I'm positive," Jase answers me and I imagine Romano's ugly snarl of a smile as I punch his teeth in. I can practically feel the way the tight skin of my knuckles would split as his teeth broke under them. "I got a sample from their streets, took it back and it's definitely our mix. A heavier version than what we got off Malcolm."

"Do you think Romano knows why the pharmacy pulled it and the side effects?" I ask Jase as I push my office door open.

We acquired a banned drug, manipulated it, and just started selling S2L, street name Sweet Lullaby. It was designed to help with anxiety and insomnia. It can aid in weaning off an addiction to harder drugs. But S2L is the most addictive because of the way it calms you, assures you and your entire being that everything is just as it should be and lull you into a deep sleep. Thus, the name, Sweet Lullaby. The undesired side effects were too great to risk… for them. Not for us.

"I think they know exactly what it is," he says with a touch of anger, "seeing as how they fucked with the formula." The door practically slams shut from the weight of his push. He doesn't look me in the eyes until he's seated in the chair opposite mine. It's only when he says the next sentence that I finally fall into mine. "They made it more potent. It's practically lethal with the way it numbs the senses, slowing the heart and forcing the body into a deep sleep."

My thumb brushes against my jawline as I consider what Romano is up to. "He stole our drug; he's selling a version that's deadly on his territory…" I think out loud, not bothering to hide my string of thoughts from Jase.

Jase is the one who got a hold of the drug from an asshole who owed us a debt but had secrets within the industry. Malcolm was useful enough that we let him live. For a little while.

"He's selling on his territory. Sweet Lullaby but the lethal version is going by ST, Sweet Tragedy. He must not have enough, or else we wouldn't see the increase in demand."

"The thing about demand is that those who are addicted are still living."

"Unless it's being used on someone else."

"So, he's selling it as a weapon? Not as a drug?" I have to admit the thought occurred to us as well, but until we have a preventative drug that renders the deadly version useless, I wouldn't dare to even hint at the possibility.

His fingers tap, tap, tap with a nervousness on the armrest. "The thing that doesn't fit though… What doesn't add up… is that there isn't a rise in the death toll. There's no sudden spike in murders or people dying in their sleep."

"They're either buying and not using, or they're selling it elsewhere. Maybe overseas?"

"I think the Romanos aren't keeping up with the production of S2L, they have a small demand, but word got out that we're the suppliers. So, Romano decided to up the ante, make the potent version which got someone's attention. Someone who wants control of the market. Whoever it is, he's buying every drop he can of the potent version, and every bit of ours so he can make the change himself, concentrating it and making an untraceable weapon."

"How could Romano be so fucking stupid?" The words are pushed through my clenched teeth. We sold the drug as a relaxer, a way to ease pain and keep people from

ODing on the deadlier shit. It's the perfect way to make an addiction last. And Romano's greed had to fuck it up.

I'm silent as I consider Jase's theory.

"Whoever's gathering it is on his side, not ours. Someone who wants his territory, maybe?" he suggests, and I can only nod in response. Whoever it is isn't doing a good job of hiding their whereabouts and intentions. Unless of course, they wanted it to be known. My thumb brushes along my chin again as I consider every asshole I know who could want Romano's place. Maybe they wanted us to know.

"I want Mick's crew on the south side, tracking the information of every buyer and to find a connection. I want to know who's fucking with it and if they're selling anywhere else."

"It's expensive shit, this potent version. And whoever is buying in bulk has to be waiting to resell."

"Maybe they think Romano will lose the war, and they'll come in to a territory with a built-in high demand, already supplied with the drug?"

Jase nods at my prediction, clucking his tongue and still tapping his finger on the chair. "That's not a problem for us," he adds.

"You think they'd stop at the Romanos?" I question him and like the intelligent fucker he is, he shakes his head, the small grin ticking up his lips. Jase loves a challenge. He lives to snuff out those who think they can threaten what we've worked so fucking hard to build.

"So, we don't tell Romano?" he asks me.

"Not a word. He stole from us." I look him dead in the eye as I come to the conclusion with my brother.

"You still want to do the dinner next week?" he questions me.

Romano thinks it's a celebratory dinner.

Talvery is weak. It's almost a letdown at how easily everything is crumbling around him. There's already a crack within his own factions, or so says the word on the street. Half his crew is taking bribes from Romano. I'm reluctant to let my guard down. Looks from the outside can be deceiving. I know that all too well.

Nonetheless, Romano will come here to this celebratory dinner. And I'll have the utmost enthusiasm as his host and partner in celebrating the fall of his longtime rival. Long enough to lure him in at least.

"Yes." I can't stress my words enough as I stare at the box under the bookshelf on the right side of the room. "Next week he'll be here, at our table, in our home."

"It's not about the war or the drug though, is it?" Jase's question brings my gaze back to him. "It's about her?"

His intuition freezes my blood. I have to remind myself that he's my brother, that he would know because he's been so close for so long. I have to remind myself that there isn't a way another soul could even begin to guess the truth.

"Yes," I reply cautiously as our eyes lock and I wait for his reaction. Once again, I fall prey to the ticking of the clock as he carefully chooses his words. "She's part of it."

"We could give her money and let her run," he offers. And he assumes wrong.

"She'll run right back to her father, and you know it."

"Then let her," Jase says and shrugs as if it's no concern to us if she were to retreat back to her father.

"And have the Romanos and everyone else think we're so weak that we just let a girl walk away?"

"Since when did you start caring what they think?" he asks me, still feigning that this conversation is a casual discussion that means nothing.

"They need to *think* that I don't care what they think. But how they see us matters more than anything. For us to control what they do, we have to know what they think. We have to be able to manipulate it for us to know what they'll do next."

"You can say you grew tired of her." Jase continues to make suggestions and this time it spikes my anger. I've grown tired of him pushing me to let her go, to eliminate her from the equation. She's too valuable to me.

"Never," I answer in a single breath without thinking.

"Never?" Jase asks questioningly, only now dropping his guard, his grip tightening on the leather armrest and letting an inkling of anger show.

"I wanted her… before."

"Before Romano offered her?" Jase's interest is piqued.

I only nod in response, feeling the confession so close to coming to life.

"Why?" he asks me, and I don't answer him. I can't. Instead, I offer him a small truth. "He didn't offer her. I told him it would be her or no one," I say softly, to ensure the words will vanish by the time he can hear them.

"What are you going to do to her?" he asks me again. My brothers keep asking me that and it only pisses me off.

"She has to fear me… for a while." My thumb nervously runs along my bottom lip. "It won't always be like this."

"You need to give me more," he demands, and I quickly spit back, "I don't need to give you shit."

A beat passes and the rage slips into my blood. The memories and everything I've worked for, everything we've become turns to hate and ruin.

"This conversation is over," I tell him. He only smiles. A coy knowing smile, and nods. The tension evaporates and without another word, he leaves the office. Although I know he's left with far more than he gave.

As I watch him leave, the ticking of the clock won't stop. Tick tock. Tick tock. Tick tock. My gaze moves from the box to the laptop with a black screen staring back at me.

Deep breaths. In and out. Deep breaths bring me back to her.

When I flick the monitors back to life, to see what my little songbird is doing, she's already asleep.

It's been so long since these memories have haunted me, but they come back slowly as I turn off the lights in her cell.

Memories that made me. Memories she's a part of, even if she doesn't know.

The memory of the day I learned who Talvery was and what fear could really do to a person.

There comes a point when it doesn't matter what the last punch broke or how much blood you've lost. It's a point where you can't feel anything anymore.

Your vision is blurry, and you know death is so close that you pray for it. It's the only thing that will take it all away.

Nothing makes sense. Even as my head snaps back and more warmth bubbles from my mouth, the pain is nothing. And knowing the end is near, it provides a comfort. The chains holding me to the chair fade away and I can hardly feel them digging into my skin.

But even in all of that, she meant something. I knew it instantly. She had the strength to destroy the hope that it would all end soon.

Her small fists banged on the door that was so close but so far away.

Her voice called out and broke through the fog of reality.

I couldn't hear what she screamed, but it was something so urgent, her father put down the wrench. I remember the heavy metallic sound of it falling onto the floor mixing with her sweet feminine pleas for him to help her through the closed door.

I was so close to everything being over, and she saved me. Even if she doesn't remember it. She never even saw me.

It took years before I let myself think of her again. And of that day.

I almost had an out. I was so close to leaving this life a good soul. Maybe not pure, not perfect, but a better man than I am now and an innocent soul.

She's the reason I lived and turned into this.

I don't just want her at my mercy.

I want everything she has.

I'm not going to stop until I have her and her everything.

CHAPTER 12

Aria

I THINK IT'S BEEN TWO DAYS SINCE CROSS CHANGED THE RULES. IF I'M RIGHT, IT'S been almost two weeks since I've been here. And two full days of not eating anything. I refuse to eat from his fingers like a dog. I'm not his pet. The way he looks at me like he'd wish for nothing more than for me to kneel between his legs and accept each morsel is riddled with both desire for me and desire for power over me. The combination is heady, and it plays tricks with my mind. I'm addicted to the hunger in his eyes but I'm afraid of what's to come if I give in.

I don't want to submit and kneel in front of him. At least, that's what I keep telling myself. Each ache I have reminds myself of this. As the loneliness stretches and the boredom makes me wonder if I'm going crazy, I have to remind myself. It's always a reminder.

The thoughts make my breathing heavy and my stomach rumble. The sickening part of all of this is that I'm looking forward to him opening the door. I want him to come in tonight like he did last night and the night before. With a silver platter of temptation.

I'm starving and I know I have to give in. I know I will at some point. He's right. I will eat. I'm already praying for him to open the door, even as I curse him and clench my hands into fists, swearing I'll be strong enough to refuse him.

He's going to win. I can feel it.

I'm praying for him to come, so I can have something to eat. Whatever he brings, if he were to come right now, I'd accept. No matter how much I wish it weren't true. I would do anything to eat right now. To eat anything at all.

My eyes lift from the ground to the door as it creaks open. I don't lift my head and I stay on the dirty ground, stiff and unmoving.

I can feel his eyes on me, but I can't look at him. The only thing that holds my attention is the tray balanced in his right hand and held at his chest. I can't see what's on it yet, but I can smell it.

My eyes close slowly and I nearly groan from the sugary scents that flood my lungs. When I finally open my eyes, cued by the sound of him moving the chair across the floor and closer to me, I see it all. I see the tasty treats that will be responsible for my pathetic undoing.

The tray is full of the sweetest things. Berries and chunks of mango and fresh pineapple.

It's all brightly colored and arranged beautifully. Like I said, a silver platter of temptation.

"How's your hand?" Cross asks me and it's only then that I even acknowledge him.

"Fine." My short answer is rewarded with him pulling the tray closer into his lap. "I think it's bruised," I offer him in an attempt to give him what he wants.

"You were banging your fist on that door for over forty minutes." My teeth grit at his response.

"Well, you heard me at least," I say, although I can't deny that it hurts. I'm so fucking alone. And tired and sore and aching with pains. But so alone more than anything else.

"I did," is all he says.

There's a routine that comes with Carter Cross. He likes things to be done a certain way, maybe so that it can appear that he's predictable but I'd much sooner think it's so he can force my own behavior to be predictable for him.

In these sessions, the ones where food is offered, he attempts the semblance of a conversation before offering food. And today, I know I'll talk back. I know I'll do what he wants. I'm that desperate.

"You're dirty," he tells me with what seems like sincere sympathy. "You don't wash yourself like I'd hoped you would."

I bite my tongue at the perverted comments, but I can't hold it all in. "I'm not a dog to be bathed." I can't hide the anger. I should fake my tone like he does, but I choose not to. He'll feed me regardless. I hope. He only smiles at me in response and it nearly makes me back away from him. Not because of the way he's looking at me, but because of how my body reacts to the smile. How he seems to enjoy it when I don't hold back. It's dangerous. *He's* dangerous.

"You're tired."

"It's difficult to sleep on the floor." Even as I answer him, I can feel how heavy the bags are under my eyes.

"There's a mattress at least," he quips, and those piercing eyes stare deeper into me like he can see through the wall of defense. Just the way he looks at me makes me question everything.

Time evades me as I stare back at him, feeling those same walls crumble deep inside of me. I try to suppress the hate I have for him in this moment, just so I can get this over with and eat.

"You look weak, songbird."

"You keep calling me that," I bite back.

"I've never called you weak," he says, and his answer is just as stern as mine.

"I meant 'songbird.' You keep calling me songbird." My voice cracks. I don't want him to call me anything. Not my name, not a sweet nickname. It doesn't reflect how he truly sees me. It's meant to weaken me, make me soften. "Stop calling me that."

"No," he says in a hardened voice. "Now come here, songbird Come kneel in front of me and let me feed you."

This is the second part of his routine and the one where I've told him to go fuck himself over and over again. But today, I slowly move my body and get on my hands and knees. I swallow my pride and it hurts. It physically hurts. I didn't know pride was a spiked ball until I move one knee in front of the other. My body is hot with embarrassment and shame as I stop at his feet.

I can't open my eyes until his rough hand brushes against my jaw. I wish I didn't feel the need to lean into him. Loneliness consumes me every day. If I could pause this moment and pretend I'm somewhere else, with someone else, I'd lean into his strong touch. I'd allow myself to enjoy his warmth and comfort.

But as it is, I'm staring into the dark eyes of a man who's held me like this before. And then so quickly shown how easily he could hurt me.

Swallowing thickly, I wait for the third part. Only seconds until he tells me to open my mouth.

As if reading my mind, Cross lets his thumb brush along the seam of my lips. It's a gentle caress that ignites something primitive in me, heating my core and making my heart beat furiously inside my chest. My knees inch forward, obeying the command from my body to move closer to him.

Closer to the man who controls my freedom. Closer to the gentle touch.

"Open," he commands me, and I feel my lips part of their own accord.

My eyes stay closed until his hand moves away, and his warmth is replaced with the chill of the air in the cell.

My heart flickers with fear until I watch him pick up a chunk of strawberry and lift it to my lips. I'd be ashamed at how greedily I eat the small piece of fruit if only consuming it didn't make me feel as though I'm starved. The sweetness falls into a pit of hollow hunger pains. And again, my body moves closer to him.

He doesn't say anything or hint at anything other than his desire to keep feeding me. And I accept every piece with a hunger that only seems to intensify. My hands find their way to his knees, gripping him as I swallow the next piece he's offering me.

It takes me far too long to realize I'm touching him. His groan of approval is what cues my awareness, but as I try to pull away, he does the same to the fruit in his grasp.

"Stay." He gives me the simple command, and so I do. I cling to him for more.

The part that's truly shameful though is how much hearing him tell me to stay made me crave more of him. His hand on mine, watching him watch me.

A moment passes where I realize he knows my forbidden thoughts.

My greatest fear is that he'll voice them and bring them to life. I force my fingers to dig deeper into his leg and I open my lips wider, silently begging for more, so I can hide the temptation that grows hotter between us.

I think he's doing it slowly on purpose. Picking up the bits of sweet fruit and taking his time before he slips them between my lips.

"Open wider," he commands me and it's only because my stomach pains with the need to eat that I obey him, that's what I tell myself. I close my eyes, holding back every other thought.

"Look at me," he commands as I swallow the small morsel and his strong hand cups my chin, forcing my head up. The juice from his fingers wets the underside of my chin in his grasp. He's so close, his dark eyes swirling with an intensity that holds my gaze captive. "You're so strong," he tells me, and I hate him for it. "You don't believe me, but you are."

The rough pad of his thumb brushes against my bottom lip and I almost bite him, just to spite him. To prove to him that whatever he assumes I'm thinking is all in his head. I catch the broad smile growing on his face as I look back up at him.

He offers me another piece and I take it in my mouth. I have to wait for him to pull his fingers away, but he doesn't.

My gaze moves back to his and he lowers his lips to my neck, his fingers still in my mouth and the juice of the fruit tasting even sweeter. His short stubble brushes my collarbone and then he whispers in my ear, "See how strong? You'd love to bite me, but you know how to survive."

His hot breath tickles my neck and sends goosebumps down my body. Shamefully, my nipples harden and my back bows slightly. "Such a good girl, Aria," Cross says, and I pull away from him, leaving the fruit between his fingers and brushing my ass against the cement as I scoot backward, putting distance between us.

The fear is alive within me, but it's changed. I fear what I'm capable of and how much I'd enjoy it.

The vision of him pinning me down on the ground flashes before my eyes and cruelly, it only makes me hotter. I swallow thickly, feeling my cheeks heat with a blush.

Cross doesn't move from his chair. "You're all done?" he asks me. I can't look him in the eye. I don't even trust myself to speak. Maybe this is what it's truly like to be broken.

"Is it because you've finished, or because you're wet for me?" he asks me in a husky voice that only adds to my desire for him.

"Fuck you," I say beneath my breath, narrowing my eyes and letting my blunt nails dig into the cement.

Cross lets the trace of a smile play on his lips, but it doesn't reach his eyes as he stands up, towering over me. "I told you I wanted you, Aria. And I get everything I want. Just remember that."

CHAPTER 13

Carter

SHE HASN'T EATEN, SHE'S BARELY MOVED SINCE SHE GAVE IN LAST NIGHT. I'VE COME in twice since then and both times she's denied me even though in three days all she's eaten is a handful of fruit.

I can feel the tension between us. I know she's at war with it as much as I am. But she spends her nights screaming and barely sleeping. The little bit of progress during the day is erased and there's nothing I can do about it.

She's going to cave again and I can feel it on the horizon. I've never been so eager to come into this cell as I am today.

I have to hide my smile as she slinks from the mattress to the floor. She never stays on the mattress when I come in. At least, she hasn't yet.

My heart beats hard as I watch her expression fall.

There's no tray tonight. No offering for her.

It's easy to see her breathing pick up as she registers I'm here for something else.

I intentionally let the chair drag along the floor as I make my way to her.

"I don't have anything to say," she tells me as I sit down only a few feet away from her. Far enough so that she can crawl to me and kneel. The crawling part I'm not interested in. She decided to do that on her own, but I don't care how I get her on her knees in front of me. So long as she submits.

"That's interesting that you would start the conversation then, isn't it?" She doesn't respond. Her collarbone looks more prominent today than it ever has. I couldn't see it on the monitors, but three days of barely eating is starting to show and I don't like it. Starved is not how I want her.

I should feel remorse, not anger at the observation.

"Why make it harder on yourself?" I question her with a deep tone of disapproval.

And once again, she doesn't answer.

"You'll cave again. You can't help yourself. You realize that, don't you?" She's a smart girl. Anyone with any bit of intelligence knows that starvation is painful, and the instinct to survive will kick in over pride.

"Just let me go," she says weakly, brushing under her eyes and hiding the tears. So close to breaking. So, fucking close.

"I'm getting tired of hearing you make that request."

"Then both of us are tired," she says softly, picking at her dirty clothes. I would give her everything if only she'd obey me.

"You wanted me," I remind her, and she huffs a pathetic sound of disgust.

Her eyes narrow as she looks me in the eyes and tells me, "You aren't what I want."

"What did you want then?" I ask her, leaning forward in my seat so quickly that I startle her. I'm only inches away and so close I can feel the heat from her body. She turns away from me, looking toward nothingness on the blank wall.

"Answer me," I say and there's little patience in my voice. My body tenses as I move forward in my seat so I'm as close to her as I can be. I don't like what she does to me, but even more, I don't like that I don't know what to do with her. I don't want her like this. I need her to break now, her mind before her body.

She looks at me with a stare of contempt before barely speaking the words, "I don't know what I wanted."

"You wanted me to fuck you," I tell her in a voice intended to be seductive. I practically whisper. "I'd feed you, care for you, fuck you and put you to bed used and sated." She's silent as I move back to a relaxed position in the uncomfortable chair. "That's what you wanted."

"I just wanted my fucking notebook back!" she screams at me with a bite of anger I know must've hurt. Swallowing thickly, she looks away from me as her eyes turn glossy.

My heart pounds hard, just once, then stops for a moment as she wipes her eyes.

"You want a notebook?" I ask her, although I don't know what the fuck she's talking about.

Her chest rises and falls steadily as she looks at me. Each breath deepening the dip in her collarbone. "Tell me," I command her.

"My drawing pad," she murmurs softly, anger and contempt forgotten. "That's what led me to the bar where those assholes got me," she whispers with defeat. "I just wanted my drawing pad back."

"A specific one?" I ask as my brow raises slightly. It's not going to happen. I can get her a new one, but I'm not risking what's already been set in motion to find something she's left behind.

"Yes," she whispers and parts her lips to tell me something else, but I can't and won't hunt down any of her possessions.

"It's gone," I say flatly, cutting off her words.

I watch as she swallows and note the way the sadness returns to her eyes. "Any would do." Her eyes search my face warily as she sits back against the bed, making it dip with her weight. She's frail with a look of submission brimming close to the surface.

"A drawing pad. What else do you want?" My fingers itch to trace along her jaw and force her to look at me. To force her to make this easier on herself and both of us.

She peeks up at me through only slits, her dark lashes barely letting me see any of her eyes. But in the small bit she offers me, I see nothing but rage.

"You have something to say?"

"Fuck you," she spits.

I've never felt the urge to kiss her until now. In filthy clothes and all. It's quiet between us as I imagine gripping the nape of her neck and taking her lips with mine.

She'd bite me. I know she would because she thinks she should, and that only makes me harder.

"That mouth of yours. That's what's going to get you into trouble."

"As if I'm not in trouble already," she answers me through clenched teeth, lifting her chin at me.

"You will be if you don't obey me." Each word comes out heavy, making my chest clench with a tightness of what's to come. My breathing is shallow, and my blood burns a little hotter.

I can see her lips twitch with the need to speak, but she bites her tongue.

This is the version of Aria that I want. The raw anger of knowing and accepting that she's at my mercy.

"Tell me what you really think, Aria," I say softly although the words ring out loudly in my ears. My gaze is locked on hers. My blood rushing in my ears. All I can do is wait for her.

One beat. Two beats of my heart before she whispers in a cracked voice, "You're a monster."

"And why is that?"

"Because of what you want from me," she says quiety, but she doesn't break eye contact.

"What is it that I want from you?" I ask her as I grip the edge of the chair tighter.

"You want to fuck me." She doesn't hesitate to answer but the anger in her expression morphs to pain as she rips her gaze away from mine.

"Of course, I want to fuck you," I tell her in as calm a voice as I can manage. My gaze slips down to her curves and I have to force them back up to see her doe eyes back on mine as she scoots farther back on the bed. She's searching for comfort and safety, but all she's doing is making me want to pursue her.

I lean forward, resting my elbows on my knees. "The second I saw you, I wanted you." My confession comes out a whisper and the memory of her weeks after that night happened years ago flashes through my mind. I had to know the face of the angel who'd saved me. If only she had known then what she was doing, if only she'd known I wasn't worth saving. The hate and love I've had for her has warred for years within me.

Silence separates us for a moment. And then another.

"Just get it over with," she breathes the words but doesn't look up. The tone of defeat rings false.

"Is that because you want me too, but you don't have the courage to admit it?" I dare to challenge her and again that anger comes back full force.

"Fuck. You." She leans forward as she says each word, practically spitting them. And the rage and defiance only make my cock more eager to thrust deep inside of her.

"You will, little songbird." Lust pumps through my blood as she inches back on the bed yet again, her gaze fixed next to me as if she's watching my every move but doesn't want me to know it.

That only makes the hint of a smirk on my lips grow.

The chair scoots back as I stand and the sound of it scratching the floor frightens Aria. She sits up a little straighter, a little stiffer and watches me with wide eyes as I take two steps closer to her.

"You want to get it over with?" I ask her as I reach for my belt. I want her to see how hard I am for her. And teach her a lesson.

My belt slips through the loops of my pants, leaving the sound of leather brushing against the fabric to sing in the air. My blood is laced with adrenaline and lust as I watch her breathe heavier and faster.

The metal of the buckle clinks on the ground as it lands and then I unzip my pants. A flush travels up Aria's chest and into her cheeks.

"Come here," I give her the small command with the bit of breath left in my lungs as I grip my thick erection through my pants and she watches. I swear her lips part and her thighs clench as she watches.

Her wide eyes dart from my cock to my eyes.

"Come here," I tell her again when she doesn't move. I know she wants me. Maybe not like this, but I have to show her what power she has. Until she submits, all she has is power over me. "Get down on your knees in front of me," I add and palm myself again. "Aria." Her name comes out hard on my lips, but dripping with sin and desire as I add, "I fucking want you."

I don't miss the small gasp from her lips as she hesitates another second.

I watch every small change in her expression. From how her nails dig into the mattress, to how her body tenses and makes the bed creak as she inches forward as if she's going to listen to me. She swallows so loudly I can hear it as she slowly climbs off the bed. She stands on weak legs before dropping slowly in front of me, down onto her knees.

My pulse quickens but I don't know how. All the blood in my body feels like it's in my dick.

"If I leaned down and shoved my hand between your thighs," I ask her, holding back a groan from the thought, "how wet and hot would your cunt feel right now?"

Her eyes widen, and she leans back, but with the way she's seated, with her knees under her, she can't lean back far without being off balance.

"Do you know what it will feel like when I finally shove myself deep inside your tight little cunt?" I ask as my dick pulses with need and I have to stroke it once more.

She breathes out heavily, nearly violently and avoids my gaze.

"You're going to scream my name like your life depends on my mercy." I stroke myself again and again. Fuck, I'm so eager for her touch my dick is throbbing so hard it hurts. "I won't show you mercy, Aria, I'm going to fuck you like you're mine to ruin."

She whimpers and struggles to remain still in front of me. Her thighs clench as I kick the chair behind me, so I can crouch down in front of her.

Her hazel eyes are wide and filled with desire.

"I want to give you everything," I whisper as I lean forward, letting my lips trail along her jaw. A ripple of unease runs through me as I realize the truth in those words.

She shivers, and I watch her nails dig into her thighs. "You have to tell me what you want, and when I ask you how badly you want my cock, you better tell me the truth."

I pull away, letting my fingers trace down the right side of her face, and then lower, to her neck and collarbone. Then lower to her chest. "I want to see how you react when I pinch and bite these," I tell her as my fingers travel to the peaks of her breasts.

"Do you think you'll enjoy it?" I ask her. And for the first time, she admits a small truth, nodding her head once and then ripping her eyes from me.

Her breathing is chaotic, and I know she's ashamed.

"I desperately want to feel you cum on my cock," I admit to her, whispering in her ear since she still has her head turned. "Tell me what you want."

All I can hear is our tense breathing mix in the hot air between us.

"Tell me, songbird," I say, willing her to give in.

Time seems to stretch on forever.

"A drawing pad." Blinking away the haze in her eyes and still denying what she truly wants, she utters useless words.

And I leave her just like that, wanting and panting and flushed with need.

She'll learn to ask for what she wants. Or she'll stay here forever.

CHAPTER 14

Aria

I'VE NEVER FELT LIKE THIS BEFORE.

Like there's nothing left of me but a shell of a weak and pathetic person. I'm on the edge of loathing myself and the way my body begs me to give in to Cross.

But most of all, I pity myself and that's what's driving the hate.

My father isn't coming. Nikolai isn't coming.

I was worried that they were dead, but Carter told me yesterday that they're still alive and the war is only getting started. I don't know if he's lying to me or not. If he wanted to offer me hope so he could crush it. I don't know anything anymore and nothing gives me hope of getting out of here.

Even as the thought hits me, I crumple forward and bury my face in my grimy hands. They smell of dirt but as I struggle to breathe and maintain any sense of composure, I don't give a damn. No matter how many times I bathe myself with the warm water that waits for me when I wake up, I feel dirty. The kind of dirty that doesn't wash away.

I'm alone. A prisoner. And I don't see any way out of here. There's no white knight planning on barging in here. I'm not worth it. If I was, they would find me, they would come for me. They would save me and make Cross pay for keeping me here to starve and torment with thoughts of being his fuck toy.

Fate sent a dark knight after me instead. With dinged and scratched armor and a taste for something that I shouldn't crave. My face is too hot when I pull my hands away, calming my breath and leaning my head against the wall behind me.

Exhaustion has taken over and I know it's because I don't eat.

But I could, a little voice whispers in the crevices of my mind. The same dark corners where the memories of yesterday send a warmth through my body.

My teeth dig into my lip as I remember how his skin felt against mine. How everything felt. It was… everything.

Like electricity sparking through every nerve ending all at once, with a heat and fluidity that made me want to rock my body.

Yes, the dark knight is good at what he does. He's damn good at making me want to cave and give in to both his desires and mine. I lick my lower lip, wincing at the cracked skin as my back stiffens and I glare at the steel door that refuses to budge.

As if knowing I was thinking about him and what he could do to me, the door to this prison opens and my hardened expression shifts to one of worry, curiosity, and eagerness.

I hadn't realized how dark it was in the room until the bright light from just beyond the cracked door makes me wince. My tired eyes sting with the need to sleep.

I suck in a small breath, but I don't cover my eyes or leave them closed for long. Pressed against the wall, I wait with bated breath until my eyes adjust.

I expect to hear the door close, but it stays open.

And the man I thought was coming in? It's not him. It's not Carter.

Thump, thump. My heart slams hard in my chest as Jase takes a step inside. Still the door stays open and my eyes have to glance at what's beyond it.

A hallway and nothing discernable, but I know it's freedom. That barely ajar door leads to freedom.

"Now don't make me regret this." The deep voice seems to echo in the small room and I swallow thickly. It's only when my throat stings and I feel as if I could choke that I realize how dry my throat is.

"Jase?" I chance a word and it makes the man smile. I remember him from the night I was taken. That's what Carter called him. He put the rag to my mouth. He's one of them.

He gives me a sexy lopsided grin that should frighten me. But instead, his charming looks put me at ease. He must be younger than Carter. His eyes are softer. But I remember them all too well, for the wrong reasons.

"You remember me?" he asks me and takes a step forward, grabbing the chair that Carter uses. He's just as tall as Carter, but leaner and in only a white t-shirt and faded jeans, he looks less threatening.

But looks are deceiving.

My lips part to speak, but I can't get out a word. A million questions are running through my head.

Why are you here? Where's Carter?

Are you going to let me go?

I can only nod.

"You're looking a little on the rough side," he says and then his voice drifts off as he looks behind him. I follow his gaze to the open door, but quickly my sights are back on his and the chair in his hand that scratches along the concrete. Turning it backward, he sits on it. As if he's deliberately acting casual.

He is. This is a setup for something. In my head, my words are strong and demanding, but when forced out they sound weak and desperate.

"What do you want?" I swallow, and this time the scratchy sensation in my throat is almost soothed. But the pain in my chest grows with every thump in my heart.

Jase breathes in deep and turns to look back over his shoulder, toward my freedom, and then points to it with his thumb. "He doesn't seem to be taking care of you, is he?"

Thump. Another thump.

"Is this a trick?" My question is meager at best.

Jase's chuckle comes from deep in his chest and his smile widens, showing his perfect teeth.

He shakes his head. "No tricks. I just know he can be stubborn and sometimes he gets in his own way." He's being far too kind. There isn't an ounce of me that trusts him.

My gaze falls to my feet. My dirty feet and scraped knees. And then to my nails, the dirt beneath my fingers that doesn't seem to leave.

My teeth dig into my lower lip to keep me from spilling all the desperate pleas begging me to come up, but it hurts. "What does he want?"

"You." Jase's voice is soft and at ease. As if the answer was simple.

"What about me?" For the first time, my voice is as strong as I imagine it would be.

Resting an elbow on the back of the chair, Jase places his chin in his hand and considers me. He parts his lips but then closes his mouth.

"Just tell me," I beg him.

"I don't know. This…" Jase trails off, then clears his throat and looks away from me for a moment before looking me back in the eyes to continue, "isn't something he does."

"This?" I ask sarcastically, and like a madwoman, a grin forms on my face and I swear I could laugh. "Which part of this?" I dare to spit back at him. And for the first time since Jase has walked in here, pure fear pricks down my spine at the sight of his expression.

That cold, heartless look in his eyes is there and gone just as quickly as it came.

He stares ahead of him, at the cinder block wall and ignores me for a moment. I almost speak but I don't know what to say. And even if I asked the questions that keep me up at night, Jase wouldn't know the answers.

Mindlessly, I pick under my nails. Maybe if I begged him, he'd let me go. The huff of a genuine, but sarcastic laugh gets Jase's attention. I can feel his eyes on me, but I don't look up until he speaks.

"Carter said to buy you a drawing pad. But I thought maybe you'd want something else as well?"

"Sleeping pills," I answer him without thinking twice. I'm hungry, but more than that, I need to sleep. "It's hard to sleep in here."

When I peek up at him, Jase is looking at me like I'm trying to fool him and that thumping in my chest beats harder and faster. "I need to sleep," I beg him. "I take them at home. That or wine some nights. Please, I'm not trying to drug anyone or OD or anything. I just need to sleep, please." My voice cracks and that pathetic feeling that plagued me only moments before he walked through the door comes rushing back to me, hard. It nearly makes me bury my head between my knees with shame.

"I just want to sleep," I plead.

"Sleeping pills… any particular brand?" Jase's question eases the anxiety slightly.

Composing myself as best as I can, I brush my hair behind my ear and answer him, "I've tried a lot of them. There's a pink box at the drugstore. I forget the name," I say then close my eyes tight, trying to remember it. Trying to picture the box that sits on my nightstand.

They open quickly at the sound of the chair scratching on the floor.

But Jase is just leaning back, grabbing his cell phone and typing into it.

"Do you want anything else?"

"Tarot cards," I blurt out without really thinking and the expression on Jase's face tells me that I'm being stupid or naïve or weird. I don't know. I mean, even if I am losing my mind I do realize it's an odd thing to ask for. "I've been bored out of my mind and I like to think with them. It's just something I like." With each sentence, my words come out softer.

Every day I read my cards. The damn things didn't tell me this was coming though.

"Maybe clothes?" Jase asks me, giving me a pointed look and my cheeks flame with embarrassment.

"Clothes would be nice." I haven't thought much about my actual clothes; I know I'm dirty and covered in filth. The only place I've sat or slept is on this tiny mattress and I know I smell.

"I could use a lot of things-"

Jase cuts me off. "I'll get you some toiletries and you know… those things."

I nod my head, swallowing down every bit of humiliation that threatens to consume me.

"You're very nice for a prison guard," I tell him although I stare straight ahead at the empty corner of the room.

He huffs a short, humorless laugh and asks, "Food?"

"Carter said he has to be the one to feed me," I answer Jase immediately and then close my eyes as my empty stomach tightens with pain. I should have eaten before. I have to be smart. But how many times have I told myself that, only to end up in the same place with no change?

"That sounds like something he would say."

Everything hurts at this moment. My body from exhaustion, my heart from hopelessness. Starvation is only third on my list.

"What else would Carter say?" I ask him, just to continue talking. To get to know him. To make him feel like I want him to stay. My heart flickers with the hope that he may hold the key to me leaving.

"Carter would say he's sorry it had to be this way." I'd laugh at Jase's words if they didn't hurt me the way they do.

"I don't think I believe that," I nearly whisper.

"He never wanted any of this," Jase tells me. "He was only a kid when everything escalated, and it was kill or be killed." The silence stretches as I imagine a younger version of Carter, one who hadn't been hardened by hate and death.

"You always have a choice," I manage to speak, although I find it ironic as I sit in this cell, without a single choice of my own.

"It's a nice thought, isn't it?" Jase offers. There's no sarcasm, no sense of anger or sadness. Only matter-of-fact words.

"I'd like to leave this room," I tell him although it comes out a question. As Jase nods, hope rises inside of me.

"It will happen," Jase says. "I know it will."

"Would you let me go outside at least? Or by a window for some fresh air?" Jase tilts his head and narrows his eyes as if to ask me if I think he's stupid.

"I promise I wouldn't run or anything like that. I swear." My throat tightens as he considers me.

"I'll see what I can do," is all he says to my racing heart. But it's something. It's a tiny piece of hope.

"Why are you being nice to me?" I stare into his dark eyes, willing him to answer me but inside, I hope for a lie. I want him to tell me everything is going to be okay. That he's going to get me out of here. But it's all wishful thinking.

"I'm not a nice guy, Aria, so get that out of your head." He stands abruptly and then looks back at me as he opens the door wider, so he can leave.

My blood pounds in my ears at the sight of the wide open door, with Jase's figure blocking it. His shadow fades into the darkness of the room.

Smart. I repeat it over again. Be smart.

Now is not the time. *Be his friend.* The thought hisses and I listen. He could help me. He could have mercy on me where Carter doesn't.

"I'm just following Carter's orders."

I only nod once and force myself to look elsewhere. Anywhere but toward the false sense of freedom beyond the door. He'll be back. Next time I'll be more prepared.

And with that, I'm left alone again.

CHAPTER 15

Carter

THREE HOURS HAVE PASSED, AND EACH HOUR SHE'S MORE AND MORE COMFORTABLE. She hasn't stopped drawing since Jase left the cell. And I haven't taken my eyes off of her. There's only one camera in the room and without being able to zoom in, it's hard to see her features.

A pile of clothes and her blanket are neatly stacked and folded on the bed. But she stays on the floor, scribbling away. One page after another as if she's obsessed and unable to stop.

I need to know what she's writing down. Especially if it's some sort of account of what's happened in the last few days. A message, maybe? Maybe it has something to do with why she screams in her sleep nearly every night.

Unease creeps up my spine at the memories. I'm not surprised the first thing she asked for were sleeping pills. I can't fucking sleep anymore either. Every other night, she cries out in terror and it's only getting worse.

I thought things would change after the other day.

Another paper flies across the floor, but before its fluttering has even stopped, she's already sketching on the page that was beneath it.

Change is necessary. Even if I have to force it.

The walk from my office to the cell takes too fucking long. My fists clench tighter and my heart beats faster as I get closer.

I keep the door open and leave the chair where it is this time.

As she scoots back onto her ass and away from the piles of paper to get away from me as I approach, I lower myself to them, crouching down and picking up the closest one.

There are still a few feet between us, but the expression on Aria's face is of complete fear. Not the defiance I've grown to expect.

"Caught you off guard?" I ask her, cocking a brow. Maybe she thinks I've come to steal her gifts, or maybe the lack of food reminds her of what happened the other night. I know she ate every bit of that tray Jase gave her with her new possessions earlier today.

I wonder if she thinks it's a secret he kept from me.

"You look scared," I add when she doesn't answer my initial question. Her doe eyes are wide, and the colors stir with so much thought and curiosity.

She doesn't answer me. She looks like she isn't even breathing as her eyes glance from the paper in my hand to the open door.

"Don't think about running, Aria. I don't want to have to take these away the second you got them."

Slowly, her chest rises and falls. Her stiff body loosens although she stays back. With her head lowered, she only peeks up at me. It's an interesting difference, the way she looks at me compared to my brother. I fucking hate it. But fear and control are everything. One day Jase will see that.

With my jaw hardened at the thought, I look down at the paper before turning it over in my hand to see what she's drawn. It's upside down at first and it takes me a moment to realize that.

It's drawn with pen, but it's beautiful. Fine little lines and sketches that depict a bleeding heart with three knives stabbed through it. The background is a storm and the ink smears only add to the emotion clearly evident on the paper. Although the knives seem to pierce through the heart easily, the rain behind it is so violent, it detracts from the knives a little.

"What is this?" I ask her without looking at her. I know she's looking at me; I can feel her careful gaze. She doesn't like to look at me when I'm looking at her. Although it's a habit I need to break, I'm more concerned with getting answers than obedience.

"The three of swords," she answers in a small voice and it beckons me to look back at her. For a moment we share a gaze, but then she drops it, focusing on the paper in my hands.

"One of your tarot cards?" I ask her and then straighten the paper in my hand, noticing how it resembles a card.

"Yes. Jase said he bought me a deck online but until they arrive I thought I would draw them myself."

I consider her for a moment. Of everything she could ask for, of everything she could be doing at this moment, this is what she chose. "Why?"

"I like to think about things and it helps me." She nervously picks at the edge of her dirty shirt where a thread has come undone. "It's been lonely, and I haven't been able to think of anything new. It was just something…" her voice trails off and she takes in a shuddering breath. Weeks of doing absolutely nothing but living with your demons would haunt and break the strongest of minds. But she's survived.

"Do your clothes not fit?"

"They do, I just get dirty doing this. So, I thought…" she pauses to take in a short breath and then another. "I just wanted to take care of this, and then I'd planned to change and try to clean myself up."

Nodding, I hand the paper back to her asking, "What does it mean?"

She's hesitant to reach out and take it, but when she does, her fingers trace the edges of the knives. "The three of swords represents rejection, loneliness, heartbreak…" Her words aren't saddened by the information, merely matter-of-fact.

I wonder if she's lying. If the one card that she's drawn I happened to pick up, would really mean those things or if she's toying with me. She could be trying to weaken my resolve by gaining sympathy. It will never happen.

"But yours was reversed," she says, and it cuts through my thoughts of her intention.

"And what does that mean?" I ask her, expecting her to spit back that I'm the one causing it all. For her to blame all of this on me. And in so many ways it is my fault, but she's to blame as well and she doesn't even know it.

"Forgiveness," she whispers the word and then slowly inches closer to pick up each of the fallen papers, dozens of them, gathering them together and avoiding me at all costs.

The word resonates for a moment, lingering in the space between us and striking something deep inside of me.

My blood pressure rises as my eyes search her face for an indication as to what she's getting at. But she doesn't look at me and her body seems to cower more with each passing second.

The moment passes, and she neatly arranges the stack in front of her and still doesn't look up at me.

Stubborn girl. The familiar tic in my jaw begins to contract as I wait another moment. And then another before she looks up at me through her thick lashes. Instead of seeing disinterest, resentment, or whatever I was expecting, all I see is the unspoken plea for me to let her have this small bit of happiness.

But nothing in this life is free. And she should know better than that.

"When I come in here, I want you to kneel for me."

She flinches as she realizes what I've said and as her head lowers, the dip in her collarbone seems to deepen to a level that sickens me.

She's resistant to obeying, but she needs to understand. There is an expectation both of us need to meet. And what's been done can't be taken back. That's not an option. "I admire your strength. I do." I talk with her eyes on my back as I stalk to the metal chair at the far wall. I debate on leaving it there and giving her space. But that intention is quickly forgotten.

Picking up the chair, I take it back to where she's still seated, shaking her head as her shoulders hunch in.

"You keep saying I'm strong and I have to admit I don't get your humor." I'm taken aback by the severity of her tone and the venom that veils each syllable as she speaks. She offers me a smile that wavers and then adds, "Did you let him give it all to me so you could simply take it away?" Maybe the small taste of what used to be and what she could so easily have is what she needed to remember her defiance and ignite the spark between us again.

I'd love for her to fight me, but I'll only allow it after she submits.

"I'll do as I see fit," I answer simply, and she refuses to look back at me, her fingers tracing each of the papers. "All you have to do is obey me and I'll give you everything you need."

"I'd rather die." Her hazel eyes simmer with indignation as she waits for my answer. "You can have it back."

I take my time, sitting on the chair in front of her. Towering over her small frame, I lean forward and speak calmly. "My songbird, it's one thing to have the balls to say that.

I respect it. But it's another to go through with it. You've already obeyed twice. And I didn't ask much, did I?"

She huffs in a tone that's both weak and strong. A manner that reflects her tortured state. So close to having what she wants and needs, and yet so close to losing everything.

"It was a cruel joke, wasn't it?" Her eyes narrow as she gazes at the door like it beckons her.

"I don't joke, Aria. Your life belongs to me. Everything you will ever get for the rest of your existence will come from me." My words come out harsh and irritated. I'm sick and fucking tired of her denying both of us. "Get. On. Your. Knees."

"Fuck you," she spits out, and instantly my fingers nearly wrap around her throat as the rough pad of my thumb rests against her lips. I can feel the rush of her blood in her neck as I grip her tightly, her gasp filling the air along with the sound of the chair scraping from the rapid movement forward.

She stiffens with my touch but she doesn't protest, staring back at me with that burning expression as I tighten my grasp. Her breath comes out with a shudder, but she stares back at me expectantly, waiting for what I'll do next.

My heart hammers and my dick stiffens with each passing second that she holds my heated gaze. I see the moment she realizes that her hands are on my waist. Pulling herself toward me, not pushing me away.

Her eyes spark and I nearly crash my lips against hers, urging for more. Instead, I leave her there, letting a low hum of approval fall from my lips so she knows I know exactly what she's thinking.

A fire ignites between us as she grips me tighter, so tight the sound of her nails scratching against my pants is all I can hear.

"You think you shouldn't do it, simply because you've been taught it's wrong. But is that what you really want?"

"I don't want you," she says breathily, not even attempting to hide her desire.

"I won't let you ride my cock until you tell me how badly you want to cum on it." I hold her fiery gaze as I ask, "Do you understand me?"

Her body sways slightly as she holds back a strangled groan of lust.

"Humor me, Aria. I already know you're strong."

"You make me weak." Her voice breaks and the tension from the other day returns in full force. She steadies her trembling lip between her teeth.

"Is that what you're afraid of? Being weak?"

She nods her head slightly, ever so slightly. And I can see the last bit of her walls crumble for me. Crashing down to the ground in small, insignificant piles of rubble.

"I don't want you weak." I lean forward, whispering against her lips, "I want you mine."

Her eyes close and her body bends forward; she rests nearly her entire weight on me. "I will never submit to you," she says, and her words are a weak confession. As if she hates their existence.

She's close. So close. I need to offer her something.

Hope. The offer of hope is something a desperate person can never afford to pass up.

"I made a deal I shouldn't have. But I need to go through with it for as long as I have to. And it has to appear that I've done what would be expected. You're going to help me and then I'll give you whatever you want."

"What do you need me to—"

"Obey me," I say, cutting her off. "Kneel when I enter and do as I wish." My hands tingle with the sensation of feeling her so close to caving. They clench and unclench at my side.

Time passes in slow ticks as she pulls herself away from me. She can try to pretend she has somewhere else to go. But I'm her only way out of this. And eventually, she'll beg me for something. She. Will. Beg.

"Anything?" she asks, and she already knows the answer. "Like my freedom?"

"Almost anything." I don't lie to her.

"There's nothing else—" she starts, but I cut her off. "There's always something else." My words are sharp at first but I correct myself.

"There's always something else," I repeat and then add as I stand up to leave, "It's something you so desperately need, but you don't even see it."

CHAPTER 16

Aria

PART OF WHAT KEEPS ME FROM GIVING IN TO CARTER AND THE FEELINGS THAT have been taking over my every waking moment is obvious.

The fear of the past returning. The truth in the terrors that devour my nights.

And the nightmares I remember of a past monster erase everything I've felt for Carter. There is nothing that will change that.

Sometimes it's the feeling of Stephan's hands on me that wake me up screaming. It's been so long since I've felt it. Or at least since I've been aware of it.

It used to be every single night. I couldn't sleep at all without seeing his face. Without feeling him rip me away from my mother as I begged her to stay with me. She was already gone though. Even as a child I knew she was dead.

He'd killed her.

The sleeping pills the doctor gave me at my father's request worked for a little while. Then I stopped and even though everyone else would say I was screaming, I didn't remember. I couldn't remember a single dream. Nothing but darkness as I slept.

It's come back to me though in the last few months. Even the pills can't dull the nightmares anymore. They don't stop them from lingering once my eyes have opened.

It's like I've gone back fourteen years, and my nights and days are both haunted by the memories.

"Please, Stephan," I begged him. I looked up into the eyes of the man dragging me away from her. My nails scratched and bent on the wooden floors as I kicked him, falling hard to the ground.

And he snarled, "You little bitch."

My heart races and the tears stream down my face. My fingers dig into the mattress and the sweat turns to ice along my skin. I don't know if I'm asleep or awake, but I know what's coming. I can't move; I can't breathe.

I can see myself rocking, but I'm still. I'm aware of that. It's a different time, in a different place.

I'm safe, I whisper and try to will the images away. I'm safe.

But when I open my eyes and try hard to keep from crying any more tears, I remember where I am.

It's been years since the nightmares have tortured me like this. It makes sense that they'd come back now. But without a place to hide, not in my sleep and not while I'm awake, I don't know how much longer I can go on.

I can't live like this.

I can't and I won't.

I want to call out for Carter of all things. He could hold me and take it away.

The bed beneath me groans as I roll over, and for the first time since I've been here, my back is to the door. I'm conscious of it. As conscious of it as I am the feeling of Carter's hand on my jaw. The strength, the power, the heat, and fire that lick their way up my body when he holds me like that.

Like I'm his.

I remember his words, *"I made a deal I shouldn't have. But I need to go through with it."* How he said I have to help him. I've spent weeks in this cell with no hope, until now. My imagination is wild with thoughts of what could come. But each and every one of them leads back to one scene. One that makes my thighs clench tighter.

Slowly, I lift my fingers to where his were and close my eyes as the tips of my fingers tickle my skin. The memory calms me and yet, it makes my heart beat faster.

It's his hands on me that I think of as I try to drift back to sleep. And I almost do.

But the realization of how much power he has over me with something so simple as a touch meant to control me, easing my pain steals any chance I have of falling back to sleep.

CHAPTER 17

Carter

S TEPHAN. ALEXANDER STEPHAN.

It's his name screamed. He's who terrorizes her in her sleep. I know it is.

I've listened to it over and over again, each time the anger intensifying.

Last night she screamed his name.

All these nights I thought it was me causing the terrors. I thought she hated me and that she truly dreaded what I could do to her.

I've never been so fucking wrong in my life.

The door to her cell opens with a small creak, but it cries out loud in my ears as Aria's bloodshot eyes stare back at me.

"Can't sleep?" I ask her, leaving the door open and walking with evenly paced and deliberate steps to the side of her bed.

She looks so frail beneath me. Barely eating and not sleeping for more than a few hours for over a week will take its toll on anyone. She doesn't answer me. Her eyes follow me though.

"I won't kneel," she says weakly.

"I didn't come for that."

Her brow scrunches and she nearly questions me. She knows she's disobeying, still fighting a losing battle, but my guard is down. It almost makes me smile.

"I asked for pills to sleep," she says, and her pleas are desperate. But I had to know more. There would be no pills to take it away when she wouldn't share it with me. How else would I have found out? It's her stubbornness that will make her suffer.

"I want to know how you know Alexander Stephan." Even though my words come out softly, meant to be gentle, she pales in front of me and I can see the chill spread over her body as she backs away from me.

There's only so far she can run in here and I'm tempted to grab her and force her to answer me, but I already know everything I need.

I was stupid to think I knew everything there was to know about Aria. I didn't consider anything other than who she was five years ago. I didn't consider the past that made her into that girl.

I knew her mother was murdered by a now-associate of the Romanos years before our family existed in this reality. At the time, he was the right-hand man to Talvery. Betrayal is thick in this business. Her mother's murder is what started the feud years ago, but it's been quiet for over a decade. No one's made a move since the unsuccessful retaliation on Talvery's part. Each side was simply maneuvering pieces and has been waiting for the other to strike since then.

My blunt fingernails dig into my palm as I resist touching Aria. Her back is pressed against the wall and she gathers the covers closer to her chest as if she has hope that they could save her.

But there's nothing that can save you from your past.

When she finally speaks, it's anger that threatens to come out in her voice. "Don't give me to him, please."

Anger sparks through me. This girl has a way of igniting it within me like no one else.

"You belong to me." The simple words gritted between my clenched teeth make her stiffen, but her eyes show a different response. Hope, maybe.

"Any man who thinks they can lay a hand on you will die at mine. Is that clear?"

Her eyes search mine for sincerity, even as she nods her head. "I told you, you belong to me."

The shift in her demeanor is slight. The heavier breaths, the gentle relaxation in her shoulders, and the defiance that begs to come out in the gorgeous blend of greens in her stare.

"Who is he to you?" I ask her again and watch as the cords in her slender neck tighten when she swallows.

"He killed my mother." She doesn't show much emotion; she tries to hide it, to appear devoid of it. But sadness and fear emanate from her voice.

I consider what to ask her next, but I don't want her to know what I know. If she doesn't already, she wouldn't believe me.

"Tell me more," I decide to command her, rather than asking for specifics.

She brushes the hair from her face and as she does, the blanket falls from her chest. It's only then I notice she's finally changed clothes. The thin, pale blush cotton shirt complements her complexion. Her fingers wrap around the cuffs of her sleeves as she pulls her knees to her chest.

"It's not something I like to talk about," she says simply, and then rests her cheek on her knees and looks up at me. The air is different between us. The tension of the game we've been playing isn't here and so I scoot closer to her, wondering how she'll react.

And she does. My little songbird.

She keeps the space between us, shifting to the other side of the bed and straightening her shoulders to keep her eyes on me.

The corners of my lips kick up into a half grin.

"Even now?" I ask her and the defensiveness fades, but she doesn't answer.

A moment passes, and then another. Finally, she looks toward the open door. It's the first time she's done it this morning; usually her gaze flickers to it constantly.

"You screamed his name last night," I tell her and when she looks back at me, I know she's not breathing.

"I'd like to know why," I say to finish my thought.

She swallows visibly and again pulls her knees to her chest. As she does, I inch closer.

Only one. Although she stares at my hand, lying flat on the mattress and closer to her, she doesn't move away.

"I was there when he did it."

"You saw her die?"

She nods. "I was hiding. I was only playing." She shakes her head and I inch forward again, beckoning her for more. But nothing comes.

"What aren't you telling me?" My question comes out as a demand and that's when the defiance returns and the girl I'm used to seeing returns.

Her dry lips part but after several moments, she never says a word. I stand up, pushing off the thin bed and making her sway with the dip in the mattress.

"I don't like hearing you scream," I confide in her and I'm met with silence.

I turn to look over my shoulder and see her soft eyes staring at me, brimming with unshed tears.

"I'm sorry," she apologizes to me and I find it hard to swallow as she turns her gaze from me to the blanket.

This is moving too slowly. Far too slowly. She's close to breaking and for both our sakes, I have to push her. I will not let her move backward. We're so close, and time never stops its ticking.

With that in mind, I reach down and take her blanket from her. She stares up at me like a scared child and I have to push out my words, although they come out with the control and power I always have. "You need to bathe. I don't trust you. So you'll have to trust me."

CHAPTER 18

Aria

I'VE NEVER WONDERED WHAT A PRISONER WOULD FEEL LIKE WHEN LED FROM CHAINS to a feigned freedom. Like a courtyard or elsewhere. I wonder if they feel the same initial instinct to stay close to their warden, the way I do with Carter.

Or, maybe it's because I'm tired. I'm so fucking tired. Of fighting, of starving myself, of not sleeping. I'm not broken, but I am so fucking tired.

The rich mahogany furniture, high ceilings and carved molding accents move around me in a blur. Without shoes, my bare feet pad softly on the polished floors, and it's all I can hear.

I'm not sure if I should peek up and take in my surroundings, but every time I do, Carter gently brushes my shoulder and I instinctively pick up my pace, focused on what's to come. Still, I try to track everything, to pay attention to every doorway and window, every possible chance of escape.

My heart beats fiercely as he leads me to the right and I see a thin stream of light in the darkened hall from a room in the distance. The sounds of chatter and even laughter echo around me, although Carter pulls me in the opposite direction.

Adrenaline courses in my veins and my throat tightens.

There are other people here.

"Don't be stupid, Aria," Carter whispers in the shell of my ear, making my heart lurch and forcing me to jump back. I hadn't realized my thoughts were so obvious.

"Come," he orders me, offering me his hand. My own is small in his as he wraps his strong fingers around mine and leads me deeper down the darkened hall. All I can think about as he takes me closer to where he wants me, is that there were people here, all this time, and I have no idea if they heard my screams or what they would have done had I screamed just moments ago.

Carter unlocks a door, the clinking of metal keys accompanied by his rough voice as he says, "My brothers stay up late. They always have."

His brothers. Jase. Who else? There isn't enough curiosity in the world that could lead me to ask him. But deep in my soul, I'm crying for answers although I can already hear the hiss of the truth in the back of my skull.

There is no mercy here. Not from anyone.

The door opens with a muted creak and I only nod as he gestures for me to head inside. The small bit of hope fluttering in my chest is strangled. I can barely swallow, barely do anything but place one foot in front of the other through a large bedroom, until I hear the flick of a light switch.

The dim light flows across the black and white marble tile. Carter doesn't wait for me to enter before turning on the bath at the far side of the room. I'm struck by the sheer size of the bathroom. Even coming from wealth myself, I'm taken aback.

"It's beautiful," I speak softly. Although how I'm able to speak, I don't know.

The feel of the cold tile under my feet has never been so welcome.

The sight of the plush towel folded neatly on the counter makes me itch to touch like nothing else ever has.

The sound of a running bath has never felt so soothing. And yet, I'm so aware that I'm only a prisoner in a gilded cage, and this moment outside of the cell may be my only chance of escape.

My body is tired from not eating much and having terrors wake me every time I sleep. But I still feel the need to fight.

Carter doesn't respond to a thing I say, or to the next step I take into the bathroom, letting my fingers trail along the pale paisley pattern on the silver wallpaper. My gaze flows through the room easily but stops when I see the tub.

I can't take my eyes away from the steam that billows around the edge of the clawfoot tub.

Leaning over the spotless porcelain, Carter's back is to me with his muscular shoulders pulling his shirt tight, and I imagine how I could push him and run. I could shove him with every ounce of strength I have and run out of the room. I doubt I'd get far though, and I don't know where I'd go.

Now I know his brothers stay here. They're here somewhere.

No, I'm sure I wouldn't get far.

"I want to feed you before I bathe you." Carter's statement cuts through the visions of me running until he adds, "Strip down and get into the tub while I get your dinner."

The dead hope is resurrected; he's leaving me. The thought makes me more anxious than anything.

As he leaves, Carter grips the door and adds, "I won't be long."

Left with only the heat and comfort of the running water, my heart beats once, then twice.

My eyes close and I whisper, "Don't be stupid." The aching inside, the desperate need to run, it's all outweighed by the knowledge of what would come if I disobeyed.

Would I really deny myself a reckless chance of freedom for a warm bath? For food and his touch? Have I been so deprived that such small comforts would rate so highly?

My nails dig into my palms as I war with myself, and when my eyes open, all I see is myself in the mirror. My hair is tangled, although I've run my fingers through it daily. It's oily and dirty, which is to be expected.

My face is thin. Much thinner than I remember. Lifting the thin cotton shirt above my head, I inspect my body, running my fingers over my sides and down to my waist. The cell is so dim; I didn't see the bruises from when I was taken. The cuts around my wrists have left thin white scars, and the bruise on my ribs is an ugly shade of dark brown that's faded to nearly nothing.

I hadn't felt defeat until I was led from my cell, giving up the possibility to run only to see how damaged I've become.

The sound of the water striking against the surface harder brings my attention to the tub.

It's nearly full. The steaming hot water and relaxing fragrance of lavender bath oils Carter poured in it, beg me to cave. To let go and stop fighting. To be good and do as I'm told. If only so I can rid myself of the sense of failure and remember who I am again.

And I still remember those words he spoke days ago. He made a deal and I'm to help him. There is more to this than I know. "Be smart," I whisper to myself. I'm playing a game without knowing the rules. Without knowing the next phase. The little bit of hope and wonder push me forward toward temptation.

Turning the iron faucet, I realize it's the first thing I've touched in weeks beyond the few items in the cell. Something as simple as turning a knob feels both foreign and nostalgic. I never want to go back to the cell. My chest feels hollow as I think, *never*, but I know that the choice isn't mine.

It is, a small voice murmurs in the back of my head. The voice that takes advantage of my pain and promises so much hope in whispers of deceit.

Jasmine and lavender fill my lungs as I inhale the calming scents and quickly remove my shirt and shove my cotton pants down my legs. Although the clothes are new, they're still dirty. Everything in that cell is dirty.

The fabric clings to my toes and I have to kick it off and toward the puddle of clothes. Just as I do, I hear the heavy footsteps of Carter coming back.

Fear keeps me from moving for only a moment, but then I quickly place a foot into the steaming water, hissing at the onslaught of heat and causing the water to splash around the tub. Water hits the floor as I move to step with my other foot into the hot bath, the heat becoming more and more welcoming as my body adjusts to it. With my back to the door, I hear Carter enter, but I ignore him, lowering myself into the tub filled with a warmth I so desperately needed. And hide myself from him.

"How does it feel?" Carter's voice carries through the room with a powerful resonance.

Like heaven, I think as I turn slowly, careful not to splash the water, but also careful to stay under and somewhat hidden beyond the white bubbles on the surface.

I try to tell him that it feels wonderful and thank him when I finally meet his gaze, but I'm silenced by the intensity within. His eyes swirl with the danger of a man close to getting what he wants. An animalistic heat passes between us and I can only nod for fear of what my voice would sound like if I dared utter a word to him.

Thankfully, he tears his gaze from me and picks up a ceramic plate from the counter.

"You need to eat." Carter's command sounds more like a reminder to himself. And again, I merely nod.

I've had delicious food before. I've gorged myself on delicacies without thinking twice. It's one of the only benefits of my upbringing. But the food Carter brought me makes my mouth water and my grip tighten on the tub to keep me from ripping the plate from his hands.

He must see my eagerness; he always smiles that devilish grin when he knows I'm eager. Bastard.

"Open," he commands me and like a good girl, my lips part and I nearly moan when he slips me the small chunk of filet dipped in au jus with a dab of herbed butter smeared across the top. The meat melts in my mouth, the tastes singing on my lips. My eyes are still closed as I relish the food, thinking it's the most delicious thing I've ever eaten when Carter brushes another piece against my lips.

Instantly I open my lips for him, and his finger brushes against my tongue as he gives me a second piece and then another. My teeth scrape against his fingers and my eyes widen with worry that he thinks I did it on purpose, but he only feeds me more.

The fear and worry slip away, just as the time does with each slice of tender meat.

Blistered tomatoes and peppers along with roasted potatoes find themselves in the mix as Carter feeds me until my stomach is full and I can't take another bite. It's been so long since I haven't felt hunger pains. It feels like forever since I've sunk into a deep tub, covered in hot water. I rest my head against the side of the tub and pretend like everything is alright. It's only a small moment until the clinking of the ceramic plate on the tile floor disturbs me and brings me back to the present.

My body stiffens slightly, sloshing the water toward the edge of the tub away from Carter as he dips a washcloth into the tub.

His fingers brush against my skin and sinfully, I welcome the touch. It's been so long, and I've been so lonely. I want more. I need more. I find myself wishing for him to take me like I know he wants to.

Has he really broken me so easily? Or is this something I should want the way I do? The questions bring a haze to my mind and a thrumming in my blood. The washcloth travels over my body, starting at my feet and working its way upward. My calves, my thighs and so close to between them.

I know he can hear my heavy breathing; he can see how I grip the edge of the tub. But he doesn't touch me there. Instead, he tells me to wet my hair and takes his time massaging my scalp and lathering my hair. The scent of the chamomile shampoo overwhelms me, and I hum ever so slightly until I hear it and stop myself.

Everything feels so good.

"Back under, songbird," he tells me in that velvety voice. The voice I don't want to disobey, and so I don't. I do as he says. With every command he gives me, I do exactly what he says.

He massages the washcloth over my shoulders and I whimper as he kneads the pain away. I hadn't realized how much my body ached until he showed me so. A low groan of approval forces me to open my eyes and stare into his. But he's not looking at my gaze. His eyes are focused on my hardened nipples, peeking up from the water.

The washcloth makes a splash as it hits the water and slowly sinks to the depths of the tub. Carter lets his fingers trail down my chest, plucking one of my nipples and then the other. It happens slowly, his fingers determined but also giving me a warning. His rough thumb circles them first before tugging on them and causing my head to fall back and my thighs to clench. Each tweak sends a sharp spike of need between my legs, and I nearly spread them for him. My clit pulses with need. I feel it so strongly I don't think it would take much at all for me to cum for him. And I can't find it in me at all to find any shame at that fact.

The dull desire that hasn't faded, shoots through me and I welcome it.

Carter's dark eyes find mine, but instead of reaching lower, his arm dips into the water next to me and he gathers the washcloth once again.

I'm reminded of his patience. How slowly he does everything. I don't know if he finds pleasure in teasing me or if it's simply that he doesn't want this moment to end, but either way, I lean my head back as he continues bathing me, and I don't object until his hand is right where I've secretly been wishing for it to be.

He brushes the washcloth against my throbbing clit and I gasp, moving away from the intense pleasure and making waves in the tub that splash over the edge. Fear and desire mix into a confusing potion that I drank long ago. And at this moment, I'd drink the bottle again, I'd suck it dry and lick the edge of the neck where the last beads of liquid would gather. That's how badly I wish for him to do it again.

"Don't let go, Aria. If you do, I'll stop," he warns me and my lungs still. My body's on fire with need. I slowly lower myself back under the warm water, until my breasts are hidden again, and I hold Carter's eyes as I slowly reach back up and grip on to the edge. My body's still, so still as Carter's gaze flickers between my pussy and my stare. I bite down on my bottom lip as he reaches between my legs again.

His movements have been steady and slow. Careful and considerate even. But as the washcloth falls into the water, brushing against my thigh and ass, and his fingers replace the cloth, his movements are nothing but savage.

He shoves his fingers inside of me. My back bows as the sudden spike in pleasure crashes through every inch of my body.

"Carter," I whimper his name as he pushes his palm against my clit. I've never been touched like this. Air is torn from me and I can't breathe or move or do anything but grip tighter and try to stay still as he finger fucks me harder and harder.

"Carter," I cry out his name louder into the hot air and grip the edge of the tub as hard as I can. I can't let go but my body is begging for me to run, to move, to both get closer to the intense pleasure and to leave it quickly.

I know when I do cum, it will split me into pieces and he'll love how I shatter under his touch. It both terrifies me and thrills me.

I should be ashamed as I writhe in the water. I should be embarrassed as he hisses when my pussy clamps around his fingers and my orgasm tears through me, coming faster and harder than it ever has before.

My heart shouldn't pound for more. My body shouldn't ache for more. I shouldn't sit up so quickly with the intention of gripping his wrist and pleading with him for more. The waves are still crashing through me as he turns around, grabbing the towel and ignoring how I've just come apart for him.

My fears cloud the desire; they dim the sensation of lust that ricochets through my blood, my breathing steadying.

But when he turns to face me, I know it's alright. I know I did well to let him touch me. From the way he looks at me, it's like he's never wanted anything more in his life.

CHAPTER 19

Carter

SHE'S TOO GOOD. TOO FUCKING PERFECT.

And that's how I'll keep her so that each and every time I can ruin her. It's a delicate balance, knowing what to offer her and when to take from her.

Tonight, I've given more than enough, and I'll feel her break beneath me. I'll feel her shatter under me as I take every bit of her that I want. And she'll fucking love me for it.

The water falls around her in a patter onto the tile floor. She lets it drip down her back and sides. Even the thick towel I'm wrapping around her waist can't hide her from me. I've felt every inch. Every curve is burned into my memory.

Her skin trembles beneath my fingertips as I brush them against her shoulders.

I take my time, letting each small touch catch her off guard. The gasps and sharp breaths only add to the thrill. My cock is harder than it's ever been as I lead her to the bedroom and she clings to that towel as if she'll be able to keep it.

Her small frame casts a shadow on the thick carpet, the moonlight shining through the drapes. I can practically hear her heart beating as she stares at the bed. My fingers slip over her silky skin and I let my lips fall to her shoulder, so I can whisper, "You don't need this anymore." My fingers slip between the plush towel and her soft skin. I half expect my songbird to object. To continue to pretend like she doesn't want this.

But to my surprise and delight, she lets the towel fall and gently steadies her back against my chest when I take that small step forward, discarding the distance between us.

My fingers dip into her cunt, her hair tickling my fingers as I pet her still-swollen clit. I'm rewarded with her ass pushing against my cock, her back bowing, and a small moan that's barely muffled.

"It's my turn, Aria," I say, and my voice nearly trembles at her name when I feel her thighs tighten around my fingers. "Are you ready again so soon?" I turn her around, her small breasts a beautiful flushed color and her bottom lip drops in surprise like she's been caught.

"You're eager to cum again and feel that sweet, sinful torture paralyze your body?" I take a half step forward, forcing her ass to bump against the bed.

"I bet I could make you cum just from sucking these," I tell her and pull her pale petal pink nipples between my middle and pointer fingers. I tug on both at once. Her head lolls slightly, but those beautiful hazel eyes stay on mine as she moans.

"Sit." I give her a simple command. And she obeys. I can't describe the pride, the satisfaction from watching her so eagerly waiting for another command. "Good girl," I add, the words slipping out easily, and my hand rests gently on her thigh. I move it upward until I grip her ass and toss her higher onto the bed.

"Show me your cunt." Her cheeks blaze a bright red, even in the darkness, but letting her head fall back and staring at the ceiling, she parts her legs and then bends her knees, digging her heels into the comforter beneath her so I can see my prize.

"Look at me," I tell her, surprised by my own irritation. Her eyes instantly find mine, widened slightly. "Watch me. I want you to know how I look at you. What I think of you. Do you understand me?" She doesn't hesitate to nod. And glancing between her face and her spread pussy lips, I make sure she's watching me intently.

My fingers trace along her lips, soft and wet with arousal. Goosebumps travel over her thighs and she shivers when I gently push on her swollen nub. Her back arches off the bed as my fingers slip over her entrance and then back up.

"Beautiful," I say the one word, and that gorgeous blush in her chest creeps to her cheeks. I'm careless as I rip my shirt off on my way to the nightstand.

I have two sets of cuffs, but I'll only use one pair tonight. Pulling the door open, I grab the set and grip her wrist to move it where I want it. Her inhalation of surprise is met with the sound of the cuffs tightening, one on her wrist and one on the bedpost. Outstretched, she struggles not to object.

I can tell by the way she readjusts herself that she knows what's coming. I unbuckle my pants and she stills; they fall to the floor and my stiff cock juts out. I've never known how badly my cock could ache to be inside of a woman. Until now.

Gripping it and stroking once, precum already beads at the head.

My gorgeous Aria whimpers with need.

"Spread your legs for me." Before I'm finished speaking the words, she's already obeyed.

"I've waited so long for this," I admit to her as I crawl up the bed and over her small frame. My hips fit between her thighs and my cock nestles in her pussy as I lower my lips to the crook of her neck.

I've agonized over how I'd fuck her the first time. Whether I'd make her ride me so she couldn't deny how badly she wanted me. I wasn't sure if I'd be slow and steady, making her scream for me to fuck her harder as she got closer to the edge of her orgasm.

But now that the time has come, I realize how selfish I am. How truly and deeply to the core selfish I am.

All I want to do is take what's mine. To slam myself inside her to the hilt and fuck her like she's my whore. Mine and mine alone.

And that's exactly what I do. In one swift stroke, I ravage her. Her tight pussy is already hot and wet and eager for my cock. She takes all of me and screams out a sweet sound of utter rapture. With her free hand, her nails rake down my chest as her heel digs into my ass.

The need to keep still inside of her while she cums violently on my cock is overridden by the desire to piston my hips and rut between her legs. The sweet smell of her arousal and the sounds of our flesh smacking together repeatedly are everything I'll need to justify what I've done.

She struggles under me, her shoulders digging into the mattress with each hard thrust. Every time I pound into her, she responds like she was made just for me. The tightening of her pussy, the strangled cries, and sweet tortured moans are better than I ever could have imagined.

Her nails dig into my shoulder as I keep a relentless pace. My balls draw up and my spine tingles with the desire to cum deep inside of her.

But I need more. Gritting my teeth, I fuck her harder and faster until a cold sweat breaks out on my skin.

She screams out again, but the scream is different this time. It's pain. It's reflected in her face too. My heart sinks in my chest until I see her wrist, being pulled against the metal cuff.

Fucking hell. I'm agitated and reckless as I climb over her, her arousal covering my dick as I dig in the nightstand for the key to unlock the fucking cuff.

It takes longer than I'd like and when it's finally free, I don't waste a second to grip her hips, then flip her over so she's on her knees with her ass in the air. She yells out in surprise, but it's silenced when I slam all of me back into her welcoming heat.

The sweet sounds filling the air are heaven. With every thrust, she cries out in pleasure.

I grip her ass with both of my hands, nearly cumming with her as she spasms on my cock. Her nails dig into the sheets and her thighs tremble with the ripple of her release.

I wanted her to beg for it. In the tub, in my bed. I wasn't going to let her cum until she was begging for me to fuck her.

But the best-laid plans never do work out.

And as I thrust into her with an unrelenting pace, feeling her struggle to stay on her knees until she finally falls beneath me while I rut into her savagely and she screams out incoherently with pleasure, I realize I'd rather have her beg me to stop. I'd rather take every ounce of pleasure from her until she can't take any more.

Until she's limp and spent and can do nothing but hold on to the comforter beneath her as if it can save her from me.

CHAPTER 20

Aria

I'VE NEVER FELT SO DELICIOUSLY USED AND BARED BY SOMEONE SO SAVAGELY.

My body aches as it has for weeks, but in a different way. In a way that makes me feel like my body will give in and collapse if I try to move. As I roll over in the bed, I can still feel him inside of me. Taking everything and pushing me over the edge, time and time again. The reminder sends a wanting desire through my blood.

He fucked me like he owned me.

Because he did.

He does still.

The thought makes my eyes pop wide open. My gaze travels slowly over the brightly lit room with gray walls and a tray ceiling painted even darker. The room has a sense of power to it. It's bold and dangerous even. Sharp and modern furniture and not a thing out of place.

Except for me.

My body is still, knowing I'm in Carter's room.

Not in the cell; a breath leaves me slowly, as quietly as I can allow it. I never want to go back there.

I don't hear anything. Not a sound. Another moment passes, and slowly I will myself to reach behind me, searching for Carter's presence, any sign that he's sleeping next to me.

I find nothing but the chill of empty sheets.

It takes me longer than I'd like to admit to have the strength and will to turn over, still pretending that I'm sleeping. But after moments of sensing no one else in the room, I take a chance to look around and find the room empty and the bedroom door open.

I take in his bedroom as slowly as I did the other side and wait for a sign that Carter's here. But there's no trace of him.

A pile of vibrant clothes, at odds with the bright white comforter, catches my attention.

Daring to sit up and wincing from the dull ache between my legs, I cautiously pick them up and find a silk robe and negligee that I would never wear.

It's scandalous and for the body of a model. It makes no sense that my initial thought is that he's going to be disappointed with me. That I could never do this delicate combination of lace and silk justice. Other than to justify it with the thought that if I disappoint him, he'll send me back. And I never want to go in that cell again. Never.

I don't even realize I'm clutching the fabric to my chest until Carter's voice pierces through the threatening thoughts.

"What's wrong?" he asks as he enters the room.

My head shakes of its own accord, making my hair tickle my bare shoulders as I do and reminding me that I'm naked.

I should have searched through his things. I should have tried to escape. A bulleted list of all the ways I've disappointed myself weighs heavily on my chest as I watch him pull one drawer open and then the next until he sets a pair of metal handcuffs down on the dresser.

His casual stance is a façade; power still radiates around him. Carter stalks toward me.

I'm only moving from the cell where I could deny him, to his bed where I'll be his whore.

"If you don't like it, there are more." Carter's tone is dismissive at best and I don't know what he's referring to until he nods at the ball of clothes in my hand.

I let the fine fabrics fall onto the comforter, not knowing how to answer. I'm on pins and needles as I sit here trying to decide what I need to do to keep myself safe and in the best possible position to gain my freedom back.

"I like you nervous." Carter's voice draws my eyes back to him. He looks more casual today than I've ever seen him. It's not the clothes he wears, but his posture and the way he stalks toward me. Stopping at the edge of the bed, I get a strong whiff of his scent and I hate how much I love it. Even more so I hate how my thighs clench and the twinkle of a grin threatens to pull at his lips when I whimper.

"I enjoyed you last night," Carter's voice rumbles in a way that ignites my nerve endings on fire. Reaching out to cup my chin in his hand, he stares at my lips, running his thumb along the bottom one.

And something shifts inside of me. This is a man with so much power and control, someone who could destroy me and in many ways has already. Yet all I want in this moment is for him to kiss me. He hasn't yet, and deep inside a part of me needs it.

But his thumb stops the soothing motions and his expression falls as he speaks, although it's worded as a question. "You haven't eaten?"

"I only just woke up." The words come out like an excuse with a plea coating them. The weak sound on my lips disgusts me. I was stronger in the cell. I breathe in harsher, knowing I'd bite back a quip if only my ass was on the thin mattress in the dark cell in this moment.

But I don't want to go back. I'm ashamed to know it so clearly and to hold onto that truth like I'll die if it slips from me. In an effort to diminish my hate of that pathetic fact, I remind myself that are far more chances of escape out here.

And there is nothing but agony in that cell. The ache of loneliness and starvation and sleepless nights filled with past pains.

I refuse to go back.

Carter's touch falls as he turns away from me, back to the dresser. "There's breakfast in the kitchen. If you see anyone, ignore them and they'll ignore you. Understood?" He tosses the cuffs inside a drawer and searches for something else.

I nod once when he glances over his shoulder, although inside I'm reeling. All I can think is that there may be someone here to save me. Someone to show mercy. Maybe Jase? Or else I can run.

"Verbal responses, little songbird," he says casually as if he's telling me what the weather is. The drawer shuts tight with finality and I find myself nodding my head again as I answer him, "Yes," with my eyes fixated on the metal peeking through his clenched hand.

"And you'll wear this," he tells me as he holds up a thin chain. Every inch or so there's a small pearl, alternated with diamonds. It's long, so long it would fall to nearly my belly button and as I take it in I see the diamonds grow larger as you near the end. There, in the center, is a large tear-shaped diamond.

But all that sparkles is only sin disguised in beauty.

"A collar?" My heart beats like a war drum inside my chest. He must hear the defeat on my tongue.

"You can't collar a songbird, Aria, but you can tether one or cage it. The choice is yours."

"Either the cell or the necklace?" I ask him to clarify, and just the idea that I can save myself from going back there has my hand reaching for the necklace.

Carter nods once, and my eyes are brought back to his.

"Turn around," he orders me, the fire flickering in his eyes. Steadying my breathing, I turn my back to him and feel the sweet sensation of a shiver run down both my front and back as he moves my hair to the side. My nipples harden as the cool diamonds and pearls fall down my chest and over the crook of my shoulders and neck. Carter lets his hands trail to my breasts once he's done, his hot breath tickling the shell of my ear as he whispers, "Beautiful."

But just as quickly as he's shown me gentleness, he leaves me, his absence intensifying the coldness of the air. And I'm left naked on my knees in his bed. Wearing a collar and making decisions based on fear.

Thoughts of my father and Nikolai return. Shame accompanies the image of their disapproval and disgust. As much as I'd like to lie, I loved what Carter did to me last night and I'd let him do it again.

"Why are you doing this to me?" The words are torn from the other side of me. The side I want to hide and tell to be quiet.

Walking back to the dresser, I think Carter's ignored me until he answers, "Because I can," he answers in a tone not to be questioned or defied. "A man asked me what I wanted, and I could buy anything I want, yet I saw your picture and knew I could never have you." He turns to face me, leaning against the dresser and waiting for my response.

I remember the words I've held so dearly that he spoke days ago. The words that gave me hope. How I would help him and he would give me everything. I wonder if it's a lie, or if what he's telling me now has anything to do with that deal he shouldn't have made.

"And now that you've..." I trail off, then swallow my words.

"I don't have you, Aria. Not yet. But when I do, you'll be begging me to stay." What strikes the most fear in my heart is how utterly and completely I believe him.

Walking toward me, I can see something begging to escape from his lips. Something that's maybe a secret, maybe not. But he merely runs his fingers along my lips again and tells me he'll find me when he's ready for me again before leaving me and keeping the bedroom door open.

When something is hard to the touch and so sharp it would draw blood, you have to always be careful. It's the gentleness of it that will break you. You can't ever let your guard down.

If you're smart, you avoid it and if you have to be around it, you stay away from the parts that hurt. But those aren't the parts that destroy. It's the parts that you begin to crave, the parts you don't want to resist that bring you to your knees. They make you forget or maybe they make you think the sharpness won't cut you, as if you're somehow immune or no longer prey to it.

Even knowing so, I fall helpless to the way he cups my chin like that. And I sit there for far too long with my fingertips lingering where I can still feel him.

I can't breathe as I wake up. The cold sweat that covers my skin makes me shake, as does my racing heart. The room is dark, and I can't see for a moment, but the hands gripping my shoulders and holding me down aren't the ones in my nightmare.

It's not Stephan, I try to think logically as I hear Carter's voice yelling at me to wake up.

My chest heaves as the light filters into my vision and I see him. The anger in his tone is absent from his pained expression.

My shoulders hunch forward as I try to calm down. It was just a night terror. I can't control them. I can't stop them.

"Please don't send me back," I barely push out and it causes Carter's fingers to dig deeper into my shoulders before he releases me. Stalking to a chair on the far side of the bedroom, he sits with his body leaning forward, his dark eyes staring at me through the dark room.

My skin tingles with a numbing fear. I can't go back to the cell. Tears leak from my eyes at the thought that one fear of mine, a man who destroyed my world and threatened to do more, would keep me from being safe from yet another, the cell.

"Please," I plead weakly and before the word is completely spoken, Carter commands me, "Come here."

Although my body feels weak, I force my limbs to move quickly as they fight with his sheets. I practically fall to the ground and quickly crawl to him, the rug brushing against my knees.

In nothing but a pair of silk pajama pants, his abs ripple in the faint moonlight. His body looks like it was carved in marble. Even with the fear still strongly present, I can feel the itch of my fingers to run down the carved lines of his muscles. If nothing else, he's a beautiful distraction. He can use me, fuck me into a deep sleep. And I would beg for it in this moment.

I'd beg him to use me and take away everything else.

I slow my pace as I get closer to him, the necklace nearly dragging on the ground. Its presence makes my nakedness very much at the forefront of my mind. His knees are parted, and I settle in between them. In the darkness and with that look in his eye, he radiates power as I kneel at his feet.

Slowly, I reach my hands up to his thighs in the silence. He hasn't said a word, but I'm sure I have to please him. I can't go back to the cell. Not over this.

My fingers slip between the silk fabric and his hot skin at the deep V on his hips.

My actions are cut short and my heart lurches when Carter's strong fingers grab my wrist and yank my hand away. I can barely breathe as the intensity in his gaze ignites.

The silence stretches as he stares at me and I feel helpless, not knowing what he wants.

"Get on all fours," he commands me, barely loosening his grip so I can quickly obey him. My heart thumps so hard it's all I can hear.

"Face on the floor," he tells me, and I do as he says, keeping my ass in the air. "Palms up and at your knees," Carter tells me and again I do as he says, but he repositions them. All the weight of my body is on my shoulders and neck as I lay my head on the floor and my arms stay behind me, not useful in balancing or aiding me in any way. I'm completely bared to him and at his mercy.

A moment passes and then another as Carter paces around me. I try to swallow, but I can't. The fear of him finding me less than pleasing makes my knees tremble, and he only responds by moving my legs farther apart. The moment I close my eyes, his deep and rough voice commands me to open them and look at him. Towering over me, I have no idea what my dark knight thinks of me or what he plans to do to me.

"Tell me what you were dreaming of," he finally says, and I answer him, the rug rubbing against my cheek and my breath feels hot against my face.

"I don't remember," I tell him and although it's true, I know what the terrors consist of.

"It wasn't important to you? Not important enough to remember?" he asks as he crouches behind me. I can't see him, but I can feel him. I can always feel Carter's unyielding presence.

"No," I shake my head against the ground and answer him how I think he wants me to. "It's not important and I'm sorry," I tell him, and the silence stretches.

My body jolts forward as his hand brushes against my ass. The rough pad of his thumb follows down to my pussy, gently trailing along my clit and then back up. He grips my ass cheek in a bruising manner and my eyes shut tight as I prepare for more.

Whack! His hand slaps against my ass and forces a cry from my lips. I sink my teeth into my lip and take another. The sharp stinging pain is accompanied by his hand sliding up my front, so he can roll my left nipple between his fingers. The combination of pain and pleasure is directly linked to my clit. My body rocks to the side, unable to stay still as he pulls my now hardened peak.

He instantly releases me to push down on my upper back between my shoulder blades, and he spanks the same spot on my ass again. Biting down on my lip, changes the cry to a muffled whimper and the pain that shoots up my body ignites every nerve ending in my body, heating my core and stealing my breath.

Panting against the rug, I wait for more. I can feel my pussy clench around nothing, praying for pleasure to take the pain away. His splayed hand on my back travels along my spine, leaving a trail of goosebumps. I can feel his breath against my ass before he bites down, making my mouth form an O with both surprise and something else. The pain is nothing like what I expect and my body trembles with delight at the thought of more.

Quickly, he pulls away and another sharp smack meets my heated skin, this one sending tears to my eyes. The pain and intensity have gathered into a ball in the pit of my stomach and I don't know that I can take anymore.

"Please," I whisper, but I don't know what I'm asking for.

"Why am I punishing you, Aria?" His deep voice is a soothing balm to my broken cries.

"Because I woke you," I answer him as I feel his hips brush against the backs of my thighs. He settles behind me and lowers his lips to my shoulder. He plants a small kiss on my shoulder as the head of his cock gently presses into my entrance. It's only a tease and I find myself rocking backward, praying he'll fuck me and take the pain away.

His hot breath tickles the crook of my neck as he whispers, "Because you lied to me."

I can't respond because he immediately slams inside of me and fucks me exactly how I wanted him to.

CHAPTER 21

Carter

"THERE ARE FIVE WINGS IN THE ESTATE. AND EACH HAS THEIR OWN LOCK." I glance down at Aria, listening to her bare feet pad on the marble tile as we enter the foyer. The double-doored entrance is only feet away and I know she's resisting the urge to look at it.

"There are locks everywhere, inside and out." She chances a peek at me and stills when she meets my gaze. "I often invite those who I don't consider friends here and sometimes I don't want them to leave."

She's silent as she considers what I've said. Nervousness trickles down her body. It's in the way she swallows, the way she holds her hands in front of her. The way she almost trips over her own feet. And I love her nervousness.

"The front door, for instance." I motion toward it and she turns stiffly as if she wasn't dying to look at it. "That box there, to the right of it. You need a code to open it, from either inside or out."

"I thought you said it was one or the other." Her soft voice is questioning. Her hazel eyes peer up at me as if I've wronged her. As if I've hurt her. "You said a bird can be tethered or caged, not both."

A smile tickles my lips as I reply, "Haven't you learned that all you need to do is ask?"

Her lips turn down into a frown, but she stays quiet. She knows she's caged. Wherever she goes, she will go with me, caged and protected just the same.

"I'm a prisoner," she says as her voice cracks, and she looks longingly at the front doors. The architecture foreboding in a way that seems to forbid a guest from leaving.

"You were before in your father's home." My voice is deep and echoes in the foyer. Her eyes reach up to mine in shock as I continue, "Afraid to leave. Afraid to do anything without permission."

"I wasn't afraid," she whispers, and I know she's well aware of the lie she's spoken.

"You let fear rule you. Don't lie to me." Unease trickles through me. The realization of what she truly fears could change everything.

"How do you know what I did and didn't do?" she asks weakly, denying the truth and deflecting her attention to something else.

Since she lied to me, I present a lie to her in return. "When you were offered to me,

I did my research. I have friends in your father's army of men. Eyes and ears who offer information for a certain price. I know you spent almost all of your time alone in your room. Maybe that's why it took so long for you to obey me. You're used to cells."

Her mouth parts, no doubt with a rebuttal, but wisely she slams it shut before a word is spoken.

Time passes as we move on. Both of us quiet. Both of us in our own world of denial.

"Your things can be moved to my office, den, or the bedroom. The drawing pad and whatever else you want," I offer her but still, she's quiet. Her fingers fidget with one another throughout the tour of the two wings she's allowed to enter. She doesn't seem to look at anything or notice anything at all unless we pass a window, which, as I pointed out, have locks on them as well.

"Why are there five wings?" she asks me as I lead her to the grand kitchen. She still hasn't eaten and she needs to. There's no reason for her not to and the threat of sending her back to the cell if she doesn't, is so close to being spoken to life. I'd rather save it for something else, something more meaningful. But my little bird needs to eat.

"I had four brothers and decided they should each have their own wing," I tell her and step into the kitchen. The garden is just beyond the back wall, lined with black glass from floor to ceiling. The floors are a dark walnut and polished so smoothly I can see our reflection in them.

Her eyes move across the sleek, modern kitchen, from the high-end cabinets to the white granite countertops. Everything is done in white. It's clean and modern and balances the black glass perfectly.

I anticipate her saying many things, but not the next words that spill from her lips. "I'm sorry."

My forehead pinches with a deep crease. "For what?" I question.

"You said you had four brothers. I take it that one or more have passed?" She turns to face me and her hip brushes one of the stools to the island. I can tell she's not sure if she should sit or not, and I leave her wondering. Just like I leave the pangs of regret and sadness to settle in my gut. Instead, I focus on how discerning Aria is. She's a deadly combination of beautiful and perceptive. I need to remember that.

"Carter," Jase calls out from behind me and when I turn his steps slow. His eyes drift from where I am, almost blocking Aria from view, and then to her.

"I didn't realize you were busy," he says to me although his eyes travel down Aria's body. Even with her robe tied tightly with the sash and covering her décolletage, she looks like she was made to tempt.

"What is it?" I ask him and again he looks at her. From my periphery, I watch her glance at the floor and those fingers of hers continue making tight knots around one another.

Gripping the back of her neck, just slightly, she stops her fidgeting.

They both want to know what she is to me. I can see it written on their faces as much as I can feel the tension in the air.

It doesn't matter what she is, so long as they all know she's mine.

Even more, I know Jase is questioning the way I hold her at this moment and why she's out of the cell. Maybe he's wondering how long I'll keep her out here. Or how long I'll keep her period.

I make soothing strokes with my thumb along the back of her neck as Jase tells me something about a car. I don't know what the fuck he's talking about. I don't give a damn either. I assume it's some update about the supply, but he doesn't want to speak openly in front of Aria.

My little songbird relaxes under my touch, peeking up at me every so often. I know she's wondering what he thinks of her.

"Aria," I say her name in the middle of whatever Jase was saying and he falls silent. "I'd like you to step outside, so I can talk to Jase." All I can hear is her breathing in this moment. The fear, the hope, the surprise of her surroundings. My poor Aria knows so little. But she'll learn.

She quickly nods but she doesn't move until my hand slips down her back, leaving a trail along the silk. Jase stays by the island, his hands in his pockets as I lead her to the door. It's black glass as well and blends into the wall, only opening when a verified print is pressed against the biometric security panel. Aria watches intently, but she wouldn't be able to open it if she tried and with fifteen-foot walls around the garden and a guarded fence around the estate, she won't be able to run.

I can see it on her face when the realization registers with her.

"And when I'm done with this conversation, it's back to the bedroom." I lean in closer to her and whisper in her ear, "I'm going to fuck you until I've had my fill."

The sound of Jase's footsteps lets me know he's coming as I watch Aria walk into the garden, letting the sun hit her face as if it's the first time she's ever experienced it.

"I have Jared on the lookout at the club. We'll have a list of the heavy buyers of S2L by the end of the week."

"Perfect," I answer him although I watch Aria walking deeper into the garden to lie on a patch of grass. "Anything else?"

"Talvery knows we have her."

A smile pulls my lips up. "It took him long enough. One of Romano's men leaked it?"

I turn to Jase, who's watching Aria as he nods. "It couldn't stay secret forever." He turns to look at me before adding, "He'll come for her."

"He'll want to," I correct him. "But which of his men would be willing to come here and die for her?"

"She speaks highly of Nikolai," Jase offers, and I can see the hint of a smile on his face. Aria's first week in the cell gave me plenty of information as she talked out loud to nothing but brick walls, begging for help and companionship. Nikolai's name slipped from her lips nearly every single fucking day.

"Let him come. He can be the first of them to die."

CHAPTER 22

Aria

THE SMELL OF COFFEE IS WHAT WAKES ME, AND WITHOUT THINKING I ROLL OVER in the large bed, stretching before I'm even fully awake. The soothing ache of my muscles is comforting, as is the gentle fragrance of clean linens and the hint of a masculine scent that makes my core both ache and heat.

And then I remember.

It's always like this.

I've been out of the cell for three days, and yet when I wake up in Carter's bed, it takes me a moment to remember. Maybe I don't want to admit that it's real. Maybe a part of my subconscious is far away from here. But each morning I have to remember.

Slowly, I calm my beating heart and wait for a noise, any sign that he's here. He's a sinful addiction, creeping into my blood and fueling the lust and fire for the forbidden. I crave him, his acceptance, his dominance, and yet I'm so aware that's all wrong. That small voice that whispers there must be a way out of here is getting quieter by the day. That's what scares me the most.

Three mornings I've woken up in Carter's bed, and just like the last two, he's not here.

Not physically, but he's watching. I learned the hard way yesterday, only the second day of being out of the cell. I thought I couldn't waste another day, listening and obeying. I had to try to find a way out of here. The memory forces my gaze to the dresser.

I was snooping. How could I not? He wasn't here, and I still have no way out of his grasp. No one comes in and no one goes out. The place is a fortress and I its prisoner.

And so, drawer after drawer, I slipped them open, hoping to find something. I'm not sure what. A gun or a weapon.

I'm not sure he'd listen to me if I made demands and held him at gunpoint, or that I'd be successful in rushing him or forcing him to let me go. Somehow, I find it hard to believe, but still, I had to try.

My eyes close and my body tenses, remembering his deep voice and how it shook me to the core. The drawer slammed shut as I screamed out and dared to look over my shoulder at Carter leaning against the doorframe.

"Kneel." The one word I've refused over and over from Carter brought me to my knees. My words tripped over one another as I tried to apologize or hide what I was doing.

But I've always been a terrible liar and he knew better.

"Open your mouth." Hearing him give me the command made my pussy hot and clench with desire. He throat fucked me. A punishment, I suppose, but it's not what it was for me.

With my fingers digging into my thighs, my eyes burning, and my breath cut from me, he shoved himself down my throat. And I was nothing but wet for him.

The fear was still present. It's always present. The knowledge that when he was done using me, he could send me back to the cell kept that fear very much alive.

He wasn't done with me when he pulled away and allowed me to breathe again. As I heaved for air, he forced me to all fours. Shamefully, my face turned hot as it hit the rug and he slammed inside of me. My back tried to arch as I moaned a ragged, strangled sound of pleasure.

I came nearly instantly, and Carter stilled deep inside of me. Gripping the hair at the base of my skull, he forced me to arch my back and whispered in my ear, "You fucking love what I do to you." And I couldn't deny it.

I fucking loved it. But it was a punishment and I was reminded of that and what I'd done before he left me panting and sated on the floor.

"Next time it will be the cell." His words ring clear in my head as I glance at all the drawers I have yet to open.

I may love the way he fucks me, but that doesn't change much. I don't fight the urges anymore. I want them, and they help me to survive, but it doesn't make me any less ashamed, because I know very well I'm a prisoner here and Carter can do with me as he wishes.

Although I crave my freedom, that doesn't mean I don't have desires in my captivity.

The one thing I always notice is what Carter doesn't do.

He never kisses me. Never once. And he doesn't talk to me the same way when there are people around. I've met two of his brothers and each time I anticipated being tossed aside or demeaned. But each time, Carter's talked to me as if I'm a friend, maybe. Or a business acquaintance. As do his brothers, although their words are few.

When we're alone, it's different. There's a comfort in his voice I didn't expect that's only replaced by a heavy cadence of desire when he gives me a command.

The combination of all of this is a whirlwind of chaos in my mind.

But one fact remains the same: Another day survived is another day I'm Carter's whore.

My bare feet sink into the rug beneath the bed as I slink off of it and walk toward the cup of coffee on the dresser. It's still hot to the touch.

A million thoughts bombard me every waking moment. Why is he doing this is the one that's a constant. Carter's a man of intentions. Calculated and manipulative.

Lifting the hot cup of coffee to my lips, I blow across the top and feel the heat caress my face.

He could have slipped something into the cup. He could have left it on the dresser intentionally to remind me of yesterday. My feet are planted right where I was when he punished me.

I go over every possible reason he could have had for putting a cup of a coffee within sight and leaving it for me. It's flavored with enough cream and sugar that the bitter coffee flavor is less evident. Yesterday I made a cup for myself, my first cup of coffee since I've been here. And he must have watched.

Maybe that was the reason he left this here; he wanted me to know he was watching. Maybe he just wanted me to wake up.

Swallowing the sweetened drug, I decide it doesn't matter. I could wonder all I want, but I'll never know.

The only thing that matters is that if I didn't drink it, he would know, and I imagine he would be disappointed. Which is something I don't want to risk happening after yesterday.

I'm determined to be cautious and smart with every decision.

To not go back to the cell, but also to help Carter. I haven't forgotten his deal. He said I would help him and then he'd give me everything. I'm waiting, staying in his good graces. But something is going to change. I can feel it in my bones. All I have to do is obey and wait for the time to strike. Either for his plan to come to fruition or for another opportunity to make its presence known so I can escape and go back to the safety of my father's home.

Before I even realize it, the ceramic mug is empty in my hands and I leave it on the dresser to change into the clothes he left for me on the end of the bed.

Another routine of his. It's the routines that give me comfort. Knowing what to expect, and how to react. That's something that doesn't frighten me, if nothing else.

The fabric is thicker today. Nothing sheer or delicate. I have to grip the shoulders of it and hold it at arm's length to discover it's a black cotton wraparound dress. It's beautiful and as I slip it on, the soft fabric tickling just above my knee where it stops, I start to feel beautiful myself.

The necklace, the dress. They're classically elegant and hug my curves. I'm tempted to brush my hair and use some of the toiletries Jase bought for me.

More than anything, I want to draw the image of the woman I used to be onto the new canvases I was given last night. A blank page begs to be covered in ink, and I feel and look so different now. Maybe not so much on the surface, but everything I think and feel is no longer a semblance of what once was.

But first, I dress how he wants me to, I'll seek him out, and then I'll bide my time hiding in the art where I can remember what used to be and hold on to the last piece of the girl I used to know.

I know I'm only playing into Carter's hand as I thread my fingers through my locks and make a braid, placing it over my shoulder and then reach for the cosmetic bag. I don't recognize myself.

But the woman in the mirror is lovely. The kind of lovely that fills other women with envy, but as I drop the mascara onto the counter, I know that no one would envy me and all I am is a pretty fuck doll for Carter.

For now. It's what I have to be. Or at least that's what I tell myself. I try to dignify it by convincing myself that I have to in order to survive. But I can't deny the thought of him commanding me to spread my legs for him sends a wave of heat and want to my core.

Stepping out of the bedroom makes me nervous. It doesn't make much sense to feel safe at all here, but there is a hint of safety in knowing that only Carter will come into his bedroom. I know what to expect. Outside of the confines of those walls are things I have yet to explore.

I know where the den is, and I spent a good bit of time there yesterday. Photographs upon photographs and beautiful art lined every inch of wall in the den. It was easy to lose myself, and take in each one, imagining I had somehow slipped away and fallen into the art, away from here.

Someone in here has a fondness for old trucks. Nearly ten photographs had trucks in them, rusted and worn down, the hoods covered in snow or blue flowers peeking out from under the tires. I've never felt so strongly that old trucks are beautiful until I felt the emotion from the photographs. Maybe I'll draw that instead. Or both. I have plenty of time for both.

I know where the kitchen is from Carter's bedroom too.

And I've ventured there on my own once, but the other times Carter's brought me there.

Yesterday he made me kneel in the kitchen. The way he said it reminded me of the punishment in his bedroom, and I quickly fell to the ground to obey.

The cold floors were smooth and unforgiving against my legs, but I stayed still and at his feet as he fed me bits of his meals. I think he truly enjoys doing it. Having me on my knees beside him and at his mercy. And I have to admit, I didn't hate it, at least not until someone came into the kitchen.

I could hear whoever it was walking in, but they didn't say a word. I remember how I stilled, how I didn't know what to do.

Carter continued to place the chunks of salmon between my lips. And within seconds, whoever had entered, left.

From what I know, there are four men living here. The only other one who's talked to me outside of Carter is Jase. But I imagine it's only when Carter permits it. And I have a mental note in the back of my head to befriend him. The more ammunition I have, the better.

But I'll be careful. I'll be smart. And for now, that means obeying.

I'm nearly to the right threshold of the grand kitchen when I see Carter leaning against the counter, an iPad in his hand and his attention focused on it.

I can't help the way I freeze. As if I could somehow blend into the rich hall and vanish before he could see me.

Even if his touch lights every nerve ending of mine on fire, I still fear Carter. That will never change. Letting out a shaky breath is my downfall; Carter peeks up from his task and sees me. His gaze is lethal as he takes in my appearance.

Slowly. Ever so slowly.

Every inch of skin where his gaze lingers is instantly set ablaze.

"Come." It's the only word I'm given. A command not to be denied, and that rapid hammering in my chest intensifies. One step after another.

My life has become a series of careful steps.

Before I've even come fully into the kitchen, he commands me to kneel and I hesitate. His voice is different. The reverence and desire are absent. Something's wrong and immediately I feel defensive. My hands feel clammy as I wonder what's changed. I nearly swear to him that I haven't done anything wrong.

I've only ever kneeled at his feet, but the power in his voice makes my knees weak and I drop to the floor where I am, feet away from him in the hall, although I'm afraid he wanted me next to him. Fear. Fear commands these so carefully taken steps.

A moment passes and then another before he glances my way, through the doorway to the kitchen. "Here, songbird. Come kneel here." There's an edge of annoyance in his voice and I nearly cry. It's ridiculous. Utterly ridiculous that his reprimand would upset me to that extent, but as I crawl the last few feet to sit beside him in a kneeling position, my body nearly buckles, and I realize why this morning Carter seems different. Harder and less interested.

"You have her trained well." The man's voice sparks anger in my blood. It mixes with the fear, confusing me and I have a difficult time managing my expression, my movements. Everything in me is screaming to look at Romano, to stare into his cold dark eyes and tell him to go fuck himself.

"There's still plenty for her to learn," Carter speaks absently, swiping the screen of the iPad and focusing his attention on it. He doesn't touch me. Not like he does around his brothers.

My head hangs low, so low it nearly hurts my neck, but I don't want Romano to see my face. I have to bite the inside of my cheek so hard that it bleeds to keep from speaking up.

Be smart, I remind myself although it doesn't soothe a damn thing I'm feeling.

"How's—"

Carter cuts Romano off and states, "I'm happy with it. Let's move forward."

With his simple words, Carter leaves my side to walk the few feet across the kitchen, passing the iPad back to Romano and I chance a peek up. In his crisp dress shirt and dark gray slacks, Carter's expensive, dominating appearance is at odds with Romano's mien. His shirt hangs baggy in the front, not tailored to be fitted, I'd suspect because of his weight.

"When does it begin?" Carter asks with his back to Romano as he stalks toward me. He catches my stare and holds it until he reaches me, forcing me to pull my chin up so I don't break his gaze.

He only looks away when his hand reaches my hair and he cups the back of my head. The satisfaction and thrill of having him hold me so gently and possessively are undeniably fucked up. But still, I nearly smile.

The more comfortable I get, the more I grow to crave his small touches and the warmth of his body.

It's not supposed to be this way, but I can feel myself slipping into this new reality.

"Next week," Romano answers him and I can practically hear his grin. "We'll start taking them out all at once. As many as we can."

Adrenaline pumps in my veins, remembering the conversation from weeks ago. He's going to kill my father's men and all I can think about is Nikolai, my first kiss and only true friend in this world. My family and everyone I grew up with.

I know, and yet I can do nothing. The air around me is suffocating as I sit there silently, remembering how easily some of them have killed before, how I've wished that those men would die so many times. But not all of them. Not my family. Not Nikolai.

Inside I scream at myself to beg for answers, to beg for mercy. But on the surface I stay calm and wait for Romano to leave. There has to be a way for me to spare some of the people I love. The only people I love. The only family I have.

Please, show mercy. I nearly whisper the words as Carter leaves me yet again, walking Romano to the door and leaving me lonely and pathetic on the floor of the kitchen.

I don't make a sound. I stay silent.

But I will beg. I will fight. I will do anything. I won't let them kill my family.

There has to be a way.

If he cares anything for me, he'll show mercy. My gaze drops to the shadows of the two of them in the hall. The saddest part of the last thought is that I already know he won't show mercy. I'm only his whore.

CHAPTER 23

THE FIRE CRACKLES. I'VE ALWAYS FOUND COMFORT IN THE SOOTHING SOUND. My songbird's humming is the only thing that's come close and whether or not she knows it, she's been humming every so often since I left her in the den.

Gripping the back of the tufted sofa, I watch the glow of the fire play across her face. The shadows only make her look more beautiful. Even though she's drawing near the hearth, she hasn't turned on the lights. The sun set hours ago, taking the daylight that filled this room with it. But she's stayed by the fire, consumed with her art.

"Aria." I attempt to keep my voice calm and gentle, so I don't startle her. But I achieve the opposite and the black charcoal in her hand leaves a mar across the center of the piece she's drawing. Surprise and fear are evident from her parted lips but she shifts her expression quickly, leaving her pad and the charcoal on the hearth to kneel for me.

She doesn't address me any other way, simply waiting for a command. Her submission is beautiful, but there's a twisting in my gut. She's faking it. It's only because of yesterday. She's only being good because I caught her searching through my room. She doesn't fool me.

"You did well this morning," I compliment her as I round the large sofa. Her eyes watch me; they watch every movement I make.

As much as I see her, I know she sees me. It's one of the things that's pulling me to her every second of every day.

I don't want to miss the little hints of honesty that she can't hide from me.

"I don't like that man," she says under her breath, daring to raise her eyes to me. "Romano." A grin pulls at my lips. "I couldn't tell," I say, toying with her.

She did perfectly. Submitting to me and showing him how I have her under my thumb. That I've gained control of her, even when she couldn't contain her contempt for him.

She's helping me set him up for his own demise, and she doesn't even know it.

"Can I tell you a secret?" I ask her as I sink into the sofa, relaxing against it as she nods once and then whispers, "Yes."

"Come here." I pat the seat next to me and watch her debate on whether she should crawl or stand to get here. Glancing at her right hand, covered in charcoal, she chooses to stand and reach for the towel on the coffee table. She's deliberate in her motions as she quickly cleans her hands and then walks quietly to sit beside me. Only the crackling of the fire occupies the silence.

As she sits, I slip my arm around her waist, pulling her closer, lowering my lips to her ear then nipping her lobe before moving to her neck.

When I'm touching her, she knows exactly how to behave. She loses that constant inner questioning and gives herself to me completely. Letting her breathing quicken and her head fall to the side. She can't hide from me when my hands are on her.

It's a heady feeling I've grown addicted to.

I imagine she doesn't realize how often she touches me. Like now, how she reaches out to my shoulder as I rake my teeth up and down her neck.

Nipping her ear once more and feeling the thrill of her ragged moans deep in my chest, I whisper to her, "I want the man dead."

Her lashes flutter open and as they do, Jase enters the doorway. He hesitates and nearly turns around, but I gesture for him to enter. Time and time again, she seizes up when another person is added to the equation. She forgets how to react and becomes a lost little bird with a broken wing. Stiff in my embrace, she struggles to know where to look as Jase enters.

Slowly she pulls her legs up onto the sofa and bows her head. I know Jase is watching me, but I can't take my eyes away from her.

"You're mine," I tell her in a voice that commands her to look back at me. "You will hold your head up high." Her eyes widen slightly and then follow my fingers as I trace them from her collar down the center of her chest. "How else will they see this?" My pointer intertwines with the necklace and she nods in understanding.

I can feel her heart racing just beyond my touch, but I let the necklace fall into place and turn back to my brother. The judgment and disgust that lingered in his eyes only days ago are gone, replaced now only by curiosity. It's all going better than I'd hoped, even if it has taken longer than I'd planned.

"It's set for next week." As the words register with Jase and he tells me the shipments are coming in early for Romano, I notice how Aria's demeanor changes again.

She already knows too much. As much as I enjoy her presence, she shouldn't be privy to the knowledge of how her father's empire will fall.

"You look lovely tonight," Jase speaks directly to her. Surprise lights up her face as the fire continues to cast shadows over her.

"Thank you," she says, but her voice is soft, too soft and she clears her throat to repeat herself. "Thank you."

"I admire your art," he adds, and I glance down at the scattering of papers on the floor. Three new ones today, and each more stunning than the last. She's not rushed anymore. She takes her time, and the beauty she creates is captivating. I never expected to feel proud of what I thought was only a distraction.

The thrill rings in my blood. She craves acceptance, protection, and a tenderness that I can't always give her. But my brothers can. Even now as she worries and struggles, his kindness makes her weaker toward me. Each small gesture of acceptance makes her more willing to obey me.

"She's talented." I compliment her as well, although I speak to Jase.

"Thank you," she says again, and the fidgeting stops momentarily, replaced by a calmer demeanor.

"We'll go over the rest tonight," I tell Jase and he takes the cue to leave easily enough. No more of this in front of her. She needs to be perfect for the dinner.

And then everything will change.

"Tonight then," Jase says and nods a goodnight to Aria. A gentle smile flickers on her lips, but she struggles to speak to him in return.

"You're doing so well," I speak to her gently as Jase leaves us. Her hair is soft under my fingers as I push the locks from her face. "Apart from yesterday morning, I mean."

The reminder makes her stiffen, but only until I trail my fingers back to the necklace, the mix of pearls and diamonds strung together on a thin platinum chain. So delicate and breakable, just like her.

"I'm sorry," she apologizes again.

"No, you're not." The words come out with a sternness that's irrefutable. "I expected as much, but you aren't sorry."

"I'm sorry I disappointed you," she says, and the statement sounds genuine, even as she closes her eyes and swallows noticeably. I take in every hint of her features, seeing nothing but sincerity.

"Aria," I tell her as I slip my hand to the nape of her neck, "you haven't disappointed me." My voice is deeper than I intended, laced with the lust I still have for her.

I thought I would grow tired of her but having Aria and playing with her has become my favorite game.

She only sighs at my statement, a soft sound that's a mix of want and need and something else.

I whisper at the shell of her ear, "I can spoil you; this doesn't have to be something you hate."

"I will give you anything," she whispers and those beautiful eyes peer into mine, searching for mercy, "Please don't kill my family."

"I had to pick a side, but they'll both die, Aria. There's no changing that." If I could steal the pain from her, I would.

"You said you wanted him dead. Romano. Why not side with my father?"

"Do you think your father would spare me, Aria? Do you think he'd allow me to live?" My voice comes out harder with each word, remembering how my life was almost snuffed out by his hands. Her gorgeous eyes turn to dark wells of sadness. She knows the truth about her father, but still, she continues.

"He would," she whispers with hopefulness.

"He wouldn't," I tell her, expecting to be angered by her naivety, but it's only pity for her that I feel. "You need to stay out of this, Aria," I command her, and she nods once, but I can see the pleas written on her face.

"I can't just do nothing," she whispers.

"You must, or you'll leave me with no choice." It's not a threat, but it's full of truth and I pray she behaves. "You're smarter than this. You know how to survive."

"I'll always be a prisoner," she murmurs, and her voice is soft but desperate. Her eyes open and she almost says something. She almost begs or pleads or questions. But she doesn't.

"I want to steal the fight from you," I say the words without thinking, without realizing how honest they are. "I will have all of you, Aria."

It takes a moment for her to respond, and when she does, it's with her eyes closed and her words are laced with pain. "I know you will."

She holds on to that pain so well. Gripping it chaotically, just to hold on to something. In a way, that enrages the very core of my being. But soon all she'll hold on to is me. So soon. I have to be patient with her. If nothing else, time will dull her pain and then all she'll have is me.

"Lie back," I give her the command and she obeys instantly, falling onto the sofa and resting her head on the decorative pillow. Brushing my hand against her inner thigh, she parts her legs for me. The cotton slips up higher, but I have to lift her ass up and push the dress up to her waist to see all of her.

"You're always wet for me," I utter the words beneath my breath as my cock hardens. My fingers trail up and down her shaved pussy. Her lips glisten with arousal and her breathing hitches.

I unbutton my collar and pull my shirt off first, dropping it carelessly to the floor. Every second that passes, Aria's breathing gets heavier. The sofa groans under me as I shift my weight to move my shoulders between her thighs.

Gripping her ass to hold her in place, I start with a single languid lick of her tempting cunt. When I look up and find her lips parted, her eyes wide and her cheeks that beautiful hue of pink, I decide I won't stop licking, sucking and tongue fucking her cunt until she can't fight me any longer.

And then I'll have her writhing under me, cumming on my cock like she was made to do.

CHAPTER 24

Aria

T HIS ISN'T WHAT LIFE IS SUPPOSED TO BE LIKE. NOT FOR SOMEONE LIKE ME. Surrounded by luxury and chained to a gilded cage, I shouldn't wake up feeling at ease.

But that's how I feel. I know that so long as I obey Carter, I'll be all right. I'll be safe and pampered even.

While my family is murdered, and I do nothing.

I can't allow it. I won't.

I have to remind myself with each kindness he offers me.

Like last night. I was holding onto a deadly combination of hate and hope. Desperate for a way out of here so I could warn my family, or a way to convince Carter to be on my father's side to present itself.

And I slipped into sleep knowing I needed to do something. That today I would act and find a way. But each kindness makes me weaker.

I'll never forget the way he held me. Gripping me to him as I lay on my side. My heart raced, and fear was real in my veins. As real as anything else. Sleep still held my eyes tightly shut until I heard his voice, recognized the deep measure of his determined words. "Come back to me." His breath was hot on my neck, his hand strong as it splayed across my belly. He held me so close and so tightly, I couldn't move when I woke up.

I could still feel the drum of my racing heart as he flipped me onto my back and buried his head in the crook of my neck, kissing me ravenously, as if he'd been deprived of it. And I pined for his lips on mine, but he didn't give them to me. I was still blinking away sleep when he whispered, "If you're going to scream a name in your sleep, it'll be my name."

I woke up wondering if it was a dream if he hadn't really taken me from a nightmare and fucked me into a deep sleep of desire. But he was still holding me the way he had when I woke up and there was no denying it was real.

"You stopped humming." Carter's deep voice pierces through my thoughts and I look up at him from the ground beneath his feet. Rolling the black charcoal between my fingers I lie to him, something I know I shouldn't do.

"I'm just thinking about what I'd like to draw next."

He knows my response is a lie. His eyes narrow, but he allows it. I don't think he wants me to go back to the cell any more than I do. Although part of me wonders if one day he'll start fucking me on that mattress and I'll be confined there.

The only thing that relieves that thought is the knowledge that Carter enjoys others seeing how I've become his. How I obey him while he gives me this freedom. If you can call it that.

My gaze wanders across Carter's office and lands yet again on a bench that doesn't belong. It peeks out from under the bookshelf across from me and it simply isn't supposed to be there.

The wood is old and unfinished, at odds with the dark polished shelves housing beautifully covered books.

The hinges have a hint of rust. I tap the charcoal in my hand against the paper and stare at it. Wondering why Carter would allow it to stay.

"Where did the bench come from?" I ask him on a whim. I haven't asked him anything. Not for a single thing. Nor have I initiated conversation. But if I have any hope of changing his mind about my father, I have to be able to speak up. And it starts right now, with that bench. Craning my neck to look at him over the desk, from where I'm seated on the floor in front of him, I wait for his reaction.

"Bench?" he questions, although I already know that he knows what I'm referring to.

Pointing straight in front of me, I answer him, "It doesn't look like it belongs."

I can hear his chair creak as he leans back, and I know he's debating on telling me something, although I don't know what. It's only an old, beat-up bench.

"Do you want to see what it can do?" he asks me, and the tone of his words catches me off guard. He must sense the hesitation because as he rises and makes his way to the bench, he adds, "It's a safe box."

The charcoal in my hand makes a small thud as it hits the paper and I watch Carter open the lid to what I thought was just an old bench.

"It's bulletproof, and it can only be locked from the inside."

"Someone could just pick it up…" I state my thought absently and he gives me a small, sad smile.

"If they knew you were in there, they could try, although it's heavy. So heavy I couldn't lift it with Daniel the day I got it."

I let my eyes graze over Carter's shoulders then back to what I thought was only a bench. I take a quick breath, ready to ask him if it was from his childhood. It's obviously far too small for him. Although I know I could easily fit. But I don't question him.

"The lock is here," he tells me and fiddles with something inside of it that clinks. I have to stand up to see and since I'm standing, I walk closer to him and to the contraption.

"Is it really safe?" I ask him and he's quiet until I look up at him. His eyes question mine. "As safe as a box can be."

Now that I'm closer to it, I'm certain I could fit inside. It would be tight. As if reading my mind, Carter tells me, "You'd fit. You'd be safe."

My eyes drift to the brass locks on the inside. There are only two, but they travel along the entire top edge. A long rod of steel falls down and slips into place when locked. I imagine you could open it with a welding torch, but with all this metal, the person inside would be burned, scarred, maybe killed before the box would actually open.

"Can you breathe in there?" I whisper my question.

Carter nods and runs his finger along small slits in the box, designed so they can't be seen from the outside, but light filters through them.

I swallow thickly as Carter places a hand on my lower back and asks, "Do you want to get inside?"

I should say no, the fear inside of me is there at the forefront, screaming that the small space is dangerous. It may look like safe, but the cell was much larger, and it was instrumental in my downfall.

But the fear is so minuscule. So quiet. It's hard to be scared of something so… insignificant when my life is in the hands of a man like Carter. And I think he'd like it if I got inside.

I nod once and as I do, I'm already lifting my right leg. With Carter's hand to balance me, I slip inside easily.

"The locks are here, but you'll have to feel for them when the lid is shut, it'll be dark."

"Are you going to close it?" I ask him and my heart pounds. I don't want him to leave me here. He towers over me and answers, "You'd be the one to close and lock it, Aria."

"Right. Of course," I say then shake my head and reach for the lid. As if it's the obvious thing to do. It strikes me then as odd that he would grant me this, a safe place to be away from him. But I could only stay in here so long.

This box is meant for hiding. The thought occurs to me as I lower the lid. It's meant to hide, to stay quiet and not be seen.

My heart thumps once as the lid shuts tightly and a tiny ray of light shines through. It's filtering in through a small slit. One that can't be seen from the outside, but I can see it clearly.

My fingers trace the locks as they slip into place, a heavy thump from the steel rod falling causing my body to react by bucking back.

Thump, thump. My heart hammers.

It reminds me of the door being kicked in when I was hiding in the closet.

My throat closes and my eyes water as I clearly see my mother through the slit. Just like I did when I hid in the closet. The memory is vivid. It's too real.

"Stop!" I scream and struggle against the lid. Panic consumes me. *I can't stay here, I can't be quiet and let him murder her.*

Screams rip through my throat. "Stop it!" I scream and it's only then that I hear Carter. His fists pound above me.

The tears that stream down my face seem to burn my skin as I fumble for the locks.

"Carter, please!" I beg him.

"Lift the locks!" he yells at me, but I can't. I can't see them. All I can see is him holding my mother down, stabbing her over and over. The blood was everywhere. He was too fast. I couldn't save her.

"Please," I beg him and feel the entire box lift from the ground only to fall hard on the floor beneath me. Jostling me and reminding me where I am.

"Open it, Aria!" he yells at me and I try to find the locks. It takes me a long moment. Each second, images of my mother pass before my eyes. The way she tried to fight him. The way she tried not to scream. I know she didn't want me to hear or to see.

But you can only hide so much.

Finally, the locks slip back into place in my shaking hand and the mechanism opens with a loud thunk. Carter practically rips the top open. His strong arms pull me up and I'm safe in the light of the office. The images fade and I find myself huddled in his arms, feeling foolish and unable to explain what happened. My body won't stop shaking.

I hate the box. I hate it. I hate it more than the cell.

"Shhh," he shushes me and brings me to his chair. I think he's going to set me down in it, but he doesn't. He keeps holding me tight in his arms. My body shudders and I wish I could calm myself down and take it all back.

I can't stop crying.

I haven't had a panic attack in so long. It's only been night terrors for years.

"I'm sorry," I mumble the words and brush my tears away furiously. They're hot and I can already feel my eyes becoming puffy. I can hardly breathe.

"I hate the box," I push the words out as if I could blame it.

"It's okay." Carter's answer is soothing. He doesn't ask what happened. He doesn't push me for anything.

He only holds me and comforts me, running his hand up and down my back. His warmth and strength and scent surround me. And I want more of it.

I would die for more of it.

A knock at the office door startles me. "Hush, songbird," Carter whispers against my hair before calling to the door, "Come in."

It's Jase. It's almost always Jase.

He stands in the doorway, gripping the knob and not letting it go. I get the sense that he doesn't like to stay when I'm around. Like if I wasn't here, he'd have taken a seat. A shudder runs through my body, and I bury myself deeper into Carter's arms, wishing I could go back to just a minute ago.

"I just wanted to let you know, the dinner is set to go as planned."

Seeing Jase, reminds me of everything once again. Like being woken from a deep sleep. Back to realizing all of this is wrong and there isn't a piece of it that should feel right.

Back to the fact that I'm nestled in the arms of the man who's set to destroy everything I am.

The thought of dying for more of Carter's touch is still vibrant in my mind. And it withers like the petals of a broken flower in the scorching heat as the sane side of me remembers what I really am and who he really is.

"He's coming?" Carter asks and there's a deep rumble of anger hidden beneath his words. It's enough of an edge that my body stills in his embrace.

Jase nods, his gaze moving from me to Carter. "He's coming."

"And are we still on for tonight?" Carter asks Jase in a tone quite different. A tone that makes me curious. Curious enough to peek at Jase.

Jase's gaze flickers to me again before he answers, "Yeah, we're on for tonight." Patting the doorframe, he nods toward Carter and leaves us alone.

The tears, the flashback, and panic, they seem foolish now. It was only a glimpse at the past. Carter loosens his hold on me as my body stiffens and I hold my arms to my chest.

Why does he hold me and comfort me, when I'm nothing to him but a play toy? It's so he can make me weak. I know that's why. I'll fall powerless to him so easily. And he'll use me up and throw me out.

I can already see it happening.

"I'll be gone tonight." Carter's voice seems deeper, rougher even. The sound forces me to look at him as he speaks. It's odd to be at nearly eye level as I sit on his lap.

His gaze is so sharp, I can barely look him in the eye.

"You can get yourself dinner. And wait for me in either the kitchen, den, or bedroom." I stare at the knob on one of the drawers of his desk, nodding my head in obedience and feeling awkward and too afraid to speak.

My body shudders as he lays a hand on my upper back, between my shoulder blades and working his way down to the small of my back.

"Maybe you need a drink?"

When I turn to him this time, I want to yell at him. I want to hide. I want to cry.

The question is on the tip of my tongue, *why are you doing this to me?*

But I already know the answer. It's why Carter does everything.

Because he can. Because he wants to.

CHAPTER 25

Carter

THE RED ROOM WASN'T MY IDEA. IT WAS JASE'S, OF ALL PEOPLE. HE'S QUIET, KEEPS to himself, but he created a club that's the perfect cover-up and a successful business at that. He always stays in the back, where other business is conducted, but nonetheless, Jase's creation is something he's proud of. And every time I come here, I'm reminded of that fact.

The music thrums in my veins before the large red glass doors even open. In a gray tailored suit, I don't exactly blend in with the nightlife. Not like Jase does in his faded jeans and crisp, button-down, open at the collar.

I prefer a suit. Jase prefers to blend in. Each method has its advantages.

"Welcome back, sirs," Jared greets us as we step into the club, the music at full volume and the smells of alcohol and sex appeal hit me instantly. With the dark red paisley wallpaper that lines the walls and black chandeliers hanging from the sixteen-foot-high black ceiling, The Red Room looks like a nightclub of sin at first glance.

As the alcohol pours throughout the night and the bodies grind against one another, sin is an accurate description. The money flows as easily as the liquor.

Walking past the grinding bodies and kitten eyes from several women holding drinks in one hand and their clutches in another, I ignore it all, listening intently to what Jared has to say.

I stopped everything to come down here with my brother. All because Jared, the club manager, and head of business while we're away, said he had a girl who would talk.

"You sure it's her?" Jase asks him.

"Yeah," Jared nods as we pass the second bar and make our way around the edge of the dance floor to get to the backroom. "She comes in every week asking for it."

"What'd you tell her?"

"Nothing. Just that the delivery is on a delay." The DJ starts a new set and the dance floor roars so loudly the ground shakes as the steel doors to the backroom push open and then close softly, finally silencing the distractions of the club.

"Thanks for waiting for us," Jase tells the two men in the back of the room. Mick is one of them; I don't know the name of the other, but Jase does. This is Jase's place to run. Everyone knows him, and he knows everyone, so I let him lead and stay quiet.

Quiet is dangerous, and that's exactly how I want them to see me.

"Of course, Mr. Cross," Mick says and nods his head at Jase then quirks a smile at me as he adds, "and Mr. Cross."

The small girl seated at the lone table in the room grips the plastic cup of a pink drink that's probably got just as much sugar in it as alcohol. Her lips part open with a hint of disbelief and then she licks them, smiling although it's thin and withered. Just like the state of her body under the too-tight tube top.

"You're waiting for the delivery?" Jase asks, looking to the left and right as if he doesn't want to say it out loud and get caught by someone. I'd laugh at him and his display, but he's damn good at what he does, and I do enjoy a good show.

The girl imitates him, looking over her shoulders at the two hired men of ours in The Red Room t-shirts and black jeans before she nods. "You guys have the best sweets."

"Sweets?" I ask, and she grins at me like she knows a secret she can't wait to tell me.

"It's what the streets are calling it now," she says and bites down on her lower lip, letting her body sway. Jase and I pull out our chairs across from her, the legs scraping across the floor. Sweets. Plural. Because that fucker Romano has his version out. I keep the small hint of friendliness firmly in place. But I'm nothing but pissed at the reminder

"Sweet Lullaby, you mean?" Jase asks, lifting an eyebrow. And again, she nods.

"You're buying a lot of this stuff," Jase tells her although it comes out a question. Her nails scratch down her arms as she glances all around us. She's jittery and the chair legs beneath her keep rasping on the floor.

"I just need it, okay?" Her words are rushed. The air changes around her instantly.

Noting her hollow cheeks, dead eyes, and pale lips, the humor, and vibe that she's down to have a good time have vanished.

"Is it really what you need?" Jase asks and leans forward to stare into her eyes. "'Cause we've got some other stuff you might want?"

She's in need of a hit. That's for damn sure and if I had to guess her drug of choice is heroin. Maybe coke.

"I just need to grab it and get back," she answers, but her voice is breathy and uncertain. I wait a moment, glancing at Jase as we both hear her swallow over the muted sound of the music playing in the club.

"I think we have some coming, sorry about the wait, miss...?"

"Jenny. Jenny Parks," she answers him and then reaches into her purse for her phone. The two men behind us make a move for their guns, and the little blonde doesn't even notice.

"Fuck, it's already past nine," she says and her face crumples with a mix of anxiety and fear.

As she slips her thumb into her mouth to chew on her nail, Jase asks her, "Hey, is there anything I can get you while you wait?"

"Anything to calm you down a little? Another drink or something stronger?" I add.

Her breath comes out harder. "Yeah, maybe," she replies as her eyes dart from me to Jase. "I just wanted to come in and get the stuff. It'll be here soon?" she asks again, looking down at the phone to check the time. "Like, how soon."

"It could be a bit," Jase says and shrugs, looking at Mick and she watches him shrug too. "We've got other stuff while you wait," he offers but she's already shaking her head, still biting that thumbnail.

She speaks over the finger in her mouth. "I need the sweets first."

The problem with a junkie is that they have a one-track mind. They want the drug. And it's obvious that she gets hers when she delivers our drug to the real buyer.

Jase shrugs again. "An hour, maybe?" He glances at me and I nod my head.

"Fuck," she mutters and cradles her face in her hands.

"You want us to drop it off somewhere else?" Jase asks, and she peeks up through her lashes. We're getting the address of where this product is going. Either from her telling us or from us following her. Whatever the fuck we have to do.

"I have to get back. I'm sorry," she rushes her words as she slides her phone off the table and into her purse.

"We can get you something to take the edge off while it comes in and we can talk a little?" Jared suggests to her from where he's standing guard by the steel doors. She seems to get it then. The reality of what's going on hits her like a ton of bricks and she's shit at hiding it.

"It's just… it's my brother. You know? He needs it, and he doesn't like me to be late."

"Your brother?" Jase questions and I glance at Mick, standing behind the seated blonde, who shakes his head once. Little Jenny doesn't have a brother.

"Yeah, and he doesn't like people to come around, you know?" Again, her words are rushed and she looks at the men behind her then at us.

"I can just come back another time," she mumbles. Her breathing is sporadic as she pulls her purse to her chest.

She takes a second to stand up, but Mick's hand on her shoulder makes her pause.

A second drops between us all, heavy with the consequences of what's to come.

She's buying for someone else and lying to cover it up. Someone who keeps her doped up and someone who scares her enough to give her the strength to resist her next hit from us.

Her head turns slowly so she can see Mick's large hand gripping tighter onto her shoulder. The fear that drifts from her is palpable and sickening.

"You tell your brother we're sorry we couldn't get it to him tonight, Jenny," Jase speaks up and instantly Mick's grip on the girl loosens.

I can practically hear her heart beating as she looks at Jase wide-eyed. She's frozen still until he leans back in his seat and tells her with a wink, "We'll have it for you next time."

"You let us know if you want to talk anytime now, you hear me?" Jared says as he opens the door to the club and the music flows into the small back room.

Jenny nods her head furiously, stumbling into the empty chair next to her before taking off out of the room without another look back.

"Follow her," I tell Mick and with a single nod he's gone. Jase's blunt nails tap against the table as the door closes and the sound of the nightlife beyond it is muted once again.

"You let her off easy," I say quietly under my breath.

"Girls don't need to be dragged into this shit." That's his only answer and he doesn't bother to lower his voice like I did.

The same table he's tapping, I've covered with blood in the past. It wouldn't have come to that with the blonde, but a little lie to get her talking wouldn't have hurt her. Showing our cards that we know she's buying for someone else, well that might have gotten a word or two from her. Maybe a name.

"Maybe he's sending girls because he knows you're weak for them," I suggest. All of us have our limits. And women happen to be the common thread between us.

"Fuck you, I'm not weak," he tells me although I can see him considering it. It's in his eyes.

The corners of my lips tip up into a smirk as Jared lights up a cigarette. But with a puff and the words that come out of his mouth, the smile vanishes. "With the Talvery girl shit, they should know we aren't pussies when it comes to women."

The silence stretches in the room for a moment with neither of us commenting.

"The Talvery girl," I say beneath my breath and it gets a comment from Jared, but I don't bother to listen to him. "She's mine," I tell him, cutting off his joke or whatever the fuck was coming out of his mouth.

I stand abruptly, letting an anger I haven't felt in a long time dictate my words. Staring into Jared's eyes, the words rip from my mouth, "The next time someone refers to her as that, *the Talvery girl*," I practically spit out the name, "you tell them, she's all mine."

My teeth grind against each other so hard, I swear they'll crack.

Jared doesn't speak, doesn't move. I don't think he's breathing, although the cigarette in his mouth stays oddly still with the glow of amber making his expression look even paler.

My muscles coil, waiting for him to call her that again. She's not *the Talvery girl*. She doesn't belong to them.

"What's her name?" I ask him, tilting my head and that cigarette wavers in his mouth. "Take out the fucking cigarette and tell me what the fuck her name is." My eyes pierce into his as he drops the cigarette from his mouth, barely catching it between his fingers and swallowing thickly. The cords of his neck are tight, and I can hear him swallow.

"I—I—" he stutters, and I lean in closer to scream in his face, the words of my question scratching and ripping their way up my throat, "What's her name?"

"I don't know," he says in a quavering admission.

"It's Aria," I say then pat his shoulders with both of my hands as he struggles to look me in the eyes. The anger wanes as I feel his sweat beneath my hands.

"It's Aria, and she doesn't belong to the Talverys anymore." My words are calm, eerily so.

"Of course, she doesn't," Jared shakes his head slightly, his lips turning into a hesitant smile. "She's yours. Aria is yours and she's called Aria."

He won't shut the fuck up, the poor prick.

"You let anyone who calls her otherwise know," I tell him, nodding my head once toward a spot on the brick wall. The bricks are redder, newer and don't blend in.

"I'd hate to lose it and have to blow some fucker's poor skull open because he pissed me off."

"Yeah," Jared's answer is a whisper of fear. "Aria, and she's yours."

Jase's hand hitting the back of my shoulder is the only thing that rips my gaze away from Jared's.

"Keep up the good work, Jared." Jase adds, "Good job tonight," and pushes the door open to go back out into the bar.

He holds it open for me and I move around Jared, still very much stuck in his place and only nodding his response as if he's scared to speak. As I take a step to leave, I glance down at him, the disgusting smell of piss overriding the scent of cigarettes. The fucker pissed himself.

I wish I could smile or feel any sense of pleasure from knowing how deeply rooted the fear goes. But all I can think is that these assholes are calling my Aria, *the Talvery girl*.

She's so much more than that.

"You've got to back down with that," Jase tells me as we walk side by side through the club. There's no one around us that could hear, but still, I want to tell him to fuck off.

"I don't have to do shit," I respond in a grunt, the rage still looming, but even as the words are spoken, I know he's right. They could use her against me. She could so easily become known as my weakness.

"What's the point of doing that?" he asks me, cutting off my train of thought.

But I don't have an answer ready. There's always a reason. Everything I do has a purpose. It takes the entire walk through the club for me to respond, and not until we're out of the front doors where the cool air greets us, and the moonlight lingers over the parking lot.

The wind whips against my face, and Jase slips his hands into his pockets as the valet pulls our car up to the curb. "The point is that they've forgotten she's mine when they call her a Talvery. I won't have anyone forget she belongs to me."

CHAPTER 26

Aria

CARTER HAD ME DRINK A GLASS OF WHISKEY WITH ORANGE BITTERS BUT somehow it tasted like chocolate. I don't know what it was exactly, but it's still humming through me. He left me with a second drink in his office and it's the second one that did this to me.

Even as I stand in the kitchen, busying myself with something to take my mind off everything that's going on around me, I can feel the alcohol numbing the pain. As if I'm spared from what's going to happen, and it's everything else that's moving. I'm just standing here.

But I hate it. I don't want to be helpless and beg for mercy from a man who won't show it. I don't want to seem helpless, but I have no choice.

The refrigerator is full of nearly anything I could want. Fresh eggs, deli meat, fruits, and vegetables. Most of the meats for dinner are frozen, but there's plenty to satisfy me.

I'm not hungry in the least, but Carter told me to eat and so here I am.

It took me a while to get started, long after Carter had left.

Instead of doing anything at all, I stared at the door. And then each of the windows I passed. And the windows to the garden. I wish I could leave and tell my father they're coming, but I'm sure he knows. That's the only comfort I have in this powerless state. My father must know they're coming for him.

The knife slices through a tomato. It's so sharp the skin splits instantly without any pressure at all. I suck the taste of the whiskey from my teeth. I can't do anything, but I need to do something.

The thunk of the knife on the cutting board is the only thing I hear over and over again.

"What are you making?" A deep voice from behind me makes me jump. The knife slips from my hand and I'm too scared to jump away from it as it crashes to the floor. I stand there breathless with anxiety shooting through my veins.

"Shit," the voice says as my heart races and pounds in my chest.

It's Daniel. I've seen him before and I know that's his name. But he hasn't said a word to me. He never even looks at me. Yet, now I'm alone with him, and Carter's nowhere to be seen. In dark jeans and a black t-shirt, he runs his hand through his hair with a shameful look on his face. "I should've come from the other direction, huh?" There's a sweetness about him, but I don't trust him. I don't trust any of the Cross brothers.

"I'm just keeping an eye on you," Daniel says easily, and his lips quirk up into a half smile. "A salad?" he asks.

"Yeah," I say, but my answer is a whisper. It's odd to be a prisoner yet remain free to move about. Even odder to have a conversation with someone as if there's nothing at all wrong with my position.

I force myself to swallow and bend down slowly, keeping him in my periphery, to pick up the knife. My body trembles as I turn my back to him just enough to walk to the sink and rinse it off. "Avocado, tomato and Italian dressing. I was craving something like it," I tell him as the water pours down onto the sharp edge of the knife. The light reflects in the water and my heart thumps again.

"Salt tooth?" he asks me, and I nod, eyeing him but trying to just have a conversation. I wonder what he thinks of me. What he thinks of Carter for keeping me here.

All I can look at is the knife in my hand, the alcohol is thrumming, my nerves are high, and I don't know how to survive anymore.

The idea of an escape plan is forming, but the anxiety is so much higher.

His footsteps give him away as he walks to the other side of the counter, closer to where the chunks of avocado and freshly cut tomato wait for me. My mind is highly aware of where he is. And who he is.

He knows how to get out of here. He could be my ticket to freedom.

"Did you find the bowls?" he asks me as I turn around to face him, the knife feeling heavier in my hand.

With the water off, the room is silent. Eerily so. Or maybe it's just because of the thoughts running through my mind. The counter is hard against my lower back as I lean against it to keep me steady as I watch him open a cabinet and pull out a bowl.

He smiles at me like he's my friend or my companion, and not a guard to keep me here. And he lets me hold the knife. He doesn't even look at it. I have a weapon and I'm a prisoner here, yet he doesn't care in the least. *Why would he, you weak girl?* the voice in the back of my head taunts me and laughs.

"Thank you," I say, and my voice sounds small and weak. Gripping the countertop behind me, it feels so cold, so unforgiving in comparison to how hot my body is right now.

The ceramic bowl clinks as it hits the countertop and Daniel smiles at me. A handsome, charming smile with his hands up in the air as he says, "I'm not going to hurt you; I promise."

I'm the one with the knife.

I keep thinking it as I take each small step toward the counter.

My bare feet pad on the cold floor.

I offer him a small smile, but I don't say anything and neither does he.

Until that knife slices so easily through the tomato again. I imagine the way it would go down, but it's hard to focus. I couldn't kill him. He'd have to push in the code and then I'd run.

"Is he treating you alright?" he asks me, and my grip tightens on the knife. He could so easily push in a code and grant me freedom. And then I could tell my father they're coming.

Raising my eyes to his for the first time, I ask him, "What do you think?" I'm surprised by the strength, but I crave more of it.

His gaze flickers to the door behind me and then back to me.

Silence descends upon the kitchen.

"He's in a difficult position," Daniel offers me when I start to cut the slices into chunks, trying not to think of what would happen if I failed. What Carter would do to me if I tried to escape and failed. My chest hollows and my stomach drops at the thought. The cell. Or worse, the box. He knows what that box would do to me if he put a lock on the outside of it.

My blood runs cold.

"He's not a bad man," Daniel says, and I watch as the knife in my hand trembles as it hovers over the remaining slices.

Bad man? He's not a bad man? If only Daniel knew what I was thinking.

"Good men don't do what he's done," I tell Daniel without looking at him. "I begged him last night to spare my father. My family," I say and my voice cracks.

"I'm sorry, but you know he can't do that." It's his only response and I crumble inside. My heart twists in a painful way. It's a horrible ache that I can't explain when I hear Daniel turn to walk away.

He's leaving me. Because he can. Because it doesn't matter if he leaves me to wallow all alone. All I'll ever be is alone and pathetic if I don't even try.

My fingers wrap around the knife until my knuckles are white and I cry out for him. "Daniel!" His tall, lean body stiffens, the muscles in his shoulders rippling as he turns around.

He's maybe five feet from me. But the kitchen island separates the two of us.

Be smart, I remind myself. But at this point, nothing I'm about to do is smart. Lowering the knife to my side, the blade nearly caresses my skin when I clear my throat.

"I'm sorry," I offer him although I can hardly hear myself over the furious pounding of my heart in my chest. "Could you show me where the seasonings are?" I have to swallow before I can add, "Please."

Daniel's mouth is set in a grim straight line; his eyes pierce deeply into me like he knows exactly what I'm about to do. But he walks toward me. He walks to my side of the island. Inside I'm screaming that it's a trap, that he knows. My blood rushes in my ears and the sweat from my hand nearly makes the knife slip.

Five feet becomes four, becomes three, becomes two.

And he turns his back to me, reaching at eye level to open a cabinet before turning around and finding that knife pointed at his throat.

The sweat that crawls along my skin is sickening. It covers every inch of me as I try to speak, but my dry throat won't allow it.

Stupid girl! I hear the voice yell at me. Regret and fear are instant, but the knife is in the air and I can't take it back. My hand feels as if it's shaking, but the knife is steady.

I can't go back. "Get me out of here," I breathe as he stares at me with disdain.

"You don't want to do this, Aria." Daniel's words are so genuine, so sincere, that I almost regret taking the step forward and nearly pressing the blade to his throat.

"I want to leave." I somehow push the words out. How strong they sound, although I'm panicked.

Daniel's eyes turn sympathetic, or maybe they just look back at me as if I'm the pathetic one. I can't tell. He deceives me so.

"I can't help you with that." My heart plummets and races at the same time. This is my only chance, my only hope.

"Open the front door." As I give the command, I step forward and my trembling hand pushes the knife closer to him, slicing the skin of his upper neck, just slightly. A small nick, but it cuts him. *I cut him.*

The horror of seeing the bright red blood distracts me for a moment, a moment long enough for Daniel to shove his hand in front of me and try to grip the knife.

He may be fast, but my fear is faster. The knife pierces through his shirt and bicep, easily cutting into him, slicing his arm as I stumble back.

My heart beats so hard I swear I'll die from terror alone.

The hot grip of his hand burns into my forearm even after he's let go. My back hits the counter and I jump slightly, but I keep the knife up and sidestep slowly around him. The adrenaline is higher than I've ever felt before.

This is bad, my heart screams in terror, *this is fucking bad*. And I've lost the advantage of surprise, the threat of the knife minuscule compared to what it was a moment ago.

"Let me go!" I yell at him as he seethes at me. His grimace grows to something else. Something that looks hurt for me once again. And I want to sneer at him and his pity, but I feel sorry for me too. And there's nothing lower than that.

"I said let me go!" I'm too afraid to get closer to him and every step feels like my knees may give out from the pure adrenaline pumping through me.

"Even if I opened the door, there are two guards at the gates and I'm not leaving anytime soon. They know that." His voice is stern, and he takes his eyes from me to look at the cut. "Damn, you got me good," he says, still not even bothering to look at me. As if I'm not a threat.

"You could hide me in your car." My voice skips over my words as I struggle to think about the next step.

"And be scared of your knife that's with you in my trunk?" he asks and my head sways. My body threatens to sway with it. I failed. I already know I've failed.

Stupid girl, the voice says, but even she pities me and the earlier anger from her is absent.

My heart sinks and it doesn't stop like it's in a never-ending free fall even though I can already feel it in the pit of my stomach. "Get me out of here, please. You can get me out of here," I say although my voice cracks and I take a step forward with the knife. "Please," I beg him.

He finally glances up at me and says, "Put the knife down." That's all he says, in that disinterested tone that all of the Cross brothers seem to have. A tone that's utterly dismissive.

"Fuck you," I almost cry as I tell him off. I have to step closer to him, I have to go through with this. He nearly got the knife from me last time and if he does this time, I'm going back to the cell. Fuck. My throat closes in on itself.

As if hearing my thoughts, Daniel tells me, "I could grab my gun, Aria, don't make me."

His words kill the last bit of hope. What would I do? Throw the knife at him if he ran to get his gun? "Put the knife down."

"Please don't," I plead with him. Tears prick my eyes at how stupid I am. At what's to come.

The cell. I'll be in the cell tonight. And for however long it takes for Carter to let me out after.

The heavy knife feels heavier and I want to point it at myself. A very big part of me thinks I could get farther if I would threaten to hurt myself. But I don't want to be in pain. "Please help me," I barely get the weak words out.

Daniel's response is immediate, his steps deliberate and powerful. My body shakes as he comes close enough to grip the knife, but this time when he wraps his hand around my forearm, I loosen my grip and the knife falls from my hand to his other hand and only then does he let me go.

I cower like a disobedient child or worse, a dog who knows he's about to be beaten.

Silent tears fall, and I wipe them as I listen to the knife drop into the sink before Daniel turns on the faucet to clean his cut. The cut I gave him.

"I'm sorry." My words are choked, and I try to repeat them again but fail. My breathing comes in shallow pants. "I can't go back. Please, I can't."

"Hey, it's okay." Daniel's voice is soft as he approaches me, but fear is the only thing I have to give him until he says, "We don't have to tell Carter."

His words make me stare into his dark eyes. They're so like Carter's. But the heat and desire aren't there. Just sincerity.

"I won't tell him, okay?" His comforting voice soothes the fear in me. "This will stay between us." The relief that replaces the anxiety nearly makes me throw up.

"Why would you do that?" I question him. "I hurt you."

"Because I would have done the same." His simple answer is comforting, but it doesn't give me any hope.

"I'm sorry," I mumble my apology and have to clear my throat. I'm choking on my words. "I didn't want to… to hurt you."

"Why'd you have to do that?" I shake my head, wiping under my eyes. He adds, "I would have done it, but I thought you were smarter than that."

"I'm sorry." It's all I can say. "I need to get out of here," I insist, and my words bleed with despair.

"It's better that you're here," he tells me. "You're not safe at your father's and I know Carter may not seem like the best person to you right now, but I know there's a reason for all of this."

"My father." The words tumble from my lips. *I'm failing him.*

"You need to eat," Daniel says, backing away from me and not acknowledging me. It's the same thing Carter told me. I just need to eat. And obey.

"You're going to kill him," I say and it's a statement, not a question. I can't even think about eating. The thought is repulsive.

Daniel opens the fridge and ignores me, although he angles his body so he can see me in his periphery.

He closes the door to the fridge with his elbow as he twists off the top to a beer and takes a quick swig, making the dampened shirt of blood glisten in the light and that bit of red on his throat stare back at me.

I almost tell him I'm sorry, yet again. Even with knowing his plans for my father. It's a sickening feeling to not know what's right and wrong, but regardless, you have no choice.

The bottle smacks down on the counter and he finally answers me. "It was going to happen whether or not we stepped in."

"What was?" I ask him in a hushed voice, cautiously, barely raising my eyes to meet his gaze. The only thing I keep thinking is that I need to be nice to him, so he doesn't tell Carter.

"War."

The one-word answer forces my gaze to the polished tile floor. It's quiet while he drinks, and I clean up the mess of the cubed vegetables I won't eat.

"You won't tell Carter?" I feel selfish for daring to bring it back up, but I need to know he won't. If Carter were here for that… I can't even begin to think of what he would do.

"Look at me," Daniel's voice beckons and I do as he tells me. "I am not going to say a word to Carter. Not one word." His voice is soothing, but I find it hard to be anything close to being okay.

"Thank you," I tell him and press my hand to my face to cool it down.

He finishes the beer, all the while I stare at the spot on the floor until I turn instinctively at the sound of his name being called out by a feminine voice.

"Shit," he says under his breath. He's quick to grab me by the arm. His grip is tight, demanding and catches me off guard with that fear returning and spiking through me.

"Go to the den," he demands beneath his hushed breath and attempts to push me out of the kitchen from the other threshold. My feet slip across the floor as he pushes me toward the den.

"Daniel?" the voice calls out again, this time closer and he urges through clenched teeth, "Go."

My shoulders hunch forward and I feel like nothing. Like absolutely nothing. Worthless, pathetic and a weak thing to be pushed around at anyone's whim.

"Don't do it again, Aria. You're smarter than that," he tells me before turning his back to me and walking briskly to the other side of the kitchen.

His words numb me for a moment, even though my feet move of their own free will.

I'm supposed to be smarter than that. Maybe I used to be, but a mix of desperation and the feeling of falling into a dark abyss is all I can see anymore… that mix is deadly to any semblance of intelligence that I have.

My hands tremble and I struggle to breathe, but I try to remember Carter's words from what seems like so long ago. I try to remember what he said that made me feel like I had hope. I try, and I fail.

It doesn't matter what they were. Everything is insignificant when there's nothing you can do to change your fate.

And now that I've been so fucking stupid, he's going to put me back in the cell.

I shouldn't have done that. A heavy breath nearly suffocates me. I need to listen.

With my eyes closed, I whisper, "Daniel won't tell him." But the words have little mercy on my pain, because I know I won't be able to hide it from Carter. He sees me. He sees all of me. And he watches everything.

"What the hell did you do?" A woman's voice carries through the kitchen with shock and worry, startling me and cutting through my thoughts. As quietly as I can, I slink to the side of the doorway, so I can listen but won't be seen.

I didn't know another girl was here. But the way she's talking to Daniel make it obvious that she's with him. Not a prisoner of him. Jealousy and fear mix inside of me and I don't know why I'm so scared of being seen by her. Maybe the trickle of shame as I grip the doorway is indication enough.

"I was drinking and cutting up shit and I thought it would be cool to toss the knife." I hear Daniel give an excuse that's not at all believable. But the girl believes him.

"You could have killed yourself," she reprimands him, although her voice carries a tinge of disbelief. Guilt seeps into my blood. And a part of me knows it's ridiculous to feel sorry for trying to save myself. But so is all of this.

Daniel chuckles. "Of all the ways to die, I don't think it's going to be this, Addison." I can hear him take a drink before telling her, "I got you a beer." I almost walk away, but Addison's next words keep me planted where I am.

"We need to talk." The severity of her tone is sharp.

"Not right now." Daniel talks to her differently than the way he talks to me. Differently than the way Carter talks to me. There's an edge of comfort in his voice and I don't expect it.

"It's always not right now," she responds. "Something's going on." Her tone softens, pleading with him. "Why can't I leave?" she asks him with desperation clinging to every word.

"It's just better to be safe," he replies so lowly I hardly hear him. The thrumming of curiosity flows through me. She can't leave either?

A moment passes and another, I can't see what's going on and I inch forward, hoping to get a peek before the conversation continues. Hoping to see this woman.

"You don't need to know," Daniel says firmly and with that I creep around the corner to see Daniel leaning against the stove. I see him and a beautiful girl around my age shaking her head so hard that her dark wavy hair falls around her shoulders. She covers her face as she gasps, "You keep lying to me." Pain is etched into her ragged voice.

Daniel makes a weak attempt to wrap his arms around her before she pushes him away, his ass hitting the stove and she leaves the kitchen, heading back the way she came. Small sounds of her crying linger behind her. Daniel opens a large drawer that blends into the cabinet and he drops the empty beer bottle and cap into the trash, with a wretched pain in his expression that tears at my own heart.

As he turns to leave, I creep further back into the kitchen, but he hears me and peeks over his shoulder.

Not hiding his pain and then leaving me to mine.

CHAPTER 27

Carter

I CHECKED THE BEDROOM FIRST. THE DEPRAVED SIDE OF ME HOPED SHE WOULD BE waiting for me, already warming my bed.

But it was empty.

The den was next, after assuming I'd see her drawing on the floor of the hearth like she enjoys doing.

But the fire wasn't burning, and the room was silent.

Then the kitchen. The empty fucking kitchen. My teeth grit as I pull up the security monitor and cycle through the cameras.

My pulse races and I can hardly see straight as the monitor flickers from one to the next, each proving to be useless in showing me where my Aria is.

I told her to wait for me in the kitchen, den, or bedroom. Those were the only rooms she was permitted to be in, yet my obedient Aria isn't in a single one of them.

My heart pounds and my temperature rises.

She didn't get away.

I only left for three hours. Just enough time to drive to the club for the meet and then back. Daniel was watching her. I have to remind myself that she's still here somewhere as the cameras loop back around to the beginning.

"Fuck!" My anger gets the best of me, but as I spit out the word and feel the tension in my shoulders and chest rise, I both see and hear her at the same time.

The wine cellar in the corner of the kitchen passed in a blur on the screen the first time, but there she is, in the corner, cross-legged with a bottle in her lap. And the sweet sound of her humming travels through the kitchen.

I walk quietly to the cracked door, only a sliver of light shining into the kitchen.

Listening to the cadence of her soft voice, her humming rises and a word slips out, but I don't recognize the song. The melody is somber, somewhat melancholy.

I inch closer, careful to be quiet and slip the door open as a bottle clinks against the tile floor, notably empty judging from the hollow sound.

Aria's dark locks fall back away from her face and chest as she lays her head back against the wall, her nose pointed toward the ceiling as she hums a little louder.

It's addictive, listening to those sweet sounds. Her voice has always captivated me and I suppose it always will. What saves you from the darkness is something extraordinary.

"This isn't the kitchen," I say and break up her melody. The green and amber colors swirl into a deadly concoction of fear in her gaze as she takes in my words. I watch her throat as she swallows; I can practically hear her tense breathing as she seats herself in a kneeling position to tell me, "I didn't know."

She still doesn't look at me when she speaks. Sometimes in the evenings, she'll peek at me. But she doesn't like to look me in the eye.

Her cotton blouse is loose and baggy, offering me a glance down her shirt, although her hair lays in the way as it hangs in front of her. Even still, I catch a glimpse of her breasts and the pale pink of her nipples. My dick hardens, and I stifle a groan.

"I thought this was a part of the kitchen," she says and I hear the drunkenness on her words. Her thick lashes flutter as I stay standing in the doorway to the wine cellar, silently.

I wait for her to peek up at me, and when she does I hold her captive with my stare. It's never made sense to me before why the expression of 'doe eyes' exists. But right here, right now, I understand. It's a glance you can't break. One that pauses time and holds you still. That's what she does to me in this moment with that gorgeous gaze.

"I swear I didn't realize," she breathes the words and licks her wine-stained lips.

"From one cell to another," I tell her and my little songbird bites down on her bottom lip to stifle a smile. "You find that funny?" I ask her as my own lips threaten to tip up.

"I would prefer this one," she tells me as a flirtatious blush creeps into her cheeks. "If you saw fit to put me in a cell again, the wine cellar would be a bit more my style."

A genuine grin pulls at my lips and I find myself walking toward her and crouching in front of her small, delicate frame. Although she seems sweet, engaging even, the nervousness is still present.

I almost ask her what's gotten her into such a pleasant mood, but the empty bottle of wine to her side and the mostly empty glass sitting next to it answer my question. Her pupils are dark and large, but the beauty and desire behind them are enticing.

"You've enjoyed yourself while I've been gone?" I ask her while cupping her cheek, but instead of leaning into me, she pulls away and moves to sit on her ass. She pulls her legs to her chest.

She shakes her head once, and the happiness leaves instantly, chilling the room and my blood.

"I have something I should tell you," she speaks to her knees with her head buried in them, "but Daniel said he wouldn't." Some of her words are slurred. And even with the cuteness of her tipsy demeanor, knowing Daniel was housing a secret with her steals any sense of humor from me. "But I should."

"Yes," I tell her as I sit on the floor in front of her, "you should." A vise grips my heart as I creep closer to her. Secrets can't be tolerated. Secrets destroy all they touch. And Daniel would keep a secret from me?

She scratches behind her ear and glances at the door before looking back at me. Her lips part, but then she simply licks them, still trying to find her words. I can hear the steady beat of her heart in rhythm with mine.

"Tell me, songbird. It will be much worse for you if you don't." A crease of sadness mars her forehead and her eyes darken with worry, but the threat was needed. And with it comes her confession.

"I cut him," she says quickly and then clears her throat. "Daniel. I held up the knife and threatened him to let me go but I didn't mean to cut him, I swear."

"You want to leave me?" I ask contemptuously. The anger has come so easily tonight, my emotions getting the best of me. And it's because of her. It's all because of Aria.

"No, I just," she swallows thickly and pushes the hair from her face. "I don't know why, but when you left me… it's different when you aren't with me." She struggles with her words and I wait a moment in silence for her to go on.

"I was angry. I wanted to leave to tell my father." She doesn't see how my body tenses and rage creeps into my expression at her confession. She will never leave me. Never. And her father can burn in hell for all I care.

Gritting my teeth, I let her continue.

"He came to talk to me, and I had a knife. I was drunk and it was stupid. Or maybe just tipsy? I'm so sorry. I didn't mean it. I'm just a mess and I don't know what's right or what I should do and I…" She trails off, her breathing and words chaotic at best.

Has Daniel really gone so soft that he would let her threaten him? The sense of disappointment in both of them is mixed, but so much stronger with Aria. She wanted to leave. I have to resist every urge to throw her back into the cell and keep her there where she doesn't have an ounce of escape.

It's only the genuine sadness in her eyes that dulls the anger and brings out the curiosity I felt when I first watched her from the monitors.

It takes a moment of heavy breathing and silence between us for me to realize that it's my fault. She wasn't ready to be left in someone else's hands. I should have known better. But things will change quickly. I nod at the thought, although my gaze stays on Aria. Soon.

"He let you cut him with a knife?" I ask her, wondering how reckless Daniel must've been.

It's because she doesn't fear him. Fear changes everything.

"Only a little," she answers in a meek voice while lifting those gorgeous eyes up to mine and I find it humorous. With a gentle smile tracing my lips, I clarify, "You cut him… but only a little?"

She dares to let the peek of a smile show, but it's quickly gone. "I feel awful for doing it."

"You would have killed my brother?" I ask absently, making a mental note to watch the tapes of her while I was gone.

"No, but I know you'd kill mine." Her words are a well of sadness, but also of acceptance.

"You have no brother," I tell her as if her statement is irrelevant, but she's right. There are no limits to what I've done and what I'm about to do. There is mercy for her, but not for anyone else.

"You really tried to leave me?" A spike punctures through my chest as I voice it out loud. Earlier, I was more concerned that she shared a secret with Daniel. But the fact remains that she tried to run away. That she wanted to leave me and was willing to kill to do it.

"It was an awful attempt," she tells me as if it makes it better. And a part of me softens at her response. "I'm sorry. I'm sorry about it all. I think I'm going crazy," her words come out breathily as she drops her head back to lean against the wall. "You've made me crazy, Carter. All I am is sorry. It's all I know how to be anymore."

With my hand cupping her jaw, I wait for her to look at me with glassy eyes on the verge of tears. "No, my songbird. All you are… is mine."

"Yes," she says simply. The acknowledgement giving me a headier rush than I've ever felt.

My head nods on its own. "I didn't think you'd dare to be so bold while I was gone."

"I'm sorry." Fear traces her whisper.

"I didn't want to punish you tonight of all nights," I tell her, letting my fingers run along the necklace she wears, "I had different plans in mind." My dick is already hard as I consider what to do with her. "But you tried to leave me and there's no greater sin than that."

"Please," she whimpers as I shush her. "I don't want to go back." She doesn't cower from my touch; she welcomes it as I rest a hand on her bare shoulder, my fingers skimming under the fabric of her shirt. Her mesmerizing hazel eyes stare into mine and beg me for mercy.

"Didn't I tell you your next offense would lead to the cell?" I remind her with a question and her face crumples. She inches toward me, both of her hands on my thighs as she begs me, "Please." Her fingers slip across the expensive fabric of my pants as she crawls between my legs, begging me for forgiveness. How I've dreamed of her like this. Just like this.

"What would you do to stay with me?" I ask her, wanting to give her the mercy she begs for. I've never felt it so strongly before.

Her chest rises and falls heavily. "Anything," she answers me quickly with desperation.

"Not to stay out of the cell, but to stay in my bed. There is a difference, Aria."

Her expression falls and she struggles to voice what she's thinking. Dread seeps into my gut as she fails to answer me, but with that soft voice of hers, it leaves me at once.

Her fingers lace through the necklace as she says, "It's only when you're gone that I remember."

"What do you mean?"

Her voice wavers as she tries to explain. "I don't want you to leave me. It's harder for me when you do."

"I asked you what you would do—"

"And I said anything," she cuts me off and I can feel my brow pinch together as I look over every inch of her expression to gauge her sincerity. "When you're with me, I know that I can't leave, and I don't want to even try. But when you're gone… it's harder. So, I don't want to leave you. I don't want you to leave me."

She's a siren. I see it so clearly. It's her beauty, her broken strength, her denial, and her acceptance. It all calls to me and I will do anything I can to wrap my grip tighter around my songbird while she sings beautiful lullabies.

"Tomorrow night, you'll come to dinner with me. Kneeling beside me. You will obey. You will sit beside me, proud to be mine." She nods her head as if she's accepting a punishment, but this is so much more than that. "You'll do as I say. Every fucking thing I tell you to do." I emphasize each word, my finger running up and down her throat. "In front of my family and guests, you will show them how willing you are to obey me."

"Yes, Carter."

The way her breathing catches and she swallows the eagerness of accepting the punishment, almost makes me feel guilty for what I say next. Almost. "And tonight, you will sleep in the cell for daring to take advantage of the freedom I've given you."

"Yes, Carter," she replies although her words crack and her eyes close in agony. Her thick lashes flutter, as she opens her eyes again and she stares deeply into my own, waiting for more. The deep well of loneliness is already settling into her gaze. The look of sadness is something I've seen before, but in her eyes, it looks so beautiful.

"You'll stay there until I feel you've learned your lesson."

She nods and wipes the tear from under her right eye, but dutifully answers, "Yes, Carter."

My own breathing quickens at the thought of having her to myself before sending her away. "As for right now, you'll lie across my lap, feeling my hard cock dig into your belly as I punish you, spanking your bare ass and playing with your cunt until I feel you've paid enough for the offense of trying to leave me."

"I will," she says softly and raises her head to meet my gaze. When her eyes meet mine, she nods in agreement. "I will," she repeats breathlessly.

The command falls instantly from me. "Tell me that your cunt is mine to play with."

"My cunt is yours to play with." And her obedience falls from her lips just the same.

"And your ass?" I prompt.

"It's yours." There's no hesitation in her voice.

"And what about these lips of yours?" I question her in a deep voice ragged with desire as my thumb traces her pouty lips.

"Whatever you'd like to do with them," she whispers against my touch.

"Lift up your dress and lie here," I tell her as I sit on the ground of the wine cellar, too eager to have my hands on her to move us to the cell.

Her movements are rushed and reckless as she pulls the cotton dress up and moves to my lap. Her hips are balanced on my right thigh, but I move her ass to the center, forcing her to yelp as she tries to brace herself with her hands.

"Behind your back," I command her, and it takes a moment. Her hair is everywhere, but I slip it over one shoulder, taking my time to gather it together before grabbing both of her wrists in one of my hands. My fingers easily slip down her panties, the lace fabric almost tearing, but I'm careful with it, letting my touch send goosebumps flowing over every inch of her skin.

She moans slightly, already enjoying her punishment. But I'll enjoy it more.

With my hand rubbing a circle on her ass cheek, I tell her, "I think you misbehave just so I can punish you."

She shakes her head, writhing over my lap and making her hair toss slightly. "I don't want to upset you." Her words are soft and saddened, but her whimpers speak of nothing but pleasure.

The first smack is light and followed by my grabbing her ass and then smacking the other cheek harder. Her body bucks, but I don't even get a gasp.

Leaning to my left, I see her eyes shut tightly and her teeth digging into her bottom lip. I let my fingers slip to her cunt, and my cock aches with the pain to be inside of her.

"So tight," I tell her with reverence in my tone and then rock her, so she can feel my cock.

She only moans and waits for more, but her teeth let up slightly while I take my time with her.

"How many do you think, my Aria?" I ask her and just as her lips part, my hand pulls back and I whip her ass with an open hand that leaves my skin stinging with pain. She cries out, throwing her head back as the pain and pleasure mix and my fingers dip back to her cunt.

"I asked how many?" My voice is calm but deadly. Inside I'm burning hot with a desperate need.

"How many—" she starts to answer me, and I spank her other cheek even harder than the last, forcing tears to her eyes. The sharp, sweet pain travels from my palm up my arm. Gripping her reddened skin, I wait for her to answer but with her eyes watering and her breath taken from her, all she does is part her lips to breathe.

"Answer me, Aria." Before my words are finished she says as quickly as she can, "However many you'd like."

A beat passes where she hangs her head to suck in a breath. Another beat passes where I pull my hand away from her skin and watch as she tenses on my lap.

The rapid succession of my hand hitting her tender skin over and over again until my arm is screaming with pain and my hand feels nearly numb passes in a whirlwind.

Her cries get louder as she fights me in my lap, naturally wanting to pull away from me. I nearly lose my grip on her wrists, but I manage to keep her steady and where I need her to be, so I can fulfill her punishment.

Her ass is bright red and my skin humming with a delightful sting by the time I slip my fingers back to her soaking wet cunt. Her body shudders and her yelp of pain turns to a sinful moan.

Over and over I spank her viciously, the underside of her ass, the right cheek, the left one… and then her pussy. My hand's wet with her arousal as she trembles beneath me.

My fingers dip into her pussy with each smack, giving her only the tiniest bit of penetration. The intensity of the teasing bends her back even farther and her lust-filled gaze stares back at me with her strangled moans of pleasure and pain echoing off the walls of the cellar.

"Good girl." I praise her and watch as she peers up at me with a wondering look in her eyes and her cheeks tearstained.

"Tonight, I'm going to fuck you into that mattress on the floor like I should have the moment I got my hands on you."

Her pussy clenches around my fingertips and I reward her by pushing them in deeper and stroking her front wall.

Her back arches and I have to push her shoulder down to keep her right where I want her as I pull my touch away from her in order to leave her wanting. Her small moan of frustration is met with another slap of my hand on her bright red skin. Smack!

Her head flies back and those gorgeous lips of hers part with a deep gasp of longing. It's no longer pain. She's too close to the edge of pleasure to feel anything but.

Soothing the pain of the smack with my hand, I rub her right cheek and then pull back for one more strike.

"You would have learned sooner if I'd been rougher with you, wouldn't you?"

She moans her answer with her eyes closed and her body still, knowing another punishing blow is coming, "Yes, Carter."

Her answer is absent of sincerity. She'd tell me whatever I wanted to hear right now as she sits on the edge of pleasure and pain.

The days come back to me. Each of them and what I'd planned to do with her is in such stark contrast to what I've done. I let the fingers of my right hand trail over her ass, my blunt nails gently scraping along her tender skin and making her squirm on my lap. My left hand grips her throat, finally releasing her wrists, and I pull back, forcing her to look at me.

Her hazel eyes are filled with longing and lust. The haze is a fog in the forest. Unable to see, but so tempted to go forward.

"I should have fucked you so much sooner."

I remember that first day, how she screamed and cried for me to let her go, back when I hated her and she hated me.

Even with my tight grip on her throat, with my touch sending sparks through her body, she forces her head to shake, not taking her eyes from mine.

"No," she whispers, and my dick hardens, even more, begging me to punish her for daring to defy me. But then she adds, "This is how it was supposed to be."

Her breathing is heavy as she closes her eyes, her body bowed on my lap. She's completely at my mercy and her pouty lips are there for the taking.

All of her. Every piece of her is mine and she knows it.

Mine.

CHAPTER 28

Aria

YESTERDAY WAS FULL OF REGRET.

The moment I saw Carter again, I wish I'd taken back those hours he was gone. He always keeps his word. And true to form, he took me back to the cell and fucked me on the mattress. Maybe it was the drunkenness, maybe it was something else, but the fear of the cell was absent and instead, I did everything I could to please him. My body begged me to.

Not because I felt the need to obey.

I wanted him to kiss me.

I needed him to. And every time his lips trailed down my neck, I tried to capture them. Tried and failed. He knows I want him though. A shudder runs through my body at the thought and it's met with the dull ache between my thighs.

He fucked me until I couldn't move anymore and even as I laid on my belly on the mattress, unable to grip onto it, unable to keep my back arched as he commanded me to. Even then he rutted behind me, pistoning into me and giving me a punishing fuck.

Last night I was his whore. He balled my hair into his fist and pulled back so he could rake his teeth along my neck and force my body however he wanted it.

And I wanted nothing more.

The realization should startle me more, but instead, all I can think about is that he knows I want him to kiss me, and yet he didn't let me.

It's different when he's with me. The security I have with him is everything.

The sane part of me knows it's not healthy and that I should keep fighting, but the sane part of me is the only part of me that's held captive in this reality. If only I let it go, I feel free.

Free enough to feel safe for another day.

Free enough to know that what happens in the war will happen regardless of whether I'm here or not.

Free enough to slip on the dress that Carter's laid out for me and stare at the image of a beautiful woman in the mirror. One who I envy. One I can't believe is me.

With my hair smoothed and clipped at the side, the bit of makeup adding a definition of beauty to my porcelain skin, I feel so much like a songbird who sings soft melodies of hope, with her wings clipped in a gilded cage.

My fingers graze over the delicate lace and my eyes close, remembering last night.

The bruise on my ass sends a reminder of the pain through me as I smooth the soft lace down my curves. The sensation is directly linked to my clit and instantly my body begs for more. For me to put an ounce of pressure against the bruise.

A soft breath leaves me, a wanting one at that, and when I open my eyes, Carter is standing in front of me.

My heart slams and then does a soft trot. As if it's galloping toward him, even though he's the one walking toward me.

Each step is deliberate, but with a softness I've never seen from him and it captures every bit of my thoughts.

"You look beautiful, songbird," he says, and his voice is like velvet as he rounds me. His steps echo in the bedroom as he walks in a half circle and stops at my back.

I can hear his breathing hitch as he pulls at the lace, sliding it up my backside and sending a thrilling shiver up my body. His fingertips trail ever so gently along the marks. "Beautiful," he remarks before hiding them under the lace once again.

"Thank you," I dare to whisper, meeting his gaze as he walks to stand in front of me. My fingers slip to the hem of the dress, toying with it to hide the anxiousness of wanting to touch him as he's just touched me. I'm not allowed to today. When he opened the door to the cell, he told me if I obeyed every wish of his today, I would never see the cell again.

One day, and the rules of the game change forever.

A million thoughts are scattered through my mind, but only one of them matters.

"I'll be good tonight," I tell him in a voice I don't recognize. One of obedience, but also strength. "I won't disappoint you." A past version of me would slit my throat before letting herself hear those words. There's only a faint blip of pain in my heart at the realization.

The earlier version of me was foolish.

This version of me will survive. And this version has the audacity to admit that I enjoy it. Every fucking bit of it. To be wanted by a man so powerful who wants for nothing is a heady feeling.

"Aria," Carter says my name in a way that makes fear blossom deep in my gut. "You're going to want to defy me," he tells me, and the worry shows on my face. I can feel it tugging my lips down as it dries out my throat. He stalks in a circle around me, occasionally picking at the lace of the dress. They're cages. Each of the pieces of lace is a birdcage. And there's never been a dress that's adorned my body as beautifully as this one does.

"You may even hate me," he says in a purely seductive cadence. His hot breath tickles the bare skin of my neck as he whispers at the shell of my ear, "But you will obey me."

I nod my head and then croak out, "Yes, Carter." It's so silent in the room with neither of us speaking, moving or even daring to breathe. It's so silent I swear the darkness itself could whisper and I would hear its threatening tongue.

"Your necklace suits this dress perfectly," Carter says out loud although I don't think the words were meant for me.

Absently, I roll one of the pearls between my fingers and then feel the thin chain slide under my thumb as it moves to the diamond teardrop. It feels heavier tonight. Everything feels heavier when Carter looks at me like he is now.

With dark eyes that pin me in place and keep me still, right where he wants me. It's a silly thing, how the same gaze that once caused fear to ripple through my body now only heats my core and begs me to bend at the knees for him.

"Thank—"

Carter places a finger against my lips, silencing me. The small touch is addictive and the tension of the dinner tonight amplifies.

"Remember what I told you last night." He speaks as he toys with the necklace, holding the large diamond and lifting the weight from me. "You will kneel beside me, and you will obey every command."

Instantly my body heats. I worry my bottom lip between my teeth, wanting to ask him so many questions, but I already know he won't answer. There's only one thing to say. "Yes, Carter."

A moment passes, his eyes searching my gaze for something and I can hardly breathe.

"After tonight, no one will question that you're mine." His eyes darken and the flecks of gold that are buried beneath the coal there turn to fire. A fire that ignites my own and soothes the worries.

"Come with me," he commands me as he reaches for my hand.

CHAPTER 29

Carter

MY WALK IS CALM AND STEADY, EVEN AS ARIA FREEZES.
The cocky smirk stays plastered on my lips, even as sickness stirs in my gut. Every bit of my body is screaming to act, but this is for her. It's all for her.

"Come," I command Aria as she stares straight ahead at the entrance to the dining hall. Her chest rises in slow motion as her lips part with the hint of a shaky breath. "Aria," I say, and her name slips from me like an admonishment, "I said come." The demand is there, but the look she gives me in return is one of defiance and betrayal. There's so much hate in the dark greens and ambers of her eyes that I almost regret this.

But she needs this. That hate for me won't be there for long.

Stephan and Romano's shared rumble of deep laughter is the only sound in the large room as they see her. With the blood-red velvet curtains shut tightly, the only light in the room shines down from the scattered crystals on the chandelier.

The smell of beef wellington, seated beautifully at the center of the table, greets us as we enter the room. The light shines off the butcher's knife beside it.

Aria's walk is hesitant but she obeys me, even if there are tears in her eyes.

"I was beginning to think I'd have to come up and get you," Jase says as I take Aria's hand in mine and motion for her to kneel beside my chair across from Stephan. Her palm is clammy, and her grip tight as she lowers herself to the floor. The pain I feel for her is nothing compared to what she'll have in only moments.

As quickly as she can, she tears her hand from mine. And again, laughter from the two guests echoes off the walls.

"Still so defiant." Romano's eyes sparkle, but I ignore him, taking my seat.

I hate that for the moment I can't keep my hand on hers, but soon I'll have her again.

"No need," I tell Jase, meeting his gaze and forcing a smile on my lips that grows as I turn my attention to Stephan, nodding a greeting and then turn to Romano. "Thank you for coming, gentlemen."

"The pleasure is all mine," Stephan says at the same time as Romano nods his head, the thin smile growing on his lips and turning wicked.

"It's a delight to see you've taken a liking to our gift."

Anger burns deep in my chest at the memory of him having his hands on her only weeks ago, but it stays where it is as I return his smile, placing my hand on the back of Aria's head. She remains stiff, not leaning into my touch, which only intensifies the fire inside of me. But I will have patience, even if she tests me.

"I wish I could see her better," Stephan says, sitting up from his seat for a moment and making a comical face. Jase gives him a bit of laughter, I'm sure because he knows what's coming. He'll enjoy this, but not nearly as much as I will.

"No sense of humor?" Stephan speaks to Daniel and then glances at Declan, both of them quiet. It's only the seven of us in the room, although the kitchen is abuzz with the sound of dishes being plated. And the men waiting for my order.

"I know a few jokes," Daniel says wryly, but then he picks up his drink and leaves the unspoken words hanging in the air. Romano's shoulders stiffen and a hard gaze meets his eyes.

"Come up here, Aria," I say and pat my lap and then glance at Stephan. "I'd like for our guests to see you better."

From the corner of my eye, I see Romano's tension ease. The room is silent, so silent I can hear my songbird swallow as she stands up on weak legs. I'm quick to pull her into my lap, pressing my hand against her ass and reminding her of last night. Her eyes widen, and she gasps, thrilling the men she doesn't dare look at.

"Excuse her," I speak to no one in particular. "She's not used to company."

With all eyes on her, I place her exactly how I'd like her, nestling her ass into my crotch and wrapping my arm around her waist. "Relax," I whisper into her ear, knowing full well the other men can hear me. Her hair tickles against my jaw and shoulder as I move it from one side of her back to the other so I can expose her neck.

"You can't say hello to an old friend?" Stephan asks.

"If I recall, she's more fond of begging." Romano's comment doesn't go unnoticed.

"She's a little frightened," I say before kissing the crook of her neck and feeling her body relax for the first time, although I know the moment will be gone before I'd like.

"One of the many Talverys who will fall to their knees," Stephan gloats and raises his glass to toast, but I don't reciprocate.

"I thought she would, but she betrayed me last night," I tell them and reach for a goblet of water.

"Betrayed?" Romano's voice is low.

I nod and look to see how my brothers react to my words.

"I thought she was doing well?" Jase comments and leans forward in his seat to look at Aria, his stare commanding her to look at him, which she does, but only for a moment. Her head is held high, but her glassy gaze stares at nothing.

"She tried to kill Daniel," I tell Jase and he gives me a look of shock but then turns to Daniel, who's smiling.

"Kill you?" he questions Daniel.

"As if she could," he says, leaning back in his seat. Aria struggles to breathe as we talk about her in front of her like her presence is a meaningless joke. But everything has a purpose.

"It was only a knife." Daniel looks at me as he answers, and I reach for the one in front of me.

"This one?" I ask him, and Aria rocks forward a moment, her ability to stay strong being questioned. When I peer up at her, her eyes are shut tightly. "Look at me, Aria." My words are lethal on my tongue.

Instantly, her eyes open and a scattering of tears lines her lashes. Instead of wiping them away, I hold up the knife and ask, "This one?"

She shakes her head gently. "No," she says, the word a mere whisper. I can feel the pounding of her heart.

"Take it," I demand as I grab her hand and put it over the handle of the knife. "Would you like to use it on him now?" I ask her.

"No," she says and her voice trembles, but again she shakes her head and answers me. "How about on me?" I offer her. "Would you like to slit my throat, Aria?"

"No." Her answer is a barely spoken breath and her grip on the knife loosens.

"I told Daniel this morning," I begin, addressing Romano to my right and giving him my full attention, "that it was his fault. There was no fear of him and what he'd do to her."

Romano considers me, his brow raising and his lips turning down into a frown before he nods in agreement. "Fear is powerful."

"I choose other tactics," Daniel speaks up and then looks at Aria as he adds, "I let her do what she thought she needed to, so she could at least feel that she'd tried." His voice is neutral, devoid of the empathy I know he has for her. It's all a show. That's the real difference between us; Daniel likes to hide behind an image.

I am the image of what's to be feared. It exists in my being and there's no hiding it.

"Do you remember me, Aria?" Stephan dares to ask her, leaning across the table to be every bit closer to her that he can.

"Oh, she does," I answer for her as she struggles to respond. "My poor Aria, I know this is hard for you," I say and hold her tighter, although she's stiff doing her best to stay seated on my lap.

"I imagine it is," Stephan says and then adds, "She's grown to be just as beautiful as her mother."

My blood sings with both rage and vengeance, and it's a feeling I adore. A smile creeps across my lips as I confide in him, "She sings for me, but the memory of you is strong enough to stop it." I turn to Aria, letting my finger trail over her shoulder to slip a lock of hair to her back and then turn to Stephan. "I can't have that."

Confusion mars his face for a moment and I let time pass for a moment in deadly silence.

"I could give her a different memory to hold onto," Stephan suggests and the laugh that creeps from Romano's gut is tight with tension.

"I don't believe Carter enjoys sharing," Romano comments, but I hold up my hand to stop him, speaking only to Stephan.

"I do believe she needs a different memory. I'm tired of hearing her cry out in her sleep." As I speak, Aria's expression crumples and I pull her closer to me, forcing her back to my chest and whisper in her ear, "Should I let Stephan fuck you?" I don't let them see the anger, the hate, the deep-seated pain of watching my songbird relive the memories in front of her tormentor. They can't see yet, but they will suffer. I swear they will pay.

Deep in my core, I have the fear of breaking Aria, of pushing her too hard, but she needs this.

"Carter," Jase warns, and I only shoot him a gaze of contempt. If this is to go as planned, Romano is the witness whose testimony matters. His perception is the only one that matters.

Aria breaks down at the mere question, her reality again failing her. Each bit of her shatters with hope fading from her very existence. It's then I know I've truly broken her and the beautiful shards of what used to be Aria Talvery can fill the crevice of my soul she broke long ago. And I can use those pieces how I'd like. Creating perfection in her from what's been broken.

As she gasps an answer, a plea from her lips that only I can hear, I pull her tighter to me, feeling her warmth and her small body pressed securely against mine. The knife is still in her hand, although weakly held.

"You still have the knife, Aria," I remind her. "Would you like to cut me now?" As I ask her the question, her hazel-green eyes strike me with every ounce of pain she feels at this moment. "Why are you doing this to me?" she asks, her small voice revealing her agony.

I let my fingers slip up her dress as Romano says something I don't care to listen to.

Letting my lips trail along the back of her neck, I whisper just for her. "Do you think I'd let him fuck you?" I ask her and press my fingers to her clit, forcing her to push back and feel my cock on her bruised ass, hard at the very thought of what's coming. "That I would let him even imagine taking what's mine?" The hiss of my voice travels throughout the dining room, but I'm certain no one could know for sure what I've asked her.

Her eyes, still shining with unshed tears, finally meet mine and stare back at me as she whispers, "No."

A smile threatens to pull at my lips and I let it as Romano and Stephan cluck their tongues in disapproval, as if they have any control at all over her. As if they know what's coming.

I rock her into my lap again and the sweet gasp that parts her lips brings a light to her eyes. A light that I've given her. Only me.

Bringing my lips to the shell of her ear, I whisper, "Do you think I'd *ever*," I stress the word, "let him touch you?" As I prompt her, the demeanor of my guests change.

"No," she says with the strength of realization. My sweet girl. I watch as her breathing calms and she glances at Stephan and then Romano before looking back at me and answering me again, her head shaking and letting those locks play around her bare shoulders. "No," she repeats softly.

"She's rather bold, don't you think?" Romano asks Jase, who doesn't respond to him.

"I love how strong she is," I say aloud, ignoring the comments from Stephan at the end of the table for a moment before adding, "Her will was difficult to break, but it was worth it."

Declan speaks up, tired of the show I imagine. He has no patience and he states pointedly, "The dinner is getting cold."

"Of course." I lean back in my seat and splay my hand against Aria's stomach to push her small body against mine. "Would you like to carve the meat, Aria?" I ask her and glance behind me toward the kitchen. "Bring out the plates in just a moment," I call out and catch Romano's gaze. "This chef is to die for."

"I can hardly wait," he says beneath his breath.

"Aria," I tell them, "will cut the wellington and serve us, I think." A half grin ticks up the corners of my lips as Romano smiles.

"I didn't expect this from you," he tells me, and I cock a brow at him. "I didn't think you enjoyed this as much as you seem to."

My grin widens. "You have no idea how much I enjoy this." Tonight, my songbird will be changed forever. And I'm the one who will give it to her. She will never fear anyone but me ever again.

"You have her sit at the table?" Stephan questions me with a glint of humor in his eyes. His thin lips twitch into a smile and I manage a smile back, remembering that this is for her. She's the one to do it. My grip on her waist tightens, to keep me from ruining everything.

"You do as you'd like in your home, but do not question me in mine." My words are sharp and not to be taken lightly. They force the smile off his pale face while Romano coughs at the head of the table.

"I think he only means that we were expecting to see her on the floor… where slaves belong."

Picking up the large butcher knife on the table, I put the knife firmly in Aria's hand and command her to carve the beef wellington. She can barely reach, and I do my best to balance her as she reaches over the table, the sharp blade piercing the puff pastry shell with a slight crack that's audible in the silent room.

My breathing comes in harder and harder, knowing what's next. I can taste the sweetness of it already as the meat falls onto the platter.

"Carter has a soft spot for her, I think," Jase offers, and he and Daniel share a look. One of my brothers on each side of me. Both of them ready for when I cue the kitchen.

"I want a nice meal, for fuck's sake," I say with a touch of humor to break the tension and put both Stephan and Romano at ease. "We start a war tomorrow. And technically, shots have already been fired," I say, and shrug then place a small bit of meat onto the platter as Aria's movements become strained.

"Yes. Here's to victory," Romano says, raising the glass of champagne in front of him. The bubbly liquid rises in the air, and with it, both of his hands. It's like I'm watching in slow motion as I turn my attention to Stephan and see him do the same. An empty hand palm up on the table and his other raised in the air, holding a glass.

"Cheers, bring out the dinner," I call out as I raise my glass, not bothering to reach for my gun.

My voice rings out and our men from the kitchen bring out the serving dishes. My closest men, disguised as servers, quickly make their way around the room with their trays.

They unveil each of the covered platters at once to reveal their guns, aimed at both Romano and Stephan. All while Aria's carving the meat with shaky hands.

Stephan and Romano both suck in a breath but keep their hands raised even as curses fill the air, as do the sound of pistols being cocked.

Aria drops the knife on the table, her shoulders hunched and a squeal of both terror and surprise forcing her backward and into my arms. I wish I could have warned her, but Romano is going to live to tell the tale.

Her shoulders are cold in my embrace as I pull her close and whisper, "You're all right."

All three of my brothers raise their loaded guns, but I keep my hands on Aria, still trembling. Declan, seated at the opposite head, keeps his gun pointed at Romano and my other two brothers keep theirs pointed at Stephan as they face him.

"What the fuck is this?" Romano is quick to speak with indignation and attempts to lower his arm. My eyes pierce into Stephan's, who's staring straight at me with a bitter hate that I'm used to seeing from men I've fucked over. It's always followed by the milky gaze of dead eyes. He doesn't dare lower his arm. Because he knows the truth better than Romano does.

I hear the distinctive sound of a gun with a silencer going off, but I don't bother to look and verify that the bullet landed just behind Romano as a warning shot. My eyes stay fixed on Stephan's. Just as his are on me.

"This is a show for you, Romano," I finally speak when he stands abruptly. "Help him sit, Jase."

Without a word, my brother rises and I can just barely see Aria in my periphery. My sweet, haunted girl. She grips the table and watches intently as Jase pulls out the chair for Romano, waiting for him to sit a few feet away from the table where his hands can easily be seen.

Jase stays behind him, his gun still trained on Romano although now he could easily shoot Stephan as well. But his death is for Aria, and Aria alone.

"The knife, Aria." I address only her. She's so small on my lap as she looks at me and then slowly around the room. She's hesitant to pick the knife back up and the cursing yell from Stephan nearly startles her into dropping it again.

The rage in my blood turns from a simmer to a boil. "Even now he holds a fear over you, my Aria," I tell her in a low voice of reprimand. "I won't allow it."

I can feel her skin turn cold as she waits for my command. She's barely breathing, still scared and confused. With the knife in her hand, I pull her back into my lap, taking my time to calm her so she can see clearly.

Fear can cloud everything, turning reality into falsehoods.

"Are you mad at me, songbird?" I ask her gently, cupping her jaw in my hand. I can feel her swallow tightly and peek back at Stephan before looking at me. "Why?" she asks me with such sadness.

"You needed this," I whisper against her lips, nearly pressing mine to hers in an effort for her to understand how crucial this moment is, both for her and for us.

Her bottom lip quivers as tears prick the back of her eyes. "I thought you were giving me to him," she confesses as her voice cracks and her shoulders shudder.

Gripping her tighter I speak clearly, loud enough for everyone in this room to hear. "You are mine and Romano lied to me when he gave me to you," I hiss.

"Bullshit!" Romano dares to interrupt me and my hackles rise, the anger brimming. But I'll deal with him once I'm through with Aria. She will always come first.

"You were damaged." Her expression crumples at my words, shame filling her hazel eyes as I add, "You were so fucking broken I couldn't have my hand in it." I turn my head to sneer at Stephan. "Not when someone else has such control over you."

"I'm sorry," she whispers, and the tip of the knife hits the table as her grip loosens.

"Did I tell you to drop the knife?" I ask her and instead of taking the hint and holding it tighter, she drops it to the table, covering her face with her hands and leaning into my chest.

"I really thought..." she pauses as her chest heaves and I give her this moment. I comfort her and make the men wait. They will wait for her. And so will I.

For this I've waited so long already, another minute can be spared for her pain.

"I thought," she continues to stammer, and I kiss her hair, rubbing her back as she tells me, "I thought you were done with me."

Pulling at her shoulders, I force her to arm's length in my lap. "Never," I tell her with all sincerity, feeling the truth down to my core, coursing through my blood and in every thought I could ever have.

Aria's breathing calms as she stares into my eyes, while a softness I've never felt drifts over me. "You scared me," she whispers.

Running the tip of my nose against hers, I whisper against her lips, "It's a gift for you."

When I pull away, her eyes are still closed, but slowly they open and I nod toward the knife.

"Kill him, Aria."

Romano curses, but one of my men presses the barrel of his gun to his head.

"Pick up the knife and end him."

I watch Aria's shaky fingers pick up the knife, and then she stares at her prey. He scowls at her, but she doesn't back down. Her chest heaves again and the way she holds her chin up lets me know she's scared but doing her damnedest not to be.

Fear can never hide though.

"I won't be with you if you don't," I tell her and instantly regret the words. Her eyes widen, and she sucks in a breath. "I can't let you continue like this," I tell her, wishing I could take back the first words I gave her.

Her eyes flicker from me to Stephan and she nods her head slightly, but still, she doesn't move.

Even knowing she has the knife in her hand, I lean forward and rest my head against her chest. "This is for you, Aria," I whisper in the hot space between us. "It's all for you."

Inhaling her scent and feeling her body against mine, I kiss her throat and move to the crook of her slender neck. Her nails dig into my shoulder as she gasps.

It's an apology for the threat I just made that never should have left me.

My lips slip down her shoulder and she moans softly, relaxing into me as my hands travel up her waist.

"Kill him, Aria," I command her and continue kissing her neck, my touch turning ravenous.

Raking my teeth down her jaw, I worship her.

My brothers are witnesses to what I'd do to have her be completely mine. Romano and the dead fuck Stephan watch with a series of slurs and profanity.

Let them all see. Let the entire fucking world see.

My cock is hard when I pull away, seeing her breathless and in need.

"First, you take care of him." I nod toward Stephan and then tell her, "And then you will be truly mine."

Aria's nod is swift and she's quick this time to leave my lap, although her touch lingers on my shoulder as she steadies herself.

Three guns are pointed at Stephan, but he's only looking at her as she rounds the table. I follow her at a distance, giving her this.

Stephan's smile is grim and unnerving as he sneers, "She'll never do it. Just shoot—"

Before he can get the last word out, Aria whips her hand through the air, slicing his neck open and forcing blood to pour from his neck. As his hands reach up to his throat, she screams a bloodcurdling sound, slicing again in the same pattern. Only this time, it cuts through his hands, nearly severing one of his fingers.

She doesn't stop. She stabs frantically into his chest, hitting his arm, his shoulder, his throat again. Her aim is reckless, and my men take a step back, blood drenching his shirt and spraying from his cuts.

She's savage in the stabs. Chaotic even. For a moment, I want to tear the knife from her for fear of her cutting herself.

She screams out as the knife pierces through the expensive fabric and into his soft flesh, the blood seeping through his clothes. The cry from her is sickening. Not because of the piercing scream, but because of the overt sadness. She kills him with her pain.

"Let it out," I say without conscious consent. I can see Daniel turn his attention from her to me, but I ignore him. None of them matter right now.

She needs this more than anything.

Romano stands from his seat, backing away and it's only then that I break my focus on Aria.

"Sit," I practically snarl. The anger is mostly because he dared distract me from this.

He grits his teeth and feigns irritation as he slowly obeys me, but he can't deny the utter fear I can see in his gaze.

With both hands on the armrests, he slowly takes his seat and I can focus on Aria again.

Her energy has waned and she's silent as tears stream down her face. Her small body looks weaker and weaker, but she doesn't stop stabbing into Stephan's lifeless body. She's obviously exhausted, but she doesn't stop.

Not until I give her the command, my low voice foreboding and dominating in the silent room. "Aria. Give me the knife."

Her wild eyes glance at me, only for a moment as the knife trembles in her hand and she shakes her head, no.

"Aria," I raise my voice, forcing it to echo in the room. The only sounds I can hear are the blood rushing in my ears and Aria's ragged breathing as I grit my teeth and tell her one last time. "Give. Me. The knife."

HEARTLESS

At first, his words were harsh and his touch cold.
I knew he was a dangerous man and he could destroy me if only he wanted to.

That's not what he wanted though. It's not what he needed.
It's not what I desired either.

It's so easy to get lost in the touch of a man who's powerful and unattainable.
A man who wants for nothing… except me.
Soft touches and stolen glances made my blood heat and my heart beat in a way I never knew it could.

Yes, it's easy to fall into a haze of lust and desire.
But there's a reason his reputation is one of a heartless man.
And I should have known better.

PROLOGUE

RAIN IS COMING. THE KIND OF RAIN THAT MAKES YOUR BONES ACHE. THE DARK gray sky is streaked with dry lightning that splinters the crack of pain even deeper. There's only so much a man can take. Only so far he can be pushed to the brink and still want to survive.

First, my mother lost her fight with cancer.

Then Tyler, my youngest brother, was struck and killed by a car.

And now, my father has been murdered in cold blood.

The blame for my father's death is easy to place. A group of thugs who wanted the highest high, and they were willing to do whatever it took to chase it.

They didn't fear my father. Not like they fear me.

I know that's why they waited for him to be the one on the street corner, instead of me dealing from the back of the truck. When my mother died, selling drugs was what we needed to do to pay the bills. But months have passed, and it's more than an income stream now. Dealing, and the fighting that comes with, it is now my obsession.

I'm not just peddling dope or selling off stolen prescriptions. The drug trade is lucrative beyond anything I could have ever dreamed.

But Talvery taught me more than anyone else could.

He taught me where the boundaries were. Taught me what fear is capable of.

He showed me what it takes to make the pain go away and replace it with something more addictive than heroin. Power is everything.

And I feel it flowing through my veins.

Crack! Lightning strikes again, followed by a boom and shaking of the ground.

Rain is coming, but I'll stand here for as long as it takes.

The priest's voice is a dull monotone and the cries from distant family members, who I've only ever seen a handful of times in my life, numb me.

The casket in which my father's body lies reflects the first droplets of water. The sprinkling is just the beginning of the downpour threatening to fall any minute now.

He would still be alive if they'd had the same fear of him that they have of me. If he'd learned the hard lesson Talvery had taught me months ago.

Revenge will come for the pricks who killed my father. Not because I love him. Or *loved*, rather. I think I hated him in the last few years. Truly and deeply despised the piece of shit he became when my mother got sick. The realization is freeing.

That's not why I'll hunt down each and every one of those assholes and take a baseball bat to them in their sleep, or a gun to the side of their heads as they creep through dark back alleys, or a knife along their throats in the restrooms of their favorite bars. One by one, I'll kill them all.

It's not because I want revenge or because I don't want my father's death to go unanswered.

No. I'll murder them because they thought they could take from me. They decided it was worth the risk to take from me. Anger rises in my chest, heating my blood and forcing my hands into white-knuckled fists. I have to clench my teeth in an effort to hide the rage.

No one will ever take from me again. They won't take more of my family. They won't take a goddamn thing from me. Never again.

The day my father was laid to rest, the demon who had long slept inside of me awakened and destroyed whatever bit of goodness that had lingered in my heart. From that day forward, I decided that everyone would fear me. Simply because it was easier to survive that way, obsessing over the power that fear would bring me.

I craved their fear the way I used to pray for the pain to go away.

It was all-consuming and only the tiniest slivers of this new armor ever broke off. Only when painful memories forced me to confront who and what I used to be. But even the smallest shards of my armor were so easily replaced by the blood of those who dared to threaten what I'd become.

So long as everyone feared me and those closest to me, I would not only survive, I would thrive.

They needed to fear my brothers.

And now they need to fear her. *My songbird.*

They will. I refuse to let anyone take her.

No one will take her away from me. No one.

CHAPTER 1

Aria

I CAN'T STOP SHAKING. MY ENTIRE BODY IS CONSUMED BY FEAR AND I'M TREMBLING all over. My hands are shaking chaotically, and I can't make them stop.

The heavy knife is gripped tighter than I've ever gripped anything in my life. I don't even feel like it's my hand holding the weapon. Another person's hand, on top of mine, is forcing it to stay in my grip. To hold it tighter and tighter until it hurts so much that my body begs me to fall to my knees in agony.

I won't allow my body to betray me. I can't drop the knife. I can't stop myself. The fear and rage are mingling into a concoction that's far too powerful to deny.

The blood on the blade drips down onto my hand and feels like fire on my skin. The tension, the anger, the pure rage, and terror all boil in my blood as I stare at the dead, milky white eyes of the monster in front of me.

I can't look at Carter. I can't rip my gaze from the motionless stare of Alexander Stephan.

I'm waiting for him to blink. To jump up and grab me. The fear I feel is paralyzing, but the adrenaline coursing through me is going to burst my veins. He's limp in the chair, his throat split wide open although the blood isn't gushing anymore. It's only a slow trickle at this point.

It reminds me of the way my mother's throat was slit. *The way he did it.*

I remember it so clearly. That scene has haunted my dreams for as long as I can remember. How he stood behind her after he'd abused her. How he didn't do it slowly; instead it was vicious and violent. It was all I could think to do to him here in this chair and at my mercy when Carter handed me the knife.

"Aria," Carter's voice breaks through my terror and the memory as he commands, "Give. Me. The. Knife." His words mix with the sound of my heavy breathing.

Carter's voice is demanding and on the edge of anger. I barely peek at him, the fear of Stephan waking and taking the knife from me is all too real. Blood seeps into his shirt, and his mangled body is unmoving. But I know he's going to take the knife back. Stephan will take it and do to me what he did to my mother.

I squeeze the steel handle harder. I won't let him.

Tears prick my eyes as Carter yells at me, his voice booming in the silent room and sending a violent vibration through my chest. It hurts. It all hurts.

My head shakes in defiance. I shouldn't disobey him. Bad things happen when I do. *The cell.* At the thought, my shoulders hunch and my knees go weak, ready to surrender and kneel to the man who's held me captive yet given me this revenge.

Given me the means to avenge my mother's death.

But I can't move. "I can't," I say, and my words are weak and fall from my lips like a pathetic whimper. "I won't." Those two words come out harder and I reach out, swinging my arm violently in the air and slicing into Stephan's throat again. In my periphery, I see a man back away, and then another.

A small cry slips through my lips unbidden as Carter wraps his hand around mine, his other hand on my shoulder and keeping me steady as he pries my fingers back. The murmurs of the other men in the room barely register. All I can hear is Carter shushing me, and all I can focus on are Stephan's eyes. The depths of his irises never seemed as dark as they do now.

The steady shaking of my shoulders turns violent as I try to move backward, away from the monster, away from his grasp. To run and hide like I did all those years ago.

But I can't. Carter won't let me.

It's Carter, I tell myself. Carter is holding me. Focusing on regulating my shaky breathing helps steady me back to reality.

My left knee falls to the ground first and it makes my right knee slam against the ground.

"Shh," Carter shows me mercy. Stealing the knife from me but guarding me against my fears.

"It's over," he whispers as he finally pries the knife from my grasp. And I let him. I let him take it, but I won't move until I know Stephan is dead.

"He'll come for me," the scared child inside of me speaks. He can't be dead, because then it would be over. And with Stephan, it's never over. He's haunted me for as long as I can remember.

"She's fucking insane." The sharp and disgusted voice of Romano cuts through my thoughts. *Thump, thump.* My heart beats harder as I remember where I am. "This is insane," Romano says with anger.

"Shut up." Carter's voice once again tears through my body, thrumming through my blood and for the first time, I close my eyes. But then I remember Stephan is only feet from me, and they fly open again.

The room falls silent, just as Carter commanded. His fingertips are gentle on my shoulders, one hand on each as he lowers his lips to my ear and tells me, "Go upstairs and wash yourself off."

My head shakes on its own, my eyes not moving from the body in the chair in front of me.

"He's not dead," I speak softly as if it's my excuse. Logically, I know he's dead. He must be. But the fear that he's not is so real, so visceral that I can't contain it. I can't shut it down.

Carter's grip on me tightens as I hear him breathe heavier before huffing a low sound mixed with a grunt of anger. The second he moves away from me, all I feel is the chill of loneliness.

With one heavy step, Carter kicks over the chair, sending Stephan's heavy body to the floor with a thud, and again the men back up while Romano says something I can't hear. It all turns to white noise as Carter kicks the limp body. Stephan's head falls to the side and I have to move to my right, my knees rubbing against the unforgiving floor as I look into his eyes. Still open, still staring aimlessly.

"He's dead, Aria. He's fucking dead!"

My head shakes as my pulse quickens, the palms of my hands sweaty. "He can't be," I say but my words are weak.

Carter leans over the dead body, gripping my chin in both of his hands and pulling me closer to him, but I react quickly, terrified that Stephan could reach up. That he would get me if I dared to take my eyes from his.

"Un-fucking-believable." Carter's mutter sends hatred through me. Hatred toward myself and my cowardice. How many years have I woken in sheer horror at the vision of the man lying dead at my feet? Enough that logic betrays me, making me think there's no way that he's dead.

"I'll give you his head," Carter says and not understanding, my eyes lift to his for only a moment, but he's already crouching down, the knife in his hand. He lifts it high in the air and strikes it against the open wound in Stephan's throat. His muscles tense in his neck as he hardens his jaw. Anger is evident in his strained expression as he strikes again and again, taking his frustration out on Stephan's neck.

He holds the knife in place, sweating and panting with both anger and exertion. Carter's shoe slams against the slick side of the knife. Over and over each thrust of his leg is accompanied with more power, more anger—no, outrage, that Stephan's neck doesn't split beneath the blade. My body jolts with each impact, and the awe of watching Carter destroy Stephan by tearing his head from his body slowly helps restore my sanity.

A crunch that makes my gut twist and turn echoes through the room, as does the deep growl of irritation that rumbles from Carter in a snarl. As Carter lifts his blood-stained shoe, Stephan's head rolls backward, parted from his body.

My erratic heartbeat settles as Carter stands tall in front of me. His usually impeccable suit is a wrinkled mess against his tanned skin. He drops the jacket to the floor and rolls up his sleeves one by one, taking his time as he steadies his breathing. I watch every bit of him morph back into the controlled man I know him to be. With blood splattered on his shirt, his hard jawline seeming even harder in the light from the chandeliers above us, Carter has never looked more dominating as he towers over me.

Men talk around us, but they don't exist in this moment. Not when Carter's dark eyes pierce through mine and the shards of silver in them hold me hostage.

"Upstairs." The word slips from my lips before he opens his mouth. I watch as his tongue wets his lower lip and he considers me. His eyes leave mine to trail down my body and then back up, and it's only then I remind myself to breathe. "Upstairs to wash myself," I repeat Carter's command from a moment ago, letting my gaze move to Stephan's beheaded body.

When I raise my eyes back to Carter's, I know he was waiting for me to look back up at him.

I've left him waiting.

I've disobeyed him.

Everything moves around me slowly as I regain what little composure I have left.

Carter steps over Stephan's dead body and grips my chin forcefully in his hand. I can't breathe as he lowers his lips to mine, his eyes never leaving mine and tells me calmly with a voice loud enough for everyone to hear, "He'll never have power over you again. The only thing you have to fear, is me."

CHAPTER 2

Carter

"**W**HAT THE FUCK IS THIS, CROSS?" ROMANO FEIGNS ANGER IN HIS VOICE, but the terror is unmistakable.

Picking up Stephan's untouched and still neatly folded cloth napkin from the table, I wipe the blood from my hands and arms.

My shoulders rise and fall as I go over the last ten minutes. So little time for so much to happen. Romano isn't meant to die tonight, but I lost my composure. If he doesn't pull his shit together over Stephan dying, I'll have no choice but to kill him.

Or, if I think he'll speak a word that could ruin everything I've built and everything I have planned.

I can't hide what she does to me. I can't disguise the power Aria has over me when she doesn't listen.

Romano knows too much.

The thought forces my neck to tilt to the side and crack. And then to the other side as Romano asks again, "You set me up?"

The indignation in his voice is sickening. As if I owe him any loyalty. Dropping the napkin to the floor, I walk toward Romano, my shoes crushing fallen glass underfoot as I near him.

"He's a traitor," I say simply. "He *was* a traitor." Romano swallows and his hands ball into fists and then loosen. His gaze shifts to each person in the room. All of them with me, and none of them with him.

I could so easily destroy him. Take him out and be done with him. And then I wouldn't have to worry about the impression I've left him with. I wouldn't have to worry about him telling anyone else what Aria means to me.

But at that very thought, I know I'll let him live and walk out of my home unscathed. *I want them all to know.*

My eyes close at the realization. As I take a deep breath and fall into the calmness of my decision, I hear Jase's voice cut through the fog.

"We received some information from our leak at the Talvery headquarters," Jase says and then adds, "Stephan couldn't be trusted." His voice is calm. Calmer than Romano's as he replies with some sort of defense. I can't focus on what he says; all I can do is replay each moment in my mind, trying to decipher how Romano viewed it. How my brothers saw me. How the men who work for me watched me lose control.

They'll all know what she means to me. What she can do to me. I want every one of those pricks to know.

As my eyes slowly open, I see Romano and I grin at him, a slow methodical grin.

"Relax, Romano," I tell him as I reach out and grip his right shoulder. I give his shoulder a firm squeeze.

I listen to his breathing hitch and watch as his pupils dilate. I've seen this look so many times before. The look of fear and hope mixing in the eyes of my enemies is undeniably familiar to me.

"He had to be dealt with, and I know you had a soft spot for him," I tell him evenly, giving his shoulder another slight squeeze as I force a faint, but kind smile to my lips. "I didn't want anyone to think you had a hand in this." I release him and add, "I know you two were close."

With my back to him, I survey the room, and a few of my men are cleaning up the evidence already. This isn't the first time blood has been shed in this room and they're more than capable of making it go away. The glass clinks as it's swept up.

"I don't have any room for traitors in my alliances," I speak to Romano, although I still have my back to him.

"I could have been informed," he responds, and I finally turn to him again.

"I thought you would enjoy the show. I was told you have a fondness for theatrics." A flash of fear sparks in his eyes and I have to school my expression to keep the sheer delight from showing. The only thing that makes this moment better is knowing that Aria is upstairs, and she'll be waiting for me.

"Next time, I'll be sure to tell you in advance." With my final words, I nod to Jase.

"I'll show you out," Jase says to Romano with a smirk and heads to the door, not waiting for his response. I merely stare at the old man and his ill-fitting suit that's rumpled and marred by a small splatter of red up his arm. His eyes narrow and his chest rises once with a heavy breath. I can only imagine the taste of blood in his mouth as he bites his tongue.

"Next time," are his parting words and they're followed by the hollow sound of his footsteps as he leaves the room.

"You want to keep any of him, boss?" Sammy asks. He's a young kid, but smart and eager to learn. Crouched near Stephan's body, he gestures to the head. "Or trash it all?" He looks up at me without any fear, but in its place is respect. I think that's why I like the kid. A very large part of me envies him. He never went through the shit I did. He didn't have to learn the way I did.

"Burn all of him. No trace. I don't want a single piece of that prick left in here."

Sammy nods once and immediately gets to work.

"How long until he turns on us?" I hear Jase's question from behind me and I turn to face my brother.

"He'd already turned on us, remember?" I remind him and Jase only smirks at me.

"He was still willing to deal with us while ripping us off. But I imagine that's going to change now." He leans against the wall and slips his hands in his pockets as he watches the men clean up the room.

"Both Talvery and Romano will come for us. You know that, right?" Daniel asks as he moves to join us. Declan follows and the four of us form a circle in the corner of the room.

"As long as they don't join forces, it doesn't matter," I respond without thinking. My thoughts immediately go back to Aria. Consequences be damned; this was for her.

"What's to stop them from doing that?" Declan asks. He wasn't concerned before tonight. Of all four of us, he's the least interested and the least informed. Because of that, I imagine he was the most shocked as well.

"A decade-long feud, greed, arrogance?" Jase answers.

"All of this, and for what?" Daniel's question comes out harder. "It was for her, wasn't it?"

Silence engulfs us for a moment as I watch my brother.

"There was no reason to go about it like this. To make a scene and piss off Romano like that."

"It had to be done." Jase is quick to answer and firm with his response.

"But we didn't have to make Romano an enemy. Not now, not when Talvery is coming for us." Daniel's anger is evident, but more so, he's scared. Scared because Addison is here with us.

"She's safe," I tell him, moving to the heart of his concern.

My brothers are quiet as I take in Daniel's stance. He's tired and anxious. "I want this shit to end, but now we've added gasoline to the fucking fire."

Jase answers before I can. I'm struck by the fact that I never considered Addison. I didn't care what the cost was for giving Aria the revenge she so desperately needed. "The guns are in, we just have to spread them and hit them hard."

"Who are we hitting? Talvery? Or Romano?" Daniel asks Jase, but then all three of my brothers look at me. All of them wanting to know.

Daniel doesn't hold back his concern as he says, "I know you've been lying to us. And now you brought war to *our* doorstep for her."

"I never lied," I mutter, and my words are a harsh whisper. Anger seeps into my blood as I watch the chaos in Daniel's eyes heat.

"What does she mean to you?" he asks as if my answer will assuage all of his fears.

Only if I answer truthfully.

Jase's gaze moves to the men behind us and then back to me with a subtle unasked question and I nod my head.

"Leave us," I call out and wait to speak until the sounds of men shuffling out of the room subside. My brothers are patient. Not speaking and holding back until we're left alone.

"She's getting to you," Daniel speaks softly. "You're making calls for all of us, but she's clouding your judgment."

His words feel like a knife in my back.

"You're questioning me?" I ask him, not holding back the bite of anger, but deep inside I know it's for me. I'm angry because he's right. My brow pinches and I force in a deep breath and then another, staring behind my brother at the soft gray wall where bright red blood is smeared.

"She saved my life," I tell them while turning to look away. Guilt washes through me. I know I was thinking of her, not of us. But this was meant to happen. I can feel it ringing inside of me like a singular truth never has. "And I hated her for it." The confession comes out with a gentleness and careful touch.

The silence from my brothers begs me to look at them. To know for certain their reaction to my confession. Although there's a hint of shock in Daniel's eyes, there's something else there too. Something I can't place.

"Why didn't you tell us?" Jase asks. "She saved you?" he adds for clarification.

"It was years ago, the night Dad had to call his friend in." I know they know what I mean by the reference. There was only one night Dad called in a favor for me. One night where I almost met death.

"Shit," Declan bites out and runs his hand down his face. He was only a child. It was so long ago.

"As long as I'm living and breathing—she will be mine." My response is brutal and unmoving. "Whether she likes it or not."

"You took her because you hated her for saving you?" Daniel asks although there's no confrontation in his tone, nothing but genuine curiosity and concern.

"I wanted her to know what it was like to wish you could just die and not have to live another day with the person you've become." I almost tell him I didn't know that I loved her. But I change the words as I add, "I didn't know that I cared for her. Not until she came here."

She gave me a new reason to live. Not only all those years ago when she saved me, but also this past month when I finally got her beneath me.

The silence stretches between us and it feels suffocating. I've never felt shame for what I've become, because everything I am and everything I've done is for the three men who stand in front of me, judging what I've told them.

"And Stephan?" Declan asks. He's the only one of the three who didn't know why I was letting Aria kill him. He didn't care to know, like so many other things he'd rather not be aware of.

"He raped and murdered her mother. She cries at night in her sleep because of him."

The dark pit of sadness that narrowly exists within me expands at the memory of the first night I realized the power he had over her. "I had to give her this," I explain and my last word hisses from my lips.

Jase is the first to nod in agreement, followed by Declan and then, finally, Daniel.

"They're all going to be coming for us now," Daniel says, but this time his voice welcomes the challenge. The moment of wondering what my brothers think of me, what they think of *her*, ends as quickly as it came.

I answer Daniel the only way I know how. With the only acceptable answer there is.

"Let them come."

CHAPTER 3

Aria

I DON'T KNOW HOW LONG I'VE BEEN SHAKING. MY HAND TREMBLES AS I REACH FOR the faucet and turn the scalding water even hotter. My skin is bright red, but I can't feel anything. Everything is numb and out of my control as I lean against the tiled wall. My knees quiver and my body begs me to heave. The heavy diamond on the necklace ever present around my neck hits the tile of the stall and I hold on to it as if it can save me or take me away.

Is this what it feels like to kill someone? I've only seen two people die in front of me before.

My mother was the first. And the second ruled my life until the fateful day Carter changed my life forever.

I remember thinking about that second time when I watched someone's life being taken in front of me, right as I stood at the side of the bar. Completely unaware that when I entered, my entire life would change forever. I just wanted my notebook back.

I suck in a deep breath of the hot steam as I lean my head back against the tile and close my eyes. The memory takes me back to only weeks ago, but that memory is far better than the reality of my bloodstained skin.

Shoving my hands in my pockets to keep them warm, I let my fingers trace over the keys to my car. It's the only weapon I have.

And keys are a weapon. I've seen someone slice a hole in a guy's throat with a key. I stood there numbly as the man's hands tried to reach his neck, but my father's men gripped his wrists and pulled them behind his back. Blow after blow, each one puncturing his skin as he was restrained and unable to defend himself.

A chill flows over my skin at the memory and it takes me a minute to realize I'm not breathing.

I remember the sound of sneakers kicking small rocks across the pavement. The sound of the busy street at the other end of the alley.

Three men my father employs were supposed to be escorting me back home from the studio I wanted to rent, but they decided to take a detour.

And I stood there in shock; it all happened so quickly.

Mika was with me then. His thin lips tipped up into the evilest smile I'd ever seen. That smile held pure joy. Joy at my shock? Or my horror? Maybe my pain, because I knew the man they'd killed.

Mika's dark black hair was slicked back. His beard was shaved off and it was only stubble that caressed his skin that night. Conventionally speaking, Mika's a good-looking man with a deep, rough voice that can bring any woman to her knees.

But I've seen who he really is. And knowing he's the man I've come to see and make demands of, sends a spike of fear through me.

But I won't let anyone steal from me. I can't let them push me around and let them think I'm weak. And like my father says, it's time for me to demand respect. It's what the Talverys do.

My eyes slowly open to the sound of the water hitting the bare tile. Every movement, every noise, makes my body tense.

I try to steady my breathing, ragged from the memories. The one of the night I was taken, and the other of that night two years ago when I saw a man murdered. I didn't leave home for a long time after that, and I never moved out. My father wanted it that way anyway.

I thought I knew what fear was before I walked into that bar. I was wrong.

Staring at the lifeless corpse of a man whose existence has tormented you for years is true fear. It wasn't until his head rolled away from his body on the carpet, that I could even consider the possibility that he would never hurt me again.

My gaze drifts to the pool of water at my feet. The water contains dark red splotches until it swirls and morphs to pink as it flows to the drain.

First, I watched my mother's death.

Then the death of a man who betrayed my father.

And now I've killed the man who betrayed both of my parents.

I wait for a sense of relief, or victory—righteousness, maybe. But nothing comes. There's only a hollow emptiness in my chest and a flood of unwanted memories.

The sound of the glass door to the shower sliding open nearly tears a scream from my throat.

Mika, my father, Stephan… of all the men responsible for me leading a life riddled with fear, none of them compare to the man standing in front of me. The steam billows around him as it exits the shower stall, allowing the chill of the cooler air to leave goosebumps along my skin.

Carter's gaze narrows as he assesses me, glued to the wall and still shaking, still struggling to do anything. I've never felt so weak in my life as I do right now.

Killing Stephan may have felt freeing during the moments the knife sliced into him, but I've never been so chained to memories as I am in this instant.

"What are you doing?" His deep voice comes out a question, but I don't think he expects me to answer.

"I can't stop shaking," I tell him in a staccato cadence that reflects my inability to do anything clearly. Each word is forced out as I grip my wrist with my other hand and will it to stop, finally letting go of the gem.

Carter doesn't answer me. Instead, he steps into the stall, still clothed. He hisses through his teeth as the hot water batters his arm and splashes along his bloodstained shirt, now sticking to his skin. He turns the faucet, cooling the water until it's only warm and no longer scalding hot.

The cool air feels refreshing as it caresses my skin more and more the longer he stands in front of me with the door open. My head feels light and the panic that was all-consuming only a moment ago, wanes.

In one breath, Carter strips from his shirt. In another, he closes the door behind him and pulls me into his arms. The warm water gently splashes along my back in time with Carter's soothing strokes. It takes a moment for me to return the embrace, to wrap my arms around him and press my cheek to his bare chest.

His heartbeat is steady as he holds me and it's calming. *So calming.* The trembling subsides quicker than I could imagine.

My eyes close and I welcome the darkness of exhaustion until Carter clears his throat, startling me from the comfortable silence.

"I'm sorry for telling you that I wouldn't be with you," he says and his voice rumbles up his chest. I stay tense against him, caught off guard. I barely remember his words from earlier. Everything happened so quickly; of everything that happened tonight, the last thing on my mind is the threat he gave me before I knew his intentions and every piece of the puzzle fell into place.

An apology is something I would never expect from him.

Carter is never sorry. Carter is unapologetic in everything he does.

Without an answer from me, he continues, "I shouldn't have said that. And I'm sorry for it." Another moment passes, and the cloudy haze slowly dissipates until I can peel myself away from him. My nakedness and the reality of what I am to him are slowly coming back to me.

Today has been a whirlwind of emotions. The most prevalent being pain.

I swallow thickly before stepping away from him and out of the flowing streams of water to tell him it's okay.

I don't know what else to say.

Pushing the wet hair from my face, I look him in the eyes and the intensity in his gaze sets my body on fire.

"It's not okay. And it won't happen again," Carter replies as his eyes darken and he moves in the suddenly small shower, stalking toward me to place both of his palms against the tile wall on either side of my head.

His broad shoulders eclipse everything else as he towers over me, and the sheer power that radiates from him forces a deep urge of need down to my core. The pulse is uncontrollable and threatens to overcome my senses.

It would be so easy to fall into his arms. To get lost in the lusty haze that is Carter Cross.

"I forgive you," I tell him in a single breath and try to swallow down the desire. Suddenly, I'm hotter than I was before. All over, and all at once.

My nipples pebble and my fingers itch to reach out to him, to spear my fingers through his hair and pull his lips down to mine.

But Carter doesn't kiss me. He never has. My gaze stays pinned to his lips as he lowers them, oh, so slowly, but they pass my own and travel to my shoulder. His rough stubble grazes my neck and makes my pussy throb. His tongue sweeps along my skin and a heat flows through me that I can't deny.

If I could hold on to this moment and hide from the pain of my reality forever, I would.

Just as I dare to reach up, to let my fingers travel along his shoulders and then higher, a sudden knock at the door cuts sharply through the moment.

The white noise of the shower dims as Jase's voice carries through the door, calling out to take Carter away from me.

Don't go, my heart begs me to plead with him. I can't be alone right now. *I'm not okay.*

Carter nudges the tip of his nose against mine, letting a soft hum of approval vibrate up his chest before telling Jase that he's coming. He lowers his voice and looks me in the eyes as he tells me, "Finish here and wait in bed for me."

The command and heat in his eyes is something I could never refute. "Yes, Carter," I answer obediently, and it only makes the heat between my thighs grow hotter.

It's not until he's gone that I realize how much I want him.

How much I need Carter Cross right now. I have no one else.

And how much that very fact scares me.

CHAPTER 4

Carter

"**H**E SAID HE'S COOLED OFF, BUT THE FUCKER'S ALREADY TALKING." Jase updates me the second I step into the den. The adrenaline from tonight had subsided. The ringing in my blood had dulled.

Until I saw Aria still shaking.

One look at her delicate form trembling from the aftershocks changed everything. The normal rush of triumph was replaced instantly by something else. Something I don't care to look farther into right now.

I need a drink. A strong one, at that.

"We knew we couldn't trust him," I answer my brother as the ice clinks in the glass. I fill it with three fingers of whiskey and let it sit on the ice to chill. The amber liquid swirls as I consider every aspect of what we could face from Romano.

I know his friends. I know his enemies. And most owe far more to me than they do him.

"Do we need to send anyone a reminder?" I ask my brother as I lift my eyes to his and throw back the whiskey. If anyone wants to prove themselves to Romano, I need to shut down that train of thought before it turns into anything tangible. A small reminder of what we're capable of could silence any ideas anyone has of turning on us. It's best not to entertain any delusions of grandeur they might have.

Jase shakes his head but doesn't return my gaze. Instead, he taps his finger against the back of the chair he's standing behind before continuing. "He messaged Talvery," Jase tells me as the whiskey burns its way down to my gut.

I cock a brow at his statement. "Is that intel from our informant?"

"From one of them," Jase answers with a confidence I respect.

"So, he told Talvery that I allowed his daughter to kill her enemy. That's interesting, isn't it?" I can't hide the amusement that plays along my lips.

"Not exactly. He only confirmed that we have Talvery's daughter."

A sneer of cynicism comes out as a grunt. "Of course, he did," I say absently as I fill the glass once more.

"And then he left a message for us." I don't breathe or move until Jase tells me, "He says he understands and that he enjoyed the show."

"Fucking prick." I let the words slip out before downing the alcohol in a single gulp. He's a coward. Pitting Talvery and me against one another while pretending to stay by my side. Revenge will be sweet when it comes time for that.

The whiskey is still burning down my chest as my brother asks, "Are we still with him? The guns have shipped. We have the upper hand. We can still pull back from our deal."

"Or side with Talvery?" I ask him and Jase tenses. "We could drop Romano and give the guns to Talvery."

"Why would we do that?" Jase asks with a glimmer of distrust in his voice as he walks closer to me and then settles against the side table, leaning against it and waiting for me to answer. The adrenaline returns full force as if knowing it would be a fatal mistake to put any trust in Talvery. His greed knows no bounds and to aid him could backfire immediately.

I watch the ice in the glass, seeing nothing but Aria. Hearing her pleas to spare her father.

The way she molded her body to mine in the shower was intoxicating. But she's still holding back. I would do anything to have her completely. This could be it.

But the risk is considerable.

Give it time, I hear a voice urge in the back of my head, but it can't be mine. Patience can go fuck itself.

"Of course… Aria." My brother answers his own question given my silence and then runs a hand down the back of his head. It takes him a moment before he reaches for a glass and then takes the bottle of whiskey from my hand.

I let him. I already know she's making me think differently than I should. Making my actions unpredictable. She has a control over me that's undeniable and more and more apparent each day.

"You've never let anyone come between you and business before." He downs the first shot, not waiting for a reply. Sucking the whiskey from his teeth, he asks, "Why her?"

Silence descends upon us. I've never told anyone the complete truth. About how I wanted to die all those years ago. I was so close, and she stopped it.

Before tonight, I hadn't told them that I'd hated her for it. I didn't tell anyone that I'd prayed for it all to end. That at my greatest moment of weakness, I'd given up.

Until she stopped it all.

Jase considers me for a moment. He's my second-in-command. My partner in all of this. And I never told him. I didn't want to speak the truth to life. "I need to know what she means to you at least."

"Everything." I don't hesitate to answer him, although my voice comes out lowly and full of possessiveness.

"And she wants you to side with Talvery. The man who tried to have us all murdered in our sleep? The man who set our house on fire?"

"She doesn't know." I'm quick to defend her and even I feel the irritation of it. As if it seeps from the tone of Jase's voice straight to my head.

"She doesn't know shit," he responds with slight agitation, but one look at him and he looks away, staring at the liquid swirling in his glass.

"She's loyal."

"She doesn't owe him her loyalty." He finally looks at me. He's not telling me anything I don't know already. "Does she know about her mother?" he asks.

"It's a rumor. We can't prove it." Even as I answer him, I know I'm merely playing devil's advocate. I'd do anything in my power to give her hope for the one thing she wants. Mercy toward her father.

"I'd planned to torture it out of Stephan," I tell my brother, reminding myself. I'd intended to give her truth tonight, along with the vengeance she so desperately needed. "I lost sight of that goal."

Jase only huffs, although when I glance at him there's a shimmer of delight in his eyes and a smirk on his lips before he sips the expensive whiskey.

"She'll never believe me." As I give Jase yet another excuse, I feel a vise around my heart. Squeezing it tight. "She would never side with me over her father." The truth is damning.

"I don't mind telling her." The ease with which he speaks catches me off guard. He must see it in my face though because he shrugs and adds, "I'll be gentle, but I'll make her understand."

"I don't want you getting between us." The rise of anger is something I didn't expect. Clearing my throat, I return to the whiskey. One more and then I go back to my Aria.

"She's fucking with your head," Jase says with a hard edge before adding, "I've never seen you like this."

"Like what?" I ask him, daring him with my tone to question me. Although, I already know the answer.

"Indecisive and emotional. We should have already annihilated them. You're taking your time and stockpiling more weapons and men than necessary."

"I don't want her to hate me." I expect to see shock in Jase's expression. Maybe even disgust. She's a weakness I never intended, but one I refuse to give up.

Although he's taken aback, he doesn't argue, and a tiredness sets in his dark eyes. The weight of everything I've been feeling is settling down on his shoulders now.

I propose to my brother, "We have to choose. Talvery or Romano."

"I'll die before siding with Talvery," my brother confesses without a hint of emotion. It's merely a fact. And one I can support and respect, given everything Talvery has done. "I'd rather take them both out."

Feeling the heat and buzz of the liquor slinking its way into my thoughts, I merely nod and then roll my tense shoulders. I'm tired. Not just of tonight. But tired of fighting.

There's no way to make it end though. The moment a man stops fighting in this business, is the moment he's executed.

"We've pissed them both off, so it's better to choose a side and make sure they don't put their past behind them to take us on together. Just because Romano slipped him intel doesn't mean anything more than he's fueling the flames between them… but he knows what he's doing. He's redirecting Talvery's hate."

Jase's head falls back as he downs the whiskey and sets the glass down heavily on the tabletop. He breathes out long and low as he nods his head in agreement.

"We can't let that happen. But between the two, Romano is the best choice." He stares at me, making sure I listen to his final words. "You already know that. Siding with Talvery will be the end of us."

He's not wrong. And dropping my gaze, I give in to what I'd already decided. To what I knew had to happen. Romano can't be trusted, but he can be manipulated and used. Talvery would slit our throats the second he got a chance. He's already tried to wipe us out before and failed. And for that reason alone, allowing him any mercy would be a sign of weakness.

Instead of answering my brother, I give him a short nod and turn to leave him, to head back to Aria.

"How is she?" he asks me, changing the subject before I can depart.

"Handling it well, all things considered." The image of her trembling form in the shower reminds me that she's not well. "Today was hard on her. I should go back."

"You should," he says beneath his breath, although he speaks so quietly I'm not sure if the words were meant for me or for himself.

"It had to be done," I remind him, and he nods his head in agreement.

Feeling the conversation is over, I start to leave, but he calls out for me one more time. "Carter…"

Looking over my shoulder, I see the sincerity in my brother's expression when he tells me, "Be gentle with her."

The moonlight filters through the slits in the curtain and washes over Aria's curves, hidden beneath the covers. Her hair is a messy halo, still damp on the pillow as she lies on her side.

My cock instantly hardens, remembering how I left her. Naked and wanting.

She's a good girl, my little songbird, so I know she'll be naked with the exception of my necklace around her throat. She'll be ready for me to take her.

The words from Jase still ring clear in my head. *Be gentle with her.*

Jase doesn't know her like I do, but he knows women far better than I ever have.

The images of me slamming into her and rubbing her clit until she's screaming my name push me to forget Jase's advice. To continue fucking Aria into obedience… until the moment I come closer to her.

She's still trembling. Her hands clutch one another in front of her and her eyes are closed tightly. As if she's praying in the bed.

Her breathing is a mess of stutters.

Not all of us are made to be killers. I knew that when I gave her the knife and set Stephan up to be her victim.

"It's the adrenaline," I tell her quietly, cutting through the hushed night with my tense words. Her body jolts under the sheets and she stiffens, but her hands and shoulders still tremble.

I watch as she swallows and then her lips part. The look in her hazel-green eyes is a mix of utter sadness and fear.

"I can't stop," she says, and her words are a whisper.

The need to make it all go away rides me hard as I quickly crawl into bed with her, pulling back the sheets and letting her fall into my arms. "Please, help me," she begs me.

"Shh," I hush her, petting her hair and pulling her closer to me. Her small body clutches at mine as if she can't get close enough. "I shouldn't have left you," I whisper out loud and into her hair, feeling the wisps tickle my jaw.

She only responds by moving her hands to my chest and burying her head beneath my chin. She's so frail in my embrace.

Which is anything but the Aria I know.

Maybe I've finally broken her. I already knew I was a monster, but the smile that begs to creep onto my lips at the thought is a validation of that fact. I'm not worthy of a single breath, let alone the woman in my arms.

She's not broken; a woman like Aria can't be broken. A voice whispers deep in the back of my mind, where it hides in the crevices. And the smile that begged to come out before forces its way to my face. I can only hide it by kissing her hair as I rub soothing strokes up and down her bare back.

"You're fine, songbird," I tell her, and I know she can feel the hum of my deep words with her face pressed so firmly against my chest. "It's only the adrenaline."

She doesn't move from her spot, but her lashes tickle my chest as she opens her eyes and then blinks. Her breath is hot and her nails scratch lightly against my skin, but she doesn't ask the question on the tip of her tongue. *How do I know?*

Her hands continue to shake as she attempts to inch even closer to me. With her refusing to let go of me, I reach down and pull the covers tighter around her before telling her my story.

Not all people are made to be killers, but sometimes even the sweetest of creatures have to murder. I may not have ever been innocent, but there was a time when I wasn't the callous and brutal man I am today.

"The first man I killed was a bartender named Dave," I speak quietly without pausing my strokes along her back. Kissing her hair again, I stare at a sliver of light that flits across the bedroom floor. I only know Aria is listening because of the flutter of her lashes again. "I was sixteen," I confess to her as I'm taken back to that night.

"My father didn't deal with my mother's impending death all that well." A huff of ludicrous laughter makes my shoulders shake and her body moves with mine. "He was a coward, I know that now, but to face the deaths of the ones you love… well, I can't blame him for being a coward, but I can blame him for bringing me down with him."

"What happened to your mother?" Aria asks gently, and her soft breathing is steady. It's only then that I see her shaking has turned into a slight tremble.

"She had cancer. It took two years to kill her." The memory makes my chest feel tight, but I continue with the story, the one that makes me angry, not the one that I don't have the strength to face. "My father couldn't stand to see how she deteriorated. So, he drank himself into the man he was without her."

My gaze drops to the comforter. "I swear he was a good man with her, but knowing he was going to lose her changed him." My voice lowers, and I force aside the emotions that come with her memory. To vanish into the back of my mind where they belong.

"One night, my father got himself into trouble and my mother was barely breathing." The image of her on the hospital bed they'd sent to our home for her hospice care causes my voice to crack, but I don't think Aria can hear it.

"He hadn't been home in nearly twelve hours and I knew she wasn't going to make it much longer." He knew too. He had to have known. We were only boys and even we knew she was going to die. "She died while I was away looking for him."

Aria's grip on me loosens, her nails trailing on my chest as her head lifts to look at me. I can feel her gaze on me, but I don't return it.

I can still hear the way the fall leaves crunched under my sneakers and feel the way the water from the earlier rainstorm seeped into a hole on the bottom of my sole as I trawled through the alleys looking for him.

"He used to go to a few bars I knew." I was young, but the bartenders knew me by name at that point. Aria doesn't stop looking at me, and I feel vulnerable and exposed under her eyes.

She makes me weak.

"I found him in the bathroom, beat up pretty bad. He said it was the bartender. I forget what excuse my father had, but then he cried and said he couldn't move. He cried and that's something he never did. He always drank away his pain. They beat him up and then cuffed him to the radiator, so they could come back and do it again. And again. All the while my mother waited for him."

Aria sniffles against my chest and whispers an apology.

As the memories come back to me I tell her, "My father was a poor excuse for a husband. And even a man. But what they'd done…"

I can't explain to her how the anger spurred me on. In the moment that I thought I was going to lose both of them in one night, the anger is what kept me from breaking down.

Licking my lower lip and trying to play off the hoarseness in my voice as anything but emotion, I continue. "The bartender knew my mother was dying. He knew we were on our own. He could have done a lot of things. He could have called the cops to remove my father. He could have locked the doors. But he wanted to humiliate him. He wanted to have a punching bag as payment for the debt my father owed him."

I remember the way Dave looked at me that night when I left my father where he was and walked behind the bar to demand the key. He had a smile on his smarmy face. I knew he was a dick the moment I saw him, from his slicked back hair and the glint in his eyes. I'd heard around town that he liked to get the young women who came to his bar drunk and take advantage of them. I didn't want to believe it though, not when I saw my father laughing with him other nights I'd come to get my drunkard of a father back home.

"I went to get the key and Dave tried to punch me. He was piss drunk. I was only a kid."

"You never should have had to—"

"In the streets where I grew up, it wasn't uncommon, Aria." I cut her off before she can show me sympathy or even begin to suggest that I was too young for what I saw and what I was involved in. I'm not the only one who's gone through this shit and I won't be the last. Everyone leads different lives and there are no pretty promises or mercy for some of us.

"I grabbed the chair and I didn't stop hitting him with it. The other guys there never got up when Dave went after me, but they did come for me. Not at first. Not the first time I struck him with the metal legs. The ring of the metal bashing into his head was louder than the basketball game playing on the one TV in the corner of the bar." Aria remains silent, and I continue.

"They didn't even get up when he fell to the floor. I didn't stop cracking his head in with the chair. I couldn't." A lot like Aria tonight. I hadn't made the connection until the thought hit me.

I remember how I didn't even think I was breathing. I didn't think it was real. I didn't want it to be.

"I didn't kill him that night," I tell her and then kiss her hair. My grip on her shoulder tightens and I pull her back into my chest. "The other assholes there dragged me away from him, but the minute I was free, they let me go. I got my father after leaving Dave on the floor bloodied up and moaning."

I can see each of their faces now, full of fear and disbelief that a scrawny boy had nearly killed the man on the floor. My chest heaved but the adrenaline took over.

I killed him a week later after my mother had died and we'd buried her. He came to get money to cover the hospital bills for his broken nose. Money we didn't have, but he expected we would from the life insurance that didn't exist.

No one else was home and I wasn't supposed to be home either, but the guilt of leaving my mom that night kept me from going anywhere for days.

My mother died while I was gone, and I know if I had to put the blame somewhere, it should be on my father.

I know that Dave wasn't the reason that my mother died. But as he stood in the doorway of our home, telling me that the life insurance money from my mother's death was going to him, I lost it. I already knew there was no life insurance. There was no money. There was no helping my father, a man who didn't want to be helped. There was no bringing my mother back.

I knew all of that. I also knew that the man in front of me didn't care.

He didn't care about any of that. And so, I let him into our home, grabbing the pistol my father kept by the door as I closed it. I walked Dave into the kitchen where my mother died on the hospital bed under the pretense of retrieving the check sitting on the counter. I shot him in the back. Just once, with shaking hands. But once was enough.

I didn't stop shaking, not even hours after Sebastian had helped me throw Dave's body into the river. He was the only friend I had and the only person I could turn to. He was older than me, stronger than me and he was there for me when I had no one. He didn't stay for long though. He had his own demons to run from, and plenty of them.

I couldn't stop shaking. If it wasn't for my brothers, I don't think I could have continued living. In a way, it was our first act together that led to this empire. Nothing can bring you closer to someone than death can.

I remember how I didn't want to bury Dave like Sebastian suggested because I couldn't stand to see upturned dirt after watching my mother being lowered into the ground only days before. I threw up as Sebastian dug a hole. I couldn't take it. I couldn't deal with what I'd done and what I was capable of.

And so, we tossed the body in the bed of the truck instead after covering the partially dug shallow grave, and Sebastian disposed of the body in the river. All while I uselessly rocked myself in the passenger seat of the truck, loathing myself and what I'd done.

"When did you kill him?" Aria asks me, breaking up my thoughts and bringing me back to her. I blink away the memories and the heavy sadness in the pit of my chest.

It takes me a minute to realize I hadn't voiced the last bit of my story. She thinks I just lost it at the bar. She doesn't know that I did it days later and that I led him into the house knowing I wanted to see the man die.

"Does it matter when he died?" I ask her, wanting to keep the truth from her and thinking that it makes it better if it was just heat of the moment. But nothing makes being a murderer better.

She doesn't answer me, she only lowers her cheek to my chest and I continue holding her, remembering how I shook that night after ditching Dave's dead body into the river. "The shaking will stop," I whisper.

Time passes slowly, neither of us speaking until I finally feel the weight of the day and tell Aria to sleep.

"I don't want to sleep," she tells me wearily and then forces herself to swallow. "I'm afraid I'll see him. He'll be there waiting for me."

"Shh," I hush her again, cupping her chin in both of my hands and gently placing a kiss on her forehead. I notice then how calm her body is.

It's amazing what a distraction can do to a person. It can make you forget about everything.

"He's gone," I remind her, although her prolonged fear worries me.

Killing him was supposed to set her free.

It will, the voice hisses and calms the worry creeping up on me. Nodding as if in agreement with the voice, I kiss her once more, pressing my lips to her smooth skin and then pull back, waiting for her to look at me.

"I told you. All you have to fear is me."

Aria's hazel eyes are deep with emotion, swirling with an intensity that pulls me in and pins me down until her lips part and my gaze drifts to them.

The yearning to press my lips to hers nearly wins, but instead, I remember yet another aspect of tonight that I'd planned and forgotten about.

"Wait here," I command her, and disappointment causes her gaze to lower, but she releases me for the first time since I'd crawled into bed to be beside her.

As I walk to the dresser, I strip off my shirt and pants before grabbing the case with a syringe in it and a bottle of oil from the drawer. I haven't needed it for so long, but she needs it tonight. It will let her sleep if nothing else.

Standing next to the bed, I motion for her to come to me before telling her to turn around and get on all fours. I've come to expect a lot of things from Aria. Her sass and her mouth, her questions, and defiance.

But tonight, all she does is obey, and that stirs up something inside of me. Both the pure and the depraved desires. She doesn't even ask why.

My hand gentles on the curve of her ass then moves up to her waist and back down before I give her the shot, making her jump slightly before she steadies herself and then I can push down the plunger of the syringe.

"Birth control," I tell her and then smirk at the thought as I add, "it's better late than never."

Aria only murmurs a response, placing both her hands flat on the sheets and her cheek follows as she turns her head.

"I have this for you too," I tell her after setting the empty syringe down on the nightstand and pushing on her hip. "Sit up," I command her, and she obeys easily, wincing slightly as her ass presses against the comforter.

"It should help you sleep," I explain as I pull the liquid into the bulb syringe. The oil is clear, a pure drug that will hit her hard the first night. "Have you ever heard of Sweet

Lullabies?" I ask her, and she tilts her head with a crease in her forehead indicating her confusion.

"Lullabies? I know a few-"

"No, the drug."

I don't expect her to. We've only just started selling the adapted version that's marketable. She shakes her head, proving me right although the confusion in her expression stays in place.

I lift the syringe to her lips and she obediently opens her mouth, tilting her head back slightly for me. I admire how the moonlight reflects off her slender neck and plays with the shadows down her body as the liquid hits her tongue.

"Suck it down." The command I give her makes my dick stir, but she'll be out soon. Within minutes, I would bet.

"What is it?" she asks me, and I debate on telling her how it came to be and how it's responsible for so many of the reasons I am who I am, but she yawns, cutting me off before I begin.

"Just lie down," I tell her gently, and pull back the covers for her to nestle in beside me. I've had her in my bed a number of nights now, but she's never readily slept this close to me.

With the rustling of the sheets silenced, I let my hand rest on her hip and rub soothing circles there. I breathe in the scent of her hair and leave a small kiss there as I listen to her steady breathing and know that sleep has taken her before I could even begin to admit what this drug really is.

CHAPTER 5

Aria

I USED TO DREAM OF THINGS I'D BET ALL GIRLS DREAM ABOUT.
I would dance so beautifully, my hair swinging in the air as I landed a perfect pirouette. In my dreams, I could be and do anything. I'd dance in a ballet center stage, and amidst a crowd of thousands, I'd perform beautifully.

I'd climb the mountains and find a magical field of flowers where they came to life like the story of *Alice in Wonderland*. I could talk to the animals and drink tiny cups of tea that would make me small enough to follow the rabbits down the rabbit holes.

I could be anyone I wanted to in my dreams. But those visions were from long ago. It's funny how they come back tonight.

Each of the scenes flashes through my head as if on fast forward. I see myself as a young girl performing the arts I wanted to before I realized my insecurities would keep me from even trying. I watch as I remember a dream I had of kissing a boy in my class. I imagined my leg would kick up behind me as he deepened it.

But even as the memory of my dreams from long ago comes to life before me, I'm aware that they're only dreams. I never kissed Paulie. I never had the courage to and if I had, I know it wouldn't have happened the way I pictured it.

For a moment, I question if I'm dreaming or awake. Everything is so vivid. So real.

But the scenes keep going. They don't stop for me.

The hairs at the back of my neck prick as I know what's coming. They're all in order, like a timeline of my hopes as I watch the scenes play out. I know I'm getting older. I know what's to come, and I want it to stop.

My head shakes. Make it stop.

But they don't.

I watch as I dream about my mother and me in the park. She's there with her friend like she always is. And I'm there drawing instead of playing with the other girls. I dreamed of drawing something that day, but when I look down at the paper it's blank. I can't remember what it was. But it doesn't matter. All I can focus on is her face. This is the dream that turned into a nightmare. The first dream of so many I had over and over again.

Make them stop. My throat closes, and I want to scream. It's too real, too vivid. And I can't stop it.

I can feel my nails digging into the sheets. I'm awake, but I can't open my eyes. I can barely move, and I can't stop the images.

My heart races as I see myself in the closet.

Please stop, I whisper in my dreams, but my throat doesn't feel the words. Not like my chest feels the pounding of my blood.

There she is standing with her back to me, facing the door. My mother's standing there and I'm terrified. Why did she tell me not to leave? Not to scream. Not to move except to hide.

Terror races through my veins.

I wish I could move and go to her. To help her.

Please make it stop. I don't want to see it again.

I don't want to see him push the door open and force her down on the ground. She barely fought him and now I know why.

I can feel the tears leaking down my cheeks and I try to scream, but my words are voiceless.

Stephan looks so young. So much younger than he did when I stabbed him. When I murdered him and put an end to the sick smile on his face.

I can't watch, but I can't close my eyes. I can't turn it off. There's nowhere to run in your dreams.

Please, I don't want to see this. I don't want to remember.

The pain grows in my chest and it paralyzes me. The shaking overwhelms me as he pulls out the knife. It's only a small knife, one like Daddy has for fishing.

Run! I try to scream to myself. *Save her!* I will my limbs to move, but I'm victim to my dreams.

She's still on the ground with her back to him. She's crying so hard but trying not to. She's pinned beneath him as I cover my screams with my hands over my mouth in the closet.

Please, Mom, run, I want to say, but my plea is only a whimper. I know she won't. I have no control here and I've seen this nightmare so many times. The memory haunts me in my waking hours just as much as it does in my sleep.

I didn't know what he was doing to her. Not when he held her down and pushed himself inside of her and not when he pulled out the knife. I didn't know it was over until he sliced her neck open. I knew what death meant and when I saw the bright red blood leaking from her and the way she covered it with her hands as she tried to keep it from flowing, I knew what was happening.

But what he did to her before, I didn't know. It wasn't until a month later when I told my cousin Brett that he explained it to me with a pained expression I'll never forget. I told him everything, but he didn't want to hear. He said Talverys don't cry, we get revenge. He was wrong about both of those things.

Nikolai would listen to me though. He let me cry and didn't make me feel ashamed of that fact.

Even the thoughts of Nikolai don't stop the visions before me. Of my mother with her hair pulled back by Stephan as he slit her throat, of her looking toward the closet where I hid when the life left her.

Her lips are moving.

I can't hear what she's saying.

She's saying something. A chill flows down my arms. This isn't what happens. This isn't what I've dreamed before.

Is this real?

The hairs on my body stand on end. My breath is caught in my throat. I don't watch Stephan like I have before. I know the look of triumph on his face as he wipes off the knife on her bare back. I know what he does next. But my mother is still alive as her face falls to the floor. The blood pools around her cheek like it always does. But this time she blinks slowly and looks at me.

"Mom," I whisper, wanting to move but not able to. *Move*, I will myself hopelessly.

My mom blinks again and she speaks. I know she does. *"I can't hear you, Mom. Please. Please don't die,"* I beg her.

Is this real?

Am I breathing? I can't tell anymore.

I watch her lips, the right side of them covered in her own blood.

But the movement from the man standing behind her steals the attention from her.

Stephan stole what used to be and I can never have it back. Him dying doesn't mean anything.

No, I whisper and shake my head as my small fingers of the child I was, reach out and grab the closet door. I can feel it. I can feel exactly what the edge of the closet door felt like.

My shoulders shake violently; this isn't what happens in my dream. The chill leaves and I feel hot, too hot. "Wake up!" I hear Carter's voice and it begs me to open my eyes, but before they obey, I hear my mother's voice say, "You can't forget me."

I suck in air as my eyes shoot open and I stare at the ceiling of Carter's bedroom through a haze of tears. The lights are bright, so bright it hurts, and I close them just as quickly.

With both of my hands covering my eyes, I feel the wetness and try to rub it all away.

My chaotic breaths are matched with Carter's as I slowly come back to reality. Back to Carter's bed. Back to the safety of this moment and not the nightmare of the past.

It was so real. Again, those goosebumps flood every inch of me as I reach Carter's gaze. His eyes are dark as he stares back at me.

His lips part, but he doesn't say anything for a long moment.

"I was screaming?" I ask him, although I know it's true. My throat feels raw and my words are hoarse.

"For almost half an hour," he tells me with nothing but concern and then visibly swallows as my blood chills. "You wouldn't wake up."

It's been years since I've slept through the entire nightmare. Or even since each second played out as if it were an eternity.

Years have passed, but I know the terror was never like that before.

"I don't know what you need," Carter intimates to me, sealing me from my thoughts like he's confessing a sin. I watch his throat as he swallows again. Pulling his arms around my chest I try to lie back down as if this is normal. As if this is okay.

"Hold me," I tell him although I stare at the ceiling, seeing the vision of my mother looking at me in the haunted memory. Her still alive on the floor even though I know she was dead.

"Please, just hold me," I plead with him and turn my head, so I can look at him.

Confusion mars his face, but he doesn't say anything. He only climbs closer to me on the bed and pulls me tighter to him.

I need him to hold me more than I've ever needed anything. Other than my mother to come back to me.

CHAPTER 6

Today is the first day I see Aria as stronger when she's with me. And I can't shake that thought as I enter the den.

I've only left her for a few minutes here and there. Staying quiet behind her and watching her every move. But she knows I'm there and each time she's started to break down, she comes to me.

Of her own free will, she comes to me, asking me to hold her as if my touch could take her pain away.

My poor songbird hasn't realized my touch only brings pain, and I hope she never does.

The drawing pad shows a clean page. Not a mark lays against the stark white.

With a pen in her hand, she lies on her belly on the rug in front of the fire and stares at the blank sheet as if it'll speak to her.

I would stay there longer, standing behind the sofa, listening to the crackling of the burning wood, and waiting for her fingers to move across the page, but with a shift in my stance, the floor creaks beneath me and breaks her focus.

With lack of sleep, she's slow to move, but she does. Sitting up on her knees she faces me, waiting for whatever it is that I have to say.

It's funny to me how she says when she's with me she forgets, and life is easier.

When I'm with her it's the same until she asks questions, and then I remember everything.

"It's time for the question game again," I tell her, and she drops the pen, letting it roll off her thigh and onto the floor. The frown that's marred her tired expression all day stays in place.

"It feels like forever since we've played this game," she says absently. Her tone, her body language, everything about it is off today. It feels dampened, depressed even. More so than I've seen her before.

Clearing the tension in my throat and letting my hands clench and unclench I remind her, "It hasn't been that long since you've been out of your cell."

A smirk tips her beautiful lips up and she stares at me as if defying the fact. "I said it *feels* like it's been forever… there's a difference."

Her soft gaze trails across the sofa and then back to me. "Am I staying here?"

"You can move wherever you'd like."

"You haven't come near me today like you usually do," she comments and my gaze narrows at her. I recount the day and each and every time she's come to me. The thrill of her choosing to approach me is dulled by the fact that she realizes things have changed between us.

I search her expression for what she's thinking. For a hint as to how this will modify her behavior. But I can't predict her. Not when it comes to what's between us. And thus, it's time for me to question her, to try to gauge what she's thinking based on her own questions.

"That's not a question," is my only reply to her.

She shrugs as if it doesn't matter, and tension spreads through my jaw. "It wasn't my turn to ask," she says simply with a calmness in her voice that only increases the strain.

Be gentle with her. I remind myself again.

Jase offers me a lot of advice though, and my typical response is for him to fuck off. Aria watches me as I walk to the sofa and take a seat on the right side. She decides not to move from her place, but she adjusts to sit cross-legged.

There's a sudden crackle from the fire and she barely acknowledges it. Just like the tension between us.

"How are you feeling today?" I ask her and tell myself it's because I want to get into her head, not because the last twenty-four hours have changed everything.

"Tired," she tells me and the small bit of strength she's shown since I've walked in wanes. She picks at the fuzz on the rug beneath her and answers with a catch in her throat, "I don't know how to feel right now. There's so much…" her voice trails off and I ask her, "So much what?"

The smirk on her face is nothing but fragile as she asks back, "Isn't it my turn?" The walls around her are toppling down. I can see it. I can *feel* it. She's too weak to hold them up any longer, but the girl beneath them isn't what I imagined. She's a girl who's been left alone far too long. A girl who should never have been left alone at all.

And the realization tugs at me like nothing else ever has.

I force my lips into a straight line and give her a small nod.

"Why did you do it?" she asks me in a whisper. Still picking at the imaginary fuzz and only glancing at me occasionally. As if she's afraid to catch my gaze and see something there that could ruin her.

"Do what?" I ask her, although I already know what she's referring to.

Why did I bring her to the dinner? Give her a knife. And let her kill the man who's hurt her so cruelly.

"Why did you… give me the knife?" she finally asks, and her words are twisted and tortured. As tortured as she's been all of today and last night.

"Why did I let you kill him?" I clarify for her, making her come to terms with the truth. She sucks in a heavy breath and pushes the hair from her face as I speak. "Why did I give you a knife so you could kill Alexander Stephan?"

The sofa groans and the fire hisses as I sit back and release what sounds like an easy breath. "Because I wanted you to do it," I tell her and almost elaborate, but the sarcastic huff that spills from her lips as she looks away from me and toward the door stops me from giving her more.

"What did you dream of last night?" I ask her, and I can't help that my body leans forward, eager for her reply. She hasn't been forthcoming, but she always answers me when I give her the opportunity to ask whatever she'd like.

She licks her lower lip, still shaking her head from my non-answer.

"Dreams," she answers with a hint of indignation in her retort. The words I wanted to speak moments before nearly come to life, but then she adds, "I dreamed lots of dreams," shaking her head with the smallest of movements. Her voice is small, and she speaks as if she's not even talking to me.

Like she's validating what she saw with herself.

"It was like my life sped forward in the form of the dreams I had growing up."

My brow furrows as I listen to her. I expected it to be only nightmares with the way she screamed. The memory of her shrill screams and the terror of her cries sends a bite of cold down my back that slowly rolls through every limb.

I couldn't do anything but listen to her and I've never regretted a damn thing in my life as much as I regretted giving her that knife like I did last night while she screamed.

Licking her lips, she continues and then that crease in her forehead returns as she looks at me. "And then I dreamed of the night he killed her."

My head nods on its own. I knew to expect it, that seeing him would elicit those fears for her, but I expected her to be different after she killed him. For the realization that he's dead, to free her in a way she could never be while he was allowed to live.

Give it time, the voice hisses again and the irritation I have for it shows on my face, silencing Aria.

"You can keep going," I tell her, fixing myself and then adding, "if you'd like."

But the moment has passed and instead she takes her turn.

"Are things still the same?" she asks me.

No. The answer is instant and obvious in my head. Strong enough that I feel the word echo through my veins. "Do they feel different?"

"That's not how this game is played," Aria answers with the trace of a smirk on her face although the tiredness has never been so evident in her eyes as it is now. "I asked you first," she tells me and waits for a reply.

"Kneel," I command her, wanting to prove that the power I held over her before is ever present. Even if the fear she held for me has vanished.

The realization that is what's different sends a spike of regret through me, but it's fleeting. I harden my voice as I tell her again, "Kneel and then ask me if things have changed."

The heat ignites in me as Aria narrows her gaze, the hazel reflecting the flickers of the flames that linger behind her in the fire.

Her lips part and she squirms in her place, but as her eyes close, she only smiles at me while shaking her head.

"I don't want to," she dares to defy me.

My dick hardens instantly, but my knuckles turn white as I grip the arm of the sofa.

Everything inside of me is at war. It seems fitting, since my little songbird seems to be in the same predicament. Her body begging to bend to my command, yet her strong will preventing her from giving in.

"I don't want to punish you today. Not when you need comfort. Don't mistake my gift to you for anything other than what it was." I push the words through clenched teeth, not wanting this tension between us to end. I love her fight. I love it, even more, when I can take it from her.

"And what was it?" she asks me, her eyes sparking with the desire for the truth.

The grin on my face grows as I realize she's set me up, seeking the answer I wouldn't give her when she asked her first question. *Why did I do it?* The tension in my body eases slightly, although the thrill of punishing her is still ringing through me.

"Taking away the fear you had, so I could end it and be the only thing you have left to fear."

"I think you're lying," she bites back although her voice is teasing, sensual even. Not believing me for a moment. Her gaze doesn't waver as she challenges me. I love that she knows better, but if she knew the power she had over me, I could lose everything. She's still loyal to the enemy. There's no denying that.

The thought makes my gaze drop to the fire behind her and it only returns to her when she adds, "But I don't know why you're lying to me."

"Because you don't need to know," I tell her simply and at first her lips part, ready to tell me off, but then she questions herself.

"You're biting your tongue so hard that I imagine you can taste blood," I point out and try to force a smirk to my lips.

"I've asked you two questions and you haven't answered either truthfully," she tells me and then glances at the fire behind her. "What's the point?" she asks no one in particular with a faint whisper.

"Maybe you're asking the wrong questions," I offer her although my entire body is alive with fire. Yesterday was hard on her and she performed exactly as I wanted, but her defiance today is uncontained, and I have no idea how to handle her. Not when she needs me to give her comfort. I wish I'd had her when I was in this same position years ago.

Even knowing that I've had enough of her insolence.

Those hazel eyes pierce through me at that moment, as if she heard my thoughts. The turmoil inside me twists into a knot until she asks the one question that solidifies my decision to leave her on her own for a few hours, so she can feel the need for me once again.

"Are you still going to let him kill my father?" she asks me. Her voice is steady, with maybe even a hint of provocation there.

Let him.

Let Romano.

She doesn't know that if I could do it myself, I would. If I could be the man to pull the trigger, I'd do it without a second thought.

The silence is only broken by the burning wood, now cracking and hissing. As our conversation continued, the sun has set and with the dimming light from the windows, shadows play along Aria's small form.

"I have to go out tonight."

"That doesn't answer my question," she's quick to reply, not taking her gaze from me.

"The game is over." My voice hardens, the anger pushing through.

She is mine. She will obey. Or I will risk everything to reign over her. There is no question in my mind what will happen if she doesn't take her place beside me.

"How convenient," she responds and that's when I meet my limit. There's only so much she can push.

It only takes three large steps until I'm towering over her. One swift motion and my hand is around her throat. My fingers press against the pulse in her veins as her fingers wrap around my hand. Her eyes widen but not with fear, not even with shock. They widen with hate, with anger… They widen with a spark of fight that rivals the roaring fire behind her.

She's never looked more beautiful to me than she does now.

Her nails dig into my skin, but she doesn't pry them away. She just wants to hurt me. She wants to show me what she's capable of.

Oh, songbird, I already know. She's the one who's only just now realizing what she's capable of.

I lower my lips to hers, deliberately placing a knee between her thighs. Invading every inch of space that separates us.

With the heat of the fire igniting the tension, I whisper against her cheek, "You've forgotten your manners, Aria."

"Manners," she bites out as if the word disgusts her and with the small bit of movement, I squeeze a little tighter. She can breathe, she can speak, but my grip on her is unyielding.

My other hand roams her body, drifting down her waist as I nip along her shoulder and then the fleshy bit of her earlobe. My fingers trace down her thigh and then back up, pulling up her skirt as I move back toward her waist until I let my fingers slide to her inner thigh.

And she moans.

She fucking moans, closing her eyes and letting her head fall back slightly. Even with the fight in her, she craves pleasure more than anything.

"What should your punishment be, songbird?" I whisper against the shell of her ear. The shiver that it ignites in her makes my dick harden to the point that it's painful not to thrust inside of her.

Her answer is a muted moan followed by an attempt to swallow. I don't loosen my grip to aid her; instead, I force her to look at me, to open her eyes and answer me.

"How should I punish this mouth of yours?" I ask her in a low and deep voice, not bothering to contain my desire for her.

"Fuck you," she barely pushes out and then licks her lower lip. Ever the defiant one.

"You would love that, wouldn't you?" I whisper against her lips, letting the words mingle with the heat from the fire and the lust between us.

Her hazel-green eyes swirl with a concoction of everything I know she's feeling. The anger and fear, but more than anything, the longing to be pleasured and cared for.

"Get on your back so I can play with your cunt," I command her the moment my fingers loosen on her throat, nearly making her fall backward. But she catches herself, then lies down as I told her to, one elbow at a time, her eyes never leaving mine.

"You obey so easily when you know you're going to get off, don't you?" I toy with her and the hint of a smirk pulls at the corner of her lips. Her intuition will be our downfall. She thinks she knows who she's playing with. But she doesn't realize what's at stake.

A gentle push on the inside of her thighs has her pulling them apart for me. My pointer trails up the thin black lace of her panties, dampened at her core with her arousal, and then to her swollen clit. Her head falls back, and her nails dig into the threads of the rug as she attempts to hold back the moan that threatens to spill from her lips. I can already hear it though. She's so fucking close. So in need.

"You need to get off. I should have done it last night."

The lace tears easily as I hook my thumb through it, ripping it from her sweet cunt to give me full access to her. With a quick intake of air, she lifts her head to watch me.

All that anger means nothing when I can give her this.

I shove two fingers inside her ruthlessly. Her hips buck and her lower back comes off the floor with the sensation it elicits.

I splay my other hand across her belly and push her back down, not stopping the brutal strokes against the ridges of her front wall.

Her head thrashes and she bites her lip. "Fuck," she says but her plea is only a whimper. Her fingers move to my hand on her belly and then up my forearm. Never stopping, pulling, and searching for something to hold on to.

"Let go," I tell her and for a moment she lets go of my arm, but that's not what I meant. "Give me your pleasure. Let go of everything holding you back from falling," I whisper in the air above her as I watch the light dance across her face. Her lips are parted and make a perfect O although her forehead is scrunched with the strain of holding back her strangled cries of pleasure.

The scent of her arousal permeates the air and precum leaks from my dick, begging me to slam inside of her.

With my cock pressed against my zipper, I finger fuck her furiously, pushing a third finger inside of her and my thumb against her clit. "I'm not going to stop until you cum on my hand, Aria. I'll fuck you like this until you can't think straight if you don't give me what I want."

Her head thrashes from side to side and then her back bows. I have to push harder with my hand on her hip to keep her down and strum her faster.

"You want another finger?" I ask her and then kiss the inside of her knee. She's so fucking tight I don't think I could though. It's an idle threat, but the idea of stretching her to the point where I could fist her cunt and give her undeniable pleasures she's never felt, has my hand moving harder and faster in unrelenting strokes and I don't stop.

Even as she cries out my name.

Even as her pussy spasms.

Her body rocks with the force of her orgasm and I don't stop, drawing it out and taking every bit of pleasure from her that I can.

It's not until her breath comes back to her and her eyes find mine that I pull away, sucking each of my fingers while she watches.

"Your cunt is so fucking sweet," I tell her and watch her reddened cheeks blush even more violently.

"I'm growing to love your punishments," she says breathily with her eyes closed and the power I feel vanishes. My dick, still pulsing with need, begs me to push her onto her stomach and rut between her legs. She'd cum again. And again.

The worst thing a man of power can do is to issue a false threat. Yet, I've done it with Aria. More than once.

My goal isn't to punish her though; I only want her to obey.

Just as I begin to unbutton my pants, my phone vibrates in my pocket, the timer going off.

Time is up.

With her eyes closed and an angelic look of content on her face, I question leaving her, but I have to.

"Clean up and make yourself dinner." I stifle a groan as I stand, hating that I won't be able to get lost in her touch for hours.

"I'll be back later." I give her the parting words and start to leave. Each movement makes my hard cock ache even worse, but I'll have her tonight.

"Carter?" Aria's soft voice cuts through the air and stops me just as I've started to leave.

"How long will you be gone?" Traces of fear and loneliness linger on her question. This is the new side of her I'm not used to.

The side I've only seen since last night. Back to being the girl behind the broken wall instead of the woman who's angry at being left alone for so long.

"A few hours, maybe."

Her expression falls as she slowly picks herself back up. She only nods in understanding as she covers herself again.

"Do you want anything while I'm out?" I ask her out of instinct, wanting to see her eyes on me again. Wanting her to show me more of this vulnerability. I can offer her so much more than she ever dreamed.

The very thought spikes awareness through me.

She's the one with control. Topping from the bottom. Sly girl. I need to take it back, for her own good. She needs me to have control, even if she doesn't want to give it to me. Even if she has no idea how much she needs to give it to me.

"No," she answers me with a small shake of the head. "Thank you, though."

"Manners and all," I say to play with her as I leave the room.

Her sweetness numbs the thoughts of demanding more from her, but only so much.

CHAPTER 7

Hours have passed since Carter left. The smell of garlic is still fresh on my fingers as I head into the dimly lit wine cellar. With a flick and a click, the cellar lights up and a beautiful array of wine bottles shines in the light.

An easy breath leaves me at the thought of getting lost at the bottom of a bottle. One glass or two, and I'll still have my wits with me.

But the wits can go fuck themselves tonight. I don't know what to think or feel. I don't know anything anymore. The memories of what once was and what I am today are playing tricks on my sanity.

I'm acutely aware of it but helpless to do anything about it. That's the worst part.

That, and how I feel about Carter.

It's an ever-changing relationship, but I'm fully aware of the cracked wall between us. He's pretending it's not there, and maybe I'm a fool to think something has changed, but I see the pain and sadness behind his eyes. He can't hide it any longer.

He's broken. It takes a broken soul to know one.

Even what I've been through in only the last twenty-four hours, pales in comparison to how broken and shattered Carter's been for years. And I desperately want to heal him. I want to take his pain away more than I've ever wanted to heal myself.

Deep inside, there's the inkling of some other part of him. If only I could show him.

The pain that claws at my heart only grows at the thought, but with a deep breath I let it all go. I don't know what I am to him anymore. But I care for him regardless, especially after last night.

And until I know what haunts him for sure, there's not a damn thing I can do to change anything. And so, wine it is.

I crouch down at the first row, gripping onto the steel bar of the rack and glancing at each of the labels. Pinot noir. Burgundy. Each of them. I love a good glass of red with spaghetti and Bolognese, and right now, I prefer Cabernet. The next row makes my lips curl up, for the first time in God knows how long.

I can pretend that there's nothing wrong. I can pretend for a short moment. I'm good at doing that. At continuing to go through the motions even though deep inside, I know nothing is okay and there's no way to right the wrongs.

The heavy bottle of dark red wine means I can have a moment. A small, seemingly insignificant moment, to simply breathe.

Well, only while I stay in the kitchen. The thought steals the happiness from my lips and as I stand, I feel my muscles tense once again. At least, until Carter comes back.

When Carter leaves, I'm scared to go anywhere other than the four rooms I'm familiar with. The den, his office, the kitchen, or his bedroom. This place is huge and I'm curious to see more of it. But his brothers are here. Somewhere. *And they're the enemy.*

It's easy to forget when I'm with Carter. He has a compelling power over me. Just being in his presence sets my body on fire and I move with him. Every step, every breath.

But the moment he's gone, I'm so very aware of everything.

"I just need to eat, to drink…" I whisper as I flick off the light and head back with the bottle in my hand to retrieve my dinner from the kitchen island, the aroma wafting to greet me as I shut the door.

But the second I hear the door close, my heart drops at the sound of another person in the kitchen.

"Damn, this smells good," Jase says as he walks closer to the large pot sitting next to the stove. I've already mixed the pasta and meat sauce. He towers over it, picking up the serving spoon and smiling down at my dinner.

My grip nearly slips on the bottle; my palms are so sweaty.

"You make enough for all of us?" he asks me with a charismatic smile.

A truly charming expression graces his face. With his stubble growing out longer than I've seen before, he looks different, but the similarities between him and Carter are still striking.

I can feel myself swallow before I attempt to answer him, but just the sight of him reminds me of last night. I can see him sitting in the chair to my left, smiling while my gaze drifts back to Stephan.

My heart pounds in my chest like it did last night in the shower. I can feel the anxiety and adrenaline mix and it takes everything in me to stand up straight.

"Whoa," Jase says as the spoon hits the steel pot and he practically jogs around the island to come closer to me. As soon as I register that's what he's doing, I instinctively take a step back, my shoulder hitting the closed cellar door. Every time I blink, I see Stephan. Sitting at the table, glancing between Carter and me. Waiting for me to kill. Waiting for me to become a murderer.

He knew. They all knew. And they let Romano walk away.

With both hands raised, Jase widens his eyes and slows his steps, even dropping his stance a few inches and crouching down. "You look a little dizzy," he says softly. "You already have a bottle?" he asks me and to my disbelief, a short huff of a genuine laugh leaves me.

Of course, he would think that I'm drunk and that's why seeing him would cause me to react with significant panic.

It's not that I saw him only last night, a few rooms away as I murdered a man who'd haunted me for years and continues to do so. It's not that I'm still forced to stay here even though I so badly wish I could run home and hide in my room from all the terrors that plague me. My body heats with anxiety, but the knowledge that I have a grasp on the present gives me much needed strength.

He takes another step closer and I shake my head, pushing off of the door and going around Jase. One of my hands grips the neck of the bottle, the other runs through my hair. "I'm just having a moment," I finally answer him weakly although my back is to him as I walk back to the counter where my wine glass is.

My heart races again. It won't fucking stop. Off and on all day, it's been like this. *I need Carter.* The bottle hits the counter hard and it's only then that I risk a look over my shoulder at Jase.

Jase's eyes are narrowed and he's still standing where I left him. I can't take my eyes away from his as he pins me in place with his gaze. Much like Carter does, but Jase is assessing me.

I have to give him something, but all I can think of is to answer his earlier question. Whether or not I made enough food for everyone else.

"I made the entire package, so there's definitely enough." With the answer coming out easily, I turn back to the wine and opener. Easily uncorking it as I talk to him although I can feel my hands start to tremble again, and my heart threatens to trot out of my chest.

"I wasn't sure if anyone would want a plate, but I was going to save it for leftovers if not." I can hear Jase walk back toward the pot slowly, even though he's still assessing me. The second the wine glass is full, I lift it to my lips.

"So, wine is your therapy?" Jase asks as he stalks over to stand only a few feet from me but leans his lower back against the counter.

"We all have our vices," I offer him and lick my lips. The sweet taste offers little aid to the chaos coursing through my blood. But his soft expression does something to me. It loosens something hard and sharp that was lodged deep inside of my chest, suffocating me.

"I get it," he tells me, his forehead smoothing as he turns and reaches for another glass in the cabinet. "Mind if I have one?"

The shake of my head is weak, but not because I don't want to share. I don't mind at all, especially, if it will give me a chance to win over Jase. I remember a thought I had that feels like forever ago, a thought about using Jase to gain my freedom. Or maybe to ask for mercy for my family.

No, the shake of my head is weak because Declan joins us, striding in as if I called a meeting.

Jase stands beside me, glass in hand as Declan takes Jase's former spot, repeating the motion Jase did when he first walked into the kitchen. "Oh, damn," he says over the pot with a reverence in his voice. "You made us dinner?" Declan asks with a boyish grin.

That's not exactly the truth, but I don't deny it. "I wasn't sure if you'd like it, but there's plenty."

Declan grabs the plates, the clinking ceramic filling the room as Jase gives me space, walking to the other side of the U-shaped island and leaning against it, opposite me. The thought of being in the room with Carter's brothers scared me literally only minutes ago. But an ease washes over me as I watch Declan make a plate and then point the spoon to Jase, who answers the unspoken question.

"Yeah, I want one, I haven't eaten yet."

I lean forward a little off the counter, ready to ask him to make me a plate too, but Declan speaks first.

"You didn't poison it, right?" Declan asks with a shit-eating grin. "You know I've got to check," he jokes and then makes Jase's plate.

And there goes the sense of ease and the smile that graced my lips. It washes away like a lone shell on the shore before the tide.

I'm still the enemy. I will always be the enemy. And that's what they'll always be to me.

I offer him a tight smile and force down the well of sadness and pity. "Not yet, you got here too soon." A tight knot forms in my throat, but I drown it with the wine as Declan chuckles, still piling spaghetti onto the plate. Bastard tears prick at my eyes and all I can think is that I wish either Carter were here or that I was back at home, under the comfort of my blanket.

"I don't think she's eaten yet," Jase tells Declan in a tone that has no trace of the humor I forced into my response. He grabs the two plates Declan's made and motions for me to follow him to the small table to eat in the kitchen. Declan looks shocked at Jase's reaction and the seriousness in his tone and objects to him taking both plates, one of which was his. His forehead creases with confusion… until he sees me.

I've always been shit at hiding what I'm feeling. My father used to tell me I'd fare better in this world if I could learn to lie.

My body moves unwillingly to follow Jase, but at least I grabbed the bottle. I can't look at Declan as he watches me. I know he sees through the faint humor I veiled my emotions with in my response.

"Are you okay eating here?" Jase asks. The legs of the chair make a scratching noise on the floor as he pulls it out for me. I stare at the chair for a moment, marveling at the kindness while questioning his intentions.

He feels bad for me. That's all I can think. He's being nice because I'm wounded. That's all this is.

"I'd rather be alone," I finally answer him, finding my voice and feeling the cords in my neck tensing as I look back at him. I have to force my words out of my dry throat and they hurt as I do. "I just need to be alone for a moment." My breath shudders and the back of my eyes prick as I see the visions of last night again. Only three rooms down. The grand dining room is only three doors down from here.

"Please," I say quickly in a whisper and place the wine down on the table with as much grace as I can.

With both hands on the table, he looks over his shoulder and says something to Declan, but I don't hear what.

"You going to be okay?" he asks me as I hear Declan's footsteps leaving the kitchen.

"How long does it take to be okay after murdering someone? Even if you feel it was justified in every way?" I ask Jase and he merely looks past me at Declan's exit before bringing his eyes to mine.

Jase doesn't answer me; he simply looks back at me as if I hadn't spoken at all.

I start to think he'll leave me like that, taking his plate with him, but instead, he asks me his own question, "You want me to grab another bottle?" to which I can only nod in response.

He's kind enough to grant me both the loneliness and the second bottle I desire.

CHAPTER 8

Carter

YOU WERE SUPPOSED TO BE GENTLE WITH HER.

Agitation leaves me in a singular deep groan. I don't respond to Jase's text and I don't intend to. He doesn't recognize the severity of the situation. He doesn't know shit about her.

He doesn't know what she needs.

The bitter thought stays with me as I shut down my phone and quietly enter the kitchen. I know she's still sitting where she was an hour ago and just as I expect, she doesn't see me come in.

She never does. She always gives me the opportunity to watch her, to see what she's like when she doesn't know I'm looking.

I'm hardly ever disappointed, but watching as she fills her glass again, the pleasure of being in her presence again is dulled.

It's becoming a crutch. If she knows I'll be gone, she drinks. It's only happened twice, but still, I notice. Part of me recognizes her condition. Her situation. I realize it may be easy for her to give in to a vice and let herself slip somewhere where the pain is absent, and the choices are meaningless. But I don't want it to become a habit.

With a twist of her finger, she pulls my necklace she wears up closer to her lips, letting the diamonds and pearls play there in between sips of wine and absentminded hums.

Her lips part slightly as she sways in her seat and stares at a black and white photograph that's in the hall. She hums against the gemstones and I wish I knew what she was thinking. The sadness and tortured stare tell me she's still there, my little songbird with clipped wings.

I don't recognize the song that she hums. I never do. Sometimes it sounds more like a conversation than a song.

I follow her gaze as I walk closer to her; the black and white photograph is a picture of the side of our old house. The one that burned down. The one that *her father* had burned down, expecting the four of us to be inside and sleeping.

I feel a sudden pinch along the edge of my heart, reminding me the damn thing is there.

"What are you thinking?" I ask Aria, ignoring the pain in my chest and causing her to jump from the tone of my deep voice.

Her expression is soft, as are her eyes when she turns in her seat. There's even the hint of happiness on her lips.

"You're back," she says and there's a lightness in her statement. She can't hide the relief that slurs with her words. And that bit of disappointment I have at her drunkenness returns.

"I said I'd be back tonight." It's all I offer her as I pull out the chair next to her, letting the feet drag across the floor noisily.

"What were you doing?" she asks me with a pleasantness that seems genuine.

She's naïve to think I do anything pleasant this late at night.

I was ending the life of a thief. A drug addict who bought more and more of SL and wouldn't answer a simple question.

What was he doing with it?

It's a rare day that Jase can't get a response from someone. He's good at what he does. He left the junkie to bleed out and waited for me to come. It's my name they fear the most.

If pain and the threat of death can't get an answer, true fear is quick to provide one.

And it did. The only word the prick spoke before life slipped from him was a name. *Marcus.* All I got was a name. But it was all I needed.

It's a name I'm growing to despise more and more as the days go by. Daniel used to have a good reputation with Marcus, a man who lives in the shadows and never shows himself. But that was before he found Addison again. Since then Marcus has yet to be found, but apparently, he's been busy.

"Work," I answer, and my short response tugs her smile down.

"There are leftovers," she offers me even though the smile's vanished. I can feel how the sweetness inside of her has hollowed out.

As she reaches across the table to play with the stem of her glass I ask her, "You made me dinner?"

"If you didn't all look so alike, I'd know you are brothers by the way you react to a damn meal," she offers with a somewhat playful nature.

I can't pin down what she's thinking. Or what she thinks of me as I stare at her.

"It's been a long time."

"Since you've had Bolognese?" she asks as if my words are nonsense.

"Since someone's made us dinner," I tell her and think of my mother. Once again, Aria looks at me as if she's read my mind. The pretending to be happy and acting like things are normal slips away.

"I'm sorry," she whispers, and I choose not to respond. Sorry doesn't take anything back.

"I like to cook," she offers after a moment, breaking up the silence and tension. "If you'd like… I don't mind cooking more?"

I used to avoid the kitchen and dining room when my mother got sick. It's where she died. None of us liked to go to the kitchen. It was better to be in and out of that room as fast as we could. In a way, I should be thankful Talvery burned that house down. It was nothing but a dark memory.

Her slender fingers move up and down the glass and I expect her to drink it, but instead, she pushes it toward me. "Would you like some?"

I shake my head without speaking, wondering if she knows what I think about her habit.

"I don't like it when you're gone," she says before pulling the glass toward her again.

"Why's that?" I ask her, grateful to talk about anything other than the shit going on outside of this house. Enemies are growing in number each day.

"I start thinking things," she says quietly, her gaze flickering between the pool of dark liquid in the glass and my own gaze.

"Is that right?" I ask her, pushing for more.

"It's better when I don't have a choice," she admits solemnly. "At least, for the way I feel about myself."

"What's better?" The question slips from me as a crease deepens in my forehead.

"My thoughts are better," she states but doesn't elaborate.

"How's that?"

"If I'm with you, I don't worry about my family, the fighting…" her voice cracks and her face scrunches. "That's awful, isn't it?" She shakes her head, her flushed skin turning brighter. "It's horrible. I'm horrible." And with her last word she picks up the glass, but I press my hand to her forearm, forcing the glass back down to the table.

"You're many things," I tell her evenly as I scoot the seat closer to her, "but horrible isn't one of them."

"Weak. I'm weak," she answers with disgust on her tongue. Her gaze leaves mine, although I will her not to break it. Instead, she stares at the stem of the wine glass. There's still a good bit in her glass, but from what I can tell, this is her second bottle. "I'm so weak that I want to have no choice," she says disbelievingly. "How fucked up is that?"

"You're in a difficult position, with few options and severe consequences." I've never been good with comfort, but I can offer reason. "And deep down inside, you know whatever you do, it won't change anything." The truth that flows easily from me is brutal and it causes Aria to visibly cower from me.

"Thank you oh so much," she says with a deadpan voice as she lifts the glass and then downs all the remaining alcohol. "I was beginning to feel pathetic and like my life had no meaning whatsoever." She raises her hand in the air and then slaps her palm down firmly on the table. There's a bite of anger to her words that pisses me off. The glass hits the table before she looks me in the eye and tells me with an expression devoid of any emotion but hate, "Thank you so much for clearing that up for me."

"I do enjoy your fight, Aria. But you'd be wise not to speak to me like that." My own voice is hard and deadly, but it does nothing to Aria.

"Would I now?" A simper graces her wine-stained lips. "I'm not sure there's a single wise thing I could do, is there, Mr. Cross? Other than obey your *every* command."

Her defiance is fucking beautiful and only makes me hard for her. My cock stiffens and strains against my zipper as I lean back to take her in. It feels as if we're picking right back up where we left off and I couldn't be more agreeable with that situation.

My breathing quickens as she stares at me, daring me to disagree with her.

"You love being angry, don't you?" I ask her, although it's not a question. "There's so much more power in anger than there is in sadness." The statement makes her lips purse.

"You have no idea what you're capable of," I tell her a truth that could destroy me. "Women like you were made to ruin men like me."

"Oh?" she asks. "Us women who aren't capable of changing anything?" She seems to remember her fight as she adds, "You'll have to clear that up for me. I'm either too drunk or stupid to understand."

"Or too blinded by your past?" I offer her. "So consumed with changing something that's meant to happen. That *will* happen, so much so that you can't see what lies ahead."

"What's meant to happen? As in?" she questions as she noticeably swallows. Her hands grip the edge of the table as if she needs to hold it in order to sit upright.

"You know exactly what I mean, Aria."

"If it happens, if what I think you're referring to right now happens, there will be no future for me. The willing whore of the enemy who could do nothing to save the people she loves. What kind of life is that to lead?"

My blood runs cold at her words. Numbly I watch her reach for the remains of the bottle closest to her, only to find it empty.

Would she kill herself? Is that what she's saying? My blood pounds in my veins at the thought of her leaving me, let alone leaving me in such a manner. I can barely look at her as she sags back into her seat and turns to give me her attention again. "If you were me, what would you do?" she asks with genuine curiosity.

I'm still reeling from her earlier confession to answer quickly, but I finally find words that have a ring of truth to them. "I'd take care of myself and my own survival."

"My own survival?" she asks with a sarcastic huff of disbelief. "If they're dead, then who am I?"

My breathing becomes ragged, tense, and deep at her question. "You are mine." My answer is immediate, stern, and undeniable. Each word is given with conviction.

But all they do is turn her eyes glossy. "And that's all I'll ever be. A possession."

The sadness is what destroys my composure. She unravels me like no one else ever has. She'll devastate everything I worked for, everything I am, but so long as I have her, it will all be worth it.

"I was meant to have you. I only fucking lived to have you." I've never spoken truer words.

Her breathing is shallow as her chest rises and falls. "Carter?" She says my name as if I'll save her from what she's feeling, from the truth breaking down every bit of her own beliefs.

"You were made for me to have. To fight. To fuck. To care for," I say as I lean closer to her, my grip tightening on the back of her chair as I lower my lips until they're just an inch from hers. My eyes pierce into hers as she stares back at me with a wildness I crave to tame. "Do you understand that, Aria?"

"You're a very intense man, Carter Cross." She speaks her words softly with tears in her eyes that I don't understand.

All I can do at this moment is crash my lips to hers, to silence the pain, the agony, all of the questions she has. The kiss isn't gentle; it isn't soft and sweet. It's a brutal taking of what's mine. What's been owed to me for years.

The instant I capture her lips, she gasps, and I shove my tongue inside of her mouth, pushing myself out of the chair and hearing it bang on the floor as I take her face with both of my hands. My tongue strokes hers swiftly and she meets my intensity with her own. Her fingers spear through my hair and her nails scratch at my scalp, pulling me to get impossibly closer.

She moans in my mouth as I pull away, desperate to breathe. In one movement, I pull her down to the floor while shoving her skirt up her thighs, maneuvering her beneath me. Her belly presses to the floor and my erection digs into her exposed ass.

"You're such a dirty girl, not bothering to cover this." I cup her already wet pussy as I ask her, "Aren't you?"

My other hand grips the hair at the base of her skull and pulls back hard enough to make her back bow. Her lips part with a sweet gasp of both pleasure and pain as I ruthlessly rub her clit.

"You're mine, and nothing else. You'll let go of everything but what I command you to do and be." My words are whispered against the shell of her ear. They mingle with her moans as I stare at those gorgeous lips. Desperate to take them again, I give in to what I want. Removing my hand from her cunt, I grab her throat from behind and crash my lips against hers.

"Carter," she heaves my name the moment I break the kiss and without thinking twice, I release my cock and slam inside of her.

Feeling her hot, wet walls spasm the moment I enter her drives me insane. She's so fucking tight, but she takes all of me to the hilt with a strangled cry.

My hips piston with a relentless pace to claim her and everything she is. Everything she'll ever be.

"Mine," I grunt out and release her throat and hair to grip her hips with a bruising force.

Her arms barely bracing her as she cries out her pleasure.

Over and over I fuck her as hard as I can. And each one of her strangled moans, combined with her hopeless scratching at the floor beneath her, only fuels me to fuck her harder.

"Mine." I push the word through my teeth as she cums violently beneath me. My own release follows, my balls drawing up and my toes curling as thick streams of cum fill her pussy.

She lies there panting, her small body sagging as she desperately tries to support herself and breathe at the same time. Both efforts seemingly in vain.

My cum leaks out of her as she whispers my name again and again. Bracing one forearm on each side of her, I rake my teeth up her neck and nip her chin before kissing her again.

And she kisses me back, reverently and sweetly. Her hands find my chin and her fingers brush along my scruff to keep my lips pinned to her own.

My chest heaves in air as I fall to the floor next to her.

The cool air relieving my heated skin.

The only effort Aria makes is to inch closer to me, to have both her bare and clothed skin touching mine.

"I've been waiting for that," she says softly as she nuzzles next to me, content with being held.

"For what?" I ask her, still catching my breath.

"For you to kiss me like that."

To kiss her. The memory of her lips hot on mine begs me to kiss her again, but her words stop me.

"It was worth the wait." The words fall easily from her lips, the same lips that look swollen and reddened from our kiss.

The reality comes back to me in this moment.

This isn't what this was supposed to become.

I don't know what the fuck she's doing to me, but it can't continue like this.

I'm ruining everything.

CHAPTER 9

Aria

I'M SURPRISED I SLEPT AS WELL AS I DID.

No terrors, just a much-needed deep sleep. From whenever Carter brought me to bed, until nearly 2 p.m. this afternoon.

There isn't enough sleep to mend the exhaustion I feel, but I'm grateful I've gotten through one night undisturbed.

As I shift on the wooden floor in Carter's office, the ache in my muscles intensifies and I wince. I'm so fucking sore from last night. From this whole past week, maybe. I don't know if this is normal or not, but I hurt. Every moment of the day, I feel him inside of me still and it takes me to the edge of both pleasure and pain.

Both physically and emotionally.

There's no denying Carter is a broken and lost soul. And there's no denying that I want to make all the wrongs in his past right.

My mind is a whirlwind of what I wish could be undone, but there are no answers that take pity on me and provide me with clarity. All I can think to do is offer him kindness. To obey, to be good for him. And maybe he'll feel something other than the anger and hate that cloud his judgment.

I can only imagine the world he grew up in. The small pieces I've been given are jagged and harsh.

I shouldn't pity the monster he became.

I shouldn't love what he does to me.

But I do.

The short piece of chalk rolls back and forth between my fingers as I study the paper lying on the floor. I can't remember what I drew at the park. The questions I had in my dream from not last night but the night before, are still alive and vibrant in my mind.

I can't help but to think there are answers in my subconscious. Answers in my dreams.

But I can't remember what I drew that day.

Instead, I keep drawing the same thing, the house from the photograph in the hall. It's quaint and small, with rustic features. It's definitely a backroad setting but there are other houses beside it. Close to each other.

The brick was old, and the mortar seemed even older. The weeds that grew up the side of it felt as if they belonged there like nature was intent on reclaiming the structure.

Whoever took the photograph captured the beauty of the home perfectly, but why does it call to me? Why do I keep drawing it and only changing the flowers that grow around it?

"There are four steps." Carter's voice breaks into my thoughts and I glance up at him, not registering his words. He takes his time rolling up the crisp, white sleeves of his dress shirt. I can't help but admire the corded muscles under his tanned skin and remember how his hands gripped me last night, leaving bruises on my hips that still ache to the touch.

He gestures to the drawing. "The front porch had four steps."

It takes me a moment to comprehend and I offer him a small smile before asking him, "This was your house, wasn't it?"

He nods and adds, "You make it seem more alluring than it was."

My heart tugs and a small knot forms in my throat as he returns to his laptop. Maybe if he grows to care for me, everything can be okay. It can be made right.

What a naïve thought.

"What are you thinking?" Carter's question brings me back to the present again.

"I keep drifting into thoughts I shouldn't," I answer him without much conscious consent. Maybe I've rested so much that the sleep refuses to leave me, making me drowsy and my thoughts hazy.

"Like?" he prompts.

"Like, wondering why I love this house so much," I answer him cautiously although my gaze stays on the paper.

"I hate that house," Carter says after a moment and I move my eyes to his. The coldness in his eyes is ever present and it sends a chill down my spine.

"You hate everything," I tell him absently.

"I don't hate you," he says pointedly, and his rebuttal sends a warmth flowing through me.

"How do you feel about me then?" I ask him and busy my fingers with the piece of chalk.

His words are softly spoken and it's the first admission from him of any kind. "The very idea that you're mine makes me feel as if there isn't a thing I can't conquer. But actually having you is... everything."

I don't know if he realizes how powerful his words are. How intense he is. Just being around him is suffocating. Nothing else can exist when he's with me.

"What do you remember about last night?" he asks me, and I blink away the trance he held over me.

"Everything," I answer him as if it's obvious. "You came home. We had a conversation and then more on the kitchen floor..." I trail off and my teeth sink into my bottom lip at the memory. "And then you took me to bed."

Carter nods slowly as if gauging my response. "You don't remember what you told me when we got to bed? Do you?" My heart flickers once, then twice as I try to remember.

But I don't.

"I fell asleep," I tell him as if it's an excuse.

It's quiet for a long moment and an uneasiness washes through me. Like I've said something that I should regret but I don't know what it was. Swallowing thickly, I steel myself to ask, "What did I say?"

But he doesn't answer me, he only tsks in response.

A pounding in my chest and blood makes me feel on edge until Carter rises and stalks toward me. He looms over me, owning me with his presence as he likes to do. My eyes close as he lowers his hand to the crown of my head gently and then twirls a lock of hair between his fingers.

My heart races with his touch and I don't know if it's from fear or lust.

"All I want to do is fuck you until there's no question in your mind who you belong to." His admission forces my thighs to clench and that tender ache returns.

The tension and fear dissipate with each small touch he gives me.

"If you gave yourself to me, everything else would fall into place."

His fingers trail lightly along my collarbone and up my chin then move to my lips, tracing them with a tender touch that I would have once found difficult to believe belongs to Carter.

"Is that all? Just give myself entirely to you to use as a fucktoy? That would solve everything?" My comeback is weakened by the gentle way the words flow, the flirtation that I can't deny in their cadence.

His cock is right in front of my face, obviously hard and pressing against his pants. My mouth parts and my fingers itch to reach out and take him.

The throbbing between my thighs intensifies and I struggle to remind myself that I'm his captive, his fucktoy, his whore, and nothing more. All I can think is how much I want to pleasure him like he did me last night.

I want to bring him to his knees and make him weak for my touch like I am his.

"I want to…" I have to stop myself and swallow my words, feeling dirty.

He crouches in front of me, his gaze penetrating mine with an intensity that begs me to lean away from him, to run from the beast of a man who isn't hiding anything from me.

His darkly said words are whispered from his lips. "Tell me what you want, Aria."

"I—I—" I stutter. Like an insignificant unequal.

It takes every ounce of courage in me to raise my gaze to his, to inhale a breath, and on the exhale confess, "I want to suck you."

"You want to wrap these pretty little lips around my cock until I cum in the back of your throat?" he asks easily with a huskiness that comes from deep in his chest, moving his pointer to my lips and tracing them once again.

I nod, forcing his finger to alter its path and graze against my cheek instead. I'm breathless, full of desire and want, numb to everything but him.

What has he done to me?

The thought hits me as he leaves me panting on the floor to grab one of the chairs in front of his desk and move it directly in front of me. He wastes no time, performing the task quickly.

He doesn't speak as he sits down, both of his hands resting easily on his thighs.

My hand is shaky as I lift it to his zipper, but he catches me before I touch him. His grip is hot and demanding and steals my attention and breath just the same.

I'm pinned by the lust in his eyes as he asks me, "Have you done this before?" He tilts his head to ask, "Have you done anything before me?"

"Yes," I answer him although it feels like a half-truth and just thinking that I'm partially lying to him makes my pulse quicken and body heat. It's not the same. What I did with Nikolai wasn't anywhere close to this. We were young, and I needed someone to offer me comfort. Nikolai was the only one there for me. I kissed him first, and I begged him to touch me.

I loved him, and I knew he loved me. Even if he would only ever be a friend.

But my father could never know about us and when Nik moved up in the ranks and I grew bolder, my father grew suspicious. I don't think Nikolai ever wanted to risk his position for me.

And I didn't want to risk our friendship.

What I had with him was nothing like this.

"Who was it?" Carter asks me. "More than one?" His head tilts as he releases my hand and my heart beats like a war drum.

"None of your business," I tell him playfully and grab both of his wrists to move his hands to the armrests of the chair. "Let me play," I tell him as if it's a command, but the words come out as if I'm begging.

He doesn't answer me, but his fingers wrap around the armrests and he doesn't say anything to stop me.

I fumble with the button, my nerves getting the better of me as I move to my knees in between his legs. The sound of his pants rustling and the deep hum of desire from Carter's chest fuel me to ignore my nerves.

He lifts his hips to help me after I unzip his pants and his cock juts out in front of my face. Shock catches me off guard. It's larger than I thought. Veiny and thick. Instantly, I wonder how he fit inside of me. Squirming in front of him, I know he knows what I'm thinking. The rough and masculine chuckle gives it away.

I glance up at him as I wrap his dick with both my hands. I can't possibly close my fingers around him, but the part that worries me is how I'll fit him in my mouth.

I imagined taking all of him and pleasuring him to the point where he couldn't control himself, but now I question if I can take a fraction of him without gagging.

Slowly, Carter lifts his hand as if asking for permission and moves it to the back of my head. "You can lick it first," he offers low and deep, not hiding how his breathing has hitched.

The bead of precum at his slit entices me to lick it, and so I do. A blush and pride rise to heat my cheeks as the man seated in front of me shudders at my touch.

His large hand splays and brings me closer to him, urging me on for more. But I tsk him, grabbing his hand and placing it back where it belongs on the armrest.

He readjusts in his seat, but his eyes never leave mine. They're darker than before, which only makes the silver specks stand out even more. The heat there leaves me wanting and I lean forward, finding my pleasure by covering the head of his cock with my lips.

The salty taste of precum and the feel of Carter's thighs tightening under my forearms as I brace myself, make me moan with my mouth full of him.

"Fuck," he groans, and his hips buck slightly, pushing him further into my mouth, moving against the roof and down my throat. And I take him easily, although my teeth scrape along his dick.

Using my lips to shield my teeth, I put pressure on his cock, taking every inch of him that I can.

My eyes burn as I lower myself more and more, and each time I get hotter and hotter for him. The thought of getting on top of him and taking my pleasure from him crosses my mind, but I resist. I want to show him I can give him pleasure like he gives me.

My nails dig into my thighs as I feel the head of his dick hit the back of my throat. It takes everything I have not to react. To not pull away and gasp for air as he suffocates me when his hips tip up and he shoves himself just a bit past my breaking point.

I sputter slightly, forcing him out of my mouth so I can breathe. I lean back but I don't stop. Even knowing there's saliva around my mouth, I keep working his cock with my hand and quickly take him back in and try to deep throat him again. The deep, gruff groan that Carter unleashes as I hollow my cheeks makes me feel like a queen. Like a powerful queen able to bring this man to his knees.

Through my lashes, I peek at him. At his stiff position and his blunt nails digging into the leather of his chair as he holds onto it instead of reaching out for me. My eyes drift upward as I take him deeper, trying to swallow. And at that moment Carter breaks.

"Enough," he bites out and stands up, pulling his cock from my mouth and leaving me on my ass in front of him. My palms hit the floor hard, but I don't care. The only feeling in my body I care about is the throbbing pulse between my thighs.

I can barely control my breathing as I look up at him. Carter Cross. Unhinged and unable to give up control. "I want you," I plead with him from beneath him.

It's true. I want him, and I'm unwilling to hide that fact any longer.

He turns his back to me, his pants sagging around his waist until he shoves them down, showing me his tight ass and muscular thighs.

His forearm braces against his desk and in one swift motion he clears it all to the floor. The phone, pens, his laptop, the papers. They flutter and crash to the ground all at once, but none of those things matter. The only thing I can do is stay victim to the intensity of Carter's needs.

"I want you to ride my face. I need to feel you cum on my tongue." His words make the ache between my thighs even greater. My need to feel him come undone even stronger.

My legs feel weak and ready to buckle as I stand, but it doesn't matter. Carter grips my hips and forces a yelp from me as he lies across his desk, his still-hard cock jutting out as he lets me sit on his chest.

Before a single word is spoken in between my gasps for breath, Carter shoves my skirt up and shreds my panties.

As I watch the tattered lingerie fall to the floor, Carter reaches for my blouse, ripping it from the top and exposing my breasts. He tears at my clothes like they're nothing. And they may as well be, judging by how quickly and easily they fall to his whim.

He said he wanted me to ride him. But Carter's a fucking liar. His fingers grip the flesh of my hips and ass and he keeps me right where he wants me. He drags his tongue from my opening up to my clit, where he sucks to the point of me falling forward with a blinding pleasure that lights every nerve ending on fire.

My breasts hit the desk above his head and as I scream out, the door to the office opens.

I cover myself and try to hide, but Carter's still ravaging my pussy when I catch Daniel's shocked expression.

"Fuck," is all he says, and he turns as quickly as he can to leave, reaching behind him for the doorknob but failing to grab it. I'd laugh if I wasn't petrified, knowing I'm about to cum. The pleasure swirls into a storm in my belly and threatens to ride through every limb, moving to the tips of my fingers in waves.

"I'm going to cum," I cry out to the ceiling as Carter lifts me off him, shoving me down against his hard cock where it brushes against my ass, so he can see who the hell opened the door.

The door slams shut finally, and Carter sits up, making me fall back against the desk while his thick cock runs along the length of my pussy and I cum. The feel of his cock just barely brushing up against my entrance is what does it.

I cum violently, with my face and every inch of my body heated. I can hear Carter grabbing his pants and pulling them up his legs even as the pleasure rolls through me, paralyzing me and heating my body all at once.

Daniel Cross, brother to the most powerful man I've ever met, just witnessed me riding Carter's face and taking my pleasure from him.

I shudder as my hand reaches up to cover my breasts. I can barely breathe as I hear Carter pull up his zipper.

I should feel shame of some sort. But I can't bring myself to do it. I feel nothing but sated, breathless and fulfilled.

"I have to see what Daniel needs. Leave one heel on each side of the desk," Carter commands me while grabbing each of my ankles and spreading my legs apart on his desk. "Wait for me."

He grips my hips, pulling me closer to the edge of the desk as I nod. My skirt is rumpled around me and my hands instantly move to my pussy.

"If you want to touch yourself, do it." His command comes in between his ragged breaths. "Cum as much as you want while I'm gone."

I lie there, my back on his desk, my ass directed to the seat he rules in and my chest heaving as he leaves me.

I'm still catching my breath when I hear the door close.

Touch yourself, I hear his words again and moan just from the command. From the deep voice and cadence that can only come from a man's voice filled with desire.

My fingers trail over my clit, but I can't do it.

I'm so sensitive to even the slightest touch that I have to stop my movements before pushing myself over. I can't do it. It's so intense, I simply can't bring myself to the edge.

I clench around nothing, I picture Carter between my legs, on top of me, smothering me with his weight as he pounds into me and I have to scissor my legs. My hands fly to my hair, pushing it from my face and trying to get a grip.

When I open my eyes, I stare at the blank ceiling, accompanied only by my heavy breathing and the ticking of the clock.

It doesn't stop ticking, but with each stroke, my needs diminish, and my sanity comes back to me.

I lie there for what feels like hours, and when I check the clock, it's accurate. Over an hour has passed, my back is stiff and the desire I had is all but gone, subdued by concern, replaced with a feeling of rejection. As I sit up, everything hurts. My back, especially. I stare at the door, willing Carter to come to get me. But he doesn't come back.

Not this hour and not the next.

Any bit of power I felt, fades to nothing, which is exactly what I feel like when I slink out of the room, covering myself with the torn shirt.

I haven't stopped staring at the clock in the bedroom and wondering if I should go back to the office. I can't possibly lie there waiting for him for hours. I'm almost certain he didn't expect that when he left me.

But every minute that passes warns me to go back. To stop defying Carter and show him that I can be what he wants, and maybe that would convince him to do what I want. To spare my family.

The pride and thrill are long gone and in their place only uncertainty.

All I'm doing is worrying as I restlessly wait in Carter's bed.

The moment I hear the click of the door opening, I sit up straight in bed, getting on my knees, clutching the sheets to my chest.

Carter walks in slowly, his gaze on the floor. He looks exhausted and beat down like I've never seen him. I can't get a word out, shocked by the sight of him in this state, but the excuses I've drummed up and rehearsed in the last few hours don't matter anyway.

He apologizes. Carter apologizes to me for the second time in only a matter of two days.

"I'm sorry I kept you waiting this long. I didn't realize…" his voice trails off as he heads to the dresser, carelessly dropping his Rolex into a drawer and then taking his time to strip down.

The muscles in his shoulders ripple as he undresses with his back to me.

"Is everything okay?" I ask him, daring to pry.

His five o'clock shadow is thick, and his eyes look heavy. It's only then that I wonder if he slept at all last night.

I barely sleep as it is, and Carter's always awake when I drift off and always out of bed when I wake up.

"Daniel isn't in a good place at the moment," he tells me in a single drawn-out breath before climbing into bed.

"Problems with Addison?" I can only guess.

Carter's gaze turns curious, but also guarded as he watches me scoot closer to him. I wonder how much of this is an act, and how much of this is really my desire to get closer to Carter as I let my hand fall to his chest. It's awkward at first for me to lay my cheek on his bare chest while my fingers play with the smattering of chest hair that leads lower and lower. But the more he allows it, the more he wraps his arm around me like I belong there, the more comfortable I feel taking what I want from him.

"What do you know about her?" he asks me, and I feel the words rumble from his chest.

"Just that she's with Daniel," I tell him and then remember the first time I saw her. How upset both of them were over something I wasn't privy to. I add quietly, "I think they love each other."

I don't have to look up to know that Carter's smiling, but I do. But the small smile is weak; the bleakness can't be hidden even by Carter's handsome lips.

"She's not handling lockdown well," he confides in me. Lockdown. I've heard the term more than once. I know what it means, and it reminds me of the reality. My father would often leave me in the safe house for days at a time if he had to leave during lockdown. It was better when he would only be gone for hours and I could hide in my room, which I did regardless of whether we were on lockdown or not.

The words are barely spoken as my chest tightens. "I can imagine."

"You stayed in your cell for longer than I thought you would without submitting to me. You have a mental strength that most don't." I don't know how to take Carter's statement. It's not a compliment, although it feels like it.

"Still, I can see her wanting to leave. To not be..." I try to think of the right word, a word that won't upset Carter and ruin the conversation. My fingers weave around the thin chain ever present around my neck. The expensive necklace that's truly a collar.

"Tethered?" Carter questions and I can only nod, my cheek brushing against his chest as I stare straight ahead.

The silence lasts longer than I'd like it to, but all I can do is listen to the steady rhythm of Carter's heart until he speaks.

"She's safe here. She's cared for." The way he says his words is careful, yet tense. That, combined with the way his heart picks up its pace, makes me think we're not talking about Addison anymore.

"What would you tell her then?" I ask him, wanting an insight into Carter's thoughts. "The moment she's alone and the thoughts of leaving race back to her?" I have to know what he would say. "What would you tell her?"

Carter moves for the first time since I've settled next to him. He lifts the arm wrapped around me and lets his fingers slowly trail along my skin as if he's carefully considering his answer. He kisses my hair once, then twice before using his other hand to lift up my chin and force me to look at him. His touch is gentle. So gentle it could break me.

"I'd tell her she has someone here who loved her before she even knew the darkest levels to where love can take you. And that there's no better protection from the shit life we lead than that."

My heart stops. I feel it cease to beat as he continues to stare at me, and I can't will it to move again. There's nothing but sincerity in his gaze and the last bit of guard I have crumbles.

Love. The word love breaks something deep inside of me.

"I need this one for me," Carter says before I can respond. He rolls over, pinning me beneath him and fucks me roughly, kisses me ravenously and then holds me to him, my back to his chest. All the while I break more and more. So much so, that I know I'll never be the same again.

CHAPTER 10

"**W**HAT'S THE UPDATE?" I ask Jase, leaning against the wall in the hall. My eyes stay pinned on the carved glass doorknob with my thoughts on what's behind it.

"Same as before." Jase's answer comes out low as we both see Aria and Daniel making their way toward us. They're far enough away that she won't be able to hear. Her fingers twist around one another as she walks quickly to keep up with Daniel's pace.

I don't know what Daniel tells her with a wide grin, but it cracks the solemn look on her face and she smiles back at him.

"Romano's ready to strike when we are. As far as everyone knows, it's the two of us taking out Talvery."

"And the drug? What about the buyers hoarding it?"

"They're all saying Marcus. But it's only a name." I know what he's getting at. When a man is close to death, he'll tell you anything you want to know, either to make his ending quick or to try to save himself. Four men now, each hoarding the drug we know to be lethal and each only giving up a single name in their last breath. Those are the only four buying in bulk, except for the girl I saw a week ago. I'd rather not seek her out, but our options are dwindling.

"Why not give more information?"

Jase's palm presses against the wall and I can feel his gaze on me as he leans closer. "What does he have on them that they keep his secrets even as they die?"

"Maybe they don't know anything else," I offer, but Jase shakes his head. I only glance up at him because of Aria. She sees his expression and the bit of happiness Daniel provided her instantly vanishes.

Jase looks worried, angry even with a scowl plastered across his face.

"We'll talk about it later," I tell him lowly, but he doesn't stop.

"They didn't give me anything. Not a drop-off point, not a procedure or any details at all." He leans in closer to me to emphasize, "Only a name."

Our gazes are locked for a moment longer than they should be.

Daniel clears his throat at the same time that I hear his and Aria's footsteps come to a stop behind me.

"Then we have a name," I tell Jase and a small twitch gathers on the corner of his lips.

"Later," I remind him. "We'll talk later." He nods, pushing off the wall and finally nodding a hello to Aria.

"I hope you like it," Jase tells her, and she glances between the two of us, not knowing what the hell he's talking about.

As Daniel and Jase walk away, heading back the way Daniel and Aria came, she tells him, *thank you*, to which she's given a smile from both of my brothers.

Her nervousness is still visible as she barely glances toward me and continues to run her fingers along the seam of her blouse. Anything out of the normal routine causes this reaction in her.

I wonder how long that will last.

The drunken comment she made the other night hasn't left me. That night, as soon as she was asleep, I made arrangements.

She said she's going to leave me one day. That she's going to run away and hide in her room until the war is done with. She was drunk, but she said it as if it was a fact.

She doesn't remember saying it, but that doesn't change anything.

I won't let her leave me. She's never allowed to leave me.

I asked her why she'd leave me, and she said so simply, that sometimes she just wants to breathe but can't even do that without overthinking everything.

I won't give her a bedroom, but she can have a room to run to.

I can hide what's going on from her until her questions fade and all she has left is me.

"What is this?" Aria asks as the door opens.

"It was a storage room," I answer her with one hand splayed on her lower back and one hand on the door to push it open as far as it'll go.

"And now?" she asks aimlessly as she takes a step into the brightly lit room. Her face is filled with awe as she steps further into the lushly decorated room.

Other than a gray paisley wallpapered wall to the left, where one would presume a bed to sit, the remainder of the walls are a soft blush, nearly white.

The chair at the vanity is lined with a matching gray striped fabric and beyond it are glass vases and a matching glass standing light.

Gray and blush are the only two colors. The decorator referred to the color scheme as mineral tones, but it looks feminine as fuck to me. I wanted Aria to know this room was designed for her, so every piece of furniture and item contained in this room was meant to ensure she knew it belonged to her.

Everything else, from the plush white rug in the center of the room to the sheer curtains, is white. A glass table and mirrored nightstands allow the light to shine through with no obstructions.

It didn't take long for the company to put it together. Her room is at the other end of my wing, farthest away from my bedroom. It was Jase's suggestion and the only reason I agreed was due to my impatience. I needed it done quickly considering we're only days away from all-out war.

"What do you want in return?" Aria asks me hesitantly.

My expression turns hard for a moment while I consider her. "This isn't a negotiation or a game, Aria. It's a gift." Her beautiful hazel eyes widen slightly and her lips part to apologize, but I interrupt her to ask, "Do you like it?"

"It's beautiful," she says reverently as she admires the details of each of the pieces, only taking small glances at me to keep track of how I'm assessing her as she reacts to the room.

"There's no bed?" she asks quietly with a touch of confusion as she stares toward the wall where one should obviously sit.

"You can sleep in my room…" I almost add, "or the cell," but I choose not to. She seems to hear the words regardless, her eyes drifting to the floor as she swallows thickly.

"This isn't a room I'd like you to consider your bedroom." My words bring her gaze back to me. Choosing my words carefully, I tell her, "You belong with me, but this is a place for you to go if you need… space."

She only nods, and I think that's all the reaction I'll get until she peeks up at me, her fingers trailing along the patterned wallpaper, and says softly, "Thank you." The gratitude melts the tension between us, and it soothes a deep need inside of me for her to want what I can give her.

I watch Aria walk hesitantly to the vanity, intricately carved and an antique, but stunning. She barely touches the cut glass knobs before pulling out the drawers and finding her things there.

Not the ones she had at her home, but new ones to replace each item she had.

Her hand hovers above them for a moment, almost as if she's afraid she'll be bitten by something inside if she moves too quickly.

Her pace is quicker as she moves to the closet, filled with all kinds of clothing. From expensive dresses and lingerie to nightshirts I was told she prefers.

"I enjoy picking out what you wear," I tell her and catch her attention as she turns to look at me, although her hand is still caressing the silk of a deep red blouse.

"And you choose red," she says beneath her breath before turning back to the closet. "There's certainly a theme."

"Red complements you well," I answer her although she doesn't respond. I take a single step toward her, but she continues to examine the room, taking in each bit with care.

"If you'd like something changed," I tell her as she opens a nightstand drawer, "it can be arranged."

She stares at me as she shuts the drawer. There's an edge to her movements.

"How did you know?" she asks, and her question is laced with tension.

"Know what, exactly?" I ask her, my muscles coiling from the tone of her voice.

Her gaze shifts to the open door before her eyes land on me. Her fingers play with the edge of her blouse in a nervous fidget.

"You have a lot of things here." She licks her lip and debates on continuing, but she doesn't need to.

"I asked for a list," I answer her before she can ask how I knew what she'd want.

"There's a rat," she whispers, and her posture turns stiff.

"How did you think Romano knew when and where to acquire you?"

"Acquire… is that what you call it?" Her voice rises as she stalks toward me. Slow, deliberate steps and I can feel the tension rolling off of her shoulders. "The rat told you where to acquire your whore and what to fill her room with?" she asks me with shaky breaths and tears in her eyes.

"I wanted this to be nice for you." The hard words linger between us as my throat tightens. Anger is written on my face; I can feel it like stone, but I can't change my expression.

Of every smart comment and tiny bit of anger she's shown me, this is the worst.

Distrust is clearly evident. I didn't earn her distrust. I'm not the fucking rat.

"How did you expect me to react to being told someone was spying on me?" she asks with genuine distress as her lower lip wobbles and she catches it between her teeth before turning her back to me. I thought she already knew. She's a smart woman, but I forget how trusting she is. How loyal.

Her arms cross and uncross as she debates on how to handle the revelation. She paces from the dresser to the vanity. Already pacing in this room. I have to fight the urge to smirk as I watch her pace back and forth over the white rug, which is exactly how I pictured her in here.

But not so soon, and not like this. This room is better than the cell if nothing else.

"I thought you would have assumed," I tell her honestly and nervousness prickles my skin as she glares back at me. It's unsettling and I debate on leaving her here, but I refuse. She's not going to take her anger out on me. Not when it belongs to someone else. "It wasn't supposed to upset you. I wanted you to have everything you could have possibly wanted," I admit to her and try to keep my voice even and calm, but the anger toward her response still lingers.

The nervousness grows inside of me, and I'm sickened by it. I thought she would appreciate this. I thought she would be excited to have everything she had before. Or at least grateful. I thought wrong.

I should feel irritated or pissed, but that's not what I feel at all. I've done this to her. She can't accept a gift without being cautious of my intentions.

With a growing pit in my stomach, I speak without meeting her eyes. I stare straight ahead at the hanging curtains that are only meant to add beauty to the locked windows that will never open for her.

"I wanted to make you happy," I tell her and clear my throat of the spiked knot. "I thought this would make you happy," I pause to run my hand over the back of my head, feeling the ever-present crease that reminds me how shitty I am at knowing what she needs beyond a good fuck and finally look into her thoughtful gaze that's already softening, "or at least provide you comfort."

My heart beats faster as she stares back at me with a kindness she hasn't before given me. "I'm trying to be gentle," I confess to her.

"I'm sorry," she whispers in a choked voice. The second I feel myself wavering and losing the man I am to this woman, she wanders toward me and wraps her arms around my waist, her hands splaying on my shoulders as she hugs me.

It takes me a moment to hold her to me and when I do, I kiss her hair and bury my face in it before she pulls away.

Her eyes are glassy but she doesn't cry; she sounds strong, although a few of her words crack as she says, "It's just a reminder… of everything that I'll never have again." She gestures to the room and exhales deeply before adding, "It's beautiful and it does give me comfort. You have no idea how much I love this. I do." She swallows with her eyes closed and then runs her fingers through her hair. I wait patiently for her to continue.

"I'm sorry, it's just… there's always something that happens that proves I know nothing and I'm lost."

"You're not lost." My response is immediate, and my tone is one I expect from myself. It's not to be questioned. "You belong here, with me."

Her shoulders steady as her breathing calms and her formerly emotionally-distraught features calm once again, but it's an act. She's brimming inside with a mixture of fear, betrayal, anger, and confusion.

"You're only lost because you want to be," I tell her low and deep, reaching out and pulling her small body closer to me.

Her hands land on my chest and she gasps slightly before looking up at me.

"I can give you everything. I can give you what you never even dreamed of before." I mean every word. I can and will.

Her long hair shines in the light as she nods, making it swish along her collarbone. She's compliant, but her wide eyes are full of questions. Questions she doesn't ask me. Some of them I'm grateful I won't have to answer.

"If you want to run, you run here."

"Carter, there are things you can't replace." She looks straight ahead at my chest as she speaks and her shoulders shudder. "Money can't replace—"

"I'm fully aware of what money can't replace. Nothing can erase the past. Nothing can bring it back." The sharp edge of my words and the pain and anger I refuse to hide in them erase her desperation to beg me for what I will never give her.

"I'll give you what I can. Everything that I'm able. But sometimes what we want most is impossible to achieve." My throat tightens with emotion and just as it does, Aria props herself up on her tiptoes, gently caresses my face and kisses me.

It's short and only a peck. Only a small kiss. Nothing like what we've shared before.

It feels different than it has before. Her touch is hesitant. A different kind of fear is in control of her and shows in her eyes. The kiss is meant to put an end to the conversation. She's hiding in that act.

"Tell me what you're thinking," I command her although the edge of desperation is evident to me. I don't think she can hear it. I pray she can't.

Her answer doesn't come quickly. She tries to leave me, and I cling to her, but she grabs my wrists and pulls my touch away as she tells me, "I'm scared."

"You don't have anything to fear if you obey me," I tell her, pinning her gaze to mine.

"You don't understand," she whispers.

The unspoken words between us are causing a crack in the delicate balance of what we have.

The reality that she's still my prisoner.

The truth that I won't rest until her father is dead.

The fact that she won't forgive me for killing everyone she's ever known and loved.

And the fact I never want to be without her and I think she feels the same about me. If only she could accept what's to come.

The Talverys will be massacred. And she, the sole survivor of her name, belongs to me.

CHAPTER 11

Aria

I**T'S TOO MUCH, I THINK WITH MY THUMBNAIL IN BETWEEN MY TEETH AS I LIE IN** *the soaking tub.*

Every day, something changes, and I never know how to react or what it means for us. What it means about me.

How could I not have known someone was watching me?

It must have been Mika.

He was always watching and taunting and teasing, but I thought it was just because he was an asshole on a power trip.

I lower my hand back into the steaming water and try to settle against the edge of the tub. My foot slips up to the faucet, feeling the hot water splash against it.

I can feel my fight leaving. The urge to keep fighting and keep holding on to the girl I was before Carter *acquired* me is trickling out of me day by day.

He's going to kill my family. My father. Nikolai. I know Carter will, no matter how much he cares for me.

That's the most painful part. I think he does care for me, but Carter is ruthless and there's nothing I can do to stop him. There's no point in trying.

The hopelessness presses against my shoulders, threatening to push me under and drown away my sorrows.

I wish I was numb to it all. There's nothing worse than being fully aware yet having no way to change any of it. Without fighting, I feel like a traitor. I'm not just surviving any-more. I'm living, and I don't know how I can forgive myself for having feelings for the man who's responsible for so many horrible sins.

Just as I feel tears pricking at my eyes, Carter's voice startles me. "You're tense."

I try to hide my sniffling and feel pathetic that I'm crying at all. Carter ignores it though, offering me that small bit of mercy as he strips down and slowly sinks into the tub, scooting me forward so he can lie in the bath behind me. The water sloshes and rises higher up my body as he sinks into the tub.

His touch is gentle, and I don't fail to notice that he's hard already. Just the thought of his cock makes my thighs clench and the dull ache that never leaves sends a wave of want through me.

Maybe that's why I don't want to fight him. The only thing that takes away the pain and anger is the one thing he gives me constantly. And that makes me a whore of the worst kind.

The water sways and a shiver runs down my spine as Carter's large hands press against my shoulders, pulling me into his chest. His fingers drift down my body, over the pearls and diamonds of his necklace that I always wear because he told me to, and the faint touch hardens my nipples and leaves goosebumps in his path to the hot water.

"What are you thinking?" Carter's deep voice rumbles just as I close my eyes and I open them to stare at the tiled wall and answer bluntly.

"I was thinking I don't want to kill you anymore because you fuck me so often." The truth spills out easily, not even questioning my answer to him.

His rough chuckle almost makes me smile as he reaches for the sponge and then dips it into the steaming water.

"I'm so tired," I say absently as Carter runs the sponge along my shoulder and down my forearm.

"It's late. Later than you usually stay awake." I spent hours in the gilded room. That's what I'm calling it now. That's all it is. Even if it is beautiful, and I do love that he had it built for me and I'm grateful to have my things back… or replicas of them.

"When do you even sleep?" I ask him. "You're always awake when I go to sleep, and awake when I wake up."

"I don't like to sleep," he answers me. "I can sleep when I'm dead."

His even tone and lack of humor make my heart tense. Like it doesn't want to beat when he talks like that.

Readjusting, I watch the film of bath oils move on the surface of the water and nestle my foot under Carter's calf.

"You know we could have started this way," I say weakly, not sure if I should broach the subject, but what do I have to lose?

"What way?"

"With you giving me a room and being less of a monster." The words slip out easily and Carter's ministrations pause at the last word. But then he keeps going, continuing to wash me.

"And what would you have done? Destroyed the room and used the shards of glass to kill me?"

He's not wrong. I could easily see that happening and the reality makes the small hairs on the back of my neck stand up.

What happened to that fight? To that edge I'm fully aware would have come out had the situation been different.

Nothing has changed. Carter stole me, keeps me prisoner and he's going to kill my family.

None of that has changed. Yet here I lie against him, loving his touch and finding my heart being ripped into two.

"We should talk about something else," Carter suggests.

The sound of the water falling from my shoulder to the tub is calming. Which is anything but what I should be feeling. The sponge is still hot, and it soothes my tired muscles.

"I could fall asleep in here," I murmur absently. All I want to do anymore is sleep. I don't know if I'm depressed, worn out, or if that's what happens when you lose your fight.

"Can I wash you?" I ask him, wondering if he'd let me.

A moment passes and then he dips the sponge back under; I expect him to give it to me, but that's not what happens.

"I like washing you," he whispers against my ear, his warm breath creating a wave of want that flows through me. But my eyes stay open.

Of course, he wouldn't want me to wash him. He couldn't even let me suck his dick. A small huff of feigned humor leaves me, and I readjust in the water so that the sound of it splashing will drown out the huff, but he hears it anyway.

"What?" he asks and leans forward to look at my expression, pulling my shoulder against his to keep me from avoiding him.

I meet his dark gaze, the grays and silvers seeming to take over in the bathroom light. "Nothing, it just feels good. It's nice to feel cared for."

Without speaking he leans back, kisses the crook of my neck, and moves the sponge to my neck and chest.

"Did you think it would be this way from the beginning?" I ask him. Truly wanting to know what he thought back then, only weeks ago. The reminder of the cell, of me starving and dying of both boredom and fear should make me angry, but all it does is make me pity Carter.

"I didn't know what to expect from you. I only knew I wanted to have you."

"To have me," I echo and settle my head in the crook of his neck. The movement makes my breasts rise above the surface of the water for a moment and the chill is unwelcome until I settle back into the water.

"Your choice of words always seems to amaze me." My voice is flat, and I wish I could take it back. Silence stretches, and I wonder how long I've been in the water.

You can't wash everything away, but I wish I could.

"How did you think this would end?"

"You're asking a lot of questions tonight," he says instead of giving me an answer and places the sponge back on its shelf rather than answering me.

"Oh, and I see I've found the question that crosses the line," I tell him with a smile although a deep pain courses through my heart as I shut my eyes. Each beat feeling harder and taking more of me just to keep going. I can only imagine what Carter wanted to do with me.

"It all changed when I saw how much you wanted me. When I saw how much you craved my touch… how much you needed me." I open my eyes as Carter's fingers reach for my chin, the water dripping into the tub as he forces me to look into his eyes.

"I need you to want me still when this is over." Carter's words hold an edge of sincerity that's too much to handle.

I almost ask why, but I'm afraid of the answer I'll get. I'm afraid what I feel for him isn't reciprocated. I've been foolish before, and I'm almost certain I am now.

"I'm not afraid of you," I confess to him, wanting to at least hint at the depths of what I feel for him.

"You should be." He doesn't try to make his words gentle in the least. "You need to be."

In his presence, my body turns to fire. He ignites something inside of me like no one else ever has. I doubt anyone else could ever affect me the way he does. Some moments, I hate him and who he is, and what he's done and will do. But unless those thoughts are on the forefront of my mind, the hate fades and it's replaced with a lust that clouds my judgment and demands my body bow to his. To show him love like he's never seen and the power of what it can do to heal him.

What's more? I crave it more every day. I'm addicted to Carter Cross. And the shame of that fact, although present, has quieted.

But the voice is still there and picks away at me. It's relentless, but so is Carter.

CHAPTER 12

Carter

Some moments, I feel closer to her.

Others, more distant.

I wish I knew what to make of her tonight. Nothing went as I thought it would and that puts me on edge.

She fell asleep in the tub, and as I carry her small form wrapped in a towel to bed, I can't help but notice how peaceful she looks.

Tonight, was like knowing you're in the eye of a storm. She's calm and placated but beneath the surface, everything she's truly feeling rage inside of her. She needs to let it go.

I have to set her down and pull the comforter from underneath her before she can bury herself into the mattress.

As she nestles into the sheets, she wakes calmly.

Rubbing her eyes, she comes to and asks, "Is it morning?" She practically hums the words.

With her damp hair a mess and sleep lingering in her expression, she's fucking gorgeous.

I cup her cheek and plant a soft kiss on her lips, to which she lifts hers up and deepens it. I'm growing addicted to the way she kisses me. How she doesn't hide her passion in her touch.

Unlike in her gifted room today. I want them all to be like this one.

I've never kissed a woman before her. Never let myself fall for anyone or given them that part of me. So, every peck, every time she deepens it, it means so much more than I thought it would. I need more of *this* from her.

"Not yet, songbird." Whispering against her lips I tell her, "You fell asleep in the bath."

She slowly sits up as I climb into bed next to her.

"Well, I don't feel tired now," she tells me and sits cross-legged.

Exhaustion sweeps over me as I lie down and pull her close to me. "Good, I can have you then," I tell her, letting my lips drag against her neck to leave a trail of open-mouth kisses. I rock my erection into her hip and then pin her under me. "I wanted you in the bath."

I'd planned on putting one heel on each side of the tub, just as I'd told her to do in the office, but her questions were more important. More insightful, even though I didn't like where they were going.

It feels like she's slipping from me, slowly. I'm losing her, and I don't know how or why.

But I'll get her back. She has nowhere else to run and no one else.

She only needs to accept that.

Her hand sweeps behind my neck and she pulls my lips to hers, taking and demanding. "Make me forget," she whispers against my lips and my chest aches at her words.

I need to forget, just as she does. It's so easy to get lost in her.

My fingers trail down the dip in her waist slowly until I find her cunt. Already hot and wet and needy, she rocks herself into my palm and I smile against her lips.

Nipping her lower lip and guiding my cock to her entrance, I tease her, "You're always ready for me."

"Always," she mewls just before I slam into her to the hilt.

"Fuck!" she yells out as I pull out and then thrust into her slowly, taken aback at the tone of her strangled cry.

Her palms press against my chest, pushing me away as I kiss the crook of her neck and she moans a painful sound. "Carter," she whispers my name with agony. Her brow is etched with a look of pain.

"It hurts," she gasps, arching her neck as I pull out of her completely. "It hurts," she repeats, trying to close her legs. Shit. My body tenses concerned that I hurt her. Fuck. Not like this.

"Shh," I whisper against her neck and kiss her lightly as my fingers find her clit. She needs to feel good under me. I can't have her any other way.

Instantly, she moans that sweet sound of pleasure I love hearing. "I was wondering how much I could fuck you before you'd be too sore." She only replies with a quick inhale and the buck of her hips which does nothing but give me slight relief.

"Look at me," I command her, and her head turns instantly to face me. Her gorgeous hazel-green eyes burn into mine. My thumb rubs ruthless circles around her clit and Aria bites into her lower lip, desperate to keep her eyes on me but knowing the pleasure will rock through her soon.

Her back bows slightly and her breaths turns to pants, but instead of letting her get off, I lower my fingers, trailing them through her lips and gathering the wetness to bring it lower.

"I could always take you here," I say lowly, pressing my fingers against her forbidden entrance.

Aria's answer is to open her mouth wider with a look of shock, but more than that, sinful curiosity.

A smile stretches across my lips as I say, "Not tonight though. I have to play with you first." Her eyes light again with curiosity and the guilt I felt a moment ago diminishes. I bring my fingers back to her clit then down to her entrance, pressing them inside her gently, but even that makes her wince.

I have to pull the covers back to look at her slick folds; she's red and swollen, well used.

That doesn't mean I can't give her pleasure and that I can't have mine in return. If I've learned anything about Aria, it's that the more I give her pleasure, the more compliant she is.

Her eyes stay pinned on me as she looks down her body and waits for what I'll do to her.

I run my tongue up and down her pussy and then suck on her clit. She's so fucking sweet. The taste of her on my lips makes my cock twitch with need. With her hands in my hair and her heels digging into the bed she finds her release, screaming out my name.

She curls on her side as I move back up the bed and lie next to her, not waiting to position her just as I want her. With one hand on her breast and the other pushing the hair away from her flushed face, she's still reeling from her orgasm when I move my cock between her thighs.

"Arch your back," I tell her, and she obeys instantly, jutting her ass out. And it tempts me. The curve of her waist and the round flesh of her ass are so seductive. I can just imagine gripping on to her and rocking into her as she screams in ecstasy.

She's not ready for my dick to take her ass though… not yet.

I settle on pushing the head of my cock inside her, only the head and wait for her reaction. A small moan escapes her lips as she rocks gently, finding the aftershocks pleasurable. I know there will be a bite of pain, but there's nothing better than when pain and pleasure mix.

"Grab my cock," I give her the command, and she reaches around to take my cock and stroke it. "Harder," I say then put my hand over hers and show her how to jerk me off. She only has a grip on the base of my dick, but her unsure hold and the lust in her eyes are enough to get me off. Even without her pussy clenching around the head of my cock.

"Fuck," I groan as she rubs me and slowly pushes more of me inside of her. With my hand on her hip, I stop her from pushing more of me inside of her. Even with her getting off, it'll only make her worse off and all I need is this.

"I want you every night, however I can have you." My words are tense as I sit on the edge of my release.

The air between us is different now. There's a raw quality neither of us can hide, although I'll never admit it.

Her pressure is firm, her strokes even and deliberate, and then her pussy spasms around the tip of my dick as she cums again from me rubbing her clit.

But it's the way she's looking at me that gets me off. Like I'm hers to play with. I'm hers to fuck, to use.

Like she owns me, as she strokes my dick and I cum inside her.

My eyes beg me to close them as I revel in the sweet burst of satisfaction and I mark her again. But her gaze stays on mine, our breath mingling, and I'm forced to get lost in her hazel eyes. I'm still cumming when she releases me, turning and kissing me hard, crashing her lips to mine and devouring me.

My cum leaks from her and onto the sheets, but she doesn't care and neither do I.

Her heart races as she presses her breasts to my chest and belly to mine. Once again wanting to get closer to me, and I feel for the first time today I have her back. She's mine again.

The day I stop fucking her will be the day I lose her. She needs my touch like I need the air she breathes.

"I think I might be able to sleep now," she whispers and then smiles against my lips.

"Sleep well." I keep my voice calm and soothing, rubbing my arm up and down her bare back as she settles her head on my chest, a new habit of hers. One I approve of.

Looking up at me with her head resting on my arm she tells me, "Sweet dreams."

I kiss her gently as she drifts off to sleep in my arms with the faint taste of lust still on her lips.

⁕

Addicts will get high on anything. My father's words ring in my ears. The white lights are too bright. I wince.

Where am I? My head lolls to the side; it's so heavy I can't lift it. *Everything hurts.*

Slowly, I feel each of my limbs. My wrists won't move, pinned against a metal chair. The same with my ankles and every inch of me is in pain, but the worst is radiating from my stomach.

I heave up a breath that squeezes my chest, coughing up blood.

Fuck.

My right eye is swollen, and I try to open it, remembering how my mother's pills fell into the gutter. No, we needed that money.

My father said the addicts would buy them, but hardly any of them did. I stayed out all day, and only two buyers paid me anything. And then the men showed up. Talvery's men.

"How long was he there?"

I hear someone from across the room ask the question and open my eyes to see a swinging light and a man in a crisp suit with long black hair slicked back tossing my wallet across a metal table littered with tools.

A groan tears from me as I try to move. Try to get away. I know he's going to kill me. I know it.

But it's hopeless.

"I'm sorry," I spew and more blood spits up. "I didn't know," I try to say but my throat is so dry and feels bruised. I don't think they heard me, so I repeat myself, pleading for mercy. "I didn't know."

"You didn't know what, kid?" a man hisses in front of me. Pain spikes at the back of my scalp as he grips my hair and shakes my head to look at him. "You didn't know you were dealing on my turf?" His eyes are a pale blue and ice cold. "The whole east side knows it now. So, you're fucked." He spits out the words then leaves me, picking up something from the metal table.

Every crunch of bone, every rip of my skin, every deep gouge pushes me closer and closer until I'm holding on to life by a thread.

I even cry out for my mother.

They all laugh in the room. But still, I cry out for her. Praying she can't see this and what's happened only weeks after her death. Shame and regret and pain make my head feel light and slowly I feel weightless. So close to death.

Please, just end it. I don't want to live anymore. I can't.

Bang. Bang. Bang.

At first, I think they're guns that wake me, stopping me from drifting to lifelessness.

Bang. Another bang at the door so close to me, yet impossible to reach.

"Please, I need you," someone says, and her voice sends a chill through my body, but at the same time, warmth. "I need you." The words are feminine and soft, but with a plea that begs me to listen.

She needs me.

The pain is still vivid with every move of my limbs, but I can hear her if I listen.

The voice turns harder, colder and the air goes frigid.

"I need you, Carter," she says again but this time there's no negotiation in her tone. "I need you!" she yells at me.

The anger rising and a storm brewing around me, she screams at me, her voice reverberating in the room, "I still need you!"

CHAPTER 13

H IS ARM FEELS SO HEAVY. I CAN BARELY HEAR MY GROAN AS I WAKE UP AND try to push away Carter's arm.

I struggle, but he only squeezes tighter.

My shoulders twist and I push against his arm, but the muscles are coiled, and his grip is too much. I can't breathe.

My eyes shoot open, realizing this isn't a dream.

"Carter!" I cry out in a strangled breath, fighting his hold and letting the anxiety rush through my blood to make me kick backward, shoving and heaving to get him off of me. "Wake up!" My heart pounds harder.

I struggle to breathe. My voice croaks and my lungs burn as I yell, "Carter!"

My chest flies forward as he jolts awake, instantly releasing me and leaving me breathless and crumpled on the bed. The mattress dips and groans as Carter gets up. I push the hair from my face and then try to steady my ragged breathing.

It was only a moment—a small moment—maybe a minute in time, but I thought he was going to kill me, he held me so tight.

"You scared the shit out of me." I barely get the words out, my eyes still burning.

Without an answer, I turn to him and it's then I see he's breathing just as heavily as I am. With both palms against the wall, he leans over and tries to calm himself down.

My blood runs cold at the sight of him. "Carter?" My voice carries across the room to him, ignoring how my muscles are screaming still from fighting against his grip.

Getting onto my knees, I crawl to the edge of the mattress. His shoulders are tense, and he won't look at me.

Cautiously, I climb off the bed and go to him. "It's okay." I try to keep my voice soothing, but my body hasn't caught up to the fact that he needs me. "I'm okay," I say, trying to reassure him.

With my heart hammering, I gently place a hand on his arm but he's quick to rip it away and stalk to the bathroom, leaving me with a pounding fear racing through my blood.

"Carter," I say hesitantly, but he doesn't respond to me at all.

The question is clear in my mind, go to him or let him be? I'm still catching my breath

If I've ever seen a man who shouldn't be left alone, it's Carter. He's too broken, and there's no telling what he'll do.

"Was it just a nightmare?" I ask him innocently, wanting him to give me anything. I can feel the rug end and the wood begin as I walk toward him in the dark.

He flicks on the light in the bathroom and runs the water. And I walk toward the sound and strip of light from the bathroom that guides me.

"Carter?" I ask him softly as I push the bathroom door open and see his back to me again. His muscles ripple as he washes his face.

"Please, talk to me," I whisper weakly when he still doesn't answer me. Even after he's dried off his face. "Are you okay?"

I can see him swallow in the mirror. I can see the weary expression of a man who's led a horrible life. The fatigue in his eyes. The pain etched in the faint scars on his back.

He presses his palms to his eyes and breathes in and out. "Go to bed," he commands in a harsh tone I don't expect, although, I don't leave as asked.

My heart squeezes with pain. I won't leave him like this. "I don't want to," I tell him with barely any courage, the words coming out shaky.

"What happened?" I ask him in a comforting whisper. "It was just a dream," I tell him, hoping they'll have more comfort for him than those words do for me.

For the first time, he looks at me in the mirror, and the sight of him sends a chill down my spine. The power, the anger, the man who rules and gives no mercy expecting none in return, pierces me with his gaze.

"Don't tell anyone." His words are soft and they hang in the air with a threat. An unneeded and ridiculous threat.

"Tell anyone what?" I question his sanity at this moment, only to realize he doesn't want me to tell anyone that he had a nightmare. "I wouldn't. I would never." My words come out quickly as tears prick my eyes. "That's not why I'm here, Carter."

"Go to bed," he tells me again, although this time his words are softer.

"Are you okay?" I ask him, taking another small step toward him, but still not sure if I should touch him. All I want to do is hold him, pull him close to me and tell him it's all right. Just like the way he's held me over the past few weeks. But I don't even know what happened.

With his grip on the edge of the sink and his head lowered, his voice comes out quietly and nearly menacing but more than that, heart-wrenching.

"Look at me, Aria." He speaks to me in the mirror, his eyes bloodshot as they stare back at me. "Look at who I am. Nothing about me is okay."

I stand there shaking, my words and breath caught by the intensity of the man in front of me. Even as he turns off the light, leaving me in darkness as he walks around me, his skin barely grazing mine, I tremble. His pace is ruthless as he leaves me, slamming the door and I'm left stunned and shaken. More than anything, I'm saddened by everything that just happened and so aware of how alone I am as I cry myself to sleep.

CHAPTER 14

Somehow, I fucked up.

She's the one who was supposed to change when I gave her the knife.

She's the one who should need me.

Not the other way around.

I can't shake last night or the knowledge that every day Aria seeps deeper into my blood and every thought that I have.

I'm consumed by her. I can't deny it. She brings out a side of me that should have stayed dead.

"Are you listening?" Daniel asks me, tearing my eyes away from the drawing Aria made yesterday.

He looks as worn out as I feel. It's because of Addison. She's not okay being back here. She didn't realize what this family became after she left. Time changes everything, but she didn't know. She couldn't have. And this lockdown leaves us nowhere to hide.

"She needs more than this. She's not handling the transition well. She needs… she needs to not feel trapped." Daniel hunches over in his chair, both hands on the back of his head, his elbows on his knees. When he looks up at me, I feel like I truly am the monster Aria calls me for putting him through this. For putting both of them through this. With tears in his eyes, he tells me, "I'm losing her. I don't want this for her."

"You're protecting her," I remind him. She's the one they went after and tried to kidnap, to kill, to do whatever they wanted with. She may have been safe if he'd never chased her. If they hadn't realized he loved her. But you can't change the past.

"She doesn't care," he tells me as he swipes his eyes with the heel of his palm, hiding his pain with a look of anger and annoyance I know is just a ruse. "She thought at first I was overreacting. That it was all in my head and over the incident at her place." He shakes his head silently before looking me in the eyes. "She said I was being ridiculous. She had no idea. So, I had to tell her."

"You told her what?" I ask him, just now realizing he's told her more than she needs to know.

"That men are going to die, and those men want us dead first. I told her we're at war. She still wants out. She doesn't like this. And I don't like keeping her here against her will."

My voice feels tense and catches in my throat watching him in pain over this.

"She didn't agree to this. This wasn't what it was like when we were kids. She had no idea, and I brought her back blindly. I was selfish." His words are laced with regret. The last sentence comes out in a harsh whisper. "So fucking selfish." The pain radiates off of him. "I can't lose her again."

"You can't risk her safety either," I reply and I'm firmer with him than I usually am. We're at war, and Talvery and his men will attack us the moment they can. "If I were them," I tell Daniel, "I'd be waiting and any chance I could take to strike first, I'd take it."

"I know," he murmurs and hangs his head. "They know they're dead men; they have nothing to lose. And they'd kill her just because I love her."

"It'll all be over soon," I say to try to offer him comfort as he rests his elbows back on his knees and steeples his fingers, keeping them against his lips.

"I don't know if she'll still love me then," he whispers his pain.

"I know what you mean." The words slip out and I can't stop them. Daniel's eyes hold a question, but he takes a moment to ask it. Waiting and stretching the silence.

"Have you thought for a moment, that maybe keeping her locked up is putting her more at risk? There's only so much you can control for someone until it turns on you."

"What choice do I have?" I retort, and his gaze moves to the floor again. "We're all prisoners of war," I remind him. "But it will be over soon."

"When it's done with… she'll stay? Aria will stay with you?" he questions me.

I search his face for the intention, why he would even consider her leaving.

"She won't hold it against you?" he asks me as if knowing what I needed to hear him say in order to answer.

"I don't know. She's mine. And she'll stay with me. Forgiveness will come."

He starts to say something, readjusting his footing but then he shakes his head.

"I came in to tell you something else, although I'm not sure you want to hear it," he tells me and straightens in his chair.

I gesture for him to go on. Although, I don't know why I'm in a rush. I've barely spoken to Aria this morning and I'm not sure I'm ready to, not after last night.

I expect him to tell me the same shit Jase has been saying, that Marcus is up to something. Marcus is going to strike. That we have three enemies now, not just one.

Without any proof other than the word of dead men. A single word. The enemies will fall in order: Talvery, Romano, and then Marcus. When we have more proof. I'm not in the habit of starting a war over a single word from the lips of a soon-to-be-dead addict.

"Nikolai is asking around for her," Daniel tells me and that catches me by surprise.

"Is that right?" I ask as my thumb taps against my lip. Resentment stirs inside of me. He brings out a side of jealousy in me that I've never felt before. *He had her first.*

Daniel nods with the hint of amusement at his lips. "Ever since Romano confirmed it."

"And what's he asking?"

"How he can get her back." He doesn't hide the thrill in his eyes from delivering this news to me.

"You're a prick for loving this as much as you do."

"It certainly adds an interesting dynamic, doesn't it?" he asks and a mix of curiosity, hate, and jealousy mingle in my blood.

"He has nothing to bargain with and even if he did, there's nothing I'd want in her place."

"He's already been told that and that it would be pointless to even ask you, but he *demanded* you be told."

"Did he?"

I can't blame Daniel for being so amused. "He seems to really care for her."

"Is this the first or second time I've told you I want him to die first?" I ask Daniel and he only snorts a laugh. Every night in the cell that Aria spoke his name, my hate for Nikolai grew. And she did it often. I'm fully aware of how *close* they were. Too fucking close for him to keep breathing when all of this is over.

"You really think she'll forgive you?" he asks with a cocked brow. I don't think he realized what his question would do to me.

She'll have to forgive me. There's no other way.

I don't like leaving Aria or being away from the estate right now, especially knowing that every moment I'm away is a moment that threatens to make her question what she should do. That's a dangerous thought to leave her with; all she should do is what I tell her, but I have to be present for this.

There are times when it's required to be seen. This particular instance is one of those times. With slicked-back hair and a sharp suit, Oliver looks younger than I remember him. Maybe it's the wide grin on his face that adds to his youthful appearance. Maybe it's the shot of what looks like whiskey that he clinks against Frank's beer and then throws back as he takes his seat. Neither of them sees me, but the security and Jared notice the moment I enter. They tense as I let the back doors close easily behind me, listening to Frank's hard slap on Oliver's back in congratulations.

Frank's all right I guess. He's a little older than me, only by a few years, but he's perpetually twenty-one. A punk kid with no goals in life other than making a buck on the streets and letting everyone know he's proud of it. I don't give a fuck what his motivation is, so long as he listens. I catch his light blue gaze and he slides back in his chair with a broad smile. "The boss is here," he utters but his jovial words are slurred.

"Your mom waiting up for you, Frank?" I ask him, hiding my grin as I walk toward the table they're sitting at in the right corner of the room.

Glancing over my shoulder, I take notice of who's counting the money down the hall. All the drugs come in and out of the Red Room, Jase's nightclub. As does the money.

"Ma can wait up all she wants." He blows off my comment, not taking the hint that he should make his way out.

"I think there's some business," Jared points out and gestures between myself and Oliver, his head tilted as he tries to convey to Frank that he should get the fuck out of here.

The shot glass sounds heavy as it hits the table and Frank pushes out his chair. "All right, all right, the big guys gotta talk." He mutters without looking at me, "You don't got to tell me twice." As he's putting on his jacket, I lay a hand down on his shoulder and wait for him to look at me. I stand close to him, catching him off guard and creating a thick tension that's undeniable. Fear looms in the depths of his eyes as I tell him earnestly, not breaking eye contact, "Thanks for understanding."

"Can we get another?" Oliver asks, the happiness not at all dampened. He doesn't see how Frank stumbles backward; he doesn't notice the change in the air. Frank does, and all he says on his way out is, "Of course, boss."

Yeah, Frank's an all right guy.

As I pull out the chair across from Oliver, letting it drag across the floor, Frank leaves, entering back into the club, bringing in the pounding music. It's quick to fade as the door closes with a resounding click.

"Thank you, thank you," Oliver thanks Jared, who's pouring out another shot of whiskey in front of Oliver and then filling the empty glass Frank just had.

"To finally snuffing out the fucking Talverys." Oliver's age finally shows as he raises the glass in the air and doesn't hide the hate on his face. He's new to the crew. Not at all like Frank, who started with me only five years ago. I picked up men as I took over street by street. Giving the men who ran them the option to come with me or die.

Oliver came to me though. Pissed that Talvery didn't want him, he offered up his services as muscle on the street. If it wasn't for Jared's word, I never would have hired him. Too old. Too cocky. More than that, he's too eager to make a name for himself.

With a nod of my head, the old man throws the drink back, clicking his tongue against the roof of his mouth as he sets down the glass and shakes off the burn of the shot.

"I heard everyone's ready to get it over with," I tell him, resting both of my arms on the table. A sly grin kicks up his lips. "Couldn't be more ready, boss."

My own grin shows itself. An asymmetric smirk as he calls me boss.

The dumb fuck should have remembered that earlier today.

"So, what happened," I ask him easily, motioning with my hand palm up for more, "give me all the details."

He's grinning from ear to ear as he tells me what I already heard, what *everyone* heard.

"There were four of them right across the street from Dale's bar, on Sixth Street. I saw them walking in and knew they'd be there for a few."

In my periphery, I see Jared stiffen; he knows me well enough to realize that this isn't going to end well for the man he stuck his neck out for to get on the crew. I bet he's wondering what that means for him. If I was him, I'd be wondering too.

Oliver still hasn't caught on. He's nothing but proud as he tells me how he walked in and shot all four of them before they ever grabbed their guns.

"All on Talvery's turf? That takes balls." I compliment him although inside my heart is pounding, adrenaline raging inside of me and the tension building. I've been needing a release for all of this pent-up anger. Wiping the smirk off old Oliver's face might be exactly what I need. That, or falling back into bed with Aria.

Just the thought of having her makes me want to speed this shit up and get back to her.

I've already been gone long enough.

"No one's making a move, but they were right there," he says and emphasizes his words, shaking his hands in the air. No one's crossing lines, and no one's made a move, not even Nikolai. But this dumb fuck thought he could do it and get away with it.

"How many shots have you had so far?" I ask him, my foot tapping against the ground as my impatience grows with every thought of getting Aria under me tonight.

"This is my fifth since Jared brought me in." He sways slightly in his chair as he tells me, but the smile only widens.

"Two for each of the four," I say loud enough for everyone to hear me and stand up. I have to walk around the table to pat him on the shoulder as I tell him, "Three more, all on me."

The smell of whiskey hits me hard as he reaches up to return the pat on my arm. His touch is firm with the first pat, but I don't stay in place, making the second one turn to a tap. My gaze is on Jared as Oliver says something behind me. A thanks and another cheers to killing the Talverys. I don't fucking care what the dead prick has to say.

Pausing in front of Jared, I keep my voice low as I tell him.

"It's on you to slit his throat when he's done those three shots."

On cue, Oliver calls out for another. The blood drains from Jared's face, but he nods and with a low voice he answers, "Of course."

There's not a hint of anything but remorse on Jared's face. He's tense, but he had to know it was coming. "No one does a damn thing until I say so." My shoulders stiffen, and the anger threatens to show itself, so I reach out, straightening Jared's tie and then add, "If there are any other dumb fucks who want to show off and not wait for my orders," I look Jared in the eye to tell him, "don't bother me and make me come in here. Kill the pricks where they stand."

CHAPTER 15

THE FRONT DOOR IS OPEN; IT'S NEVER OPEN.

The soft pads of my feet patter against the marble floor as I make my way to the entrance, following the bright light of day.

I can already smell the fresh air and the warmth before I step outside. The grass in the front yard is lush and although it's fall, the weather is lovely.

I haven't stepped on the porch at all. Not once since I've been here, and the thought seems too odd to be a reality, but it is. I was carried inside, and I've only ever looked through the etched glass of the windows but I don't try to do that often as it is. It just seems cruel to tease myself like that.

I glance behind me, down the foyer, and then peek outside, but I don't see anyone. Not at first. Not until I take a step onto the smooth slate porch and then another.

I hear him first, Jase. With a phone to his ear, he walks around the side of the house and then back up. There's a hitch in my breath and a slam in my chest; I freeze, but only for a split second.

I'm walking outside.

I'm not trying to run away. Although I have to force my limbs to move, I do just that. Staring Jase in the eyes, I walk to the stairs. They're grand and massive, just as you'd expect for an estate like this. Not to mention beautiful. Everything about this place looks expensive and each detail intricate, from the trimmed bushes and groomed flower beds to the arched driveway paved with cobblestone, reflects an elegance from whoever lives here.

I nearly snort just thinking about Carter choosing all these details. Carter is anything but elegant.

I hold Jase's gaze as I slowly sit on the steps. A large column blocks me from his view and I can imagine he'll come running.

So sorry to interrupt his phone call. The captive is fleeing; call the guards, call the guards!

A genuine laugh makes my shoulders shake at the sarcastic thoughts. As I lean against the column, enjoying the sun that dances across my skin and the fresh breeze, Jase comes running up the yard, just as I anticipated.

Rolling my eyes, I give him a face. A face that says, *are you fucking kidding me?*

"I'm on break from being the prisoner. I called in a temporary replacement," I mutter

His lips twitch like he wants to smile, but he doesn't. He doesn't say anything, not to me and not for a few minutes. I can hear the sound of someone speaking from his phone although I can't make out the words. He doesn't seem to pay attention to them at all.

My heart beats a little harder and anxiety trickles slowly into my veins. My foot nervously taps on the stone steps, but I hold my ground. Even as I start to get emotional, knowing that I can't even step outside without someone losing their shit, I stay right the hell where I am and enjoy the fucking porch.

"I'll call you back," Jase finally speaks, although it's still not to me. My muscles get rigid and my teeth clench together. *If he thinks he's taking me inside...* I swallow thickly at the thought. What am I really going to do? I can at least kick him. One good hard kick, maybe in the shin. I nod my head faintly at the idea, keeping my eyes on a few leaves that have turned a beautiful shade of auburn as they sway in the gentle wind. If he puts a hand on me to force me back inside, I swear I'm going to kick his ass.

A soft grin tugs at my lips. It's nice to feel like a tough girl at least. And like I have a choice.

"You picked a good day," Jase says, and I lift my gaze to see him slipping the phone into his pocket before he climbs the first few steps to sit by me but on a stair lower than mine.

I'm quiet for a moment, gauging how he looks so comfortable and acts like this is normal. Just like he did in the kitchen.

"It is nice." I nip at my lower lip before adding, "I used to have a balcony off of my bedroom. I liked sitting out there."

He glances back at me for a moment but ends it with a short, almost sad smile and then he leans back, bracing his forearms on the step behind him.

I guess my guard has decided to pretend to be my friend and just sit by me.

"Who designed this place?" I ask him, wanting a distraction and to think of anything but last night.

I woke up alone and that's exactly how I've felt all day. Miserable and alone.

I could sit peacefully in silence on my own, but Jase interrupted that. If he's going to babysit me, then he's going to have to talk to me. A punishment for a punishment. I smile at the snide remark in my head and think about raking up all the good lines I've had since I walked out here. I guess I'm in a bitchy mood. *Good luck to my adversaries.*

"We did," he answers with a smirk that doesn't hide his pride.

"No, you didn't." I don't even hesitate to call him out on his bullshit.

"Why would you think we didn't?" he asks me, a quizzical look on his face.

"You're telling me that you chose lilacs and peonies for the front yard?" I question him, challenging him to tell me that any of the Cross brothers wanted those plants.

Jase's expression turns guarded and he clears his throat as he looks toward the very bushes that give me my argument.

"Our mother wanted lilacs and peonies." His admission is spoken simply, flatly. "She asked for them for Mother's Day, but she died just before," he tells me, and his voice dims toward the end.

"I'm sorry," I say and keep my tone gentle. "I didn't mean-"

"It's fine," he says and waves me off. "I get what you mean, but yeah, we designed it. A few years back." A gust of wind blows by, sweeping some of my hair in front of my face and some behind my back, leaving a chill in its wake and reminding me that it is, in fact, fall.

"Well, it's beautiful," I tell him genuinely. I ignore the chill in the air and wrap my arms around myself. Goosebumps threaten, but I'm not ready to go back inside and the sun feels warm. I could lie in the sun all day, but it looks like I barely have an hour before the trees on the edge of the estate will hide it from me.

"You aren't planning on running, right?" Jase asks me and turns around to look at me with a stern look on his face. "I'd like to keep my balls, and I'm sure Carter would take them if I let you leave."

Laughter erupts from me just because of how serious he looks. His expression changes to one of humor and I find myself surprised by him yet again. Shaking my head, my hair tickling my shoulders I tell him, "Daniel told me it's useless with the guards." I shrug as if it's all a joke.

That's what my captivity is apparently, a fucking joke. Yet, there's only a modest pang of despair from that thought.

Jase huffs and looks over to the right side of the yard. And the way he does it makes me think Daniel's lying. Like Jase is hiding something from me.

"There are guards?" I question him. "Aren't there?"

He looks me up and down for a moment like he's considering telling me something.

"Yeah," he nods and tells me, "we have a few posted along the fences."

I acknowledge what he said with a small nod, but don't respond. Instead, I think about taking a walk to clear my head, but I'm sure Jase would follow me like a lost puppy and I wouldn't be able to think anyway.

"We told them to just taze the pretty brunettes, though."

I give Jase's joke a small laugh and lean forward to run my hand down my legs before considering if he was being truthful. "You're joking?" I ask him, and he shrugs like an ass-hole with a shit-eating grin on his face.

"You're in a good mood today," I mutter sarcastically.

"Right back atcha."

Time passes easily for a moment, but much to my dismay the clouds come in and capture the sun before I'm ready for the warmth to leave me.

"You want a blanket?" Jase asks me, and I glance at him, watching as he stands up, stretching his back and wincing as he holds his ass. "You might want to bring a chair out too if you're staying longer," he tells me, and I can't help but smile.

"I may go in; I don't know," I tell him and that's when my dumb heart reminds me that I'll have to see Carter and that he's being weird and distant… and stupid and guarded and a fucking dick. My throat goes dry and I let out a distressed breath. I can't look at Jase when I do. I know he saw, though.

"You know he has it bad for you, right?" he asks me and that dryness in my throat travels higher, making me feel like I'll choke if I speak, so I don't.

"Don't hurt him," Jase tells me, and I whip my eyes to his, craning my neck since he's standing up now.

"Me?" I ask him incredulously. "First of all, I don't hurt people. Secondly, he won't let me close enough to even think of hurting him. Whatever we have is very one-sided and," I try to keep going, but my words crack, and I hate it. I hate that I'm emotional over this. I hate that I'm close to admitting how much I feel for him and that whatever he feels for me isn't even close to being the same. I get why Beauty fell in love with the Beast, but it doesn't change who Carter is. There's no magical rose or kiss that will turn him into a prince. All Carter will ever be is a beast.

That ragged breathing comes back, and I stand up, ready to make a cup of tea and go hide in the den, or maybe the new room, the white room, the pretty room with the replicas of what I used to be in it. Whatever the hell that gilded room is. My hideaway room.

"Hey, hey," Jase's voice is comforting, and he takes a step closer to me, but doesn't touch me as he says, "He's had a hard time."

"Yeah, well, so have I." I bite out the words and surprisingly keep the bitterness in my voice to a minimum.

"He's had a decade of hard times, of people he loved dying, his only friend and brother leaving him, and then other fucked up shit. It was a never-ending cycle until he became the person he is now."

I glance up at Jase, but only for a second because I don't want to cry. He looks sympathetic at least, and genuine, but right now I need to know something will change. I don't need excuses; they're never good for anything.

"What are you doing out here?" Carter's sharp voice makes me jump and I nearly fall backward on the stairs but catch myself. My heart pounds and for the first time, I feel real fear since coming outside.

"Are you crying?" Carter asks me with disbelief and then turns to Jase with a look that could kill.

"She was just talking about you, actually," Jase answers Carter slowly, and the two stare at each other for a long, hard moment.

"I wanted some fresh air for a minute," I say to break up their *moment*, not holding back my anger as I continue. "I got lucky enough that my cage door was open." With those parting words, I step past both of them, brushing against Carter as I do and hating that I breathe in his scent, feel his warmth, and love them both.

I need a cup of tea, a good book if I can find one in my new room, my hideaway room, and some time to ignore the world.

But Carter doesn't give me that. I make it two steps inside the door before he snatches my elbow. I rip my arm away and he looks at me like he doesn't understand. Like I'm the one who's acting out of the ordinary.

"What's wrong?" he asks me, concern lacing the demand to answer him.

"Are you fucking serious?" I don't contain my outrage even though I should have. Carter's eyes narrow and darken, but I don't let it stop me. My heart races and it hurts harder with each thump.

"You're being an asshole. An even bigger one than usual."

"Be gentle," I hear Jase say quietly as he shuts the front door, hiding the last bit of light from the day and leaving us with the sound of his trailing footsteps. Part of me wonders if he's talking to me or to Carter.

"I'm sorry," Carter says through clenched teeth, almost like those words weren't meant to come from him in this moment. He shifts his weight from his left to his right and looks down at me with a look that elicits both fear and that dark desire I can't deny.

A rumble of low irritation settles in his chest as he tells me, "Mind the way you speak to me."

"You should do the same," I bite back without thinking. But it's true. His eyes flash with anger, but he doesn't speak. His jaw is held firm and I bet if he were to clench his teeth any tighter, they'd break. "You treat me like a child," I tell him and then swallow thickly, feeling the knotted ball grow tighter in my throat. "You don't want me near you, you don't talk to me. And last night…" I can't finish because again I feel like I'm going to cry, and I swear I'm not going to. Not here.

He doesn't let me love him. But it's because I'm his whore. I already know that's the answer. It's why he didn't kiss me for as long as he did. I'm meant to be his whore and nothing more.

A moment passes where I'm just breathing. Staring into the eyes of a man who can make me feel so much, but right now it all hurts. I want him to hold me and let me hold him back. I want to slap him and tell him he's an asshole and that I hate him. I want him to tell me that he loves me, and he doesn't think of me like I think he does.

In a matter of seconds, I go through a fantasy where everything will be okay.

"Give me your hand," Carter commands me. I jut out my chin, hellbent on telling him to fuck off, but he has a pull over me. The depth of pain in the hollows of his dark eyes makes me bend to his will. Slowly, I bring my hand up for him to take it. Even if I am just his whore, obeying his command.

I watch as he presses my hand to his phone, flattening it and then turns his back on me, walking to a panel by the front door.

I can feel my eyebrows pinch together.

Carter already said he's sorry once. I doubt he'll say it again. At this point, I don't even know what I want him to say. His words aren't the problem, it's his actions.

"If you're going back outside, grab a coat." His words are stern but there's a trace of melancholy there. *Press your hand here,* he demonstrates. He gave me access. My heart flickers to life, and I hate that it does. It's the things like this that make me question what I am to him.

"I wasn't going back out tonight," I tell him weakly. Wanting more from him, but not knowing how much to push him. My eyes dart from his to the door. Carter's a hard man and maybe he's had a hard life, but I need more than what he gave me last night and today.

I don't know if I'm in a position to ask for it, to demand it, or if Carter is even capable of giving me more than this. And if he goes through with his plans, all of this is for naught.

"Well, whenever you do," Carter tells me but when my eyes reach his, he moves his attention back to his phone.

I glance down at what he's doing only to find him exit whatever it was and that's when I see today's date.

And that's when this little truce no longer matters.

Nothing matters.

CHAPTER 16

THE MORE I GIVE HER, THE LESS I HAVE HER.

The moment I let her have access to outside, she stormed away from me. Not with the anger I expected given her outburst, but with a heartache that's inexplicable.

The color drained from her face and she ran from me. Literally ran away from me and straight to the white room. She ignored me when I called out to her and tried to muffle her cries.

Everything shattered in front of me. There was no sign, no warning.

It's my fault; she wasn't ready. I can't push her to move faster when the final deed has yet to be done.

That's the only thing I can think of that would make her run from me like she did.

Her door is locked, a feature I considered excluding, but I know I could knock it down if I needed to.

I haven't moved my eyes from the monitor on my phone but watching her cry hysterically on the floor was brutal. It was fucking torture.

It's been nearly an hour since she's stopped, but she hasn't moved from the floor. Sitting cross-legged and picking at her nails, she's just sitting there, rocking on and off, humming and crying. The only saving grace I have is that my necklace is still around her neck. She hasn't taken it off since I put it on her.

I told you to be gentle, Jase's text message interrupts the feed and I click over to it. He's the only reason I haven't lost my shit. Although I'm on the verge of ripping the door off the hinges of that room and demanding she tell me what set her off.

I fucking was. I quickly text him my reply and then add, *How much time has to pass before I can go in there?*

You can't. He answers immediately and even though a part of me knows he's right, a bigger part of me knows she needs me. She needs someone, and I want to be that someone.

What if we side with Talvery? Over Romano? I'm grasping at straws just to keep her.

It will be a sign of weakness. Jase's response is swift, and the next question is quick to come to my mind. I know no one will understand or respect why I'd allow Talvery to live. Not unless it's clear why. And undeniable.

What if I married her? I type the words, but I can't send them. The thought of her as mine truly, in every way, sends a thread of hope passing before my reach. So close, and so delicate, just like the necklace around her neck. And I think maybe she'd do it. She'd agree if I agreed to spare her family.

But being a wife to a monster only makes her vulnerable. The hope dies as quickly as the flame of a fire only meant to have an ember.

She's not feared, not respected. My enemies would kill her the first chance they got, just to hurt me. I know they would. Just as they tried to take Addison from Daniel.

Jase sends me another text. *She needs to tell you what happened.*

He's right. I need something to fix. Some way to control what went wrong.

If it's her family, you're fucked. Jase texts me again before I can text him back and I almost fling the phone at the wall when it shows on my screen. Instead, I flick to her monitor, but she's not there.

She's gone.

Just as I abruptly stand up, ready to hunt her down wherever she's gone off to, I hear her walking down the hall and slowly she comes into view.

Adrenaline spikes through me and I try to stay still. Because if I move, she might change her mind. She might go back to that fucking room, but I can't let her. I swear to God, I can't let her.

She enters the bedroom with bloodshot eyes, the hair on the side of her face damp from her tears and her face reddened. Fuck, I've never felt pain like this. Even in the cell, she didn't cry like this. She's never cried like this.

It's as if she's mourning.

I can barely breathe, but I swallow the pain down as she steps into the room, refusing to look at me and then glancing at the bathroom.

"There's no bathroom in the other room. The hideaway room," she says, and her words are roughly spoken, but she doesn't cry.

"Come here." The command is soft, an attempt to comfort her. I know she likes being held and I can do that.

I can hold her better than anyone else can.

She walks numbly and when I wrap my arms around her, she doesn't react. She doesn't hold me or lean in. She doesn't stiffen either. She's just there. Her entire body feels frozen under my touch and I instantly pick her up, cradling her in my arms to put her into bed, to force her to rest and lie down with me. Everything will be all right in the morning.

But the second I take a step toward the bed, Aria jolts and slams her palms into my chest, kicking at the same time and deliberately falling out of my arms and crashing onto the floor.

"Fuck," I grunt out and reach down to help her up, but she scampers backward, crawling away from me before standing up again and facing me like a caged animal intent on running.

A thousand shards slice into every bit of me. Into my numb skin, making their way inside my blood and up my throat.

"Aria, tell me what's wrong," I demand but she only shakes her head, pushing her hair away and then rubbing her hand against her tearstained cheek.

"You already know what's wrong," she says woefully, and I know I've failed her.

"You'll forgive me," I speak lowly, my hands clenching into fists.

Her eyes reach mine and they gloss over as she whimpers, "I know." She sniffles once and turns to go to the bathroom, but I can't let her.

"Tell me something," I say, raising my voice but she stops and then slowly turns. "Ask me anything," I add.

A moment passes where she only sways in the knee-length sleepshirt she's changed into. She almost says something twice, but in the end, she only shakes her head.

Finally, she asks me something I hate, but I know I deserve.

"Will I ever be allowed to leave?" Her question reflects her hopelessness.

"Yes." I want to tell her more, that I'll take her wherever she wants to go, but I'm afraid if I speak too much, she'll break down again. Every word has to be spoken carefully.

"When?" she asks.

"After the war is over," I tell her firmly. "There's no exception to that."

"And when will that happen?" Her words are small, nearly insignificant, reflecting exactly how she must feel.

"Soon." I try to be short, not wanting to hurt her any more than she already is, but also not wanting to lie.

"I would like to at least say goodbye," she whimpers and her voice cracks.

"He knows where you are. If he wanted to say goodbye, he could."

"He knows I'm here?" The shock in her voice is unexpected and I feel like a prick. She's going to have the same reaction she did yesterday when she learned I had someone spying on her.

"Yes." I swallow thickly, but at least she's talking to me.

"And he hasn't come for me?" she asks with such sadness, but it only enrages me. Doesn't she know the man her father really is? He wouldn't risk his life for anyone. Not a damn soul. "How long?" She visibly swallows and hardens her voice as she asks, "How long has he known?"

"Since the dinner," I tell her and then count the days. "Four days."

Aria's face crumples and she covers her mouth with her hand, looking impossibly more dejected somehow.

"When you're at war, you eviscerate them first. I'm sure he has plans…" I want to lie to her, to tell her he has plans to get her after he's killed me. But I don't believe it. Talvery would bomb our estate, killing her with me, if he thought he could get away with it.

"Where does that leave me?" Aria asks in a weak whisper.

"What do you mean?"

"You're going to *eviscerate* the Talverys… where does that leave me?" she asks with surprising strength and tenacity.

"You belong to me." It's the only answer to that question. And the truth she already knows. She's already accepted it. I know she has.

"What would you do if I told you no? That I don't want you?" She steadies her breathing as best as she can and straightens her back. "That I don't want to be your whore anymore?"

"I would know you were lying. And you're not my *whore*." My heart pounds accompanied by a prickling along my skin.

I expect her to come back with some quip asking what she is to me then. But she doesn't. Instead, she tries to destroy what little goodness she's given me.

"What if things changed, and I didn't want you at all?" she asks me with each word clear and just as sharp as the knife it feels like.

"Why would you? Why would you *lie?*" I dare her to tell me it's the truth. That she doesn't want me anymore.

"You would have sent me back after the bath if I'd said 'no,' wouldn't you?" she asks me and I have to take a minute to realize what she's even referring to.

"Our first night? You didn't sleep with me because you wanted to stay out of the cell," I practically spit the words out of my mouth, brimming with outrage. "You didn't even know you weren't going back." My voice rises and I feel it scrape up my throat. "Your heels dug into my ass that night, spurring me on. You fucked me because you *wanted* me." I emphasize each word, taking a steady and dominating step closer to her with each one until I'm so close to her, I can feel the tension radiating from her. "You wanted to know what it would feel like to have my cock inside of you." Lowering my lips to hers I whisper, "Or am I wrong?"

She stares into my eyes and I stare into hers. The mix of greens and blues and golds are vibrant and alive amongst the shards of blotchy red and white.

"Did you want it or not?" I harden my question just as my gut twists with disgust and I start to question if she never wanted me at all. If I was so fucking obsessed with her that I was wrong all this time.

"Yes, I wanted you!" she screams at me although her last word crumbles before it leaves her lips. "And I shouldn't still want you." She doesn't hide the pain when she tells me, "I should hate you."

Relief, sweet relief, is short and minuscule, but there's so much relief in her admission.

"Why's that?" I ask her softly, wanting her to keep going. To work through this because, in weeks, this fight will be meaningless. She'll forgive me. She already knows she will.

"Because you're going to kill my family and everyone I love. That's why." The fight leaves her with the last sentence.

"Yes." I keep my voice strong, although I don't know how. "I am."

"Please don't," she whispers her plea and I wish I'd already done it. I wish I'd already shot the bastard, so she would stop this.

"Is your father a good man?" I ask her, knowing this is going to hurt her, but she's already so low, there's not much lower a little more truth can take her. "Do you think the men who protect him deserve to live long enough so they can try to kill me?"

"They won't," she tries to tell me, shaking her head vigorously and reaching out to take my hand with both of hers but I rip it away. I won't let her beg for his life.

"They've already tried," I say, and my nostrils flare as I tell her. "Right after his drug addicts killed my father. They murdered him for forty dollars and a bag of pills." I remember how my father looked on the metal table in the morgue. How his knuckles were bruised from fighting back.

"And your father was pissed that I dared step onto his turf to kill them. To get revenge. He protected them!" I scream at her and wish I hadn't. Tears flood from her again and she gasps for air. "Your father sent four men to our house. Our rundown, piece of shit house. The house my mother died in. The house you love so much." I can't help but sneer at the thought. "We weren't there. Thank fuck we weren't there."

She's barely breathing through her hands that are covering her face as if they can shield her from the hard truth as I tell her, "He had them burn it down with incendiaries. I should have killed him then, but I couldn't get to him. I sure as fuck can get to him now."

"I'm so sorry," she whimpers, and tries to calm herself down. And I almost reach for her, to hold her, because I want to. Right now I need to hold her too. But then she speaks.

"Things have changed," she offers weakly, wiping the tears from her eyes although they don't stop flowing.

"How can you still defend him? After all this?" The pain won't fucking stop. I'm bleeding out the pain.

"The odds of me allowing your father to live are slim to none. Even if I want you to be happy, you know why he has to die. I bet you even think he deserves it," I tell her. "A small part of you has to think he deserves it."

"You said you'll kill them all, but all of them don't deserve it," she continues to plead with me, not offering me any comfort as I try not to break down remembering the soot and ash that stood in place of the home I'd grown up in. "It's not just my father who will die. Nikolai was my only friend. And my family will stand with my father. You can't kill everyone I've ever loved."

"If they stand against me, they deserve to die."

"Not all of them-"

"Like who? *Nikolai*," I sneer his name with disdain and she flinches.

"Please?" she begs me, but the loss is already clear in her eyes.

I turn my back on her, feeling lonelier than I've felt since she came into this house as I say, "You can make new friends."

CHAPTER 17

Aria

IT'S MY BIRTHDAY, BUT IT WASN'T UNTIL I SAW CARTER'S PHONE THAT I KNEW WHAT the date was.

No one here knows it's my birthday; why would they? They also don't know that yesterday was the anniversary of my mother's death. The day before my birthday.

And for the first time, I didn't go to her grave.

I start to cry again, and I don't know if I'm crying for my mother, for my family, or for Carter and the boy he used to be. I could cry forever, and it wouldn't be enough for the tragedy our families combined have suffered.

My back leans against the wall of the bathroom. To my left, the door is shut and in front of me, the shower is running to drown out the sounds of me crying. I wanted a shower to wash it all away. A hot, scalding shower.

Instead, I'm crouched on the floor by the door. I can barely stand, I'm so lightheaded and exhausted. I don't trust myself in the shower. I don't trust myself or anyone else anymore.

I know my father is a horrible man. A godawful man condemned to hell. I didn't know what he did to Carter. I had no idea. "I didn't know," I whisper to no one. I was so blind for so long and I wish I could go back. I hate all of this. I hate all the pain. I hate that there's no way to go backward.

I can already accept my father's death, as cruel as it sounds. For what he's done, there's no mercy in his death. More than that, he lived when my mother died. And he knows I'm here, yet he's done nothing. Nothing was ever done for my mother's murder. I'm sure my father would do nothing to honor my death.

Flames along the side of the house I've drawn flash before my eyes. I can't forgive him. I can't forgive my father, and I don't even want to know when he's gone. I don't want to give him the honor of mourning him.

But it's not just him.

It's Nikolai too. Why hasn't he come for me? Please, he can't be the same man my father is. A staggering breath leaves me. I know he's not, and I can't accept it.

I won't.

I've never felt so torn—no, so ripped apart.

But I'm sick of crying. I'm sick of dealing with death, time and time again. I'm my father's daughter. I live in a world where attachments are limited and mourning only fuels hatred. I've stayed hidden and quiet, attempting to go unnoticed for years and stay out of the way, and therefore, out of the sights of men who would see me as a bargaining chip. Yet, here I am, in the hands of a man hellbent on murder and vengeance.

But as I thought about how every anniversary of my mother's death, Nikolai brought me to her grave, I started to despair. How every birthday, I woke up finding a text from him and a note that he would take me wherever I wanted to go.

And how that didn't happen this time.

And how it never will again, and there was no way I could stop it.

There's no way I can save him.

I mourned the death of a man who still breathes. Not being able to hear him today or talk to him and let him know how I miss him and wish I could do something to stop it all, is a death in and of itself. And in its place is what I've been taught to hold my entire life. Hate.

It's as if Carter's already killed him; he's taken my only companion in this world away from me. And the anger in that realization grows by the second. Hardening my heart.

Maybe next year, when I visit my mother's grave, Nikolai's will be near.

The thought and visions of an old gravestone next to a newly carved one bring a new flood of tears.

That's all I can do. To mourn them.

To mourn us all. And to cling to my hate for a man I'm growing to love.

A soft click causes my eyes to lift to the doorknob and I watch it slowly turn. Haphazardly wiping my eyes, I slowly rise to my feet, leaning against the wall as Carter opens the door. Steam that fills the room drifts to the open space and the hot air makes my heated face feel that much hotter.

Carter stops after one step in the room, staring at the empty shower for a moment before turning to me when I let out a heavy and broken breath. The look in his eyes showed true fear until it settled on me.

I saw fear in the eyes of a man who does nothing but revel in it.

Still, I feel like nothing beneath him as he stares down at me. "I thought you were in the shower." His eyes roam my face, searching for something.

I try to swallow, but I can't. Instead, I shake my head softly and pray for him to leave. I should have stayed in the hideaway room.

"I don't like to see you like this." Carter's statement sounds genuine, but all I can give him in return is a sick and sarcastic huff of a laugh. It croaks from me and I can barely breathe in after. Reaching for the tissues by the sink, I turn my back to him. My shoulders are still shuddering with the mess of sorrow that weighs down on me.

His large hand settles down on my shoulder, carefully, gently, and he tries to pull me close to him. To hold me like he's done before. With half a step forward, he attempts to hug me from behind, he even closes his eyes and lowers his lips to kiss my bare shoulder.

But I'm quick to turn, push him away and step out of his embrace. He can't hold me and think it makes it all go away. Not anymore.

The tissue is balled in my fist as I push him again, shoving him away.

He doesn't let me comfort him, so I won't let him do the same to me. To use my pain against me. So, he can do as he pleases, regardless of the consequences they hold for me.

"No, you don't get to touch me." My words come out sharply with a fierceness I didn't know I still had in me. Rage heats in his dark eyes as his expression hardens and he stills where he is, his jaw tense and his shoulders rigid.

"Tell me now that you don't want to throw me back in my cell." Again, emotion cracks my words. I stare back at him, waiting for a response. It's difficult not to see the sorrow and fear in his gaze that he's showed me before.

"The only place I want to throw you is on my bed to remind you of what I can give you." He speaks quietly, in a deep tenor that sounds raw to my ears. "You still belong to me," he reminds me.

My lips twitch up into a sad smile. Sad for him that he thinks he could possibly ever have me the way he wishes. It will never happen.

A flicker of anger, the cluck of his tongue, one step toward me, and Carter morphs back into the man I recognize from weeks ago. Cold and calculated.

But you can't go back. He, of all people, should know better.

"Kneel," he commands but I can hear the desperation in his voice. He may want to pretend but he knows can't control me when I'm like this. I can barely control myself.

"Send me back to the cell." My demand comes out strong and with defiance, no one could deny.

I'll be better in the cell. Better there than the hideaway where I'm simply avoiding him. The cell leaves me no options. I need it. I need to get away from the man standing in front of me.

If Carter touches me, I'll cave. I know I will. I'll forget the pain and the anger. I'll forget to mourn. There will be nothing of me left but what he wants there to be.

I'm weak for him. "I need to be away from you," I whisper with harsh anger on my tongue.

"No." His denial of my request should only strengthen my resolve to disobey. But my limbs feel weak, and I so desperately need to be held. I want him to be the man to do it.

"Do I need to try to run?" I ask him in an obstinate breath, not daring to look him in the eyes.

"As if you could get away from me." His answer comes out softer than it should. And with more comfort than I can resist.

"Fuck you," I spit out at him in a last-ditch effort.

"You really want to go back to your cell, don't you? I could always keep the door open if you prefer. So you can pretend I'm the monster you want me to be."

I could always keep the door open. The words force tears to my eyes. He would take it away. Take away the pretense that I have absolutely no choice. Instantly, I hate him for doing this to me.

"I hate you," I spit at him, every bit of anger and sadness mixing into a deadly concoction.

Carter's eyes blaze with heat in the mix of all of this as he steps closer to me. With each step forward he takes, I take one in reverse until the back of my knees hit the edge of the tub.

"Admit it," he whispers so closely to me I can feel how hot he is. The hot water sprays down behind me, filling the room with white noise and heat. I can't take my eyes from Carter's as he leans in closer. His shoulders cage me in and his angular jaw holds nothing but dominance as he tells me, "Admit that you understand, and you know this has to happen. Admit it," he asserts.

"There's always a choice." I barely get the words out as he touches me. As he lays a finger, a single finger on my collarbone and lets it travel lower. His touch is fire to my skin. And I'll be damned if I don't want more of it. When my eyes reach his again, my heart twists with unbearable pain. The sadness conveyed in his expression reflects his low tone as he utters, "It's comforting to think we have choices."

When his eyes lift from my throat, where his finger travels up and down in a soothing stroke, the pain in his expression vanishes and once again the hardened man commands me, "Admit it. And admit you're mine."

Slap! I can't explain why I did it, even as my hand stings with severe pain, my lungs refuse to move, and fear overwhelms my body. A bright red handprint marks Carter's face and slowly he tilts his head back up to face me.

I slapped him. I struck Carter Cross.

One breath and he grabs both my wrists and shoves them above my head.

"Carter." The way I say his name is like a plea although I don't know what I'm begging for. I'm in over my head, feeling lightheaded and full of nothing but fear. Fear of him, of what's to come. Of everything.

"Aria," Carter's voice is strangled and reflects exactly how I feel. I open my eyes to beg him for forgiveness, to apologize, but his eyes close and he crashes his lips to mine.

Pressing them deeply to mine with a savagery I need to feel, nipping my bottom lip, devouring me until my own lips part and my tongue seeks his.

Fuck. I need this. I need him.

His fingers tighten around my wrists and he stretches them higher as his other hand roams down my body.

I don't know at what point the mourning and defiance changed to this. To the absolute need to be fucked by him, worshipped by his body. The feel of his powerful hold and brutal touch that turns soft the instant I need it to be, is addictive.

It's worse than any drug.

His left hand nearly releases my wrists, but the second I try to move, he tightens them again. "Carter," I say, and his name is a strangled moan as I squirm against the hard wall while his right hand finds my panties and shreds the lace. The thin fabric falls down my leg, tickling me in its wake and during all this, every nerve ending in my body is on edge.

"Aria," Carter moans my name, his scruff scratching my shoulder as he breathes against my neck. I'm so hot. Everything is hot and ready to be lit aflame.

His thick fingers drag along my pussy, the moisture there aiding in how easily they travel up to my clit then back down to my entrance. Pausing each time to tease me and bring me closer to the edge.

"Tell me you don't want me, that you're really done with me and I'll stop," Carter whispers and then drops his head to the crook of my neck. All I can hear is the mix of our heavy breathing and the white noise of the shower behind us.

My eyes open as I shudder and try to breathe, to make sense of any of this, and that's when I see us in the mirror. A sad, ragged girl with red eyes and nothing but pain reflected in them. Pinned to the wall by a man built to consume and bred by this world to hate.

And my heart breaks.

It breaks for both of us.

I don't want to cry anymore. "Please," is the only whimper I can manage, and I don't know what I'm pleading for.

Maybe just to take the pain away, if only for a little while.

Carter's strong chest presses hard against mine, trapping me and overwhelming me as he shoves his fingers deep inside of me while ravaging every inch of exposed skin with his lips.

I heave in a breath; my neck bows and my body rocks with the immediate pressure building deep in my belly. It rocks through me like waves. So close and threatening.

My nipples harden and my toes curl, my hips threaten to buck, to move away knowing the heavy hit is coming. But with Carter, there's nowhere to run. And the pleasure is an onslaught, an unforgiving bliss I'm submerged in.

My body is paralyzed by the blinding pleasure, and it's only then that Carter releases me. He doesn't let me sag against the wall, he immediately grabs my body, hugging me to him until he can lower me to the floor and shove his pants down.

He fucks me like it's the only thing he's ever wanted.

He takes his time, although each thrust is punishing.

I claw at his back and he bites my shoulder.

I scream out his name and he screams out mine.

Neither of us breathing, save the air from each other's lungs.

The heat, the passion, the need... it's all undeniable. I can admit that. Of everything Carter wants me to admit, I can admit that he has a part of me I didn't know existed and a part of me no one else will ever have.

"How can I hate you and love you at the same time?" I ask him in staggered words as I struggle to breathe. My eyes open wide, realizing what I said, but Carter either doesn't hear or doesn't care as he climbs off of me, his cum leaking from me as I lie on the cold floor, panting.

A part of me cracks as he stands and runs his hand over his face and then down the back of his head. Standing with his back to me, a part of me shatters. I'm such a fool. A foolish girl at the whim of a monster. Lost in my pain until he can overpower it with pleasure.

He carried me to his bed. Wordlessly.

He wiped between my legs with a warm, damp cloth and then carried me to his bed. I can't look at him; I can't do anything but lie here. And every tick of the clock makes me wonder if I should climb out and go sleep on the floor of the hideaway.

My heart hurts too much.

At least he's not touching me. Every time the bed groans and the covers shift over my naked body I tense, thinking he's going to hold me, but he doesn't.

I replay the last twenty-four hours over and over again.

"Why did you look scared when I wasn't in the shower?" I finally ask him, breaking the silence and the pretense that I could even try to sleep. "I don't understand." I give him the reasoning for the question as it came seemingly from nowhere. They're the only words that have been spoken between us since the slap, apart from the confession that went unheard.

"Jase had a lover once," Carter answers me, softly spoken, but rough and deep. I can hear him breathe heavily, feel it even with the dip of the bed and then he adds, "She killed herself in the shower."

My lips part, although I stay lying on my side, my back to him. More pain. More tragedy. I wonder what Jase did to her that made her kill herself. I didn't think he was capable of such a thing. The question is on my tongue, but I don't ask it.

Carter had fear in his eyes when I wasn't standing in the shower because for a moment, for one brief moment, he thought I was lying dead in the tub.

CHAPTER 18

I WONDER IF SHE REALLY LOVES ME.

I'll never forget the way she said it. It gutted me. She may grow to love me, but she'll always hate me.

I can't blame her for that, but I want to hear the words apart from the hatred. So, I can pretend it comes without a caveat.

I want her to say it again, and this time to mean it. Those words shouldn't have fallen so recklessly as I pushed her to the edge of pleasure. They're addictive and they did something to me I can't describe.

She's drawing so slowly today. Lying in front of the fire in the den, she's only been working on one picture. One single piece of art for the last three hours. I'm still not sure what it is, all I can make out is a field of flowers, but there's something beyond the black smudges of petals.

I don't have time to question her about it though. Other questions are too precious to be wasted by another moment of silence.

"What do you want more than anything in the world?" The fire crackles once my deep voice has broken the void of silence between us. The tension is still there, but it can't exist forever. I won't let it.

Aria's hazel eyes lift, and she peeks at me through her dark lashes, not bothering to move from lying on her elbows. She glances back at the drawing and visibly swallows before shrugging slightly and looking back up at me as if she doesn't have to answer.

At this point, she doesn't. I don't care what she does or how she treats me with the door closed, so long as she doesn't run or hurt herself.

"I want my family to be untouchable," I confess to her.

"That's quite an ambition," she answers, crossing her ankles and still staring at the drawing pad in front of her. She's still cold.

"Isn't that what you want, too?" I ask her. "That would seem to be especially desirable given the current environment." I can't keep the smug tone from my voice to cover up the pain from her reaction. If she would talk to me, she'd see. She has to see that there's only one way for this to end. And once it's over, it will all be better. I'll make it better for her.

"I want everyone to fuck off and leave me alone," she answers with a bite that tips the corner of my lips up into a half smile. I love the fight in her. She'll live, she'll survive. A girl like her knows how to survive if nothing else.

"Anger is something I didn't expect. And someone like you shouldn't be left alone," I tell her.

"I don't want to cry today. So, I'll settle for anger." Her answer comes with muted irritation. She throws down the stick of charcoal onto the paper and then meets my gaze to ask, "Why shouldn't I be alone?"

"It's one thing to say you want to be alone. It's another to truly be it. You pretend like you don't exist in the same world as I do. Locking yourself away and acting like that's what you want. But you belong here. You were born to this life. You need to accept that. And loneliness in this world leaves you vulnerable and that's a life neither of us can afford."

"I was alone in the cell," she says solemnly. I don't think she slept at all last night; I know I didn't. "I survived."

A melancholy huff leaves me. "You weren't alone. The first night you slept, I'd drugged your dinner to make sure you would. So, I could tend to your wounds and the cuts on your wrists."

"You did?" Her eyes are filled with shock. "Why?"

"You were mine to take care of." My shoulders stiffen, as does my gaze and she drops hers, falling back to the smudges of charcoal. "I knew you would live. And you would break quickly. Everything needed to happen quickly."

"Why?" she asks me, and I don't know how she can't know at this point.

"I'd intended to show how willing you were to be mine to everyone who was watching. So, there would be no question where you stood in the war."

Her eyes close and she chews the inside of her cheek at my admission, trying to keep her emotions in check. I know the truth of the situation is raw for her. An open wound. But she needs to see it all. She has to accept everything for what it is.

"Instead, there's no question where I stand when it comes to you. I never liked Stephan. Once a traitor, always a traitor. But giving his death to you, allowing you to have vengeance? It spoke more words than I realized it would."

Her face scrunches with the painful memory and then she hangs her head, avoiding my gaze and rubbing her cheek against her shoulder. She pushes the hair out of her face and when she speaks, she doesn't look up.

"But you're still going to…" She doesn't bother finishing her question. I know she already knows. She'll come to accept it.

"Your father doesn't deserve what he has. He's not half the man Romano is. And Romano is a pathetic excuse for his title. They'll both die. Along with everyone who fights for them."

"Please. Not everyone. I'll do anything." Her words are spoken with conviction and she lifts her hazels up to meet my dark gaze. "You want me to kneel at your feet? I'll kneel."

She still doesn't get it. And my heart aches for hers.

"What if I wanted you to stand at my side?" I ask her, my heart racing in my chest. It's a risk to give her more. Every time I do, she fails to cope with it. But I need her to know what I really want from her. What I desire more than anything.

"You would tower over me," she answers.

"That's not how it works, songbird. And it's not what I want. You've only ever had broken wings, but I can show you what true freedom is."

"You're still going to kill my family?" she asks me as if that answer is the end all, be all.

"I'm going to do a number of things you're going to disapprove of. You need to accept that." My answer is hard, leaving no room for any intolerance. "I'm not a good man."

"Is this what it would be like to stand by your side? To have no control and to simply accept what you do?" I'm surprised by her answer but eager to discuss terms.

"On some matters, you'll never have control, and you'll have to accept what I choose. Whether or not you want to know about them is your decision." I know part of her despair is because she knows everything, yet she's a casualty with little recourse.

"I'm sorry you know as much as you do," I tell her and then almost take it back, thinking she'll take it offensively and that's not what I intended.

She doesn't though. Instead, she cracks, showing me the side of her I love. The raw vulnerability.

"I don't want this life," she whispers, slowly pushing the art away so she can rest her head against the rug. The light from the fire licks along her skin.

"We don't get to choose," I remind her. I've told myself so many times that I wish things were different, but you live the life you're given.

"You're wrong," she tells me as if she has another option.

"Do you love what I do to you? How I fuck that pretty little cunt and force you to scream out my name?" I'm crude and harsh with my question.

She doesn't answer me, but she doesn't have to.

"Then no, you don't have a choice. I had a choice once. I chose wrong."

"You'll get tired of me," she whispers, her eyes seemingly vacant but the depths of them harboring pain. "One day I won't be a shiny new toy. One day, you'll want someone to fight you and I'll have none left in me." Tears pool in her eyes. "One day, the idea of shoving your dick inside of me won't interest you in the least."

She has no idea how wrong she is. I'm only growing more obsessed with her. Breaking every rule to satisfy her.

Risking everything to heal the broken pieces of her she refuses to acknowledge.

I'll never let her go because she isn't a toy. She isn't a challenge. She isn't the fuckdoll she thinks she is and secretly loves being.

"Will you let me go then?"

"Never."

She turns to face the fire and I whisper to her, "You're so wrong, Aria. If you weren't so set on hating me, you'd see."

"You give me every reason to hate you," she tells me. In the reflection from the mirror above the mantel, I see the fire dancing in her eyes.

She'll never know how much her words hurt me. Or maybe she does, and that's what she was after.

"Why are you doing this to me? Why me?" she asks me in a single breath and I offer her a singular truth in return.

"Your father set a series of events in motion," I reply, remembering the night his men took me from the street.

I remember how the pills spilled into the gutter even as they slammed their fists against my jaw and I fell to the cold cement. With her, I only see what lies ahead. But she's caught in the past. And that's what will destroy us.

"So, it's my father's fault?" she asks me with a sadness in her eyes, as if I've robbed her of some fantasy.

"No, it's mine." My confession confuses her for a moment, but before she can say anything else, I continue.

"I thought I loved you," I tell her with a bitter hardness that forces the words to sound violent on my tongue. Her eyes widen as she turns back and stares at me. Her stance changes to one of prey, realizing it's stumbled into its worst enemy. The shock in her eyes fuels me to push her farther. For her to realize the man I truly am.

"For a long time after I left your home, when they kicked me back out onto the street after brutalizing me, I thought I loved whoever belonged to the sweet voice that stopped them from killing me." Aria's expression changes to one of fear and knowing.

I tell her to break whatever thoughts she has of love. And whatever thoughts I have of it. Weakness crushes down on me as I tell her what I used to think. What I expected this to be when I stabbed the knife into her picture and told Romano to bring her to me.

"I knew I hated your father, and eventually I hated everything. I hated you for letting me live." Aria is silent, waiting with bated breath to see what else I'll say.

"I'm condemned to hell. Of everyone on this Earth, God knows I deserve to burn. And it's because I was allowed to live. It's because of you."

"It has nothing to do with me. My father—"

"It has *everything* to do with you," I tell her, feeling the rage from the memory take over. "You're the one who banged on the door and pleaded with your father. I was so foolish. For a long time, I thought when you were crying out, 'I need you,' that in some fucked up way, you were calling out for me."

As I take another step closer to her, the wildness returns to Aria's eyes, the fear I know and love swirls within them. Her cunt is still feeling the pleasure I give her, while her heart beats with the knowing fear of me.

"I didn't—" she starts to protest, and I stop her.

"You're the bird in the forest who lured the child out of safety until he fell into a black hole he could never get out of. And still, the bird sings so beautifully, taunting the child as he becomes a man of hardness and hate, stuck in a hell he didn't know was coming. Do you know what that man dreams of more than anything?" I ask her, remembering the moment my gratitude changed to hate for the very girl who sits in front of me.

She barely shakes her head, not taking her gaze from me.

"First to get out, for the longest time, just a way to get out. But when he realizes he can't, that there's no changing who he is and where he's damned to, he searches for the songbird. Eager to capture it. Just to silence the song forever. That's why I wanted you."

I lean forward, pinning her with my gaze as I tell her, "Aria, that was before I held you. No matter how much you choose to hate me, I swear I'll never let you go. You mean so much more to me than I would dare to admit to anyone."

CHAPTER 19

BANGED ON THE DOOR.

The stove ticks with the flame licking up from the burner and I turn it to medium before setting the pot of water on it.

I can't get over Carter's confession.

I would never go to the half of the estate where my father does his business. My mother died on the second floor in that half of the house and I swear I can still feel her there.

Whatever he thinks happened, didn't.

I never interrupted my father's work or even attempted to be anywhere near his business. I never banged on the door. I never called out that I needed anyone for anything.

I wouldn't dare.

Carter chose wrong. The woman who called out to him and saved him… she wasn't me.

I'm not his songbird luring him into the forest. I'm not the girl he thought he loved yet grew to hate.

It was never supposed to be me.

The hollow emptiness I've felt since he left me there in the den all alone, is unexplainable. I should be happy; I should tell him how wrong he was to take me. I should confess that voice he heard didn't belong to me. Instead, I swallow the dark secret down and let it choke me as I watch the pot of water boil.

"What are you making?" Daniel asks me and disrupts my thoughts. "Damn, you look like hell," he says, scratching the back of his head. In bare feet, faded jeans, and a plain white t-shirt, he looks relaxed, but he can't hide the exhaustion in his expression.

"Ditto," I tell him and spoon the potatoes into the pot. I've already cut everything else I need to make potato salad. Now I just wait. My mother used to make the best potato salad. I swear it's better the day after though, once it sits in the fridge for a full night.

I'm not hungry at all. I'm simply going through the motions, pretending the truth of my situation doesn't destroy every fiber inside of me.

Daniel opens the fridge as I spoon in the last few chunks. With the door open and his face hidden from me as he reaches for something, he asks me, "Want to talk about it?"

A genuine, yet sad smile tugs at my lips.

"You want to talk about *your* problems?" I ask him back.

"I asked you first," he says with a hint of humor, shutting the door and revealing a jug of orange juice.

"You sound like your brother," I tell him absently.

"Well shit," he tells me, pulling out a glass. It clinks on the counter as he smiles at me. "Don't go offending me left and right there, Aria," he jokes, and I let the small laugh bubble up although it sounds subdued and futile.

I stir the hard potatoes even though I know I don't need to. But I completely forgot the timer, and the realization makes me lean forward to start it.

With the beep of it being set, and the numbers counting down, I take a step back and lean against the counter.

"What'd he do this time?" Daniel asks me, mirroring my position as he leans on the other side.

"Nothing new," I tell him and the honesty in those words is what hurts the most.

The soft smile that lingered on his lips vanishes at my reply, and so I focus on the numbers, watching them as if I could speed them up if only I stare hard enough.

"Why won't he let me leave?" I ask him in a whisper.

Because he thinks you're someone else. Someone who saved him.

My throat dries, and my words crack as I tell him, "This isn't right."

It's silent for a long while, with only the sound being the water beginning to boil again.

"Because he cares for you," Daniel finally says, and I look him in the eyes, letting him see the real effect Carter Cross has on me.

"What a way to show it. Killing my family is just the cherry on top." My sarcastic response makes Daniel's expression harden.

"I have opinions of your father as well," he tells me softly, in a tone I haven't heard from him yet. My heart slams once and I'm forced to look him in the eyes. "I'll keep them to myself though," he tells me and then opens the fridge to put the orange juice back.

No doubt so he can leave me. So he doesn't have to tolerate my self-pity.

"And what about everyone else? Everyone I've ever known and loved?" I can barely breathe as I push him for justification.

"If you knew the truth," he tells me, facing me after shutting the fridge doors, "you wouldn't blame him." There's so much sincerity from him, I almost question my resolve.

"It's not just my father. So, I can, and I will blame him," I respond despondently, although I'm undecided on whether or not I believe my own words. When I look up at Daniel, my heart races chaotically and my body freezes.

Addison walks into the kitchen slowly, glancing from Daniel to me before offering me a small smile.

I can't breathe, and I don't know what to do. Anxiety pricks at my skin as she takes me in. My hair is still damp from the shower and I'm wearing a sleep shirt. I know my eyes show the lack of sleep and I look like a fucking mess.

More than that, I know Addison doesn't know who I am. She's normal. She's not forced to stay here like I am. Not the same way, at least.

Daniel plays it off far better than I do, wrapping his arm around Addison and giving her a soft kiss that forces her eyes back to him.

Shifting my weight, I glance at the timer and consider just leaving. I don't know what I'd say to her if I could even look her in the eyes right now.

Hi Addison, I know all about you and I know you don't know anything about me. I'm Carter's whore and he's going to kill my entire family soon, so I'm not allowed to leave. Nice to meet you.

Although that's not quite true. He admitted I mean more to him. *But it's because he thinks I'm someone else.* I've never felt more shame than I do right now. Every time I remember his words, I want to cry. Because he never wanted me and the moment he finds out the truth, he'll throw me away.

"Addison," Daniel's voice breaks up my spiteful thoughts as he says, "This is Aria. She's with Carter."

She's with Carter.

His words echo in my head as Addison smiles sweetly, pushing a lock of hair behind her ear and giving me a small, but friendly wave while staying where she is. "It's nice to meet you," she says kindly although she glances back at Daniel, no doubt wondering what's wrong with me.

"Hi," I offer up a single word and it croaks. I'm not *with* Carter; I'm against him. Except of course when I'm writhing underneath him.

"She's having a hard day," he tells her softly. My heart thumps in the way that hurts. The way that makes it feel like it's a tight ball that needs air and without it, it only gets tighter.

"Sorry." I swallow and tell her, "I'm not usually this weird." I roll my eyes and force a huff of a laugh up to ease the tension.

"You're not weird," she says and shakes her head at my words. "Just looks like you're having a hard day. That's totally reasonable," she adds with her hands waving out in front of her. "No judgment here."

I get the feeling that Addison is lonely from her tone, from her awkwardness. Or maybe I'm just projecting what I feel myself.

"Let's get back," Daniel says and the tightness in my throat grows. At least I got to meet her, and he said I'm with Carter. It's respectable. Well… to some. I'm sure to her it is.

"Sure," she tells him softly, with an answer spoken so low it's just for him, but then she raises her voice and speaks to me.

"Do you want to come with me to the gym tomorrow?"

I blink at her question. I'm surprised by it and not sure what to say.

"I just took a shower, so…" she starts to say and then rocks on her heels, wrapping her long hair around her wrist nervously.

I don't know if I'm even allowed to talk to her alone. Anger rises inside of me. I don't need permission. And one day, she'll know what I am and why I'm here. I can't hide it forever. Then what will she think of me?

"I don't know," I offer her. My gaze flickers to Daniel, but he stands easily beside Addison as if nothing's wrong. Like none of this is abnormal. The way the Cross boys do.

"Come on, we can drink wine while we do the back thing. It feels good," she says playfully. "I don't even like working out," she says and then looks at Daniel as if looking for permission, but not waiting for any. "But being locked up here is killing me and it's at least something different to do."

I watch the happiness drain from her and the smile only staying where it is because she's forcing it. "If you want company, I could really use some girl time," she says softly and then rolls her eyes as the emotion plays on her face. "Sorry," she huffs, shaking her head and leaning into Daniel as he holds her close. "I'm having a bad day too."

"I can work out," I tell her immediately, saying what she wants to hear just to take away her pain. I bite my lip as my heart sputters, wondering if Carter will stop me from going.

"I'm not a runner though," I warn her, trying to lighten the mood and force a small smile to my lips.

A genuine happiness lights up her face and she nods enthusiastically. "Oh, yeah, for sure." She laughs a little and breathes out easily, "If you ever see me running, you should start running too because there's someone behind me trying to get me," she jokes and doesn't see how Daniel responds. How his lips turn down and then press into a thin line. She's oblivious to it, but when she glances at him, he's quick to hide it. To offer her a peck of a kiss and then tell me although he's still looking at her, "I'm surprised she's using the gym at all."

She shrugs and points out, "There's not much else to do."

"We could just drink in the den?" I offer, grasping at a way to make it more acceptable. Carter knows I go to the den, so if Addison happened to come in there, he couldn't blame me for that. Well, he could. He'll probably find some way to stop it from happening as it is.

"That sounds perfect," she tells me with a broad smile. Daniel drags her away just as the timer goes off on the stove.

With a genuine smile and a short wave, she says sweetly, "I'll see you tomorrow."

It's kind of her, but I have no idea if I will.

Seeing how blind she is to everything, I'm reminded of how little I knew in my father's house. Even being oblivious to everything else, she still has a sad smile. I guess there's not much difference between knowing the truth and being blind to it. The effect is still the same.

CHAPTER 20

She's so lost, my Aria. I can't take my eyes from her as she stares at the comforter, her fingertips barely grazing it before she pulls the sheets back. Her expression is a mix of emotions. Sadness, confusion, the barest hint of anger. As the seconds pass, her chest flushes, and the lust of knowing what's to come takes over. But her brow stays furrowed as the bed groans with her small weight and the sheets rustle.

I don't think for a second that she's gotten over her anger, but it's not as raw as it was hours ago, let alone where she was yesterday. I still don't know what set her off at the front door, but I'm going to find out. She can't hide from me forever and I don't buy that bull-shit that there was nothing in particular. I watched the surveillance cameras over and over again. Something happened. I just don't know what.

I loosen my watchband, feeling the slick metal brush against my wrist before placing it back in its spot in the drawer. My gaze is still pinned on Aria, who's looking anywhere but back at me, her fingers fiddling with her necklace. Another second, another heavy breath.

The internal war is waning, but war leaves casualties, and I know she's taking record of everything she's lost and what's left of the woman she once was. I watch as she swallows, her chest rising higher and her breathing quickening.

She's so close to submitting everything to me. So, fucking close.

She doesn't even see it.

"You can't stay mad at me forever," I tell her as I pull my shirt over my head, grabbing it by the back of the collar.

I kick off my pants and ready myself to join her in bed, wondering if she'll tense when I wrap my arms around her. It's only fair that it guts me every night when she does it. I'm more than certain I deserve a harsher punishment.

"Do you know Addison spoke to me today?" she asks me with an edge of anxious-ness rather than acknowledging what I've said. She doesn't seem to have taken my confes-sion in the den earlier to heart, but she's more guarded now than she was before. Maybe she doesn't remember, but I thought it would change something between us. For the better.

My lips twitch with the hint of a feigned smile. "I do," I tell her, and she finally looks at me with a pleading expression.

"And?" she asks with clear curiosity but the desperation weighing heavier.

"And what?" I ask her as if I can't comprehend her line of questioning. Addison knows who I am, and I agree this situation is less than moral, but if she were to learn the truth, she would still love my brother. She'd still be family. She'll forgive me. Daniel's sins have been substantial, and she's forgiven him, mostly.

"Are you going to let me go?"

Her bottom lip wavers, but she waits patiently as I drop my hand to hers, thinking carefully about my next words.

"You'll like Addison," I tell her genuinely. "I won't stop you, and I won't be there to control you; I don't have any interest in it either."

"So, you don't care?" she questions.

"I care, but not in the way you think. Why would I want to stop you two from getting to know one another?" I ask her and then add, "My brother won't either. You two should get to know each other." I don't let on how anxious I am to hear what she tells Addison and whether or not she confides in her.

"I could tell her you're holding me hostage, that you trapped me in a cell for weeks…" she answers me with a cocked brow although she can't hide the sadness that still lingers in her expression. I can see so clearly that the very idea of how we became what we are now, tortures her.

"Would you really want to bring her into this?" I ask her pointedly. "She's having a hard time, and you and I both know she wouldn't react well to that."

"What if I say something I shouldn't?" she whispers quietly with genuine concern. I watch as she picks at the blanket, clearly on edge with the prospect of saying something that would cause more problems for our already delicate situation.

"Don't," is the only answer I have for her. "Be careful with what you say."

The silence stretches for a moment and I consider her.

"Maybe it's best you forget all this for a moment, and just talk to her as you would have anyone else a month ago."

I have to be so delicate with her. Ever so delicate. She doesn't answer, although the careful tiptoeing around her words slips away as she adjusts under the covers.

"We have other matters to discuss," I tell her as my thumb runs along the stubble of my jaw.

Although she nods, a heavy sigh leaves her in a staggering way, the sleep showing in her expression. She's overwhelmed and exhausted. Neither of us slept last night. Even after crying half the night, she woke every hour.

"What happened yesterday can't happen again. You have a choice. You can take your punishment now, or you can have it after your date with Addison."

Her body tenses and she struggles to form words, her lips parting and strangled breaths taking the place of whatever her question is.

"You won't be sending me back to the cell then?" she finally asks, her voice as strained as her body is stiff.

"That wouldn't do you any good." I wrap my arm around her, comforting her and leave a small kiss on the crown of her head. I whisper, "I told you, you shouldn't be left alone. This punishment is to benefit us. I promise you that," I tell her and feel the weight of everything looming in my thoughts.

I can see her swallowing her words. Practically reading her mind, I can see how she wants to tell me that we would be better if I would let this war go or let her go, but she doesn't dare speak it.

"What is it?" she asks me.

"I haven't decided yet," I tell her honestly.

"Tomorrow then," she tells me softly with defeat in her expression and it shreds me, but tomorrow she'll see.

"Is this what it will always be like?" she asks. "I do something you don't like, and I'm punished for it and then fucked until I forget I hate you?"

I don't think she meant her question to be humorous, but a short chuckle makes my chest shake. Running my fingers down her arm, I decide to tell her more, to set boundaries. But with them comes new rules.

"In the bedroom, I want you to obey. Anywhere else," my blood pumps harder and hotter as I finish, "I want you as mine."

"There's a difference?" she asks with feigned sarcasm. That mouth of hers is going to get her in trouble. Her disobedience shouldn't make me as hard as it does. As much as I love it, tomorrow night she'll be punished. There's no mistaking that.

"You already know there is," I say and although my voice comes out deep and foreboding, I try to lighten it. "It's time for a new game, Aria."

"No games." Her voice rises, and she has to lower it before adding, "I'm done playing games with you, Carter."

"You'll never be done with me." My words whisper against her skin. "You already know that."

Her fingernails dig into the sheets, pulling them tighter as she continues to avoid looking at me. I know why she doesn't want to meet my heated gaze. It will make hers fill with desire, too. She can't deny what she feels for me and how much power is in the tension between us. The push and pull that drives me wild does the same for her. The difference is that I can admit it; even if it will destroy me, I can fucking admit what she does to me.

"What do you want?" she asks me although she stares straight ahead, her expression flat and indifferent. "Tell me what you want from me," she says, and a spike of anger plays in her tone. "Tell me what it means to be yours," she asks through clenched teeth and I merely stare back at her. She already knows. We both know that she knows exactly what it means.

"Here you fuck me… you punish me like you did before." I don't miss how her eyes darken as she gazes around the room, looking to where I've spanked her, throat fucked her, made her cum harder than she ever had before.

"Yes," I tell her and watch as her pupils dilate and her legs scissor to ease some of the heat growing between her legs.

"And what do you expect outside of this room?" she asks and when she does, her voice wavers. She knows how much is at stake.

"For them to fear you." Her eyes flash to mine and suddenly my songbird is very much interested. I continue, "The way they fear me."

She laughs a sad and pathetic sound, ripping her gaze from me as she shakes her head. Her soft lips part, but no words come out and instead, she continues to shake her head and stares at the knob of the bathroom door across the room. Looking anywhere but at me.

"Fear is easy to attain," I tell her the simple fact. And it truly is. Keeping it is the curse that never fades. But I can bear the weight of that burden. She only needs to play the part. They have to believe it.

She shakes her head gently as if I don't understand. She tells me, "I want to draw. Maybe own a studio one day. That's my ambition. Or sell some of my pieces to people who would love them the way I do. I want them to feel what I feel when they look at them." I can see the light of hope in her eyes as she tells me a dream of hers I would never have known otherwise. I can give her that, so easily. All she had to do was tell me. "That's the only thing I've ever wanted beyond being happy. Having a family and making them happy."

A family.

I can give her that too, and the thought of her swollen with my child makes me force back a groan of want in my throat. Closing my eyes, I remind myself she needs time. All in good time. Once the war is over, everything will change.

Opening my eyes, I ask her, "And what does any of that have to do with what I've asked of you?" My question catches her off guard. "You forget the world you live in." A family, a gallery. It's all so easily attainable. But only when we have control. And that requires fear. They *must* fear her.

I ask her, "You want that studio? A gallery? Children, Aria? Do you think your name alone is one that wouldn't put a target on your back?" She flinches at the question and I can see the doubt and worry play across her face. Her lips turn down as her breathing picks up. It doesn't matter if Aria stands beside me or not; the minute she was given the name Talvery, her entire life was at risk.

"Anything that gives you pride or happiness is a weakness waiting to be exploited. But only if anyone would dare to cross you. And Aria, if you haven't noticed, the stunt I pulled the other night will lead to whispers of what you mean to me. And that makes you a far greater weakness to exploit than you ever were to your father."

"So, that's what I am? A weakness?"

The tension grows between us as her expression softens but stays riddled with curiosity. She whispers a question I know has been torturing her. I watch her soft lips as she asks, "What do I mean to you? *Me.* Not the girl you thought I was."

I replay her words that one of her greatest ambitions was to make her family happy, feeling my heartbeat slow as if time is forced to pause for me to consider how to answer her.

The mere idea of ensuring her happiness is becoming a greater ambition to me than anything else has ever been. If I spoke those words to her now, she'd laugh in my face. She doesn't see what I see. She doesn't know what I know. I could never tell her. I don't have the words even if she was ready for them.

She doesn't have the forgiveness to offer me for what I've put her through and what I'm going to put her through.

She wouldn't believe me if I told her this is for her. That it's all for her. And if she did, she'd still use it against me. She doesn't even realize the woman she can be. The defiance and stubbornness that makes her perfection in my eyes.

"I'll show you what you mean to me, Aria." My voice is rough and deep but holds nothing but sincerity. "Until then, the new game has started. This room is for fucking you, punishing you and giving you pleasure beyond imagine. And outside of this room, you will be mine, and you will demand respect and earn the fear that's owed to you."

Her hazel-green eyes brim with something I've yet to see.

"Carter Cross," she whispers my name. "I don't know that I'm the woman you think I am." Her words are etched with sorrow as if she really believes what she says.

I lean in closer to her, resting my lips against her shoulder and running the tip of my nose along her skin. My lips caress her jaw where I kiss her gently and then nip the lobe of her ear.

I whisper along the shell of her ear, watching goosebumps form down her shoulder and across her chest, pebbling her nipples. "You have so much to learn and so much to accept, but Aria," I open my eyes to stare into hers before I continue, "I know you won't disappoint me."

My gaze focused on her lips, I speak more to myself than to her, "It's all been leading to this."

CHAPTER 21

I HAVE THREE HOURS AND A SINGLE BOTTLE OF WINE. I SHOULD'VE GRABBED A SECOND bottle, knowing Carter will be waiting for me in his bedroom when this rendezvous is over.

There's a tension in my chest, a faint flicker of life in my heart with the nerves of what's waiting for me.

The idea of running back to the hideaway room flutters into my mind every so often. Carter held up his word that he wouldn't come for me the first time I fled there, but what are the odds he'll do that again? If I try to avoid the punishment and him, I have a feeling everything will only get worse. There's a single distraction I'm grateful for though. Someone to talk to and someone who doesn't know what I'm going through. I'm indebted to Addison, even if she has no idea. In fact, I'm grateful she has no idea.

Popping the cork out of the bottle, I stop pretending as if hiding will do anything at all. I may fear Carter at times, along with the thoughts of punishment, but there's a darker piece of my soul that craves it.

I can't deny the idea of being throat fucked or tied up by the most powerful man I've ever met has every nerve ending in my body lit like a fuse waiting to go off.

Even as I pour the wine, listening to the sound of it, I think of every way Carter's punished me before. How hot and eager he made me for more as he played my body against my emotions. Even still, I'm numb with grief.

It makes no sense. Save the fact that my heart is truly torn and in disarray.

The dark liquid swirls as I set the bottle down and lift my glass to my lips, breathing in the dark blend to fill my lungs. Maybe I've truly lost it all. Maybe I'm crazy at this point.

I need something to give. Everything is about to fall apart in front of my eyes and just out of reach. But how do I change any of it? What I truly need is mercy from a heartless man dead set on revenge.

"There you are," I hear Addison before I see her and my heart attempts to leap up my throat, beating chaotically as if caught in an unspeakable act.

"Hey," I breathe out and my voice wavers. The wine in my glass swishes from being jostled and to steady it, I hold the stem with both hands.

"This kind of feels like a blind date, doesn't it?" Addison jokes with a genuine smile.

Her mood is greatly improved from yesterday. She almost seems like a different person from what I've seen before.

Carefree and excited. There's a sweetness about her and the air around her as she walks into the room. Without hesitation, she picks up a glass and fills it.

"It kind of does," I agree with a dry laugh and a half-smile and the awkwardness wanes. My hands are clammy as she lifts up her glass for a cheers and I do the same.

"To new friends." She tilts her head with the same smile on her lips, but it's softer as the glass clinks.

Sighing, she settles into the sofa, making herself comfortable. "I've only been in this room the one time," Addison starts talking although she's not looking at me at all. She tucks her legs up under her as she sets the glass down on the end table and stares at a black and white photograph framed just to the right of the mantel. "Carter wanted to show me he'd hung my pictures," she says softly and then glances at me. "I think he just wanted to make me smile and feel welcomed, you know?"

My brow raises in surprise. "These are yours?" I ask her, finding the conversation a wonderful distraction for the well of emotion that constantly pulls me into the tide of depression I've been feeling. The idea of Carter doing anything for her just to make her happy has questions drifting in the forefront of my mind, but I swat them away. No thoughts of Carter or anything else. I've proven to myself I'm incapable of processing it all.

Every few minutes, my mood has changed today. Whether I think of Nikolai and his impending execution, my father and what he did to Carter and the Cross brothers, the fact that he hasn't come for me, or Carter himself and the cruel things he says and the murders he has planned.

Yet the prospect of falling into his arms for him to soothe all the painful twists and turns this week has given me, somehow clouds my judgment and that's where I want to stay. Accepting a comfort and turning my back on reality.

Maybe that's why I'm growing to hate myself. Yes, I truly think I'm going insane. And I'd blame Carter if only I could remember what he's done and what he plans to do when he kisses me and takes all the pain away.

"All of them but those two," she says and points out two abstract watercolor paintings behind us that straddle the entrance to the den. Tugging my skirt down, I clear my throat and smile. The kind of smile I've given others before when I know that's what they expect to see.

Sometimes that smile turns into a genuine one, and that's what I hope this turns into. I pray that's what it will be.

"You're very talented." I have to admire her work yet again. It's not the first time I've noticed them. "They're stunning."

Her fair features blush and her shoulders dip a little as she waves me away and jokingly says, "Aw shucks," causing me to let out a gentle laugh. "That's kind of you."

"I love art," I tell her and for some reason the generic statement makes me scrunch up my nose. "I love the ones that make you feel." My hands gesture in the air toward my chest to make my point. "Like with yours." My words fail me, and I have to close my eyes, shaking my head for a moment, so I can put the right words in order to get out exactly what I mean. "It seems so simple, even with the black and white taking away even more of what we'd see normally. But in the simplicity, there's so much more there that speaks to a raw side of your soul like you can feel what the photographer feels, or any artist by focusing on an object that would have such little meaning if you saw it in passing. In the art, it begs to tell you a story and you can already feel what the story is about."

"I knew you were a girl of my own heart," Addison says and offers me a kind smile. "I have to admit," she leans forward, hushing her voice, "I've seen your drawings and I could say the same right back to you."

"Thank you," I tell her, feeling the happiness of a shared interest, but also realizing the ice has been broken and the questions she has for me are probably similar to the ones I have for her. The questions beg to slip through and bring me back to the train of thought I was on moments ago.

It's too easy to just be friendly, to sit on the surface of the world we live in and pretend that everything is just fine.

"So where are you from?" Addison asks me, taking another sip, her lips already staining from the wine, and then she reaches for the throw blanket. I finally take a seat on the armchair I've been leaning against. The leather groans as I sink down in it and sit cross-legged to be comfortable.

"Close to here," I tell her and ignore how my heart beats harder, my fingers tracing along my ankle to keep them busy while I carefully avoid details. I can't look her in the eyes as I wonder if she knows where I come from and who my family is. My throat dries but before it can cause my words to crack, I quickly ask her, "What about you?"

Glancing at her, I can feel the anxiety course harder in my veins, but her expression stays casual and easy. I get the impression that Addison is more laidback than I am. Harder to shake. Stronger in a lot of ways. And for some reason, that thought weighs against my chest heavily as she answers.

"I grew up around here, but left and traveled for the past, like five years, almost six years now?" Her voice is light as she continues. "I've lived all over."

"That's amazing," I say with wonder. I've never left home. I've never ventured outside of the parameters I was given.

"Did you live on your own?"

Addison nods with a sly grin and then clucks her tongue. "I was kind of running away at first," she says, and her voice is lower as she shrugs and then takes a heavy gulp of wine. She licks her lower lip and stares at the glass as she says, "It was too hard to stay." She peeks up at me and her piercing green eyes stay with mine as she says, "It was far too easy to just keep going, you know? Rather than staying still and having to deal with it all."

The jealousy I felt only moments ago instantly turns to compassion. Her tone is too raw, too open, and honest not to feel the pain of her confession.

"Yeah, I get that," I tell her and settle deeper into the seat. "I really do."

Time passes quietly as I slowly pick through the questions, one that won't open up a raw wound unless she cares to go there herself. "What brought you back?" I ask.

"Daniel." She rolls her eyes as she says his name, but she can't hide how her smile grows, how her cheeks flush and she pulls her legs into herself as if his name's only home is on her lips. "We bumped into each other a few towns over and he brought me back."

My smile matches hers as she continues her story. "We grew up together—kind of. I kind of grew up with him and his brothers I guess. It's a complicated story," she says then waves me off, wine glass in her hand, although she takes a long minute before sipping it again, staring past me at the mantel.

"This one is delicious," she says before finishing it off.

"I love the dark reds." My statement is spoken as absently as she spoke hers.

"They're the best," she says wide-eyed and then reaches for the bottle for another glass.

"You two getting along all right?" Daniel's voice carries through the den before he's even taken a step into the room.

My skin pricks with unease, being brought back to reality when I'd been slipping into a hiding place of Addison's story. I keep my smile plastered on my face as he glances between the two of us.

I wonder if he thinks I'd tell her why I'm here and what happened. That I'd warn her away from Daniel and expose that he knew. That I'd beg her to help me and frighten her.

My heart feels like it collapses in on itself as the two of them go back and forth in lighthearted banter although a touch of tension is obvious.

"Always hovering," Addison says although there's a quiet reverence there that Daniel doesn't seem to grasp. He sighs and runs his hand down the back of his head before saying, "I just came to see if you two needed anything."

Addison playfully slaps his arm as he stops behind the sofa where she's sitting. "Liar. You came to eavesdrop."

"You got me," he says and lets her shoo him away with a simple, "Get out," but not without a kiss.

Addison lifts from her seat, making the blanket around her waist fall as her ass lifts up. "Love you," she whispers and then gives him a peck. Then another and another. Three in quick succession.

With the tip of his nose brushing against hers he says with his eyes closed, "Love you too."

And there isn't an ounce of me that doesn't believe them both. My smile falls and there's no way I could fake one in this moment. Love exists in their exchange; it breathes in the air between them.

It's undeniable and nothing like what binds me to Carter. It's not lust, it's a meeting of souls, the two of them needing one another and recognizing that truth.

"You need anything?" Daniel asks again as my gaze drifts to the side table. The edge of the carved wood grants me a small escape from their display.

"Aria," Daniel's voice is raised as he addresses me directly. "You need anything?" he asks me, and his eyes carry his real question, *Are you okay?*

"I'm fine," I tell him as evenly as I can and then clear my throat before reaching for my glass again.

It takes a long moment after he's left for the tense air to change.

"So, you and Carter?" Addison asks me, cocking a brow to be comical. She sips the wine but keeps her eyes on me and the expression on her face makes me laugh.

"Yeah, me and Carter," I tell her tightly, but with humor.

"He's keeping you trapped here too, huh?" she asks and the easy interaction that existed before turns sharp.

"You could say that," I reply but my voice is flat. Chewing on the inside of my cheek, I consider telling her the truth for a split second, but there's no way I ever would. Not because I don't trust her, but because I'm truly ashamed in this moment.

I've given up. I'm lying in bed with the devil. And as much as Addison appears to like me, there's no way she'd ever respect me if she knew the truth. I don't even respect myself.

"I'm guessing he chased you?" she asks speculatively. "The Cross boys tend to chase."

"Again, you could say that."

"When I first I met Carter," Addison starts to tell me a story, realizing I'm not open to sharing my own Carter tale, while her thin finger drifts over the edge of the wine glass, running circles around the rim of it. "He was different from the other brothers."

"How so?" I ask, watching her finger as my shame eases.

She glances at me for a moment with a pinched expression. "He wasn't around as often, and he was always quiet when he was around, but you knew the moment he was in the house. He *was* the authority."

"What do you mean?"

"Like their father wasn't the best, you know? After their mother died, he took it really hard." She swallows as if a painful memory threatened to choke her if she continued, but she goes on. "So, if anyone needed anything, it was Carter who was asked. Carter who made the rules. Carter who got whatever was needed."

I watch her expression as she tells me their story.

"This one time, it was so stupid." Her eyes get glassy but she shakes her head and brushes her hair back. "These kids stole our bikes," she tells me, forcing strength to her voice.

"Tyler took me to the corner store and we left our bikes outside, and these assholes stole them." She laughs the kind of laugh that you force out when you want a release from the need to cry.

"You knew Tyler?" I ask her, feeling a chill run down my skin, leaving goosebumps along their path. Nikolai told me once that when you have that feeling run through you, it means someone's walked over your grave.

She only nods, her eyes reflecting a sad secret, and then continues. "It had to be these guys, they were older and there were like six of them. Grown ass men who had nothing better to do than steal bikes from high school kids." She breathes in deeply before smoothing the blanket down across her lap and telling me, "We walked home and the last ten minutes it rained the whole way. We were soaked when we got back."

"Daniel wasn't there; Tyler went to him first because he didn't like to bother Carter. None of the boys ever liked to bother him with petty stuff, you know?" she asks me, and I don't know how to respond but she doesn't give me time to regardless.

"So, Carter was there and asked what happened. He was quick to anger back then, so much different from now," she tells me, and I look at her as if she's crazy, but she doesn't see. She picks at the blanket and continues. "He and Tyler left together in the truck, Carter told me to stay back and within hours, both bikes were in the back of the truck safe at home. Tyler was never one to fight. He was a lover and a kind old soul, but he said those guys wouldn't mess with us anymore. I kind of wish I'd seen what Carter had done." She says the last words like a spoken thought that had just come to her. All I can think is that she's probably better off not having witnessed what Carter did to those men.

"I guess that's not the best story," she says and shrugs. "Sorry, I kind of suck at telling stories."

I offer her a soft smile and say, "I liked it."

"Anyway, that's what Carter does. He takes what he wants and doesn't take any prisoners or put up with any bullshit."

Her words strike me in a way I can't explain and the same tears that she'd wiped away haphazardly at the start of her story, threaten to fall from mine.

"Are you okay?" she asks me, although judging by the way her smile wavers, I could ask her the same.

My lips part ready to do what I've always done, to tell everyone that I'm fine. To pretend like nothing's wrong.

"Only if you want to talk," she quickly adds, practically tripping over her words. Even her hands come up in protest. "I'm not usually this weird, I've just been on edge lately and it's so nice to be able to talk to someone else. Someone who's not...," she stops and holds her breath, searching for the right words but none come. I can see it in her eyes that she's suffering like I am. Something's wrong and I can only guess that it's because she's trapped here. Trapped like I am, but for such different reasons.

"I'm okay, and I get it... I do." My attempt to reassure her falls flat. She offers me a weak half smile that doesn't reach her eyes.

"I wish I could tell you something," she whispers and then shakes her head as if she's losing her mind. Maybe I'm not the only crazy one in this room. Wiping under her eyes she looks to the door and exhales a harsh breath. "I should go." Maybe she had a curfew time too. Or maybe she just doesn't want to break down in front of a stranger.

Glancing at the clock, I see nearly three hours has already passed. I feel like we've only just sat down.

"Yeah, I should too." I clear my throat and try to think of something to say that's comforting for her even though I hardly know her. A piece of her though, her heart and soul, I know well. "I'm here if you ever want a drinking buddy," I offer.

"Or to binge-watch something good on Netflix?" she offers, and the genuine happiness lights up her expression.

"Sure," I offer her a smile with my upturned voice and imagine the loss I can already feel doesn't exist.

"This might sound weird," Addison tells me as she picks up her wine glass and downs the last remaining bit before looking me in the eyes, "but you look like you could use 'a somebody.'" She sets the glass down, the clinking of the glass breaking up the white noise that drowns me when Addison stares down at me, standing up on her way to leave. She pushes the hair off of her shoulder and tells me solemnly, "I didn't have 'a somebody' for a long time. And I know how it feels."

It's hard to describe the pain and hollowness of having a stranger seem to see through you and when they look there, they want to help you, to be there for you with a genuine kindness. When you look back at them, you see it too. It's so obvious but speaking the truth would make it real, and it's so much more comforting to run and hide or pretend like everything is okay for at least a little while.

I have to clear my dry, scratchy throat before I tell her, "I might take you up on that."

CHAPTER 22

Carter

THE FLOOR CREAKING ALERTS ME TO HER COMING. THE BATHROOM LIGHT IS STILL on and the soft yellow light filters into the room, casting a shadow where she stands. Aria's never looked so tempting and radiant. Licking her lips in defiance even though there's fear and defeat in her gorgeous hazel eyes. Naked, with her skin flushed from the prospect of what's coming, she stands there caught in my gaze.

I've never been so hard in my fucking life. I know she needs this. We both need it. The last few days have been large steps back with only meager steps forward.

She stands before me as my equal, daring, and relentless, although on the opposite side from where I stand.

"Come," I command her as I sit on the chair and run my hand down my right thigh.

She walks in from the bathroom hesitantly, her body stiff but still she comes to me, stopping in front of me and waiting.

"Sit," I tell her, and she instinctively reaches for my hand as I pull her ass down to nestle in my crotch. She stiffens her back and continues to pretend she doesn't need this. She knows better if only she'd open her eyes.

"I've thought a lot about what's causing tension between us." The statement comes out deep and husky, unable to deny my desire for her. I let my middle finger slip along her shoulder and watch as it makes her nipples pebble. Her beautiful skin both flushes and at the same time pricks with goosebumps.

"The first thing I'm going to do is punish you." Her lips part with a quick breath, but she nods her head in understanding. "The second is to give you something you want, and something you need…" I pause my movement and wait for her beautiful hazel-green gaze to meet mine before adding, "If you take the punishment well."

Her breathing quickens, and I can see how her blood pumps harder in the veins of her neck but still, she nods in obedience. Her eyes continue to flicker to mine with questions, but she doesn't ask them.

"Lie across my lap," I tell her gently. There's no need to be firm, knowing what's to come. Nervously, she obeys but tries to hold on to the chair as her balance is off and her legs dangle aimlessly.

I adjust her, so she's positioned perfectly, her hip on my right thigh and she gasps in protest, but it's short-lived.

"Hands behind your back," I command her, and she obeys, although she's awkward in my lap, trying to balance herself. It doesn't matter though, the second I grip both her wrists in my left hand and press them to the small of her back, she's steady. And that's how she'll stay until I decide this punishment is over. Her pussy is already glistening; the mix of fear and desire is a powerful thing.

My blunt fingernails trail over her pale, supple ass as I give her a simple command. "Tell me why you ran from me when I gave you access to the front door." My chest feels tight with worry that she'll never see. I won't allow her to question my control. Not again. Never again. She needs to know in every fiber of her being, that I can take control from her but that more than that, she needs it.

"I need to know what set you off, Aria," I say clearly enough to be sure she understands how much this means to me when she doesn't answer.

"I don't know," she tells me with a tense voice before blowing a strand of hair out of her face.

The lying will come to an end shortly.

Slap! My hand stings all the way down to my wrist as the bright mark lands on her right cheek and Aria cries out, her hips bucking uselessly as I hold her down with a firm grip and do the same to her other cheek. Moving to her center, I slap her there and then again on the right cheek. All the while, she writhes in my lap and cries out with muffled screams of protest.

My heart hammers and my dick hardens when my fingers drift lower to her cunt. Her breathing hitches, and her entrance clenches around my fingertips but she gets no reward for lying to me.

I speak softly as I gently lay my hand on her hot cheek, rubbing soothing strokes over the sensitized marks. "Tell me the truth." My command falls into the silence that mixes with her strangled moans as the pain and pleasure combine. I dip my fingers to her cunt, letting them run through her slick folds. My middle finger trails down to her clit and I circle it once, tempting her and rewarding her obedience as she stays where she is, where she belongs on my lap. "Tell me, Aria."

With a shaky breath, Aria's back attempts to bow and her thighs clench. She visibly swallows, and I know she's going to cum, so I stop. My finger is still pressed against her, but without the movement, she lifts her eyes to mine, breathing heavily with her lips parted.

"I don't know," she answers, her mesmerizing hazel eyes begging me to believe her. I don't wait for her to prepare. I spank her other cheek and then move back to the right before returning to the left repeatedly, feeling a burn that runs up my arm as my hand goes numb.

Aria's scream echoes in the room as her body stiffens across my lap. She seethes, sucking in air through clenched teeth as tears prick her eyes. My own breathing rages from me as I land the last blow and keep her steady where she is.

Gulping for breath and hanging her head low while attempting to fight the need to struggle against the hold I have on her, she turns her head away from me. But I see the tears.

Instantly, I place my hand over her heated skin, ignoring how she jumps and applying enough pressure to soothe the pain. My heart skips once, then twice as she struggles to maintain her composure, the tears falling freely as her face reddens.

"I've got you," I whisper to her and she turns to glance up at me, a look of pure hate on her expression. "Tell me what happened, and it stops," I offer her again, and watch as her bottom lip wavers. "I won't let you go until you tell me."

Her face crumples and she sobs out, "It's stupid," before letting the tears fall again.

I continue rubbing soothing circles, occasionally squeezing her ass to keep the blood flowing and the nerve endings on edge. The endorphins flowing in her blood will make her pleasure that much greater. Both the body and mind always prefer pleasure to pain.

And I'll give her both. Although she hates me now, she'll love me when this is over.

My fingers drift to her core this time, pressing inside of her and I'm instantly rewarded with her arching her neck, her eyes closed as a small moan of pleasure drifts from her reddened lips. Her cheeks are tearstained, and a few droplets still linger on her lashes.

Her cunt clamps around my fingertips, begging me for more.

A strangled moan fills the hot air as my cock hardens even more and presses against her belly. Fuck, I want her. I *need* to have her tonight and claim her again. To remind her of how much she belongs with me.

"Tell me now, Aria," I demand, my voice deep and rumbling with the need I feel alive in every cell of my body.

She only whimpers, and then defiantly shakes her head. "I don't know, I swear I—"

Before she can even finish, I slap her ass as hard as I can. The pain that had numbed brightens back to life. Under her ass cheeks, on her ass, on her pussy. I spank her in a new spot each time, rotating between them but the pace is ruthless, the slaps unforgiving. My jaw clenches and the pain rips up my arm as she screams out.

"Stop lying to me," I barely get the command out through clenched teeth as I stop the punishment, forcing myself to breathe and instantly soothe her reddened skin.

She heaves in a breath and then another. A shudder runs down her body that morphs her sobs to moans. She's close to this being so much more. But what I want are answers and she won't cum until I get them. I'll make damn sure of that.

The hair on the side of her face, wet from her tears, is stuck to her skin as she says, "I saw the date."

Her upper body rocks and she tries to move away from me, groaning with a pained expression before telling me, "I saw the date on your phone." Her words are spastic at best, but I know I heard her right.

My breathing is still erratic, my hand stinging with pain and my lungs refusing to move as I take in what she's telling me.

My fingers loosen on her wrists slowly as I wrap my arm around her waist, careful not to touch her ass until I'm ready to set her on my lap.

She winces and seethes, not moving her arms even though she freely could.

Bringing her into my chest, I let her collapse in my arms. Her hands lift to my shoulders as the tears soak into my shirt. The feel of her cheek on my shoulder as she buries her head in the crook of my neck is already a soothing balm to me.

"You saw the date?" I prompt her to tell me more. To explain it to me as I comfort her.

"The day before was my mother's—" she gasps, not finishing and I run my hand up and down her back, letting her cling to me.

I shush her, letting my warm breath whisper along her hair and I wait for her to settle.

"You missed the anniversary of your mother's death?" I ask her, feeling a pain inside me crumple every bit of strength I have.

"Yes," she croaks and tries to climb closer to me as if she wasn't already pressed against me. "It was the first time," she says in between breaths, "that I didn't go to her grave."

Holding her while she cries, knowing the pain she's feeling could have been avoided so easily. I could have done something to help her, even if it meant gathering dozens of men to protect her while she saw to her mother's grave. I could have done something if only I'd known.

"I'm sorry." I try to put every ounce of compassion into my apology. "Please believe how sorry I am," I say and kiss her hair, her shoulder and then pull her away to kiss her swollen red lips.

She buries herself back into the crook of my neck and then cries out as her ass brushes against my pants.

"Thank you for telling me," I say as I maneuver her on my lap, so I have access to her cunt. "Hold on to me," I command her, and she does instantly. She needs someone to hold and someone to hold her, I've never been more sure of it.

"This will make the pain go away," I tell her, although my words are hollow. Pleasure can hide only one specific kind of pain. I rub her clit first, letting the intensity from the unique pleasure that comes after both pain and mourning flow through her.

She bites down on my shoulder, her fingernails digging into my skin through my shirt. She writhes on my lap, so close to the edge already, although each time her ass brushes against the fabric of my pants, her voice hitches, and her grip on me tightens.

Pressing my fingers inside her, I stroke her ruthlessly and butt my palm against her clit. Her back bows and I have to hold her closer to me, laying my hand against her shoulder.

"Cum for me," I whisper in her ear. My cock is hard and desperate to be wrapped in her hot cunt, but I can't take my pleasure from her like this.

It's all for her.

"Carter," she gasps my name as her body rocks with pleasure and her head falls back. I don't stop until she's trembling, and her cries have stopped completely.

My heart races against hers, sweat covering my skin and every muscle in my body coiled.

Time passes slowly as I wait until she's calm and coherent. And each second, I carefully select the words she needs to hear.

With weak balance, she finally lifts her head to look me in the eyes. Her expression pinches as she leans back, feeling her raw ass brush against my pants once again, but this time her lips part and another orgasm threatens from the faint touch.

"I need more from you," I tell her, breaking her moment and forcing her hazel eyes to stare into mine.

"I have you here," I say as I let my fingers fall to her pussy and then cup it, watching as she gasps, throwing her head back and rocking herself into my hand. My lips drop to her throat, whispering against her skin, "So needy."

Before she can get off again, I stop and wait for her eyes to reach mine, dark with desire and lit with lust. "I'm getting to you here," I tell her and smooth her hair back on the crown of her head.

A moment passes with a tense beating in my chest before I drop my fingers to her chest, between her bare breasts and ask her, "What about here?"

My eyes flicker between where I'm touching her and her own gaze, now swirling with a hopelessness and sadness I wish I could take away.

The ever-present vise tightens on my heart as she asks me in a whisper, "If I gave you that, what would I have left?"

It tightens further, and my heart refuses to beat. The answer is so obvious. "You'd have me." I watch her expression remain unchanged and I have to look away.

Breathing in deeply, I ignore whatever I'm feeling, every last bit of it, knowing logically, she's close. I know she is.

She comes and goes, and that's because of her father. If he wasn't in the picture, she would be mine completely. And Nikolai…

"You know what I need, Carter," Aria finally speaks and when she does her voice cracks. Tears linger in her eyes. "For you to have my heart, you can't destroy it. You can't kill them."

I cave. Knowing what this could be, I offer her something, just to have a chance to break through the wall that guards her heart. "I'll call him, but you'll be silent."

With a look of shock and gratitude, she leans in closer to me and starts to speak but I press my finger against her lips, silencing her and halting her movements.

Fear is power. And every day, I fear her never loving me more than the day before. I've given her the power and I don't know how I let that happen.

"I will call your father and you'll listen only. Is that clear?"

Although she nods, she doesn't speak until I move my finger away. "Yes, Carter."

It occurs to me how little she obeys unless she has hope. I instantly regret telling her I would call her prick of a father.

I need to give her hope in something else. Because when this war is over, her father will be dead, and she'll have to find forgiveness or be miserable and hate me forever.

CHAPTER 23

Aria

I DON'T KNOW HOW I SLEPT AT ALL.

I keep wondering if he's really going to do it. If Carter is going to call my father and if he does, what would he say? I almost ask Carter if I can call Nikolai, just to tell him I'm safe but I don't know how Carter would react, and I don't want to push him when he's given me this hope.

If my father knew Carter gave me Stephan to kill, literally forced to stay put with a knife placed in my hand, wouldn't that offer some sort of truce between them?

My hands are shaking so much from the anticipation and anxiety of what they'll say that the picture in front of me is blank, not from lack of inspiration, but from the inability to create even a simple line.

An hour has passed with me sitting on the floor of Carter's office, listening to the tapping of keys and the steady tick-tock of the clock. All the while, I can't focus on anything. Not a damn thing except for when Carter's going to call him like he said he would.

Glancing up at Carter, I catch his gaze and I know the look in my eyes is pleading and expectant.

"You need more." Carter's voice is deep and low, and it booms through the office. Or, maybe it's just that I'm on high alert and everything is thrumming to life as I wait for what's to come.

My throat tightens, feeling the dejection once again for the one thing that could change everything, but I stand on shaking legs and go to him.

It doesn't escape me that he has me under control again. That my only desire is to obey him, so he'll give me what he claimed he would. He may have given me false hope.

My heart flickers like a candle so close to its flame going out. He wouldn't do that to me. I refuse to believe it. I know he feels something for me. He must. I can feel it in the very marrow of my bones.

Carter pushes the phone farther away from him, an old desk phone, and I stare at it as I hear him push the laptop and stacks of papers out of the way.

It's right there. *Just call him.*

Pat, pat, he pats the top of the desk and I take the hint, lying on my belly, knowing he's going to lift the dark red chiffon dress up my thighs and bare my backside to him.

My cheek presses against the hard desk and I can feel my heart hammer against it. Gripping on to the edge of the desk, I wait for the cool gel to hit my sore ass. There aren't any bruises this time, but somehow it hurts more. This morning I nearly cried waking up to the pain until Carter used the ointment.

Sucking in a deep breath, my eyes close and I feel Carter rub the soothing balm into my hot skin. It's tender still, but even more so, it makes me crave more of his touch.

A soft hum of gratitude and want leaves my lips, and it's met with a rough chuckle from Carter. Opening my eyes, I glance up at him, although I have to push the lock of hair out of my face.

My heart does that flickering again.

"It looks much better than how it was last night and this morning."

"It feels better now too," I tell him easily, watching his expression as he pays close attention to where he's rubbing the balm.

"You didn't tell me the entire truth last night," Carter says before opening a drawer and then closing it. My heart thumps once, thinking of what I left out but having nothing come to mind.

I don't know if he just put the gel back or if he's taken something else out.

Before I can answer, Carter tells me, "You forgot to mention your birthday."

He finally meets my gaze and there's a softness there that I hardly ever see from him, but it's the side I pine for most.

"I didn't think it was important," I try to speak, but my words are whispered. Of every reason I'm breaking apart, that fact is meaningless and even speaking it as if it could contribute to this pain is disrespectful to the tragedies that surround us.

He's gentle as he repositions me on the desk but doesn't pull my dress back down. It's bunched at my hips and that's what I'm thinking about when I hear the first cuff open and look up at the feel of metal grazing the skin on my wrists.

"Your other hand," Carter commands and I give it to him although I'm riddled with a slight fear.

"Carter?" His name comes out as a question as he handcuffs me to two metal loops on the side of his desk. Again, he repositions me, sliding my body down so I'm stretched on my belly across his desk.

"I don't have a gift for you at the moment," he says absently as he steps away from me, leaving the cool air to hit my ass which is still very much exposed to him. "But I'll have to find something nice for you."

The flicker instantly morphs into a thrumming with a slight fear of the unknown.

I try to turn around and look at him as he fiddles with something on the shelf. I don't see what he has but whatever it is, he has it in his hand.

"Carter, I'm sorry." My first instinct is to beg my way out of another punishment. My ass is still so sore. But even as the adrenaline spikes through me, I can't imagine he'd do it. That he'd punish me for not telling him it was my birthday. "Please," I whimper.

"Hush," he says, and his voice is calming as he lays a hand down on my lower back. His touch is an instant salve to my nerves. The rough pads of his thumbs rub soothing circles and that alone calms me. "This is for pleasure, songbird."

A slick oil drizzling between my ass crack makes me jump, but I'm held down by his hand and the cuffs. Again, he chuckles, deep and low at me, ever amused but I love it.

I love that sound.

"I need to spread you, and then you need to push back," he commands, and I force myself to swallow, feeling the pressure of a cool metal object press against my forbidden hole. I'm instantly hot and tense. The nerve endings come alive and the heat spreads like wildfire through my body and along my skin.

The thrumming intensifies, my heart slamming and lust consuming the ounce of fear that lingers.

A shudder of pleasure and a hint of stinging pain make me clench everything, but the second the tension is gone, Carter pushes the plug deeper inside of me. Oh. My. God.

I can barely breathe as the new sensation takes over. My nipples pebble and rub against the desk as I squirm beneath his ministrations. He fucks me with the butt plug, pushing it in and out, over and over.

"Carter," I moan and then whimper, feeling close to cumming so soon. I feel so full. So hot. The little hairs on the back of my neck rise as my head thrashes.

"Your cunt is clenching around nothing," Carter observes, and his deep voice forces my eyes open. Just as I feel the need to raise my ass higher, Carter pushes the plug in deeper and stops everything, leaving me feeling full and hot and on the edge of desire.

"Arch your back," Carter demands as he presses his fingers against my inner thigh, spreading my legs for him even though they tremble with the threat of an orgasm so close.

I swear I can feel it in my pussy. The arousal is there even though I'm so aware that nothing's inside of me… not there.

The metal of the cuffs digs into my skin, my ass is in the air, and each wrist bound to the desk. A soft moan escapes and the heated blushes rise up my face to my crown as Carter brushes his fingers across my clit and then up and down my pussy. "Should I tell your father the truth?" he asks me.

"Should I tell him I wanted you so badly that I was willing to start a war to keep you?"

While his words force a moan from me, they push my emotions over the edge.

It wasn't me he wanted.

The little voice in the back of my head reminds me, and I have to close my eyes tightly, pushing away the immediate sadness and dejection.

I feel tense and on edge in more ways than one. The swell of both emotion and lust beg me to tell him, but Carter's silent and his touch absent. I force my eyes open to see him watching me. His dark eyes staring deep into mine, searching for something.

I know I should tell him, but if he knew the girl who banged on the door calling out that she was in need wasn't me, would he want me still? I can't bear for that answer to be no.

"Do I need to gag you?" Carter asks. My heart hammers and my pulse quickens.

"For what?" I ask in return, but then immediately assure him, "I can be quiet," for whatever he's thinking. I'll do anything he asks.

"It's time to call your father," he tells me, and a mask slips over his face. An expression of indifference that makes the angular lines of his jaw look that much sharper. I can see the moment he changes into the Carter I first knew and hated. It happens right before my eyes; I see the darkness take over.

"You can stay on edge for it." His voice is a hum of both desire and amusement. "Think about how good it's going to feel when I fuck you and finally let you cum."

CHAPTER 24

ALL I CAN THINK ABOUT AS THE PHONE RINGS, IS HOW MUCH CONTROL I'M GOING to need not to fuck Aria senseless until she's screaming my name while her father is on the line.

I press the numbers slowly, one at a time, remembering the look of absolute agony on her face when I mentioned starting a war for her. I didn't mean for it to break her.

It's only the truth.

Putting the phone on speaker, the tension boils inside of me as the phone rings and Aria struggles on the desk.

Ring.

I trail my finger down her backside all the way to her knee, and she whimpers. "Hush," I tell her, watching goosebumps form along her smooth skin.

Ring.

"You don't want your father to hear you," I say and don't bother to whisper. The sound of her breathing hitching begs me to look into her eyes. They're pleading with me, and I swear I'll try to give her something from this call.

Something that will help her.

I'll show her what kind of a man her father is.

Ring.

The third ring is only partial, followed by a low click and a pause before I hear the voice of my enemy. "Cross," he answers the phone.

Anger erupts up my throat at the sound of his voice. I can only concentrate on Aria's tempting body sprawled on my desk to calm me. Oh, and she does. Letting my fingers delight in her soft touch, I drag them up her wet lips and slowly push against the plug in her ass.

The suppressed moan tugs a sick smile onto my face as I answer, "Talvery."

Continuing to fuck her ass with the plug and reveling in the faint sounds of the metal clinking as Aria tries her damnedest to both hold still and quiet the sounds of pleasure gathering inside of her and threatening to go off at any moment, I speak clearly, "I thought you may want to have a conversation?"

There's silence on the other end as Aria's lips form a perfect O and her lower back and thighs tremble. She's so fucking close. Slipping a finger inside of her cunt, I use enough pressure to get her off.

"Maybe about my arrangements with your daughter?"

Her leg raises and slams down on the desk, twice. Two loud slams that jostle the phone as her face scrunches and she bites into her lip.

That's once.

"You son of a bitch," Talvery sneers at me, oblivious to what I've just done to his daughter.

Aria's eyes pop open, although her face is still flushed and she's struggling to breathe quietly.

"Don't you know you should have more respect for women than that?" I tell Talvery and drag my fingers back down to Aria's clit. The shiver that runs through her makes it all the more thrilling.

"How did you get her?" Talvery's question makes me pause, taking my fingers away from her to consider his question. His *first* question. Not whether or not she's well or safe, but *how* did I get her.

Two options exist. He knows of the informant and wants it verified, or he truly has no idea.

"She was a gift," I explain to him evenly, my eyes narrowing on the phone and waiting for his response to give me more insight.

The sound of Aria's sharp inhale reminds me of my songbird, and that she's listening. Leaning forward, I plant a kiss on her thigh, one meant to soothe whatever pained thoughts are running through her head.

"From Romano?" he asks me, breathing heavier into the phone. "Is that what you expect me to believe?" he sneers, and Aria raises her head on the desk, ready to object and speak up, but I silence her, gripping her chin and shaking my head once. I know my expression is hard as fucking stone, which is what makes her flinch, but she cannot be allowed to speak to him.

I won't let her be any more involved in this war than she already is.

"You can believe what you want. You asked a question. I answered."

She's tense on the desk and she's facing away from me, trying to look at the phone, as if there's anything there to see.

She scissors her legs, to turn her body so she can see the phone, and again my lips tug into a smile when she moans softly.

He can't hear her as he tells me, "I've been informed."

I don't give him much thought. I know what he's been told, and he can go fuck himself with that misinformation, while I fuck his daughter.

I move back to her ass, teasing her and fucking her with the plug. Her nails scratch against the table as she tries to fight the desire to moan out loud.

I hit mute for just a moment, ready to hear that sweet sound I love. Her father continues although he can't hear us in return.

"What'd you do to her?"

I whisper to Aria, grabbing her ass with my other hand and forcing that beautiful sound to spill from her lips. The mix of intense pleasure and sting of pain too much for her to control. "Look at me while I fuck your ass, Aria." Her eyes widen with fear and I smirk as I explain, "He can't hear you, but I'm unmuting now, so be quiet, songbird."

Those beautiful lips part with both a sigh of relief and then a quiet whimper of pleasure as I go back to teasing her pretty little cunt. Her eyes nearly close, but she whips them open, obeying my last command to look at me.

"I'll kill you if you touched her." Talvery issues a false threat as I unmute the conversation.

"How could I not touch her?" I ask him.

I hear a small whimper of protest from Aria and feel like a prick that I'm goading her father in front of her.

With apprehension coiling in the pit of my stomach, I speak. "I've given her everything she needs. She's having hard days." Although her father is listening, these words are just for her as I add, "She seems to be fitting in well, and at times she even seems happy."

Her hazel eyes soften and nearly gloss over, her eyes never faltering from my gaze.

"What do you want, Cross?" Talvery's harsh and bitter voice forces my jaw to clench.

I think about telling him how she told me she loves me. But repeating those words to him and using them like that would be a travesty.

She's calmer, wide-eyed and waiting with bated breath for my answer.

"Just to talk. I have someone here who wanted to hear your voice."

I push my fingers into her tight cunt and my thumb presses against the butt plug. The clinking of the handcuffs is loud enough for Talvery to hear and knowing that, a conceited grin stretches across my face.

"Let me speak to her," he says but his demand is pathetic. I'd never do anything because he ordered it. I'd go through hell just to spite him.

"She's a little tied up at the moment," I tell him, feeling the arrogance surge inside of me, but wanting to contain it enough to keep it from hurting my Aria. I circle her clit ruthlessly, knowing she gets off so easily with this touch. I'd rather she be in such blinding pleasure that she can't hear or even comprehend the conversation.

"I'll fucking kill you," he says, and he doesn't hide the anger in his voice.

"You keep trying to do that," I retort and the anger seeps into my voice with every passing moment. And although concern is clearly written on Aria's expression, her thighs tremble with the upcoming release and her teeth sink into her bottom lip so hard she'll be tasting blood if she bites any harder.

I mute the conversation again for only a second to command her, "Cum for me, Aria." And then finger fuck her harder.

Her back bows and a soft, strangled cry slips by her lips just as I tell Talvery, "I promise I'm being good to her. I know how to treat a woman."

At my words, she cums, hard and violently. Her entire body showing the tremors of pleasure that race through her.

"Did Romano tell you what she did?" I ask Talvery, more to remind myself. This strong woman is mine. I'm fucking proud to have her as mine.

"Stephan?" Talvery asks as Aria's eyes meet mine and I whisper harshly in response, irritated by his interruption, "Yes."

Breathing heavily, Aria tries to look up; she tries to will the phone to give her more of a response from her father.

But nothing comes.

There's nothing but silence on the other line.

And I hate him for it. Truly hate him for the tears he brings to her eyes.

"You didn't come for her." I have to swallow the spiked ball growing in my throat. "How long have you known?"

When he doesn't reply, the edge of hate comes on thicker and I say, "I know Romano spilling a little secret wasn't what tipped you off."

Her face crumples and I lean forward, kissing every inch of the curve of her waist.

"Give her a message for me," Talvery says, but I ignore him in preference for the sweet sounds of gratitude I can barely hear from Aria.

"I couldn't tell her before this, but I'm telling her right now."

"I'm listening," I tell him, only to mute the phone again as I kiss Aria's reddened skin on her ass and gently move the butt plug in and out once again. She's so close already.

"Tell her I said, 'Stay quiet while I'm gone and stay in her room.'"

Unmuting the phone, I answer him quickly, "I'll be sure to let her know," and then hang up the phone, done with him and this conversation. And ready to hear her scream my name.

Moving her legs off the desk and fueled by her gasp and the sounds of her nails scratching along the desk, I unleash my cock and shove myself all the way in her to the hilt.

"Fuck, yes," I groan as my limbs tingle. "Fuck, I need you," I whisper along her back as I lower my lips to kiss along her skin. I stay still inside of her, letting her adjust and waiting to make sure she feels nothing but pleasure.

"You have no idea how much I want him to know you scream my name every night."

"Is he—" Aria asks before throwing her head back with a strangled cry of pleasure as I slam inside of her again.

Still, she turns to look at the phone, with her face scrunched and struggling to stay quiet, and I know she's wondering if he can hear.

Even as my cock is inside of her heat, she worries.

I won't fucking allow it.

I bang the phone down over and over, so she can hear. One hand on the phone, the other with a bruising grip on her hip. I fuck her in time with the violent banging until she can register the dead tone.

Shoving the phone off the desk, I tell her, "He doesn't matter. Nothing else matters." My words come out with a hard grunt as her pussy spasms around my thick length. "There's only us," I push the words out, pistoning my hips and feeling my balls draw up once again.

As I pound into her, I ask her, "How does it feel to have your ass and pussy filled at the same time?"

"Carter," she whimpers my name as she cums again. And then again. As I ride through her pleasure, each one harder and stronger than the last, I beg my body not to give in.

I want to stay in this moment forever. Her chained to my desk, feeling nothing but the heat of my desire and the thrill of me fucking her until her legs are weak and shaking.

But I have to. And on the third time her cunt grips my dick with her orgasm, I thrust myself as deep inside of her as I can, and cum harder than I ever have in my life.

I'm breathless when I pull the plug from her, giving her yet another wave of pleasure. I'm panting when I uncuff her and pull her into my lap to feel her heated skin tremble against mine.

The sound of our mingled breathing doesn't last long. Aria's hair tickles along my shoulder as she pulls away from me, reaching for the phone.

Her shoulders shake with her ragged breath and her eyes look lost in the distance.

"It's fine," I tell her, the swell of rage and worse, disappointment, brewing inside of me.

"Can I call him back?" Her question is immediate and laced with a mix of fear and worry. "Just me, please?" she begs me in a broken whisper.

Watching her swallow, I gauge her desperation that seemingly came from nowhere.

"I don't trust your father," I tell her honestly.

"You can trust me," she suggests weakly, the pleading tone still present.

I give her silence as I search her gaze and the desperation transforms to anger when she adds, "You didn't have to taunt him like that," but her voice cracks.

She's worried. Something's wrong

"Please let me call him back," she begs again. "I promise it's okay. I just want to tell him I'm all right." She worries her bottom lip between her teeth as she looks me in the eyes, both of her hands gripping on to me.

"No, what's wrong?" She won't look me in the eye at my response, so I grab her chin, forcing her eyes up and searching for the truth inside of them.

"Why does it have to be like this?" Her words crack, and tears leak from the corners of her eyes.

"What the hell happened?" My eyes narrow as I watch her lose it. Losing every ounce of composure. "What's wrong?"

"I love you," she answers with pain. "I'm sorry," she whimpers, wiping her eyes and trying to get away from me and out of my hold.

"I would never hurt you," I tell her as my heart races, knowing I can't give her the same words back. "You know that?" Going over everything that happened, all I can think is that it's the way I spoke about how she came to me. The way we started and the arrogance I showed. "The way I was talking-"

She stops me, pressing her fingers to my lips, "I would never hurt you either."

My phone going off distracts me; the message is from Jase. *You need to see this, now.*

Pressing a kiss to her soft lips, I try to end her worries. She attempts to deepen it, but I pull away, pressing my forehead to hers and wishing I didn't have to leave her right now.

I whisper against her lips, "Wait for me in the bedroom." I open my eyes to see the longing in hers and a well of emotion that knows no depths.

She only nods, loosening her grip as I set her down on the ground and stand up with her.

"I have something to take care of and then I'll come to you," I tell her, but her expression is absent of accepting a thing I'm telling her. One day she'll understand that I'll take care of everything so long as she trusts me to.

But she goes just the same and I watch her walk away from me as I stand outside the office door, wondering if she holds the same opinion of her father now that she did hours ago.

She glances behind her one last time, giving me a sad smile before disappearing around the corner to the stairwell.

I don't make it down the hall before Jase is up the stairs, full steam in his gait until he lifts his head and sees me.

"We need to talk." Jase's voice carries down the hall with an edge of urgency. "Now."

"What's going on?" I ask him, feeling my forehead crease and the adrenaline pumping harder.

"There's been a breach. Looks like we're going to have company." His eyes reflect the welcome of a challenge and my lips curl up in agreement.

"Talvery?" I ask him, wondering if her father was already in motion before the call, or if he stupidly acted off impulse.

Jase nods, but worry lines his expression. "There are only six."

"Six men?" I question. "Talvery isn't that fucking stupid."

"One's an informant and probably how they got past the first gate. Two are her blood."

"You think someone helped him?" I question Jase, thinking the informant was aided by someone he's spoken to, but he shakes his head quickly.

"We were alerted the second they were spotted. Where's Aria?" Jase questions and I'm quick to answer, "She's safe in my bedroom. She won't leave."

My throat dries and tightens, thinking about them stealing her, but worry and fear will only bring my downfall.

"There's no way he thought he could succeed in doing anything but sending his own men to be killed with only six."

"There's definitely something off," he adds and pulls up the feed on his phone. Six men along the inner tower, fully armored. I watch with him as he asks me, "We could question them?"

My chest tightens as I recognize the face of one man. "Nikolai."

He dared to come here. To try to take what's mine? Anger fills my blood and a seething mix of jealousy and vengeance turns my vision red.

"I was thinking we eliminate the three that don't matter but bring the cousins and Nikolai in for questioning." His statement is spoken in a low voice as he looks behind us, back to where Aria waits for me.

I lick my lips, knowing that Talvery is fully aware all six would die in an attempt to infiltrate and kill us, to rescue Aria.

"Nikolai is foolish and desperate. If he came because he knew she was here, I could see him only being followed by a few men."

"They're all high ranking," I say quickly, knowing each one of them. Recognizing a few who have killed on my streets.

"There's no way they came without Talvery knowing."

"Did they come to kill? Or to take her?" I ask Jase but had I waited for a second longer, I wouldn't have had to ask at all. I watch as one of them drops a grenade on the edge of the garage, followed by another a few feet farther down. *They came to kill.*

"They left explosives lining the gate. A scan shows they have enough on the bags strapped to their backs for the entire estate if they could get through it." My lips twitch with menace. "The same as before?" I ask Jase, remembering the site of the ash and rubble my former home was made to be. "You think it's the same men?"

Jase and I share a look, but he doesn't answer me verbally.

A call to Jase's phone replaces the surveillance on his phone. The moment he answers, my own phone rings to life in my pocket.

"It's Aria," Jase tells me before I answer my phone. He doesn't hide the nervousness as he tells me, "She's not staying in the bedroom."

"Where is she going?" I ask him, but then realize it doesn't matter. If she sees, she'll have to choose.

"Let her be, let her come if she chooses." My heart races as Jase tells them my orders and my phone dies in my hand. She'll see what they're capable of and what I need to stop, what I need to protect.

Let her see, let her choose.

"Have them kill the three, now." My voice is hard although inside tremors of rage grow. The three bodies will drop the second the command is given, leaving the other three scrambling but trapped on our estate. "Bring the other three to me."

CHAPTER 25

Aria

IF ONLY CARTER WOULD LET ME CALL MY FATHER OR GO TO HIM. MY SKIN PRICKS with goosebumps that won't leave and the constant chill I feel is at odds with the heat boiling my blood.

I can convince my father that there's another way.

I heard what he said. The message for me. He was speaking in code. He's coming. In only hours, my father is coming for me.

Stay quiet while I'm gone and stay in your room.

My father would tell me that before leaving for the night when we were on lockdown, but only when he would be gone for a few hours. If it was any longer than that, he'd have me go to the safe house.

There's no way those words were a coincidence. I'm sure of it. He wouldn't have said it if he wasn't coming for me. He wouldn't have said *those words* if something wasn't happening by tonight.

My heart hasn't stopped racing. My throat is tight with guilt and fear. It can't happen like this. I don't know exactly what he's planning, but those are words said in times of war. Something bad is going to happen. I know it. I can feel it in the pit of my stomach. It's going to change everything.

I can do something. But I need time that I don't have.

Pacing up and down the corridor to Carter's wing in the estate, I try to formulate an excuse for my father or a reason that would justify Carter not reacting to my father's threats. I can't go into the bedroom and just wait. I refuse to simply stand by.

The conversation that was just had on the phone repeats itself over and over again in my head and I start to debate if I heard my father right.

Tension squeezes my chest so tightly I can't breathe.

After days, my father decides to come. After weeks of me being missing, he's finally coming for me. And there's nothing I can do to stop him.

My hands are shaking horribly, and it does nothing but piss me off. Forming a fist, I slam it into the wall. How could he do this to me?

Both of them.

Carter's not innocent. He knew that conversation would piss my father off. He was goading him, practically laughing in my father's face.

And I took pleasure in it.

Every bit of that pleasure I wanted. There's something sick and twisted about how I craved Carter pushing me to the edge while my father spat hate at him.

Carter has proven there's a side to me that desires depravity and a sense of justice that's sinful and warped.

I should have known better. We were playing with fire but after weeks of being with Carter, of being his, of growing to love him made me feel invincible beside him.

I've always been foolish like that.

Brushing the hair away from my face, I rid myself of the regret and focus on the now and the present.

I have to tell Carter, but I don't know how I can save my father if I do. And I know it won't be my father coming. He won't storm Carter's castle. It'll be hired men, or worse, Nikolai. Telling Carter will only ensure that his guns will be ready and whoever is coming will be killed before they even come close.

"Fuck." The word slips from my lips in a strangled breath.

I was so full of hope, so eager to have this call happen, and instead, my worst nightmare has come to life. I've brought the war to me and to Carter's doorstep.

A moment of clarity comes over me, and my eyes whip open.

I start moving before the thought is even clear.

He's not in the office. Carter is not in the office where the phone is. *And I don't remember him locking the door.*

I'm well aware that Carter has cameras everywhere, and that's why I walk as if nothing's wrong. My shoulders are square, and I try to keep my expression impassive even though tears prick at my eyes and my chest hiccups with the need to break down.

These men will kill me before they get a chance to kill each other.

The doorknob rattles under my grip, but it turns, and the door pushes open easily. I don't waste any time, knowing Carter will come if he sees me, and I fall to my knees, gathering the phone still carelessly tossed on the floor from earlier.

My finger shakes as I press the buttons, but I do it. I grip the phone with both hands as I hold it to my ear and watch the door. If he doesn't know already, he'll know soon enough.

Ring, ring.

Every pause of the ring grips my heart harder.

My throat feels as if it's closed up, clogged by something unseen when the call goes dead. Not unanswered, but dead.

Clank! I slam the phone down over and over again, just as Carter did before, feeling the heat of anxiety roll over my skin. My teeth are clenched as I slam it down again before bracing myself over the desk.

Deep breaths. I need to stay calm and find a way.

Not another second passes. Not another tense breath heaves from me before I pick up the phone and hit redial again.

To no avail.

Tick-tock, tick-tock, the clock on Carter's office wall taunts me. Showing nearly fifty minutes have passed since Carter left me.

The only other number I know by heart is Nikolai's. I don't know if he would listen. Or if my father would listen to Nikolai. I don't know anything for certain, but still, I dial in his number.

One number at a time.

And he doesn't answer.

The phone goes to voicemail, but the inbox is full. A ball of barbed wire seems to unwind in my throat as hopelessness steals the breath from me. With every breath, I swallow more of it and it pains my chest. My fingers dig into my shirt right over my heart, gripping and trying to pull the spiked pain away. But it only grows.

Tick-tock. Tick-tock.

I try my father's number again, putting it on speaker this time, giving up any pretense I had before. If Carter walks in, I'll tell him everything. There's not any other light of hope left in the dark clouds that settle around me.

With the sound of the dead tone coming from the phone, I set the phone down, politely resting it in its cradle, and collapse into Carter's seat.

I try Carter's computer. It's password protected.

I type in Tyler. Rejected.

Cross. Rejected. I would try birthdays and old exes if I knew any. But I don't have a damn thing to work with.

My mind wars with itself, the stakes growing higher and higher as the seconds pass. Pulling open his drawer and flipping through files I try to find anything that could hint at his password, but I come up with nothing.

Tick-tock. Tick-tock.

The clock plays tricks on me. An hour and a half has passed.

My pulse is so fast; I can't hear anything else. I feel dizzy and lightheaded as I stand up and I have to brace myself to keep from falling over. The desk feels so cold and hard and the edges of it sharper than they did before.

I squeeze them so tightly that I think I may have cut myself but when I look down, there's been no blood shed.

"I have to tell him," I whisper to no one.

I can't balance myself as I walk. I have to rest my head against the wall for only a moment to catch my breath and think of the right words to say, the only words to say.

My father is coming. Men are coming to kill you.

I fight back the rush of oncoming tears and force myself to move. *Or maybe only to rescue me.*

I shut the door behind me and take in a shuddering breath.

I walk down the hall toward the stairwell, feeling cold and numb.

Deep breaths, one foot in front of the other. That's how I'll end my father's life and all those who stand with him. My cousins, my uncles. *Nikolai.*

God help me, please.

I pray as I grip the railing tightly and take each step carefully as my knees feel weaker.

Show me what to do. Please.

I'm halfway down the second set of stairs, toward the back half of the estate I never venture to, when I hear a gun cock. I freeze.

The sounds of a slap and a grunt mix with a cry of agony. My knees nearly buckle. *They're here.*

I'm too late. *No, please no.*

"Fuck you." I hear a voice I think belongs to one of my cousins and another hard smack as my knuckles go white from gripping the railing.

I can't breathe as my bare feet pad on the cold floor and I sneak closer to where the voices are coming from. My heart is beating so loud, I think they'll hear me.

How could I have let this happen?

How could Carter? The thought goes unfinished, but either way, my heart breaks.

"We'll take it from here," I hear Carter's voice as I see the backs of two men leaving, walking out from an open doorway, and heading to the rear exit. Both dressed in black and carrying guns. Not handguns or pistols, but automatic weapons. I nearly fall backward on my ass trying to take cover in the closest doorway, so I go unseen.

The sound of metal scraping against the floor can only be guns being kicked away.

Guns and questioning. It's an interrogation. My heart races and I struggle with what I can do to stop this.

"Where is she?"

Nikolai. I grip the wall, just around the corner from the front room where the voices carry from. The mix of adrenaline, fear, and betrayal riding through my veins in waves and overwhelming my ability to even think.

"I'll ask again, nicely. What were your direct orders?" Jase's voice is cold. Colder and harsher than I ever could have imagined. "Or did you not have any?"

I can barely breathe and when I do, it sounds so loud. My heart's beating out of my chest when I peek around the corner, getting low to the ground and praying no one will see me.

"Did your boss really send you to your death on a whim? Six men against an army?"

I cover my mouth with both of my hands and nearly fall forward at the sight in front of me as I round the corner, the rushing of my blood drowns out the voices of the interrogation, but the sound of a gun smacking against skin and crashing into bone rings clearly.

With my eyes shut tightly and a sickness stirring in my stomach, I force my eyes open. I force myself to see everything.

Nikolai makes up one of the three. The other two are my cousins, Brett and Henry. They're brothers and years older than me. We've shared every holiday. I was a bridesmaid in Brett's wedding. Every event we've been to together for years flashes before my eyes as I see Brett spit blood onto the floor. The left side of his face is already bruised and the black chestplate of his armor is covered in blood.

My heart squeezes. I don't want to see this. I can't. I can't watch, but I have to do something.

"We're not telling you shit," Brett sneers and Henry struggles next to him. With their wrists bound behind their backs, Henry sways. His right eye is swollen and that's all I can see, but he's not well.

What did they do to you? My heart bleeds at the question.

Jase and Declan have guns pointed at the back of their heads, with all three of them kneeling in a row in front of them.

"You want to join your friends sooner, rather than later?" Jase questions them.

I've never felt so betrayed. So sickened. Bile rises in my throat as my gaze drifts across the three men I've known all my life so close to their lives being over if only a trigger is pulled.

"Fuck you," Nikolai grunts out, pulling my focus to him. Although he stares at Carter with nothing but hate, his eyes show his pain. And it's my undoing.

The war has never felt so alive as it does now.

That's when I see a light shine, directing my eyes to what matters.

Carter's gun is tucked in the back of his pants. It's staring right at me, the light from the room reflecting on it. And the guns on the floor behind him. Three guns and one I recognize as Nikolai's.

He took their guns, he kicked them away from my family. And now they kneel in front of Jase and Declan, waiting for execution. The sound of a gun being cocked pushes me forward and leaves me no choice.

My hands shake as I crawl toward the guns. One scratches across the floor as I try to pick it up and I know at that point they see me. So, I do the only thing I can.

I point the gun at the enemy who doesn't have a gun.

I stand on weak legs and grip the gun as tightly as I can. Aiming it at the back of Carter's head. Knowing I've made a choice and hating myself for it but fueled by the need to protect my only friend and family.

"Carter," I call out his name and feel the eyes of everyone else in the room on me as Carter turns slowly around to face me.

His eyes flash as he lets out a breath, but he doesn't retreat, he doesn't even seem to take me seriously. He looks at me the way you'd look at a child playing dress-up. Non-threatening and as if they're simply being cute. It cuts me in a way I didn't think was possible.

He really cares so little for me. He's really going to kill them all and expects me to fall in line, obeying and submitting to his every whim.

As he steps toward me and I pull the trigger back even though my hands tremble, his expression morphs, and the damage I've done is so clear to me in this moment. His firm expression of disapproval and irritation changes to one I've never seen. A mask of hardness and sharpness that makes his chiseled features look even more dominating and villainous.

I can hear him breathe as he stops in his tracks. Everything about him is terrifying, save the look in his eyes. Those dark eyes with bright specks of silver still shine with something else. Hope, maybe? But it vanishes when I call out to him, feeling the tightness in my throat and chest squeezing the courage from me. "Let them go," I force the words out and they come out strong. I don't know how because at the moment I feel nothing but weak.

I feel like I failed the boy still hurting inside of Carter. I've lost the trust. I can see it as Carter's eyes glaze over and the darkness overwhelms them. I've never hurt so much in my life as I do now, but what else was there for me to do? I'm in a hopeless situation and there's no possible way for me to win.

My palms are so hot and tingling with the rush of adrenaline and mix of fear that controls my every move, and I nearly drop the gun but somehow, I hold it steady and keep it pointed on Carter.

"The girl we've all been waiting for," Carter says without a change in his expression. No arrogant smile. Nothing but a menacing look of hatred and disgust.

His head tilts and he says a word low and deep in his throat that sends a sickening chill down my spine. "Talvery."

BREATHLESS

Her lips tasted like Cabernet and her touch was like fire.
I was blinded by what she did to me. I so easily fell for something I
thought I'd never have.

I was weak for her and should have known better. I should have known
she could never love a man like me.

She brought out a side of me that I wish had stayed dead.

I won't make the same mistake twice.
I don't care how much she begs me.
I don't care that I crave her more than anything else…

This is book 3 in the Merciless series. It picks up right where book 2, *Heartless,* left off.
They must be read in order.

Dedicated to Bethany.

Thank you for reading my cards.
And everything that came with it.
xoxo

A special thanks to my editing team and betas who make my books what they are.
Donna, Chris, Becca, Teresa, Katie, TJ, and Sophie—I couldn't do this without you.
#TeamWillow

CHAPTER 1

Carter

IT'S BEEN A LONG TIME SINCE SOMEONE HAS DARED TRY TO KILL ME IN MY OWN HOME.
Even longer since someone has pointed a gun at me and lived to tell the tale.

I can barely hear a damn thing due to the ringing in my ears. I've waited for this moment, but this isn't how I thought it would go.

She loves me, I remind myself. She fucking loves me. I know she does.

Aria's face is flushed, and her hand trembles as she fights to hold the gun steady.

I take one step toward her and she cocks it. The click fills the room. Whatever remaining semblance of a heart I had shatters in my chest, the small shards shooting waves of pain through my body.

The sick grin on my face wanes even as I struggle to hold it in place, focusing on those gorgeous hazel eyes. Eyes that drew me to her, that begged me for mercy, that made me feel more than I've felt in years.

Eyes that fooled me.

"Drop your guns," Aria demands, her voice shaky but clear and loud regardless. It's fucking insane that in this moment she strikes me as utterly gorgeous. In her strength, she's at her most beautiful.

"Drop them!" she calls out more strongly and the gun wavers. It's obvious she's never held one before, or at the very least, never fired one.

Yet, she's pointing it at me. It could go off accidentally, killing me. *Would she regret it?* I question and feel a strong tug in my chest. A well of emotion threatens to break my composure. Every inch of skin is numb as I stare at the barrel, feeling everything crumble around me.

In front of the enemy.

In front of my brothers.

In front of her.

"Carter?" I hear Jase without seeing him, asking if they're to listen to her or not.

Two of my brothers, Jase and Declan, are behind me with guns pointed at three men kneeling on the floor. Two of them are her cousins, and the third man is her former lover and friend. The name she prayed to while in the cell, the one name I'm tired of hearing her speak, belongs to him.

All three are men who wanted to kill us only moments ago. Men that Aria is protecting, and willing to kill me to save.

Those fucking shards dig deeper into whatever wound they've gouged in my chest.

Swallowing the knot in my throat along with the distress I'm feeling, I answer Jase although I don't take my gaze from Aria. "Drop them." Instantly, relief shows on Aria's face, and she even relaxes her grip on the gun until I add, "But don't let those fuckers have them. No one holds a gun," I swallow thickly and add, forcing a smirk to my face, "but Aria."

The control is still in my demand. They'll listen to me, everyone who's worth a damn in this room will… but as time passes, I can feel it slipping away. I can only imagine what her family thinks, but it's what my brothers are seeing that fucking shreds me. They know I love her.

And now they're watching her betray all of us.

"Let them go," Aria commands in a weaker tone, one filled with a plea. Visibly swallowing, she finally breaks my gaze to look at them. Her startled, sharp intake of breath at what she sees destroys me. Her mercy and compassion for them are sickening.

They came to kill me. She fucking knows that.

She might kill me yet.

I loved her. I know I loved her, and that was my first mistake.

Anger rises and rings in my blood. My sanity finally comes back to me, hardening me and reminding me of who I am and everything I've worked for.

It's all going to crumble. All because of her.

I would have done *anything* for her.

"Let's go." I hear Nikolai's voice, low and riddled with pain. The blood is still bright red from the split on his lip and a bruise has already formed on his face. My knuckles turn white as my fist tightens. All I need is one moment to take out every bit of my aggression on him. I want to break his jaw for daring to speak those words to my Aria.

I've never felt rage like I do now as he reaches for her like he can take her away from me.

Because he can.

Because she's willing.

"Go," she says, and Aria's voice is strong as she glances at him. Again, the gun is slack in her grip. She doesn't seem to notice how loose the gun is in her hands. I could take it; I could chance it. But it would risk putting her in danger, and my gaze falls at the thought.

"Now," one of her cousins hiss, tugging on Nikolai's arm. The shirt tightens around his neck as the fabric is pulled. Peeking at him from my periphery, I'm disgusted, as is Nikolai, judging by his expression.

"Come with us," Nikolai urges, raising his voice to command her, but also beg her, and I take my focus from Aria, staring at the man Nikolai is.

He reminds me of the boy I once was.

Foolish and reckless. But he never went through the shit I did. He was bred into this life, he wasn't thrown into it and forced to fight to survive every fucking day.

Yet he thinks he can take her.

"I'm staying," Aria says with authority before I can say anything. Her declaration makes Nikolai flinch. A small bit of hope flutters in my chest. My throat tightens, and my chest aches, feeling as if it's on the verge of ripping wide open. *She's staying.*

"We don't have time for this!" one of her cousins yells out, glancing around the room as if any minute now, I'll change my mind and kill them all.

He'd be right if it wasn't for Aria.

She wanted them. She chose them.

"I'm not leaving without you," Nikolai growls and stalks to Aria, ready to take her. That's my cue to reach for my gun.

Their reunion has lasted long enough, and I refuse to let him take her. No one will take her from me. No one.

Adrenaline races through my blood, my breathing coming in heavier as my jaw clenches. The gun is hot in my hand. Hotter than it's ever felt before. It's pointed at Nikolai; Aria's is pointed at me.

My voice is deep and rough as I tell the three of them, "You have two minutes to run."

"Carter," she says, and Aria's voice is a desperate plea, but she has no room to bargain and I have no mercy remaining, not even for her. I ignore her, feeling the rage from what she's done seep into the marrow of my bones as I finish stating, "and then we'll open fire."

My brothers move slowly, reaching for their guns as Aria's expression crumples with pain and she rocks backward toward the wall, with her nervousness evident.

Nikolai's jaw is tense, his light blue eyes sparking with hate. "Come with me," he says beneath his breath. "Take her!" he commands his allies.

But they run, leaving him alone and leaving her behind. "She had her chance!" one of the men yells behind him. Their sneakers squeak as their footsteps pound on the freshly polished floor. Cowards. Talvery men are cowards.

"Aria, please," Nikolai begs her as if it breaks his fucking heart. Fuck him.

"One minute," I grit between my teeth and he finally looks at me. My grip tightens on the gun. One squeeze of the trigger and I'd be rid of him forever. I'm so close to pulling it, just to end it all. He looks me in the eyes and I wish the look I give him back was enough to kill him.

"Go," she whimpers, her eyes flickering from my gun to him. "Get out of here!" she screams at him.

"I'll come back for you," he tells her as if she's his long-lost love.

I hope he does come back for her. My nostrils flare and my chest aches as she gasps for breath watching him leave. *Come back for her, Nikolai. Come back, so I can break your fucking neck.* I bite my tongue, tasting the metallic tang of blood in my mouth.

I will kill him if it's the last thing I do.

He's still running away from her. My blunt nails dig into my palms as my fists tighten and the anger and jealousy mix into a deadly concoction. Red bleeds into my vision and it's all I can do not to pull the trigger as it follows his movements.

"I wanted to tell you," Aria sobs as the sound of Nikolai running away fades in the hallway. "I didn't think—"

"Tell me what?" I ask her.

"That they were coming," she says with a pain in her voice that matches the one swirling in her eyes. She's breaking apart, barely breathing and I can see the regret, the remorse. But only one thing resonates with me.

"You knew?" I question her and feel a chill rush through my body that sinks all the way to my bones.

She never loved me. She never did. You protect the ones you love. Always. And she didn't protect me.

I was a fucking fool and she isn't the woman I thought she is. She's a fucking liar.

"Are we really letting them go?" Declan's question slices through the haze of disbelief and treachery.

"You knew?" I ask her again, my temper coming back anew.

"I, I…" she stutters over her words, her gaze darting over my face, fear and pain causing her hazel eyes to glass over with tears. She lowers her gun all the way down, not daring to point it at me anymore and I drop mine as I move closer to her, each heavy step sounding more foreboding than the last.

"Carter?" Declan yells my name, demanding an answer.

With each step closer to her, she takes one in reverse until her shoulders hit the wall.

I holster my gun before ripping hers out of her hands, although she doesn't put up a fight. "Carter," Declan calls out again, not caring at all that the woman I loved set me up. She knew they were coming to kill me, to kill all of us, and she did *nothing*. "Are we letting them go or not?" Declan asks.

With one hand braced on the wall above Aria's head and the other pinning her hip to it, I look her dead in the eyes, ignoring everything about her gaze that draws me in. She can't have that anymore. I'm taking that power away.

Feeling the dominance of hatred flow through me and wanting to hurt her as she's hurt me, I answer Declan in a deep voice that's barely audible. "Kill them all."

⊷•⊶

Jase

I'm quick to follow Declan out of the room, even though I know it's a mistake to leave Carter alone with Aria.

I'll be fast. I have to do something to stop this.

"Declan." Raising my voice, I call out to my brother and the sound of his footsteps echoing in the hallway stops instantly. He turns to me, anger and tension still rolling off of his shoulders.

He can barely look me in the eyes.

"Yeah?" His voice is tight as I make my way to him, closing the distance as quickly as I can.

I keep my voice as low as possible and ignore the banging of my heart against my ribcage as I look over my shoulder to make sure no one followed, to make sure no one can hear me defy my brother's orders.

"Don't tell them to shoot to kill." I start to talk before I've even fully faced him. My words are mixed with my tense breath from the adrenaline flowing through my blood. "If they shoot, tell them to make sure they miss."

Declan hears me; I know he does by the shock on his face. The roar of anger coming from the foyer behind me reminds me of how unhinged Carter has become. He's going to do something stupid. Something he'll never be able to take back.

"I'm going back to them," I tell Declan and turn away only to have him grip my arm and pull me back to him. He doesn't say anything at first, but I can see the question in his eyes, the feel of betrayal from him.

And it shreds me.

"You know he loves her," I tell him, feeling the ache of sadness rising inside me. It hurt Carter, but it's more than that. She betrayed us all.

"Not after that," Declan nearly whispers. Shaking his head slightly with a defeated expression on his face, he continues, "Not after she—"

"It's not her fault she had to choose," I push the words through my clenched teeth, knowing in my gut that she's fighting with what's right versus where her loyalties should lie. "She never should have known."

The tension in Declan's gaze wavers, and he looks behind me before reaching my eyes again.

"She made a choice to stay. Let Talvery know that. She chose to stay. It'll fucking kill Nikolai and make the crack in their factions that much deeper. Nikolai has to live."

I know Carter will be pissed at me, but he'll get over it. He'll thank me when it's all said and done. It has to go down like this. I can't let him ruin everything.

With a tight nod, Declan runs his thumb over his chin but doesn't say a word.

"Tell the guards to let them go back to Talvery. But make sure they all know she chose to stay. She chose Carter."

CHAPTER 2

I'VE ALWAYS KNOWN CARTER TO BE A BEAST OF A MAN. BARELY CONTAINED AND waiting for an outlet to release his rage. As his chest rises and falls with each heavy intake of breath and his muscles coil, his shoulders get more and more tense. With each ragged second of anxiousness passing between us, I know there's nothing holding him back.

"You chose them." His words are calculated, spoken with control although he looks anything but in control. The tension winds tighter and my body grows hotter with every hard thud in my chest.

"No," I try to tell him although my throat constricts to the point where I think I can't breathe. I start to shake my head, but he lets out a snarl, flipping the front table over in one swift movement. The carved wood antique crashes into the wall with a loud bang that forces my body to tremble as he screams, "Get out!"

The rough cadence of his voice carries through the room and I back away from him, my shoulders hunching as fear consumes me.

Tears prick my eyes and I try to speak, to tell him I didn't have a choice. I just did what I thought I needed to. "I'd never have—"

He turns to me, taking three large strides forward, the cords in his neck taut and bulging as his dark eyes pierce into me.

"Shot me?" he questions me with nothing but disbelief and rage burning in his eyes.

The intensity of his stare alone makes me cower.

"Carter," Jase speaks up from behind us, but Carter doesn't turn away from me. He stares at me like I've betrayed him. As if what I did was the ultimate sin.

Has he forgotten that they're my family? That I've begged him to spare them and yet he was going to execute them? Did he forget that he stole me from them and locked me in a cell for weeks?

He stares down at me as though he hates me.

I feel it. It's raw and palpable.

At this moment, I feel he truly hates me. And that's what breaks me.

Because no matter what he did to me, I never hated him. *I love him.*

Tears flow from me easily as Carter informs Jase in the most unfeeling manner that I'm to be removed from the premises.

My heart hollows and collapses, but my feet move, my body shoves me forward. And Carter follows, blocking me from running down the hall to the bedroom.

"I thought you loved me," he sneers at me and I cover my mouth with my hand to hold back the agony.

I do love him. I do.

I swear I love this man.

Even if he hurt me and even if I hurt him just now.

I can't voice a single word as his warm breath covers my face and my body wracks with a sob.

"Carter!" Jase yells, grabbing his shoulder and forcing him to look at anything other than me.

The moment he does, I bolt. I turn to run past Jase. I don't dare try to run past Carter. He could block me, catch me, and throw me away. He could see to it himself to banish me from his home.

The hideaway room is past the bedroom, so that space isn't an option either. And given the state Carter's in, I don't trust him to keep his word and let me recover from what's happened, so I can try to explain.

Instead, I run as fast as I can, on shaky legs and with adrenaline coursing through me, in the opposite direction. The muscles in my thighs scream with pain as I take the stairs two at a time. The pounding of my heart and footsteps are overwhelming. I'm hot and sweating and not okay in any sense of the word. I have to make him understand somehow.

He starts chasing me, although at his own slow and teasing pace. The second I hear Carter behind me, I slip. My elbow and hand crash on the hard, wooden stairs as does my knee, sending shooting pains through my body. I could cry, and I hate myself for it. I did this. This is my fault. I look behind me and see Carter start to climb the stairs. A mask of anger and dominance appears set in stone on his handsome features.

The cell.

The thought hits me at that moment. I force myself to get up and run to the cell. I know it's behind a painting. He wouldn't be able to get in if I ran to the cell and locked myself in. It'll take him time to get a key; time I desperately need. He needs to calm down and I need time. Time so I can figure out how to explain things to him in a way he'll understand.

Running up the stairs and using that momentum to push off the wall at the top, I careen down the hall.

Which one is it? My breathing is unsteady and a cold sweat breaks out along every inch of my skin. My heart won't stop racing; pounding chaotically. I can barely see straight.

There are six large paintings in the hall and my fingers fumble around the first, trying to heave it to the side, but it's not the right one. I tremble as my gaze is whipped toward the sound of him coming.

The second painting I push so hard that it falls, nearly toppling over on me. It's at least five feet long and four feet high. And it's not the right one either. The frame splits and cracks and I have to high-step over it, scraping my shin as I go, but I don't care. *Where is it? I need to find it, please.*

"You can't run from me." Carter's deep voice reverberates through the hall, and glancing behind me, I see his shadow as he climbs the stairs.

Thump, thump, my heart pounds harder and harder. I can barely breathe.

I don't know which one is the cell. I don't know.

The box.

The very thought has me sprinting down the hall to the last set of stairs. Up one more floor and on the left. I run as fast as I can, gasping for breath. Just the idea of Carter not giving me a chance to even speak to him, to explain, to ask for forgiveness, is crushing me with every step.

He just needs time. He has to understand. I can make him understand.

Visions of his face when I pointed the gun at him flash through my mind as I run.

Carter, seemingly over the desire to move slowly and let me run from him, picks up his pace as I get to the hall. I can hear his footsteps pound up the stairs, so I run as hard as I can, nearly slamming into the closed door of his office. Tears prick as the hurt and betrayal of what I've done set in.

I scrabble with the knob so clumsily in my own chaos that I think it's locked, but it's not.

It's open and a wave of relief runs through me although it's short-lived. Nothing is okay at this moment. Not a damn thing is all right.

I don't waste any time; I don't bother to close the office door either. Sprinting to the box, I rip the top open and practically fall into it, scraping my thighs and back. A scream is ripped from me, but it's merely instinctual. I don't care about the pain; I don't care about anything other than shutting the lid and locking myself in.

I have to reach up to get the top of it lowered and when I do, I see Carter in the doorway. Fear paralyzes me when I see his face, contorted with a look of outrage and red from running. My skin is ice cold as I reach for the lid. My fingertips feel numb as I slam it down.

There's a snap, I hear it, but I don't know what it is. It comes with a tug at the back of my neck that's accompanied by a sharp pinch I try to ignore as my fingers slip along the edge of the lid searching for the lock.

Shrouded in darkness, I struggle to find the lock, hearing Carter's footsteps getting closer and closer, but my trembling fingers find it and the multiple clicks assure me I'm bolted in.

All I can hear is my staggered breathing for a moment and then another.

With a deafening roar of anger, the box lifts off the ground only an inch, if that. Through my tears still streaking down my hot face, I can see Carter lifting it with all his strength, but it's meant to outlast such acts and so it does.

Crouched in the box and gripping on to myself, I hold my breath knowing he can't do a damn thing about it.

It's only then that I hear the rolling of the beads. It's only then that I feel the pearls rolling around me. I shriek in terror at first, thinking that something is alive and in the dark place with me. But it's only my necklace. The beads that have fallen off the broken chain.

Tears leak freely at the realization.

My chest hollows as I cover my mouth to keep from crying harder.

The box moves a little more and I close my eyes until he drops it, making my body sway and tumble in the small amount of space I have. A small yelp escapes me, but I focus on calming down. I'm on the verge of a panic attack or worse.

My eyes are closed tighter than they've ever been. Shock and horror still threaten to suffocate me as I struggle to inhale.

A few minutes pass and all I can hear is Carter's chaotic breathing. For a moment someone comes in, I think Jase, speaking quietly and trying to tell Carter to calm down, but the door closes shut with a loud click and then there's silence again.

Nothing but silence and the slamming of my own heartbeat and the rushing of blood in my ears.

It's going to be okay, I try to reassure myself. *He has to understand.* Even the thought is fleeting in my mind. All Carter knows is that I chose them, my family and his enemies. I pointed a gun at him and cocked it.

Oh, my God. My head spins as the memory comes back to me.

I threatened the life of the only man I've ever loved.

When I finally open my eyes, Carter's are fixed directly on mine. As if he can see me, even though I know it's impossible. His dark eyes pierce through me, pinning me where I am and eliciting a new kind of fear.

His deep voice sends a jagged spike of despair through me as he says low beneath his breath, "You can't stay in there forever."

CHAPTER 3

Carter

I'VE NEVER IN MY LIFE FELT LIKE THIS BEFORE.

The clock ticks as time passes. I can count on one hand every time I've been betrayed, but it's never felt like this because none of them were close to me. I've never let anyone in.

Not the guards I've depended on, not the boys I took in to help. I didn't feel betrayed by them when they only stole from me or tried to bargain with someone else who wanted me dead.

I've never let a soul close to me other than my brothers. So, no one can hurt me.

No outsider has ever been close to me... except for her, the only woman I ever loved.

A chill rolls through my body like the unrelenting tides of the ocean. The adrenaline has waned as I sit here in the chair, staring at that fucking box. My knuckles are bruised and cut, but I keep putting pressure on them, to keep me from thinking of a different pain, the aching in my chest.

Every time I blink, the barrel of her gun is there, staring back at me.

"Carter." Daniel's voice breaks me from my thoughts and brings me back to this reality. It fucking hurts; every piece of me hurts. Sitting up slightly in the chair, I finally take my eyes away from the box, away from Aria. I tilt my head as I take in my brother and the man standing next to him. Eli's one of our guards and head of security.

"Eli's finished the walk-through." He's struggling to keep his eyes on me; I can see it in the way he swallows visibly and clenches his hands. Even his voice is strained.

She did this. I know Daniel cared about her. And she betrayed him like she did me.

Eli steps forward to speak, telling me about each of the bombs they found and disposed of and where exactly the Talvery men ran. No surprises and nothing I give a fuck about at this point. Not when the woman who caused all of this is still right in front of me, but safely hiding in plain sight.

"All of them?" I ask just to pretend to be present, pressing my sore back into the chair and still staring at the fucking box. I can barely see Eli nod in my periphery as he answers, "Yes, sir." With his shoulders squared and his hands behind his back, he looks like the soldier he used to be.

But he defied me.

"You let them live," I say flatly, turning my attention directly to him for just a second, so he can see how pissed I am, hardening my gaze and my scowl. Then I look back to the box. The box I took from a man I refused to show mercy to. Aria's breathing picks up and she moves within its small confinements.

"I ordered Eli and the guards to let them live." Jase's voice sends a cold trickle down my neck. It's hard to swallow as my blood heats with anger.

One by one, they're all turning their backs on me.

Aria moves inside of the box again; I can faintly hear her crying. It's then that Eli catches on to the fact that she's in the box. Glancing at him, I can see his expression fall, the puzzle in his head forming as each of the pieces fall into place.

It takes a moment for him to fix his fucking face and wipe the look of disgust off of it.

She did this. She will suffer the consequences.

I gave her a chance; I would have given her anything had she simply chosen me. I was stupid for ever loving her. Or for thinking she loved me.

"Leave," I bite out the command, feeling the raw word scratch against the back of my throat. Eli's the first to turn around sharply and leave at once. Daniel and Jase step forward rather than retreating and my muscles tense, my teeth gritting as I lean forward in the seat I haven't left for nearly an hour now.

"Carter," my brother says, and Jase's voice is strong and demanding. Not like the way Aria's been saying it as she whimpers in the box, begging me to understand. I won't hear it. There's no excuse.

"Fuck off." It's all I can say back to him. The rage blisters inside of me, eating me alive that they all defied me.

"Carter." Daniel's tone is softer, more placating. "Just relax for a minute. Calm down," he tells me.

I can barely inhale, refusing to believe everything that's happened.

"Did you hear that, songbird?" I ask her rather than facing my brothers. The legs of the chair scratch against the floor as I lean forward, searching for a seam in the box where I think she can see me. I stare at it with an unforgiving bitterness as I tell her, "I just need to calm down."

I can feel the depth of emotion roaring inside of me as Jase speaks, "It was an unfortunate event, but we can use this to our favor."

"Unfortunate?" I can't hide the disbelief and venom in my voice as I stare back at him, finally rising from my seat. The force of the abrupt movement shoves the chair back. All I can hear is my heart beat in time with my heavy footsteps as I move closer to my brother.

Same height as me, the same determination in his voice.

"Knock it off," Daniel says and walks between us, separating us with a hard hand on both of our chests. "What about Aria?" he says quickly as he pushes me back. His glare pleads with me to think about something other than her apparent betrayal. "She's not okay." He lowers his voice to tell me the obvious and then lets his gaze move to her before looking back at me.

"What about her?" I ask him in a hardened tone. My hands form fists so tightly, I can feel the skin across my knuckles nearly crack and the cuts that are there split even wider.

A whimper from the box catches the attention of my brothers, both of them looking toward her as I stare at them.

"What the fuck do you even care for?" I sneer at Daniel. I raise my voice to remind them of the hard truth, "She chose them."

The sobs return from the box behind me and it enrages me. "Now she cries," I say, talking to her more than to them as I walk closer to where she is. The box is off-center now, crooked and making the end of the rug uneven from my useless attempts to open it even though I know it can't be done.

"She wasn't crying when she held a gun to my head!" Everything turns to white noise. Whatever my brothers say, the relentless crying from the woman I loved as she hides from me for fear of her own life, all of it.

I hate everything at this moment. I hate everyone. But I hate myself the most.

"She wasn't crying when she found out her family was coming to kill us. To kill all of us!" The last bit comes out louder and harsher than I can control, and I reach above the box to the bookshelves, shoving aside a row of them. The hardcovers and pages fly into a flutter before slamming down on the floor.

"I was!" Again, I hear her cry out, "I was!"

But all it does is fuel me to continue wrecking every shelf above her. All of the books falling around her, some of them slamming against the box, only make her cry out louder.

I hate her.

I hate them all.

I hate everything.

It takes both of my brothers to pull me back against the office window and away from the shelves. As I catch my breath, I think about destroying all of it. Wrecking every piece of this rich interior. It mocks me. It's a façade of control and I have none anymore. Not a damn shred of control.

"You never loved me!" I scream at her. "I should have kept you in that fucking cell until you knew better than to defy me!"

"Please, Carter, let me explain," she weeps.

"I was too fucking good to you," I sneer at her as loud as I can, feeling my composure deteriorate just as any ounce of mercy has. I scream at the top of my lungs, wanting to shred something apart. Every last bit of my humanity will do.

"Stop," Daniel says, his head close to mine. As he uses all of his strength to push me against the cold glass window, he's so close that I can feel the burn of his body heat.

"It's okay," he tells me as Jase grunts, his expression strained and his face red with exertion. Every inch of my skin is numb with a pain I've never felt before.

I want to tell them all nothing is okay and that I'll never stop. Never. There's nothing left of me but this shell of a man. But before I can tell them that I'll find the men they let get away and I'll rip out their fucking throats before they can breathe a word of how Aria betrayed me, a small voice comes from the doorway.

"Fuck." Daniel barely breathes the word before releasing me to run to her, to Addison, but he's too late.

I don't know how much Addison saw, or what she saw, but her face is pale.

Aria's still crying uncontrollably, and it's going to be obvious. It's obvious I'm hurting her and that she's scared. She's scared of me because I've fucking lost it. Nothing else matters.

There's no hiding now. Not from my brothers, not from the Talverys. Not from Addison, the one connection I still have to my brother Tyler.

Shame and disgust are a painful cocktail to swallow, but I choke it down.

"What the fuck are you doing?" Addison's voice vacillates between strength and panic as she stands in the doorway to my office. Her eyes dart from me to Daniel.

"How long have you been standing there?" Daniel asks Addison.

"Long enough… to…" Addison struggles to even look at Daniel. "You're hurting her," Addison barely glances my way.

Aria's sobs are punctuated with hiccups as she breathes in heavily, like she's desperate to stop, desperate to quiet her cries.

"Aria?" Addison's tone reflects a despair I've never heard from her before and inside I shatter. Whatever bit of anger that lingered, fragments and scatters in the pit of my stomach. Sucking in a deep, shuddering breath, her eyes go wide with fear and she takes a half step back.

"Daniel," she says hesitantly, her eyes wide with shame and disbelief as her body shakes so strongly I can see it from across the room. "You can't be okay with this?"

Fuck. Fuck. It's all fucked!

I straighten my stance as Jase lets go of me, moving out of the way and taking a few strides closer to Aria, away from me and out of sight from Addison. But the movement makes him that much more obvious to her.

"Get her out," she says, and her demand is strained by the veil of fear. She's pointing to the box but doesn't dare to let it steal her gaze from Daniel.

"Addison, stay out of it," Daniel tells her as he takes another step closer to her, his hands held in the air.

"Are you fucking serious?" As each word cracks with disdain, pain grows on her face. "Daniel, help her." The last word comes out in a croak as she backs away from him, further into the office and closer to the shelves. She nearly trips on the fallen books but manages to keep herself upright. She only takes her eyes off of him to see where Jase and I are. Neither of us is moving as she struggles to get closer to the box, closer to Aria who's quiet, and for a moment, I worry if she's all right.

"Why did he say cell?" Addison asks, and I can't even begin to think of when I said that word or how I used it. All I can see is red and my memory is a white fog.

"Addison, please," Daniel begs her.

"He's hurting her, putting her in a cell?" she shrieks and then turns any bit of remorse or disgust into anger. "You're allowing it! You knew!"

"She put herself in there," I say, cutting off the interrogation directed at Daniel and feeling the need to defend us against Addison's unspoken, yet all too clear thoughts. "Tell her, Aria." I raise my voice, feeling my cold blood fill my veins and praying to hear her voice.

"What did you do to her?" Addison's breathy words are filled with accusations.

"Nothing." Aria's voice is finally heard, although it trembles and is minuscule compared to ours.

With a hardened jaw, I dare to stare back at her, narrowing my gaze and not allowing her to blame this on me.

"She ran up here and hid because she held a gun to my head." Each word comes out harder, but I stay where I am as Addison inches closer to Aria.

"Addison," Daniel says as he tries to reason with her, keeping his voice low, but not to be denied, "get out."

"Fuck you," she spits at him and then finally lays a hand on the box.

"Aria," she calls out to her, banging the palm of her hand on the box behind her, although she still faces Daniel with a defiant expression on her face.

Aria whimpers for Addison to go, to leave her alone and stay out of it.

"I'm not going anywhere," Addison's quick to reply, tears leaking down her face.

"Don't cry," Daniel pleads with her, stepping forward and trying to reach out for Addison. The resulting slap is so hard, so vicious, I practically feel it against my own skin. Daniel's cheek instantly turns bright red, his head rotating back slowly to face her as Addison screeches at him, "Don't touch me!"

"Addison, you need to." Daniel barely gets another word out before Addison loses her shit entirely. Her voice three octaves higher than it should be, her entire body shaking with a new kind of vengeance, she's only getting more agitated.

"What did he do to her?" She sways in anger as Aria's sobs are echoed in Addison's voice.

What did I do to her? To Aria?

I loved her the only way I knew how. My head feels light and everything I think I know means nothing.

I should have known it would never be okay. I'm too fucked up to keep a woman like her. To keep anyone at all. What did I do to her? I drove her to betray me, to threaten to kill me.

"What happens between them—" Daniel starts to try and defend himself, not me. Not the relationship I had with Aria. Because there is no defending that. I know it deep in my gut.

I try to take a step forward, toward the door to get out, but stop when Addison shrieks at Daniel, shoving him away as he tries yet again to go to her.

"Please, just go!" Aria begs her and that only makes Addison more adamant at getting her out of the box.

As Addison screams at Daniel, I force my heavy and numb legs to move forward. "You knew! You knew what he was doing to her!"

The ice in my veins freezes my blood, and my heart refuses to beat without the warmth. "How could you?" she wails.

In a single day, everything has fallen.

Even as I walk out of the office, shutting the door behind me and hearing the faint screams leak into the barren hall, I know everything is ruined and nothing will be the same.

Everything is broken, and I have no way to fix a single piece of it.

It's all dashed beyond repair.

CHAPTER 4

Aria

THEY WEREN'T GOING TO KILL THEM. I WANT TO THINK CARTER AND HIS brothers would never do that. They wouldn't execute my family in front of me. It's all I keep thinking as my eyes burn in the darkness of the box.

Nikolai would do it, though.

He would kill the Cross brothers, all of them, to set me free. But he doesn't know them and everything that happened. I haven't had a chance to convince him otherwise; all he knows is that I was taken. With every second that passes, I calm my panic, knowing I have to talk to Nikolai and stop this. I need it all to stop and for them to listen to me. For one of these thick-skulled men to just listen to me.

None of this would be happening if they listened to me.

A shuddering breath forces my body to tremble against the rough wood and my neck arches with a sudden deep breath.

I don't know if it's a panic attack or a sharp break from reality that's making me shake like I am.

Or the fear. The raw and paralyzing fear of what I know Carter is capable of and what I think he's going to do to me when I step out of this box.

"I love you," I whimper again, closing my eyes tightly and forcing the words out. I wish I could take it all back, but the alternative was watching my family die right in front of me. Watching Nikolai get shot in the back of the head. I cover my hot face with my hands, shaking my head like a lunatic at the thought.

"I don't want anyone to die." My strangled words are barely heard as the box shakes and then a hand bangs against the top.

"Aria, please." Addison's tone is desperate and I'm so ashamed. I don't want to leave this box. I feel like a child again, hiding in the closet and telling myself it's not real if I don't come out. If I stay here, none of this is real.

"He hurt you?" she asks, but her question is more of a statement. The question comes from a friend to a friend. Directed at a woman hiding from someone, someone she loves and crying hysterically. A grown ass adult, hiding in a box. I know exactly how this looks, but I don't know how to explain it to her, so she'd understand. She's not from this world. And she doesn't know Carter like I do either. Although, none of that makes this right.

None of it. "How long has he been doing this?" Her voice breaks at the question and I hear her cry for me.

I wish I could die right here.

"Come out!" she screams to me, her voice sounding ragged as she thumps on the box.

I know we're alone; Jase made Daniel leave and I heard the door shut what feels like hours ago but is probably only minutes. It's only Addison in the room now, crying as she holds the box and apologizes to me as if she's done anything wrong at all.

"He wouldn't listen to me," I whisper to no one in the darkness of the box. Every time I tried to explain, he wouldn't hear me out. He'd cut me off and tell me to get out. Just like she is. At this point, I don't think there's a defense I could possibly have that would make what I did forgivable in Carter's eyes.

"Get out!" she yells even louder. Her voice sounds hoarse at this point, and I hear her lay her body over the box heavily, falling onto it and crying. "How could he do this?" she whispers and then sniffles. I don't know if she's talking about what Carter did to me, or how Daniel allowed it and defended it. I know to see him in this light... it changed how Addison sees him, and that fucking kills me.

"I never meant for this to happen," I tell her weakly, closing my eyes and feeling them burn from hours of straining to see in the darkness and shedding hot tears.

I can hear her move again, but I don't know what she's doing, and her voice doesn't travel far. "I'm so sorry. I didn't know... I didn't know."

Reaching up slowly, I force my numb fingers to unlock the box with a loud click that makes my heart pump hard, so hard it feels like it'll stop beating altogether.

As I lift open the top, the light filters in and I squint. It fucking hurts. My eyes feel like they're burning, but I force the top open further as Addison stands up in front of me on shaky legs and wraps her arms around me. I hold her back tighter, gripping on to her and bunching the thin cotton of her shirt in my hand as she pulls me hard into her chest. "It's not your fault," is all I can say, and the words are so flat, so lacking to my ears, that I harden them, pulling her back and staring into her forest green eyes.

"You did nothing wrong," I tell her.

She stands there with a troubled expression, wiping away her tears and shaking her head. "What did he do to you?" she asks me softly, still holding on to me as I climb out of the box on shaky legs, staring at the closed door. I feel cold; it's so cold.

There's not a piece of me that doesn't think Carter's watching. I know he must be. My first instinct when thinking he knows I'm out of the box is to hold myself. To wrap my arms around my shoulders and wait for him to punish me. I can barely stand looking at the closed door.

Addison grips me with a bruising force, shaking me until I stare into her eyes. "What did he do to you?"

I just want to cry. I don't know where to start, but the shame clogs my throat and keeps me from speaking at all.

"It's okay to tell me," she whispers although the words barely come out. Fresh tears leak from the corners of her eyes as she speaks so calmly to me. "Whatever he did, you can tell me. It's okay."

"It's my fault," I start, and an awful gasp leaves her as she covers her mouth. It hurts, everything hurts, but the way she looks at me like I'm wounded, and I don't know any better, I can't explain the pain it causes.

She shakes her head violently, staring back at me.

"You don't understand," I try to reason with her but my voice cracks and all I can think is to keep repeating that it's my fault. It is, truly.

"I knew he'd hate me. I knew…" I can't finish the sentence as the door to the office opens. Fear spikes through me and I jump back, hitting the back of my legs against the box and nearly tumbling in. Addison guards me against whoever enters as if she's my protector.

"Get out!" she sneers at whoever's entered and with equal amounts of curiosity and terror, I peek over her shoulder. Even though I'm feeling weak and pathetic, my fingers numb and my chest heaving in air.

It's only Daniel.

"Addison, please." Daniel's eyes are red-rimmed, and I'm shocked. "Let's get out of here, okay?" He talks softly with his hands held up, approaching us like the two wounded animals that we are. "We can leave," he offers her.

"I'm sorry," I say and can barely get the words out, seeking Daniel's gaze so he knows I mean it. "I'm so sorry." My voice is wretched.

"Look at her." Addison's voice ricochets in the office as she steps toward Daniel. "Look at her!" she screams in his face and he lowers his head, shaking it and trying to speak. Addison doesn't understand; all she sees is the pain. And there's so much of it.

"It wasn't my place," Daniel tells her sternly, but his expression is begging her to understand. How can she, when she knows nothing?

"She's not okay and your brother did this to her." She takes another step forward and points to me, still standing behind her. Her bottom lip trembles as she shouts, "You did nothing!" I grip on to my shoulders tighter and feel so small. It's hard to know what to think anymore, but I know what she sees, and it breaks my heart.

"He didn't have a choice—"

"Bullshit!" she cuts him off, screaming louder and louder, "You let him hurt her!"

Silence compresses the time, forcing the clock to tick faster. The moment passes quickly as my head feels woozy and I can't stop my breathing from coming in just as fast.

I hold onto myself tighter, struggling to remain upright.

"I'm leaving and I'm taking her with me." The anger is gone; there's only resolve in Addison's voice. "So help me God, if you stand in my way, I'll never come back to you. Never, Daniel."

"You're leaving me?" he asks, the look in his eyes hardening, the silvers sparking even as the tremors of intense emotion run along his hard jaw. His determination is still there, still unyielding.

"How could I stay with you?" she asks, trying to disguise the misery in her tone as she hurriedly wipes away the tears. "How could I stay here, knowing this?"

Any semblance of anger vanishes from Addison, the realization of what she's doing breaking through her rage and disgust. She's leaving him.

"Don't do this," I finally speak, pushing forward and grabbing Addison's arm. I plead with her, "You don't need to get in between; you don't need—"

"It's not about what I need to do," Addison speaks so softly, but with an evenness that's at odds with her disheartened expression. "It's about what I want to do." Her voice doesn't waver as she turns to Daniel, grabbing my hand in hers and telling him once again, "I'm leaving and I'm taking her with me." With a quick intake of air and tears brimming in her deep green eyes, she hesitates but then adds, "Don't follow me, Daniel."

"You know I will," he tells her with no remorse, but also with no objection to her leaving either.

My hand feels so cold in Addison's and I try to speak again, but she shushes me. "Please, don't make this harder on me," she speaks to me although it sounds like a desperate prayer.

It's quiet for so long, the agony lingering in the air. My gaze darts between the two of them; he's staring at her, but she's staring at the open door.

"I need to leave," she tells him again, squeezing my hand and I squeeze back, for her. I keep praying to hear Carter's footsteps or his voice. Any part of him to come to me and fix this. To fix the mess I caused.

"I don't want this to happen," I say, and the words are rough beneath my breath as I tug at Addison's hand for her to look at me. And she does. I can feel Daniel's eyes on me, but I don't look at him; instead, I beseech Addison, willing her to believe me. "He didn't know," I lie. I'd tell a thousand lies to keep it from tearing the two of them apart.

I can see Daniel shift uncomfortably out of the corner of my eye, but I don't react. Addison's expression turns soft and sympathetic as she squeezes my hand again. "You don't have to lie for them." Her voice is coated with a sadness that claws at my insides. She gives me a soft smile that's false and it falters when she tells me, "They're big boys and they knew what they were doing." Turning to Daniel she adds, "He knew I would never be okay with something like this." The emotion wrecks each of her words and in turn, the hardness of Daniel's gaze. I can't bear to look at him, watching as her words destroy them and whatever love was left between them.

"It's over. And I want out," she says in two breaths that linger between them. "Let me go, Daniel. Please. You need to let me go this time." Even as the tears fall down her cheeks, she stands strong. I look past Daniel, refusing to look at either of them as my vision blurs with tears. The pain I feel for them magnifies as I realize she's taking me with her, and Carter isn't here at all.

He's not fighting for me.

He doesn't want me anymore.

I cover my face, pulling my hand away from hers and letting out the tortured sorrow of leaving him, but in the back of my mind I hear the voices hiss, he won't let it happen. She won't be able to leave so easily.

They're silenced with Daniel's only parting words. "I'll have Eli take you."

He doesn't touch her; he doesn't wait for a second longer. Instead, he simply turns and leaves us without another word, which only makes the pain grow stronger.

Carter, please, come take me. Please.

Addison struggles to control her composure, watching Daniel leave without even a single goodbye.

"I'm so sorry," I tell her again, hugging her back as she hugs me tight.

"You keep apologizing when this isn't your fault." Her words are soft and interrupted by the sound of footsteps.

I barely peek at the man named Eli, dressed in a fitted gray suit, no tie or cufflinks which makes it seem more casual, and with worn black dress shoes that are scuffed but somehow suit him.

It's his gaze that forces me to look away. Sharp pale blue eyes that have nothing but sympathy in them.

I don't want it. I'm ashamed as Addison leads me behind Eli and another man called Cason.

He's shorter than Eli, but not by much, and with bulging muscles that make him seem larger. He's the one who carries two bags he says are for us, but I don't know what's in them. Addison cries harder although she nods her head. Her strength at this moment is something I admire. I wish I could move forward, to make the decision to leave even knowing what the Cross brothers are capable of.

With Cason behind and Eli in front, our footsteps echo in the quiet hall. At every corner, I both hope that Carter is there to stop me and pray that he's not, so I can escape and hide away from him.

Every second closer to the door feels like it pulls on my torn heart.

Carter never comes, and that makes the chill from outside that much colder.

The peonies have died from the season's passing, they never last long, and the pale moon is full, illuminating every bit of the path to the sleek black sedan waiting for us even though the night is still early.

As I stare up at the house, searching for Carter in any of the windows, Addison waits for me to get in the car with silent tears still falling. He's not there. He's not watching.

"We don't have to leave," I tell her softly once more, desperately wanting Carter to come out and say he understands and that he forgives me. As I do him. In every way.

For what happened in the cell. For what happened today. It's all fucked up and there isn't an ounce of good in any of it, but I swear I love him. And love is forgiveness, isn't it?

I forgive him for anything he's done. I just want him back. I want him to love me again.

Please, Carter.

But not seeing him here… Him knowing that I'm leaving, and not bothering to say goodbye or try to fight for me in the least, I know he doesn't want me. It crushes me.

That thought is what forces me into the car, my back hitting the leather with a forceful blow. The sound of the trunk opening and the murmurs from Addison and Eli speaking mean nothing.

I don't know where I'll go or what I'll do.

My skin is numb, and I can barely breathe.

How many times have I tried to run? Yet here I am, and I would give anything for Carter to stomp toward us and rip me from my savior to throw me back into the cell.

The leather seats protest as Addison gets in and buckles her seatbelt. I talk over the click. "I love him," I say, swallowing thickly. "I love Carter."

She barely glances at me, her eyes red and blotchy and her cheeks still flushed from crying.

"I love Daniel too." Her voice is hoarse as she leans her head back, resting it and staring at the ceiling of the car. "But love isn't enough sometimes. They can't do that to you."

I'm ashamed at her reply. I'm ashamed that I need saving.

I'm ashamed that I allowed it and with a single moment, she's seemingly put an end to it.

I wish I could rip my heart out and never feel love again. How easy life would be if you could truly be heartless.

Hours ago, I was in love with a man I know I should never have let near me.

And now he's watching me leave with zero objections, and it destroys me. I've never felt pain and regret like this. It doesn't matter what happened between us today; I would be feeling this tear in my soul regardless of what I'd done.

I should have known the concept of a happily ever after would never come to fruition when my last name is Talvery.

CHAPTER 5

S HE'S REALLY LEAVING.

She walked away. Straight through the front door. Never would I have seen it happen that way. She was always running and hiding in the shadows. I knew she'd leave one day, deep down in the pit of my stomach, but I never imagined it'd be like this. I never imagined it would fucking hurt like this either.

Swallowing thickly and ignoring the pain, I pick up another book from the floor, a hardback of *Lord of the Flies*. It's a collector's edition and I watch as I trace the spine of it with my fingers while asking Daniel, "Did you call Sebastian?"

He's leaning against the windowsill, but I can't fucking watch them leave like he is.

I won't watch her walk away from me.

"He knows already." His voice is low, not filled with the resentment I keep waiting for him to throw at me.

For being the hard man he is, Daniel always has forgiveness for his family. I wish I felt the same.

"How is that even possible?" I ask him while placing the book on the shelf and reach down for another. Someone else could take care of this and clean up my mess, but I don't want them to. I need to do something mindless before I deal with the consequences. Every time I bend down is another deep breath. Every book on the shelf is a piece put back into place.

I need to do this before I can deal with Jase going behind my back and everything that's happened over the last few hours. No one will come out unscathed. No. One.

Grinding my teeth together, I keep my back to Daniel as he answers me.

"Addison was ready to run; I could see it." He looks full of guilt and remorse as he stares out of the window, watching the car lights die in the thick of the forest as they move farther along the road.

Taking them away from us.

Taking her away from me.

Even glancing at the lights, so small and faint in the distance, shoves the knife deeper into my chest.

"So, I called him and asked if he would mind." He shrugs, attempting to refute the devastation of what's happened. It's clearly written in his expression, but he continues, "He's never used it and it's close, it's contained, and easily defended."

"Do they really think we'd let them go?" I ask him, feeling a surge of control again. She's never leaving me. Never.

"I'm sure Addison knows better." The urgency in Daniel's voice compels me to look back at him. He's leaning against the window now, facing the door to my office and staring at it aimlessly. "She'll try to leave, so we need to watch for that too."

"Always watching…" I mutter and then add, "For enemies coming and for our women leaving."

"Look at you, even now you care about her," he points out and Daniel's remark catches me off guard. "More than you admit to her."

"I just don't want them to have her."

A withering, sad smirk tugs at Daniel's lips, making him look even more miserable. "Our women." He repeats my words and the tension tightens around my chest. "Is there a difference with what's between Addison and me, and Aria and you?" he asks me in a voice laced with accusations.

"I love Addison," he tells me before I can answer, his breathing quickening as he struggles to hide the pain of watching her leave him.

He looks at the floor for only a moment, shoving his hands into his pockets before looking up at me and asking me outright, "Do you still love her?"

A beat passes, but only one. A single beat inside my chest and I know the answer. I breathe the word at the same time as the door opens and one of my men enters.

"Boss," Jett calls out my title while knocking on the open door.

"Do you have an update?" I ask him with an eyebrow cocked, looking at his knuckles on the door and wondering why he fucking bothered to knock.

Nodding his head and straightening his shoulders, Jett answers me without hesitation. Daniel's restless, leaning against the window then kicking off of it as he listens to the soldier. Jett's one of Eli's men. Eli's a lieutenant, the rank given to the men we trust implicitly to lead other men in our crime family. And Jett's the soldier he left behind to see that everything fell into place with him gone.

The four of us, my brothers and I, we each have two lieutenants and the area we claim is split four ways. It keeps things clean and organized. All of the men who work for us call me boss though. I'm the one and only boss.

Yet this motherfucker listened to Jase. Jase gave an order that directly countered mine, which should have been absolute, and this asshole listened to him.

A tic in my jaw starts to spasm as I remember, feeling the heat and anger of what happened only hours ago stir hate into my blood once again.

I can see the moment Jett realizes I'm not over that little stunt. His pupils dilate, and he stutters over a word before talking faster. That's what happens when you're fucking scared.

I have to remind myself that they didn't know. Jase is the one and the only person responsible.

"Eli and Cason are in the first car, and there are three decoy cars even though there's no trace of anyone watching or following." He swallows, and I can hear the dry gulp of his throat as I imagine tearing it out.

Jase defied me.

They followed his orders and didn't know of mine.

I remind myself of that fact, bending down to snatch another book off the floor and rein in the rage. Someone needs to have the piss beat out of them for what happened.

Slamming the book on the shelf, I see Jase's face. He let them go. Everyone will know that she put a gun to my head because of him.

"Would you like me to help—"

"No," I cut him off in a single, low breath, devoid of any emotion.

"Does 'anyone' include Romano's men?" Daniel questions and I watch for Jett's reaction, setting another book on the shelf. "Or better yet, who knows where Aria and Addison are going and that they've left the premises? Name every single man."

"Eli and Cason's men, the ten of us," Jett's quick to answer him and then stands silently at attention again. His gaze darts between the two of us, waiting for any other question or orders. The way he stands is firm and upright, same as Eli. But there's a nervousness about him that I don't like.

"I want thirty men spread out on the blocks surrounding Sebastian's place on Fifth," Daniel tells Jett, although I know he's talking to me. "The Red Room is on the northern side, so that street is already handled, but the other three sides of our territory are lighter on men and closer to Talvery than I like."

"We need fifty," I correct him. The east and south sides need to have a second row. If Talvery's going to come for them, if my enemies find out where Addison and Aria are, I want more men.

"We can do fifty easy," Cason answers as if it was a question and not a demand. He continues, "We just need to pull back on the lower east side, closest to Crescent Hills." Jett licks his bottom lip as he looks past me, using his fingers to tally up men absently.

I take a moment to really consider him as he tells me that "place" is always causing problems, but if we back off the problems take care of themselves anyway. As in the people we tend to have to control in Crescent Hills, simply kill the people that cause them issues if we don't step in.

I know that he's right because it's where I'm from and that's how it was when I grew up, but it pisses me off. The idea that we can move out of areas we've only just begun to take over and let them kill each other off because it's not worth it… it hits me in a way that it shouldn't.

Only because it's a place I used to call home. I know that's why, but it doesn't help control the rage that boils inside of me.

"Fifty then," Daniel answers and crosses his arms. From here I can feel him looking at me, but I'm still focused on Jett as he rambles on about which men can go where. I'm going to start calling him Mr. Calculus if he doesn't shut the fuck up soon. My jaw is clenched so tightly I think my molars will crack from the pressure.

I could see me taking out my displeasure on Jett. I can already feel how his jaw would crack under my fist. It would take more than one punch without my brass knuckles.

"Carter," Daniel says, and it breaks the vision of me beating the piss out of this entitled fuck. An asshole who didn't grow up the way I did and doesn't give a fuck about anyone in that city.

"What?" I don't hide the irritation as the word comes deep from my chest.

"Put the poor book down," he tells me, glancing at the book I'm practically ripping apart in my hand. Slamming it into its place on the shelf, I run my hand down my face and then brace my hands against the carved wood details of the bookshelf. I stare at the empty place still waiting for the books to be replaced.

"Ever the fucking comedian," I mutter under my breath, trying to relax and shrug off the need to let all my rage out.

"Keep a watch on the two of them and tell us if they want to leave," Daniel gives Jett his orders, but what the dumb fuck says next pushes me over the edge.

"What if Aria wants to go home?" Jett asks, concern evident in his gaze.

"What's that?" I can feel my own gaze narrow in on him as I push off of the bookshelf. The room feels hotter, smaller, and adrenaline races through my blood.

The soldier doesn't pick up on my anger. He doesn't get that what he's suggesting is going to get his head bashed against the fucking wall.

"Get out," Daniel speaks up as I take two steps toward my prey.

Jett goes still at Daniel's command, looking back at him as if wondering if he heard right. "She's not going anywhere," Daniel tells him as he stalks forward, pushing his hand against my chest for the second time tonight. The harder, darker side of his soul shows as he grabs Jett by his throat and pushes him against the wall. So hard I hear a crack, although I'm not sure what it was that made the sickening sound.

Jett's body sags in Daniel's grasp.

"Both women will be there temporarily." Although they're of similar height, it feels as if Daniel's towering over Jett as he nods and quickly agrees with Daniel, staring him in the eyes and making sure his voice is clear.

"Of course. They're there temporarily. I know that."

"Make sure you don't forget that." Daniel's parting words are sneered as he releases Jett and the man struggles to steady his feet. "Get out of here." Watching him yell in Jett's face eases some of the tension. Only some of it.

Jett doesn't pause or wait for anything else from either of us. He must have some sense in him after all.

"I wanted to bash his head in," I tell Daniel as the sound of that fucker racing down the hall to get away dims.

"I know," Daniel says with his back still to me as he rolls up his sleeves. "That's why I had to do it."

The ticking of the clock marches steadily between his last words and his next. "With the war coming, we need all the men we can get."

CHAPTER 6

Aria

WHEN I HEARD ELI SAY WE WERE GOING TO A SAFE HOUSE, THIS WASN'T what I was expecting.

It's on the far end of the city, away from the hustle and bustle, in a quieter area and close to Main Street with a few shops within walking distance. There are a few quaint houses that line the street, but nearly a quarter mile separates each of them on this street.

This isn't like the safe house my father has. This house is in plain sight, but it's built for war if only you look closely enough at the exterior.

The three-story building is made of stone, with a concrete fence around the property, covered in beautiful ivy. The front door is all steel but beautifully etched with what looks like a Celtic pattern. I only got a brief glimpse before I was led here to the second floor, and each floor seems to be self-contained, so multiple families could live here and never even see each other. I'm in absolute awe, although it doesn't take the pain away in the least.

The kitchen is open to the living room. The center of the room is focused around a stone fireplace with a darkly stained, reclaimed wood mantel. Its ruggedness matches the iron and spicewood chandelier. But it's at odds with the clean sleekness of the all-white kitchen, just behind us.

We're stuck here, with a large L-shaped chenille sofa and matching armchairs that hug the fireplace until the guards say otherwise.

"Only a few minutes," is what Cason said. But more than a few have already passed as we linger in the beautiful gilded cage.

I'm biting my tongue though; I don't dare say a word to Addison as I pace behind the sofa. Addison's still pissed, but it seems fake to me. Like she's just trying to be angry at being locked up here rather than being brokenhearted over what happened.

She's been staring for the last ten minutes at the clothes she dumped on the sofa, trying not to cry. I can't stand seeing her on edge like this.

I'm an asshole, but I'll admit I'm grateful to be distracted by her. If I was alone, I'd be huddled in a ball crying on the floor.

"This is bullshit," she grits out the words, still staring at the clothes. "This isn't what I meant when I said I was leaving!" she screams to no one.

"He said it would only be a week or so, right?" I ask her carefully, trying to calm her down just the slightest.

She nods and visibly swallows before rolling her eyes, seemingly remembering that she's annoyed with being held here rather than given free will to leave.

"For our protection." Addison picks up a dress and balls it in her hands before throwing it back down on the sofa. Pushing her hair out of her face, she leans her head back and takes a deep breath. She does that a lot, the leaning her head back and deep breaths. I've seen her do it a few times when she gets worked up.

"Is that like a meditation practice or something?" I ask her, wanting to change the topic if I can, to something… less devastating. I'm exhausted from crying, but tired of being exhausted from crying. I don't want to hurt right now; I need a distraction for just a moment. Just a moment to breathe before I face my reality again.

She nods her head, barely moving from the position and takes a moment before telling me, "It's a yoga thing, really, I don't know that I can meditate." She reaches for the duffle bag on the floor and picks up the clothes on the sofa, one piece at a time, to toss them back in. "My mind is always wandering, and I have to get up and do something."

I nearly smile, happy that she's talking to me about something else. It was silent in the car ride here and the tension has been suffocating me.

"Yeah, I get that," I answer her. "I tried meditation a while ago and it was not my cuppa."

"Cuppa?" she questions with her brow furrowed, and I stifle a small smile at her curious expression.

"Cup of tea." I shrug and add, "It wasn't my cup of tea." Staring at my own duffle bag on the armchair, I add casually, even as I feel the weight of my heart seem to grow and sink into my stomach, "I like tarot cards better."

"Oh!" The excitement in Addison's voice is not at all what I was expecting. Maybe she's better at pretending life is all right when it's in shambles than I am. "And like palm readings?"

I have to smile at her enthusiasm.

She keeps talking as she finishes gathering the clothes. "I went to see a gypsy in New Orleans once." She peeks over at me as I walk closer, taking a seat on the far end of the sofa. I have to, so I can hear her over the sound of the guards still walking through the safe house to make sure everything is in place. As in, cameras. I know those fuckers are putting up cameras.

I have to keep my mouth closed, my teeth grinding against one another at the thought, and keep the anger from showing as she tells me her story of the woman she met by Café du Monde. I swallow thickly as she tells me about New Orleans, a place I've never been.

She's still feigning an upbeat attitude and I'm trying to keep up. I wonder if she can pretend like this when she lies down. When there are no distractions and sleep evades her. Just the thought of what my mind will do to me tonight, makes me grab the throw blanket on the sofa and wrap it around me as if it could protect me.

"I wanted to get my coffee grounds read and all that too, but I didn't have time."

"Seven kids?" My brows haven't moved from their raised position since she casually mentioned that little fact the palm reader told her. "She said you're going to have seven kids?"

I didn't hear the rest of what she said about the reading as I stared off absently, pretending to listen but really thinking about tonight and how I know I'll cry again. I feel helpless, hopeless, and pathetic.

Addison's expression pales and she purses her lips before she carefully says, "Pregnancies." She doesn't hide the pain in her eyes when she clarifies. "She said seven pregnancies. She also said they wouldn't keep."

Fuck. I can't even look her in the eyes as I struggle to tell her I'm sorry. She only shrugs it off before pulling up on her bag to close it.

The sound of her zipping up the bag is accompanied by the sound of Eli walking back into the room. With his dress shirt sleeves rolled up, the tattoos on his arm are on full display. They're all in black and white with lots of detail. A compass that fades up his left arm catches my attention, but the tone of his voice brings my gaze up to his.

"The rooms are ready. We'll be downstairs at all times." Eli's blunt and has a hint of some accent. Irish or British maybe, I can't tell. It's subtle, but it's there.

"I don't want to stay here," Addison tells him again. Her shoulders rise and fall quickly as her breathing quickens. "I'm not with Daniel anymore." Her voice cracks, but she continues, "And I don't need a safe house. I need to leave."

Eli's expression is unmoving. I almost question if he's heard her as the silence stretches between them. The only sounds are from the other men behind Eli in the hall as they walk downstairs to their section of the safe house. "I understand." Eli's initial response takes Addison by surprise. She even flinches slightly, but then he adds, "There are some precautions that need to be taken first. But in one week, give or take, we will take you to wherever you want to go, and leave you alone."

Alone.

I hate that word.

"So, we're supposed to stay locked up in this fucking house?" Addison's anger rises as she asks the question, each word getting louder than the last. I watch as her blunt nails dig into her palms as she fails to rein in her anger.

"Main Street has several shops and a few restaurants. We have no objections to you walking the block… however, someone will be with you at all times."

My mind has been reeling all night with everything that's happened. I've been here for nearly two hours, and I'm only just now realizing why we have to stay here under house arrest with guards for one week. *And then we can go free.*

One week.

"He's going to kill them." With my gaze fixed on the sheer curtain, draped in the moonlight from outside the window, the crushing feeling in my chest returns. "One week until the war is over."

Addison turns slowly to face me, and I sink back further into the sofa.

"I'm being held hostage until my family is dead." My throat closes slowly like it's suffocating me, and my eyes burn hotter as the pain diffuses through me.

I've lost Carter. I've lost the chance to influence him because I failed.

And now I'm trapped in this beautiful place while everyone I love is murdered. My vision is blurred as I picture the house I grew up in, the blood on the walls, bullet holes in the doors. Licking my lips, I taste my salty tears. "Eli, can you answer me a question?" I ask him with a short breath I'm barely able to hold on to.

The lightheadedness floods my mind as he nods his head, yes.

"Is there someone to clean up everything you leave behind?" I struggle to breathe as I look him in the eyes and continue, "Or when I ask to go home in a week, will I be the one who has to clean up the bodies of my family?" My voice shakes on the last word, but he hears me. I know he does.

I picture my cousin, Brett, and his wife and their baby. In a moment, they're right where I last saw them during the holidays. And in a blink, they're lying dead on the floor, their eyes staring back at me as if seeing me for who I really am.

And I hate what they see.

Some of my family may be cruel like Carter, but not all of them are and so many people will die. I know what to expect. I've seen it before. I can't sit here and do nothing.

I refuse.

Eli stares back at me, assessing me and judging me, but I don't care. As long as I can hold on to the strength of my mentality, I don't care what he thinks. Knowing I can't and won't sit by and do nothing is all that matters.

"I know it's war, but I would rather be with them right now," I tell Eli, brushing the tears away as I realize that's where my place is. "I think it would be best if you sent me back to my home."

"Maybe when the week is over, you'll want to go somewhere else," is all Eli gives me.

It's not until he's gone that I realize Addison is silently crying.

She can't even look at me, but I don't care.

I don't care about anything anymore.

"It's what this life is like," I tell her solemnly, remembering all the nights the men would fill the kitchen downstairs, clinking their beers and patting each other on the back. "I had an uncle named Pierce." I haven't thought about it in forever, but now I'm reliving a certain night when I was fifteen years old. The night that marks the first time I fully grasped what my family did for a living and began to really see the consequences that came with it. I can feel how raw my throat is when I pause to swallow. From screaming, from crying.

"I came downstairs while he was holding something up in the air and everyone else in the room was cheering." Their voices echo in my head. "I remember smiling, so happy that my father was in a good mood." I don't know if she's listening, but I keep talking.

"My uncle was so happy to see me." I remember the way his grin widened before putting down whatever it was he'd been holding and hugging me like he hadn't seen me in years. "I felt like a part of the family that night. My father even gave me a small glass of wine despite the fact I was only sixteen." I remember the way it tasted, and how I felt when he poured from his bottle and gave me the glass in front of everyone. "He said, tonight we drink. Tonight, we celebrate Talvery. And everyone cheered again when I took a sip."

I peek over at Addison, who's listening intently and waiting for the punch line.

"It wasn't until a few days later that Nikolai told me it was a human tongue. The tongue of a rat who was murdered, and they were celebrating because the charges were dropped with no witness living to testify." I had to beg Nik to tell me; he told me I wouldn't want to know, but I pressed him. After he told me, I knew I could trust his opinion if I ever wanted to know something again.

I stare at the fireplace, wishing it would crackle with a soothing flame, but it's empty and there's no wood here to start a fire.

"Talverys and the Cross brothers are the same. And they'll both kill each other or die trying." It's a truth I've wanted to avoid for so long, but now it seems as if I can only try to limit the damage they'll cause.

"That's not the way they grew up," Addison tells me with tears in her eyes. "They were good people."

"My family is full of good people too." My gut churns from trying to defend this life to her. To someone who didn't grow up in it. "They just do bad things. Like my uncle. He loved his wife, he loved his kids, and he would have done anything for me if he were still alive."

It's quiet for a moment as Addison slowly sits down next to me, holding onto herself like she'll fall to pieces if she doesn't.

She doesn't speak for a long time; neither of us does. But neither of us gets up either. "I don't understand how Daniel got into this. This isn't what they were like before. I swear to you. They were good and… and… I don't know how this happened." She looks lost like she had no idea. I've seen women before who are in denial, who turn a blind eye. But she's truly shocked. Maybe she didn't realize how real this life can be. How close to death it is.

"I do."

My response grabs her attention and she waits for more, but I don't know how much she really wants to know, or what she needs to know.

"For the longest time, there wasn't anyone south of Fallbrook. That's where I'm from and basically the territory my father keeps. My father talked about taking it a lot." I remember back when I was little, how I'd sit in his office coloring and he'd have hushed conversations about the developments in Back Ridge. "There wasn't anyone living there, no businesses, but then," I clear my throat and tell her, "then developments grew and there were more people. More opportunities, as my father called it."

"He and Romano had two territories side by side, and both wanted it. But the areas are like a cross, sort of." Four quarters, I draw it out on the blanket on my lap, the way Nikolai explained it to me. "Carter's area is the bottom left, but his portion is bigger now. The bottom right is Crescent Hills and it's not claimed, just a shit town with no one policing it, no one protecting it. Carter and his crew keep moving closer and closer, but they only take it little by little. My father has the upper left and Romano the upper right. They both wanted the territory where Carter is now, but while they waged a cold war against each other because of my mother…" I swallow a dry lump not knowing if she knows but not in a state to explain. "Carter took over. One by one, killing the men who worked for my father who tried to stop him, or, sometimes, Carter took on my father's soldiers, proving he would be ruthless and that the area was his, but he had mercy for those who stayed with him."

"So, it was Carter?" she asks, and I can see in her eyes she doesn't want to believe Daniel was involved.

"I've heard Jase and Carter's names a lot." I almost say more, but I hold it back, swallowing my words. "But Carter is the one name that everyone knows. It's either Carter or the Cross brothers."

Addison's brow is pinched but her expression is riddled with anguish as she says, "I don't know why Carter would do that. I don't know why he'd want to live this way."

Again, I almost say, "I do," but I don't. It's because my father knew what Carter was capable of. He knew they would take over. My father tried to kill them before they could become the powerful family they are now, but he failed. His failed attempt is what made Carter who he is.

The truth, and facing the truth, causes a coldness to flow across my skin and I pull the blanket more tightly around me.

"I understand if you could never be friends with someone like me. Someone whose family makes a living through death and sin. Someone who…" I trail off, pausing for a moment before what I'm about to say next. I have to close my eyes to say, "Someone who broke you and Daniel up."

"Stop it," Addison breathes the command with a seriousness I wasn't expecting. "You didn't break us up and you're still my friend." She grips my hand in both of hers as I stare back at her, hoping she still feels this way in the morning. Because I have no one right now and, in a week, I may have even less than no one.

"It's going to be okay and we're going to look out for each other. You have to look out for the ones you care about. You know?" Her gaze begs me to agree with her, to stay strong. But I'm not like Addison.

Tears beg to run down my face, but I bite them back, refusing to cry any more tonight. Instead, I nod my head and force out my reply, although the words are strangled. "I'm trying to. But what can I do when the ones I care about want each other dead?"

The silence comes again, but she's quick to end it this time.

"Let's have a drink." She's off the sofa before I can even tell her how badly I need one.

I can only nod my head in agreement, still wrapping my head around the spiral of horrific events that led me here.

I can't think about anything but Carter as I hear her open a bottle of wine and the glasses clink on the counter. Instead, all I can do is picture Carter's face the exact moment I lost his trust and he lost his fucking mind.

It's going to haunt me forever.

If not that, then the sight of my family in coffins.

There was no way for me to win.

I don't want to do this anymore. I can't deal with this anymore.

I need to stop this.

CHAPTER 7

Carter

I T'S QUIETER HERE THAN I THOUGHT IT WOULD BE. SEBASTIAN PICKED A NICE AREA. He had the place built two years ago but never came back. I don't know if it's the memory of him or everything that happened tonight that makes my heart twist like someone's wringing it out from inside my chest.

The whiskey didn't make the pain better. Not the first glass, not the second. Not when I threw the bottle at the window, shattering it and filling the room with the smell of liquor. Earlier, I spent too long sagging against the wall while sitting on the floor of the office staring at the box. The box that's still open, empty, and pushed up against the rug. I can't move it back. I can't bring myself to move it back as if she was never in there.

Everything is telling me to let her go.

Logic and reason. She will never love me because of the way we started. She will never love me after I kill her family. She will never love me, because of the man I am.

I know it all to be true.

But the idea of letting her leave fucking hurts.

"Do you want me to go in with you?" Daniel asks me from the driver's seat, ripping my gaze from the front of the house and cutting through my thoughts.

"Are you sure you're okay to see her?" he asks me the real question.

"I'm not going to hurt her," I tell him as I stare back at the house, praying I'm telling the truth. I want her to feel this pain. I want her to know how much it hurts.

"What are you going to do?" he asks me, his hands sliding down the leather steering wheel.

"I'm going to give her what she wants," I lie. I'll never let her leave me.

My brother's voice is stern and loud in the cabin of the car as he says, "You're making a mistake."

I'm taken aback by his criticism, staring at him as the dark night sky gets darker. "You can do what you'd like with Addison; I won't judge you. But stay out of it when it comes to me and Aria." It's all I can tell him because I don't know what to do with Aria. I don't know what I can do with a woman who would betray me like she did.

"Are you really going to let her walk away?" When I don't answer his question, he pushes me by saying, "She'll have no one when this is done with. No one."

I raise my voice to reply and end this conversation. "I said I'm going to give her what she wants. I didn't say I'd let her go." My blood rushes in my ears as Daniel's eyes narrow in the darkness.

"Are you coming in?" I ask him, refusing to let him continue.

"No, she's not inside. She walked down to the liquor store for more wine when Aria went to bed." He settles back in the seat and looks straight down the road to add, "I'm going to drive up there and keep an eye on her from a distance."

Pausing, he looks at me before adding, "Cason's with her and there are eyes are on her, but still…"

"She must know you'll be watching her," I say absently, remembering everything that happened months ago.

His nod is solemn. "I know she does. I'm sure she hates it too."

Giving him a tilt of my head to part ways, I grab the handle to open the door, but Daniel's words stop me. "I wonder if she'll know when I get to her."

With my fingers wrapped around the handle, I still, then ask, "What do you mean?"

"She used to know somehow. Years ago, when Tyler died. Every time I came close to her, she'd turn around as if she knew I was there. It didn't matter how far away I was or how many other people were around us. She always knew, back then."

He finally looks over at me, the sorrowful smirk still on his face. "I wonder if it'll be the same even now."

I don't know what advice to give my brother. I can feel his pain and there are no words to help him.

"Just make sure she's safe," I tell him, remembering all those years ago and everything that happened between them… between all of us.

"Always," he tells me and smacks the back of his hand against my arm. "Don't fuck it up." He forces a weak smile to his face, although it doesn't reach his eyes. I can't give the same back to him.

The sounds of the night greet me as the car door opens and then shuts easily. The crickets and the wind are all I can hear. The men posted on the side of the building see me and I acknowledge them with a simple nod. I button my suit jacket and walk up the sidewalk and onto the porch. With every step, the anxiety over my fears grows. The fear that I've lost her forever. That she never loved me, and I never really had her. The fear that tonight has destroyed anything and everything that's between us.

There's no turning back from what's happened. There's no denying that she's clouding my judgment and keeping her means losing the confidence and respect from my men.

Helplessness is something I haven't felt in so long, but it's with me now as I stalk toward the safe house.

Eli's been at the front door all day with his earpiece in and the phone displaying the monitors. He stands up straighter with the smack of my boots on the stone steps as I make my way toward him.

"Aria's in the north bedroom on the second floor. Addison's at—"

"The liquor store," I finish the sentence for him.

"Boss," he says and rewards me with the barest flicker of a smile. "Of course, you'd know." He opens the massive front door; it's solid steel eight feet high and three feet wide. The bright light from the foyer reflects off the freshly polished wood floors. It's been a while since I've been here and the memory of standing on this threshold with Sebastian makes me pause.

Chloe, Sebastian's wife, is the one who chose everything for this house. She wanted to come back. I really thought they were coming home years ago when this house was built, but they didn't.

Standing there, I remember my childhood like it was yesterday, back when I was a different person. Back before all that shit happened with Aria's father; before my best friend left and my mother passed away, leaving me on my own to take care of my drunkard of a father and my four brothers. I've never thought back on it and felt ashamed. But as I stand here, I think back to who I used to be and know I would hate the man I've become. I would hate who I've turned into and what I've done.

You can't go back though. You can never go back.

"Is there anything I can do for you?" Eli asks quietly, carefully.

"How is she?" I ask him. I've known Eli for four years now. He helped me take over the majority of this territory and he's the only reason I've moved deeper into Crescent Hills, where I'm from. There's no law in Crescent Hills, so moving my empire there is a task harder than most, and the income doesn't justify it. It's a hellhole no one wants, but I thought Sebastian would eventually come back and help me take it. I thought wrong.

"She's been crying on and off since Addison left." Eli's gaze doesn't stay on mine as he reports on Aria to me. He looks down at his shoes and swallows before looking me back in the eyes. "She saw some of the news. I'm not sure what she's most upset about. Leaving you or losing her family."

Anger is a slow simmer. I shouldn't have waited to pull the trigger. "If they were already dead, I wouldn't have this problem."

Eli nods in agreement. "We're ready when you are, Boss."

"Romano's already taking down the streets in the upper east."

Eli nods again and says, "It's been all over the news today. I imagine Romano will hit them from the south side this week."

"Talvery will be expecting it though."

"That's good for us here. Chances are good he'll take his men on the northernmost streets up there and hit him harder."

"They both react predictably."

"And they'll both fall... predictably." The grin on his face would be reflected on mine, but all I can think about is how Aria will truly hate me then. She was willing to threaten me to save them. Deep in my gut, I know the idea of vengeance is something that will cross her mind. And it fucking kills me.

"I don't know that I can ever trust her again," I speak the revelation out loud and regret it immediately. What the fuck is wrong with me?

"She'll get over it. I overheard her explaining things to Addison; she understands why this has to happen."

The night air clings to me, holding me here at the threshold instead of moving forward to face Aria.

"Where did you find that dumb fuck, Jett?" I ask him to get off the topic and remind him who I am. His fucking boss.

"He's a good shot, just a little shit when it comes to his mouth. I think he has Asperger's or something." He looks past me and into the night for a moment before continuing. "He's not too good at reading social clues, but in the war, he waited three days to get a shot on the insurgents in Afghanistan. Three days he stayed in the same bunker, barely bigger than a shack. He didn't fucking move until the three on his hit list were in his sights." He huffs a short laugh although it lacks genuine humor. "They came out for a smoke, thinking they were in the clear since it'd been quiet for three days. It only took him twenty seconds to get all three of them in the skull."

"I still want to rip his fucking throat out," I tell him absently, although my respect for Jett grows as I picture what he's been through.

Eli shrugs. "I've told him before that he could still shoot his gun if I cut out his tongue." He chuckles and adds, "Jokingly, of course. I owe him my life."

"I'll keep that in mind the next time I want to punch his face in." My words come out dull, lacking the conviction I had before.

"What'd he say?" he asks me.

"Nothing," I answer him, knowing I don't want to have this conversation with him. I respect Eli, but he's not my friend. This is business.

He nods once, opening the door just a hair more and the soft sound of it creaking is loud in my ears.

"Tell the men not to go in and to stall Addison until I'm done in here," I say, staring at the spiral staircase that leads to the second floor where my little songbird is now caged. "I don't want her to hear this."

"Yes, Boss."

I pat him on the shoulder as I walk in, but I don't look him in the eyes. Even though I'm staring at the staircase, all I can see is everything that happened hours ago. The gun she pointed at me, the box she ran to and hid in. The sight of the car as it pulled away and how she didn't object.

My throat's tight and the hammering of my heart gets faster and more painful as I climb the stairs. The railing is slick under my hot palm.

She's mine.

She's going to know I fucking own her when I leave her tonight.

Even if she still leaves me, she will always belong to me.

Always.

The thought makes the rushing of blood in my ears that much louder. Each step closer to the door my cock gets harder, thinking of every reaction she'll have to me.

Anger, hate even.

Or maybe she'll beg me to forgive her.

I close my eyes, resting the flat side of my fist against the wall to the right of her bedroom door at the thought of her begging me for mercy. Something she refused to do in the cell.

My eyes open slowly at the sound of the bed creaking from just beyond the door.

Aria

I heard his footsteps before the door opened.

I can't explain why I prayed for it to be Carter. The last time I saw him, all I had was fear of him.

With the window open, the wind drifts in, shifting the curtains out of place and letting the moonlight drape over Carter's dominant form.

My heart flickers in a weird uneven beat and I'm reminded of the first time I ever saw him. The same fear races through me, but so does the feeling that he could save me.

If only he wanted to, but from the sharp look in his eyes, that's not what he has planned for me at all.

At this point, I'm okay with that. He can do what he'd like to me because I already know I'll submit to him. I already know I still love him. No matter how fucked up it is.

"Carter," I whisper his name as I sit up in bed, letting the sheets fall into a puddle around me. A shiver graces my skin as the wind tickles my shoulder.

The floor creaks with his heavy step and the shadow across his face moves, hugging the sharp lines of his jaw as he stalks toward me.

"Get on your knees," he commands me in a rough voice. That's the only greeting he gives me and it reminds me of what life was like in the cell with him.

Defiance runs deep in my blood and it spikes anger high in my chest as my jaw clenches.

"That's what you have to say to me?" I question him with my voice wavering. Anxiety and heartbreak are equally present, making my toes curl and my fists bunch the silk sheets. I can barely breathe as I bite back the words, "You didn't come for me."

He pauses at the end of the bed, but only for a moment, a single beat of my wretched heart. He speaks softly, yet forcefully as he slips off his jacket and lays it carefully at the end of the bed.

"I have many things to say to you, Aria Talvery," he practically spits my name and I snarl back, "Fuck you," feeling the hate for him intensify.

I've always known he was my enemy, but I never felt as if he saw me that way. The tides have changed.

His deft fingers unbutton his shirt and my eyes leave his to watch as he strips.

"I told you to get on your knees," he reminds me in a voice that drips of dominance and sex. He tosses his shirt on top of his jacket, losing the control he had a moment ago.

My eyes are drawn to the leather of his belt as he unbuckles it and then quickly pulls it from its place, letting the leather hiss through the air.

My pussy clenches as he bends the leather into a loop and waits for me to obey him. "You've already questioned me, defied me, and lied to me today. Are you really going to disobey me again?"

I swallow thickly, knowing I want his punishment, and I want this. But I didn't lie to him.

"I've never lied to you and I never will," I tell him quickly, feeling my pulse quicken.

"You didn't tell me the truth. That's lying," he says, his voice louder and he doesn't hide his anger in the least.

"I won't…" I pause and trail off. Biting down on my lower lip, I hate that the one conflict we have that will tear us apart, again and again, is one we will never agree on. "I won't sit back and let you kill them. I won't."

Carter's movements are faster than I thought possible, sending a spike of fear through me. The belt hits the bed as he grips my chin and lowers his lips to mine. My heart races and lust mixes with terror. "You don't have a choice," he whispers against my lips.

I question myself even as the words leave my lips, "You're wrong."

I can feel his heat; I can hear his heart hammer in his chest as I stare into his dark eyes. I could get lost in them forever and at this moment, I wish I could. "I wish things were different," I tell him as his silence grows.

"They will be soon," he says. The darkly spoken words come with a threat. "On your knees, songbird."

It's his nickname for me, his grip on my chin, his lips so close to mine and the rapid pace of his heart, that all make me move.

I keep my eyes on his for as long as I can as I get onto all fours and let him slowly strip my pants from me. He pulls them down slowly, teasingly even as his fingers brush down my sensitive skin.

The cool air is all I can feel for a moment and I know the belt is coming. I brace for it, but there's nothing for what feels like forever.

"Do you think you deserve this?" he asks me with his voice low and not an ounce of resentment that I expect.

I breathe the word easily, truthfully, "Yes."

The belt bites the flesh of my right thigh from behind and I scream out in agony. He didn't waste a second.

My thighs tremble as I try to stay on all fours.

Smack! The edges of the belt scrape against my ass and send a wave of pain through my body while burning where they slice across my skin. I can't control the sob that claws its way up my throat. My toes curl as I grip the sheets tighter and fight back the tears.

I jump at the soft touch of Carter's hand against my heated flesh, wishing I'd said no, but then I would be the liar I claimed not to be.

"Do you know what happens to men who point a gun at me, Aria?" Carter's voice is laced with a deadly threat as he bends over me, his hard cock digging into my ass and just the feeling of it sends a deep-rooted desire to surface in my blood.

The lust nearly drowns out the pain. It's so close, and I wish it would, but Carter isn't finished punishing me yet.

His lips brush the shell of my ear as he tells me, "They don't live to pull the trigger."

I have to swallow before I can answer him. My skin alternates between pain and pleasure on the places where his hand still rubs soothing circles. "I never would have pulled it," I answer him in a soft voice while rocking my hips back against him. I've always been a whore for him. I bow to him and love it. Some sick side of me desires it. I imagine I always will.

"You don't care that everyone saw, do you?" he asks me and the weight of what I've done feels heavier.

"I'm sorry. I didn't want to do it." I swallow thickly, conflicted by my exhaustion, my pain, my greed for more of his touch. "You left me no choice."

He pulls away instantly, leaving my body feeling the chill of the air between us. I can hear the metal buckle of his belt clink and see him raise his arm in the shadows that play on the wall in front of me.

I close my eyes tightly but it doesn't help in the least.

Smack! The belt bites at my left ass cheek, and then immediately moves to the right.

I bite down as hard as I can on nothing and try to hold back my cries as the belt screams in the air and lands blow after blow against my tender flesh.

My arms buckle as the pain rips through me. Tears leak uncontrollably from the corners of my eyes.

Carter fists the hair at the base of my skull and forces me to look at him.

His eyes are dark and swirling with tortured emotion. "I need to see you, Aria. You can't hide from me."

My head shakes before I realize I've moved, the stinging pain making even the small movement of brushing my thigh against his absolute agony. "I can't," I whimper.

I've never felt a pain like this. I try to hold back the tears as my shoulders shake, but they come regardless.

"You can take this," Carter tells me, grabbing the reddened flesh of my thigh and squeezing it. The pressure forces the pain to shred every last piece of control I have.

With his right hand on my thigh, he cups my pussy with his left.

My back bows instantly and I'd collapse to my side if he wasn't holding me in place. The pleasure is unimaginable. Every inch of my body feels it. My nipples pebble, but my neck arches and my body begs for more.

"You can take this, Aria." Carter's voice is gentle, soothing, and deep as he rubs his fingers against my sensitive clit. From the way he sounds right now, I almost wonder if the lust he once had for me is now gone, but I know that can't be true. That can't be the case from the way he starts to touch me.

He pinches my clit and a lightning bolt of pleasure thrills every nerve ending in my body. I'm hot and cold at the same time. Quivering beneath the man who gives me pain I can't bear and pleasure that's as equally consuming.

And I crave more of him. I need his fingers inside of me.

He pulls away as the numbing pleasure races through me and I see him reach for the belt again.

"Carter," I whimper a plea. I love the pleasure, but the pain is terrifying. "Please," I beg him.

He hesitates. With my cheek on the pillow, staring up at the broken man who only knows how to break others, I beg him again. "Please, forgive me."

"I've already forgiven you," are the only words he gives me before gripping the belt tighter.

I close my eyes, waiting for more punishment, waiting for Carter to take me how he thinks he needs.

Instead, a soothing hand runs along the dip in my waist, and as much as I want to pull away, knowing his gentle touch is going to cause where he's struck me to flare with pain, I stay still for him. I let him caress where the belt met my skin, and bring the pain to the surface even more.

"I just want you," I whisper into the pillow. It feels damp beneath my cheek, soaked from my tears. "Please, Carter."

"This is me, Aria. This is who I am."

His words are a fire that licks along the wounds of my heart, split into two halves of who I am. The first half of me is a woman who's broken and in love with a man who's been hurt more times in this life than I could possibly bear. And the other half is a woman who wants to be strong and refuses to allow her will to be ignored any longer.

"You don't know who you are anymore, Carter. No more than I knew who I was when I held the gun," I tell him in a shuddering voice. "Take from me what you want," I concede. Closing my eyes, I bury my head in the pillow but then remember what he said. And so, I position myself on all fours again, even as my legs shake. "I'll give it all to you."

The belt drops to the bed with a thud and before I can turn my head to look over my shoulder at Carter, he plunges deep inside of me, his cock filling me and stretching me without mercy. One of his hands grips my hip to keep me upright as the force of his thrust nearly shoves my body into a prone position from the blow. Fuck! It's too much so quickly. The scream that's torn from me is silent.

With his other hand, he pinches my clit hard and the force of the pleasure tearing through me makes my back bow as I scream out his name.

His thumb rubs my clit relentlessly as he rides through my orgasm, fucking me like it's the last thing he'll ever be able to do.

And I take it all. Biting down on the pillow to mute the screams and writhing beneath him from the mix of pain and pleasure that confuses my body, I take all of him.

Over and over again.

I take it until I think he'll break me. Until my body begs me to flee, but even then, he doesn't stop. He's a brutal man, with brutal instincts and I don't know that he'll ever have mercy on me again.

I'm barely sane, barely coherent when I feel his thick cock pulse inside of me. The head of his dick is pressed deep inside of me, and I've never before wanted a moment to last forever like I do now. Feeling the most intense orgasm I've ever had while Carter groans my name and then lowers his lips to kiss my shoulder.

He breathes heavily as he lays his chest on my back, moving one hand to brace himself and the other to hold my belly, keeping my skin pressed to his.

The last kiss he gives me is a long one, his lips to my shoulder. Like he doesn't want it to end.

"I fell in love with the idea of you," he whispers after pulling his kiss away from me. "Then I fell in love with fucking you." There's an agony etched in his words. It sounds like he's telling me goodbye and I've only just now realized it.

"Carter," I say as I turn in his embrace, ignoring the pain from the belt which is still present, bringing my hands to either side of his hard jaw and try to kiss him back, but he pulls away.

"I thought I loved you." Every bit of the man who brings terror to all who defy him is gone. There's a softness in his eyes that begs me to accept it all, to bow down to him and bend to his will. No matter what it is.

But I can't. Not anymore. Not after what happened, and I saw the truth of what's to come. And if that means this is the end…

I gaze into his eyes as he stares into mine, and I can feel the unspoken words. Either I submit to him, or I'm his enemy.

"I love you, Carter. But I won't be your songbird anymore. Not when you chose to ignore the one thing I need from you."

"You want me to surrender and that's something I can't do." He swallows thickly, the hard edge to his tone growing rougher. "You're making it impossible for us to be together."

The tension between us is too real, so thick and so suffocating. "So are you," I tell him. "I love you, but I will go to war against you." My words are shaky as they leave my lips. "I still love you, Carter. And I still want you." The last words come out rushed and I beg him to believe me.

"I will kill every man of the army that backs you, Aria. I will destroy them all until there's no reason left to fight." He doesn't mention anything about love. Only war.

"I will die to protect them," I tell him the truth. They're my family. And they've protected me. "I have to," I plead with him to understand.

He doesn't conceal the pain my answer causes him. And that only makes my own suffering grow. "Where is that loyalty for me? For my brothers?"

"I will never hurt them or you." The thought of them dying at the hands of my own family clutches my heart in a vise. My voice cracks as I speak, "I only said I would protect my own."

"Little naïve songbird… I wish you could."

CHAPTER 8

Aria

EVERY TIME I MAKE EVEN THE TINIEST OF MOVEMENTS, THE ACHE BETWEEN MY legs consumes my body.

I both hate it and love it. I love the reminder that Carter came for me; I hate that I'm again faced with the reality I can't outrun.

I've been watching the news and listening to the guards. I know blood has already been spilled. Yesterday I got a glimpse of it, but I wasn't sure. Today Addison's kept the news on and I know for certain the war has begun.

I recognize the names of some of the men in my father's army. The soldiers. Men who have gathered in my kitchen late at night. Men who have shared dinner with my family from time to time.

Men who have been kind to me.

Men who have looked after me when my father wasn't there.

Men who have children and wives.

And the names I don't recognize from men who live on the east side of the state… I imagine they have families too. Or did. Before this happened.

My father made me go to the funerals whenever someone died. Always. I've never missed any of them. He said they were family and deserved that respect. As much as I've hated my father and as much as I think I'm nothing but a bother to him, or maybe a bad memory of my mother, I always respected the dead and their families.

This time I won't be able to, and for some reason that hurts me deeper than I think it should.

Two names that haven't come up are Nikolai and Mika.

The first, a man who I've loved in more way than one.

And the second, a man I've dreamed of killing myself.

In this world, there are men who are good, and there are men who are evil. I won't be convinced otherwise. In war, both types of men die. And both types of men populate every army.

"How are you doing this morning?" Addison's question pulls my gaze from the coffee maker to her. I meant to turn it on and never did. I can't concentrate on anything else but the war.

She looks like she didn't get any sleep at all. The dark circles under her eyes are a dead giveaway. "I came in to check on you last night, but you were already asleep."

My lungs seize thinking how grateful I am that she didn't come in while Carter was there. I've never felt so torn in my life as I did last night. It's an impossible situation.

"Yeah, I passed out." I offer the lame excuse and it feels fake on my tongue knowing I'm hiding the truth from her. I finally hit the button to start up the machine but then have to check to make sure I added water. I did.

All the while, Addison heads to the fridge as if it's any other kitchen, knowing Eli fully stocked it last night.

I almost tell her Carter came over purely out of guilt, but I swallow my words. She won't understand. She clears her throat and speaks before I can confess though.

"I saw Daniel… that's what took me so long."

Unshed tears shimmer in her eyes and she slams the fridge door shut before tossing the butter on the counter so she has both hands free to press her palms to her eyes. "I'm sorry."

"You have no reason to be. Out of everyone involved, you have no reason to be," I say and wish she could understand how empathetic I am to her. "I get it. Let it out," I tell her while putting my hand on her shoulder and running it back and forth to try to soothe her.

"I just can't believe he'd be okay with the way Carter treated you. That he would do nothing."

I let out a long breath, understanding why she's standing so strongly against Daniel, but hating that I'm a part of that reason.

"I've come to terms with two things," I tell her, hoping it will help her. "One, I love Carter even if he hates me." The first confession brings her eyes to mine. "Two, I'm not going to sit back and do nothing. I won't ever let him do something that will hurt me or my family without fighting him."

"How can you be with him, knowing…?" She doesn't finish, but she doesn't have to.

"I don't know how. I honestly don't. And I don't know if any of it really matters." I lean my back against the counter and grip on to it from behind. "I can't stop this war. I can't protect everyone. I can't stop the people I love from dying." As I say the last part, my mother comes to mind and I try to block her out. I'm already spent with emotion and trying to balance right and wrong, love and war, that any mention of her will be my undoing and it's not even ten o'clock in the morning.

"This life is brutal," I whisper and then clear my throat to face Addison again. "But it's my life. And I want to be in control of my own decisions."

"You know we're still locked up, right?" Judging by the hint of a smile on her lips, her words are meant to make me laugh and they do, a small breath of a laugh.

Reaching for the butter and content to let the conversation die, she adds, "Let's eat before we think of how we're going to escape."

"I can hear you," a voice says from behind us and scares the shit out of me. Eli's in the doorway, a smirk on his lips and if he was closer I'd be tempted to smack it off his face.

"I'm sure you all can," I answer him and look toward the ceiling. "I haven't found the cameras yet."

He doesn't respond to my jabs as I watch the coffee maker sputter the last bit of my caffeine addiction into a ceramic mug. Instead, he tells me, "You have a message."

He's so tall, it only takes four strides for him to close the gap between us and reach me, holding out a folded piece of paper.

"Did you read it?" I ask him before taking the small piece of parchment.

His stare is hard and unforgiving as he answers, "Yes." Pissed off from the lack of privacy, I easily toss the precious piece of paper onto the counter. I have no idea who it's from, but I continue moving around my warden to look for sugar in the cabinets.

"Does Carter know?" I ask him when I finally find it. I close the door slowly, holding the box of sugar tighter than I should.

"Yes."

I nod and then ask, "Is it from him?"

I would be surprised if it was, since he didn't have much else to say last night, and Eli proves my assumption correct with a single word.

"No."

I swallow down the sudden pang of anxiety, wondering who it's from and what it says, but I don't dare let on to Eli.

"You don't have to hate me," he says as I continue to walk around him and Addison as she fries something on the stove.

"You don't have to hover," I answer him immediately.

Without another word, he leaves, and I feel guilty although I know I shouldn't.

"What are you cooking?" I ask Addison after he's left, staring at the piece of paper without reaching for it.

"Eggs, do you want some?" she asks, peeking at me and then at the paper. I'm surprised she doesn't ask about it; I can see the question in her eyes.

"Sure," I answer just to be friendly. I don't think I could eat if I tried though. I'm already sick to my stomach.

"How do you like them?" she asks before flipping her own in the pan.

"Over easy, please, and thank you," I tell her, trying to keep my voice upbeat and waiting to open the note until I'm alone.

"Yolk?" Addison makes a face. "Eww. Really I don't know if we can be friends anymore." She's only joking though. I know she is, but the thought of losing her sends a wave of nausea through me.

"Fine," I tell her back in as playful of a voice I can manage, "I'll eat them however you're making them. I like eggs however they come," I lie. I've only ever had eggs over easy. I don't even eat hard-boiled eggs. I can't justify why I lie to her or why I'm so nervous and feeling so alone. But I do and am.

"I can make them how ever." Addison shrugs and then adds, "Over easy is the easiest way anyway. I just don't like the taste of yolks."

Her easygoing reply settles the nerves still racing through me, but I glance back at the note and notice when her gaze follows me there. Still, she doesn't ask questions and I get the feeling that's a learned habit of hers.

I watch as she cracks two eggs on the side of the pan, then takes a bite of hers from a plate on the right side of the stove.

"I can totally cook them if you want to eat," I offer, feeling guilty. I can't shake all these awful feelings running through me.

"I like it," Addison tells me and then takes another bite. The pan sizzles as the tension runs through my shoulders and the note stares back at me.

"Can I tell you something else?" Addison asks me, scraping her fork on the plate rather than looking at me. When I don't answer she peeks up at me and I'm quick to nod my head.

"I like that they're here in a way."

"Who?" I ask her, feeling my forehead wrinkle with confusion.

"Eli and Cason." She doesn't hide the guilt in her tone. "I know they're basically keeping us hostage but seeing all those people on the TV this morning," she pauses and visibly swallows. "Hearing the update on the death toll in this gang war?" She rolls her eyes as she repeats what the reporter called it. Looking over her shoulder at me and then reaching for another plate, she tells me, "At least I know we're safe."

I can only nod and accept the plate. I've been 'safe' all my life. There's no such thing as safe, only the illusion of it. Telling Addison that won't help her though.

My fork shuffles the eggs around on the plate while Addison watches, but she doesn't say anything about it. I try to take a bite and then another, but it's flavorless and it only makes the pit in my stomach feel heavier.

"Are you going to read it?" she asks me and then tilts her head toward the note.

I nod once and finally reach for it, but after I read it, I don't tell her who it's from. I don't tell her what it says either.

All I know is that Eli read it and I don't know what that means for me.

Aria,
Meet me tomorrow night. I just need to see you. I need to know you're all right.
Meet me at the candy shoppe on Main Street. You can walk there; I'll be there. I promise.
Tomorrow. Eight at night.

Yours,
Nikolai

"Are you all right?" she asks me as I feel the blood drain from my face.

The sound of my fork abruptly scraping against the plate drowns out my answer to her. I mutter, "I just need a second," as I walk past her with the note clenched tight in my hand. It feels like a betrayal of Carter to see Nikolai. But I need to. I have to see him. I have to know he's all right.

My steps are deliberate as I walk as quickly as I can toward the stairwell, intent on searching out Eli. I don't have to look far; he's waiting for me at the top of the stairs.

"Eli," I speak his name quickly like I can't get it out fast enough. The uncertainty I'm feeling makes my skin tingle as I hold up the note.

"Aria," he says my name back easily and as if nothing's wrong.

"You read this?" I ask him even though he already told me he did.

He only nods.

"Are you going to stop me from seeing him?" I ask him, the strength in my voice threatening to vanish at any moment.

"It depends."

"On what?" I ask him with no patience at all.

"On what Carter tells me to do," he answers, and I stand here helplessly in front of him.

"Are you going to kill him?" It's the next logical thought.

He hesitates, and I plead with him, "I won't run from you if you let me go to him. I need to see him."

He only takes a moment to respond, "I'm waiting to hear Carter's decision," and I can't contain my frustration any longer.

"You go ahead and wait. My decision is made." I know my words mean nothing to the cadre of soldiers surrounding me. It's a false threat, but I'm done playing these games where I'm some damsel trapped in a tower.

"Before you storm off," Eli begins with a straight face before I can turn my back on him and do exactly as he thought I would, storm off.

He holds out a package and I stare at it cautiously rather than take it. "What is it?" I ask him.

"You don't trust me now?" he asks with a hint of an asymmetric grin.

I don't respond. This isn't a game to me, it's my life.

"It's from Carter." He holds it out to me and I finally accept it, reeling with emotions I can't even begin to describe.

"What is it?" I ask him, but he only shrugs. The box isn't particularly big or small, so I can't even begin to guess what it contains.

"Tell him I want to see Nikolai… please."

With a short nod, he puts his hands behind his back and takes his position as if guarding the stairwell was what he was told to do. And maybe he was. Maybe Carter thought I'd run down the stairs and out the door the moment I got a note from Nikolai.

I don't wait to get to the bedroom to open the package. I peel back the tape as I walk, and force open the box.

Inside is a phone, simple and black, and art supplies, a drawing pad, and colored pencils.

Such little things, but I stare at them on the bed for far too long in silence, wishing I hadn't grown up in this world.

CHAPTER 9

HOURS HAVE PASSED, BUT SHE HASN'T MOVED FROM THE BED. OCCASIONALLY she flips open the sketch pad, but she doesn't draw like she did before.

Mostly she looks at the phone, expecting it to ring.

She's waiting on me. She's waiting for my move, but I don't know what the best action to take is.

Every time my phone rings and I'm given intel on where the men are and where they're going, my orders are immediate, confident, and not to be questioned. All who stand in my way will fall.

But what Aria wants… I sit back in my seat, observing her as she stares at the pad in her lap. I don't know how much leeway to give her. Free of her cage, my songbird might very well never come back to me given what I'm planning to do. And I can't have that. Aria is mine.

"How many men did Romano send in there?" Daniel asks as he walks into the office unannounced. No knocking whatsoever. I guess some things don't change.

Taking a deep breath that stretches my back, I answer him, "Four."

"And he wants us to send a dozen?" His tone is incredulous, but I had the same exact reaction and I give him a look that says as much.

Turning my attention to Daniel, I take in his dark eyes and the rough stubble that's overgrown on his jaw. He's still in the same shirt he was wearing yesterday too.

"Did you sleep?" I ask him, and he shakes his head no, but he moves the conversation back to business matters. Back to busying himself and ending the bullshit that keeps him from having Addison back.

"Jett went down late last night to Carlisle. He said this morning that he counted at least twenty-two Talvery soldiers that come and go down the block."

"That's right inside the northern border between the two of us, not between Romano and him."

"Right," he answers me, but I didn't need him to say a damn thing, I just needed a moment to think.

"Are the rest of the areas high density like that?"

"High density?" he echoes, not understanding. He hasn't been back long and he's still catching up.

"Instead of spreading his men out, he's keeping them heavy and clustered in one area? Or is this the only street like that?" Crossing my right ankle over my left knee, I lean back in the chair and pick up a pen to tap it against the desk as I think.

"It's like that three blocks from the divide between Romano and Talvery on the upper east side. Bedford, I think it is."

"Where are the rest of them?" I ask him. "I want a count and whereabouts of his men at all times."

"We need more eyes out if we want that intel. Jett can't move if he wants to pick them off."

"Then get them."

"Most of our men are surrounding the safe house…" For the first time since beginning this conversation, he lowers his voice to confess, "I don't want to move them."

"So, we need to take on an army with only a handful of men."

"Skilled men hired for this express purpose. Men who have been waiting for this for how long?" Daniel reminds me. Most of the men we picked up came with us for a reason. Hate is a better motivator than fear is and Talvery's made more enemies in his decades of reign than I'd like to give him credit for. As he grew older, he grew harder.

I wasn't the first boy he nearly beat to death for dealing in his territory. The others had families though, families who knew exactly who was responsible. Families who came to me, knowing we shared a common enemy.

I glance at the monitor, at my songbird who's staring at nothing and consumed by her helplessness. For a split second, I wonder if she knows everything her father did. But I already know she doesn't.

Daniel continues the conversation, hellbent on coming up with a plan. "Jett thinks we could use eight men total, two on each corner of that street and the other four on the other side to clean up that area."

"Eight men, to take on their twenty?" My voice is flat, my gaze pinned to his, but all I can see is how this will go down. How we can take out each of them.

"Romano's supposed to be sending down four in the next two days to go in, since he wants clean kills to avoid the news and having to pay off more cops. But I think we should hit them tomorrow night with the automatic assault rifles we just got from the docks."

I nod my head in agreement. Clean kills take more time, time that they'll use to react. "Why wait until tomorrow?" I ask him.

"It's Sunday," Daniel reminds me. A huff leaves me, somewhat sarcastic, somewhat pathetic. There are rules in this industry if you can call it that. No women, no children. Give peace at funerals. And leave Sundays for families. They're signs of respect and boundaries. The only reason they're kept is that sometimes enemies become allies and it's easily justified by saying that the enemy always gave respect.

I know only one man who defied the laws and my little songbird stabbed that fucker to death. Not a soul defended him. And who would when his death was justified for breaking a sacred rule?

Well, that man… and then myself. I took Aria from Talvery.

"Tomorrow night then." Daniel's eyes shine brighter with the challenge of pulling this off.

"Jett can stay where he is and take out any of Talvery's men that survive the hit. We need the police to stay back for at least eight hours. Instead of going in to see who's still breathing, we let the men try to come out to read the situation, and Jett will pick them off."

"They'll be easy to pay off. I know Officer Harold will hold them back for a grand a minute."

Daniel considers it and then offers another plan. "The alternative would be using explosives. But the street is a good location and that's a mess that'll bring too much attention."

"Hit them tomorrow night with the automatics. Pay off the cops for four hours and we'll hit the Talvery line up north as a distraction with the RDX, my explosive of choice courtesy of the shit Talvery put us through. Set off the explosives there at the same time as the hit on Carlisle Street. Let them focus on the bombings while we destroy their front line."

Daniel nods in agreement, relaxing into the chair, although his foot doesn't stop tapping on the floor, giving away his anxiety.

"Who all is there?" I ask him as my own qualms creep up on me.

"What do you mean?"

"Of Talvery's men, who…?" I pause to swallow thickly and ask my brother flat out, "Are any of them Aria's family?"

"Her cousin, Brett, comes by the bakery in the morning. It looks like their usual meet-up spot. He's been there every morning for the last three days, according to Jett. But at night, no. None of her blood. What she considers family is debatable though."

"You would think Talvery would be going out full force against Romano," I answer back instead of entertaining his thoughts on who Aria's family is.

"He was until yesterday. He moved the men to Carlisle, to our border the night after the dinner." He clarifies what night he's referring to when I give him a questioning look. "The night she killed Stephan and Romano passed the message to him. Then, yesterday, something else changed."

I close my eyes remembering that night, remembering the feeling of pride and lust I had for her growing that night she ended Stephan's life. "When it was confirmed that we had Aria."

"Yeah, that's when he moved more of his men to our side."

"So, now he's coming after us?" I can't help that I smirk, loving the challenge and the flow of adrenaline in my blood.

"There are equal numbers of men posted on the two borders. But if I were him, I'd be gunning for you."

"He knows we let her kill Stephan."

"Maybe that's why it's equal and why all his men aren't raiding our turf?"

"A man with two enemies, both pointing guns at him, who knows what he's thinking?" Daniel's tone turns morose. "I have to tell you something you aren't going to like."

"And to think… you're interrupting this pleasant conversation …"

"Look who's making jokes now."

"Maybe I'm learning a thing from you."

"What happened last night that led him to move more men closer to us?"

I ask my brother, "Is that what you have to tell me?" I tap the pen against the desk as I think about everything Romano told me about his plans to decimate them in only four days flat.

Daniel repositions himself and nods, but his eyes are full of worry. "Romano and Talvery know where the girls are." He visibly swallows and adds, "They followed us."

I only nod, not wanting to acknowledge that truth. "Are you sure?" I ask him, feeling the tension build in my shoulders.

"Yeah," he answers with a tired voice, the fidgeting of his foot finally halting as he asks me, "What do we do with the women?"

"If she doesn't come willingly… I want mine back in the cell when this is over with."

Daniel's expression hardens. His disappointment and anger even, are evident. I don't care what I told her, what promises I've made or how fucked a position she's put me in. I don't care about any of it. The possessiveness stirs in my blood and I struggle to contain myself, so I settle on redirecting Daniel. "What you do with yours is up to you."

"You can't do that to her." Daniel dares to tell me what I can do. "You can't lock her up and expect her not to fight back."

"You're just pissed this is affecting you and Addison, and I'm sorry for that, but I'm not letting Aria walk away from me. I won't allow it." The last sentence is barely spoken through clenched teeth as my heart rate quickens and my hands form white-knuckled fists.

"Do you want a prisoner or a partner?" Daniel's question catches me off guard.

"She'll never see me as her partner. I will always be the enemy." I speak the truth that fills me with dread. This war has to happen. I will kill her father. And she will never see me as anything but an enemy once it's done.

"Not if you treat her as a partner."

"I want someone who wants me back," I confess to him. "I want her to want me back, and that will never happen once this week is done."

"You're so blinded by hate that you don't see it," Daniel tells me as if I'm a fool.

"You and Addison are different. Don't look at me like we're in the same situation. And you fucking know that's true." He shakes his head but remains silent.

"I'll put her back in the cell if I have to," I tell him with finality, staring past him and at the closed door. She wanted me once and I'll make it happen again. She'll learn to forgive.

"What are you doing? I've never seen you like this." Daniel's expression is worried, but more than that, sympathetic.

"I loved her," I say, and my answer is harsh; I can feel my control slipping again. It slips so easily with her.

"And?" he questions me as if he doesn't understand. As if it isn't obvious that the woman I love is the enemy. Even when all of them are dead and I've taken her back, I will always be the enemy to her and there's nothing I can do about it. Not a damn thing.

"You still love her, so why would you do that to her?"

"I don't know what love is."

"You're being fucking stupid and this 'woe is me' bullshit doesn't look good on you, Carter."

"Fuck you," I seethe as I tell my brother off. "Addison will run, and you'll follow like a little puppy dog, but she'll come back to you because you didn't do a damn thing to her. Aria…" My throat gets tighter as I speak, threatening to strangle me if I speak the words aloud. "I'm going to kill her family. I've locked her up, I've punished her."

"What you have is different, but it's obvious to her that you love her. You'll see."

"Love isn't enough sometimes. I don't know how you've gotten stuck on some fantasy,

Daniel. I live in the real world, where I'm the villain. So, go ahead and tell me she'll love me after this. Keep telling yourself that too. Whatever helps you sleep."

Daniel doesn't answer. A moment passes and then another before he stands up abruptly and leaves me alone.

The second the door slams shut, I turn back to the monitors, focusing on them as my blood simmers and my gut starts to churn.

My body is ringing with anger, contempt, and fear. I haven't felt fear in so long. True fear threatens to consume me at the very real possibility of losing her.

Not if you treat her as a partner. Daniel's words echo in my head, but how can he say that when he knows what that means in this world we inhabit?

Aria's still staring at the phone and without hesitation, I pick up the phone on my desk and call her.

Only yesterday, she lay across my desk while I played with her cunt and her ass, knowing she loved it and thinking she loved me.

A day can change everything.

The line only rings once before she answers, cradling the phone close with both hands.

"Hello?" Just the sound of her voice is soothing. Everything about her is a balm for the burning rage inside of me.

"Do you hate me?" I ask her, needing to know.

"Have you killed them?"

A sad smirk kicks my lips up as I touch the tips of my fingers to the screen. I can see her swallow as the silence stretches, I can see her start to crumble when I don't immediately respond. And I hate it. I hate that this is what will happen to her.

"No." The moment I speak the word, her head falls forward and I hear her take in a deep breath. "But you know it has to happen," I remind her as she sits up straighter, still cross-legged on the bed.

"I know," she answers. I watch as she picks at the comforter and then readjusts but winces as she moves. No doubt the lashes from the belt are causing her pain. They barely left a mark on her. I held back, but even so, I know she's still hurting from it.

I struggle to breathe as she asks me, "So, it's inevitable that I'll hate you then?"

"That's your choice."

"I know some of the men who have died already," she confesses with pain etched in her voice. Her words are so strangled and unwilling to be spoken that I almost don't hear her. It takes me a second and then another, the ticks of the clock marking each of them.

She covers her mouth with her hand, pulling the phone to one side as she gathers her composure, but keeps the other end pressed close to her ear.

"There is always loss in this business," is all I can give her until I think to add, "I'm sorry."

"I'm sorry too," she tells me after a moment.

"This is no different than before when men standing in front of your father were shot, so to speak. They fight for him, and they die for him. It's all happened before."

"I'll tell you something that maybe you don't find obvious, Carter." Aria finds her strength and it gives me hope until she speaks. "I hated the men who killed them before. I just didn't have a face to associate with their deaths."

"Romano."

"What?" she questions and in even a single word, I feel the hope start to rise inside of me again.

"Direct your hate there, not at me." Maybe I'm a coward for hiding behind Romano while I can, but she can't hate me. I don't know what I'll become if she does.

She lies back slowly on the bed, ever so slowly, and stares at the ceiling before she asks, "This, wasn't you?

"I haven't had to do anything yet, but things have changed."

"What's changed?" she immediately asks, but her voice is even, devoid of emotion. I can hear her swallow as she asks me, "What exactly has changed?" She bunches the top sheet in her hand absently, waiting for my answer.

I question telling her for only a moment. But ultimately, I decide to give her what she wants. To treat her like a partner in this.

"The number of your father's men that have moved closer to Carlisle Street."

"Where's Carlisle?" she asks with her hand falling back onto the bed, but still gripping the sheet.

As much as she'd like to know what's going on, she has so much to learn.

"One street up from where our territories are divided, Miss Talvery." My cock hardens as I speak to her like this as if I'm negotiating with the enemy. My little songbird is playing the part of the queen. And what a queen she would make.

"I don't like it when you call me that," she says quietly, but her lips stay parted long after the word is spoken. I watch on the screen as her hand moves to her belly.

"Your father is preparing to invade and conquer and he's making it obvious."

"He's defending his territory." She's quick to reply, and I find her logic appropriate. Which makes me sit back farther in my seat.

"Remember who you are, Aria."

"I'm still figuring out who I am, Carter." The air of dominance wraps around her like a cloak when she talks to me like that, with only a whisper of submission. When she gives herself to me with no pretense, only honesty.

And I take that moment to tell her exactly who she is and will always be. "You're mine."

"Am I?" Her voice is coated in sadness as she closes her eyes.

"Yes," the word is practically hissed as I lean closer to the screen, wishing I were there with her now.

"And if I leave this place; if I leave… to see someone?" she asks me, and I know exactly what she's talking about. "Would I still be yours?" My pulse hammers in my ears and I bite back the initial response and the next.

I give her the only truth I know, "You will always be mine."

"Carter," Aria's voice breaks and she covers her eyes with her hand as she talks. "I'm scared."

"You're brave," I tell her, and she lets out a humorless laugh on the other end of the phone.

"I'm afraid I'm going to fail and we'll both be left with no one," she tells me, wiping under her eyes and repositioning herself on the bed, once again wincing. My gaze flicks to the nightstand where I left the cooling balm, still right where it was last night.

Ignoring her statement and refusing to think of that possibility, I ask her instead, "Are you still hurting from your punishment?"

Again, I'm given that huff of a laugh before she answers, "Yes. You left your mark on me, Mr. Cross."

"It's not the only mark I want to leave on you, songbird."

I hear her breathe in deeply on the other end and I lower my voice, forgetting everything but the two of us when I ask her, "Do you love it when I call you that?"

A second passes before she whispers, "Yes."

Again, I reach up to the screen, wishing I could touch her right now. But I can't. Not when I know the enemy could come at any moment. My men will stay with her and protect her. So long as she's safe, that's all that matters.

"You need to use the balm I gave you," I tell her and watch for her reaction.

She glances at it but doesn't move. The tension rises inside of me at her ignoring the request. A request made to help her.

"What if I want to feel it?" she asks me before I can scold her, and confusion runs through me. "What if I think I deserve to still feel the pain and I don't want the balm?" Her voice cracks slightly, but she holds her ground.

My poor Aria. The weight of two conflicting worlds is resting on her shoulders. And the consequences are heavier than any one person could possibly bear.

"You need to heal, so that if you disobey me again," I tease her, "I'll have a fresh canvas to work with when you do." I feel the ease of a smile grow on my face as the tension subsides with her genuine laughter. It's muted, soft, and just as feminine as Aria is.

"I guess I didn't think of that," she says before climbing to the edge of the bed and kicking off the thin sweatpants she's wearing. She isn't wearing any underwear.

The realization reminds me that I'm hard for her.

My dick throbs as it presses against my zipper and I want to lean back, to readjust, but I find myself leaning in closer to the monitor.

Holding the phone between her ear and her shoulder, she's able to grab the balm. She asks me, "Can you see me right now?"

"Yes."

I'm rewarded with a small smile on her lips as she looks around the room, searching for cameras she won't find.

"Put the balm down, Aria," I command her, feeling my cock twitch with need. I watch as she obeys me, setting it back down and standing in nothing but a thin cotton t-shirt.

"Yes, Carter," she simpers into the phone.

"Put the phone on speaker," I tell her, keeping my voice even so she won't have an inkling of my deep and heavy lust for her. She does as I tell her, and the moment she does I give her another command. "Set it on the bed and get on all fours like how I had you last night."

With the angle of the camera, I can see her pussy easily. I can even see up her shirt as it hangs around her waist and her pale pink nipples are obviously visible. "You're fucking perfect," I groan deep in my throat as I unzip my pants and fist my cock, pumping it once and then again.

Swallowing hard I watch as her fingers move to her sex, and she glistens with arousal.

"Do you like this, Mr. Cross?" she asks me with the sultry voice of a vixen.

"Miss Talvery, I fucking love it." I push my confession through clenched teeth. As I stroke myself, she presses her fingers into her cunt and when she does, her eyes close and her cheek pushes against the pillow.

Her lips part and I can just barely hear the sweet moan of pleasure.

"I wish I could shove my cock down your throat right now," I tell her as precum leaks from my slit. I rub it over the head of my dick and shivers of desire run down my spine and straight through my body, making my toes curl.

Like the good girl she is, she tells me back, "You'd make me choke on it. I love it when you do that." Her dirty words make my cock impossibly hard and I know I'm going to cum.

"Fuck yourself faster," I command her, and she immediately obeys. Pushing her small fingers in and out of her tight cunt. Her back bows and her hips sway with her impending orgasm.

"Hold still and grab your ass where I struck you while you cum for me," I tell her as my balls draw up. And she does. With her head pressed into the pillow, one hand squeezing the marks on her ass and the other fucking herself, she cums violently, falling to her side and screaming out my name.

My name.

I lose myself with her, cumming into my hand like a high school prick and wishing there was nothing that separated us. Wishing we lived in a different world.

CHAPTER 10

Aria

I T'S AN ODD RUSH OF EMOTION THAT FLOWS THROUGH ME. THE FEAR AND ANXIETY are most easily described, but there are others tangled in a knot in the pit of my stomach. Carter made it all go away when he told me to touch myself. Submitting to him makes everything go away and the feeling lasts long after he hangs up the phone.

As I walk out of the bedroom, knowing I'm doing something he'd prefer I didn't, the haze and comfort that comes from submitting to him dims. It's a consequence I accept. Before he ended our conversation, he told me what I chose tonight is up to me. He's giving me the choice, and I won't waste it.

I want to be more than I have been all my life.

A touch of shame washes over me as I think, *I want to be a woman who could stand by Carter's side.* It's shameful because this isn't for Carter. This meeting isn't for my father.

This meeting with Nikolai isn't even for him.

It's for me.

My heart pounds in my chest, as does the adrenaline in my blood. Tonight, I'll live up to my name. To be Aria Talvery, daughter of a ruthless crime lord. And a woman standing between two men waging war.

My father would have me stay willingly in my room. My lover would have me stay willingly locked in his house.

I'll stay and stand where I want after tonight until I see my end. No matter if that means I'll lose both men.

Even if the pleasure Carter gave me only an hour ago is still coursing through my veins.

I can hear Addison making something in the kitchen and I hesitate to go in to see her. I haven't told her a damn thing and it feels like I'm lying to her by keeping these secrets from her.

As I step in to tell her I'm going out, the microwave beeps and the smell of chicken noodle soup fills my lungs. Comfort food, even though there's no comfort here.

The air is easy between us, but I know it won't last when she turns around and sees me. I've been struggling with whether or not I should tell her since I got the note. I want to lean on her, to confide in her, but I also want to save her from this awfulness that rages inside of me.

I don't know what to do. I honestly have no idea what to do, but I know if she asks me, I'll tell her about everything. And I'll never lie to her.

"Dinner?" I ask her as she pulls the door open, not peeking back behind her to answer me. I wish she would. I wish I could get this part over with.

"You want some?" she asks softly, devoid of the cheeriness I anticipate from her. I watch as she sets the bowl down after removing the paper towel covering the top and trashing it. That's when she finally looks up at me.

"Are you okay?" I ask her a question first, but she ignores it, asking her own instead.

"Where are you going?" Addison's voice is thick with sleep. "Are you meeting Carter?" The deep crease in the center of her forehead is evidence enough of her concern, but she quickly fists her hands and places one on each hip as her chest rises. The act actually makes me smile and eases some of the nerves bubbling inside of my chest.

I love her and her protectiveness. I wish I could hide in it.

"I have a meeting with someone else," I tell her and feel that unease rise up higher, into my throat and bringing true fear with it as she asks me, "Does Carter know?"

"Yes," I answer her in a single unsteady breath.

Shifting her weight from one foot to the other, she doesn't respond, and I watch as the fight in her subsides. I can read the questions on her face, but she chooses not to ask any of them. The biggest two being "who?" and "why?" I was so like her once in my life.

"I'll be okay." I can at least give her that to ease her worries, although it feels like I won't be okay. It feels like I'm risking everything, and the consequences will be severe. I know it all already, I've weighed all the risks and thought of each outcome.

But I have to do this. "I have to try something to stop all of this." I give her a little more, hinting at what I'm doing, but she doesn't ask additional questions.

"You surprise me," Addison admits, her lips turned down into a frown although I'm not sure why.

"What's wrong?" I ask, ignoring the obvious and feeling my heart try to climb into my throat. I cautiously step closer, not wanting to hurt her or leave her feeling like she's anything but my friend, my closest friend.

I have to clasp my hands together in front of me to keep from reaching out to her, but it doesn't matter, because she reaches out to me first. Brushing her hand against my forearm, she gives me a hesitant smile.

"You handle it all so much better than I do, and I just…" As she trails off, her tone says it all. *She feels weak.*

I can't stand her reaction and I squash her thoughts as quickly as I can. "I don't handle it well; I barely handle it at all." I try to joke with her, but it doesn't work. She takes in a deep, unsteady breath and then looks back to the bowl of soup.

"Daniel asked me to forgive him yesterday."

The sudden change in topic startles me and I don't know if she's upset with me or not. I ask in a near whisper, "What did you say?"

"I said that I didn't know how I could. That when I fell in love with him, he was a different man."

"I'm sorry," I tell her as I grab her hand.

She's choked up and I find it contagious as she looks up toward the tallest cabinet and speaks to it, rather than me to keep from crying. "He said I'm good at lying to myself but that it's okay and that he still loves me." She sniffles, wiping under her eyes even though the tears haven't fallen yet. "Can you believe the balls he has?" Her lips twitch up into a sad smirk, but it doesn't stay long as she gives in to the tears.

"I miss him," she cries softly into my shoulder and clings to me. I'm quick to hold her tightly, hugging her as she breaks down. It fucking hurts seeing her like this. If I could go back, I'd keep her from learning the truth. I wish she'd never seen what happened. I wish she'd never peeked into this world I can't escape.

She pulls away after only a few seconds, shaking out her hands and walking away, but then comes right back. Her unease shows as she paces like I do but in much smaller circles.

"I feel crazy," she mutters and sniffles again.

"The Cross boys are good at making the women they love go crazy," I answer her in a deadpan tone with a weak smile. It takes a minute for her to look me in the eyes, and when she does, she doesn't accept the humor in my response.

"I swear I didn't know the things they do. But he told me he's always been a bad man and that it never stopped him from loving me. Or me from loving him before."

I rub her arm, feeling like it's all my fault and hating myself for it. I wish I could go back. If only I could. There's so much I would change.

"I want to leave with him, but he won't leave his brothers and I don't think I could ever ask him to do that, but together they will live like this… rule like this."

"He's not a bad man, Addie." I don't know where she's going with this, but I refuse to let her focus on something that will never change. "And what they do… they do because they have to." I swallow down the pain of the words, knowing I've had to choke on that excuse for as long as I've lived.

"How can we live like this, knowing what they do? What they're capable of?"

"We remember why they are the way they are. And we give them the love they need, so long as they give it back to us." I stare into her eyes, meaning every word.

"I know they need love. They desperately need to be loved." Tears prick at my own eyes as she looks away from me, but I see from her expression that she knows it's true. There's nothing in the world that would deny that truth.

Addison wipes under her eyes with the sleeves of her pajama shirt. She's dressed for bed, exhausted and dealing with the weight of loving a man from the world I grew up in. Part of me is jealous of her, a very small part, but it's there. "He loves you, Addie," I whisper to her, squeezing her hand.

She squeezes mine back and then lets her hand drop to her side. "I know, but if I accept it, I'm no better than he is. And I'll never be okay with what Carter did to you. I don't care if you are."

"Carter and Daniel are different men." My answer comes out harsher than I wanted, and I attempt to soften it by adding, "And I know Carter's reason, Addie." I try to tell her more, but the words won't come out. I can't tell her about what my father did and what Carter thinks he heard. If I told her that, the next logical thing to say would be that it wasn't me he heard. The voice he heard that gave him the strength to keep living didn't belong to me.

My heart plummets painfully in my chest at the thought of my secret, making me feel sick once again.

"When are you leaving me?" Addie asks, changing the subject again and moving back to the counter to grab a spoon from the drawer. The metal clinks against the ceramic as she stirs her soup. "A secret meeting in the middle of the night?" She tries to add a sense of playfulness into the chide, but it doesn't come out strong enough.

As I answer her, she lifts the spoon to her lips, blowing on the soup and then swallowing it.

"Not so secret, and I'll be back soon."

"Should I ask what it's about?"

I don't know what to tell her, and I remember all the times I was curious but too afraid to ask. I wish someone had taken my fear away from me and told me more about the world I was living in. That's what fuels me to tell her, "I'm meeting a friend I grew up with who's one of my father's men."

Her face pales as she peeks toward the doorway to the kitchen. Maybe she expects to find Eli there, I don't know, but then she whispers, "Should you be doing that?"

Her eyes plead with me to be truthful and so I answer her honestly, putting a hand on her shoulder and not daring to take my gaze away from hers as I say, "I should have done it sooner."

"What if he tries to take you back?" The raw note of fear in her voice means more to me than I could ever tell her.

I shake my head. "Eli is coming with me, and Carter knows about it. I'm not leaving you, Addison. I promise. He wouldn't let it happen."

"So, you two…?" She doesn't finish the question.

"Are… speaking, but still not okay," I answer slowly.

"Why go then?" she asks, and I know she'll understand my reasoning.

"He's my friend, and he's going to die or he's going to help kill the man I love." Tears brim, but I hold them back. It's the painful truth, and I know I need to change it. "If I don't do something, those are the only two outcomes."

"Are you…" Addie looks anywhere but at me, until she gathers her thoughts and finally asks a question I don't know the answer to. "Whatever you tell him, or ask of him… will he listen to you?"

Cason comes into view from the very doorway she was just looking toward. "I don't know," I answer her with a weak smile, although I stare back at Cason. Something thuds hard within my chest knowing Nikolai has always tried to keep things from me. He thinks it protects me, but I know now that he's wrong.

Addison's gaze follows mine and the clinking of her spoon against the bowl as she places her dishes in the sink marks the finality of our discussion. "Be safe," she tells me quietly as she leaves.

"You too," I tell her and listen to the sound of her retreating down the hall to the bedrooms as Cason steps into the kitchen. His jeans are dirty, covered in mud from the knees down.

He was doing something… and I can only imagine it involved a shovel and shallow grave.

"I heard you might be going out." Cason starts talking the moment Addie's out of the kitchen. I wonder if she stopped in the hall, holding her breath and staying as still as she can so she can listen.

I've done that more times than I can count.

"I am." My answer is hard as I look Cason in the eye. "Right now, actually."

"Are you sure you want to do that?" he questions me. The man's nearly a foot taller than me, with broad shoulders and arms that are a dead giveaway he spends too much time in the gym.

"You're the muscle." I ignore his question and ask him my own. "Aren't you?"

He tilts his head, considering me.

"You guys have a certain look to you," I explain as I walk through the kitchen and head to the living room. It's a modern house with an open concept floor plan, so he has no problem viewing me as he crosses his arms and leans against the wall.

"The scar on your chin, the tattoos across your knuckles, probably where they're scarred too," I speak to him as the vision of men my father referred to as the muscle, invades my memory. They'd come to the house every once in a while, with big envelopes stuffed full of cash they'd leave for him. As polite as they were to me, I knew what they did.

They beat the shit out of men who didn't pay up. My gaze drifts to the mud on Cason's shins… and they buried the men who didn't learn the lesson fast enough.

Slipping on my shoes, leather ballet flats, I peek up at Cason and ask him, "Do you have bullet hole scars too?"

His eyes are still assessing me as the silence drags on. It doesn't even look like he's breathing as I stand tall and make my way back to him. There's a matte black earpiece in his right ear, and I wonder if Carter's listening. I wonder if Carter's asking him to stop me because he doesn't have the balls to do it himself.

Fed up with Cason forcing me to talk to myself, I tell him, "It's three blocks down, and Eli is accompanying me. Thank you for your concern."

As I walk toward the stairway, glancing at the clock on the stove to make sure I'm on schedule, Cason decides to walk in front of me, his large chest becoming as unyielding and firm as a brick wall.

"I urge you to reconsider," he tells me with a voice that comes from deep in his throat. Towering over me, he's a man who creates fear. And it stirs in my blood, warning me to back down and simply survive the encounter. I look him in the eyes and tell him calmly with a hint of a smile and a narrowed glare, "See, I knew you were the muscle." Inwardly, I feel like I'm about to choke on a spiked ball of panic.

I stare into his dark eyes, meeting his gaze and refusing to back down. Not this second, and not the next. Never.

"I'm going," I tell him with finality and strength I don't feel anywhere else.

"As you wish." His answer is accompanied by a look of disappointment. Clenching his jaw, he moves his gaze back to the kitchen.

My body sags and I heave in a breath when Cason turns his back to me to go down the stairs first. The sinking feeling that chills every inch of my skin is something I've felt before and I hate it. It will always come. Those who are bigger, scarier, and hold an air of darkness around them will always bring out my survival instinct to run. But they die just like the rest of us.

I only peek up to Cason's back when I hear him as he grabs his ear. I can hear the bellowing that's coming from it from where I stand.

"Aria," Cason starts speaking before he's fully turned to me. "Please forgive me for trying to intimidate you." He chokes on his words as if terrified of getting them wrong and the look in his eyes couldn't be further from the look that gave me goosebumps only moments ago.

"I forgive you," I answer him slowly, questioning my own response and wanting to know what the fuck just happened. The question lingers in my words as they reach his ear. Or rather, the earpiece that's still filled with the yells of someone on the other end. An enraged Carter, naturally. My lips threaten to tug into a smile as I hear his voice, but I contain it as Cason continues.

"Your decisions are your own and I have absolutely no right to interfere. I'm only here to protect you."

It's as if he's speaking an oath. His gaze is genuinely full of remorse and I wonder what he really thinks of me. I haven't thought of that at all until this moment.

"I'll never turn my back on you again," he tells me with both of his hands clasped in front of him apologetically. He even lowers his head some, hunching his shoulders to meet my gaze at eye level. "Would you like me to take you to Eli?"

"No need." Eli's voice startles me and I'm ashamed I jump backward. Eli's smile is wicked like he's proud he got to me. With my hand on my chest and my back against the wall, he passes me a white jean jacket.

"You scared me," I tell him in the same breath I exhale. My heart still feels like it's about to leap out of my chest.

"I know," he says, grinning like a Cheshire cat before resuming his normal dominating stance.

"Carter wanted me to give this to you, in case you'd be needing it," he tells me, and I snatch it from him. It matches my outfit, which I do and don't like about this situation. I want to ask where the cameras are. I want to question both men and demand they tell me everything Carter tells them, but I don't want to give away how little I know. Not to them.

"Asshole," I mutter as I right myself and steady my breath. Cason lets out a snort of a laugh and the tension between the three of us eases some. But only for a moment.

"I'm sorry, Aria," Cason tells me as I drape the jacket over my forearm. "I have strong opinions and I know I need to keep them to myself and I'm sorry," he rambles slightly, but his tone is genuine, and his green eyes shine with remorse.

"I get it," I tell him. "I know what war means and what this means." I look him in the eyes as I answer and neither of us wavers, not until Eli speaks up.

"Are you ready to meet with the enemy?" Eli asks me, and I can't look at either of them as I answer, "I already have."

From the corner of my eye, I see the smile wane on his face, but Eli nudges me with his shoulder before walking out in front.

"Be smart, Aria," Cason warns as my small footsteps echo in the foyer. My quickened pulse increases even more and I have to walk a little quicker to keep up with Eli.

It didn't feel real until just now.

The crickets are out tonight, and the sky is lit with so many stars. More stars than I've ever seen in Fallbrook.

"How long until we're there?" I ask Eli, breathing in the crisp air of the cool summer night and ignoring the roiling in the pit of my stomach. The anxiety numbs my hands and I clench and unclench them before deciding to shrug on the jacket and slip my hands into my pockets.

Taking a look around to my left and right, this street is nothing but houses. I barely remember that from the drive up. The next street is where the houses are grouped closer together and there's something on the corner, a church or a liquor store, maybe both. I don't remember.

"Not long, he's already waiting," Eli tells me, but the playfulness, the easiness from the stairwell are all but forgotten.

He glances at me as I keep my pace steady with his, taking strides more often since he's taller than me. The sound of a car driving up the next street over makes him pause and he holds his arm out, stopping me from moving out into the street and pushing me closer to the brick fence of the house to my left. A moment passes, and the sound of the car diminishes. The voices from the same earpiece Cason was wearing make me stare at Eli. I can't hear what they're saying, but I know he's getting information about something.

Dread and panic mix together, making my legs feel weak. Eli glances up at the house, to the second floor and waits, then a sound creeps into his ear and he nods.

The nod wasn't for me and as Eli looks down at me and smiles politely, both of us know it.

"It's clear, Miss…" He stops and clears his throat then says, "Aria."

The dread's still there, making my hands clammy and causing my throat to tighten.

"I was hoping you wouldn't do this," Eli tells me and continues to stare straight ahead even as I look up at him, willing him to look me in the eyes.

Since he doesn't look back at me, I stare straight ahead as well. "If you thought I'd lie down and let this go on without trying to stop it, you were wrong."

"There's no way to stop this."

"I stood by before and did nothing while I watched family die," I speak quietly and swallow the knot that forms in my throat as I think of my mother. After taking a moment to compose myself, I tell Eli with finality, "I won't do it again."

CHAPTER 11

Carter

I HATE BEING IN THIS OFFICE. WATCHING CAMERAS AND WAITING. I DON'T MISS THE rush of being on the streets, but I hate not being beside the men who are risking their lives for me right now. Without the first move made on this side, the leaks and intel can't be trusted.

I'm waiting. The adrenaline competes inside of me with the hate and pent-up rage. And here I sit. Waiting.

"Carter." Jace's voice carries through the closed door. I haven't left since Daniel slammed it shut earlier and it's only now that I remember our fight. My brothers rotate in and out of my office, I'm used to them coming and going. And seemingly forgetting past conversations in order to handle business.

"Come in," I call out to him, and instantly the door opens.

"The Red Room, the stash in the backroom is gone, and the fucker who broke in last night to take it was found face down in the river this morning." Jace's words come out like an assault as he paces to the chair across from me, gripping the back of it and staring at me waiting for answers.

All day, this is what I do. Accept information and move chess pieces. That's how true empires are built. The bloodshed is nearly the conquering of a knight. Some poor fool dies, so the men with power make a simple move, knowing more are to come and there's more game left to play.

"Do the cops have any idea who did it?" I ask him, bringing my thumb to my chin and running the pad along the stubble there. I need to shave. Jace and I are more alike than I care to admit. The back and forth of the motion keeps me focused on Jase and this shitstorm.

Jace speaks in rapid fire, giving me all the details from his conversation with Officer Harold. No leads on a suspect, no trace of him on any city cameras once he leaves the edge of town and heads down to the woods on the edge of Jersey. Yet, he's found dead at the river next to his house hours later.

"It doesn't add up," I answer Jace, meeting his gaze as he lowers himself to the chair opposite mine on the other side of my desk. His thumb raps on the armrest as he nods.

"Someone's fucking with us. Letting us know that they can steal from us, kill on our turf, and they can get away with it."

"Marcus," I say the name without thinking. "He's the only man who's ever been able to get away with that shit."

"And only because he's a fucking ghost with no face." He takes a calming breath before adding, "Just one look on a tape and we've got his ass."

"How many decades now has he gotten away with it? Any territory, any head he wants severed?"

"Why fuck with us though? Why us?" He leans forward, letting the anger show in his voice and his posture.

"Daniel turned on him first, blaming him for what happened to Addison with no proof." Instead of indulging in the rage of having product stolen from us and the opportunity for justice torn from my hands, I consider everything logically. It's how it needs to be handled. With nothing but cold-hearted control.

"I don't know… If he set up Addison…" Jase's thoughts are left unfinished, but I know what he's thinking. If Marcus is after us, it's only a matter of time before we find out what he truly wants.

And if he went after Addison, he won't stop until he has her.

"The cameras and men have the safe house fully under surveillance?" I question Jase, although it's more of a reminder to myself. He nods with his thumb brushing across his lip.

"Yeah, there's no way he'd get in without us knowing."

"And who knows?" I ask him as the pieces fall one by one into the puzzle of how to handle this.

"Who knows what?" he asks to clarify, a brow lifting.

"Who knows we had someone steal from us and then they turned up dead?"

"Jared and two of his men. The men in our pocket at the station want to know what to do; they haven't asked outright, but they think it was our hit on the fucker."

"Good." My quick response in a hardened voice surprises my brother. He should know better by now. "Tell Jared I handled the prick who broke in. Tell the police that we're grateful for their cooperation and pay them off." Jase's eyes go wide and a look of outrage is there for only a moment. But as soon as it comes, it's gone.

"So, no one thinks we don't have this under control?" he surmises.

"Exactly."

"But we don't."

"It's about perception, Jase. One moment of what could look like weakness and our allies become enemies. The men we have under our thumb think they can wiggle free and take a shot back."

"What do I do about finding out who did this shit?"

"Put Declan on it. He needs to go through home security system footage around the river starting at the dead fuck's house. We can't rely on the city surveillance."

As Jase nods, he settles into the chair. No one steals from us or fucks with us. Even Marcus wouldn't dare. I never thought it was him when it came to Addison. Daniel came up with that shit himself because he had no one else to blame.

"I'll let Declan know," he tells me, still nodding in agreement.

"You're not going to tell me one thing and then turn around and tell our men something else, are you?" I let the words slip out with my disappointment and a trace of animosity evident in my tone.

"Don't do that shit," he bites back, shaking his head. "Tell me I didn't do the right thing, and I'll apologize."

The large clock ticks steadily in the background as my grip tightens on the armrest and a tic in my jaw spasms.

"You were… in a state where I think you would agree I needed to step in." He raises his hands quickly as my gaze narrows and the temperature of my blood rises. "It was a difficult night, and I would have never stepped in if what happened wasn't *exactly* how it happened."

My blunt nails dig into the leather armrests as I try to contain my anger, even as my brother sits there as if we're just having a casual conversation as if he's no threat to me.

"I won't do it again," he tells me easily, and then clears his throat. "I didn't want…" he trails off and looks away over to his left, to the box still on the ground and out of place. "I just," he looks back up at me and I can read the sincerity on his face, "I didn't want her to hate you."

It takes a moment for him to contain the uncertainty and pain in his expression. With each second, every tick of the clock, the truth of what he says chips away at the resentment I feel over what he did. "You've been mad at me before; I know you'll get over it. This isn't the first time I've crossed the line and it won't be the last. But I love you, as my brother and my friend, and I didn't want her to hate you. I know you love her."

I haven't seen Jase like this in years. Not since the last funeral he went to. And the second his confession is over, he starts up a new conversation, never giving me the chance to respond.

"I didn't come in here to bother you with this shit."

My throat is dry, and I reach behind me for two tumblers and whiskey before asking him, "What shit did you come in to bother me with then?"

"About Aria meeting with Nikolai."

"I know she decided to go. I spoke to Eli when they left."

"She already left?" he questions, shaking his head. "What is he going to tell her?"

"It doesn't matter," I say to put an end to his bullshit. "I let her go. She wanted to go to him." I down the whiskey in my glass before pouring myself more and then pouring three fingers into his glass and offering it to him.

He takes it but doesn't drink.

"How many men did he bring?" he asks me.

"Just him," I tell him, and he lets a smirk spread on his face in response.

"He may be young, but even I'm not that stupid."

"I know why he did it." Even though I realize I'm talking to Jase, I speak absently, knowing why Nikolai came alone and what he bargained away just for her to get the note. "He's desperate."

"He has a death wish," Jase speaks up, and I move my attention from him to the screen.

"I told Eli to let her make the decision. If she wants to go to him, let her… and she did."

"It would be easy to simply lock the door and coming from me…" Jase shakes his head and takes the first sip of his whiskey.

"I want to see what she'll do." Every ounce of me wants to control her. To demand she behave exactly how I want her to. Even as I stared at the monitor a half hour ago on the computer, watching her as she picked up a silk blouse I bought her, intending on wearing it for him, the urge to get to her faster than she could walk into that room raced through my mind. To keep her there if I couldn't convince her otherwise.

"Are you sure that you're sure?" Jase questions me again. I should feel angry that it's becoming a habit for him to question me, but I know he's thinking what I'm thinking, that she'll choose him again.

With a painful thud in my chest that numbs my body, I answer him, "Yes. She's already there, waiting."

"Waiting for what?"

"For me to tell Eli to let her in."

"You aren't going to be there?" he questions me with a look of complete disbelief.

Placing my palms on the desk and leaning forward so he can understand exactly why I'm not there, I ask him, "Do you think it would be helpful if he were in my presence right now?" My jaw hardens, and I can't help it as I tell him, "This is for her." It fucking hurts to admit, "She wouldn't want me there." He's shaking his head, and I shrug.

I tell Jase, "She's not in danger. The only thing that could happen is if she…"

"If she chooses him and tries to run." Jase finishes my thoughts and I nod once, bringing my attention back to the monitors. Jase looks like he's contemplating what to say next, so I remain silent.

"Eli will kill him if he tries?" I nod again at his question and throw back my second glass of whiskey.

"I just have to give Eli the go-ahead to let her in," I admit to him as I stare at the screen knowing I'm giving her what she wants, but not knowing how it will affect us and I can't fucking stand it.

The moment he touches her, I'll see her reaction.

I will never forgive her if she chooses him over me.

Aria

I REMEMBER THE FIRST TIME I SAW NIKOLAI. WE WERE ONLY CHILDREN. HIS FATHER worked for my father until he was killed.

The funeral home always had the prettiest flowers, and that's what I looked at whenever we went there, all of the pretty flowers. But that day, I let myself watch the boy next to the casket.

I never liked to look at the people there. They always cried, and it made me want to cry, but I wasn't allowed. We were Talverys and we weren't allowed to cry, no matter how much I wanted to.

The boy was crying. He was taller than me and in a black suit that didn't fit right, because he was too tall for it. His ankles were bare although his black shoes were new.

He looked so angry as he stared at the casket, wiping away his tears like they were nothing but a nuisance.

I never wanted to speak to anyone, not like my mother and father did. I never wanted to give anyone a hug or even be near any of them. Especially, the ones who smiled and laughed at funerals. I didn't understand it and it made me angry to see people laughing when they were supposed to be mourning. I didn't learn until years later that everyone mourns differently. Apparently, my coping mechanism is solitude.

And Nikolai's was anger.

I remember how hesitant I was to touch his shoulder and ask him, "Are you okay?"

He was the first person I'd ever talked to at the many funerals I'd attended by this point. When he looked at me, when he glanced over his shoulder to answer me, he had a look of pure rage, maybe even disgust, but then he saw me, and it softened. Not just softened; his expression crumpled. The boy bared his soul to me and I saw the pain and the loneliness. He didn't speak; he only shook his head. But then I tried to hug him, and he let me.

My father hired him to do collections, even though he was only fourteen. He said the boy needed a distraction and I was happy I got to see him every week.

And then my mother died. And I felt the grief, the solitude that begged me to hide away and isolate myself. But Nikolai refused to let me be alone. He promised me he'd stay with me. He was the first person who said it was okay to cry and he held me while I did.

Ever since that day, we were inseparable.

He was my only friend. My only lover. And the only person I ever trusted in this world other than my mother.

The door to the back room of a candy shop three blocks north of the safe house is all that stands between Nikolai and me. My fingers keep pinching and twisting the cuffs of the jean jacket. Deep inside of me, the fear that they've hurt Nikolai is very real. That he's cuffed to a chair and on death's door is likely. I've seen it before. So many times.

"He's okay, right?" I ask quietly, not hiding my fear as I peek up at Eli. He considers me for a long moment before nodding his head and each fraction of a second that passes ramps up my anxiety.

"Thank you," I whisper my gratitude, although I'm not sure I entirely believe him and look toward the door with my shoulders squared as if it'll open any second.

"You can go in now," Eli tells me from behind and I reach for the knob, but he stops me, gripping my forearm and telling me, "Let me."

Nodding, I wait with bated breath for the door to open. It's on rusted hinges and they screech with the motion of the heavy door opening.

"Aria," Nik breathes my name before I even see him, and his voice is drowned out by the sound of metal chair legs scraping against the concrete floor as he pushes away from a small card table in the center of the barren room. Barely aware that Eli is watching and that there are two other men in the room also watching, I run to him, meeting him half-way and clinging to him.

I don't care in this moment. They can all watch and judge.

All I can see as I hold him is the gun touching the back of his head and I can't get it out of my mind. Burying my face into his hard chest, I feel so much relief, unjustified relief, but it's there.

Nikolai holds me even tighter. Like if he loosens his grip on me, I'll be gone forever.

I inhale a deep, steadying breath as he whispers, "Thank God."

"Nik," I barely breathe his name as try to hold on to my composure. "Nik." I keep saying his name, but I can't help it. *He's okay*, I tell myself over and over as he pulls back slightly to look at me before hugging me back against his chest.

"I've missed you so much," he whispers against my hair, and I can feel his warm breath all the way down to my shoulder.

"How did you find me?" I ask him and pull back to look at him. The sight of his face shreds my composure. Faint bruises and a split lip are evidence left behind from days ago.

It's only then that he releases me, looking between me and Eli and then to the table. "Sit with me?" he asks as if there's any chance at all I would deny him, and it's the first time I can smile. It's a sad smile, the kind that comes with a pain that everyone else can feel.

"Of course," I barely get the words out and I have to clear my throat. Brushing my hair back and breathing in deeply to steady myself, I tell him, "I'm so happy to see you." My next words come out rushed. "I'm happy you're okay."

"Me too," he replies, but his voice is cloaked in sadness and he doesn't stop looking over every inch of me. "Are you okay?" he asks me and then reaches across the table to take my hand. His is large and warm, easily dwarfing my hand. Hands that have held mine for as long as I can remember.

I nod, swallowing the knot in my throat and not wanting to tell him or anyone else everything that's happened. "How did you find me?" I repeat my question and try to remember everything I wanted to tell him.

"I did what I had to do." His answer is short, but he doesn't stop rubbing soothing circles on the palm of my hand. It comforts me like he'll never know. He's done the same thing all my life. Every tragedy, every heartache. It's such a simple thing, but with that gentle touch, I can breathe, feeling as if everything is all right, even when I know it's not.

"Does my father know?"

"Yes, he..." Nik's voice gets tighter as he swallows whatever he was going to say. "He knows."

"What is it?" I ask him, and I don't hide the urgency in my voice when I demand, "Tell me everything."

"We have eyes on Carter. And I know," he struggles to keep a straight face, his fortitude failing him. "I know what he did to you," Nik says with a sickness at the end of words. "I'm so sorry, Aria." He breaks down in front of me, covering his eyes for a moment and apologizing over and over.

"Stop it." My command comes out harsher than I planned and I nearly rip my hand away from him. I won't be a charity case for sympathy.

"I swear I'll kill him." His expression hardens, and his eyes turn sharp. "I'll make him pay for what he did to you." I can see Eli shift his weight out of the corner of my eye and my pulse quickens, pounding at my temples, the adrenaline pumping harder and harder.

"No, you won't," I tell him quietly, grabbing his hand with both of mine. I hope he can read the message in my eyes telling him to shut the fuck up. Nik is hotheaded and reckless, but he can't be so stupid as to say that kind of thing right now. "Stop it," I warn him.

"After what he did to you?" he questions me, his brow furrowed, and forehead creased.

"You don't know what he did." It's all I can tell him, wanting to deny any of the accusations he could throw at me, even if they're true.

I know my expression is a mix of worry and sadness, but I can't help it. I can't control the emotions on my face. Not with Nikolai.

"I know enough. I'm going to kill him for it," Nik repeats his threat, the anger coming in full force and I feel lightheaded with indignation.

"I'll never forgive you," I whisper the words, feeling the ache sit against my ribcage, etching into my bone and eating away at whatever soul I have left.

"What's wrong with you?" Nik raises his voice with incredulity and backs away from me, his hands pushing against the edge of the flimsy table and inching it closer to me. He's breathing heavily as his composure crumbles. "He'll pay for what he did!"

"I didn't come here to talk about that," I say and struggle to look Nik in the eye. Belatedly, I remember what Carter told me about the men on Carlisle and what I'd planned to say.

"We're family," Nik reminds me, his tone wretched, his gaze covering every inch of my face and doesn't stay steady in the least. He's losing it. "I'll protect you!" he declares, and I take this moment to gain control of the conversation.

"Then move the men on Carlisle," I tell him quickly, staring into his eyes, although my words stumble into one another. Moving my hands into my lap, I resist the urge to fidget and straighten my back. "The war is between my father and Romano. Romano's the one who took me."

Nik's expression is pained as he says, "This isn't a negotiation, Aria."

He looks over at Eli, but only for a moment before giving in and spilling the plans my father has set in motion. He barely considers withholding the information and something doesn't feel right about it.

"The men on Romano's turf are decoys. He's letting them die and preparing to rampage Cross's territory."

I worry my bottom lip between my teeth and I struggle to breathe, but somehow manage to tell him, "Change his mind."

"Not after what Cross did to you."

I wish he could understand. I wish he felt like I do. I cannot fail. I won't live to see the men I love kill each other. I won't fucking do it!

"Then create a reason. Have Mika go up to… to…" I'm blanking on the street name that divides the territories. I've heard them all so many times before, but I rarely left the house. When I did, I never wandered far and so the street names mean nothing to me.

Whipping my gaze to Eli, I raise my voice and say, "Help me!" I stare at him as if he's failing me because he is. They're all failing me, and this is a losing cause. "The street where Romano territory meets Talvery territory."

"Bedford." Eli's response comes easily. He's not shaken in the least and I gather my composure, pushing my hair out of my face and staring at the steel table until I'm able to speak calmly.

"Bedford, move them up to Bedford," I plead with Nik, keeping the cadence of my voice soft and even. "Please," I beg him, desperate for him to understand.

"You think that will stop this war between Talvery and Cross?'" he asks me with an air of ridicule. "The men you're dealing with aren't men who have mercy, Aria." Nikolai talks to me as if I don't know them and it pisses me off.

I know firsthand how cruel they are.

"I'm not asking for mercy, Nik. I'm asking for fucking common sense." I practically spit the last few words. I lean back in the chair, keeping one wrist balanced on the edge of the table. "If they die, it's because you failed."

"Failed at what?" he asks me. "Taking charge of an army I don't control?"

"We have control. It's easy to take control," I say words my father once said to me. He said I needed to be harder, that I needed to wield my name and authority. I never imagined I would heed his advice.

"Send Mika to Bedford; he's at the top of the chain like you. No one would be surprised if he dies there, so make sure he does, Nikolai," I harden my voice, remembering my absolute hatred for Mika and all the evil shit he's done. "You know he deserves far less than an honorable death. Take him up there on a false pretense, shoot him in the back of the head and be done with him." I'm nearly shaken by the venom in my tone, by how meticulously I'm planning murder and interfering with war. "Tell my father it was Romano, and that you have to retaliate. Do it tonight."

"Mika's dead." It takes a moment to even comprehend what Nikolai said before he adds, "Your father killed him."

A cocktail of incredulity and anguish mix in my blood. "What? What happened?" My questions leave me in a single breath, a quiet one as I'm too afraid to speak any louder. As if doing so would change the truth of what happened.

Nikolai glances at Eli before leaning forward and speaking in a hushed voice. "Your father thought you ran away or that you were dead. He went through the tapes and Mika was the last person to speak to you."

With a deep breath, his eyes drift from me to Eli again before he turns his attention back to me. "He asked Mika why he was there and what he said that got you so upset."

"And?" I question him, my voice not nearly as low as Nik's, but it doesn't matter. I know Eli can hear. I know they can all hear.

"Mika didn't answer fast enough. Your father shot him in the head in front of everyone."

"Oh, my God." My heart pumps the blood coldly through my veins as I picture the scene and worry about what my father is thinking and everything he's been through.

"I won't lose sleep over Mika, but your father's losing it, Aria."

My chest feels like it's collapsing, and I struggle to grab hold of every bit of anger I've had toward my father since I've been here.

"He didn't come for me." I can barely speak the words.

"As soon as he found out where you were, he did. *We* did."

A moment passes and then another. I've held so much pain and anger inside of me at the thought that my father didn't care. Fuck. I wish I knew more. I'm losing this game. Each pawn I think I can capture has already been taken before I make my first move.

"He won't move those men or hold back against Cross, Aria. He wants justice." He adds firmly and with a conviction that sends a shiver down my spine, "We all do."

"This isn't justice. It's senseless death." I stare into Nik's eyes, willing him to understand me.

"You deserve justice, Aria."

"I'm fine, Nikolai. Carter didn't do anything to me that I didn't want."

Disbelief mars his handsome features. "You aren't thinking right," he says and slowly a look of sympathy replaces any hint of anger. "Aria, please come with me."

"I can't let that happen." Eli's quick to step closer to us, and I'm equally as quick to shove my hand against his stomach and tell him to back off. Eli takes in my expression before nodding his head and falling back into place. I don't know what he saw on my face at that moment, but he'll never know how much I needed him to side with me.

"I'm not leaving, Nik, and you need to find a way to move the men. Find a way," I implore him, but not a word is getting through to him.

"I won't let you stay here," Nikolai says then puts both fists on the table, breathing heavier and looking at Eli.

"I won't let you do this; I won't let you choose to stay with a man who hurt you."

"It's my choice." I don't defend what Carter's done. But I'll always defend myself and my ability to control my fate, now and until the day I die. "I *finally* have a choice," I tell him with a hardened voice, seeing my friend for the first time as my enemy.

"Is that what you call it?" he questions me.

"I can hide away. I can run. Or, I can know I have enemies and be prepared for what they'll do to me," I tell him staring into his eyes and not backing down. My shoulders shake from the sheer adrenaline and I can barely contain myself. "I don't want you to be an enemy."

"Aria," he breathes my name with agony. "I will never be your enemy."

"Then understand that I will not leave him." I question telling him the whole truth as he stares into my gaze. I don't want to know what he thinks of it, but I need him to know. "I love him, Nikolai."

"You're sick," he tells me with nothing but sadness in his broken gaze. "I won't let you go like this." His voice begs me to understand, but I know there's no reasoning with him. Just as there's no reasoning with me.

"Maybe I am sick," I play along with him and somewhere deep in my soul, I even agree. "But wasn't I sick all along? Hiding away in my room and afraid of everything." The defensiveness in my voice is nothing compared to the anger I feel at remembering how pathetic my life used to be. Life might be too kind a word to describe what I had before Carter took me.

"That's why I tried to save you," Nik tells me and reaches for my hand, but I pull away. His fingers brushing against mine feel like a fire that burns deep into the bone.

The cords in his throat tighten as he watches the space between us grow and he confesses, "I wanted you to be free. You deserve to live a better life than this."

His words ring in my ears and echo over and over. It fills the hollowness in the crevices of my chest. *He tried to save me?*

"You what?" I breathe the question.

Everything slows to a crawl as he answers, a look of shame showing on his face. "This," he motions with his hands, "this is all my fault." He struggles to look me in the eye when he tells me, "I knew you'd think it was Mika. I wanted you out, so you could run, but Cross lied to me."

My heartbeat ticks in slow motion. So slowly, the world tilts on its axis and I feel lightheaded. I have to grip the table to stay upright.

"He said he would get you out. He promised me he'd save you. He fucking lied to me, and I fell for it!" He contains his resentment when I don't respond, and leans forward begging me to understand, "All I ever wanted was for you to be free from this. I won't let this ruin you. You deserve so much better than this."

I can't speak. I can't move. I can't even breathe as I hold onto the table to keep me upright.

"Aria?" Eli calls out my name, but I don't look at him. I don't look at Nikolai when he begs me to forgive him. All I can do is stare at a scratch on the steel card table and try to hold on to my sanity.

"You were my friend," I whisper as tears prick my eyes. This all happened because of him. Because of the one person I had in life. The one person I thought I could fully trust.

"I love you, Aria, and you need to run." The word run makes my lips twitch. *Run.* That's how little he thinks of me. To him, I'm merely a scared girl who needs saving. A girl who should run, not one worthy of staying and fighting.

Letting my gaze find his, I peer into his soft blue eyes and whisper, "You don't know who I am anymore."

"You're innocent in this. You're too innocent for this life."

"Nothing about me is innocent, Nikolai. It's only what you all *think* of me."

"You know that it's not—" Nik tries to backpedal but I cut him off. I'm tired of being the scared little girl. I refuse to be seen as such.

"I never knew I had a choice until it was taken from me. I won't let anyone take it back."

"I can make this right, Aria," Nik reaches for my hand again, leaving his palm up on the table. And I take it willingly because I still love him, even if he's made all the wrong choices and doesn't see it. I still love him. He may not know how I've changed, but the boy inside of him is the same. My friend is staring back at me. I know that much.

I rub soothing strokes on the back of his hand as I look him in the eyes, letting my anger go and knowing he will never agree with me. My voice is hoarse as I whisper, "I'm fine, Nikolai."

"You're not. I can see you clearly, Aria. I always have." His voice begs me to listen, and I am, I just don't agree.

"I wish I was a better man, so I could save you. I tried," he tells me even though he looks past me with disappointment and regret equal in his expression. "I tried."

My heart pains for his. He'll never understand, and I don't know what this means for us, but I know this meeting was useless for this war.

"Try to move the men on Carlisle. I can save myself." My response gets his attention, and he shoots me a halfhearted smile, but one from a friend to a friend. One that warms the chill that runs through me.

"You're not doing a very good job of that, Ria." He uses the same nickname my mother had for me and it breaks the wall of strength I've been holding on to.

"It's been so long since someone's called me that," I tell him with a smile that matches his.

"I'll always love you," he tells me and he grips my hand harder. He whispers, "Always, Ria," before kissing my wrist. A move that makes Eli shift his stance once again.

His smile dies before mine does. "I will never forgive myself if something happens to you," he says, and his voice is choked. "I can't do anything now, but I promise I'll make this right, even if you hate me for it."

"I wish you would just listen to me," I tell him as the door opens behind me. The rusty hinges make it known without turning my head to see.

"I'll make it right," Nikolai says hurriedly as two men walk around the table on either side of me and take him away. I have to grip the edge of my seat to keep from reaching for him. My heart splinters, not knowing when I'll see him again and feeling as if I've failed miserably.

"Don't be stupid, Nikolai," I call after him.

He peeks over his shoulder at me with a smile that I recognize and one that brings tears to prick the back of my eyes. "I'll try not to, Ria."

"You'll let him go?" I ask Eli quickly and with a desperation that's obvious.

He doesn't hesitate to answer, "So long as he doesn't do anything stupid."

I can only nod a response, not trusting myself to speak, knowing full well Nikolai would do foolish things to save me.

The door closes, and Eli tells me we're waiting for a moment, but I hardly hear him as I think about everything that was revealed in the last thirty minutes.

I never thought much of who I wanted to be as I got older. I only knew what I was running from.

I didn't want to marry someone my father approved of, like Mika. I never wanted that, and I thought if I stayed quiet and listened, my father wouldn't marry me off as some of the whispers I'd heard hinted at that possibility.

I didn't want to be the reason the man I fell in love with died. That's the exact reason

Nikolai and I ended what we had. When my father started watching me closely, when he asked me if anyone had touched me because he'd kill them if they had, I denied it.

And when he cornered Nikolai and asked him, Nikolai told my father what he wanted to hear, that we were nothing but friends, but he would honor my father's request to leave me alone.

I knew I didn't want to be alone; I didn't want to run away. And so, I sat there in my room, quietly hiding from everything I knew I didn't want, but I never thought of what I wanted. I never chased what I knew deep down could be mine.

Nothing will stop me from chasing it now.

CHAPTER 13

"WHISKEY?" DANIEL ASKS ME AS I WATCH ARIA'S THROAT TIGHTEN AS SHE stares at the table. She did well, but still, watching it was fucking agony.

"Give her a minute," I speak into the microphone to Eli as I nod at Daniel. The amber liquid swirls in the bottle and reflects the pale moonlight filtering into my office.

Sitting back in my chair, I refuse to acknowledge how on edge my body feels. I'm on the edge of breaking down once again. My throat is dry and tight, my fingers and toes numb.

"She loves him," I admit the truth that splinters my chest in a whisper as I stare at the screen. It was clear to see in the way she spoke to him and held him and comforted him. But more than that, it's obvious he loves her as well.

That's something I can't allow.

"I don't want to hear you talk about the woman you love, not in that context. Not about her loving someone else." Daniel's response leaves no room for negotiation and I turn to him as he hands the tumbler to me.

Bringing the glass to my lips, I know what he's referring to and maybe it makes me coldhearted, but the pain that lies in between his words brings me comfort. The whiskey burns my chest as I tilt back the glass and take it all at once.

"Another?" I ask him, holding out the glass for him to refill even though his is still very much full. Three fingers' worth of whiskey is still evident in his glass.

He fills mine higher than before; the bottle that was full only two days ago is nearly empty now. As I take a large swig, I can hear his blunt nails tapping rhythmically against the glass. He leans against the window behind me rather than taking his seat.

"You have all of his files, so you could blackmail him into leaving." Daniel offers me a way to take care of the pesky problem. It's a solution that would work for most people, but not for Nikolai.

"He's irrational," I answer him, knowing all too well Nikolai won't stand down.

"You mean stupid?" he jokes, and I give him a rough chuckle in response, but the smirk that tries to tug at my lips ultimately fails to show itself.

"Do you think she'll hate me now that she knows I set her up all along?" I ask him.

The nerves roil in my gut, and I shut them up with another swig. That's what I'm truly worried about. Everything else is meaningless. But that piece of information could hurt us. Romano set it all up, technically, creating the meeting between the two of us. But I'm guilty and won't refute what he told Aria.

"I'm sure she already blamed you." Although there's a hint of humor in his answer, the truth of it causes my blood to turn to ice.

I scoff as I watch as my songbird stand, pushing in the chair and staring long and hard at the empty one across from her before preparing to leave. She doesn't stop staring at where Nikolai was sitting and every second her gaze stays there, the crack in my heart feels like dry lightning splitting the sky into two.

"She loves you," Daniel says from behind me, but it doesn't offer me any comfort.

"Will she when this is over?" The question alone causes the pain to run up my spine and I put the glass to my lips, only to find it empty. With a sigh, I place it on the desk.

The truth is, I don't think she will.

"I'm more concerned with her giving orders and trying to interfere, aren't you?" Daniel questions. Glancing over my shoulder, I watch my brother sip the whiskey although his eyes stay on mine.

"She can do as she wishes," I tell him the same thing I've told Eli. "I want to see what she'll do."

"She's different than I thought."

I feel restless as I watch his gaze flick to the screen, no longer focused on the back room and instead, watching Eli accompany Aria back to the safe house. Men are in multiple homes spread throughout the two blocks and each of them has eyes on her as they move from street to street.

"How's that?" I question him.

Bringing his gaze back to mine, he sets his glass on the windowsill and tells me, "She's… more…" he chooses his words carefully, "*involved* than I thought she'd be." The nervousness that prickles down my fingers intensifies when he adds, "I'm not sure what to make of it."

Cracking my knuckles, I don't look him in the eyes when I respond, "It means she'll be even more disappointed when all of it is over."

My brother considers me for a moment before nodding once and picking up his glass to finish off the drink.

He runs his fingers along the rim of the empty glass, watching as he does so and tells me, "I'm taking Addison out for the night." His lips pull down into a frown and his eyes reflect a well of sadness. "She hasn't been to The Hard Stone." He finally looks up to me and I nod, letting him know I heard him. The Hard Stone is the restaurant next to the Red Room. It's heavily guarded already, as is the club.

"I hope it goes well," I offer him, and it's genuine. I hate what's happened to them. I don't want to see my brother revert back to the man he is without her. There are only two versions of him. And I greatly prefer the one who is loved by Addison and loves her in return.

Running my thumb over the pad of my pointer, I think about Aria being all alone tonight and how she'll be thinking of Nikolai.

"Keep her out late," I tell Daniel, waiting for his eyes to reach mine. "Don't come back to the safe house for a few hours."

He lips are slow to pull into a smile, but they do.

"Do you have plans with your girl as well?" he asks me with a sense of humor that lights his eyes.

"I do now."

CHAPTER 14

I**T'S QUIET. TOO QUIET.**

The kind of quiet that makes you feel unsettled deep inside. Staring down at the empty glass of wine, I bite down on my bottom lip knowing full well that it doesn't matter if it's quiet or if I was in a room full of people chattering because I was going to feel like this tonight regardless.

This sick, numbing feeling spreads over every inch of me the second I'm consciously aware and not drifting down a memory I wish I could hide in.

Letting out a deep sigh, I push the glass away from me and wrap the woven blanket tighter around my shoulders as I get off the barstool at the kitchen island.

I finally ate today, but the food's tasteless and I can barely stomach a thing. Not when I feel like this.

Addison left half an hour ago, and I asked Eli to tell the guys to leave me alone tonight. Part of me regrets it. I'd like to pretend I could go downstairs and join them for a drink. Lord knows I need more than just one glass of Cabernet. I need a distraction and something that doesn't feel like my world is falling apart and collapsing on top of me, but that's all I have to accompany me tonight.

My bare feet pad softly on the hardwood floor as I make my way down the hall to the bedroom. All I keep thinking about is the phone on the nightstand. It only allows me to call Carter, or for Carter to call me. There's not even a number in the settings for me to give someone else.

I hate that he limits me like this, but I understand the need for him to control it right now. Because if I could, I'd call my father. I'd tell him I'm sorry I left and was stupidly taken. I'd tell him I'm okay. I'd beg him to stop all this.

And I'd be judged, found lacking, and a failure. I already know it, but I would still try.

Just the thought of it makes me pause outside the bedroom door, my hand on the carved glass knob as a shuddering breath leaves me. I hate this feeling of hopelessness that numbs my skin. I hate this feeling of being confined and pushed to the side.

I hate everything.

When the door creaks open, my feet sink into the plush carpet and I try to flick the light on, but it doesn't work.

My stomach drops even lower and I try it again, hearing the click but not seeing a change. It doesn't stop me from furiously flicking the switch back and forth rapidly.

"I didn't want any light tonight." Carter's voice paralyzes my body. It's a slow drip, like the venom from a snake bite. That's how my body reacts to his deep, rough tone.

It takes a moment for my eyes to adjust, but when they do, I see his broad shoulders from the corner of the room, sitting on a chair that wasn't there this morning.

"Carter," I say his name and then glance at the mess of sheets on the bed, and he follows my gaze to where I was hours ago, pleasuring myself as he ordered me to. "I didn't expect you to be here," I tell him softly and make my way toward him.

It amazes me how drawn I am to him. As if nothing matters but going to him.

Maybe Nikolai was right. Maybe I am sick. Because all that nervousness and anxiety doesn't exist anymore.

"I missed you," he tells me, and it sounds so unlike the man I knew while I was in the cell, and the man who rules with an iron fist but it's my Carter, the man who gives me everything behind closed doors. Flutters in the pit of my stomach travel up higher and lower at the same time, warming every inch of me.

"I need you," I whisper as I reach him, not hesitating to climb into his lap and wrap my legs around his waist. His large hands splay along my lower back and ass. He squeezes just as my lips brush against his and instead of kissing him like I intended, my neck arches back and I moan from the pain.

From the pain.

It's all he gives me at this moment, but sitting like this, being with him and feeling his heat is exactly what I need right now. The pain alone sends ripples of pleasure through my body.

He lowers his lips to the dip in my throat, letting his stubble drag along my skin as he plants open-mouth kisses right there and then trails up my neck.

He nips my earlobe before whispering in a way that creates a shiver down my spine, "I want you on the bed."

I take a kiss from him first. Stealing it quickly, I love that I catch him off guard and he nearly misses the chance to kiss me back.

He takes it though and then sits back as I leave his lap and lie on the bed.

"Strip," he commands, and I obey. I do it slowly, letting my fingers linger over my sensitized skin and reveling in the power I have. He wants me. He loves wanting me. And it's a heady feeling to have such a powerful man give in to the need of wanting you.

The clothes fall carelessly to the floor and the cool air kisses my skin as I writhe on the bed and run the tips of my fingers over my hardened nipples.

Carter stands slowly, and I barely turn my head to watch him stalk around the bed, stripping slowly for me as well. With the only light coming from the windows behind me, the shadows dance around him and it's intoxicating.

I can hear the clink of handcuffs before I see the metal shine in the pale moonlight, and it only makes me hotter for him. Before he commands me to, I raise my arms above my head and to the headboard made of thin planks. He only uses a single pair of cuffs, looping them through the planks and cuffing each of my wrists.

His fingers burn along my wrists and he lets them travel down my arm, tickling me, my breasts, my waist and then he dips a hand between my legs and I spread myself wide for him.

The groan deep in his throat is my reward, as is the spread of pleasure that runs through my body when he trails his thick fingers from my hot entrance up to my clit.

Writhing on the bed sends a mix of pain from the belt marks rubbing against the sheets and the pleasure from his touch.

He leaves me like that, breathing heavily on edge for him for a moment to grab something from the floor.

A tie, his tie. The silk runs along my cheek and then he tells me to close my eyes as he wraps it around me like a blindfold. My heart races at not being able to see and a new kind of excitement courses through my body.

Without being able to see, I can hear it clearly when he takes out another cuff as his fingers travel down my leg, to my ankle where he cuffs me. He does the same to the other side and I'm blindfolded and restrained for him.

My breathing comes in chaotically when I hear him walk around the bed again and the cold metal heats while the chill in the air makes me beg him to be touched. "Carter," I whimper his name.

"Tell me the truth, songbird." Carter's voice is deep. but laced with something I haven't heard from him in the bedroom for so long. A hard edge I don't like to hear.

Although my heart batters in my chest with the mix of fear slipping into my veins, I whisper, "Anything."

"You hate me, don't you?" he asks me and with his question comes a click and buzzing. My back bows as he touches the cold metal of the vibrator to my clit. The pleasure is immediate and spikes through me.

"I love you," I moan recklessly into the air as I pull at my cuffs, unable to move away from the intense pleasure.

He pushes it harder against me and I let out a strangled cry of ecstasy. I can feel myself clench around nothing as the intense waves of pleasure approach like the tide, creeping up and crashing harder and harder.

I'm so close. So, fucking close.

And then he pulls it away.

A gasp is torn from me and I try to look around. I want to hear where he is and what he's doing over the sound of my own ragged breath. But as I do, my impending orgasm slowly dims, leaving me slick with my own arousal and desperate for him to get me off.

Swallowing down the disappointment and trying not to pull on the cuffs that dig into my wrists and ankles, I wait for him.

"You hated me when you came to the cell."

I breathe in deeply, not wanting to remember how we started. My voice is raspy when I tell him, "I knew I wanted you."

His thick fingers push inside of me and I can feel his knuckles brush against my front wall. My breasts swing, and my shoulder blades dig into the mattress as he finger-fucks me. "Fuck," I moan, feeling the warmth spread through my body like wildfire as the bundle of nerves in my core heat and prepare to ignite.

"Carter," I breathe his name as my neck arches and I feel the pleasure build higher and higher. "Carter," I moan his name just before I cum.

And he pulls away before I can finish. My breathing's chaotic and I try to rip the blindfold away, but my hands are cuffed.

"Carter!" I yell at him and all I get in return is a rough chuckle. He kisses my jaw even as I pull away from him.

"I don't like this," I warn him in a voice that wavers. I can feel a sense of dread flow into my blood.

"All you have to do is answer me." His voice is easy as if this isn't a trap. "Did you hate me?" he asks again, and my voice tightens.

The buzzing gets louder and this time the vibrator hits me at full force. My head pushes back and the pleasure races through my blood. I'm so close. I'm already on the edge with only a few seconds of its touch.

And then it's taken away. Gritting my teeth, I struggle to move, feeling tears prick my eyes. "Carter!" I scream at him with unadulterated anger, but all I get is the vibrator back on my swollen nub.

Again, he takes it away just before the pleasure can consume me, leaving me with dimming fire and I can't fucking take it.

"Yes, I hated you! You hurt me, and I hated you for taking me!"

The pain that sweeps through me is like nothing I've felt before. Admitting what happened and knowing what I felt back then… I hate it. I hate that he's bringing it up. "Is that what you wanted?" I ask him, furious that he's doing this. "I hate this!" I yell at him but as the last word leaves my lips, the vibrator hits my clit and he leaves it there, my body flying higher and higher and then I fall from the sky, sending a tingling sensation to wreck my body all at once.

It lasts and lasts as I lie paralyzed and still at Carter's mercy.

"You loved me afterward though?" he asks me, his lips so close to mine and I push myself up as high as I can and steal his lips with mine. He kisses me back ravenously. I can feel his body close to mine and I wish I could wrap my legs around him and hold on to him, but I'm bound, and he pulls away from me.

I'm still reeling from my orgasm and the kiss I was too starved for to remember what he asked me, so he asks me again.

Breathlessly, I answer him, "Yes, I love you. I love you, Carter."

As his name leaves my lips, he pushes the vibrator back to my sensitized bud and it's nearly too much. I scream his name and he captures my lips with his as I detonate beneath him. The pleasure consumes me as the night sky is consumed with stars. Again and again.

I want to kiss him, but more than anything I want him to know how much I mean it when I say it. I love him, and he's all I want.

"Do you love Nikolai?" he asks me, and the question destroys the moment. I struggle to answer, but I do know the truth and I won't lie to him.

"Yes. But not like you," I answer him, feeling the high fall and my pulse slow. A second passes and another without him making a sound or touching me and fear races through my blood. "Carter?" I call out his name and he asks me another question.

"If I wasn't here, would you be with him?"

The silence stretches as I remember wanting Nikolai but being too afraid to tell my father. That girl, the one who doesn't go after what she wants and simply prays not to be seen, that girl is long dead.

"I don't know," I answer him in a breath and again he denies me, pushing the vibrator to my clit and finger-fucking me until I'm so close to my release I can't breathe.

Gasping for air, I search for some kind of relief, brushing my ass against the silky sheets, but Carter tsks me, holding my hips down.

"Just tell me the truth, songbird. I'll take care of you," he whispers in a voice I don't trust. One that's sinful.

"I don't know Carter. Please," I try to beg him, but he doesn't listen. He presses the vibrator against my clit and pulls away nearly instantaneously. My body bucks and the metal bites into my skin. "Fuck!" I cry out. I'm so close. I'm so fucking close again.

Off and on, off and on, he teases me.

The tides of my pleasure rush to the surface, igniting every nerve ending, but as soon as they're ready to go off, he pulls away and waits for the embers to die before bringing the fire back.

"If I wasn't here, would you be with him?" he asks me softly, calmly, his lips close to the shell of my ear. His breath traveling along my skin is enough to nearly get me off. I don't answer, I only bite down on my lower lip and shake my head, but I can't answer him.

And he does it again. Finger-fucking me ruthlessly, but the second my orgasm approaches, he pulls away. The smell of sex and the feel of my slickness on my inner thighs tease me into thinking there's more. But he leaves me panting and again my orgasm dies before I can get off.

It's the last bit I can take.

"Yes! I would try to be with Nikolai if you were gone." I can hardly believe I've spoken the sin out loud, much less to Carter. I know it hurts him and I hate it. I fucking hate it, but it's the truth. "I would try to be with him," I suck in a deep breath, brushing the tears off my face away with my forearms and wishing I could do the same with my shame, "but I don't know that I could ever have what we have. I wouldn't be the person I am without you." Tears leak down my face as the confession is forced out of me. "I love you, Carter. I don't want him when I have you."

He ruthlessly strokes against my front wall and I cum instantly. He pulls the orgasm from me, drawing it out and my body arches and goes rigid as the silent scream of ecstasy is ripped from me.

He doesn't stop until I'm limp and struggling to breathe.

"Carter, stop please," I beg him in a strangled voice that doesn't sound at all like me. "I hate this. I chose you! I fucking chose you!"

"Shh," he shushes me as I struggle to breathe. The touch of his splayed hand on my belly makes me jump, but he caresses my skin with soothing strokes until my entire body has calmed. With soft kisses on my neck, I beg him to stop again and let me love him. It's all I want to do right now, love him and feel the love he has for me.

"One more question," he tells me, and I stay as still as I can, waiting for it and dreading it. I can't stop crying, knowing what I've already confessed to him and worried that he won't love me because of it.

"Will you still when your family is gone? Will you still love me then?"

I already know the answer, but I don't want to say it.

The buzz from the vibrator makes me cry harder. He runs it along my pubic bone and my hips buck, trying to move away. I can't take any more.

"Tell me the truth," he whispers in a voice coated in hopelessness. He already knows the answer; I've already told him. He doesn't need to torture it out of me.

"No," I cry out. Hating him for what he's doing. I don't want to think about any of this, let alone admit what it would do to us.

"I love you, but if you do it… if you kill them, I will hate you forever," I gasp out as tears stream down my face. Agony tears through me both in the physical sense and emotional. He wrecked me. Carter destroyed whatever guard I had that protected me from this truth.

"I love you, Carter." I hear the cuffs click and then the metal leaves my skin. It's biting into my wrists and the second he unlocks them; I cradle my wrists to my chest.

I'm still crying into the blindfold when I hear the bedroom door open and shut. The hollowness in my chest collapses on itself and I refuse to believe he left me.

But when I finally take the blindfold off and beg him to hold me, he's not there.

Carter left me.

He doesn't love me. Carter Cross doesn't love me.

CHAPTER 15

I CAN STILL FEEL HER CUNT SPASMING ON MY COCK THE FIRST TIME I TOOK HER. I still dream of it.

I can still taste the sweet wine on her lips.

I can still hear her screams of pleasure and her whispers that she loves me.

I know for as long as I live, I'll remember it all. I'll remember what I had with her.

Tonight, I wage war against her family; I'll kill as many of them as I possibly can.

I'll destroy what we have together and risk her hating me forever. She was telling the truth and I can't stand it. Tonight, I will lose the woman I love.

My gaze drops to the phone on the bathroom counter just as Jase knocks on my bedroom door.

"In here," I call out to him and turn on the faucet to wet my razor. The shaving cream is already slathered on my skin. Since leaving her last night, I've fallen back into my old habits and I'm distracting myself by focusing on the war and everything else involved in this business.

He talks as I shave, ridding myself of the stubble and preparing to look the part of a man in control of an empire. "I have a proposition," he starts, and my eyes move to his in the reflection of the mirror before moving back to my jaw.

Each stroke of the blade is precise and smooth, skimming along my skin.

He takes a step forward, filling in the doorway. "I think our problem is that we've been content."

"Our problem?"

"The reason men think they can steal from us, the reason Romano is creating competition and involved us in this war." I consider him for a moment before going back to shaving, tapping the razor against the sink before bringing the blade down my skin again. I couldn't give two shits about any of it anymore. I'll kill those who defy me or stand in my way. And I'll be fucking content with that regardless of whether or not Jase is.

He tells me with a raised brow, "We aren't expanding."

"We have other ventures. The club. The restaurant." I don't know why I bother reminding him. I can see the look in his eyes. He won't stop until he gets what he wants.

"That money doesn't compare. You know, I know, and everyone else knows it." He speaks hurriedly like he can't wait to make his point, but I drag it out. Just to torture him.

"We're moving into Crescent Hills," I tell him.

"Because you want to take on that place, not because there's money there." His voice is flat, his expression expectant.

I can't argue that truth. "It'll be worth it to be closer to the docks," I tell him, and he shakes his head in disagreement. My patience ebbs as I tap my razor again on the sink and hold it under the running water.

"I think we need to go north. A true expansion," he tells me and waits with bated breath.

"Talvery territory?" I question him, my eyes on his in the mirror and he nods his head. "I already gave it to Romano."

"It hasn't been taken yet, and Romano can go fuck himself." Jase's voice is harsh and his persistence shines through. Jase keeps his gaze on me even though he's breathing harder with excitement. "We were going to give Fallbrook to Romano and he already has the entire upper east. Talvery turf should be ours."

His eyes dart over to mine, waiting for a reaction but I give him none. I didn't sleep for shit and I don't give a fuck about expanding.

"Are you that bored?" I ask him dully. I remember what it was like to take control, what was required to have my name permanently carved into this territory. The sickness of it all and the risk. It's not worth the money it makes.

"Bored?" Jase breathes out forcefully. "It's a lost opportunity." I don't respond. Instead, I finish shaving, careful not to react when Jase adds, "And what about Aria?"

I rip the hand towel from where it hangs at my right and dampen it under the faucet. It's hard to contain what I feel for her. The loss is too real. It's too close.

"What about her?" As I clean off my face, ignoring the screaming pain in my chest, he tells me, "I heard about how she's handling things." I grip the towel tighter, praying my brother doesn't say something that drives me to break his fucking jaw. Last night... I can't even think about how the truth stabbed me in the heart like nothing else has before.

He tells me, "I think she'd want this."

My brow furrows and I focus on breathing and controlling my expressions. "Want what?" Speaking hurts. Even breathing hurts. Everything fucking hurts.

"I think she'd want to still have the territory... maybe for her?" he offers, tilting his head and raising his brow. "Can you imagine how she'd react if we killed her family and gave her land to Romano?"

Using the dry section of the towel, I run it over my jaw, knowing exactly how she's going to react and hating it. I swallow thickly, knowing I can keep her here. Physically, I have the means to keep her here, but that will only add to her hate. And I want her to love me. I need her to love me.

"What if, instead, we do as little damage as possible?" He moves out of the doorway as I toss the towel into the sink and make my way past him to my dresser for my cufflinks. I'm running through the motions, focused on every mundane detail that's led me to this point in life.

"Any damage we do will break her, Jase," I tell him halfheartedly.

"I'm telling you, this is a good idea, Carter."

He stands a few feet from me, leaning against the wall with his arms crossed. "We already told Romano, but I say we hit them back to back. Talvery, then Romano and we take it all."

"With what men?" I ask him, feeling the tingling rage creep up my spine. "Do you remember the cost of it all? How many men have to die for you to be satisfied?" My voice is raised, and my pulse quickens. I swallow back the anger when he doesn't respond.

He flinches at the severity of my tone.

I add, "This isn't a game and every move has consequences."

"It's all a game, brother." He looks me in the eyes as he says, "A well-played and thought-out game."

He stares at me and I him as he tells me, "If Aria was able to convince those men to do what she suggested yesterday, we would have the upper hand. Talvery and Romano would lose men, and we'd be waiting to take out the rest," he talks with an evenness that sounds so reassuring.

"Only Aria doesn't know that," I tell him while taking a step forward and reaching for my jacket, which is draped across the dresser. "She doesn't know how many will die. And she will never be okay with wiping out her family."

The hint of a smile that was on his lips falters. "She has more to learn," is all he can say.

"Tonight, her family legacy starts to fall, and she will never forgive me, let alone rule alongside me." Jase's smile completely vanishes, and he glances at his feet before looking me back in the eyes, ready to say something else, but I don't let him. "Do you think she'll want to rule when her territory is nothing, but a graveyard of old memories and people forgotten?"

It fucking kills me knowing how she'll react. "She's going to fucking hate me," I bite out the words, grinding my back teeth against one another.

My breathing is ragged as he nods his head and runs his thumb over his bottom lip. "So, you're saying it's too late?" he asks.

That's exactly how it all feels. It's too late to keep her.

I let his question sit with me as I shrug on the jacket and button it. "I still think she would want this. Even if the war leaves a path of death to her throne, not everyone will die. She'll have some."

"Like Nikolai?" I reply with spite barely above a murmur, and it only makes Jase smirk at me.

"I have a feeling that fellow isn't going to make it," he jokes but it doesn't do anything to soothe the nerves that won't allow me to relax.

"In thirty minutes, they'll open fire," I tell him as I observe the little hand on my watch marching along steadily. "The next time you have an idea about damage control, maybe come to me sooner?" I suggest, and he huffs a laugh while shaking his head.

"The war has only started," he says, not giving up. "Just tell me you'll consider it."

Screwing over Romano is inevitable; doing it at the right time is crucial.

But the worst mistake Jase is assuming is that Talvery can already be counted as dead. I've made that mistake before, and I won't make it again.

"I consider everything, Jase."

Aria

THREE CANVASES ARE SPREAD OUT ACROSS AN OLD BEDSHEET ON THE FLOOR OF the living room. Three canvases with three profiles on each of them. Two men I love, and my mother, who's long gone make up the three. All the while, my mind focuses on the news that plays on the television in the background.

The list of names goes on and on. I can't look at the faces. I can't look at the scenes as they show them on the screen.

Addison is cuddled up on the sofa, staring blankly at the TV. The names don't mean anything to her, but to me, each name means far too much.

I'm barely holding myself together, knowing I should be at their funerals. Knowing I failed to save them. There's a mix of contempt and dread for Nikolai. I wonder if he even tried to move them. He knew, and what did he do? I remember what he said though, it was an army he didn't control.

It's only a matter of time before his name is spoken, added to the mounting death toll of the senseless murders between rival gangs, or so the reporter tells us on the flat-screen TV. Even the thought, forces me to choke on a dry sob, but I hold it down.

"Does this happen a lot?" Addison asks me, and I can feel her eyes on my back, but I don't trust myself to look at her, so instead, I place the flat brush in the cup and watch the red pigment bleed into the water.

"No, not like this," I answer her with my back to her. I am so used to death that it shouldn't break me like this. But it's the first time I tried to stop it.

And I failed.

"Do you need anything else?" Eli's voice comes from the doorway to the stairwell and I peek up at him, but I don't respond. He got me the paints from the corner store a few blocks down. The other things were in the package from Carter. I need a lot of things, I think. But as my lips pull down into a frown and my throat goes tight, I don't look back at him. Instead, I just shake my head no.

I hate him for standing by and doing nothing while men are dying. I hate myself for hating him, which is even worse.

"I want to go get them myself," I tell him as the thought hits me. I need to get out of here and go for a walk. I need to clear my head. I need something. I squeeze the cheap bristles over the cup before rinsing it again. "It would be nice to get some fresh air." I'm surprised by how even my voice is and how in control I seem. It's only because of Addison. If she weren't here, I have no idea how I would react to tonight.

The metal ferrule that holds the bristles clinks softly on the side of the glass as I tap it and then set it down gently on the paper towel.

I finally look up again and Eli's watching me closely. Addison's looking between the two of us and the air is tense among all three of us. She doesn't ask questions though and tonight, I can feel anger growing inside of me from her not wanting to know any more than whether or not this is normal.

"I want to go for a walk to the corner store, so I can buy a few things… please," I say the last word through clenched teeth.

"Give me an hour," Eli responds and then adds, "please." He mocks me, but in a way I know is meant to ease the tension. It doesn't though.

Giving him a tight smile, I nod once and watch him leave, although I still can't find an even breath. Everything is tense, and nothing is right. I feel like I'm breaking down. I'm losing it every second I sit here, guarded and watching the list of deaths grow.

"Are you okay?" Addie asks me as the sound of Eli's footsteps diminishes.

"No," I answer her honestly.

I wanted to help my family, and Nikolai ignored me.

I told Carter I loved him, I chose to stay with him, and he left me.

I'm a fool. I'm a fucking fool.

I'm helpless, hopeless and I feel like I'm at my limit.

The sofa groans as Addie slips off of it and makes her way toward me. She's quiet as she sits cross-legged next to me and leans in to give me a hug.

"I wish I knew what to say or do," she consoles me in a quiet voice and I instantly regret the thoughts I had moments ago. I'm so eager to lash out, I could see her being the misguided target of my frustrations, but I would never forgive myself.

Grabbing on to her forearm and giving her a semblance of a hug back, I tell her, "I wish I knew too."

Time passes slowly until she grabs the remote and turns off the TV. The click of the picture going black is louder than I've ever heard it before. I want it to stay on, so I'll know what happened, but I'm grateful she turned it off because I can't take any more.

"Do you want to talk?" she asks me, and I shake my head. I'm ashamed of how much of myself I give to Carter, only to have him hold back in return. I don't think I could tell her without her hating him even more. And after the night she had with Daniel, I couldn't do that to her.

"You could distract me and tell me what happened last night again," I offer, feeling a swell of jealousy and pain grow in my chest. Last night, I felt used. For the first time, I felt used and foolish for loving him.

"It was just a good night," Addie says, moving her hands to her lap. I know she doesn't want to rub it in, so I just nod and let it go. I stare at the doorway as if Eli will magically appear and let me go outside. The thought makes me roll my eyes. I'm stupid to think I had any sense of control.

Before I can spiral down the path to self-pity that kept me up all last night, Addison asks me, "Do you want to read my tarot cards?"

I watch her chew on the inside of her cheek, waiting for an answer. I'm so grateful for her that I would do anything she asked right now. For the distraction, for the genuine friendship, and so I nod.

"Let's do it," I answer her.

With a deep breath, I scoot backward and turn to her, sitting opposite her and cross-legged too as she reaches behind her on the coffee table for the deck of cards Carter got me however long ago.

"Okay, what do I do?" Addison asks, placing the deck of cards in front of her and staring at them like they'll magically shuffle themselves.

"Knock on them first," I tell her in a deadpan tone, knowing full well she's going to look up at me like I'm crazy.

"I'm serious," I say again and nod to the cards, folding my own hands in my lap. "You have to knock on them to get rid of any previous readings and put your own energy into the cards."

She does what I tell her, lifting the deck and knocking weakly on the back card although she's grinning the entire time. Already I feel a thread better. Only a thread, but it's one more than I had before.

"Now shuffle the deck and think about something you'd like insight to. Or don't." I shrug and stretch from where I'm sitting, feeling the ache from leaning over the canvases for the past few hours. Just glancing at them reminds me about everything and I'm quick to turn back to Addison.

"Is that enough?" she asks me, holding out the cards and I offer her a soft smile and then gesture to the deck. "Split them into three piles, however, you want, and then stack them on top of each other into one pile again."

"Is this how it's always done?" she asks me while doing as I say.

"No," I tell her, feeling a deep ache in my chest. "I learned to read cards from my mother. But she didn't do it like this."

"Oh, how did she do it?" she asks me, and I have to grab the cards and look at them rather than in her eyes when I tell her, "I don't remember. I just had to learn on my own when I decided I wanted to use her deck."

It's quiet for a moment, but she continues the conversation, steering it to a more positive side. "Are these hers?" she asks me as I lay out the cards one by one.

"No, these are ones that Carter got me." Somehow that pulls even more emotion from me as I set the final card down. I don't tell her that I was locked in a cell losing my mind when I was given these cards. And that Jase is the one who actually gave them to me. That day, or night, comes back to me and I nearly get sick.

"This is the horseshoe spread," I tell her as I lay out the cards, refusing to fall backward; I won't go backward. "The significator is in the center, but each place in this spread has a unique meaning and the seven other cards are spread in a horseshoe around it. The significator, this card, is basically you at this moment."

"The four of wands is me?" she asks me although her eyes are on the card I'm currently touching the edges of.

I nod and then add, "There are four suits: the swords, the wands, the pentacles, also known as coins, and the cups. They each represent something different in life and the wands represent creativity. Swords are conflict, pentacles are money, thus also being called coins, and the cups are emotional wellbeing. More or less.

"The four of wands in this deck—"

"I feel like this is a professional reading," Addison exclaims, barely holding in her excitement and I have to give her a small laugh.

"I've read a lot about cards. A few years ago, I thought it would bring me closer to my mother." I wish I hadn't said that last bit, but Addison doesn't focus on the negative. Instead, she says, "Well, this is freaking awesome." She reaches behind her for the glass of wine and then sits up at attention. "Please, continue." She gestures comically and takes a sip of her wine.

I have to let out a snicker that's almost a snort and remember where I left off. "Right," I say out loud, "The four of wands. In this deck, the four of wands is a literal marriage." As I say the last word, I breathe in deep, realizing how emotional Addison's been and watch her reaction, but she only sips her wine and listens. It takes a lot of pressure off of me, so I continue.

Some people take the cards literally, but I have a feeling Addison won't. She just wants a distraction, just as I do.

"The significator is a snapshot of who you are right now and the four of wands is a resting point. There's been a sense of accomplishment, and there's a sense of celebration over it, thus a marriage as the picture on the card. It's a deeply happy card about solidifying some sense of community. Which may not seem at all like where you are in this moment," I pause, feeling a wave of insecurity, but I continue, giving her the reading I think this card points to, "but it can also mean friendship, solidifying a friendship."

"So, it's us?" she asks me, and I try to keep my voice even and devoid of the intense emotion that rises inside of me when I tell her, "Yeah. I think this card is about us."

Addison settles into her position, an elbow on each knee and tells me, "I like that."

With a deep breath, I point to the first card of the seven that makes the horseshoe. "This is your immediate past and this card, the six of pentacles, is a card of generosity and harmony. It's a card depicting someone who was in a good place with the in and outflow of their money, but it doesn't always refer to money. It can also refer to charity and gracefully accepting or giving of money, time or safety." I pause and swallow before adding, "Like how you helped me. That's what this card could mean."

Addison only nods and takes another sip of wine, so I keep going, moving through the motions rather than thanking her again and bringing up that awful night.

"The immediate present, the next card, is the priestess card. She's a figure who has deep intuition."

"What about the suits? What suit is she?" Addison interrupts and it's only then that I really know she gives a fuck about the card reading or at least she's paying attention.

"The suits are in the minor part of the deck; the major part of the deck has figures basically. So, they aren't a part of the suits. There are basically two types of cards, suits, the minor cards, and then figures, the major cards."

"Oh." She nods and then clears her throat before looking at the other cards in the deck to see how many others are major cards and minor, I assume. "Okay, so the immediate present, is the priestess?"

I nod and then smirk as she adds, "I like that too. So far, this is a very likable reading."

My shoulders shake with a huff of laughter as I continue. "The priestess is a person with deep intuition and she's kind of a major arcana echo of the queen of wands. So, not only does she have a deep intuition about herself, but she has it about other people. In other cards, she's pictured holding a mirror that she can point to herself or to others. She's someone who has otherworldly energies and someone who can observe others for who they are. And also see what they need instinctually."

"Like how I knew Daniel was the man he is?" Addison asks me in a flat tone as she pulls the sleeve of her shirt over her wrist and then wipes under her eyes. With my mouth parted, I'm shocked by her response and I struggle to answer her quickly enough. "Ignore me, I'm sorry." She breathes in deeply and shakes out her wrists. "Sorry, I just had a moment."

"It's okay," I barely speak the words and look back down at the card. "It could mean lots of things," I tell her and then shrug. "Or nothing at all."

"I knew," she tells me with a grief that darkens her eyes. A sad smile graces her lips and she says, "Don't stop, please. For the love of God, let's move past that one."

Clearing my throat, I move on to the next card, but then decide to move back to the priestess. "It could also mean that you know what people need and I don't know your story, but knowing you, I would think you knew he needed you." Addison stares at me with glassy eyes but only nods.

My place isn't between them, so I move back the spread, to the third card in the horseshoe and the immediate future. "The king of wands is your immediate future. The kings in the deck are the last of the suits and they have control over the suits. The pages learn, the knights chase, the queen embodies and the king controls. And so, the king of wands is someone who's able to understand and empathize with creativity and life, but he, himself, is not personally creative or spiritual in a really emphatic sense. Instead, he's someone who works closely with creative or spiritual people, but he's distant from them and that's what makes him good at what he does. It's the distance that allows him to be there for others, but it also prevents him from being a part of it."

Struggling to place this card in the current context, I think back on other meanings for the card.

"The king of wands can also be a person who's charismatic but reserved. Still waters run deep in this person, but he's distant."

"So, someone who's controlling is coming?" Addison asks flatly and then snorts into her wine. "I didn't need cards to tell me that one."

I shake my head, knowing she's referring to Carter or Daniel, but this card wouldn't be either of them. It's someone else. "Someone who's distant and uninvolved," I correct her and feel a chill run along my skin. It pricks every nerve and forces each small hair along my skin to stand on edge.

I can hear her swallow the wine and instead of asking who or considering the meaning, I simply keep going to the very bottom of the horseshoe and the fourth card. She doesn't object.

"This card, your path, is the eight of swords. And in my deck at home…" I pause and almost regret saying home, but I don't acknowledge it. Thankfully, Addison doesn't press me. "In my mother's deck, the eight of swords depicts Queen Guinevere, she's tied to the stake and she's going to be executed for infidelity. And the interesting thing about the eight of swords is that often you'll see the woman is holding her own bindings around the pole.

Different decks have different art though." I take a moment to look at the deck that Carter got me and it's not obvious in this card. "You can't really see it here, but it looks like this woman is trapped to such a horrible fate in the eight of swords, but actually the only thing that's trapping her is herself. She's the one who has to be able to let go and free herself from her restraints." I look at the card again and realize it doesn't look like that on this deck and it's the only deck I've ever seen where the bonds are truly tied. I continue though, refusing to let her think she's tied inextricably to this fate.

"The woman in this card is not going to be rescued, but she's not doomed to this terrible fate either. The only thing trapping her is herself. The good news is that she's able to save herself; she's not actually tied to the stake."

I take a moment, thinking about everything as Addison finishes off her wine and doesn't say a word. *These cards could be for me.* The idea that they are sends a shiver down my spine. Addison knocked on the cards, I remind myself. Without a word from Addison and not liking where my thoughts are headed, I continue.

"The perceptions of others is the next card, the fifth spot in the horseshoe. The knight of wands is your card in this spot. The knight of wands is all about deep fire and chasing. Do first, think later. They tend to be impulsive."

Addison laughs into her empty glass as she twirls the stem of it between two fingers. "Sounds like that one could be true," she says with a smile on her lips and I can't help but smile too.

"The next card is the challenge to be faced and this is an interesting card to be sitting here." I think out loud, not censoring anything. "The nine of cups is on the cusp of culminating happiness. It's the difference between being engaged and being married. There's anticipation that there's something that's still held back. And then the next card, the ten is complete happiness and marriage, nothing left to come."

Addison nods all the while that I explain the card and I'm not sure how she's perceiving it until she speaks.

"So, there's still more to come? More that would make me happy?"

"Well this is the challenge card, so that's the obstacle you're facing." My answer tugs her lips down and her gaze moves toward the cards. "So, the challenge here is that you're almost there, but not quite and that's where the tension is." I don't stop. I don't want her to think about it right now, but I don't think she'd tell me even if she had ideas of what the cards could mean.

"The final card is the outcome, and for you, it's the queen of wands. She's someone who is safe, confident and she's able to empathize and nurture but she's also powerful and creative in her own right. She's someone who can wield power, but also stands on her own two feet. She's the fiery enchantress."

"That's my final outcome? I get to be a fiery enchantress?" she jokes but I'm so relieved the reading seems to be ending on a happy note.

With a nod, I tell her, "Yes, Addie. You get to be the fiery enchantress." I can't keep my face straight as I tell her that.

"So, when does that happen?" she asks me, and I have to snort a laugh while smiling.

"The priestess in the present position means this person often holds this role. It's also a major arcana card and that typically means it takes time, but it's in the immediate present position. That means there's something otherworldly about her, so she's always carrying this inside of her. Everything else is minor arcana so that would mean days… maybe weeks. But probably days." My gaze falls back to the king of wands and my blood chills. *Someone is coming.*

Addison smiles and bites down on the edge of her wine glass as she glances at the cards one last time.

Again, the king of wands is all I can see, and I'm focused so intently although I don't want to be. He calls to me. The distanced man who's coming and a chill flows down my spine in a way that feels like a nail raking down my back.

"If you're done," Eli's voice breaks through my thoughts and I've never been more grateful.

"Yes," I'm quick to tell him as Addison collects the cards, quickly putting them back on top of the deck. She seems to be just as absorbed with the card as well. I watch as she stacks all the cards neatly in the deck and puts him down last, right at the end of the deck.

"Do you want me to come with you?" Addison asks me as I push up off the floor, shaking out my hands and nerves, and try to shake off the uneasy feeling creeping along my skin. The tiny hairs at the back of my neck refuse to go unnoticed. They don't leave me alone; even as I walk across the room and put the jean jacket on, the chill stays with me.

"I think I'm going to try to sleep then," she tells me although I think she said it more to herself. She covers her face when she says, "I need that stuff, though."

"The stuff?" I ask her to clarify as I stop a few feet from Eli and think back to the vial of sweet lullabies. The drug he gave me to sleep.

"Daniel gave it to me because I wasn't sleeping, and I don't know what I did with it." She looks at the coffee table as if she left it there, but there's nothing there.

"It gave me nightmares. The lullaby stuff."

"That's a shame," she says with true pity. "I slept so well with it. And today has been…" she doesn't finish, she only shakes her head. I can only imagine how she's feeling. I know she wants to go back to Daniel. I could see it in her eyes and hear it in her voice when she told me all about last night at breakfast. I know she loves him. And I think she could forgive him if he wouldn't keep secrets from her anymore once this war has ended.

He's kind to her. He wants her. And I know she wants him too. The only thing that stands in the way are the names the reporter keeps talking about on the television and the fact that Addison now knows Daniel has a hand in that tragedy.

"I was having nightmares before, so maybe that's why?" I surmise and then shrug, pretending like the vision of my mother didn't just take over my mind this second. I glance at Eli, still standing there a few feet away, looking straight ahead and waiting for me. Focusing on him and not on where my thoughts were going.

"Nightmares?" she asks, and I only nod as I swallow down the memory.

"I'm sorry," Addie says, and I wish she didn't. I don't need more sympathy. Sympathy doesn't do shit.

"It's been a while since I've had them." I know I have Carter to thank for that. "Anyway, there's a vial that was in my bag in the drawer of my nightstand. If you want it," I offer her, and she gives me a small smile.

"Thanks," she tells me in a way that I know she's truly grateful as she yawns and then stands graciously.

"Sleep well, Fiery Priestess," I tell her with a small smile and watch as she picks up the cards off the floor and puts them on the coffee table.

"You too, Ria," she tells me and uses the nickname only two other people have used for me all my life. She doesn't see how my face blanches, but I'm able to fix it in time before she looks up at me with a sweet smile. "Ria, the card reader," she adds to the nickname and smiles.

I leave without saying goodbye, but it doesn't escape me that Eli keeps looking at me curiously because he saw how I reacted. Eli sees everything.

⚊⊳⬦⊲⚊

Tonight feels darker than the night before. Maybe because there aren't any stars out, or maybe it's just my perception. Either way, it's pitch fucking black.

It's colder too and as I huddle into the jacket, I find myself walking faster to get to the corner store that I saw a few shops down last night.

"You're quiet," Eli comments as the wind blows and my hair whips around my face. His faint accent comes through more now than I've heard before. I almost ask him about it, but my mind is spinning over the king of wands and who it could be. I always look too much into my cards… and that reading wasn't even mine.

"I'm always quiet," I answer him and when he gives me this charming, perfect smile, I nearly smile too. I watch him as he looks up to a house in the middle of the street and I know to wait when he does that, just like last night, so I do. Shoving my hands in my pockets, I breathe out and let the cool air flow over me, calming my anxiety.

"I had a girlfriend once who liked those cards. The reading ones."

"Tarot cards," I tell him as he rocks on his heels, still waiting at the edge of the street.

"Yeah, she liked to read mine, one a day, and tell me how my day was going to go."

A simper pulls at my lips. "Was she right?" I ask him, and he huffs a laugh while shaking his head.

"She was so wrong that I could almost guarantee the opposite of whatever she said was actually going to happen."

"They're really just to get you thinking," I tell him and ask, "Are you still together?"

He shakes his head and says, "She was fucking crazy." A genuine laugh bubbles in my chest at the expression on his face, and for the first time today, I feel warmth flow through me. I feel real for a moment… until the reality of everything going on hits me hard in the center of my chest.

"You're good at distractions," I say while pulling my hair to the side as another breeze comes by. As I do, the sound of a car driving a street or two down catches my attention. "Thank you for that," I add with as much sincerity as I can.

"I'm sorry you're in the middle of this," Eli offers me and all I can do is force a fake smile to my lips.

His earpiece buzzes with someone's voice and I step forward, ready to continue but his large forearm blocks me. "We're going back." His voice is stern and offers no negotiation.

"What's wrong?" I ask him feeling my heart race, and counting how many streets we've walked down. Three. It's right around the corner and the safe house is only three streets away.

I can barely breathe as he tells me, "Now," ignoring my question and wrapping his arm around my waist to quicken my steps.

I can't keep up with his fast pace as my body catches fire with fear.

As the muted voices come through his earpiece again, I peek up at him, trying to listen, wanting to know what's going on.

There was no one on the streets. Not a soul. What the hell happened?

Headlights come from my right. And between it all—the voices, the panic, the lights—I stumble, falling to the ground like a fool.

My knees and palms both hit a lawn hard as Eli tries to pull me along, cutting through the yard to head straight to the house, but I struggle to push him off of me, so I can stand up. I just want to stand up but he's hurting me as he tries to pull me up.

The parked car to my right roars to life, its engine turning and the sound filling the night just as I hear guns firing.

Bang! Bang! Bang! The guns going off make me scream and my heart leaps into my throat.

"Stay down," Eli grunts as he lies on top of me, covering me, but he doesn't stay there for long. The bullets aren't coming this way; they aren't even close.

I can barely see Eli pull out his gun, the cold metal brushing my shoulder before he fires a shot at the car.

There are so many guns going off. Too many to count and I don't know where they're firing, but it's not at me.

Some hit the car. I can hear them crunch into the metal. It pings and some bullets ricochet. Bullets hit the house Eli was looking at, the brick splintering and chips falling past the porch light as if snow is falling on this cold summer night.

Everything happens in slow motion as I peek up, the back of my head slamming into Eli's chest as he fires at the car again, telling me to stay down, but I won't. I need to know what's going on. I keep low, but I refuse to cover my head and not find out what's going on, so I can prepare myself if I have to.

There are four men in the car. I can see them clearly even though they're dressed in all black and hoodies cover their faces. Two are still firing at the building, rapidly pulling the triggers. Men from the building are firing back. Bullet casings hit the ground and the tinkling distracts me as another round of bullets comes closer to us, aimed at another house with men in those windows firing too. We're only separated from the car by a white picket fence that offers no protection and maybe three feet in a yard of grass.

The other two men who were in the car run as I take in the scene. Both of them run down the street to flee although they turn and fire, hiding behind cars and the brick fence. They're running closer to us.

I don't know the car they came from. I don't know the men, but one of them running falls instantly, screaming in agony and grabbing his leg on the sidewalk, the bright red shining brightly as he's bathed in the streetlight.

Bang.

He's silenced and goes still. My heart races, my pulse thrumming so hard I can barely hear the gunshots anymore.

The smacking of shoes carries down the street louder than the gunshots.

"Stay quiet," Eli tells me, intent on hiding as the fucker who's running tries to get away.

He's going to let him get away.

Anger and rage like I've never felt before war inside of me and it burns. It burns too bright. It burns too hot and I can't stand it.

I don't even know it's my own scream as I rip the gun from Eli unexpectedly and run down the street toward the coward who fired at me and the men protecting me. The coward who hid and waited to attack me. I won't fucking let him run.

I won't let him get away. I fucking refuse.

My feet slam so hard on the ground that I feel the pain spike through my thighs. He's only feet away from me and running faster, but he turns to fire at the building again, he slows and turns and that gives me a chance. With a deep intake of the cold air that pains my lungs, I lunge at him, seeing nothing but red.

His head crashes on the cement sidewalk and I hear his gun fall into the street and sounds like it hits metal... maybe a gutter. I didn't recognize him farther away and I don't know him now that I'm close up either. I don't know who he is other than someone who attacked us.

Even as the metal slams into his skull, I don't hear the gunshots stop. Even as the blood splatters onto my face, the heat of it nothing compared to the raging burn that flows through my own blood, I don't hear Eli yelling for me.

I don't stop, I can't make myself stop pummeling his flesh with the butt of the gun. I can't even see what I'm doing with the tears flowing down my face. I try punching him with the gun held in my hand and the metal clashes against the thin skin over my knuckles. It hurts, I know it does, but that only fuels me to do it again.

The footsteps are loud and they're coming closer, but I can still feel the man beneath me shoving me away. His hands pushing against my chest, my face, anywhere until they stop to cover his face.

I pause for only a second and it's a second too much as he reaches for the gun. Panicking, I lean forward, head-butting him and crashing my forehead against his nose. He screams out, but he doesn't stop.

He's still trying to reach for his gun and so I whip the butt of the gun in my hand down hard against his throat and his hot blood bubbles up from his lips as he coughs.

Strong hands grip my shoulders and then my arms, but I kick out, desperate to connect with the fucker who dared to wage war with men protecting me.

My left shoe hits his chin and his head snaps backward, bashing against the cement. Everything in my mind becomes a fog as Eli holds me close to him, telling me to calm down and dragging me away. All I can see is that man running away, getting away without any consequences while they escort me back, through the yards and straight back to where we came from.

It all happened so fast that I'm still breathing chaotically and shaking when Eli and another man, who helped him rip me away, bring me inside.

"Get her inside." I hear Eli's words, but they're slurred as I struggle to breathe.

The air isn't cold anymore. Nothing is cold. It's all hot and I feel like I'm suffocating.

The second the bright light of the foyer hits me, I shove them away. I don't want to be touched, I can't be touched right now.

I refuse to talk to them, to listen to them telling me to stop and calm down.

Calm down? How can I calm down when this is what my life is?

"I'm tired of taking orders!" is all I can yell out, my voice raw from screaming. The memory of what I've done seeps in slowly as I rock on the floor. I was screaming. I didn't realize it then, but I was screaming.

Every time I swallow, it hurts. My shoulders shudder and Eli tries to comfort me but I shove him away. Backing into the corner of the foyer, I'm only seeing the vision of me running after the man and fighting him.

Time passes slowly.

I steady my breathing and slowly calm down, watching my hands and willing them to stop shaking. There's so much blood on them and I wipe them off on my pants, but that just spreads the blood.

I walk myself to my room, gripping on to the railing to keep me upright. Eli follows but stays a good distance behind. Carefully stripping out of the stained clothes, I step into the hot shower to wash the blood away, although my knuckles are raw and cut. It will take time for those to heal.

Maybe an hour passes, and I spend the entire time in the shower. When I'm clean, I walk downstairs and open the front door to the house to see Eli, the other man, and two others standing guard.

All I want to know is his name. I want the name of that man. I don't know why it matters as much as it does, but I need to know his name.

I know I look foolish with wet hair that clings to my face and pajamas on, but still, I speak up.

"Who is it?" I ask Eli as I stand in the light of the foyer, and he stays on the other side of the doorway, bathed in darkness. "What's the man's name?"

"We'll find out soon and I'll tell you immediately," he answers me, and it only makes me angrier. How can he not know? It still hurts when I swallow and hurts, even more, when I clench my hands into fists at my side.

"Where is he?" I ask Eli with my teeth clenched, "I'll beat it out of him myself." The rage I feel is unjustified and I know I'm out of control and crossing a line, but I don't care about boundaries anymore. Not when everyone else crosses them.

The silence is only broken by the chirp of crickets from beyond the yard. There are three men in front of me and no one answers me.

I can hear Eli swallow as the other men stare at me, and still, no one answers.

"Where is he?" I repeat myself, ready to tell them to go fuck themselves if they refuse to tell me. I don't care what Carter ordered. I don't care if I'm their enemy or they think I'm just being babysat. "I need to know his name!"

"He's dead, Aria." Eli's voice is softer than I expected, and I have to take in a shuddering breath. His gaze is assessing, but comforting. "He died."

My eyes flicker over his and then dart to the other men. "Who killed him?" My voice is full of both shock and remorse for speaking to him like that, along with everything else. As time moves forward, I seem to come down, to ground myself again. As if blinking finally removed the red rage that blinded me.

One man steps to the side, another whispers something on the porch, but Eli's voice brings my attention back to him.

He answers me, "You did."

CHAPTER 17

Carter

"**D**O YOU THINK SHE'LL BE A PROBLEM?" JASE ASKS ME IN LOW TONES AS HE stares across the bar at the brunette. She stands out in the club full of women dressed in tight shirts and short skirts.

Dressed in jeans with rips in the knees and a loose black tank top designed for comfort, she doesn't belong here. More than that, she's slamming her hands against the bar and screaming across the counter at both the men working tonight.

"She's not why we're here," I remind him. "Let the bartender handle it," I tell him and walk past the crowds of people, but Jase stays behind a moment longer, staring at the deranged brunette.

All I care about are the men in the back room right now. Men who lost a family member tonight. Two of our guys were shot in the back while they were out on their runs to collect. The fucked-up part is that they were on the most southern portion of our turf. So, some fucker came into our territory, hid low, and shot them in broad daylight. Some fucker named Charles Banner who's now buried in a shallow grave thanks to Cason.

It doesn't bring the men back though. Death is final.

When I walk up to the back doors, Jared opens them immediately and the hushed voices of the six men inside are silenced. I can hear Jase pick up his pace behind me and come in before the doors close, quieting the music of the club.

Around the table, all six men have drinks in front of them, two of them with shots untouched. Cigarettes are lit and one of the guys takes the last puff before putting out the butt. As he blows out the smoke, the rest of the five greet me and then he follows.

The metal chair legs drag on the floor as Jared pulls out seats for both Jase and me and then goes back to his position to guard the doors.

"James and Logan." I swallow thickly after I look both men in the eyes. The youngest one, James, lost his brother and his eyes are still bloodshot. He can't stop himself from crying as I tell him, "I'm sorry." Logan lost his cousin, his only cousin and he's the one who brought him in. I can see the look of regret on his face and there's nothing I can do to take that back.

The other four men all lost a close friend.

Only two men have died tonight on our side, and we took out nearly thirty of Talvery's crew. It doesn't make the losses any easier to take. Not for the six men sitting here.

"What happened was a tragedy and one that needs to be rectified."

"I thought they said you got him?" A kid with a deep scar down the left side of his face and blonde hair speaks up. His lips stay parted as he stares at me with wide eyes. "They said he's dead."

"The asshole who stole the lives of my men?" I question him, bringing my hand to my chest. "The one who pulled the trigger was shot in the back of the head and buried in the back of the construction site off the highway. Tomorrow cement will cover him, and his name will be forgotten." I pause as the kid nods. His name escapes me, and I look around at the other four. I know three of them and then I come back to the blonde. Matthew. That's right. "Matthew?" I call him out and he nods again, bringing his gaze up from where it was focused on the table.

"You can call me Matty." He brightens for a moment, and it's then that I remember one of the guys who died was his neighbor. They grew up together.

"How old are you?"

"Just turned twenty-two," he tells me, and I turn around and motion for Jared to come closer. "Get him as many drinks as he wants all week. A birthday should be celebrated. Every day alive should be celebrated."

"Thank you, Boss," Matty tells me and I shake my head, not wanting any gratitude.

"The man who's responsible for your brother's death," I look to James and then to Logan as I continue, "and your cousin's death, Nicholas Talvery, will die the second I have a chance to end his life."

I pause as the memories of how he tried to kill me, how sneaky the fucker is, spring to mind. Always preparing and setting up his men to blindside the unsuspecting, like my brothers, when we were only kids. "No one," my voice hardens, "will take from us without having consequences."

My heart races as I look the two men on my right in the eyes. "He killed your family and I'll have his head for it."

"To the end of Talvery," Matty raises the shot glass in his hand and the other men do the same.

Talvery.

I'm numb as they throw back the shots and commiserate together.

"To the end of this war," Jase speaks up, grabbing another shot glass and filling his and then the others.

The guy's spirit picks up, although Logan still looks lost. James pats him on the back as Logan hunches over, shaking his head and crying again.

This war is useless. A fight between two men, Romano and Talvery, who already have enough. Greedy, selfish men who will risk lives to hurt the other.

And I supported it.

And Jase wants more of it.

And Aria lies in the middle of all of it.

"If you need anything, you know who to call," I hear Jase speak quietly to the two men on the right and then he stands, and I do the same. Buttoning my jacket and taking a good look at each of the men sitting there.

None of them blame me and that's the worst part of it. I'm bitter knowing they don't blame me when they should. I brought them into this.

For her.

I agreed to this… for her.

The sound of Jase walking ahead of me is all I can follow as I feel like I'm suffocating. Maybe that's how I'll die. I'll choke on every fucked-up decision I ever made.

I feel my phone vibrate in my pocket. It's been going off since the bar, but I wanted to get in and out and give the men the respect they deserve. That's the least I could do.

Feeling it go off again as we step out into the night air and wait for the car to come around, brings on the restlessness and unease that hasn't left me since I left Aria alone on the bed.

"That brunette's gone," Jase comments, leaning against a post by the curb that details all the drink deals inside.

As I pull out my phone, I glance at his profile and for a moment I see the look of loss in his eyes. He's looking out into the parking lot and past it to the busy street. I know what he's thinking about. I know what that look means.

"You all right?" I ask him, and he clears his throat, coughing into his fist and kicking off the post.

"Yeah," he answers and runs his hand down the back of his neck. "I just can't believe Talvery would waste a man like that. Did he really think he'd get out alive?" he questions, and I wonder if he's telling me the truth about what he was thinking, or if I was right.

The rumble of the engine and the soothing sound of my car pulling up grabs our attention and saves me from asking him and prying.

It's not until I walk around and open the door that I check my phone and see the missed calls and texts. Eli never texts, and he knows not to.

A's safe and sound but shit happened. Call me when you can.

It's the only text I've ever received from him. And I read it over and over, not breathing.

She's safe. Anxiety creeps up and doesn't leave me, forcing me to unbutton my collar as I walk around the other side and tell Jase to get out and drive. My hand slams on the roof when he doesn't move fast enough. "You drive!" I scream at him and feel raw fear at the back of my throat.

She's safe.

"What's wrong?" He doesn't object but stares at me the entire time he moves around to the other side.

With the key in the ignition, he sits there staring at me while Eli's phone rings.

"Come on," I grit out.

"What's wrong?" he asks again.

"Drive to the safe house," I yell at him, irritated by Eli not answering and pissed off that I'm here and not with Aria. But more than anything I'm scared that something happened to her. It's been nearly forty minutes since he called.

The ringing stops and it goes to his voicemail. *Motherfucker.* I lean forward, my palms on the dash and try to calm the fuck down. *She's safe.*

"Tell me again how we should take on more when this shit is out of hand," I mutter to Jase as he pulls up to a stop sign.

"What happened?" he asks again, incredulity in his voice. I stare at my brother, not knowing what to say because I don't fucking know. I need to know.

"She's safe," I say out loud but it's more of a reminder to myself and Jase asks, "Aria?"

As I nod my head, the phone rings in my hand.

"Eli," I answer quickly, feeling my pulse throb harder.

"We have a problem," he tells me as Jase makes a right and then stops at the light. He's staring at me instead of watching the road.

"Four men on First Street took a shot at our crew. They knew where they were and went for the two stations at the end of the security block. Only one of our guys took a shot, he's with the doc now and he'll be fine."

One breath out, a deep, low breath and I swallow the spiked knot of fear. *She's fine*, I remind myself. My eyes close and my head falls against the headrest.

My heart is thudding, rather than beating.

"Whose men?" I ask him, and he answers, "Not Romano or Talvery."

My jaw clenches, as does my fist. Fucking great. That's the last thing I need right now. Another asshole fucking with me.

"Anything else?" I ask him, opening my eyes and staring at the cabin of the car. The red and white lights from outside dance on the ceiling as he speaks. "All four men are dead, but they were known to hang out with the man who tried to take Addison. The one Daniel killed back when he was checking out Iron Heart. Men for hire. And Carter," he pauses and so does the beat in my chest. I know it has to do with Aria. I can feel it. "I was with Aria at the time. She was there."

I can't swallow. I try, but I can't. There's something in the way and I can't breathe.

"She's okay. But she was there, and she fucked up one of the guys."

My gaze shifts to Jase, who's asking me what's going on. I can only stare at him as I question Eli, "What do you mean, she fucked one of them up? You're supposed to protect her!" The rage is minuscule compared to everything else I feel. The shock and fear that she was there, the relief that she's safe and fine. The pride that she fought alongside my men.

I can hear him huff and it sounds like he switches ears to tell me, "She killed a guy. She got away from me, chased him down the street and beat the piss out of him."

My Aria. My songbird.

"I'll remember that the next time she lets me off with a warning," I say softly, imagining it happening but I can't. I can't see it.

"Is she upset?" I ask him, knowing she will be. I yearn for a time when she's happy again. When this is all over and she looks at me the way she did before.

"She's not handling it well, but she honestly wasn't doing that good before it went down."

"Anything else I should know?" I ask him as I see the sign for Hill Road and Jase turns the corner, not slowing down. The tires squeal as Eli tells me that's it.

"I'll be there in a minute. Gather the guys, I want to go over everything and see the footage."

CHAPTER 18

I'VE KILLED TWO MEN, YET I DON'T FEEL SORRY.

Staring at myself in the mirror as I brush out my hair, I don't feel sorry at all. I'm empty inside, and there's no sense of remorse; I don't even have anger left. Nothing. I feel nothing for the man I killed tonight. I remember his wide eyes full of fear. I can feel his hands on me, pushing me away. I can feel the thud of the gun hitting my skin over and over as it crashed into him.

And yet, I feel nothing.

Even Stephan. Thinking of him makes me feel nothing at all.

The hairbrush tugs as I pull it through a knot, and I take my time to carefully brush it away.

I think I must be sick. It can't be normal to feel nothing at all when hours ago I killed a man. My eyes drift to the mirror and I stare at the woman I've become. I look the same as before. The same eyes, my mother's eyes. The same everything as months ago.

But I'm not that girl anymore. The problem is, I don't know who I am.

Without Carter… suddenly the emotions flood back, and I have to slam the brush down on the vanity. It's an antique piece of furniture and I stare at the weathered wood top wishing it would give me answers and take this pain away.

He told me I would always be his and it gave me a freedom. But that freedom scares me now that he left me. I don't think he'll ever take me back and it leaves me feeling hollow inside. There's nothing remaining but the ache of him not loving me.

I suck in a breath, knowing I need to accept it and think about where I'll go and who I'll be once this week and this war are over.

All I know for certain is that I'll be alone. And that sounds like the worst thing in the world when you're empty inside.

I don't want to be alone.

The knock at the bedroom door startles me and I nearly jump in my seat. "Come in," I call out, opening the drawer to the vanity and placing the hairbrush inside.

My gaze catches the phone still sitting on the vanity. A phone that's been silent all day and all night.

What's the point of giving it to me if he had no intention of using it?

It works both ways. I know I could call him. But I'd rather let the tension sever what's left between Carter and me. It's best to let it slip away so when my time's up here, it'll be easier to walk away.

"You're not in bed yet?" Addison's soft voice carries into the room.

"Can't sleep," I tell her, not looking her in her eyes. I may not feel sorry for what I did, but I still don't want Addison to know. I don't want her to look at me and see the heartless killer I can be.

"I know the feeling," she sighs and makes her way to my bed. Sitting on the end of it, she pulls her knees up and pushes her heels into the mattress. "I wanted to check on you," she tells me hesitantly. Her voice is careful, considerate, but her eyes dart from her painted toenails to where I'm sitting as if she doesn't know if what she has to say should be said.

My pulse flutters. Maybe she already knows.

"What's up?" I ask her, refusing to let the anxiety take over. I am who I am. I've done what I've done. If she doesn't understand that, there's nothing I can do about it. I can't take back what's been done.

"Eli said you needed a little space earlier when I came down." I thought I heard something outside… I decided not to sleep and just shower, but when I got out it sounded like…" She picks at the fresh polish on her nails and peeks at me. "He said you were in the shower but to give you some space because you didn't seem like yourself?" she questions me, not trusting what Eli said to be true.

Swallowing thickly, I nod and then wet my lips. "There was an incident on the way to the corner store, but it's okay." I shrug my shoulders and turn back to the vanity, picking up the phone and holding it up for her to see before dropping it into my lap. "Nothing serious enough for Carter to call and reprimand me," I huff a sarcastic response while rolling my eyes, trying to lighten the truth of what happened.

Glancing at the phone, and then meeting my gaze she asks, "So you're all right?"

"Yeah." My answer is easy and I'm hoping she'll drop it.

"And you and Carter?" she asks and then adds, "If you don't want to talk, that's fine." Her voice is stronger, louder and contains no offense whatsoever. "I know sometimes people like to keep things in."

"I like to talk," I tell her honestly and then feel the tug of a sad smile. "Sometimes." My voice is low and so quiet I'm not sure she heard. "Some things I'd rather not talk about, but even still, I always like to talk about something. And when it comes to Carter…" The emotions swell in my throat, stopping the words from coming easily. "When it comes to Carter, I think maybe the best thing to talk about is how to move on from someone you love when they don't love you."

"I'm sorry." The sympathy in Addison's voice pushes the ache in my chest down to the pit of my stomach.

"It is what it is. He made mistakes, I made mistakes, but none of it matters anyway. We could never be together. Not being the people we are." The words come out easier and clearer than I imagined they would. Addison's expression remains soft as she searches my gaze for something. I'm not sure what.

"What's going to happen then?" she asks me, breathing in deeply and wrapping her arms around her legs while setting her chin on her knees. Sitting feet away from her at the vanity, I wish I had an answer for her, but all I can think is, "Maybe I'll do what my friend, Addison did once, maybe I'll travel the world."

With a hopeful smile and optimism in my voice, I add, "I'd like to be like her."

Addison's smile is less than joyous as she replies, "I heard she did that because she was afraid." Her lips pull down and she bites down on her bottom lip. "I ran away, Aria. I ran because I couldn't face what was left here."

"Do you regret it?"

"No," she answers in a quick breath and seems to struggle to say something else, so I push her to speak her mind. "Whatever you're thinking," I tell her, "you don't have to hide it from me. I won't judge you."

"I don't regret it, because it all brought me back here and brought me back to Daniel." Her voice cracks and she looks away, back to the closed door of the bedroom.

"So, you and Daniel?" I ask her and keep my weak smile in place, no matter how my gut churns. She's going back to him and I'm going to be alone.

"I love him, Ria," she tells me softly, not realizing how she's pulling at every emotion inside of me.

"I know you do," I somehow, some way, speak the truth without letting on how much pain my heart is in. I'll lose Carter because I'm not the woman he needs. And I'll lose Addison because Daniel will never let her go and she'll never let him go either. Even if that means she'll turn a blind eye to the things he does.

As if reading my mind, she tells me, "I don't agree with what he does sometimes, but I know he has his reasons. And I'm so sorry, Aria," she apologizes, and I cut her off, waving my hand in the air recklessly.

"Stop it. Don't apologize. You get it now, don't you?" I ask her, feeling winded by the question. By the idea that with her answer, she still may not understand this complicated mess of pain and love that Carter and I make together.

"I don't agree with it," she tells me with sad eyes, but she doesn't deny that she understands why.

"You don't have to," I tell her and then wipe the sleep from my eyes. "It's weird, but it makes me feel better knowing you understand. Even if it's still not..." Right. Right is the word I nearly say, but it can't be the correct word. Because I don't care how wrong what we had was, it was right for me. It was right for me.

And I refuse to call what we had wrong.

"Does it upset you that I still love Daniel?" she asks me, and I shake my head no.

"If I were you, I'd love him too. He'll fight for you till the day he dies." I almost get choked up, knowing Daniel would do just that. While Carter won't even tell me he loves me. It shouldn't matter to me as much as it does. But not hearing those words from him... it's killed a part of me that I don't think will ever breathe again.

A yawn creeps up and the exhaustion and weight from everything that happened today, every loss, every failure, makes me crave sleep.

I could sleep forever if sleep would take away this pain.

"I didn't mean to get into all that," Addie tells me, moving off the bed and brushing her hair to the side. She runs her fingers through her hair as she tells me, "I didn't sleep earlier, and I was wondering if you had that vial?"

Getting up from the vanity, I leave the phone on the worn wood top and make my way to the dresser. It's so quiet tonight, it's only as I open up the dresser drawer and hear the pull that I realize I can't hear the crickets. There have been crickets the last two nights, so loud that I had to pretend they were singing me a lullaby in order to sleep.

With the vial in my one hand, I shut the drawer with a hard thud and peek out of the window.

"It's so dark tonight, isn't it?" I ask Addison, the thin curtain grazing my fingers before I pull it back and face her.

"It is. Maybe tomorrow we'll see the stars," she says with a hint of a smile on her lips.

"Sweet dreams." The words slip from me as I pass the vial to her and she tells me goodnight.

As she leaves me alone in the quiet, dark room, I can't help but feel like it's the last night I'll tell her goodnight. Something inside of me, something that chills every inch of me is certain of it.

The covers rustle as I pull them back and climb into bed. I pull them closer to me, all the way up to my neck and stare at the glass knob on the door praying sleep will take me, but the nerves inside of me crawl in my stomach, in a slinking way that makes me feel sick and no matter how tightly I hold the covers, I'm freezing cold. My toes especially.

I almost get up to put socks on, almost. But I can't. A childish fear and feeling deep in my soul wants me to stay right where I am and I listen to that fear, I obey it.

Until my tired eyes burn and the darkness slips in.

Just as I close my eyes, feeling the respite of sleep flow over every inch of me, I think I hear the door open, but when I open my eyes, it's closed. There's no one here.

It's only the darkness and quietness... the signs of loneliness that lie with me tonight.

The screams from Addison rip me from my dreamless sleep. My heart pounds against my ribcage as I hear her scream again.

The clock on the dresser blinks at me; hours have passed, and I must have fallen asleep.

My legs feel heavy as I fight with the covers to move fast enough, to get out and go to Addie.

Heaving in a breath I make it halfway to the door before it bursts open. Addie's eyes are wide, her face pale and her hair a messy halo around her head.

"Aria," she cries out my name, pulling me hard into her, so hard it knocks what little breath is in my lungs out of me, but the way she trembles, the way her nails dig into me, I know something's wrong.

"He was here," she whispers in a voice drenched in terror. "I felt him," she whimpers, pulling away from me to close my bedroom door.

As she backs away from me, she almost bumps into me and startles when I carefully take her hand.

Her fear is contagious, and I struggle to remain calm but without any idea of what she's talking about, I have to ask her, "Who? Who was here?"

"Tyler," she tells me and then tears leak from her eyes. She doesn't blink, she stares at me, willing me to believe her as the tears freefall and cradle her cheeks. "Tyler... it felt so real. He was there, Aria. I felt him."

Goosebumps travel over every inch of me and the same coldness that pricked the back of my neck when I saw the king of wands lingers there once again.

"Tyler?" I question her, knowing Tyler's the fifth Cross brother. The youngest. The one who died.

"It was so real," she tells me as she grabs my wrists hard. Too hard. Although it hurts, I don't pull away; I can't. "He's angry," she says, and her words are hoarse and hushed. The intense look in her eyes refuses to let me feel anything but the sincerity and desperation in her words.

Rushing her words, she tells me, "At first, he only held me and I swear I felt him. I could feel him holding me so tightly." She releases me to cover her eyes as she falls to her knees crying harder and harder, but she doesn't stop telling me what happened.

"He held me and told me he still loves me. He said it's okay to love Daniel. He still loves me, and he'll stay with me. But Aria," she finally looks back up to me, with red-rimmed eyes, "he's angry we left. He was never mad. Tyler never got angry and he said we need to go back. He grabbed my arms. He made me promise." She gasps for breath as she grips her own arms, still on her knees and shaking with fear.

My own legs are weak as I lower myself to her eye level. My knees hit the cold hardwood floor. Gripping her shoulders softly, I wait for her to look me in the eyes.

"It was a dream," I tell her, and she shakes her head.

"It was so real."

"The drug," I try to tell her, but she shakes her head harder, her hair viciously flailing around her shoulders.

"He told me to tell you something." Blinking away the tears, she sniffles and tells me, "He said to hold him as tight as you can, or he'll die." My blood turns to ice as I stare into her eyes.

I remember the terror I had. It was only a dream.

It's only a dream. But I don't know how to convince her.

"He told me to leave and I have to," she tells me in a whisper of a breath. "I have to go back." The remorse in the air between us is palpable. And my heart sinks lower.

I don't say a word, I only grip her close to me, squeezing her until the sound of the bedroom door flinging open startles both of us.

My stomach's still in my throat when I see Eli in the doorway, his figure black and silhouetted by the light from the hall.

"I heard screaming and came up to your room," he breathes heavily and then steps in, a look of relief settling over his face. "When I got there, it was empty. You scared the shit out of me, Addison," Eli's accent is thick as he runs his hand over his face, sleep and worry both evident in his bloodshot eyes.

Addison doesn't let go of me, she doesn't move. All she does is look up at him in silence.

"Are you all right?" he asks her, and she shakes her head no.

Her voice croaks when she starts to tell him but then looks at me, "I want to go…"

She holds my gaze and I offer her a small smile, squeezing her hand and sitting back on my heels to tell her, "Go."

"What's going on?" Eli asks and Addison hugs me tight. The tears don't stop when she whispers, "Come with me please."

The idea of going back to Carter…

"He doesn't love me," is all I can tell her, feeling the last petal wither and die inside of me. "There's nothing for me there."

Her gaze doesn't leave mine. Even as Eli walks closer to us, towering over us and waiting for an answer.

"Tomorrow," she whispers and then hugs me one last time. I can feel her tears on my shoulder and I promise myself to remember this. We'll share a friendship forever, even if we never see each other again.

She breaks the hug before I'm ready to let go, standing and smoothing her nightgown out before wiping the tears under her eyes.

Rubbing her arm and looking sheepish, she tells Eli, "I don't want to sleep."

She walks past him before he can say anything else, slipping into the yellow light pouring from the doorway and going right rather than left, heading to the kitchen, away from her bedroom.

"Is she okay?" Eli asks me in a tone suggesting he truly needs to know; he's genuinely concerned for her.

I feel the ache deep in my body as I stand up on shaky legs, still cold, still tired, and in the depths of my bones, scared. I don't like what terrors that drug brings.

Hold him as tight as you can, or he'll die.

A chill flows over my skin and I look Eli in the eyes to tell him, "She just had a nightmare. It was only a nightmare."

He doesn't speak for a moment and I peek over my shoulder to check the time, it's past three and I just want a few hours of sleep.

"You should stay with her," I offer him, wanting to be alone and his forehead pinches with a question he doesn't voice.

He stands there a second longer than I'd like, so I look to the door pointedly and then back to him.

"I can never get a good read on you," Eli says and almost turns from me to leave, but I stop him.

"What does that mean?"

"I don't know where you stand and that makes you…"

"It makes me what?" I press him to continue, although there's a threat in the way I say it. The days of him protecting me are few. I know where I'll stand when my father's dead. He's not my friend. I'm smart enough to know that.

"It makes you dangerous. It makes me not trust you because I don't know who you stand for or against."

"I stand for a lot of people. The only ones I stand against are the ones who get in my way." Walking him to the door, I look him in the eyes and tell him, "Remember that," before closing the door and trying to shake off the sick, empty feeling that grows inside of me.

CHAPTER 19

Carter

L EANING AGAINST THE RAILING AT THE BOTTOM OF THE STAIRS, I KEEP HEARING her say the lie.

He doesn't love me.

It's a lie to me, but maybe she truly believes it.

"She certainly has a way about her," Eli mutters as he pinches the bridge of his nose and slowly sits at the bottom of the stairs.

"That's one way to put it." My expression is unmoving, and I can't control the scowl. Swallowing the knot in my throat is painful.

"I'm fucking tired," he mutters, and I tell him to go to bed then.

"You staying here?" he asks and I nod. I can't fucking move after hearing her say that. Addison's scream woke me up, but she was faster than I was. I couldn't hear everything, but I got the gist of it: Addison wants to go back, and Aria doesn't.

My heart feels like it's been stomped on, driven over by a tank, and then left for scraps in the dirty gutter.

"I don't know what to do with her," I speak out loud, not liking where my thoughts are going. I want her back in the cell. The core of my soul is screaming at me to put her there. She'll be safe, and she'll forgive me with time. She has to.

"You don't trust her?" he asks and peers up at me and waits for my response.

"I trust that I know what she'll do at this point." I focus on keeping my breathing steady as I listen to Addison upstairs, turning on the faucet in the kitchen. Our voices won't carry well, but if she wanted to, she could hear us.

Eli sighs as he nods his head and runs a hand over his knee.

I hated her father when I was a kid. I hated him for what he did to me. I hated him for letting me go alive. I hated him for what he did to my home and what he tried to do to my brothers.

But I've never hated him more now. Knowing when I put a bullet in his skull, it will kill her. I can already see how she'll look at me. I can feel her nails dig into my skin as she claws at me. I can hear her screaming.

I can already feel his death tearing her away from me. We're hanging on by a single thread and it's because of him. My jaw clenches and I breathe out low and steady, gazing at the molding that lines the stairwell even though I feel Eli's eyes on me.

The silence stretches until I ask him, "What do you think of her?"

"Of Aria?"

With a single nod, I appraise his expression, his body language, his tone. Everything. I can't explain how whenever one of my men is by her or mentions her or her name, I can't explain how anxiety races through me. She's my weakness and I want her to receive nothing but respect for her. Respect and fear.

But given everything that's happened, I don't think anyone knows what to think of her, or what to think of us.

"I think she has the heart of a lover and the temper of a fighter."

"You sound like a true Irishman," I tell him as I huff a response to his answer.

With his asymmetric smirk, he adds, "I wouldn't want to be her enemy and I think the two of you… together, is something that will be feared."

"I wouldn't want to be her enemy either," I say flatly as my stomach knots and my throat gets tighter. But I am. And I always will be.

It's not her that makes it impossible to be together.

It's not me either.

We never had a chance. My gaze falls as I control the numbness that pricks along my skin. I wanted her so badly, I didn't dare look past the desire for her and see the challenges rooted in our very souls.

She may try to love me, but she will always hate me.

"You think you know what she'll do after tomorrow? When they're all dead?" he whispers his question and I nod, feeling the unbearable knot twist even tighter. With the media in an uproar, the cops aren't holding off for much longer. We promised them tomorrow would be the last day we needed them to stay on the west side while we invade from the east. A single bullet to Talvery's head and his factions will fall.

Tomorrow, I'm going to murder her father.

"I think she'll kill me. And I think she'll hate herself for it but feel it was what she needed to do." Eli's gaze falls and my stomach sinks with it. My fingers are so numb I have to clench and relax my hand repeatedly, but it doesn't work to bring life back to it.

"That's … a…" he fails to respond.

"I'm choosing to be her enemy and to take everything from her. It doesn't matter if she thinks she loves me." The coldness spreads through my chest like ice crackling. "Hate is stronger." I'm surprised by how strong and unforgiving my words are. "She'll want revenge for what I'm going to do. I would want it too."

Eli looks over his shoulder and down the hall, toward Aria's bedroom. "Is that why you haven't gone to her?"

Not trusting myself to speak, I only nod. I can't look her in the eyes and confess how much she means to me, knowing how badly I'm going to hurt her tomorrow.

I won't do that to her. I'm not that cruel.

Bang, bang, bang, bang!

Adrenaline spikes from my toes straight up through my core, freezing my body, then heating it all at once at the sound of guns going off in the distance. My grip on the railing is white-knuckled as Eli stands and speaks clearly into the device on his wrist.

"Where'd they come from?" he asks, and I bring up the surveillance on my phone, all the while listening. It sounded like it came from blocks away and within seconds I can see two cars blocking the road and men leaning out of the windows.

"East," Eli answers but I already know. My heart pumps harder and the blood is fueled by the need to react. To grip the hard metal of a gun in my hand and feel the recoil again my palm after I've pulled the trigger.

I can hear the men screaming from down the street and the bullets firing as my blood heats. Three blocks at most.

A sick smirk begs to pull at my lips. I should have known Talvery would respond recklessly. Sending what's left of his men to their funerals.

The voices ring clear from Eli's earpiece:
Shots fired on Main Street.
Four men on Abbey Road.
Two cars coming up Dorset.

"Block off Fourth Street; make them come in on foot and don't hold back fire." I give Eli the command and he repeats what I said word for word.

The guns sound off like fireworks and Addison's hard paces carry through the hall. She's soon pounding on Aria's door.

Taking the stairs two by two, I grip the railing and get to her as quickly as I can. My lungs heave as I get to her door. "Stay in there and lock the door. Don't open it for anyone but Eli." All the words stumble out in a single breath and she looks at me for a moment, breathless and hesitant before nodding.

My heart pounds so hard, harder than it has in a long time. It takes me a moment to realize it's due to fear. The very real fear of losing Aria.

"I won't let anything happen to either of you," I say and stare into Addison's eyes and wish they were Aria's. She's just behind the door and I'm drawn to her. My body aches knowing she's so close, but I refuse to go in there.

If I do, I don't know how I'll leave her.

"Stay in her room." I barely get the command out, but Addison hears me. For a moment, I wonder if Aria heard me from behind the door. *My songbird.* The spiked ball grows in my throat as Addison opens the door before retreating behind it. She didn't say a word to me.

Not a single word.

Every muscle in my body is tight and at odds with what I need to do.

The muted sounds of a man screaming, and the continued gunfire is accompanied by Eli yelling out demands on the floor below us.

I try to calm myself and summon the ruthless side of me that will end this as quickly as it started.

The bullets ring out clearly. Automatic weapons that tear through the brick of houses and metal cars. Windows shatter and men yell out.

So, I move.

Quickly and with determination down the stairs.

My stomach clenches and it's the first time I can remember where so much was at stake. Where my thoughts are torn between tactics and emotion.

Between fighting to steal the woman I love and running as fast as I can.

"Bring up all the cars and block off every street," I command Eli while bringing out my phone to text Daniel and tell him where Addison is. The last I heard from him, he was trying to get in touch with Marcus and find out anything he can about the fucker he killed back in Iron Heart.

My heart pounds, and my muscles coil as I listen closely to every word that comes in from the earpiece as I switch to the surveillance screens and watch everything unfold.

I need to move. Standing here is fucking killing me but I have to remind myself that this is war and decoys are common. I won't be fooled like Talvery was.

Three streets on two sides are under attack, two on top of each other to the east and one furthest to the west of this house.

"They hit three streets at once."

"Do we have a count on how many men are firing?" I need numbers. Talvery can't have more than fifty men left.

Eli's earpiece buzzes and it takes everything in me not to rip it out and take it for myself. "It looks to be about thirty."

"They may be distractions, hitting the two sides and leaving the south side untouched. Don't move the men on the south side."

"Yes, sir," Eli answers, speaking into the device.

"Count of our men," Eli barks out the order before relaying what I said. I have fifty men to his thirty. Fifty well-armed and guarded but spread out.

Two men down.
One man down.
We're holding.

I stare at my phone, waiting for Daniel to reply, but I get nothing. Where the fuck is he?

"Three total, Boss," Eli's voice is tight as I grip the phone tighter and scream internally for him to tell me where the fuck he is. The cords in his throat tense as he rips the Velcro of his holster, moving it to the side and checking his ammo.

Three men dead.

Three more men dead.

"Kill them all," I grit out, feeling the rage turn incandescent. My head feels light as I take in a deep breath.

"You and Cason stay with the women," I give the command while my phone pings and Jase tells me he's close and coming up the south side and he already told the guards there.

His jaw is hard and clenched, and I know he wants to be out there, but I need him here.

"You two stay here." I harden my voice and look him in the eyes until he nods.

Shoving my phone in my back pocket, I reach for my gun and then move past Eli to the back room where the other weapons are stored as he tells me, "Yes, Boss."

I need men with them who know when to leave.

The back room has shelves of guns and I choose from the racks of metal shining back at me, picking up one and shoving it and the ammunition into the waist of my pants before picking up another.

Talvery's on the outer edge. There's no way he'll get in and this entire ground is a safe house. But every safe house can be broken into. I've done it before. Sebastian knew that when he built this place.

With time ticking, and the bullets still firing every minute, I turn my back on the arsenal and prepare to join my men. I only stop to tell Eli one thing, "The basement has an underground exit. The code is six, fourteen, eight, eight. Repeat it to me."

"Six, fourteen, eight, eight." He's quick to answer, but I can see the defiance in his eyes.

"Don't forget it, and if I—"

"We have enough men," Eli cuts me off and I struggle to hold back the anger. "There's no way—"

"If I tell you to," I say looking him in the eyes as my nostrils flare and my body heats with the need to strike back, "take them and lock the door behind you."

I don't wait for him to answer, although as I turn my back to him and head down the stairs, I hear him say he'll do it. The buzzing in my ears is like white noise as I climb down the stairs. I'm ready with a gun in my right hand as I stare at the front door.

I pray Talvery's here in the flesh and blood, ready to finally pay for all his sins.

"Carter," Eli calls out to me as I reach the front door.

"What?" I snap at him, feeling the rage, the immediacy, the fear even of losing men and protection for Aria and Addison.

"Your estate… He sent men there." Eli visibly swallows as my blood chills.

"My brothers?" I ask him quickly, my breathing coming in short pants. The gun in my hand slips and I grip it tighter, praying and swallowing down my fear.

"Jase said he's coming," I speak as I remember the text and Eli confirms with a brief nod.

"Jase and Declan are together, they're on their way and missed it."

Daniel. My heart beats slow, so slow it's painful. "Three bombs hit the east wing. And another four to the south wing and the garage."

"How many men are dead?" The question comes out without conscious consent, all I can think of is Daniel and the last time I saw him when he told me he had plans with Addison.

"Six currently."

"Where's Daniel?" I ask him, feeling the threat of a pain that can never be soothed brimming inside of me.

"We don't know."

CHAPTER 20

Aria

"Fuck, fuck," Addison's rocking back and forth on the bed, her legs tucked up under her as the guns continue to fire.

Men shout from the floor below us and farther down the streets outside.

"I've never heard it last for so long," I whisper as I peek out into the black night. I watch as each of the streetlights is hit, one by one, spraying shards of white light before fading into the darkness.

Addison's voice is strained and coated in worry as she asks, "Why would they do that?"

"So they can't see," I tell her.

"But then no one can see."

"It's a risk they decided was worth taking." I feel the numbness flow through my blood.

"Who did it? Who shot them?" she asks me as if I'd know.

Tires squeal in the distance and metal crashes against metal. She cries harder, falling apart and then checks her phone again. She buries her face in her knees, rocking harder.

"We can hide in the closet," she offers although her words are panicked, and I don't know if she means it or not. "We'll put the clothes on top of us," she gasps for breath and rocks again, "they'll open it but not see us. I used to do it when I was younger. They won't see us. They won't see us."

She's losing it. The way she rocks, the rapid rate with which she's talking and the look of terror in her eyes are clear signs. She's fucking losing it.

"We should have left," she croaks with tears in her eyes and the numbness turns to a freezing cold along my skin.

"He told us to leave."

"It was intuition, Addie," I breathe an excuse even as the gunshots sound louder, closer, the violence making its way to the finish line.

"Where's Daniel?" She covers her mouth as she cries again and struggles to breathe.

I don't know what comes over me as I watch her wither away and dissolve into nothing but fear and sorrow, but my hand whips across Addison's face and she stares up at me in shock before slowly moving her hand to cover the bright red mark.

My hand stings and my heart lurches with the fear of hurting her and losing a friend, but I move closer to her, gripping her shoulders and staring into her eyes to tell her, "We will not die like this."

Her chest rises and falls with heavy breathing as she waits for me to tell her more.

"Come on," I say and pull her wrist. "We're leaving," I tell her, but she pulls away.

"He told us to stay here," she breathes and lets her gaze dart between the door and me.

"I don't care what Eli said." The frustration, the anger, the terror, and lack of sleep, it all makes my body feel as if it's on fire and like I'm losing control, but I raise my voice to yell at her, "Come with me!" My dry throat screams in pain as I swallow and tell her, "We need to run."

The gunshots get louder from outside and steal our attention. They're getting closer. My heart pounds in my chest and the sound of the door opening behind me makes both of us scream. Addison's is shrill and so sharp it nearly punctures my eardrum.

Cason's out of breath as he makes his way toward us and says, "We're going to the basement." Addison shakes her head violently, and asks the only question she's been praying to have an answer to, "Where's Daniel?"

The pang in my chest strikes hard and I feel like I'm suffocating as I pray to know the same, but about Carter.

The phone is silent. My text to him unanswered.

Are you okay?

It's all I wanted to know. And he didn't answer.

"Basement. Now!" Cason yells just as bullets fly past us. The windows shatter, the small pieces raining over Addison, who covers her head with her arms and drops as far as she can forward onto the bed. I fall instantly, lying flat on the floor as I hold my breath, too afraid to move at all. Her shrill scream fills the room again as bullets ricochet and leave a trail of marks from left to right over the wall and bedroom door.

My eyes reach Cason as he stands up straight. He didn't move. He never had the chance to move. The bullet holes in his chest slowly bleed out, the bright red diffusing and spreading like watercolor paints on canvas.

"No," I breathe, tears pricking my eyes as his hand moves to one of the punctures at the same time as he falls to his knees. "Cason!" I scream out his name and reach for him, but it's useless.

The gunshots have stopped; it was a single string of bullets that clattered across the house. But they return again within seconds. Hitting him again in his neck and head, eyes closed before he falls to the floor.

Addison doesn't scream this time although I can hear her sobs from where I am. Reaching up for her, I pull her down and together we crawl on our stomachs under the bed.

"Daniel," Addison cries his name over and over, her hands clasped as she prays for him to be all right.

I can't breathe. It's so hot and the bullets rain down with no signs of letting up for minutes. More time passes with nothing. No signs of anything and that's when I see the gun on the floor. Cason's gun. As I crawl out, Addison grabs me and yells for me not to leave her. My heart lurches at the sound of a door being kicked in downstairs.

"Shh," I hush her, putting my finger over my lips and then nodding to the gun. With wide eyes, she watches me as I crawl out to get it. The cold beating in my veins picks up as the sound of a man coming up the steps gets louder and louder. The open bedroom door shows his shadow in the hall just as I reach the gun with my fingertips.

The cold metal slips in my grasp and the sound of it sliding across the floor rips my gaze up to the doorway. Without looking, I snatch the gun and Addison pulls me back under the bed.

The gun is heavy, so heavy in my hand. Addison's hands are covering her mouth as a shadow steps into the room. The floor creaks with the man's weight and his black boots are splattered with blood.

I grip the gun with both hands as he takes three agonizingly slow steps closer to Cason's body, right before kicking his shoulder over with his boot to see his face.

Bending down, I get a partial glimpse of the man as he steals Cason's phone from his pocket. The fear is paralyzing. I can't breathe. I can't do anything.

My gaze moves to the vanity and I can see my reflection, but I can see the man's too as he scowls down at Cason's dead body and lifts his gun to his head.

Bang, bang!

The gun goes off and Addison jolts each time, her eyes closed tight and her hands pressing harder against her mouth.

My heart hammers, praying he didn't hear her, but it doesn't matter if he did or not, because the man's eyes reach mine in the mirror. Cold and dark, with wrinkles that show his age. He's in the same black hoodie as the man I killed earlier, and I know this man is not one of my father's men.

The attacks out there, I think they're from my father. But the men who have made it to the safe house… they're not.

He's quicker than me, taking a large stride and grabbing me from under the bed. His grip on my left forearm is paralyzing and I nearly drop the gun. My back scratches against the underside of the wire bedframe and the pain forces a scream from me.

My finger is on the trigger and I can't get it to go off. I pull it again and again.

"The safety." Addison's voice is hoarse, and the words pushed through clenched teeth.

He reaches down with his other hand, grabbing my other wrist and that's when Addison rips the gun from me and fires. The heat from the barrel of the gun singes my skin and I scream from the pain.

Bang! Bang!

She pulls the trigger again and again as my left side falls to the floor with the man's grip nonexistent.

I can hear Addison's gasp and the clunk of the gun as the man's dead white eyes stare back at me.

My hollow chest is gutted as I stare at him and then to the doorway. My heart beats too loudly to hear anything and I have to swallow and blink away the fear to grab the gun Addison dropped and point it at the door.

I lie half under the bed, half out, with a burn scorching my forearm and wait. Time passes quickly, as quickly as my blood races through my veins.

"He's dead," Addison whispers a painful truth. "I killed him," she whispers.

"Shh," I hush her, "Quiet!"

The pounding of my heart slows as I realize the man almost got me and she saved me.

"You saved me," I whisper with tears in my eyes although I stare straight ahead.

"I killed him," she says back in a harsh whisper.

It's only then that I realize it's silent once again. No gunshots. Not from outside and not a sound inside the house.

I listen closely and hear cars outside a few blocks down, but they aren't rushed and the tires don't squeal. Rising slowly, I nearly scream when Addison grabs my ankle.

"Fuck," I barely get out the word over the harsh beat of fear in my chest.

"Is it safe?" Addison asks, and I tell her the truth, "I don't know."

It's hard to contain terror, even when there's no present danger. My gaze doesn't leave the doorway as I crawl to the window. Even as I rise up slowly and pull the curtain ever so softly, I don't dare take my eyes from the doorway for a few minutes longer.

No more gunshots and lights are on inside the houses that were black now. A car passes with its headlights and I see some men I recognize a street down.

"I think it's over," I whisper to her but still crawl to reach her. "Take the gun," I put it in her hand and when she objects I tell her I'm taking the dead man's gun.

"I'm going downstairs." With my words, Addison's eyes go wide and she grips my wrist with a bruising force. My breathing is still unsteady, and my heart doesn't find a normal cadence either.

"I have to make sure it's okay. I'm going to find Eli," I tell her, and the mention of Eli seems to calm her down. Her cheeks are red, and tears still linger in her eyes.

"Stay here," I whisper and put my hand over hers. I squeeze it once before leaving her, crawling past the dead man, and taking his gun with me. I don't stand up until I'm past the door. Blood coats my pajama pants from where I crawled through it. Standing outside the door and staring at the stairwell, I breathe in deeply over and over, trying to calm myself.

Small shards of glass pierce my forearms and I pick them out, wincing as I do. The pain is nothing with all the adrenaline running through me, but still, I'm mesmerized by the bright red and the evidence of what we've just been through.

The moment I close my eyes, a phone rings behind me.

Ring, ring and my heart shudders in my chest. A shuddering as if being brought back to life. "Daniel," Addison's voice rings out clear, the moment I think Carter's name.

My throat goes dry as I swallow and hear her tell him how worried she was.

Carter didn't call.

It's not Carter.

It takes everything in me to step forward. The feeling of loss runs deep in my blood and I struggle to keep it together. One heavy step after another, with the gun in my right hand and my left hand gripping the railing, I walk down the steps quietly, hearing the faint sounds of Addison from the bedroom and nothing else in the house.

I may not have felt anything for the man I killed upstairs, nothing but hate, and less than that for the other man in the same black hoodie who died earlier today, but as I stand over Eli's dead body in the foyer, I cry.

Heavy sobs that bring me to my knees and steal the warmth from my body.

I can't breathe as my trembling fingers touch his throat, searching for a pulse, but finding none.

My feet kick out and I crawl backward, away from his body until my back hits the wall.

Covering my face in the crook of my arm, I can't stop crying.

His life was wasted on mine. Cason's life wasted on mine.

How much death can I be responsible for, before I lose any love I could possibly have for myself?

The opening of the back door, the slamming of the knob into the wall forces me to go silent. I hold my breath and crawl to the other corner as the footsteps quicken.

"Fuck, no," Daniel's voice carries into the foyer as he reaches Eli. "Shit," he breathes the word with true mourning before his heavy footsteps hit the stairs.

"Addison!" he cries out her name as my head hits the wall and my breath comes in staggered, sharp pulls.

The back door is still open, the wind carries through the house and the cool air calls to me like a siren.

I'm numb as I stand and make my way to the door, with trees lining the back of the yard, it's pitch black, but I can see there's no one here.

There's nothing here.

Nothing but the dark and the quiet as I take a single step out. And then another as the cold flows over my skin. And another.

The thoughts of how life has spiraled downward ever since I laid eyes on Carter Cross run through my mind. Or maybe ever since he laid eyes on me. It's hard to know which, really.

The thoughts consume me as I breathe in the cold air.

The thoughts… and then the hard chest that slams my back into it and the large hand that covers my mouth as I scream.

CHAPTER 21

I RECOGNIZE SOME OF THESE FACES. MEN WHO HAVE STARED AT ME FROM A DISTANCE with hate but didn't have the balls to pull the trigger. I've passed so many of them on street corners as I drove past Carlisle and sometimes into Talvery territory over the years.

Bang!

I've imagined the bullet holes in their foreheads for years.

My blood is ringing with anger as I point the trigger at a man hunched behind the car and waiting with his back to me for one of my men to come into his view. He won't even see it coming. *Bang!*

Declan's iPad shows each of the streets, lined with dead bodies and riddled with bullet holes, broken glass and the shells of bullets that have stolen dozens of lives tonight.

War comes with a hefty cost and it's sickening but it fuels my need for vengeance.

"Four more on Second Street," Declan speaks into his mic.

Jase and I watch him carefully and keep an eye out on each side of the building we're stationed behind. Declan cheats at war, using surveillance that doesn't let a soul hide.

"Straight down from the street sign, head up the right side of the street and get them from the back. They're behind the—"

Shots ring out and I glance at the screen to see each of the four turning around too late. Their guns held in the air, aiming, but too slow to do anything before their bodies drop.

The night air is quiet.

It hasn't been more than thirty minutes since I've left, but the realization of how much time has passed since I've heard a word about Aria sends a tremor of terror rocking through me like a slow wave.

"We still have the two," Jase reminds me and tugs my arm to follow him.

Only two of Talvery's men are left. But he wasn't among them and neither was Nikolai.

The thought reminds me of Aria, crying on the bed as she confessed how she'll never forgive me if I killed them. How easy it would have been for the two of them to have died tonight at the hands of other men.

Swallowing the regret, I check my phone and see Cason's text that they're secured and safe. He sent it only ten minutes ago. *She's safe.* And at this moment, she's still in my grasp. That's all that matters.

I didn't realize I'd been holding my breath until I read that message and then the next, a text from Daniel saying that he was almost to the safe house.

Go straight to them, I text him and then add, *It's over. There's just a message left to send.*

Jase is peeking over my shoulder and his lip twitches as he mutters, "message to send," and then kicks in the back door, a door scarred with bullet holes. It reveals two men on their knees with a row of my men behind them.

"What are your names?" My voice bellows in the small room that looks like it was once used for entertainment. A busted bookshelf stands in the back left corner, board games spilling out over the floor and the projector screen straight ahead is littered with small holes.

Nearly every house on this block and the next will be just like this. The people were cleared out two days ago, bribed or threatened to leave, whichever method was more effective.

Jase crouches down in front of one of the two men and says, "If I were you, I'd answer my brother." The man behind him, the one pointing a gun at our captive lets out a single rough laugh and the man next to him follows.

"Fuck you," the old man says. He's on his knees and bent like that makes his stomach look even larger. He's got to be in his forties and as he spits at Jase's feet, the wrinkles on his face tighten. He nearly topples over without being able to put his hands out in front of him; they're cuffed behind his back, just like his friend to the right of him.

Jase stands up and moves to the next man, but when he does, my heart drops and a sick feeling spreads through my veins. "Where'd you get that hoodie?" I ask him and come closer to him, close enough to grab his collar and pull him up to look at his face.

He's younger with beady eyes and thin lips. He doesn't say anything at all, but there's a hint of a smile on his lips like he knows a secret I don't.

"You," my voice comes out harsh as I drop the asshole in the black hoodie and let him fall hard on the ground. He coughs up a laugh and I grab the old man's shirt, fisting it and the back of his head with my other hand.

"What's his name," I grit out the question and shake the old man, repeating myself in a scream that rips up my throat when he doesn't answer. "What's his name!"

"Fuck, I don't know!" The old man looks back at me like I've gone mad as I breathe heavily, my lungs heaving air.

"This one is Talvery," I drop the old man and move to the one in the hoodie, the one whose eyes are nothing but a well of blackness.

"This one is hired," I speak as I crouch in front of him, feeling my heart race.

"Talvery doesn't need to hire anyone." The old man speaks up until his executioner chambers a round and the click shuts him up.

"Where did you find this one?" I ask the man standing behind him. When I peer up, I see it's Logan.

He looks to his left and then to his right, stuttering to answer.

"Logan," I stand slowly, "Where did this one come from?"

"He was inside the line, shooting at the target, sir," another man speaks up.

"The target?" My heart pounds, but I remind myself that Daniel should be there.

"The safe house," the soldier clarifies.

A cold numbness runs through me as the man in the black hoodie, barely on his knees says, "My partner went in and finished what I started."

I turn to my brother, who's already on his phone. "Where's Daniel?" I ask him as my chest heaves for air. I squeeze the gun harder and when the fucker laughs at me, a deep laugh that chills the very marrow in my bones and fills the room, I whip it across his face, feeling the force of it splinter up my hand.

"Confirmed man dead in the safe house, wearing a black hoodie," Jase's response soothes the fear, bringing my rage down to a simmer.

"He's dead?" I ask Jase to tell me again as relief teases me.

"Addison said Aria shot him."

"She never fails to amaze me." As much as the pride fills me, there's nothing but rage that shows. Anger that they got close to her. To my songbird. They came close enough to hurt her. My fists clench tightly, spreading the thin skin across my knuckles as I breathe in slowly, deeply, seeing nothing but red.

"Daniel came up the south side, where there was less action and he's with Addison now."

I hear Jase's words, I know I do, but they don't register.

This man with the sick smile on his knees in front me, he conspired to hurt her. My stomach churns at the thought of how narrowly Addison and Aria escaped being hurt, or worse.

The first punch to his jaw, I don't even realize came from me. Not even as the skin across my knuckles splitting sends a pain up my arm. Again and again, I land punches across his face, listening to the cracking of bone in the deafening silence that fills the room.

The pulse of my racing blood is all I can hear. That and the sound of the man spitting blood across the floor as I grab him by the collar and roll him on his back to crouch on top of him. With his hands cuffed behind him, his back arches and he tries to roll back to his side, clenching and giving me daggers through his narrowed eyes.

"Who hired you?" I grit out the question and a beat passes, then another. He huffs a breath through his nose and the corners of his lips pick up in an asymmetric grin, displaying a ring of crimson blood around his teeth.

The fingers of my right hand crush his throat, forcing it to the ground and feeling his blood rush beneath my grip as I slam my fist into his face again. His eye is swollen and when I punch him again, I hear his nose crack and watch blood seep around his eyes, making them black although not nearly as black as the depth of his irises.

"How did you get past my men?" I scream the question, bringing my face close to his. The words tear up my throat, grating as they go and leaving a searing pain. All I can see is Aria, surrounded by men in black hoodies and before he can even answer, I slam my head into his, hearing the sickening crunch of his broken bones grinding against one another from the impact.

I have to release him, to get up and walk around him, staring at the man on the ground and picturing Aria standing over another just like him.

They got too close. Too fucking close.

"That one… that one I'd love to answer." I barely make out the words, they're spoken so softly. He coughs up blood, but then rests his head down on the floor, staring up at the ceiling. The man sways, barely coherent, but the smile still wishes to stay on his lips. It falters as he blinks slowly, his consciousness failing him.

Licking my lower lip, I steady my breath and bend down to get closer to him, gripping the back of his head. I grip onto his skull as I tug at his hair and force him to look at me.

"Tell me," I utter the demand gravely and his eyes flash with something. A look of delicious contentment. It's only then I realize how much I've shown him. How much I've shown everyone.

Aria is my everything. She alone has the will to turn me into a madman.

"Tell me," I push out the words through clenched teeth and feel my muscles coil, ready to assault him again, but he answers quickly this time.

"Every exit is an entrance."

My eyes search his, trying to register the meaning of his words. "I don't have time for—"

"Your little underground escape route… it was our way in. My job was easy, get outside and cause a ruckus, so my partner could do his job." He answers my unspoken question and seems to settle, so I grip his hair tighter, not giving him a moment of comfort.

"And what was his job?"

My heart beats faster, knowing they wanted Addison, but unsure of where Aria stands.

"Wouldn't you like to know," he mutters under his breath as his eyes roll into the back of his skull. I shake the fucker, waking him and stare into his cold gaze.

"Tell me." My command comes out low and vicious, my face getting closer to his as the life slips from him.

"I'll tell you one thing. It was only one girl a month ago, but then he upped it to two."

Bastards! My throat closes, and I struggle to stay where I am, my muscles burning to go to her. To Aria and to keep everyone away from her forever. No one will ever get to her. Never!

"Who did?" I don't know how I'm able to ask the question or to stay still as I wait for his answer.

"I'll die before I tell you," he replies, but then his head falls back. He's close to death already. Close, but not quite there yet.

"Logan," I say and raise my voice, but I don't look away from the man in my grasp. He'll soon be dead.

"Sir?" he asks hesitantly from somewhere to my right. I can hear his feet drag again the floor as he comes closer. "Brass knuckles?" I question him and then the sound of other men moving about registers.

"Someone," I say as I stare straight into my victim's icy gaze, "give me brass knuckles."

"Carter!" Jase shouts my name and rips my attention away. The warmth of blood splatters on my forearm and the man coughs in my grasp.

"What?" My question is sneered, pissed off that he would dare interrupt this. "He came after Aria!" I scream so loud; her name reverberates off the walls as I stare at Jase.

My chest rises and falls, my breathing coming in ragged and faster.

"Carter," Jase's voice is low but accompanied by the sound of the man in my grasp speaking at the same time.

"I couldn't wait to get them," he mutters beneath his breath.

"Carter!" My brother screams at me as I slam my fist into his jaw, hearing it crack as it dislocates. It dangles from his face and the sight only fuels me to take out more of my rage on him.

My shoulders are wound tight, needing more of a release as the asshole falls forward and Jase screams my name again. "Carter!"

"I'm not done with him," I grind out the words as I push Jase away from me, refusing to look at him and not the man who dared threaten my Aria. The man rocks on his shoulder, his face deformed and covered in blood. He has to roll forward to keep from choking on it or drowning in his own blood as he struggles to cough it up, but his movements are weak and slow. He's close. Too fucking close. I want him to live to see what true pain really is.

"Sir," Logan's voice is heard as a metal block is placed in my periphery. I've never smiled as sadistic of a smile as I do now.

"Should I do him the favor of killing him?" I ask no one in particular as I crouch in front of him and slip the thumb of my right hand over the brass that covers the knuckles on my left hand.

"Carter!" My gaze narrows as I peer up at my brother who's reaching out for me, reaching his hand out with a look that begs me to listen to him.

I don't take his hand, but I search his expression. He's worried, his eyes a pit of loss and despair. All the heat in my body suddenly feels doused with ice. A chill runs through me as I ask him with the last breath I have, "What?"

I barely register the painful groan the man, still barely alive, utters at my feet.

"What about Aria?" Jase asks me with a look of desperation and I finally hear the other men in the room. The war isn't over, and this place isn't safe now that it's been breached.

"I'm taking her home." I give him the only answer I can. It doesn't matter what she wants; a man got to her and that's unacceptable. Fuck! I grind my teeth and throw the brass knuckles into the torn projector screen when I remember the house was hit.

My body is shaking, vibrating with the need to protect her yet having my options limited. *I will protect her.* The very thought soothes me. She is mine and no one will hurt her. I'll never let anyone close to her again.

"I'll take her wherever I go." I give him my answer in a tone that brooks no further discussion, hiding the agony of what's devouring my every thought, but that doesn't change the look on his face. It doesn't remove an ounce of the fear in his expression.

"Where is she?" Jase asks, and my pulse slows, the adrenaline leaving me at the very thought of being with Aria tonight. Even if she hates me tomorrow.

"Daniel has her." I feel my brow furrow when I look at him, and everything slows. It slows and the world around us turns to a faded, blurred image. My heart beats once. He was just talking to Daniel. My heart beats again. "He has her," I repeat when Jase does nothing but visibly swallow and the already quiet room goes completely silent.

"No, he doesn't." I see nothing but red and everything turns to white noise as Jase tells me, "Aria's gone."

The End

ENDLESS

He holds a power over me like no one else ever could.

Maybe it's because my heart begs to beat in time with his.
Maybe it's because my body bows to his and his alone.
Maybe it's because he thought he loved me before he even laid eyes on me.

He thought wrong, and nothing has made me suffer like keeping that secret from him.
He thought I belonged to him, but he was wrong. It was never supposed to be me.

Our memories are deceiving, but my heart is not.
I know exactly what I want.
What I need more than anything.
I won't rest until he's as much mine, as I am his.
It's always been him.

My grandmother used to write. Her dream was for her stories to be published one day,
but unfortunately that never happened.

Times were different back then.

Although she's gone, she's always with me in my heart and even in my writing. Pieces of
what I remember of my grandmother have been sewn into these stories and I hope that
you've fallen in love with her, even if you've never had the pleasure to meet her. I hope
she would be proud of me if she were to see me now.

The ones we love never leave us.
Mommom, this book is for you. I love you.

PROLOGUE

Aria

I ONLY KNOW WHAT TYLER LOOKS LIKE BECAUSE OF PICTURES. BUT EVEN BEFORE then, when I first had the dream, I knew the boy was someone related to Carter. The Cross brothers all look so alike. He stared at me in the dream, his dark eyes piercing me even from across the field of blues and whites.

I should have been scared because I knew I didn't belong in this make-believe land conjured by my dream, but a soft smile lingered on his lips. Welcoming and endearing. He was kind. A kind soul among the flowers, although his words were anything but.

"She lied to you," he said casually. Words that etched confusion onto my face, but sent a prick of fear to chill my blood like ice.

It's only then that I heard my mother. I knew it was her instantly from her voice; we sounded so alike. A rustling noise came from somewhere on my right as she walked through the thick field. Her name begged to spill from my lips, rasping up from deep in my throat, but my voice was silent. And my body longed to move to her side, closer to where she was as she walked away slowly from me. But my limbs were still.

I was caught in place as they moved nearer one another, yet continued speaking to me, looking at me. As if they knew I was there even though I was held prisoner by whatever kept me immobile and quiet.

Tears leaked from the corners of my eyes and heated my skin as they rolled down my cheeks.

My father always spoke of my mother's beauty, and I knew it to be true, but she was older in the dreams than I remembered her to be. Age was more than kind to her though.

I tried to call out to her again, ignoring the boy, the Cross brother who had long since passed.

"I never lied," my mother spoke to me, but all I could feel was the way her words soothed my soul. It's been so long since I heard her voice. Too long. My fingers itched to move, to reach out to her and feel her embrace once more. I needed to be held so badly and my breath halted, imagining that she would come to me since I couldn't go to her, but she didn't.

Her hazel eyes were drenched in sorrow as she whispered, "I never lied to her." The biting wind carried her voice over the field.

As if her words were a cue, the sky darkened and dry lightning cracked it in two.

"Did you even love her?" the boy asked, looking up at her. "In all of this… did you even love her?" he asked my mother and the anger I felt was immediate, pushing the words up my throat although they still hung silent in the air. Of course she loved me. A mother always loves her children.

Even though the words had gone unvoiced, they both heard me and peered at me, judging my silent comment, but neither answered me. What I silently say to them changes each time the dream comes back, but the lack of an answer never does.

"Of course I did… I still do," she said and my mother's voice dragged with regret. "I died for her." She spoke clearly although pain riddled her words, and Tyler's expression only showed more agony as he shook his head.

With her head hung low, my mother pushed the hair from her face and delicately wiped the tears from under her eyes. The glossiness of her tears made her eyes more vivid and they called to me to ease her pain.

I've cried a thousand wretched screams, praying she could make out my words that I love her. That I miss her. But it doesn't change what happens next.

With the dark gray sky opening up and hard hail raining down on us mercilessly, pieces of the vision fall like a painting soaked in water. The colors smear and run together before fading to a blank canvas, and I'm left with nothing. Nothing but the sound of them arguing over her hate versus her love and what all really mattered the night she died. And another night… the night she changed the course of fate. She screams out that she died for me. Her confession is filled with a note of anger that burns through my veins.

But the last thing I always hear before I wake screaming, is her muttering, "We do stupid things for the ones we love."

No matter how many years pass, the nightmare never leaves me.

The first time it happened, I was in the cell. All those years ago when Carter, my love, first took me. But the visions have clung to me over the years, stained into my soul.

CHAPTER 1

"DON'T SCREAM."

With my breath caught in my throat, my body paralyzed from the rush of fear forced into every inch of my body, I hear the voice, but I don't obey.

My scream is muffled by his large hand and he holds me tighter, pulling me closer into his hard chest, his strong fingers digging into my skin.

The sound of his voice shushing me as I kick out, butting my head uselessly against the wall of muscle I'm pressed to—that sound is what calms me. I've heard it before. *Daniel.*

My body relaxes slowly, barely held up by my weak legs. Adrenaline still courses through my veins, but consciously I'm aware that it's him. The man who grabbed me and held me tight, *it's only Daniel.*

"Don't scream," he repeats, his lips close to the shell of my ear. So close that his warm breath tickles my neck and sends goosebumps down my shoulder. Too fucking close. He didn't just startle me; he scared the shit out of me.

I'm slow to remove my fingers from his forearm, one by one, knowing my sharp nails are digging into his arms. Blood is everywhere and so many stabs of pain race through my body, I'd rather be numb. Numb after everything that just happened.

It's only then that he loosens his grip and slowly moves in front of me, a hand still gripping my wrist.

"What are you doing?" The words rush from me in a single breath, but Daniel doesn't answer. As my heart pounds harder, he only observes me closely, noting my expression. The night air feels colder, and it's so much darker now that he's here than it was just a moment ago.

He looks behind me before meeting my gaze to ask, "Were you going to run?"

Of everything that he could have asked me just now, this question brings me more guilt than I'll ever admit. With Eli lying dead on the ground behind us, Addison upstairs somewhere, hiding from everything that's just happened, the fact I even thought about running makes me sick to my stomach. I could have. I could have run and left all of this behind like a horrid nightmare.

And I seriously considered it too.

"No," I whisper the word, not knowing if it's the truth or a lie. The nip of the evening air licks along my exposed skin as I stand in the open doorway of the safe house. The night is dark and unforgiving, much like Daniel's gaze. I can't hold it, knowing the emotions I'm feeling are written on my face.

Taking half a step back, I feel the pain of a small cut on my heel shoot up my leg, but it's nothing. Nothing compared to the pain of knowing what happened. All the small scrapes I got from the broken window, shattered from bullets, mean nothing.

War is here. The deafening sounds of gunshots have come and gone. But death has only just begun.

"What happened?" I voice the question with raw pain present in every whispered word. "Carter?" I ask him and open my eyes to meet his as they soften, then add, "My father?"

"Your father didn't come. Neither did Nikolai." His answer is clearly spoken and holds no pretense into what his thoughts are as his eyes roam over my face.

Before I can speak Carter's name again, feeling the familiar pain of loss already numbing my heart, he says, "Carter's fine. The Talvery men took a hit coming here. They should have known better."

Talvery men.

Men I'm supposed to be loyal to, and allies with. I don't know what to feel or who the real enemy is anymore. I just want it all to stop.

The breath I didn't know I was holding finally escapes, slipping through my parted lips as I lean against the doorway, letting the cool air drift along my heated face. But my throat is tight, the words and emotions tangled together and trying to escape me all at once.

"How many…?" I start to ask, but can't finish my question with the knot in my throat. *How many died tonight?*

"A lot," Daniel answers me and my eyes whip to his, demanding more. "Dozens, Aria."

I grip the top of my pajama shirt, balling the fabric together right at my chest, twisting it and wishing I could steal the pain away but it stays, growing with every beat.

I won't cry, even though a part of me wishes for nothing but to mourn. I've failed. And the very notion leads to a sarcastic response in the form of a hiss from the back of my mind. *As if you ever had the power to stop this.*

"Do you want to leave?" Daniel asks me, and the question is one I hold on to, craving the thought of running to take my mind elsewhere. Somewhere away from the thoughts of betrayal and mourning.

My lips part, but no words come out. Not at first. Daniel looks behind me once again, down the hall and to the front door of the large estate. He's waiting for someone to come, and I know deep in my gut this conversation needs to be finished before that person arrives. "I don't know," I answer him honestly and his gaze returns to me.

"You can go home. I'll make sure you get there safe. Or you can come back with us." He gives me the choice that's haunted me for weeks now. "There is no other way I leave you, Aria."

"Carter… he'll know you–"

"He thinks you're missing. He thinks your family took you back… or worse."

"They aren't my father's men." My head shakes vigorously, knowing he's speaking of the man upstairs and wanting to deny any ties to him. "That man was coming for us, both Addison and me, but I don't know him. I don't know who he is or what's going on, but he's not someone my father sent." Reaching out to him, I grab Daniel's jacket and he lets me, returning the gesture and shushing me once again.

"It doesn't matter. That's not the point." His words are more blunt and drenched with impatience I haven't seen from him before. Lowering my hand, I take a half step back as he tells me, "Right now, Carter thinks you've been taken by someone. But I can get you out of here, away from all this if it's what you want." My gaze falls to his throat as he swallows. The noises of the night are drowned out by the sound of my blood rushing in my ears at the thought of leaving Carter.

"You're offering me a way out?" *Thump.* My heart slams against my ribcage and I can't pinpoint which reason it's chosen in this moment to remind me it still exists. Either from the hope, or the fear of leaving.

Daniel only nods once before telling me, "Away from here and to your family, or wherever you want. You can go, Aria. I…" He struggles to complete his thought and turns away to cover his face with his hand before looking back at me. "I know you and Carter are on bad terms, and I…" He trails off again and swallows thickly before lowering his hand and looking me in the eyes.

He sees my pain, my agony; they're reflected in his dark gaze. "You can go. Or you can stay."

CHAPTER 2

Carter

Time moves too fucking slow. The drive back to Sebastian's place... every fucking roll of the tire is too goddamn slow.

If it weren't for the knowledge that I can pull the video feed from the security cameras on the property, evidence that will lead me to her, I wouldn't own a shred of sanity any longer. The phone in my hand is closer and closer to breaking as I bound up the steps and the anxiety grows. It's been in danger of breaking since the moment I first heard that Aria was missing. In danger of being splintered and thrown however far I could just to release the tension and pain still rippling inside of me at the thought of losing her.

"Where are the monitors?" I don't hide the anger in my tone the second the door is ripped open wide, Jase beside me, his footsteps barely keeping up with mine.

Before I can even scream at whoever's in here to get me the fucking tapes, I nearly trip over something on the floor. Stumbling forward, I barely catch myself. Eli. Fuck!

My throat closes and a sickness shoots through me. I can't help but reach to his throat and press my fingers against his icy skin. Even though he's cold, I still hope for a pulse. One second passes, and it hurts. Another second with nothing, and I can't fucking stand the cost of waging war. A war I choose to fight. All for her.

He's gone.

His eyes are closed and his blood is pooled around him. Jase has to step in a bit of blood to get around me and the bright red is smeared across the floor. We share a look as a few of our men come in behind us.

"Get him home." I give the command evenly, not revealing a shred of the emotions I'm feeling.

Control.

Eli dying is a reminder that I need control now more than anything. He will be missed and he will be mourned, but even he would tell me to focus on revenge right now.

"She's outside," Jase says and at first I don't understand what he's talking about until I turn to look over my shoulder. With the wind sweeping her locks off her shoulders and showing more of her skin, Aria glances at me.

She's here. She's safe. Relief is all-consuming for the briefest of moments.

I have her.

Those beautiful hazel-green eyes of hers swirl with a mix of pain and regret. Not the relief I've been envisioning since I was told she was gone.

"She's here." The words leave me without consent, buried under my breath as I slowly stand.

"Carter." Daniel's voice carries across the hall as I make my way to them. He steps in front of her, but I still see her face, not daring to break her gaze as my pace picks up.

"Where were you?" I'm only half aware of how hard my voice comes out and that it echoes in the hall. My heart thuds painfully in my chest as I brush Daniel aside to get to her, gripping Aria by her shoulder to pull her inside and slam the door closed.

Her feet don't move fast enough, but I couldn't care less. *What the fuck is she thinking?* Having the door open is welcoming danger.

"What the fuck were you thinking?" I say, and the words come out with a vengeance. Hating that she'd put herself in danger and be so fucking stupid.

"Get off," she says as she pushes me away. In front of everyone, she looks back at me wild eyed and as if I'm the enemy. Like I'm the one who's to blame for every ounce of turmoil that wreaks havoc inside of me.

A numbness flows through me as I regard her, all while she regards everyone else.

She wraps her arms around her shoulders and glances at my men behind me. It's then that I see what's captured her attention. The blood. It's everywhere. Soaked into the knees of their pants where they crouched on the floor and waited for more men to kill. Splattered on their shirts. My gaze falls to my own hands, stained with the blood of her family.

"I wasn't running…" Aria barely gets the words out before she stops and audibly swallows.

She doesn't run to me. She doesn't try to hold me. She glances at Eli and then pales.

As I look to my brother, the men behind me, and then to Addison slowly climbing down the stairs, the reality hits me.

She's still the enemy. She's not on my side. No matter how much I wish she were. *This war will break us.*

Aria's gaze travels the length of my suit, inventorying every bit of blood that's sprayed and spattered across it. Blood from men I've just killed.

I wish I knew what she was thinking. I wish I knew what to do.

Wrapping her arms tighter around herself, she looks at me with the silence surrounding us, suffocating us.

The only noise is the creaking of the stairs as Addison sneaks closer to Daniel.

"I wasn't running," she repeats. It sounds as if she regrets her words.

I don't know whether or not to believe her, but I know the feeling that seeps into my veins. Betrayal. And it comes from the woman I love, in the heart of war, in front of my brothers and army.

She left me once, and she'd do it again.

I imagined when I saw her, that she would run to me. That she would cling to me the same way I wish to cling to her.

The cold actuality is harsh and indisputable.

She's still a mistake—a drug I'm addicted to that's fucking up everything I've worked so hard for almost my entire life. I've never seen it more clearly than I do now.

If I didn't feel all of this for her, for a woman who chooses her family over mine, it would be all too easy. But why would she ever choose my family over hers? I don't know how I fell in love with her. It was nothing but a mistake.

It's in this moment I remember who I am.

A ruthless man with plans on tearing everything away from Aria's life, all because of who her father is and what destroying him does to her.

This isn't what I expected. I wanted to be her savior, her knight. But all I am is the fucking villain.

I'm as dead inside as I ever have been. And it's because of her. All of this bullshit is because of her. No, it's because I wanted her so badly I was willing to wage war, consequences be damned. Eli died, because of me.

"Whoever tried to take them knew her father was hitting us tonight." I speak loud enough for everyone to hear and leave Aria standing where she is.

A slow tide of agony fills my gut and rises higher until I taste bile in my throat. "I want to see the security feed, now." Two men run off, heading for the stairwell that leads down to the basement.

"Is the house secure?" I ask Daniel and he hesitates to answer me, his eyes narrowing as he glances between Aria and me.

His gaze speaks a thousand words, most of them begging for me not to be the man I was forced to become, but I'm the one who had to bear that burden, not him. He has Addison.

I have no one. Not until Aria has no one left but me. And even then…

Finally, he nods. "It's secure to return but it'll take weeks to repair, or longer."

"All men back there," I tell him and then look Jase and the other men in the eyes. "Fix the mess her father caused."

CHAPTER 3

Aria

"**Y**OU OKAY?" JASE ASKS ME AS WE STAND IN THE FOYER OF THE CROSS ESTATE. Everyone was silent on the ride over here. Cars escorted ours in front and back, even on the sides when the road was wide enough. The security detail was hovering close around me, but it seemed more like guarding a prisoner than protecting an ally. Every minute that passed made me feel more and more like I didn't belong.

It made me feel like I'd made a mistake not leaving when I could have.

"Hey, you okay?" Jase asks me again as the men filter out of the foyer.

"You sure you should be talking to me?" I ask him in return and his huff of a laugh soothes a small part of my broken spirit. Without a doubt, I've fallen for Carter, but it wasn't until today that I realized how much I love his family too. Even while coated in the blood of my own family.

"It's tense, but everything will be all right."

"I don't know how you can think that," I answer him and my voice cracks. I know the men departing must hear how weak I am, and I hate it. This isn't the woman I want to be. Clearing my throat and focusing on the one thing I can confide in Jase about, I tell him, "He's angry with me."

"He was worried, Aria. We all were. We thought those men took you." It takes me a moment to realize what he's saying, to realize what Carter must've felt and guilt and insecurity weigh heavily against my chest.

So guilty. What have I done to bear all this guilt that has seeped into my gut?

"Besides, Carter's always angry." Jase tries to joke, to lighten the pain of what happened tonight. It doesn't help me though. There's nothing in this world that can help me now.

"I thought things were different," I whisper. But I didn't know this would happen. Deep down I knew it was coming, although I wanted to deny it. It's all coming to a head and I know I'm going to hate the outcome either way. There was never a thing that could have helped me. Not a damn thing that would have saved me. I'm a woman born to breed pain and misery. My last name demands it.

"We're still at war. A single battle was fought and men on both sides died. It's going to cause tension."

"Tension," I scoff, although it's not meant to come out in an offensive way. It's just that tension isn't a strong enough word to describe the animosity and uncertainty stretching the space between us. The pure agony stifling both of us.

"Aren't you the one who called us the enemy?" Jase asks, reminding me of the words I told Eli only hours before his death. The memory sends a trickle of regret down my spine.

"Is that not what we are?" I ask him back in a low breath, peering into his eyes and wishing he would tell me otherwise. Even if it is a lie.

A beat passes, and there's nothing but silence. I wonder vaguely if the other men can hear. Or if Carter is maybe listening. If he even cares to listen at this point. He didn't speak a word to me in the car. He sat in the front, not in the back with me.

Jase only nods solemnly but squeezes my hand, then adds, "Falling in love with the enemy is torture." With a sad smile that doesn't reach his eyes, he lets go. I'm forced to watch him leave me, walking down the foyer, his footsteps echoing in the empty hall until my gaze lands on the photograph at the very end. The black-and-white shot of a house that feels as if it's lingered in the back of my mind. The importance of it, my thoughts long to remember.

If I had a choice, I'd go there now, just to see why the image haunts me. It has to do with Carter, I know it does. And I need to know anything and everything that has to do with Carter.

Our families and pride may be at war, but not my heart. My heart belongs to him. I know it with everything in me. It's why I could never leave him, even if the option was handed to me so easily.

But in this moment, it feels as if he's ripped it from my chest and thrown it out in the cold, leaving it there to die. Covered in my family's blood and ripping me from the doorway, slamming it shut and screaming at me as if I'm a fool wasn't at all what I expected.

Whatever point he wanted to make in front of his men, I'm sure they heard it loud and clear.

He doesn't love me.

How many times have I said, "I love you," to him and I was given nothing in return?

A parched sensation blankets my throat, so dry it's futile to try to swallow.

The sound of heavy footsteps coming closer to me from the doorway at the end of the long hall, makes my body flinch with each step. They're brutal and dominating. They belong to Carter, no doubt.

Confirming my thought, the brooding beast enters the hall, a bottle of whiskey in his left hand and a tumbler with ice in his right. He doesn't bother to hide how pissed he still is. Pissed at me, judging from his acrimonious glare. Again I find myself unable to swallow, but I can't help confronting him.

"What did I do to deserve this?" I bite out the words as he starts to walk past me, down to the hall leading to his wing and presumably his bedroom or office. "What the fuck did I do but merely exist in the painful life I didn't choose?"

My heart batters against my chest while I wish to either run with fear, or beat him with pent-up rage. I'm not sure which.

Even though my own legs feel weak and numb from everything that's happened tonight, keeping me planted where I am, Carter's move forward as he ignores my question.

How fucking dare he ignore me.

With my ragged voice raised, I scream at him until my face is hot. "What did I do to deserve this?"

It only takes three strides before Carter's powerful presence is towering over me, and I nearly stumble backward. Nearly, but I keep my ground. I'm breathing chaotically and waiting for him to give me something. Anything is better than being ignored, made to feel like I don't even exist.

"Where do I start, *Miss Talvery?*" His voice is low as he moves down until his face is eye level with mine. He practically sneers my name and it shreds me from the inside. "You pointed a gun at me. You stand with your ex-lover and your father who have tried to kill me, not once, not twice, but every chance they get. Including the time one week ago, by said, fucking, ex, in which you knew what was happening but said nothing." The last word is sneered. He inhales deeply, pausing as pain rips through me.

I worry my bottom lip between my teeth before I bite down on it hard. The physical pain is vastly preferable to the emotional pain that boils inside of me at his aggressive attitude.

Carter already knew all of that when he fucked me the other night. When he held me like he loved me. Nothing has changed for me, and I don't deserve this. I love him. I've chosen him time and time again. The fact I'm still here after everything is proof of that.

"And then you tried to run," he adds and I whip my hand across his face. It's purely out of instinct, generated by his arrogance and the way I feel used and defiled by him. My palm smacks hard against his chiseled cheek and my fingers follow.

His face is like fucking stone. My hand throbs with a stinging, burning pain and as I wince, my eyes stay on Carter's unmoving expression. It didn't affect him in the least. All of the sickness and hurt that ache inside of me, I feel it all and he feels nothing.

Nothing.

"I didn't," I tell him, knowing I didn't try to run. It was only a passing thought and I won't be accused of anything more than that. Not when everything is stacked against us and I'm doing everything I can to stay by him. Even when he stands firmly against me.

Time passes and he merely stares at me, judging me, but I let him see the pain. I want to hide myself in this lonesome tower he's put me in, but I stand in front of him with my hands in fists by my side and beg him to feel what I feel. And to take it away.

"I don't deserve this, Carter," I say and my voice is strangled. *Please just take it all away.* I wish he could do that for me. However it entails, I don't want to feel this way for a second longer.

"I thought they'd taken you," he continues to talk with a look of disgust on his face, even though pain is etched into his words. "But you were just sneaking out to run away. What a fucking fool I was," he sneers.

"You are a fucking fool." I mimic his mocking tone, refusing to give him all of me when he chooses to believe otherwise. Holding my hand, which has started to go numb, I back away from him, knowing this battle is over and both of us have lost. "I wasn't running," I tell him the truth and then add, "And I won't say it again." The strength in my voice comes from some part of me deep inside. The part of me that knows I could stand beside this man. The part desperate to do exactly that.

His gaze assesses me, scrutinizing my expression.

"I'm not lying, Carter. I have no reason to lie to you." I let my voice soften, to show him the vulnerability. "I love you. Even through all this, I can't stop loving you. Yes, I had a chance to run, and I didn't take it. I wanted to stay with you."

My heart flickers in my chest, barely holding on to life as Carter's expression doesn't change, then another second passes and another.

"You don't believe me?" I say weakly with disbelief.

"You've hurt me once. Right there," he says then gestures with his hand behind me, to the hall that leads to the room where I held a gun to his head. "How can I believe you?"

"If you didn't think you could believe me," I say to try to numb the pain growing inside of me, like a ball of bile that drops in my stomach, "then why bring me back here?" All I can think is that he doesn't love me. He doesn't anymore.

Silence.

It's unbearably silent as my stomach churns while Carter walks off, leaving me without an answer. Without telling me that he loves me, even though I'm the fool who spoke those words to him.

Carter

My phone is constantly ringing, pinging, vibrating. Constantly distracting me from life itself and reminding me that I'm in control. It never lets up. Even now, the instant I turn notifications back on I'm flooded with alerts.

Every second the car moved and she said nothing—my Aria said nothing at all, not one fucking word to me or anyone else—every second of silence that passed only made the hate for what she'd done grow. She may not have been with her father or his men. But she sided with him nonetheless.

My phone goes off again, vibrating in my hand and it rattles against the cut crystal tumbler. With the adrenaline and anxiousness still ringing in my blood, my grip tightens, feeling the hard metal of the phone digging into my flesh as I open my bedroom door.

I need a fucking minute. One goddamn minute to take control again.

The incessant buzzing in my hand mocks me and I slam the door shut behind me, feeling my muscles tighten and the air thin as I struggle to keep my breathing steady.

Setting down the tumbler and bottle of whiskey on the dresser, I glance at my phone, unable to simply shut the fucking thing off.

It's Sebastian.

The intensity dims, the heat subsides. He always has a way of showing up when I need him most.

I heard what happened, his message reads and as I stare at his text, another comes in. *I know you'll probably say the same as always, that you don't need me to come back, but I have to ask. Do you want my help?*

I stare at the last line, taking in the word "want." When Sebastian left, it was a while before we talked again, given everything that changed the very next day. The day I had my unfortunate introduction to Aria's father.

I thought you were busy with Chloe and work? I write back then press send, still staring at the word "want."

He's asked a few times, when shit got rough over the years, if I needed him to come back.

"Need" being the operative word. And back then, knowing what happened between him and Romano, I never would have allowed him to come back and risk a damn thing. Not with a girl by his side. The girl who is now his wife, not to mention very much pregnant.

The guard job is over; it was just a summer gig.

He never stopped traveling. They moved from place to place when they ran from our hometown. He had enough money to keep them afloat until they found a bed and breakfast to hide away in, located on a huge cattle farm. He's been there for a while and it took him a long time, not until last year, nearly ten years after leaving this place to come back. The farm's shut down, the land's sold, and Chloe's pregnant. He has no reason to come back, not with the money he still has and the extra he makes doing security detail work. But I know he longs to come home, especially given Romano has no control here anymore. Even if he doesn't want to admit the one thing that's really held him back is Chloe.

I thought you said you and this city just don't mix. I can't help asking, pushing him away further and knowing full well what I'm doing.

Do I want him back? Yes. I need him now more than ever. Every piece of what I've built is crumbling and a part of me, the part that's very much alive, wishes desperately that I could do what he did. That I could take Aria and simply run. To leave this shit behind, and make it just Aria and me. No one else, no problems, nothing but what we pack in a car before taking off. If I could trade places with him, I would.

But I have my brothers to look after, and consequences to suffer.

At one point, Sebastian was like the older brother I never had. And when he came here to see the safe house last year, I thought he'd stay. I should have known better. The world changed when he left, becoming darker, colder, and he didn't want it for Chloe.

I knew I was descending deeper and deeper into the pits of hell, a misery of my own making, when I watched them drive away. He said he'd be back, but it's been roughly a year. A year of messaging off and on. And a year that's changed everything.

I don't care what I said before. I want to come back, Carter. You need my help.

Aria

It takes a long time for me to move from where Carter's left me. Daniel comes to check on me, to tell me Addison's in the study if I want company. He's not nearly as soft toward me as he was back at the safe house. I appreciate it either way though.

The thought of facing Addison though, knowing how she has Daniel and I don't have Carter... I can't take it right now.

Jase comes by again, although he doesn't speak. He only squeezes my shoulders and offers me a weak smile that I return with a shake of my head.

Even Declan comes by and tells me he'll make me something to eat if I want, but I know I would throw it up if I could even manage to take a bite of anything at all.

It takes me a long, long time before I start walking down to Carter's wing. The idea of staying in the hideaway room offers a small bit of comfort. I could be alone and break down where the only person who would see is Carter, if he bothered to check on me.

But I don't want to hide—even if I do want to be alone. Time is precious and I don't want to live like this.

I'm halfway to Carter's bedroom when my pace picks up. His door is closed, and I'm scared it will be locked when I grip the carved glass knob, but it turns easily for me.

Too easily, even.

The savage man I love is standing at his dresser, the whiskey bottle still sealed in front of him. But shattered glass scatters moonlight around the room as the curtains sway from the air blowing through the vents, letting in glimpses of the light.

It looks as if he must've slammed the glass down too hard and with another step into the room, my eyes assessing his hand as I close the door behind me, I can see the cuts that line his skin.

From the glass, or from earlier today, I'm not sure. Maybe the mixture of wounds is from both. The reminder he's killed men today, men who may have protected me in the past, men who I've had dinner with, men who have fought for my father for years, settles an eerie chill in my bones as the door clicks shut and Carter's dark eyes peer back at me from over his shoulder.

There's a slam of fear in my chest, but it's gone quickly as Carter turns his head forward again toward the bottle, not even bothering to look at me for more than that split second.

And then I'm given more silence.

In that moment, I almost turn and walk away. I almost run out of the room. Almost… but I don't. I have a voice, and I'm going to use it.

"I'm not going to stay here as a prisoner. If you don't want me, I'm leaving." I don't know how I manage to say the words so clearly, but I do. I hold on to that small accomplishment as Carter answers me.

"I have a right to be angry." There's no menace in his voice at all. Merely truth.

"You don't have a right to treat me like I'm nothing," I dare to respond with a harshly spoken whisper.

"Did it even cross your mind that maybe I was dead?" he asks, slowly turning to face me. His eyes are tired and his voice wretched.

"Yes," I answer him quickly as my breathing catches in my chest, remembering all the worry the gunshots crying out in the night brought me.

"And what did that do to you?"

"It made me angry… angry that you didn't call." I swallow thickly, remembering how I held the phone. "I messaged you and you didn't bother to give me any sign at all that you were all right or that you cared." I confess a raw truth, baring more of myself to him, "And it hurt in every way possible. Every piece of me went numb thinking you were out there… that you were gone like Eli was." It feels wrong even speaking of Eli right now. His memory should be honored and not brought up like this.

"Daniel had already told me you were all right." I hope that truth eases something in him as I realize at least one of the reasons why I'm angry. "I knew you were all right and even if I was mad that you were ignoring me, I promise you I couldn't have felt more relief at finding out that you were okay." Every time I turn soft for him, I lose that hard edge that makes me his equal. I know it, yet I do it every time.

Carter's quiet for what seems like an eternity, as if registering what I may have been feeling for the first time. Please, I pray he'll understand. With so much against us, we need to understand each other if nothing else.

"I thought you were dead and I was ready to kill anyone who stood in my path to find you, Aria. And yet, when I got there, you didn't..."

"I didn't what?" I question him with a raised voice, begging him to tell me everything. With a hesitant step forward, I stop when he answers.

"You didn't react to seeing me."

"What did you want from me?" I ask him, honestly not knowing what he wanted. "You grabbed me like I was a child acting up." Instinctively, my hand moves to my forearm where he ripped me from the doorway and yanked me inside of the house.

"You didn't even ask if I was all right," he spits at me, condemning me for not comforting him when I'd just witnessed more death firsthand than I ever have in my life.

"There was death everywhere around me, and I knew my family was out there but-"

"It's your family you care about!"

I'm taken aback by the venom in his words. "You already knew I loved them and that I didn't want this-"

"I would do anything for you. I would kill for you. I feel like I would die without you. Yet when I got to you... all you wanted was for me to let you go."

"Carter, you don't understand."

"No, I don't." His answer is hard and unmoving.

"I'm sorry," I say, giving him an apology I truly mean. "I didn't want to upset you; I'm just not okay right now... and I was even worse earlier."

Carter's expression softens slightly, but I can tell he's holding on to his reservations. I know he doesn't trust me. I've lost his trust completely and it makes me feel trapped and desperate, needing him to give me a chance.

"I'm sorry. Do you believe me?" My question is pleading as I take the few small steps needed to stand in front of him. I swear he can hear my heart pounding as I dare to tell him, "If I could go back, I would. I would make sure I gave you what you needed, even as I dealt with all of this... this agony inside of me."

I'm careful as I raise a hand and cup his jaw. His five o'clock shadow is rough against my fingertips. The anger wanes from him as I rub my thumb up and down his cheek.

"I'm sorry. I didn't want any of this to happen, but I don't want to lose you." My words slip from me easily, raw, transparent and true. I mean every word of it.

Carter takes a step to his left, closer to the bed and says under his breath, "There's no room to be sorry in this life."

Crying is something I'm done with. I swallow down the spiked pain and embrace it rather than succumb to weakness. A second passes as Carter strips out of his shirt, unbuttoning it and then tossing it onto the floor.

He may have grabbed me earlier as if I was a defiant child walking out recklessly into a busy street, but right now, he's the one acting like a child.

"You just want to be angry with me, don't you?" I pause my thoughts as he removes his cotton undershirt, stained with blood too. "There's nothing I could say or do to change your mind. You want to be pissed at me."

He looks at me from over his shoulder, a derisive glance. "Why would I want that, little songbird?"

"Because if you aren't angry, you'll have to deal with everything else that's brewing inside of you. If you aren't a beast, then you have to be a mere mortal and deal with what you're feeling." I spew the words, not even conscious of them until they've left me.

"Ever the artist, aren't you?" He makes light of the truth, not willing to admit how accurate my words are as he turns to me and stalks closer, wearing nothing but his pants. His hardened muscles ripple in the dim light and his dark eyes seem bright with a challenge.

"Make light of it all you want. You simply want to be angry with me." He takes a large step forward and I take a small one back, not letting him get close enough to touch me. "And I'm fine with it, so long as you know it's bullshit and that I'm very aware of what bullshit it is." I spit out the last words, hating him for what he's doing. He's using his rage as a buffer to maintain his veneer of control. And it's not fair. "I love you, Carter Cross. I chose you." I have to add in the last statements, if for no other reason than to be honest with myself. Even now, I still love him. He's ruthless; an uncaring and brutal asshole. And I'm the fool who loves him and wants him to give up a piece of his armor, knowing I'll protect that part of him with everything I have.

"You didn't choose me," he insists and I start to respond, but he continues. "Choose me now, and kneel."

My pulse quickens at the look in his eyes. I've seen it before, so many times. And I'm grateful for the change. Hopeful to reach the man I love through this veil of hate.

I look him in the eyes as I obey him. The blood that rushes through my veins heats with desire. There wasn't a single part of me that hesitated.

He crouches in front of me, bringing him to eye level, and my gaze stays pinned to his. The depths of his dark irises ignite with power, with a primal need.

Take from me, Carter. Take what you need and what's left of me will still love you.

Spearing his fingers through my hair, he makes a fist and forces my head to tilt. My breath hitches with the sudden grip, and my body bows to his. There's barely a hint of pain; it's merely him taking control as he crashes his lips to mine. My hands reach up instinctively, bracing either side of his jaw as he ravages me.

The kiss is everything. It's warmth. It's home. It's a touch that awakens the pieces of me that have been silent and waiting for him to come back. I moan into his kiss, wishing I wasn't in this position so I could lean into his hold, so I could take more of him and show him how desperate I am for us to go back to what we were.

But there's no way we could ever go back.

You can never go back.

My lips feel swollen and bruised by the time he releases me, slowly loosening his grip. My chest heaves for air, and I love it. When I peek up at him, my vision hazy with lust, I see his eyes closed and his own lips parted as he takes in a steadying breath, then opens his eyes to pin me in place.

The gaze of a hunter, a predator even, stills my beating heart.

In the pale light of the early morning trickling through his curtains, the soft shadows line his jaw and make him look even more domineering.

He stands slowly, leaving me where I am and I can see his thick length as he does, pressing against his pants.

He paces in front of me, deliberating on what to do next, and I'm eager to find out.

"You'll pay for what you did."

"What I did?" The question is spoken with confusion. I have to blink away the desire as fear creeps in.

"Raising a gun to me. Standing in opposition to me." He doesn't hold any anger in his words. Only truth and certainty.

"I thought I already did." My voice is choked as I gasp out the words.

"You lost my trust."

I can only nod, not trusting myself to speak. I think about everything he's done to me since the first night I laid eyes on him. How he's deprived me, lied to me, locked me away and punished me with both pleasure and pain.

"Holding grudges hardens the heart," I murmur to myself, but my words are for him as well.

"I don't have a heart, songbird." His response is quick, but so is mine.

"I don't like it when you lie to me."

It's quiet for a moment. Carter's mind is made up for tonight. But we have time. I don't know how much, but there's always hope. And I know my soul speaks to his. My soul is desperate to stay with his. It's the only truth that matters. *I need him.*

"If you're staying in my bed tonight, you're going to have to satisfy me." As Carter speaks, my gaze is drawn to his strong jaw and then to his throat. I watch as his chest rises and falls and he stands in front of me, unbuckling his belt. The sound of the leather hissing in the air as it's pulled through the loops makes my pussy heat and clench.

"I'm staying with you," I tell him with a mix of defiance and the greedy need to be taken by him. I can't help but think he just needs to be touched. To be loved. To be given free rein over me and to *feel* how much I need him. *This* is what we need.

He doesn't speak as he unzips his pants and then lets them fall to the floor with a soft thud.

His cock bobs in front of me, swollen and each vein protruding. I can practically feel his thickness pulsing inside of me already. He may need this, but I know I need it too. I need to be loved. Loved for the person I am, by this man and this man alone.

"Lie on the bed on your belly," he commands me and I'm eager to move.

I want to make this right between us however I can.

And if this is how he chooses, to command me, defile me, degrade me in his bed, I'll obey him without objection. Because I fucking love it too.

As I crawl up the bed, stripping as I go and tossing the clothes on the floor, I hear Carter open a bedside drawer. I'm not sure what it is he's getting, but I don't care. I just want him. However I can get him.

With a cheek pressed to the pillow, I lie still on the bed, naked and waiting for him to do as he pleases. I know he won't hurt me. Not like this. His words are venomous, and his deprivation of affection is torturous, but here, like this, he won't hurt me. I know he won't. Whether he says it or not, a piece of him loves me more than his entirety could ever hate me.

The bed dips in time with my heart at the thought, and Carter climbs on top of me, his hard erection digging into my thigh as he leans over me. His fingers trail up my side and make my whole body shiver. He gently pulls back the hair over my ear to kiss my neck, giving me goosebumps that cause my nipples to harden and a shudder to run down my shoulders.

"You think you love me, Aria," he whispers in a threatening tone that turns my blood to ice. "Let me show you exactly what kind of a beast I can be."

Letting my hair fall back into place, he sits up straighter and the air around me suddenly feels colder without him there any longer.

My heartbeat quickens, but I ignore the lingering threat and welcome whatever he wants to do to me. He is mine, and I am his.

A click sounds in the air at the same time a sudden coldness hits my ass. It's wet and slick, and it takes me a moment to realize what it is.

Carter drizzles lube over my ass and then runs his finger down to my forbidden entrance. Heat rolls through my body and I struggle to stay still, knowing what he's going to do.

He takes his time, teasing me, stretching me, pushing himself in and out for what feels like too long. I can't take it. I can't stand waiting any longer, knowing what he wants and what he's going to take from me.

"Carter," I say and his name is a plea on my lips. My head moves from side to side as he shushes me.

He presses his head inside of me and it's already too much. I jump away from him, my teeth clenching.

"Push back," he commands me and then adds as he slips inside of me, "Push back right now."

My hips tilt up slightly, although only because of his grip on them and I do what he says, but it's so much. Too much. My body blazes with the forbidden touch.

I'm so hot. So full already. Every inch of my skin tingles as I try not to writhe underneath him. With one of his hands on my hip and the other gripping my shoulder with a bruising force, he slams all of himself inside of me in a swift, unforgiving thrust.

The pain of being stretched this way for the first time forces me to bite down on the pillow as tears flood and sting my eyes. I can feel him pulse inside of me, growing harder and larger and it's too much. It's all too much.

My body's on fire, alternated with freezing cold as he moves behind me at a slow, but relentless pace.

"Carter," I whimper his name as the overwhelming sensation begs me to move away but then, with just as much need, to push back and take more of him this way.

My clit rubs against the comforter beneath me and I moan. A single moan of utter pleasure, my body choosing it over the pain. Carter takes it as his cue to pick up his pace, ruthlessly fucking my ass and shoving my body down into the bed with each hard pump.

"Fuck," I moan out and he responds with a low groan from deep in his chest.

My fingers dig into the comforter, my nails scratching along the threads as my head thrashes and I struggle to breathe. Pleasure and pain mix in a cocktail I'm already drunk on.

He whispers at the shell of my ear, "You're such a dirty whore for me." At the same time, he shoves his fingers inside of my pussy and presses his thumb to my clit.

Holy fuck!

My mouth hangs open with a silent scream of ecstasy. The pleasure ripples through my body and paralyzes me as he thrusts behind me, pistoning his hips and filling me to the point where it's nearly too much with both his fingers and his cock. I've never felt like this. So full, so hot, so consumed by bliss.

He fucks me harder once my orgasm begins to wane. He doesn't stop, not even when he sinks inside of me so deep that I feel like he'll split me in two. I try to spin around out of instinct and push him away.

Instantly, Carter stops. Barely keeping himself inside of me, he tells me with a cold gaze, "Keep your hands down." There's no desire in his voice, no sense of mercy or love. Nothing but anger that I've dared to push him away.

It's a shock to my system. Seeing him like that while I feel nothing but desire and love is sobering. An icy gust sweeps through me even as he changes his expression, softening it and gently pushing my shoulders back to the bed.

"It's too much," I whisper and although the pain is gone, the intensity of what we had has vanished.

"Lie back down," he commands me in a way that leaves a deep fracture in my heart. I can hear it splinter as I return my cheek to the pillow.

He doesn't touch me again; he doesn't resume fucking me. He doesn't allow himself to cum.

Instead, he gets up and moves away from me. I try to keep from crying as the pleasure from my orgasm withers to nothing while he enters the bathroom and flicks on the light.

I feel alone in this moment, broken and used. Utterly alone. It reminds me of the last time we were together, of him tying me up and not fucking me. Instead he left me after torturing the truth out of me.

Is that all this was? More torture?

I stay still as he wipes me down and returns to the bathroom. My chest feels hollow and it's hard to swallow. Maybe I didn't lose him tonight. Maybe I lost him that night when I told him I would never forgive him. Maybe I lost him the moment I picked up the gun and I've only just now seen it.

All I know right now is that I feel like I've lost him.

Refusing to cry, I bite the inside of my cheek and listen to him walk back to the bed after turning off the light. The bed creaks as he gets in beside me. He doesn't crawl under the sheets he laid on top of me, and I don't move from where I am. I'll wait for him.

He loves me. I know he loves me, but why does it feel like he doesn't at all? *Why do I feel like I'm lying to myself?*

"I love you," I whisper and chance a look at him. The sun has risen and he can't hide in the darkness. His eyes are tired and his face looks older than it ever has before.

I watch his throat bob as he lies back in the bed and says nothing. He says nothing.

More silence. And that's the last bit I can take.

Licking my dry lips, I realize his intention was simply to hurt me, at least in that moment I turned around, the moment where it was too much. I'm quick to get up and move away from him, pushing the sheets aside.

His grip is hot, burning into me as he wraps a strong hand around my hip and pulls me into his hard, chiseled chest.

"You know I care for you." He says the words sternly, but he doesn't look at me. Not at first. The pounding in my chest rises to my throat until his eyes find mine, swirling with pain.

The chaos warps and twists inside of me. I'm hurting for him, a man who feels betrayed and doesn't know what to do because every time life has given him a challenger, he's simply murdered them, yet here I stand.

But I'm also in pain. For falling for a man so merciless and heartless as Carter.

"Don't ever do that again," I say, barely keeping my voice from breaking. "Don't ever treat me like I'm nothing to you."

"Is that a threat?" he asks, still not looking at me.

"No. Not a threat, a promise. Carter, look at me." My voice sharpens and his eyes find mine. "If you ever do that again, I'll leave you." It takes everything in me to tell him that, because I know it's true. And I'm worried it will happen. It feels so close to being inevitable.

"Do what exactly?" he asks me, daring to play as if he doesn't know. As if he doesn't realize how much he's hurt me tonight.

"Fuck me just to prove how willing I am for you to have me. Walk by me as if I'm meaningless in your life." I nearly choke on my last words, remembering how I felt in the foyer. "Treat me like I'm not worth sparing a glance."

"First, I wanted you. I fucked you because I wanted you." His tone is sharp until he adds, "But something… changed."

"Something?" I ask him, but he doesn't answer me. He keeps on speaking as if I hadn't voiced the question at all.

"What was it like to hold a gun to my head?" he asks, and his voice is thick with emotion. "Did you think it made me feel like I meant something to you?" He doesn't hide the pain behind a mask of cold indifference. I can hear him swallow and for the first time, he shows me everything in his expression. I've hurt him so deeply and I didn't even know.

"Carter, don't…" I start to say, inching closer to him although he stays perfectly still. "I was just trying to survive," I say, begging him to understand. "If I could take it back-"

"You wouldn't," he cuts me off, and I know he's right. Under that circumstance, I wouldn't allow him to murder my friends and family. It's fucked up how much that very knowledge guts me. There's no way for me to make it out of this alive.

"You were just surviving. Maybe pretending that you mean nothing to me is a way for me to just survive."

I'm struck by his confession, and I hate it. I hate the lives we have, and how fate has put us in each other's path.

"Please don't do this, Carter." My throat is tight as despair claws its way up. "I know we're broken, but stop this. Don't do this again. Don't make it worse."

"I can't make it better," he rebuts.

"Tell me you care for me again," I whisper, getting closer to him and ignoring the pain that still lingers. When I walked back into Carter's grasp, easily letting him take me back here, I had no idea that we were so broken. How could I have been so fucking foolish to think that loving him was going to fix it all? As if it could put a stop to the war, rewrite the past, and make us invincible for whatever lies ahead.

He tells me he cares about me after a moment, but then he tells me a truth I hadn't dared to admit I already knew until he spoke the words. "I wish I didn't. It would all be easier if I didn't."

CHAPTER 4

Carter

Every time I thrust inside of her, I remembered the confessions she made the other night. How she told me she'd be with Nikolai if I wasn't in the picture, and how she'll never forgive me. She meant them. She still does.

Being inside of her is heaven, but last night, it was hell. There was no way I could have taken any pleasure in her. Not when all I can think is how she's going to hate me when this is over. There's no way I'm going to be able to keep her. It's fucking impossible.

A numbness spreads through my hand as I form a fist, letting the cuts split open and feeling the pain rip through my knuckles. Leaning back in my office chair, I clench and unclench my hand again and again, just to feel something else.

I've never wanted to forget so much. To erase the mess I've gotten us into. To run away with her and start over.

It's a pain I've never felt and a position I never considered I'd be in. Because I've never felt this way about anyone else. No one else has meant so much to me before. Not even my brothers.

I don't know how we're going to make it out of this together. And I've never wanted anything more.

The long strand of pearls that starts out with small spheres growing in size until they reach the center, stares back at me from its velvet box on the desk. The iridescence shines off the polished pearls, stealing my gaze. They mesmerized me, as did my Aria. Anything that can keep my attention should belong to her.

I needed to replace her previous necklace with one she could wear forever. This necklace is timeless and even if she leaves me, I pray she'll keep it forever. I pray that what we had will be endless, even if us being together is only a dream I could dare to return to in my sleep.

As I hear Aria's footsteps patter closer to my office right before the door creaks open, I shut the velvet box. Aria's eyes are still puffy and red from lack of sleep, and her lips are swollen. She grips her sleepshirt with one hand and playfully knocks on the door even though it's open and our eyes have already met.

She attempts a smile, but it disappears as quickly as it came. Fuck, it hurts. I want nothing more than for her to be happy. Truly happy with me, with the man I am and will always be.

"I wasn't sure if you wanted me to dress," she barely speaks before adding, "since there weren't any clothes laid out."

I watch her throat as she swallows, and again she balls the thin cotton of her sleepshirt in her hand. She doesn't wear it in bed, only when she leaves the bedroom. The tension in the air is thick, and it makes my fingers go numb again and prick with anguish.

"You still want me to?" I ask her and she nods swiftly and without hesitation. I love this submissive side of her, this trusting side. I love that she wants this side of me. Even more, I love that I can so easily give her what she wants.

"I like it when you do things like that," she answers.

With a single nod, I stand up and make my way to the other side of the desk, swallowing down the lump and remembering that I need to be in control at all times. For her, and for the sake of my family and everyone else relying on me. Aria stands where she is, looking lost and insecure.

I hate it, even though I know I'm the reason for it all. I could easily bring her back into my arms and love her. But it would only end in her hating me, in her breaking me and destroying the last bit of my sanity.

If it ends this way, slowly, and with a growing chasm between us, it'll be easier to accept. For both of us.

"For you," I say and hold out the black box for her to take, and only then does she step forward. As the box creaks open, I move the chair to face her and take a seat, explaining as my back hits the smooth leather, "It's your birthday gift."

She forces a small smile to her lips, but the sadness lingers there. "It's beautiful," she says, although she doesn't look at me. "What happened to my other… necklace?" Instinctively, her hand reaches for her collar, to the place where the diamonds and pearls used to lay.

"It's where you left it," I tell her and then glance at the box, still pushed against the wall but not lined up exactly with where it normally goes. I don't want it to go back to where it was. I want to remember. I *have* to remember. My gut churns at the memory of how I felt, sitting in this very chair, while she locked herself in that box. I'm sickened by all the hate and anger I had, but more than that, the realization that what I wanted would never be.

"Are we okay?" Aria's gentle question, laced with both want and fear, brings my attention to her gorgeous face.

"I don't know that we'll ever be okay." My answer is instant and calmly spoken as if it's a certainty. "But that doesn't make you any less mine."

"I don't know what I can do, Carter." Aria's voice is wretched as she stares at the pearls, her fingertips barely skimming along each one. "I want to make this right."

"This was never going to be right, Aria. It wasn't right what I did, and what I'm going to do… it's not right to you." I don't like the way my words come out. As if I'm letting her go, because I'm not. I won't be the one to break things off, but I know she'll leave me.

It's inevitable.

"You don't get to decide what's right for me." Her answer is sharp, that defiance I love slicing through the painful truth even she can't deny: We were never meant to be.

"You're still angry at me, aren't you? For grabbing the gun." Her voice wavers as she adds, "I'm sorry, Carter." Her words are rushed and she barely breathes as she takes a single step toward me, closing the space until I reach out to take her waist in my hands. I could pull her into my lap, but I don't. I keep her right where she is, at arm's length.

"I know you are," I tell her solemnly.

"Does this mean you don't forgive me?" The pain isn't hidden in the least. Not in her words, or the way her hands hold on to mine, not in the shades of amber and jade in her eyes.

"It's not about forgiveness, Aria. I understand why. I respect it, even. But it would happen again. You would do it again." I speak to her without reservations. She'll come to the same realization I have. She will, even if it hurts her with the same pain it does me.

"You're the one who put me here. Who put me right in the middle, Carter. You could lock me in the cell, and then I wouldn't be in the way." She pleads with me, wanting me to take away her freedom and the woman she was always meant to be just so I can have her.

"You're the one who wanted out of your cage to fly away. Isn't that right?" I know it doesn't change anything. Giving her freedom only to be disappointed with what she does with it, doesn't change a damn thing between us.

"You're the one who didn't clip my wings," she says and the hazel concoction in her eyes begs me to fall for her. To give in and simply love her. They don't know it, just as she doesn't. I already do. I love her with everything in me. But this is all I can offer her. I'm already giving her everything I have. "You let me find you. You gave me that choice... I know you must've," she tells me and I don't deny it.

"To clip your wings... to keep you out of it all... that would have been the greatest of crimes, my songbird."

CHAPTER 5

I HAVEN'T LEFT THE HIDEAWAY ROOM IN … I DON'T KNOW HOW LONG.

The pearls are still on my pillow, where I left them. Both the strand of pearls Carter gave me this morning, and the loose pearls and diamonds I retrieved from the box in his office. He left me standing there, knowing we were broken beyond repair. And I did my best to clean it up. Picking up the evidence of my broken collar all while hot tears slid down my cheeks and fell into the box where I lay only a week ago.

I know the pain of a love being over. It's an undeniable feeling that stretches out slowly through each limb and finger. It's numbing, yet unforgivingly sharp.

My chest heaved with each sob until I fell to the floor.

Love isn't enough, and that's the worst thing in the whole world. Love is supposed to conquer all. It's supposed to persevere. Instead all it's done is caused us both unbearable pain. A pain I would do anything not to feel ever again.

I've lain in the makeshift bed, a pile of pillows on top of the plush rug, warring with myself. I've thought every possible situation through. Ranging from walking into the cell willingly and locking it behind me until it's all over, to telling Carter I'd kill my father and Nikolai with my own two hands.

And I hate the woman in each scenario. I despise her. And I also know I would never be able to live with myself. I would simply be waiting until the day I died. Living each moment with a resentment toward Carter that I don't think I could hide.

Fate is cruel, and this world is colder than I ever imagined.

My body is sore and it takes a moment when I stand up to begin to move. I haven't had anything to drink or eat in … I don't know how long. I'm dizzy and there's a pounding in my temple that won't quit.

I move slowly to the kitchen, listening to my bare feet pad softly on the floor and breathing in and out as deeply as I can. A cup of coffee is what I'm after, a piping hot cup that's mostly sugar and cream. I only need the coffee for the caffeine. But what I get are the sounds of Addison and Daniel carrying from the kitchen to the hallway.

I stop just outside the doorway, listening to Addison tell Daniel how she'll never leave him again.

"You promise?" Daniel's voice is soothing and there's a smile that's hidden in his voice; I can see in my mind the exact smile that would play at his lips.

"I don't want to run away anymore." Addison's voice is nothing but sincere. "Nothing will come between us, Daniel. If we can make it through that…"

My cheek rests on the outside of the doorway as I listen to them, feeling the love between them that's always been there.

I can't help but feel a pang of jealousy and to wish it were that easy for Carter and me.

"Then marry me." Daniel's response makes my eyes widen and suddenly I feel like an intruder. Not at all like a friend or family. I'm only an eavesdropper who needs to go away and not stain their memory, even if they don't realize it.

Her voice is soft as she tells him yes between quick kisses I can hear even as I push away from the doorway. Turning around, I feel nothing and everything all at once. Jealousy and happiness. Emptiness from knowing I'll never have what they share, and a sense of completion for accepting it.

Is this what it feels like to completely break down?

With a single deep breath, my eyes closed and my muscles tight, I take a step forward only to be hit by the heat of a hard body as I walk forward.

My pulse quickens when I open my eyes.

"Lost?" Carter's voice isn't muted like my footsteps were, and I can hear Addison and Daniel come out from the kitchen and into the doorway to the hall.

My body's stiff, and it takes a moment for me to even gather the courage to look over my shoulder at them.

I don't belong here. It's never been more apparent to me. I shouldn't be here.

"Aria," Addison's quick to call out for me, but I can't even stand to look at her knowing we couldn't be any further apart in what we're feeling right now. She doesn't need me dragging her down, ruining this special moment for her, and there's nothing she can give me in this moment that I would accept.

"I'm good," I say and barely turn to look over my shoulder at the only friend I have in here. With my hand raised, she stops where she is. "Please." The single word is a plea for her to leave me alone, and she listens.

Stepping around Carter, I leave them as quick as I can. I only glance back once to see Daniel holding Addison's wrist as she stares at me with tears in her eyes. Carter's gone; where to? I don't know, and I don't care.

I've never felt so torn in my life.

I knew life would never be easy for me. Not with the man my father is. But I never imagined I'd fall in love with the enemy. So much so that I would be here with him, willingly, while my family mourns deaths committed by his hand. Or that I would be mourning the loss of a love that never should have been.

So what does that make me?

Who does that make me?

CHAPTER 6

WAR STOPS FOR NO ONE.

Death never waits.

"Each wing is secure and the repairs are underway, sir," Aden tells me with a nod of his head as he stands outside of Jase's office in his wing. Most of the damage was done to Declan's wing, but everything is salvageable.

"What's the timeline?" I ask Aden. He's a new guard, one of a dozen. When the death toll came in, we lost more men than I thought originally. Right now we're keeping everyone close, but it's only temporary; it's just until we get eyes on both Romano's men and Talvery's. Jett's taking care of that with a small crew. Everything's waiting on him. But I fucking hate waiting.

"Two weeks tops until everything is replaced," he answers and I give him a nod, effectively dismissing him before walking into Jase's open door and closing it behind me.

Jase's office is nothing like mine. There's not a single book. There's no desk either. I only refer to it as an office because he does. The fireplace is almost always lit though, and flames reflect off of the mirrored coffee table in front of it. The mirrored surface has a thick patina that's developed over time. I guess Jase prefers it that way, or he'd polish it.

The shelves that line the wall to the right hold the rare antique weapons he collects. Mostly swords and knives. The ancient feel they have and their crude primitive backgrounds are at odds with the clean lines of the rest of the room. Overall, the aesthetic is modern and barren.

"How is she?" Jase asks me. His gaze stays on the fire until I take the seat next to him on the sleek, black leather sofa. It's only then that he looks up at me.

I don't answer him, the words fighting with my emotions in the back of my throat.

"That bad?" he asks, and I only nod.

The fire crackles in front of us while I sit with my brother, remembering how we got here nearly a decade ago. When I was only a kid, left at death's doorstep and wishing for it to come quickly. Jase is the one who made the first move. He killed each of the men who grabbed me from the street corner. He was fueled by anger alone, but when I recovered and learned what he'd done, I knew there would be far more death before that anger would be allowed to leave him.

One by one, we killed, we stole, we ruled with a fear we once had for others.

But fear has a way of changing you. And I would be a liar to say I wasn't motivated by it now.

I'm afraid I'm going to lose the only woman worth fighting for. The only woman I'm capable of loving.

The thick leather groans as Jase leans back, rubbing his thumb over his jaw and tells me, "It'll be all right when this is over. She'll be all right in time."

"Or she'll be consumed by anger," I say and give him a knowing look, but the expression on his face doesn't waver.

"She loves you," is his only response.

I break his gaze to stare at the fire, wondering how long it'll take for a flame so high and hot to burn down to nothing but ash and smolder.

"I didn't come to talk about her."

"It's all about her, isn't it?" he questions and my chest tightens. If I could go back to that moment and tell him not to fight for revenge, if I could go back and instead take my brothers and leave that horrid place, I would. I'm not proud of who we've become and I know it's because of me.

"You know what I mean," I tell him rather than lying to him and pretending I didn't get us into this shit because of a sick need to have Aria to myself.

"What did you come to talk about then?" Jase asks and then lays his head back. He picks up a knife from the table and plays with the blade between his fingers.

"What do you want to do from here?" I ask him. The fight in me is subdued and he can see it. I'm certain everyone can. I've never felt so weak in my life.

"I say we wait," he offers, staring into the roaring fire. The flames dance in the darkness of his eyes.

"We could hit them now… Let the streets run with blood," I suggest to him, knowing the day is coming soon. That's how this works. The winner takes the final blow.

"Two reasons. The first is that Sebastian is coming back."

Sebastian. My initial reaction to hearing that he's coming back is nothing I expected. I feel as if I've failed him. I'm ashamed for him to come back and see me like this. Ever since Aria came here, I've messaged him to keep him apprised. He's been my confidant ever since he had the safe house built. He's anchored me more than once. And he knows about Aria, and how badly we've fallen.

"When?" I ask and have to clear my throat after.

"He'll be here tonight, although he's going to his estate and the safe house first to see the damage."

A grunt leaves me before I ask, "He hasn't seen the extent of the damage yet, has he?"

I didn't want to believe it hurt as much as it did when he left. Over time the pain eased. But I can't deny that the memory of him leaving and then not coming back for so long fucking kills me. He was family. He still is.

"Not yet," Jase answers evenly and then adds, "Chloe isn't coming for a while."

"That's understandable," I say absently. Deep in the back of my mind, I always knew he stayed away because of three reasons:

Chloe never wanted to be here.

Romano would have him killed if he still had the power to do so.

Marcus.

When Marcus approaches people, they tend to do his bidding and then move far, far away. My brothers and I are the only ones who seem to have defied that pattern.

It's quiet as the wood splits in the roaring fire and specks of ash fly in the heated air.

"You said there were two reasons?" I remind Jase, waiting on the other reason we shouldn't destroy what's left of Talvery.

"Her father retreated," he tells me, still running his fingers along the blade as he leans back in the chair. He's simply waiting for war. I'm the reason my brothers were pulled into this life, and I fucking hate myself for it.

I hate that he refers to Talvery as "her father" just as much.

"He has to leave eventually. He can't hide forever."

"Until he does, we wait?" Jase asks and I can only nod. Every day this war lasts is a day longer that I have Aria so close, yet unreachable.

"You don't often come to me for advice," Jase comments and I don't respond for a moment.

"I'm tired," I tell him honestly, but I don't tell him everything else. How all I can think about is what I'll be when she leaves me. I'll be the shell of a man waiting to die, the way Jase is waiting for this war.

His gaze burns into me, but he doesn't press me for more. Maybe he already knows.

"Talvery called as well."

My head whips to his and my brows pinch together in both shock and anger at his admission. "When? Why didn't-"

"Just now, before you came in." I try to interrupt him, pissed off that I wasn't told, but Jase continues, "He only wanted to know one thing and then he hung up."

"And you told him what he wanted to know?" My blunt fingernails dig into the soft leather of the armrest.

"He wanted to know if Aria was still alive. If she was okay." He speaks evenly, staring into the fire before looking at me when I ask, "What did you tell him?"

"The truth."

I have to bite my tongue when I nearly ask him what truth he told Talvery. Because I know she's not okay. There's nothing about either of us that's okay.

CHAPTER 7

Aria

I'LL NEVER FORGET THE FIRST FIGHT I HAD WITH NIKOLAI. AS I SIT IN MY HIDEAWAY room, staring at the beautiful wallpaper in front of me with a blank canvas at my feet and a stick of unused chalk in my hand, I remember how I screamed at him and how he screamed back at me.

It was a quarrel of young love. But it was also the beginning of the end and we both knew it.

He'd taught me to shoot that day, letting me fire his gun. He was only seventeen and I was sixteen. I'd begged him to let me fire it. I wanted to know what it felt like and he told me he shouldn't, and that I would never need to know anyway.

I can't explain how angry it made me, but it didn't matter, because he moved behind me as we stood in front of the forest behind my home. His chest pressed against my back and his hands held mine as he taught me how to fire it.

The gun kicked back, but he held it steady in my hands. I remember the heat that spread through me when he asked me how it felt, whispering the question in my ear. We'd been seeing each other late at night, nearly every night for a while.

I knew he cared for me, but he hadn't said those three words to me that I'd confessed to him.

I peeked over my shoulder, and his lips were right there, so close to mine. I stared at them for a moment and thank God I did, because that's the moment my father stormed out of the house.

I tore myself away from Nikolai before he even saw my father.

That night we didn't fight over the gun, or whether or not I should learn how to fire one. We fought because he wanted to end what we had. He said my father would never allow it.

We fought because I wanted to run away with him, but Nikolai refused. Deciding it was better to stay where we were and to stop seeing each other, rather than to take the risk to leave and keep what we had.

He didn't want to be seen with me again, and that's why I screamed. He was all I had, and he knew it. It hurt me deeply, although I understood why he didn't want my father to find out. The second I showed him my pain, he took it away.

Nikolai kissed it away and said he would make it better. That he was doing it all for me, and one day I'd see. It took time for me to get used to not having him. And every time I cried, every time I needed him, if only for a moment, he came to me.

He never told me he loved me until after I'd gotten over what we had and only considered him a friend. But I knew he did before he told me. Because when you love someone, you can't stand to see them in pain.

Carter's not like that, though. He's not a man to soothe or be soothed. He's the type who puts his thumb inside of a raw gunshot wound and pushes harder. That's the kind of man Carter is.

There's no kissing away my pain with Carter. He wants me to live in it, because he lives in his. To stand by his side means to revel in the agony, and more so, to rule in it.

The knock at my door startles me. It's soft and although I wish it were Carter on the other side, I already know it's not.

Carter's not the type to knock so gently, either.

"Yes?" I call out from behind the closed door.

"It's me." Addison's voice carries through the door and I have to take a steadying breath before I can answer her.

My eyes are tired and burn from lack of sleep as she walks in.

"How did you know I was here?" I ask her and only then do I hear how hoarse my voice is.

As I sit up on my pile of pillows and look around, I realize how pathetic this looks. How pathetic *I* look.

"Daniel told me," she says softly, with a smile that doesn't quite reach her eyes. She looks around awkwardly for only a brief second before coming to sit with me on my makeshift bed.

I want to tell her that I'm happy for her, for what I overheard. I want to hug her and confide in her that I already know the good news, although it was an accident. I want to do many things, but Addison came with a purpose and she doesn't give me a chance to speak first.

I'm grateful for that because seeing her makes me anxious and awkward, given the circumstances.

"When I first moved here… well," she pauses and clears her throat, then continues, "close to here, when I moved to Crescent Hills, I had no one."

I pull my legs into my chest and lean my back against the wall as I watch her sit cross-legged. There's a small pile of plush throw blankets folded next to me and she takes the palest pink one, a soft chenille, and pulls the blanket up around her.

"I know what that's like," I tell her and she shakes her head no.

"I was an orphan," she tells me with her voice cracking and I'm taken aback.

"I had no idea."

"I don't look like an orphan?" she raises her brow and jokes, but the accompanying small laugh is sad. "I don't talk much about it, you know?" I nod as she talks, and I try to imagine what that was like.

"Anyway, I moved between a few different families and the one here was okay; it wasn't any better than the others in a lot of ways. They didn't care about me, they just got paid to keep me alive, you know?" Addison chews on her bottom lip for a moment and I can't help but wonder why she's telling me all this. She takes in a heavy breath and looks me dead in the eye. "I stayed because of Tyler."

"Tyler?" A freezing sensation sweeps across my skin at hearing his name. It feels as if I know the Cross brother who died. I've dreamed of him, and the words he gave Addison in her dream haven't left me.

"All of us grew up poor, and so he didn't judge me, not like the other kids at school. His father was an alcoholic, and his brothers were… well, they did what they had to in order to survive. And it scared me sometimes. But he loved me, and I loved him in a lot of ways. I also realized I loved his brother—I loved Daniel more, even if we were nothing back then. I hardly spoke to Daniel at the time." Tears cloud her vision and she brushes them away. "The Cross boys, they protected me, they looked out for me in a way no one had. Including Carter." She lets the tears fall and sniffles before telling me, "I swear to you, there's so much good in there."

She licks her lower lip, gathering the tear that lingers there and it's then I realize she thinks I'm not okay because I want to leave. Because I don't love Carter.

"I know there is," I tell her and she waits for more. For the "but" that isn't going to come from me. "I love him and I love this family." Emotions spill from me, emotions I wish I could bury deep down inside until I can't feel them anymore. "I want to be a part of this family more than you could ever know."

She tilts her head and gives me a look, and I actually crack a smile. "Well, maybe you do know." I sniff and look at the ceiling to keep from tearing up at the thought of being a part of this family, a family who has protected me and has loved me. Even if they are … the men they are.

"So you do love him?" she asks and reaches out to me, laying a hand on my knee. "You forgive him?"

I nod my head, knowing it's true. Both statements are so true.

"He doesn't forgive me." I tell her the truth that burns a hole in my chest. I have to reach into the pocket of the sleepshirt so I can pull out a few of the loose pearls from the necklace I used to wear. The beads click together softly in my hand as I tell her, "He doesn't trust me and he's not going to show any mercy, not to me or to anyone."

"I wanted to come in here and tell you something. Something that's scaring me, Aria." Addison's voice drops and her eyes darken with an intensity I haven't seen from her before.

"Go ahead," I tell her in a whisper, feeling the temperature of my blood drop. She rubs her palms on her jeans as she breathes out slowly.

"I went to Tyler's grave." Tears gather in her eyes the same way clouds do as a storm threatens, slowly and with an impending necessity. "There were so many forget-me-nots." She looks past me, to the window that's covered in beautiful linens, yet locked and will never open. I doubt she knows that little fact though. Her gaze stays there as she tells me, "I brought two packets of seeds with me before I left, and I scattered them all around his grave." Her eyes drift to mine. "It's nothing but a field of blue and white now," she tells me and a chill flows down my spine. An odd sense of déjà vu pricks its way deeper into my bones.

She lets out a steadying breath and shakes her head gently. "I've been dreaming of him since we came back. It's the same dream, Aria."

I remember a dream that's come and gone since I first got here. Since the first week I was locked in the cell in this place, but it's not what she describes.

"Tyler keeps telling me to remind you. Hold him tight. Don't let go… or else he'll die."

In the depths of my being, I know Carter needs someone to love him and someone he can love in return. He's a man in pain, a beast trapped in a castle of his own making. I'm just not convinced that I can be that woman.

Or that he'll let me close enough to be that woman.

"I know," I tell her truthfully. "But it's not all up to me."

"Try," she begs me. "Please, just try to hold on to him."

I swallow my heart, which has traveled all the way up to my throat, and only nod. She has no idea how much I wish I could.

CHAPTER 8

Carter

Last night she stayed in her room. The one I'm not supposed to go in. I sat by the door and listened to her cry softly. I don't know how much more of this I can take.

My thumb taps on the desk as I stare at the box. She fixed it. She did it. Not me. She didn't ask, and she doesn't know what it does to me. Part of me wants to rip it out. The other part is hoping it means something. Something beyond what I'm capable of controlling.

Knock, knock. The gentle rap at the door disturbs my thoughts. It's early. I've already met with Aden and Jase. We know where every enemy and ally is, and what they're planning. There's nothing to do but wait for Romano to lay Talvery to rest. He'll lose men doing it, but my side has lost enough. And I informed him of exactly that. His options are limited.

Knock, knock. She knocks again and I have to clear my throat, feeling the roughness at the back as I straighten in my chair and call for her to come in.

The door opens slowly, revealing Aria to me with sleep still in her eyes. Her hair flows down her bare back in waves, and the only thing she's wearing is a thin, black silk nightie with the white pearls draped down her breasts. My cock instantly hardens as she takes a single careful step in, quietly walking on the balls of her feet until she turns and shuts the door with her back to me.

"You look… breathtaking," I say, the words falling from my lips.

Her head turns first, bringing with it the sway of her hips, the gentle swing of her hair around her shoulders and those beautiful eyes that toy with my emotions. Her lips tip up, pulling into a feminine smile as a blush rises up her chest and climbs all the way to her temple. With her head tilted down, she peeks up at me through her lashes, brushing a stray lock from her face and murmurs, "That seems fitting … since you leave me breathless."

She takes deliberate but slow steps, so I know right where she's headed as she rounds the desk. I don't know why I turn off the monitors, shut my laptop and scoot the chair back, spreading my legs so she can easily climb into my lap. As she adjusts, her small hand slips to my groin and a muffled groan escapes my throat, rumbling my chest. Aria's eyes light with a playfulness, but also so much more. Her eyes always give me more than I deserve.

"I miss you," she whispers as her ass presses against my cock and she lies heavily against my chest. Her hair tickles my neck until she rests her cheek on my shoulder, and lazily presses a small kiss to my throat.

I have a small moment, a split second where I wonder if this is real or a dream. The tension is gone; the thoughts of what will come don't exist in this moment. She simply wants me, and I her. As her nails gently run down my throat, playing among the overgrown stubble, she swallows thickly and I have to wonder if the same thought has hit her as I see pain grow in her expression in the reflection on the black monitor in front of me.

"I didn't think you would come to me," I tell her quietly, and pluck at one of the pearls of her necklace, rolling it between my thumb and forefinger. She nuzzles against my shoulder and whispers in a sultry voice, "I thought you knew me better than that, Mr. Cross." The rough chuckle I give her in return shakes my chest, and along with it, her. Her breasts press against my chest, and I feel her nipples harden from the slight movement.

"I love you," she whispers and kisses my neck again, softer this time, leaving a touch of wetness behind. "There's nothing that could stop me from loving you. I tried. I can't stop," she tells me softly, lifting her head to look me in the eyes.

Instead of answering her, I cup her pussy in my lap, pressing my fingers against the thin silk that separates my hand from her hot entrance. She's damp immediately. Wet and hot for me.

As she reaches up to hold on to my shoulders instinctively, I maneuver my fingers around the fabric and press them inside of her. Her back arches and her breasts come closer to my face. I bend down just enough to gently nip the hardened peak of one nipple through the thin fabric, leaving a mark on her nightie.

She squeals in my embrace, jolting slightly, but she doesn't let go of me, she only clings tighter, her nails pressing deeper into my skin through the dress shirt.

"I want you," I breathe against her slender neck as I thrust my fingers in and out of her, moving some of the wetness up and down her cunt and then to her backside, around her tight hole. I need to make the other night right and fuck her there the way she needs.

"I love you," she tells me again in a strangled moan as I unzip my pants and reposition her to straddle me.

Again I don't say it back, and instead I crash my lips to hers, pressing them as deeply as I can as I shove my dick inside of her as swiftly as possible. With both of my hands on her shoulders, my forearms supporting her back, I slam her down, forcing her to scream into my kiss with an ecstasy I love to give her.

This I can give her. As much as she needs.

She's so fucking tight. Feeling her squeeze my cock with every thrust is something I don't deserve.

Her nails dig into my shoulders and she moans with each upward thrust. The soft sounds are short and come in muted gasps, urging me to push her higher and higher.

The air is hot but my skin is hotter as I feel her tighten around me. I'm close, but I don't want to get off. I don't want to take from her any more than I already have.

I can't breathe as I pound into her with a primal need to force the pleasure to rip through her, but she doesn't let go. She isn't breathing either as her head lolls back, her teeth digging into her bottom lip.

She's watching me as I watch her. With each slam of my hips I want to see her light up with unrelenting pleasure, but she shakes her head gently, barely able to speak as she whispers, "Not without you."

My grip on the flesh of her hip tightens, the threat of her holding back enraging a side of me. A part of my soul buried deep inside that wants nothing more than to give her everything.

With the back of my arm sweeping across the desk, I clear a spot for her, letting everything else crash to the floor so I can move her to lay flat on the desk. The laptop stays to one side, but the phone, the papers and journal with all the numbers, my cell—all that shit clatters to the floor. Her ass is hanging off the desk and my cock is still buried deep inside of her.

I'll make her cum. She won't refuse me.

I take a second, only a single fucking second to wrap her leg higher around my hip so I have the perfect angle to slam myself deep inside of her until she can't hold on any longer. So she'll shatter beneath me like I need her to. But in that second, her eyes widen and she reaches for me, her hand grabbing my shirt and fisting it as she leans up, her shoulders lifting off the desk. As she swallows, I see the plea in her eyes, and how tense her neck becomes.

"Please," she begs me as I hammer myself inside of her, forcing her head to be thrown back as her neck and back both threaten to arch. Even with my ruthless pace, she screams out for me to cum with her, to fall from the highest high and get lost in pieces beneath the world and the reality that plagues us.

"Carter," she moans my name and I cave. I pick up my pace and feel the tingle at the base of my spine. My toes curl and I let them.

As much as I know this won't last, I can't deny her. I won't do it. I love her too much, and that will be my downfall.

CHAPTER 9

Aria

IT'S A MIX OF HIM NOT SAYING HE LOVES ME, EVEN THOUGH I KNOW HE DOES, AND the way he leaves me after sex.

He left me panting and reeling on his desk, my nightgown torn and the pearls wrapped around me so tightly, I felt like they were holding me down. I was a mess, destroyed by him. And he left to clean up, taking his time without me to gather up his own pieces. Every second felt raw. Every moment another bit of reality intruded on the moment.

It reminds me of the time we had in his bathroom when I realized I'd missed my birthday and never went to see my mother. It feels like so long ago when we fought and fucked on the tiled floor. And when he stood, with his back to me and the look of regret clearly written on his face… I'll never forget the way it felt. And that's exactly what it feels like now.

Hold on to him, a voice whispers as the emotions try to strangle my throat. *Hold on to him.*

"I'm trying," I whisper.

"What?" Carter asks and I swallow the dry words, propping myself up on his desk even though I can feel moisture between my legs. I have to wad up the bottom of the nightgown, the bit that should cover my legs, and press it against myself to keep from making a mess. Carter only comes to help me down then. And only to help me down. The moment the balls of my feet hit the hardwood floors, he lets go of me.

I need someone to hold me too. My voice is weak as I answer him, "Nothing." The moment is broken and I feel it inside of me. The sharp edges of it dig into my chest and let the real world find its way back into my head.

Carter's gaze is like fire, burning into the side of my face as I turn away from him, the way he did to me just a moment ago.

"I need to go change." I offer up the excuse and then hate myself for it. I hate that I can pretend in the least that I'm all right.

My hair tickles my upper back as I turn to stare back at the man I love, the man whose love will kill me. With a shiver running down my shoulders and the coolness of his office replacing the much-needed heat I felt a minute ago, I tell him the truth. "It feels like you regret it almost every time you touch me now."

I have to swallow thickly after letting the words out. It is almost every time, isn't it? Each time since the safe house… he never came, not until now.

It's a slow change in his expression, as the slight concern morphs to indifference. To the mask he always wears. "Do you regret this?" I ask him. Before he can even answer, I push out more of the raw truth, saying, "I don't want to feel like this afterward. I don't want to feel…" I trail off as my hand reaches up to my chest and my fingers tangle around the strand of pearls, not knowing what the words are that accurately portray what I feel.

I feel like I lose him more and more when he does this after. But when I'm with him, truly with him, I'm whole. "I want you back." I whisper the words in a ragged voice drenched in despair.

"This isn't going to last." Those are the only words Carter gives me, but his expression says more. His steady gaze belies the hollow depths of his pain. Looking closer, the softness around his eyes shows just how tired he is, how vulnerable, even.

It's only then that tears prick, but still, I hold them back. Sorrow will do nothing for us. It only eats at the precious time we have left.

"Stop." I can only give him a single word before I have to take a steadying breath. I can feel myself breaking, but I won't. He must see it, but he doesn't come to me. He doesn't try to comfort me and I have to reach behind me, gripping the edge of the desk to brace myself.

"You said it yourself." Carter starts to give my own words back to me, and I have to look away from him, staring at the massive windows although I don't see anything at all. "You said you'd never forgive me, and we both know it's the truth and what I deserve."

With my fingers wrapping tight around the pearls, I speak calmly and aimlessly, "Such a reasonable gesture then, to pull away from me and not fight for me." On the last word, I turn to look at him. "Just end it then, send me back?"

Although it's a false threat, a cold chill creeps up my body. It slows everything—my breath, my pulse.

A tic in Carter's jaw starts to spasm as he turns away from me, leaning his hips against the desk and bracing himself on it as I am to look out toward the windows with me.

"The moment I heard your voice, I knew once I had you, I'd never let you go." His voice is low and full of solace. Inside I'm reeling with the ticking time bomb of the truth he doesn't know.

"Which moment?" I ask him.

I can't look at him, knowing what's about to spill from my lips. The revelation that could change everything. If ever there was a time to confess what I've been hiding, it's now, when there's nothing left to hold us together.

"When your father let me go. He let me live, and it's only because you called out."

"It wasn't me," I blurt out, and the words are dead on my lips, completely at odds with the emotion in his. I have to clear my throat and repeat my words when he says nothing at all. "I never knocked at the door. It wasn't me."

"I heard your voice," Carter starts to speak and even takes a half step closer to me, but I cut him off, and stare into his eyes as I confess.

"It wasn't me. I never went to that side of the house." My head shakes as my voice goes hoarse and I have to pause and swallow. My mother died on the floor directly above where my father worked. I never wanted to go back to that side of the house ever again after it happened. "I would have never told my father I needed him. I would have never interrupted his work." My heart clenches with unbearable pain at the look in Carter's eyes. "More than that, my father wouldn't have stopped what he was doing for me," I tell him a truth that causes the small part of me that still craves more love from my father to twist in pain. "It wasn't me you heard."

"You're lying," Carter speaks but there's no conviction.

"You know I don't need to lie to you." With a deep breath in and then a desperate one out, I tell him, "I love you, but if you only want me here because you wanted the girl who saved your life," bastard tears gather in my eyes but I refuse to let them fall as I swallow and continue, "if you only wanted some girl you've dreamed about…"

I can't continue as Carter's eyes narrow at me and his grip tightens on the desk behind him.

"I didn't want to tell you because I thought if you knew, you wouldn't want me anymore." A single tear falls, and I ignore it. "If you only wanted me because of that night, because you thought it was me, then let me leave." When I lick my dry lips, I taste the salt of more tears. Tears I refuse to acknowledge.

"It was never supposed to be me," I whisper as I wipe under my burning eyes and gaze at the bookshelf behind him. His own gaze is unreadable and unforgiving; the mask has slipped back into place.

"I don't believe you," he says and Carter's voice is low and threatening. With the cold air settling against my bare skin, I feel more exposed in this moment than I have in so long. "I know your voice. It was you."

My heart flickers as Carter moves a half step closer, his gaze sizing me up like when I was first in the cell.

"I'm not lying, Carter. It was never supposed to be me."

"I just don't know why you're lying." Carter continues as if I haven't exposed a truth that ruins everything he thought about me, every piece he both hated and loved before he even saw me.

"Stop calling me a liar." A small flame ignites inside of me as he stalks closer, invading my space and towering over me. My voice is firm, bordering on hard.

I can feel my eyes narrowing on his as he approaches so close I can feel the heat from his skin. The flames lick between us as he smirks at me, letting his gaze roam up and down my body.

"What did you think telling me that would accomplish?" he questions me. It's a fucking interrogation.

Rage burns in my blood. I have to quickly take in a deep breath to keep from snapping.

"I wanted to share something with you that would change things. Something that would sway the position you hold on how we've always been enemies and-"

He cuts me off and rebuts in a casual tone, "But our families have always been enemies."

His gaze is ever assessing. I'm the enemy in this moment. I'm a liar in his eyes.

"You're a fool to think I'd lie to you." My response comes with more pain than I imagined it would.

The smile that graces his lips doesn't hide his hurt. "Am I?"

"I'm not a liar." My hands clench at my sides and the emotions that crept up before crash into me suddenly, like rough waves at the shore. "And this was a mistake." I don't know if I mean telling him he's mistaken, not running when I could… or falling in love with him to begin with. Maybe all of it.

"It was all a mistake," I whisper to myself before looking back at Carter. At a version of him that's guarded and impenetrable while all I am is vulnerable to him. "I know that now." The realization is sobering.

I meet his gaze as I tell him, "I'm not who you think I am. I'm Aria Talvery and this was never supposed to happen."

With one of his palms braced on the desk, he lowers his gaze until we're eye to eye and his lips are close to mine. So close, and that side of me that wants nothing more than his affection begs me to take them with my own and silence whatever words he dares to speak. But I don't.

"You may be a Talvery, but you're on the wrong territory, little songbird." Backing away slightly, he searches for something in my expression before adding, "And even if you hate me, I won't be letting you go."

CHAPTER 10

IT WASN'T HER?

The fuck it wasn't her.

It's all I can think about as I lead her back to the bedroom. The sounds of our footsteps are heavy, but not as heavy as the beating of my pulse.

I know that night, I know her voice. That night, that moment even, changed my life forever. I know every detail. The cadence of her words. I've dreamed of them and been consumed by that moment for years.

The bedroom door closes with a resounding click as I walk to the dresser, where a new glass and bottle of whiskey wait for me.

I go through the motions, barely listening to her undressing and moving through drawers as I try to calm down.

It's an impossible task. Every second, the anger rises.

How dare she lie to me. How dare she look me in the eyes and deny something that led me down a path of violence and self-hate. How fucking dare she do that, yet claim to love me.

I've never hated how capable she is of affecting me more than I do in this moment.

I'll never tell her how much it hurts to hear her deny it. I refuse to let her know. I'll be damned if I ever give her that truth and that power.

As I breathe, the amber liquid flows between the cubes of ice. My grip on the tumbler is loose as I swirl it, but it's no use. I have no appetite for liquor tonight.

I want to punish her. It's all I can think about.

I've handled everything wrong because I've underestimated her, but now that she's shown her cards and revealed what lows she's willing to go to, I won't make that mistake again.

She was right. I should have clipped her wings.

"I don't know why you can't believe me," Aria speaks softly, so softly the rustling of the covers almost drowns out her words as she climbs into bed. Glancing over my shoulder, I watch as she pulls them up closer to her throat and looks back at me the way she always should have, as if I'm the enemy.

I bite down on my tongue to keep from replying as I breathe in through my nose heavily. I don't know why she'd lie about it. What motive is behind her lies?

My shoulders tense as I lean down to grab what's inside the top drawer of my dresser. The sound of it opening is ominous. The metal is cold in my hand as the cuffs clink together. While I walk to her, I think about how to cuff her, but the thought of touching her right now is dangerous. So fucking dangerous.

She casts a spell over me each and every time my skin touches her. I can't risk it.

I toss them on the bed as the thought hits me. "Cuff your left hand to the bedpost," I command her as I drag the chair in the corner of the room toward the bed, closer to her.

With my back to her, I wonder if she'll even obey me until the telltale snap of the closure echoes in the bedroom.

Only then do I breathe and sink down into the chair. I have her, and she's not going anywhere.

The light from the moon shines down on her soft skin in a way that makes my chest ache. She's so fucking beautiful. She brushes her chestnut locks away from her face and stares expectantly at me before resting back against the headboard.

"Are you just going to keep me here until the war is over and I hate you forever?" she asks when I don't say anything. Her voice is flat, but she can't hide the pain in her eyes. She can't hide that from me. Not when I've seen the raw agony the cell brought her, the torment killing Stephan gave her, and the sorrow loving me has stained into those gorgeous hazel eyes.

"That's not a bad idea," I remark, not hiding the exhaustion from my voice.

The huff that leaves her lips is humorless. She tries to get comfortable, but she's cuffed herself too high on the post. The cuff is between the middle and top rung, instead of at the bottom. She can reach the nightstand, where a bottle of wine and a glass from earlier lay, along with her cell phone. At least she can reach those, but nothing else is at her disposal.

Agitation quickly shows in her pursed lips as she props a pillow under her arm. Letting out a sigh, I lean forward, resting my elbows on my knees and stare her down. I wait for her to look at me to ask her, "Why lie?"

Fire smolders in her gaze as she pushes out the words, "It wasn't me."

Tick, tick. It's not the clock, it's the steady beat of my heart, on edge and wanting to know why she'd try to hurt me like she is.

"I have all the time in the world," I tell her and lean back. As I swallow, I realize how much it kills me, the very idea that it was someone else. "It was you," I say, hardening my voice, refusing to entertain the thought the voice that saved me belonged to another. I know it was Aria. Deep in my bones, I know it was her.

"I'm sorry, Carter." Aria's whisper is pained. She scoots closer to me on the bed and I watch as the cuff keeps her away from me. Fuck, I'm a goddamn wreck and she can see.

She could always see me though. Something about her simply knows who I am. Her soul knows mine.

"I didn't want to tell you," she whispers and I'm taken back to that night, to the pain, to the desperation to die.

"I wanted to die and you saved me," I tell her, knowing how true it is. It was her voice that called out to me as I felt the cold hand of death pull me closer to the ground. Not to a white light and salvation, but down to the dirty concrete floor. And I prayed for it to happen. I coveted nothing less than death to come to me and take the pain away. The torture I endured had destroyed any chance of peace and happiness a boy like me could ever have.

"I'm sorry," is again all she can say as emotion wells in my chest and then higher, up my throat.

"You're not," I speak through clenched teeth and hold on to the fact that she's lying. I know the voice that saved me. "You're a liar."

As Aria tries to wipe away her tears that have slid down her flushed cheeks, she brings her left hand up, only to have it held back by the cuff.

"And you'll stay right there until I'm done doing what I have to do." Standing abruptly, I watch her eyes widen. "You can stay there. Right there where you belong." My words are hollow, but the threat is real. I won't give her up so easily. If she thought lying to me would give her freedom from me, she thought wrong.

"Carter," Aria calls out and moves on the bed, the sheets falling around her body in a messy puddle, but her left arm is restrained behind her. Frustration joins the desperation in her eyes.

Her right hand moves to her left as if she could pry it free as I stalk to the door. "Carter!" She yells out my name to get me to stop as I stand in the doorway. I stare back at my songbird, naked on her knees in my bed, and chained to it willingly. A dull pink mark still shows on her breast from where I touched her earlier, right beneath the pearls that sway slightly down her front. She's a beautiful fucking vision. Beautiful, but wretched with sadness.

"Don't leave me here," she demands, as if she could, and then swallows visibly.

"You're not in a position to give the commands," is all I give her. I'm only able to take half a step out of the room before the shattering sound of glass at my right is accompanied by wetness along the right side of my cheek, my jaw, my neck and down my shirt. The dark red liquid seeps into my white dress shirt and I stare at the blotches, watching them spread over the fabric before looking back at Aria. The cracked bottle is in pieces at my feet, and there's a small dent in the drywall. It's surrounded by streaks of burgundy that are dripping down to the floor.

My heart races in my chest from shock, but also anger.

"Now you can't hide at the bottom of it." My words are spit with venom as control slips from me.

"Fuck you! I hate you!"

She screams it like she truly means it. Like her hate is the only thing keeping her alive, and I know that's what it is. I've been there. I hated her before she even knew my name.

"I knew you did. I know you hate me. It doesn't change that you're mine." I can't hide the lack of control, the unraveling of composure as I stare her down, watching her chest rise and fall with chaotic breathing.

"I won't let you do this to me," she speaks with conviction and the dry laugh that erupts from my lips is dark and genuine as I grip the doorknob to keep from approaching her.

"Fuck you!" she sneers as she rips her arm away from the bedpost. Not tugging, but yanking her wrist against the cuff. Pain echoes in her face and in the shriek that tears up her throat. My heart slams in my chest as I watch her do it again. And again. My body temperature drops and for a second I don't believe it. She wrenches her body away until a horrid scream comes from her lips. Tears stream down her face as her arm lays limp, and her wrist, still cuffed, is red and raw with cuts from the metal.

"Fuck you," she cries, her words low and full of suffering. She rips her arm away again, although this time she can only use the weight of her body and the action is done without conviction.

Fuck.

I'm too fucking weak for her. Her agony destroys any rational thought I have. I can't get to her quick enough, although I'm not thinking logically and I don't have the key. In an attempt to help, I grip her as gently as I can to push her back against the headboard to loosen the tension of the cuff, but Aria's hate is stronger than her reason.

Even with a dislocated shoulder, she shoves me with her uninjured hand. "Stay away," she screams at me with tears still falling freely. "Get away!" It's only when she tries to push me again that her body refuses to obey and she clutches at her shoulder.

"Aria," I start to say, ready to plead with her to be reasonable and let me help.

"I meant it, I hate you!" Her confession is sobering. Her face is red as she swallows down the pain and stares me straight in the eye. "You wanted me to be like this? To chain me up and make me pay? You can't go back. That's your thing, right?" She pauses for a moment to breathe and then backs up against the headboard, holding on to her shoulder and sniffling. "Well, you can't go back." Her breathing's unsteady and she speaks softer. "You did this. You made me hate you." Her face crumples with the last confessions. "This is what you wanted, and now you can have it."

The pain is numbing. It takes a minute and then another for me to even retrieve the key to uncuff her. She doesn't look at me at all while I put her shoulder back into place.

And when she sobs, I want nothing more than to hold her, but she pushes me away and lies on her side, her back to me and her injured shoulder in the air.

I've never hurt so much in my life.

I remember everything from that night years ago. And even that pain doesn't compare to this.

The whiskey is more than tempting this time and it goes down easy.

Each glass is easier than the last, and each brings the picture of our past to me like the way Aria paints. Each moment seems made up of beautiful strokes on her canvas. She could paint a painful past, yet make you desire to touch it with the masterful way her brush moves when she's creating art.

For the longest time, all I see are the moments we've had together.

The next glass brings out my jealousy. And the thought of sending Nikolai a video of me fucking Aria and showing him how much she loves it.

She brings out a possessive side of me I've never known. She makes me lose my control. She ruins everything, but she's the reason for it all.

She's mine.

That's the only thing that matters.

I would never do it; I'd never let a man like Nikolai see her cum. He had a chance with her, and he lost it. I fucking refuse to lose her like he did. I won't let it happen.

At the thought, the tumbler slams down on the desk. For a moment, I think I've broken it.

I haven't, but the whiskey is humming in my veins and knowing that, I push the glass away from me.

I get down on my knees, feeling lightheaded as I pick up all the shit I threw down from my desk earlier so I could have her. Placing the last few items where they belong, I let my hand rest where her lower back rested only hours ago. The hard chestnut is bitter cold and nothing like her warmth.

My gaze falls to the polaroid pictures laying haphazardly on top of a stack of papers. Pictures I brought out days and days ago to show Aria. Pictures of the house she says is so familiar. And one of them has my father and mother on the porch.

He loved her. Anyone who looked at them could see it. My father loved her with everything he had.

When she died a slow, slow death, he died with her.

I never learned how to love, only how to survive.

Maybe that's what Aria's been doing. Thinking on the past makes me reach for the tumbler again. The liquid burns as I swallow more down in large gulps and remember how she lay on the sofa in the corner of my office that first time.

She was so tired, but well fed and well fucked. The effects of what I'd done to her were still evident. Her skin lacked color and her ribs still poked through her flesh.

I did this to her. I put her in this position to simply survive.

That day she lay on the sofa, she slept off and on. Each time she woke startled and terrified until I went to her. I calmed her. I took her nightmares away.

Tears prick in the back of my eyes as I struggle to breathe. Yes, I hurt her, but I took it all away. All the pain, all the fear.

I thought it counted for more than it did.

As she slept that first day, I couldn't do a damn thing but watch her and every small movement of her body. I remember every inch of her frame. I've never felt so sickened by who I am like back then.

But I tried to take it all away.

My elbows slam down harder than I wanted on the desk as I rest my forehead in my hands and let out a heavy sigh, burdened by all the sins I've committed against Aria Talvery.

It's too much. Tonight has been too much.

I search the top right drawer for the small vial of sweets, but I don't find it. The papers are scattered by the time I'm done, but I don't care. When I slam it shut, the one below opens and I pull it ajar to find what I'm looking for right on top.

I know the liquor will numb me enough to sleep, but I never sleep long and tonight I need it. With a full vial, I swallow it all and when a moment passes and sleep doesn't come, I grab another vial and take more of the drug.

My legs are heavy as I move to the sofa she slept in and lie in her place.

I don't know if I would take it all back. I don't know how I can ever have her. All I wanted was her, and I still do. I can't help it. All I want is for Aria to be mine.

I hear her shuddering breath first. And when I lift my gaze from the floor beneath the desk to her flushed cheeks and then those gorgeous eyes, I feel a weight lifted from me.

Like the pain doesn't exist anymore. Because she's crawling to me. She's coming to me. My songbird.

"Are you still angry?" I ask and my voice feels rough, as if it's been unused for a long time. I can feel my brow pinch in confusion at the thought, and it's then that I realize I feel cold. So cold.

None of it matters when Aria shakes her head. The messy hair around her face lets me know she's been sleeping here in this room. She was waiting for me to wake up.

"I'm not angry." Her voice is soft as she reaches me, but the tears don't stop. My fingers splay in her hair as I cup my hand behind her head and pull her closer to me. I don't even remember what the fight was about when I touch her. Nothing else matters when I touch her. She clings to me, her hands on my thighs as she lifts up her lips and kisses me.

With her lips to mine, everything feels right again and the pain doesn't exist. Not until I feel the wetness from her tears on my face and she shudders in my grasp, pulling away to whisper, "Please forgive me."

It takes me a moment, the haze of the whiskey dulling my thoughts as I struggle to remember tonight. How she lied, how she said it wasn't her.

"Why did you lie?" I ask her, but she doesn't answer. She only pleads for me to forgive her.

Her voice is wretched as she says, "You never told me that you did and after so long … please, Carter. Please forgive me."

My head pounds with a pain that comes from drinking too much and it takes me a minute to register what she's said. I ask her, "What do you mean 'after so long?'"

She feels so right in my arms, and neither of us are willing to let go, but I feel so dizzy. So cold and confused. The room tilts suddenly. "Fuck," I say, the word stretched in the air and the room tilts again, as if it's trying to make me fall.

"It's been so long since I've seen you," Aria tells me as she touches her fingertips to my face ever so gently. She sniffles and adds, "Since I've gotten to talk to you."

"I just saw you." It's all I can manage to say, but Aria doesn't seem to hear me.

"I love you so much," she says, and her bottom lip wobbles when her eyes find mine. "Please tell me you forgive me. I need it, Carter." She pulls at my hand, holding it in both of hers and cradling my hand to her chest.

"Stop crying," I tell her, trying to breathe but feeling the air become thinner. It's like I'm suffocating. Something's wrong.

I don't want to take my hand away from her, but I need to reach for my collar. I can't fucking breathe. It's then, when I think about moving my hand, that I feel how cold she is against my knuckles. And how still her chest is. And how pale she is.

"Aria." Her name is whispered, but I don't know if I've said it. The chill seeps into my blood. She's not breathing.

"Carter, no. No," she tells me as if she knows what I'm thinking. "It was supposed to end like this. I could never be in the middle of war. I was always going to be the one to die."

What is she saying? No! I scream but there's no sound that escapes from my mouth. The room is silent, save her plea to me. "It's okay. When it happens… I'm okay dying for you. I just need you to forgive me, please. Forgive me and love me, as I love you. I'll always love you."

The prick at the back of my neck flows down every inch of my skin. The room darkens and I still can't breathe. I can't think. She can't be dead. Aria! I scream again, but it's silent.

"We don't have much time. Please, please, Carter. Forgive me." Her eyes search mine as I scream and it's then she sees my mouth moving but there's no sound.

She yells something at me as the distance between us stretches, but her voice is gone.

Aria! I scream her name, reaching for her and holding on to her cold hands with every *ounce of strength I have. Don't leave me! I forgive you! I pray she hears me but all she does is cry as the darkness invades every sense I have.*

The gasp that fills my chest sends a pain spiking down my back and I fall off the sofa and onto the hard floor of the office. I'm sweating and my heart is beating wildly in my chest.

My elbow scrapes against the floor as I struggle to get up fast enough.

"Aria!" I scream out, even though there's no way for her to hear me. "Aria!" It's all I can say as I run to her, to my bedroom and throw the door open to find her small form in bed. It's not enough. I can't swallow, I can't breathe, I can't do anything until I yank the covers back and see her chest rise and fall. She moans a small protest in her sleep from the cold, but even still, I lay my hand against her chest, right where it was moments ago, but there's warmth and the steady beat of her heart.

There's a suffocating lump in my throat at the sight of her. Still alive and still here with me. I fall to my knees beside her before covering her with the sheets again.

She doesn't stir from her sleep, and a glance at the nightstand reveals a bottle of pain-killers she must have found in the bathroom. It makes sense, given her arm. She's passed out after taking the last two pills I had. But she's here, and she's alive.

It was only a dream. But it felt so fucking real. I struggle to breathe on the floor beside her and even worse, I struggle to get the vision of her out of my head.

I won't sleep until this is over.

I've never hated myself more. I don't care if she lied. I don't care if those words didn't come from her. I've never loved anything or anyone in this life like I do her, the Aria I know, the woman who I know loves me in return. The girl I took and broke, then placed the splintered pieces back together as best I could.

I won't let her die.

Aria Talvery, my songbird, can't die.

CHAPTER 11

Aria

There's so much pain when I wake up, I feel sick. Literally sick to my stomach as I roll onto the wrong side, my left side, and a screaming pain shoots down my back and then travels up the front of me.

Seething through my clenched teeth, my eyes open wide as I bolt awake in the late morning and I struggle not to vomit.

I wish I could say I was drunk when I lost my shit last night. That's exactly what I did. I have lost all composure when it comes to this man.

It takes me a long time, longer than it should, to realize I'm alone in the bedroom. I expected to see him on the chair watching me, or in bed. I'm not sure why I expected it. I shouldn't have. He's never here in the morning. But we've never been like this before. So broken and each of us hurting the other.

We aren't throwing stones; we're tipping boulders over a steep cliff while the other lies helplessly in the dirt below.

I chose him. I wanted to be with him, and he's choosing to make me feel so fucking alone. The thin top sheet gathers in my hands as fists form and I struggle to hold back the pain from everything.

Waking up alone hurts more than it ever has before. I don't want to be alone anymore. I don't want to be hurting. I don't want to be the cause of Carter's pain either. And I think that's all I'll ever be. After last night, I don't know how I could ever be anything but a painful reminder to him.

Cradling my sore shoulder, I sit up on the bed and let my legs hang off the side as I test out my arm. It hurts like a bitch, but it's my own damn fault. The deep gouges in my wrist are worse though.

The floor's cold under my bare feet as I make my way to the bathroom in search of more painkillers and something I can use to clean the cuts. I don't find either, but I get ready, thinking about the bathroom located off the foyer. I bet there's some in there.

All the while I brush my teeth, I stare at myself in the mirror. As I brush my hair, my reflection does the same, watching the woman I am. There's not an ounce of happiness. There's nothing but darkness.

I read in some article a while back, that pets start to look like their owners because they learn to mimic their facial expressions. It's the same with adopted children resembling parents who aren't biological. The more time spent with someone, the more you inherit their features.

And as I stare at myself, all I see is the darkness that is Carter. The brewing pain deep inside. It inhabits me in a way I hadn't seen before.

The room is silent as I turn off the water and carefully set my brush on the granite counter.

None of this belongs to me. None of it is mine.

Every piece was a gift, comfort items meant to placate me. With a step back, it's hard to swallow. With a peek up in the mirror, it's hard to withstand the sight.

It's never been more clear to me that I need to leave than in this moment. Carter Cross is a drug I'll never kick. A drug that's seeped into my veins and wrapped its way around every small piece of me.

I'm addicted to what he does to me and he'll just continue to hurt me. He knows how much he hurts me, as do I, and yet here I am.

When I turn my back, it feels like someone else is there, someone behind me. The girl in the mirror maybe. She's watching me and it sends pricks down my neck as I slowly leave the bathroom, too cold and disturbed to dare shut the door.

Even as I dress, slowly and with a searing burn every time I have to move my left shoulder, I stare at the bathroom as if somewhere deep inside, a part of me is waiting for a person to leave it.

I can't shake this feeling. Not until I leave the bedroom. At least for a moment.

It feels too empty as I walk alone to the foyer bathroom. I'm hollow inside with the wretched truth so clear in my mind.

Leaving someone who hurts you shouldn't feel like this. Like you're losing a part of your soul. As if inside, there's a fissure that's expanding, and as it does, it's damaging whatever it is that makes a person alive. Whatever makes me feel is being scarred with every step I take.

Because the closer I get to the front door, the more I want to leave and never look back.

I could never, even for a second, look behind. I can already imagine his face and the way he'd look at me if I left him.

I can *feel* his pain.

As I round the corner, I'm careful to contain my emotions so I don't break down again.

With a quick intake of air, I stiffen the moment I look ahead of me, straight at the open bathroom door.

Even my heart stills, not wanting me to be heard or seen.

Addison doesn't see me as she pulls her hair into a ponytail. She's in her head, I know she is. I can practically see the wheels spinning as she walks down the right hall, past the bathroom.

It's only when she's out of sight that I even dare breathe.

I still don't move though. My limbs don't allow it.

How did I let my life come to this? Where I'm afraid to see the only friend I'm able to interact with because ... because why? Because I'm ashamed, and scared, and miserable with who I am and the choices I've made, and I can't tell her any of that... because she's on the side of the enemy.

That fissure deep inside of me, the one destroying everything in its path, rips me wide fucking open as I walk as quietly as I can to the small half bath and close the door.

The click sounds like the loudest thing I've ever heard as I sit down on the toilet and cover my face with my hands.

I feel hot and immediately I have the urge again to vomit as I reach up and my shoulder sends a bolt of pain down my back. *Fuck!*

I bite down on the inside of my cheek so hard, I can taste the metallic tang of blood. It was worth it not to scream though. Still, I want to scream so badly. I want to get all of this out of me.

I'm stronger than this, but it feels like there's something inside of me that's falling apart in a way where I know it will never be whole again.

There's a line in one of my favorite stories from *Alice in Wonderland*, that goes something to the effect of, there's no use to going back to yesterday, you're a different person than you were then.

I hate that line now. I used to love it. I could have lived by that sentiment, feeling purposeful and fulfilled. Right now? The very idea of that quote forces me to jump off the toilet seat so I can hurl what little I have inside of me into the bowl.

It's fucking disgusting. The taste, the smell, the burning feeling. And when I'm done, while I'm washing my mouth out with the running water, I don't feel any better at all.

Deep breaths get me through cleaning it all up. It's when I'm searching under the sink for a new hand towel to replace the one I used to wipe my mouth that I see the box of pregnancy tests.

Addison.

"Oh my god." The words leave me in a whisper and for the first time this morning I smile. It's only a hint of one, but now I have a light that's growing, if dim. She's pregnant. I fall down on my ass and lean against the wall as I hold the box of pregnancy tests and wonder what she's feeling and thinking. She's going to have a baby. And what a wonderful mother she'll be. I know she will.

The light inside of me is quick to fade though as I realize she didn't tell me. But maybe there's nothing to tell. The thick wrapper on the test I pull out crinkles in my hand and I think back to my last period... before all of this started.

The days have faded and with the shot Carter gave me, I never considered any other reason for not getting my period.

I'm constantly tired, irritated and emotional, and now sick. Sick to my stomach. But sick and tired would also describe anyone in my situation. Still, a heated wave of anxiousness rolls through me until I move to take the test.

Tick.

Tick.

Time passes and my thoughts run wild.

Tick.

Tick.

Time passes as the turmoil and sickness subside, leaving a dust to settle and a clear picture to form.

Tick.

Tick.

I don't know how long I sit there holding the box.

Or how long I wonder if it's worthless. If all of this is worthless.

I don't need a friend. I don't need someone to love me either.

I need to get the fuck out of here.

CHAPTER 12

I CAN'T GET THE SOUND OF HER PLEADING FOR ME TO FORGIVE HER OUT OF MY HEAD. The words are etched inside of me, ricocheting around the walls of every room I enter. Exactly how her words years ago followed me, but these pleas are haunting in a way I've never felt.

It was too real.

Even though I'm in my desk chair, waiting on my brothers, I can't stop staring at where she was last night. I'm still staring at the spot when the door opens and that's when I glance at the monitor, expecting to see Aria sleeping, but she's already up and getting dressed.

I don't know who's come in, but I start talking anyway. "We need to call the doctor." I let the air in my lungs leave me before seeing Jase and Declan walk in and each take a seat. Jase sits easily in the chair in front of the desk on the right. Declan leaves the one on the left, presumably for Sebastian or Daniel.

Sebastian got in late last night to his place, where he slept, going against what I recommended, and he's on his way here now. I need him here. I need my friend to help me figure out what's wrong with me.

Declan leans against the bookshelf, slipping his phone into his pocket and letting his head fall back against the wooden slat to ask me, "The doctor?"

His brow is pinched and I take a moment to really look at him. He's aged so much in the last few years.

I can hear Daniel's heavy steps sounding down the hall as I nod at Declan, feeling my throat getting tighter even though I attempt to relax and lean back into my chair. "Aria hurt her shoulder last night."

The pain in my chest radiates. "Last night was difficult." I can't look my brothers in the eyes, and Daniel walks in just then. The door closes quietly as I peek back to the sofa I slept on last night and then to Daniel, who asks for the time.

"We have six minutes," Jase answers him and quickly gets back to me and my lost thoughts. "What'd she do?" he asks me.

Shame is bitter. It tastes so fucking bitter.

"Is she all right?" Declan asks, and Daniel is quick to ask what's wrong as he takes the left seat across from my desk.

"Aria hurt her shoulder last night is all. She's fine," I say. It's a lie and with how silent the room is, my brothers know it too. I can't tell them what happened though. I can barely stand to look at myself, knowing what happened last night.

"Five minutes." Jase breaks the silence, lifting his arm to check his watch. The light glints off the shiny metal and I welcome the distraction. I wish I hadn't brought it up at all, but I'm not used to hiding anything from my brothers.

"When we're done, I'll handle that, but this call will hopefully give us something."

"Just so you know, we gave the last case of guns to Romano and pulled everyone."

"So they have everything they wanted?" Daniel clarifies with Jase at the news, and Jase nods.

We've been involved enough, and Talvery doesn't have the men to threaten us anymore.

"Good," Declan remarks, "Let the two of them kill each other."

My grip tightens on the smooth leather of the armrest as I stare at Jase and tell him, "All I want is to keep them all away from here." He nods easily at first, in complete agreement but when he looks back at me, his expression becomes more serious. "No one gets close," I say, and my voice hardens, thinking about keeping Aria safe. I won't let her die.

"Of course," Jase tells me, his gaze searching my face for what's changed since I last spoke to him yesterday about pulling everyone. I know I'm still shaken and out of everyone, I know Jase can tell something's off.

I'm saved from his inquisition as the door opens, and Sebastian comes in. His hair is longer, his scruff now a short and neatly trimmed beard. His eyes have aged, but the man I once knew like a brother, walks into the office and I can feel the tension start to leave my body almost immediately.

"Sorry I'm late."

"Welcome home," I tell him, meeting his gaze, but my own words are drowned out by those of my brothers. When we were younger, Sebastian was all we had to guide us.

My body's stiff as I make my way around to greet him. Seeing him is bittersweet. Time has passed, and both of us have changed. But in this cruel world we live in where you have to fight to survive, there's nothing like a friend who's been there every time you've needed them.

In Sebastian's case, every time but one, but there's no time to dwell on the past. Again my gaze shifts to the empty sofa as I head back toward my seat.

I'm still so fucking cold, and for a moment I feel like I can't breathe again.

"It's good to see you guys again," Sebastian says and then takes us in one by one.

"I wish things were different," I tell him and no words could speak more truth.

"It's only a little bloodshed," Sebastian offers, smirking and leaning back against the wall.

"You all right?" he asks me, and he doesn't hide the concern in his question. He never has, and with those words I'm taken back to when I was only a child and all the times he asked me the exact same thing.

"I'm ready for this to be over," I answer him and we share a knowing look.

"I guess it's good that I came then." His answer is firm, but comes out in a way that makes me feel slightly relieved.

I give him as much of a genuine smile as I can as he walks over the spot Aria was in last night and then back to the door. *It was only a dream.* I have to remind myself.

Sebastian asks Declan as he leans against the closed door, "Are you all set?" My brother gives him a nod, and an arrogant smirk in return.

Declan stalks from the bookshelf and walks closer to the desk, his eyes on the telephone seated in the left corner as he says, "Tracers are on and these are new. Even if he's bouncing his signal off multiple towers, or the call cuts off in seconds, I can find him."

My back is stiff with tension… but also the creeping feeling of danger. We're going to hunt down the grim reaper, one of the names Marcus goes by.

"Are you sure?" He nods at Daniel's question and then all of us stare at the phone, preparing to get answers we've waited far too long for as it rings, as if daring Declan to be right.

Ring.

I can feel the desk vibrate and the small shaking movements of the phone as I reach for it.

Lifting the handset up and putting it on speaker, I let Marcus know we're all here.

"The Cross brothers," he speaks. Marcus, the grim reaper, the ghost… whatever name he goes by, he's finally gracing us with a call. My teeth clench when I hear his voice, and my blood goes cold.

His voice has always reminded me of a snake. Not a snake you can easily kill by cutting off its head, but the kind of snake that myths make immortal.

It's the way his words linger in the air and settle into your bones.

"It's been a while," Marcus comments and Daniel's quick to reply, "Not because of our doing."

My left hand raises silently in the air, quieting Daniel although I can see the anger rising inside of him as he's barely grounded in the chair. He knows Marcus has answers, and he's refusing to give them to us.

"I believe our desired outcomes may no longer be aligned, Marcus." My heartbeat quickens, but I keep my voice even and remain calm and in control. "Is that why you've been quietly avoiding us?" I question him.

Silence. For one beat, and then another.

I can feel my brothers watching me, their eyes boring into me, but I stare at the phone, willing Marcus to answer.

And finally, I'm given a response. "Not necessarily," he answers me and then adds, "You made a change that I didn't necessarily agree with, Cross."

"You'll have to be more clear on which of us you're referring to," I tell him as I rest my elbow on the table and my chin on my fist. My thumb runs along my stubble as I glance at Declan, who's watching the tablet in his hand with an unyielding stare.

"I suppose you're right…" Marcus says and then pauses before adding, "Two of you have in fact, gone off course."

Daniel's eyes meet mine at the same time I look at him.

"What exactly changed that you decided we were no longer allies?" I ask Marcus, feeling hotter and growing irritated. Marcus is an unparalleled force, but he aggravates the fuck out of me with how cautious he is. When I can use him to my advantage, which I have in the past, I think highly of the man. I've both feared and admired him.

But to be on the other side of his temper is … enraging.

"I needed to make a deal with Nicholas Talvery." Marcus surprises me with a straight answer.

I surmise, "And my interfering was…"

"Unappreciated." Marcus finishes my sentence and I merely nod, my mouth set in a grim, straight line.

"What happened with Addison?" Daniel asks, and Marcus ignores him.

"I want Aria Talvery." Marcus's demand gets a reaction from me that he can't see. My brow raises and a smile wavers against my lips.

"No." I'm surprisingly calm as I answer, "That's not going to happen."

The ever-present ticking of the clock passes in the silence until Marcus responds, "I didn't anticipate your response to be so…. shortsighted."

"Daniel asked you a question," I remind Marcus and watch my brother. "Why was she involved?" I'm not positive that Marcus is behind what happened, but I know that he knows the answer.

"Why did you try to take her?" Daniel's question comes with a raised voice behind clenched teeth and barely contained anger. His inability to keep calm is understandable, but ineffective.

"I didn't. You already know who did."

I barely contain my irritation, watching Daniel come unhinged as Marcus continues to skirt around the one thing he needs to know.

"If we knew, we wouldn't be asking you," I tell Marcus pointedly.

"Who tried to take Addison?" Daniel speaks up with the only question he wants answered. I have so many I could drown in them, but he only has one.

I expect a single name. Or the denial of information entirely. Instead, Marcus continues to evade the answer, but he also surprises me.

I don't like to be surprised, because it means I'm lacking in information, which means I'm lacking in control.

"The same man who hurt you years ago and started all this." *Years ago?* His words repeat in my head. In the decade since we've taken power, no one has dared to hurt us until recently.

Marcus continues and this time, he places a small clue in his response. "She wouldn't be yours if it hadn't happened."

"If what hadn't happened?" Jase asks, speaking for the first time. And now I'm left wondering if Marcus is referring to Addison or Aria.

"The first hit your family took," Marcus says, giving more information to solve a riddle rather than providing an answer that would be so easy to give.

"You talk in circles and riddles," Daniel sneers and then slams his fist down before raising his voice to tell him, "I just want a name."

"And I just want Aria," Marcus answers, ever calm in a way that makes my blood turn to ice.

My brother looks at me, desperate for information, but before I can respond, Daniel narrows his eyes at the phone and tells Marcus, "If all you're after is Aria, this conversation is useless. We will never give her to you."

The line clicks dead and the moment it does, I stare at Daniel, who won't take his gaze from the silent phone. With his jaw clenched and every emotion written on his face, I feel nothing but sorrow for him. Maybe shame as well. I'm ashamed I brought my brothers into this, and I don't have a way to fix it.

"Years ago?" Sebastian repeats Marcus's words and opens the door as Declan moves to leave, looking pissed off.

"Did it-"

Before Sebastian can even finish his question, Declan's fist slams against the door-frame, splintering it with his rage.

He doesn't speak; he doesn't even slow his pace. Declan's the first to leave and Daniel follows.

"Can I have a minute with Sebastian?" I ask Jase, letting go of my thoughts of figuring out what Marcus was hinting at. With a nod, Jase is gone, leaving only Sebastian and myself.

"Don't let anyone close to this place and only trust us," I tell Sebastian, not wasting a second as he stalks to where Jase was just sitting. With both hands wrapped around the back of the chair, he looks at me closely.

"Are you all right?" he asks me again and the sad smirk comes faster this time.

"No."

"What has to happen?" he asks, and I'm grateful for that question rather than the obvious, *why?*

"She needs to be kept safe. Aria Talvery."

"Because he wants her?" he guesses and I keep my expression still and unwavering, but after a short moment, I shake my head. "It has nothing to do with Marcus. She simply needs to be kept safe."

His eyes search mine, and I hate his hesitation.

"You know what she means to me," I speak with desperation and hate that I have to say it at all. It was his idea to give Stephan to Aria. Between my brothers and Sebastian, they know all my secrets. Loving Aria isn't a secret anymore, and Sebastian knows it.

"I don't care what happens, as long as you keep her safe. She can't be hurt. In any way."

"So you want me to … be her guard?" he offers and I hadn't thought of it like that, but I nod, knowing I need someone to watch over Aria.

Sebastian nods and tells me we'll talk more in detail soon before turning and leaving. And that's the end of this very short meeting.

After he leaves, I wish he hadn't. I'm alone in the room with the memories of last night, and riddles I don't know how to begin to solve. The world feels like it's closing in on me, and years of sin are mere seconds from destroying what's left of me.

"I had a thought," Jase speaks and I open my eyes, realizing that I didn't even hear him come back in.

"I need to check on Aria," I tell him, not wanting to deal with more shit. She has to meet Sebastian, and a strange sensation curdles the bit of bile in the pit of my stomach at the thought of what she'll tell him about me.

"Just listen for a minute."

"One minute," I say. I focus on the phone, on the conversation that keeps repeating itself in the back of my mind as Jase tells me we should meet with Nikolai and let Aria see it all. Let her watch as Nikolai shows himself to be the man he is in front of her.

"What if she saw him the way we do?" he suggests and stares at me expectantly.

"I can't even begin to understand why you would think that's a good idea."

"Let Aria see. Let her see you give him the chance to walk away, and show her the side of him she doesn't know about."

"Why-" I almost question my brother's sanity until I realize he thinks I'm fucked up today because of Nikolai. He has no idea what weight I'm carrying today, but his first guess is that it has to do with Aria and Nikolai.

"You think that she'd be all right with him dying then? You're wrong." I don't give him a moment to respond.

"I don't give a fuck about Nikolai, and I've resigned myself to the fact that Aria is going to hate me for what I'm about to do. What she knows and doesn't know is irrelevant."

Defeat crosses Jase's expression when I tell him a truth I wish didn't exist.

"She loved him first, I know that. And she loves me now." I swallow thickly and then tell him, "A part of her will always love him, but a part will always love me too."

"I'm struggling here," Jase says and runs a hand through his hair. "Something's wrong."

How could he not see? How could anyone not understand?

"I don't know how this is supposed to end any other way but with us apart."

There's no way for this to end other than for her to hate me, or for me to die.

"She understands-"

"And I understand she'll hate me when it's over," I cut him off with my rushed words. "What everyone needs to understand is that even if…" I have to pause and take a deep breath, staring past my brother at the closed door as I continue, "Even if she leaves… Even if she decides she can't live with…" I've thought of this ending so many times, but I've never fully accepted it until this moment.

"Even if she doesn't want me anymore when this is all over, I want her protected. I want her safe. Even if she can't live with being my wife, my lover, my … everything. Even still, I need everyone to know that she's protected and that she'll always be mine."

CHAPTER 13

Aria

CARTER NEVER CHANGED THE LOCK.

It's funny how regret sweeps through me as I open the front door. My hand is heavy with it and as I look over my shoulder, back down the hall, so are my legs. When I put my hand to the scanner, I didn't expect for it to work. I didn't think it would be so effortless.

Saying goodbye is never easy. Especially the kind of goodbye that's final. The kind that hurts to say out loud, but it hurts even more when buried deep down inside.

I only stand in the doorway for a moment before I feel the breeze in the early evening air. I'm surprised no one's running down the hall when I close the door behind me.

Even more surprised when I wrap my arms around myself, careful with my left shoulder, although it's feeling better now with the pain pills I found in the half bath's medicine cabinet.

The wind brushes my hair from my shoulder, exposing my skin to the cold. Goosebumps flow over my skin as I take each step down, each step farther away from Carter.

Part of me wonders if he's watching. Another part knows that he is.

He won't let me get far. I already know that, but I need to know how far he'll allow before someone will come and scoop me up to take me back to him.

Whether it happens today, or tomorrow, or a week from now, I'll never stop trying to leave. I repeat those words in my head as I take another step.

I don't think of the reasons. There are too many at this point, and only the outcome matters.

I can't stay here any longer. This isn't the life I want. It's never been more clear than it is now.

My pace doesn't slow until I get to a metal gate at the end of the drive. I hadn't seen it before through all the trees, and I guess it was open last time the cars drove through.

I can't imagine they keep anything out but vehicles, because the gaps in the intricate metal are plenty wide enough for a person to pass through.

And I do.

My fingers grip the cold iron and I duck my head as I turn to slip through the bars.

Peering back at the house, I know he's watching and when I turn back to the remaining driveway that carries on for at least a quarter mile and then weaves through a thick forest, I know he's going to stop me soon. The cameras at the top of the gate swivel, following me.

My heart flickers weakly. The stupid thing doesn't understand. It's still filled with hope.

There's no hope though. There never was.

CHAPTER 14

Carter

MAYBE IF SHE'S NOT WITH ME, SHE WON'T DIE FOR ME.

The thought comes and goes quickly, but as I watched her walk down the porch steps, it was there for a moment.

That I could let her go to save her.

She can't die for me, if I'm not with her.

The thought is only a small blip in my consciousness, but it keeps coming back. Even as Sebastian runs into the room to tell me she's out front. I don't have time to question fate and what I've done. I can't leave her unprotected. That's not an option. I won't allow it.

"I know." The words come out even but low, with a threatening menace I can't hide.

"We've got an eye on her." He's catching his breath, his chest rising and falling with heavy pants, but his demeanor is calm. His words though, are prying. "Does she normally walk out past the gate?" He's careful not to ask outright if she's trying to escape, which is something I'm not used to from him. I can see the change in the way he looks at me. Time's changed many things since the last time we've done something like this together.

It takes a moment, another moment before I can even breathe at the realization. A decade has passed, and I hate what I've become.

I didn't want to be this man. I didn't ask for this life.

As much as I wish I could, I can't go back. My gaze centers on Sebastian, holding the authority I've fucking earned. "Lock her up." Every syllable comes out hard, and each word is accompanied with a slamming in my chest.

She can't die then. She's safe here.

"Everything is barricaded, guarded and armed. No one is getting close and no one is going to hurt her." The words echo in the room and Sebastian is silent. He already knows I'm merely reassuring myself.

"Just snatch her up?" Sebastian asks easily, as if there's nothing at all wrong with what I'm doing. I nod, feeling a knot wind tighter in my stomach, twisting unforgivingly at the fact that she's trying to leave me. Willing to leave me.

"I know she's angry." I try to justify the fact that she's leaving, but I swallow my words. "I'll make it right with her," I say as I turn away from Sebastian and move to the window to see how much farther she's gone. "Don't let her get much farther than the gate."

"You think she'll go all the way down the drive?" Jase questions from behind me. There are men lining the estate, past the drive although it's still not safe. I don't bother to turn to him as the sun sets beyond the trees, where it's least protected. The light blue in the sky instantly darkens as the auburn leaves weave patterns with the remaining light.

"Just get her." The knot climbs up my stomach and twists and turns inside of me. It's a pain I haven't felt before.

Last night plays out as I look at myself in the reflection of the window. I love her. I love her completely and without hesitation. But the man I am is one who destroys.

The fact that some part of her loves me, only means she's setting herself up to be ruined. Every piece of her broken… by me.

As I swallow down the thought, my hands move to my pockets and I vow to fix this between us. I don't have another option. I won't let her go.

"You all right?" Jase's voice brings me back to the present and as I turn to him, I look back to the sofa. Empty. Just as the floor is in front of my desk. The visions of last night pass like another blip.

Sebastian's gone, and Jase has taken his place. Time is moving like the flickering images of an old movie reel with some of the frames missing. I don't know how long Sebastian's been gone or when Jase came into my office.

"No," I answer my brother honestly and my next words come out ragged. "I've never been like this. I've never," I pause to pull my hands from my pockets and run them over my face. Staring at the drawer to my desk, I remember taking the sleep aid last night. It's only a drug and it's never affected me like this. It has to be the drug. *The sweets.* The last time I took it was years ago.

"She's just angry," Jase says then looks over his shoulder before shutting the office door and coming to take his seat opposite me.

"I don't want to sit," I tell him with agitation before he can sink into the chair.

I watch his knuckles tighten as he grips the back of the seat. "I want this over. We need to end it." My words come out harder and faster as the desperation to move past this with Aria takes over.

"We're letting Romano-"

"Fuck Romano!" I slam the back of my clenched hand against my chair, needing to feel something other than this pain that's creeping inside of me. Needing to do something other than wait.

"We can't do both, Carter." Jase's voice is calm, but full of reason. He doesn't move from where he is, but his eyes watch me with increased interest. "We can't guard the estate and also attack Talvery's." He finally moves, backing away from the chair although his hands still grip it. "You can't have it both ways."

Time marches on as I consider my brother. The one thing he's always had is an opinion. Constant fucking ideas. Constant pushing. Yet as I lean forward, breathing in to steady myself, he's quiet. He's not pushing either way.

"What would you do?" I ask him, not looking at him, but instead staring at the closed door behind him.

"I can't answer that," he tells me and I fucking hate him for leaving me with nothing. The back of my jaw clenches as I peer down at the screen. She's at the gate.

She's leaving me.

It was never supposed to be me.

Her words from last night, words that wrecked me and caused all of this shit. Those words come back and as I watch her, I believe her.

"She told me," I swallow before finishing my thought, questioning telling Jase any of this but deciding I need to tell someone, "She told me it wasn't her all those years ago."

It takes Jase a moment before his expression registers what I'm talking about. He knows about that night. As well as Declan and Daniel, Sebastian too. That night changed everything. For her to deny being a part of it… I can't fucking stand it.

"Who else could it have been?"

"No one." My answer is immediate and unforgiving, joined with a similar pain in my throat as it tightens. My eyes close as I think to myself, *how would I know? How could I possibly know if another woman was there?*

"Carter," Jase's voice cuts off the memory of that night. "What happened to her shoulder?"

"I cuffed her to the bed. Well, she did, because I told her to." Jase doesn't waver as I lick my lower lip, hiding the shame. "I told her she could stay there until it was over." My eyes lift and I find his as I explain, "And then she ripped her arm away until it dislocated and I uncuffed her, but she…" I can't even finish.

"She did it to herself?"

"Physically… yes." It feels like a lie on my tongue. I'm the reason it happened. It's my fault.

Jase's nod of understanding is short and then he peers past me to the window. "Well, that explains why she ran."

"She'll always run," I tell him as the knowing defeat gets the better of me.

"Stop lying to yourself." Jase's calm voice catches me off guard. "You love her. I know it. And she loves you. Don't let anything come between you."

Love isn't always enough, I think, but I don't say it out loud. Instead my gaze turns to the floor in front of my desk, last night still reeling in my mind. The image of her lying there comes and goes with the blinking of my eyes. "You need to help me keep her safe." I don't know how I even speak. My body is stiff and my limbs are frozen.

"You're scaring me with the way you've been today." Again Jase's feet and posture shift, but his grip remains stiff, keeping him where he is.

I look back to the sofa while I tell him the one thing that's responsible for how I've been today, "I don't want her to die."

"It's not going to happen." Jase's answer is nothing but confident. I wish last night hadn't stolen that same certainty from me. I almost tell him about the nightmare. About how real it was, and how it's fucking with me.

"Whatever's gotten into your head," he starts to say, the concern etched in Jase's words making me look back to him as he finishes his thought, "get it out."

"I just didn't sleep well." I give him a half truth.

"Well tell Aria you love her, fuck her until she forgets why she's angry and sleep. Both of you need to sleep."

"Is that all I need to do?" I question him to lighten the tension, but it does just the opposite.

"You can start with showing her more respect than you have in the past. More love. Tell her you love her."

"She's not leaving because I don't say it back to her." I scoff at his suggestion.

"I think that's exactly why she's leaving. That, and the fact that you told her what to do." His words register one by one. "I think she would let you destroy everything in her world but you, so long as you showed her how much you loved her and told her often."

I don't know when my brother became the voice of reason, but everything he's saying sinks in deep and slow, numbing the anger, the need to fight. Numbing the guilt and the worries. It all seems to fade at the very thought that I can keep her. That it's possible.

"If she felt the love you have for her, she wouldn't leave. No one would give that up." His dark eyes shine with a memory of something else. Something I know has nothing to do with me, but his next words are exactly what I need to hear at this moment. "She doesn't feel loved, and I know you can make her feel it."

How can she not feel everything I feel for her? How can she not feel *this*?

Just as the question consumes me, the phone rings and it's the same number as before. *Marcus.*

CHAPTER 15

MAYBE A QUARTER MILE.

The driveway to the estate is miles long. Miles. The cast iron streetlights that line it cast a pale yellow glow down the paved road that winds through the woods, and I got maybe a quarter mile from the gate before I heard the gravel kick up as tires moved behind me. Gazing to place where the woods begin, I think maybe they're another quarter mile away.

The car heading toward me isn't driving fast and I merely walk to the side of the road and stand there crossing my arms when I hear it approach. I imagine I look like a petulant child, but it's only because I'm cold. The evening air in the shade is bitter and unforgiving.

My shoulder is numb, and so is all the pain. I'm ready for it to end. However it comes, I'm prepared for what's next.

The thought makes my throat tighten and that's when the window rolls down. It's Sebastian, not Carter. It takes me a moment to even recognize that it's him. Addison told me about him when we were at his safe house. She showed me a few pictures of Carter and his brothers with Sebastian in them. I know it's him, but that doesn't dampen the disappointment that Carter didn't come himself.

"Carter sent you?" I ask beneath my breath. Hating that I even expected Carter to bother with acquiring me. Of course he wouldn't. With the car idling, I wait for the man to speak.

He's obviously older, but his features are classically handsome. He's the type of man who could get away with whatever he wanted; he could charm you into anything. Even if there is an air of danger that surrounds him.

"Will you do me a favor and get in easy?" he asks me and a handsome smirk shows off his perfect teeth. "I'll do you a favor in return," he offers.

Kicking at the driveway, I let my gaze fall and then feel the chill in the breeze before I ask him, "What's that?"

"I'll drive; we can drive a bit until you calm down?" he offers. "You can tell me why you're upset."

Although he's seemingly kind, I loathe what he just said. "Upset?" I swallow thickly after speaking and Sebastian puts both of his hands up in defense.

"I don't want to make anything worse or step on anyone's toes, Aria." His voice pleads with me as he adds, "Just help me make this better if I can."

The sky darkens as I wait a moment. Watching this man and finding myself envious of him. He knew Carter. The boy before he turned into what he is now. Curiosity overwhelms any anger with that thought.

My legs move on their own and I find myself climbing into the car. The door shuts with a dull thud, silencing the faint sounds of the forest.

"I'm Aria," I offer him even though he already knows. "I'm sorry we had to meet this way." My manners seem to come back to me as he lets off the brakes and we move forward.

The locks in the car are automatic and they slam down, sounding far louder than they should and reminding me what all of this is for me, a prison.

"I've met people under worse circumstances," he tells me. He keeps his word, driving slowly on the long path. So slow I could walk faster than this, but I'm simply grateful to be heading away from Carter's castle of heartlessness.

"I don't want to go back," I say absently. I don't expect it to make any bit of difference. As the confession leaves me, I stare at the lock on the door, so easily lifted if only I were to reach out.

"You know I have to give you back to him, right?"

My pulse races and then seems to frost over as I remember Daniel offering me an out only days ago. I could have run, I could have accepted Daniel's offer, although who knows if he truly meant it or not.

"I've never seen him like this." Sebastian starts to say something else, but then he shakes his head and waves off the thought. "I don't want to get in between you two," he tells me.

"Everyone else is," I answer flatly and then really look at him until his eyes dart to mine. "Everyone has always been between us." That's the sad truth. If it were only us, there's no question I'd be by his side.

Parts of Sebastian remind me of Eli, or maybe I simply long for someone to confide in, someone who understands and respects the situation the way Eli did. The thought brings a swell of emotion up my chest and I stare out of the window, at the dark green leaves strewn in between the dried-up amber ones.

"Hey." Sebastian's voice brings my focus back to him.

"Have you talked to him today?" The concern on his face seems out of place as he waits for me to answer.

"I just got up, and…" I trail off to swallow the sickness rising up my throat, remembering what happened when I made it to the bathroom. "I haven't." There's nothing left to say. That's the truth of the situation, but I don't bother to voice it.

The silence in the car is awkward. Sebastian asks questions I don't want to answer.

"What's wrong?"

I don't bother to even give him a response to that one.

"Do you like the quiet too?" he asks me after a moment passes with neither of us talking.

"You like the quiet?" I ask him to clarify and he shakes his head no.

"Carter always did."

Again I turn to the window. It's not shocking that the brooding man prefers silence. And the way that little fact tugs at me makes me wish I hadn't climbed into the car.

"Although some days he'd turn up the radio just to numb it all out." He clears his throat and turns the car around. As he's making the three-point turn to head back to the estate he tells me, "When he'd stay with me, back when his mom was sick, he always wanted it to be quiet. He used to say the quiet was his safe place, but then again, he grew up with four brothers and the only time it was quiet was when he wasn't home… so…" He shrugs.

"What was he like back then?"

Sebastian regards me for a second and slows down as we near the estate.

"Stubborn, ambitious," he answers me and then says, "loyal to a fault."

He stops in front of the gate and I ask him to go around just one more time. My hands feel clammy as my gaze flicks to the lock and then back to him. I don't think he saw though.

"So he's always been like this?" It comes out as more of a statement than a question, but Sebastian refutes it.

"Carter wasn't ever like this. He wasn't brutal, he was fair. He didn't…" Sebastian stops his thoughts again and this time a darker set of emotions plays on his face. "I should have never left," he confides in me and I give him a weak smile.

"If I could go back," he starts to say, but I cut him off, stating, "You can never go back."

The moment ends with silence as the car continues to move farther away. Closer and closer to the point in the road where I've chosen. The place where he turned around last time. Where he slowed down the most, and the farthest down the drive that he'll go.

"Why did you leave?" I ask Sebastian, more to distract him than anything else.

Sebastian doesn't even spare me a look as I reach for the lock. He's too busy pinching the bridge of his nose to keep whatever emotions are haunting him at bay.

Click. I shouldn't have turned to look at him, wasting the split second but also feeling guilty from the look of surprise and hurt on his face when he sees me rip the handle back and push the door outward.

He hears the lock click up though and his fingers wrap around my wrist, my left one with the deep gouges from the cuff last night. Fuck! The pain travels quickly and in a single electric motion. I hiss from the sudden jolt of pain as I rip my arm from his grasp, nearly falling out of the car until I have both feet on the ground and run as fast as I can. I don't stop. Not for a moment. Not when he cusses and puts the car in park. Not when I nearly trip moving from asphalt to dirt as I enter the woods. Every breath hurts my lungs as I heave in air.

A few men's voices are carried into the woods. I know there are more men who guard the estate, but I don't know where they are. Somewhere they saw, which means they're close.

My legs are far too weak, and I can hear Sebastian's car door open and then his hard steps on the pavement as I whip past branches. More men shout and the tree limbs lash out at me as if to punish me, and I take it. I take every bite of the thin boughs and when I get to a sudden edge, I fling myself over, eager to get away. To fall hard, and that's exactly what I do. Landing on my back, I hit the cold dirt and roll.

My palm braces against something at the same time my legs bash into the rough trunk of a tree. The bark tears at my legs and I bite down to keep from screaming in agony. It hurts to stand up, but I do. Feeling lightheaded and weak, I stumble at first but keep moving. The voices sound farther away now. I hope they are.

I don't know which way is which, but I run as fast and hard as I can. I can't outrun

Sebastian; he's far too big, and I've never been a runner. But I'll hear him when he comes, and I can at least hide.

"Fuck!" Sebastian's voice reverberates in the forest and it sends birds flying out of the treetops. Their sudden movement makes my heart lurch, and I'm staring up at them as I run into something hard.

Something with hands.

Something that grabs me.

The scream in my throat is held back by a large hand over my mouth.

My heart thumps and my anxiety spikes wildly until he shushes me, holding my small body close to his and hiding behind a thick tree.

"Shh, be calm, Ria." Nikolai's voice is the most comforting thing I could have asked for in this moment. Tiny cuts on my arms and face sting as I cling to Nikolai. Tears burn in the back of my eyes.

"I've got you now."

CHAPTER 16

Carter

"I THOUGHT THERE WAS NOTHING TO TALK ABOUT?" I ANSWER THE PHONE WITH Jase across from me. He's slow to take his seat in the chair but quiet as he does it. There's not a sound in the room other than my own heart beating until Marcus answers.

"I forgot I wanted to mention something," he tells me over the phone. "Are your brothers with you?" he asks me and then adds, "They may be interested to hear this as well."

"I've just messaged them," Jase answers and sets his phone down on the table. It vibrates with a response and then another.

"I'm glad you're here, Jase," Marcus says and I can hear the smile that must be plastered on his face. His voice carries through the space and over to the door as it opens, bringing Daniel into the office. He's still catching his breath and slowing his pace after taking quick steps into the room.

"And which one is that?" Marcus asks as Declan comes in next, his tablet in hand. "Is it the one attempting to track me?" Marcus asks and instinctively I move my gaze to Declan. He merely stares at the phone on my desk, not answering.

"Of course we're trying to track you," I answer Marcus, slowly taking my seat and ignoring my own phone going off. "It's only fair, and you know it." He gives a low chuckle, but says nothing.

"What is it you want to tell us?" I ask him and glance at the monitor to see Sebastian's car parked in the street. I know he was talking to her. The nagging voice in my head is only concerned with Aria, but she's not even back yet. This call is going to be quick. First I'll handle this, and then I'll deal with Aria.

Soon. Soon I'll have her back, and I'll take Jase's advice.

"I have more information regarding the first time the lines were drawn in the sand," Marcus says. "Lines you failed to see."

"No more riddles." I cut Marcus off and grit my teeth before telling him, "I'm tired of games. Tell us who tried to take Addison and Aria." I harden my voice as I add, "I want names."

It's quiet for a second and then another, but Marcus eventually speaks.

narrows as he stares at the phone, not with anger, but with recollection. And we all look to him.

"About Tyler?" Jase asks and instantly my blood turns to ice. "The articles about the woman who hit him?" Jase clarifies and my mind races.

Lines drawn in the sand.

The first hit our family took.

"Tyler's death was an accident," Daniel speaks up and then visibly swallows, walking closer to the edge of the desk and daring the voice on the phone to deny that truth.

It was five years ago. Almost six now.

Tyler's death was before all this. Years ago. After I went against Talvery, once I started making a name for myself, yes. But I was no one. It's only in the last few years that my name has become synonymous with fear. Jase and I had barely gained ground, let alone anything worth the attention of hurting Tyler.

"His death was an accident," I say steadily, repeating Daniel's words.

Still, the coldness doesn't leave me. Slowly the memories come back of my youngest brother. He was the only good soul of the five of us. If ever a death was cruel, cutting his life short was just that.

"What were the articles?" I ask Jase, but Marcus answers instead.

"About her addictions…" Marcus's voice drawls until he says, "About her sudden death while waiting for her sentencing."

Daniel's face is pale and his eyes are glazed over. He saw it happen. He was there when Tyler was struck by her vehicle.

"What are you getting at?" I question Marcus, keeping my voice even and not letting the emotion get to me.

"She died in her sleep," Jase speaks over me and Marcus responds without hesitation, to say, "She was murdered."

"A name, Marcus," I remind him. "You wanted to tell us something, so tell us all of it. A woman being murdered in jail means nothing."

"No, but the name of the contract hit she was given, does. A hit I denied. The name was Jase Cross." Overwhelming nausea rises inside of me as Marcus weaves a tale and paints the picture of my past differently than I've ever seen it. "A small-town thug from Crescent Hills. A boy who was getting in the way and needed to be taken care of before he and his brothers gained too much ground. But she knew too much and had to die once she did her bidding."

"What?" Jase's voice carries disbelief as a growing numbness covers my skin with goosebumps.

"A hit?" Declan questions. Incredulity is written on his face.

I can't move. There's so much tension in every part of my body.

"Tony Romano came to me first." Hearing Romano's name sparks the need for vengeance, but I won't act quickly. I'll listen first, and assess. But imagining my youngest brother, only sixteen years old and dead in the street, proves that task to be futile. "He said either of the two would do, but settled on Jase." Marcus continues to tell his story while I wonder if it's possible. If it's true.

If Tyler was murdered all those years ago. If he took the place of Jase.

"The article I sent to Jase in particular was the biggest clue of all. His picture was there. What was he wearing, Jase?" Marcus leads Jase with the question, and it's only then that Jase's face crumples with torment. "Your hoodie." Marcus answers his own question, and I can hear Jase swallow.

"It was meant to be Jase, and she saw a boy who looked like him, on a rainy night in the same sweatshirt she was looking for. She wasn't a drunk driver, she was an alcoholic and drug addict hired by Romano because I refused."

"That's why you were there?" Daniel speaks up, his voice loud enough for Marcus to hear over the speaker. "You knew it was going to happen?"

"I thought it was going to be you. I wanted to save you. I had other plans for you." My throat's tight as I listen to Marcus, finding it harder and harder to disagree with his version of what happened. No matter how much I want to deny these revelations coming to light, years later.

"He wanted to end you, but instead he delivered a death that fueled both of you to conquer without remorse."

"Romano?" Declan questions, and we share a knowing look.

"Romano," Marcus confirms.

He's dead. He's fucking dead.

"Why now?" Daniel asks, not hiding the emotion in his voice. "You were there. You knew all this time and you didn't tell me back then, you didn't warn me… but now?"

"Why tell us this now?" Declan repeats Daniel's question.

"For one, you asked who tried to take Addison and Aria. I'm giving you an answer. But the other reason, the much bigger reason, is because I knew Carter would listen. I knew I'd have his attention." Marcus's voice lacks the same depth it had during his tale. Like he's snapped back to the present and he's no longer interested.

"You would've had my attention whenever you wanted it, Marcus," I tell him honestly.

"Yes," he answers, "but I didn't want it back then. I wanted it now." And with that, the line goes dead.

None of my brothers speak after the click fills the room.

He didn't want it back then?

Another riddle. I let the words sink in, but they hardly mean anything. Marcus has never lied. Romano had my brother killed. Romano has taken his last free breath.

"He's a dead man," I speak out loud although none of my brothers react.

Jase hasn't moved. He's as still as he can be, and Declan keeps looking between him and Daniel.

"It wasn't your fault," Daniel offers Jase, but Jase only shakes his head.

Mourning the loss of a loved one is the worst feeling in the world. There's no drug that can take that pain away, because there's no drug that can bring them back. They're simply gone forever.

But to learn the truth of a tragedy, to learn that there was more to the story, more than what you were told before and to still have no control, it adds salt to the wound.

And for Jase… he's in fucking agony, knowing it was supposed to be him.

The vibrations from my phone are a muted distraction. I don't even know how long it's been going off—Jase's is going off too —and I'm eager to pick it up, only to realize what Marcus meant.

He didn't want my attention back then. He wanted it now, because he didn't want my attention elsewhere.

Anger ignites inside me like never before as I read the message out loud. "Aria's gone."

I'll kill them all.

CHAPTER 17

M Y HEART WON'T STOP RACING. IT'S ALL MOVING SO FAST. ONE DECISION COULD change the course of everything. I didn't know when I walked through that gate that it would happen like this, moving easily from one side to the other. I was foolish to think I could just run away from this life. The thought echoes in the chambers of my mind as my left foot crunches the twigs on the ground and my right side leans heavier into Nikolai. He's walking so fast, pulling me in closer to him. It's all moving too fast.

There are small scratches everywhere. My jeans are torn and covered in dirt and my arms are smeared with blood. What's worse is that I can't stop shaking. I think it's just the adrenaline, or maybe it's due to anxiety. I don't know which, but I can't stop shaking and it makes Nikolai hold me that much tighter.

The branches crack beneath our feet with every step and I keep looking back. They must hear us. It's darker with every passing moment, and I don't know where we're going but it doesn't matter; Nikolai leads me away. *Nikolai will be the one Carter blames.*

Every small sound behind us makes me jump, but even then, I'm not given a moment to stop; Nikolai doesn't let up. I can hear his heart pounding, and I know he knows he's dead if Carter's men catch us before we get out of here.

I don't think he'd hurt me, but he'll kill Nikolai.

"He can't find us together." The words rush from me as I reach up and grab Nikolai's shirt, forcing him to stop and think. "He can't think you took me; he'll kill you. He can't—" the words don't stop tumbling out of me, but Nik hushes me.

"I have you, and I don't care if he knows it." He's surprisingly calm, and justified in his response. "I've waited too long to get close enough to save you." My thoughts race, wondering how he even got through Carter's security, where they are and how long Nikolai has waited out here for this moment.

"How did you know?" I ask him, my eyes searching his for all of the answers.

"Someone told me to come. He told me I'd be able to save you." As he speaks, Nik's voice is full of so many emotions. "I'm sorry it took so long, Ria," he says, his voice cracking as he grips my waist and urges me forward. I stumble, refusing to move and waiting for him to look back at me. I need him to realize how serious this is.

"He's going to kill you," I say and stare deep into his light blue eyes, knowing it's true. Before I can urge him to run, he tells me, "Not if I kill him first."

"Don't talk like that." The words are torn from my throat, immediate and raw, just as instincts are. Betrayal flashes in Nikolai's eyes and I wish I could take the words back, if only to ease his pain, but I can't. He's stunned and pained, crushed from my words, but it doesn't last long.

The sound of heavy footsteps behind us forces me to crush myself into Nik's embrace. Gripping onto his shirt, I beg him in a whisper, "Run."

I can feel his large hand splayed along my shoulder, pulling me closer to him as he whispers against my hair, "Never. Never again."

My face is buried in his chest when I hear my name called out behind me. For a moment I imagine any way that I can barter my life for Nikolai's, but I don't believe for one second that Carter would negotiate with me. Not when I have no control and nothing left to offer.

The moment is short lived, because I hear the voice again. So familiar, yet it feels as if it's been forever since I last heard my cousin Brett.

Shock forces me to pull away from Nik, but again everything happens so fast. Even as he grabs me in a bear hug, Brett drags me along the edge of the woods to a dirt road where an old, beat-up truck is idling. There are two other men with us, but I don't remember their names and with Brett clinging to my side, I don't have time to ask.

"I'm so sorry, Ria," my cousin keeps saying as we move to the truck. "I'm a bastard and a coward, and I'm sorry."

"It's okay," I tell him repeatedly, not knowing what else to say or how to comfort him. Or where the fuck he came from. "I told you to run," is all I can settle on, but he shakes his head, remorse flooding his eyes.

"Two in the back, armed and ready." Nik gives the command as the truck door swings open with a creak that carries through the woods.

"Ria." Brett says my name reverently before hugging me one last time and helping me up into the truck. The dried leather seats are cracked. I've never seen this car in my entire life.

"Don't worry, it's sound, just made to look like it's something to be ignored," Nik says, as if reading my mind. My gaze finds his as the truck sways with Brett and one of the other guys climbing into the back and under a tarp, guns slipped through inconspicuous holes. This truck was made for getaways. The quiet hum of the engine is all I hear for a moment.

It's only then that I feel like it's real. Like I'm actually leaving Carter and going home.

Going back to my father and his men.

The two other men I can't place, although their faces are so familiar, but their names still elude me in this moment. I can feel their eyes on me as they climb into the back, assessing, judging, and questioning. Wanting to know what happened and more importantly, whose side I'm on, I'm sure.

He let me get away. It's all I can think. Carter let them take me. That's the only way it could be this easy.

The thought brings a swell of emotion up my throat and I feel like I'm going to be sick again. The dry heave forces me to open the door and lean out of it. The air is cold against the sudden heat spreading through my body and traveling up to my face.

Everything is quiet as the sickness leaves me. It's disgusting and leaves an acidic burn in its wake. But even when it's over, I can't bring myself back into the car fully. I lean out of it, feeling the cool air and wishing I could leave as easily as the wind can.

It's all too much. It's all too fast and I hold my belly, not knowing what to think or what to do.

It's only when Nik gently rubs my back and whispers that we have to leave that I resign myself to the fate I chose.

"I didn't plan for this," I confess to Nikolai as he pulls me back into the truck and gives me a napkin to wipe my mouth.

I didn't plan to leave the man I love. I didn't plan on him allowing it.

I didn't plan to run back to my family, to his enemy.

And I didn't plan for the small life I wanted to protect from all of this.

I needed to run to get away. Not to fall back into the same game, only to find the color of my pieces have changed.

"He's going to hate me," I cry out softly and once again, Nikolai pulls me into him. The truck is still idle and I know time is ticking. Precious time.

Nik calls out for one of the guys to come drive and scoots to the middle so he can comfort me, even as I cry over Carter.

As the other man gets into the driver's seat, giving me a look of sympathy, Nik reaches behind the seat and pulls out a thick, wool blanket.

"It's all right," Nik tells me, not taking the moment to curse Carter or question my sanity. "We're going home."

⸺•⸺

For the first ten minutes, I kept expecting bullets to fly out of nowhere. I was ready for the ping of steel to slam against the truck. And then I thought maybe Carter would just appear in front of the truck. Standing in the middle of the road like a madman.

It took too long for me to swallow the jagged pill. I've truly left Carter. He's not coming to take me back.

"You don't have to tell me now." Nik's voice slices through my thoughts. The man at the wheel, a man named Connor, glances at me. I know he's curious. I can't imagine what everyone thinks of me, knowing I chose to stay with Carter when they came to rescue me.

Shamefully, I consider making up a lie, just so they won't know how I've fallen for him and how I betrayed them by doing so. The idea comes and goes with the rumble of the truck being carried into the fall air.

"You don't have to tell me right now," he repeats and I gaze into Nik's eyes as he continues, "but I need to know everything you remember." He nods slightly, as if wanting me to agree to such a thing.

"You don't want to know, Nik," I answer him, feeling the painful fissure again in my chest. My cheeks heat as I stare down at my hands and pull away from him. I start to tell him that I love Carter and that I only ran because he doesn't love me in a way that's healthy. I only ran because I can't bear to think of a child growing up in this world we inhabit. I wanted to run away from it all, but as the truck jostles over a bump, I know I only ran into another hell.

"You're safe now," Connor says calmly from his seat. It takes me a long second to re-member who he is. To place his face and his voice. Turning around in my seat, I remember the other man from when we were younger. The memories pooling together and remind-ing me who I am.

"How about I tell you a secret?" Nik offers. He sets his hand on my thigh and rubs a soothing circle with the pad of his thumb. He's so much taller than me, I have to crane my neck to look up at him after watching him swallow.

The air changes instantly, tensing and becoming thick. Too thick as Nik starts, "Do you remember the day we met? At my father's funeral when we were just kids?"

My pulse feels weak as I answer him, knowing deep inside of me that Nikolai will never hurt me, but also feeling that whatever he's about to tell me, whatever it is, is going to cause me pain. It's the look in his eyes. I recognize it too well.

"You have to wait for me to finish," Nik presages his confession, and I nod. "Tell me you will. Promise me, Ria," he commands me, his voice hardening.

I glance at Connor, who cautiously looks back to us before I tell Nikolai, "I promise." With a quick breath I add, "I'll let you finish."

Butterflies flutter in the pit of my stomach as Nikolai says, "I was working for Romano at the funeral. When my father died, I was working for Romano."

The words hit me over and over. *Working for Romano.* A revolting wave of nausea spreads through me as Nikolai swallows and peers down at me, waiting for a response. I can't breathe.

Romano. The man who took me and traded me for a war. The man who would have seen me dead that night I killed Stephan rather than to have his ally murdered.

My body stiffens and I can't control it. I've never feared Nikolai, not until this moment.

"Romano told me your father had my father killed. That's why I was so angry when you touched me. When you came over to me as if you had any right to."

I can't swallow and I struggle to breathe.

"I don't know what my father—" I battle the need to explain, to defend, to do what-ever I have to do to survive with the anger that slowly rises. Lies. My life has been built on so many lies and with so many men I can't trust.

Nikolai cuts me off. "It doesn't matter. None of it matters, Ria."

I have to bite down on my lip to keep from screaming at him not to call me by the name my mother called me. The betrayal and rage stir inside of me, brewing a cocktail I'm not sure I can control.

My best friend. My only friend. Deceived me for years. He was a rat. A fucking rat!

"Your father told me that it was Romano who'd done it. That Romano had my fa-ther killed. And I didn't know who to believe. I had no one, yet both of them had hired me. I was only a kid; I was angry and more than that, I was scared and so fucking lonely."

The truck moves steadily along until we're out of the brush and dirt road entirely, headed down a back road of thin asphalt.

The day at the funeral comes back to me slowly with the quiet rumble, the picture painted in a different hue than I've seen it before.

"I'm still the same, Ria. You have to understand. I was a kid, and you don't say no to men like your father... or to men like Romano."

"Did my father know?" I manage to ask him as the anger wanes and the boy in my memory looks back at me. I remember his face. I remember the anger and I remember how he held me in return. How I needed someone just like he did. He was my someone. But the lies… I'm so sick of the sins and secrets.

"No." His answer is solemn. "Romano wanted me to keep eyes on Talvery, and Talvery hired me to do shit work. I figured one day, one of them would kill me." Nik's voice is resigned and flat, with no motive revealed in his words other than survival. "Romano would kill me for not telling him everything. Or your father, for being a rat. I didn't want this. I was only a boy."

Through my lashes, I peek at Connor, who doesn't respond. That's when it hits me that Connor knew too.

Adrenaline spikes through me, numbing me as Connor's gaze catches mine.

"I don't work for Romano," Connor tells me before I have to ask. "But I've known what Nik has—all of us have—for years."

My gut churns. My throat's tight as I look up at Nik. "You didn't tell me?" The words are merely whispers.

Nik doesn't speak, he only looks down at me with regret, but Connor answers in his place. "Your father will kill us if he finds out we know, Aria." I can barely tear my gaze from Nik to look back at Connor. "You didn't deserve to be put in the middle."

The irony of his words aren't lost on me.

"I had to stay and as everything happened, I did what I had to do to survive."

"You didn't have to stay," I argue.

"Yes, I did."

"Why did you stay? You could have left any time and just run." I push the words out, containing my anger that's dimming, and remembering all the times we've been together. At one time in my life, he was my everything, and yet, he held onto secrets that could have destroyed me.

It's quiet for so long, I start to think I didn't ask the question, until I look up at him.

He stares back at me with such pain in the depths of his haunted eyes. Pain that I don't already know, yet somewhere deep in my soul I did know. I've always known.

"I could never leave you, Ria," he tells me and then rips his gaze away to look straight ahead as his eyes gloss over.

"Then why let them take me?" I ask him and swallow the hard lump growing in my throat. "You gave me to Romano!" My voice raises and I can't help it, but as it does, Nik grips me tighter and peers at me with a fierceness that's undeniable.

He told me that he's the reason I was taken. It's Nikolai's fault all of this started. If he loved me so much, why would he dare risk it?

"No, I didn't. He fucked me over, and he'll pay for that." Nik's jaw is hard and his eyes dark with anger. The kind of anger that I've seen before. Anger that comes with revenge.

"I wanted you away from this life," he confesses to me, his shoulders relaxing as he stares out the window behind me. "Your father is getting older. Everyone knows his time is coming to an end. What do you think would have happened to you?"

I don't answer Nik's question.

"He promised he'd save you. I lured you out, taking your notebook, and I knew you'd try to retrieve it. I knew you'd think it was Mika. And Romano lied to me. I'm sorry, Ria. Your father doesn't have long, and I needed to protect you. I needed you away from all of this."

"It wasn't your decision to make," is all I can say to him. My notebook. It's an odd feeling to have an object mean so much in a life where nothing is meaningful anymore.

"I can't believe it was all you."

"I had to save you," he tells me and settles back into his seat, apparently done with the conversation.

It's hard not to blame it all on him. Everything I've gone through. I struggle with all the emotions running through my blood.

"You love him, don't you?" he asks me with a hint of disgust in his tone. "He's brain-washed you." He gives himself an explanation without waiting for my response.

"I do," I say, staring Nikolai right in the eye. "I love Carter Cross…" I have to swallow before finishing. "But I'm not dumb enough to think we'd last… Because he doesn't love me. Not how I need."

My heart does this awful thing just then. It pumps, but it's lifeless. It beats, but there's no sound. It gives up on me in this moment, and I can feel it as it happens.

It's a lie on my lips. I hear a whisper in the back of my head.

I have to remember why I left. I have to remember this life and what it does to people.

"I need to get out of here," I murmur beneath my breath, not to Nikolai or Connor, but to myself.

"I can help you," Nik is quick to tell me, pulling me close to him although I'm still in his grasp. "I'll make it right. I'll get you out of here, Ria. I just have to do one thing first."

CHAPTER 18

Carter

"**O**F COURSE HE'D BRING HER BACK TO HIM." THE WORDS ARE ACCOMPANIED by silence as we watch Nikolai and his crew pull up and wait for the gates of the Talvery estate to open.

She didn't run to Nikolai—or even to her father. I fucking know she didn't. She ran, and she had good reason with the way I treated her, but she didn't run to him.

I saw the footage.

"I'm sorry," Sebastian says from the back of the Grand Cherokee SRT. The black SUV sits in the shadows. With tinted windows and an engine that can hit sixty miles per hour in four point eight seconds, it's our go-to vehicle, armed and equipped for anything coming our way.

We got it years ago so we could haul ass after making hits.

As we sit idle along the forest two miles away from the Talvery estate, I don't give a fuck about speeding away from anything. Not without Aria.

"She was going to run however she could," I mutter under my breath at the driver's seat, excusing Sebastian.

"Still…" he mumbles, running his hand through his hair. He can barely look at me and I hate it. It's not his fault she ran. It's not his fault she got away. It's mine.

The wheel is hot under my grip and everything inside of me is pushing me to get out and storm the front doors of her father's estate.

Which would leave me dead on the polished marble front steps.

She's so fucking close, but out of my reach as the neatly trimmed bushes that line the path to the door sway with the wind on the screen. I've only been closer to this property once in my life.

At the mercy of her father when I was just a boy.

I swallow down the memory as the car door opens and several men with machine guns approach Nik's beat-up truck.

That fucking prick.

My heart slams in my chest when I see her. Her brunette locks tumble around her shoulders. Her shirt's torn and there's still dirt covering half of her ass all the way down her leg.

She doesn't carry herself like the girl she used to be. Her head is held high and her shoulders are straight, but the fear is still there, dancing in her doe eyes.

As much as she can't hide that she's a woman meant for this life, she can't hide the fear it brings her to be caught in the middle of a war either.

Aria doesn't stop looking all around her as Nikolai ushers her into the front door, looking over his shoulder in the direction of the camera we've hacked into. As if he knows we're here.

It's only when the men surround her, that I realize how quiet it is in the SUV.

The shame and regret hardly register anymore. Shame from the way I've treated her. And regret for it all.

"I'll do better by her," I tell them and still not a damn man speaks up. I see Sebastian nod in my periphery and I have to close my eyes and take in a steadying breath before opening them to see Nikolai's hand on the small of Aria's back. And then the large front door closes.

"It'll be different when the war is over," Jase offers and Sebastian agrees. As if any of it is because of the war.

"It'll be less complicated." Daniel chimes in.

"Less need to fight," Declan adds.

It was never the war though. It's my fault.

Knowing Nik's with her eases some of the strain coursing through me. The jealousy is present as always, but I don't have time for that. He'll protect her, and that's the only saving grace I have right now. Nikolai won't let a damn thing happen to her, and I owe him for that. I know more about Nikolai than any other Talvery man for one reason. He's the one who was always with Aria. He's the one I wanted every detail on. And he does love her, I know he does. I owe him more than I'll ever let him know.

He can be her hero for the moment. He can protect her.

I don't give a fuck if I'm nothing but the villain who captures her.

The villain who holds her against her will until her will changes.

The villain who will put an end to this war and to the empire her last name gives power to.

The villain who will stop at nothing to have her completely.

And the rest of me, whatever is left, the rest of me will belong to her. Always.

I don't have a choice; that is all I'll accept.

And she'll learn to accept it too.

"We already know the place, and we have the count on the men." Jase is the first to get to business. Tonight, Talvery will finally fall.

There are eight men at the front entrance. Another four towers along the tall brick walls that surround the property. Each of them with a handful of men armed and ready.

There will be even more men inside. They'll have to die as well.

"Wherever we hit will be a distraction," Declan says as if he's thinking out loud, "but they'll also send Talvery into the safe room."

"We need to contain him and Aria too if we can," Jase responds to Declan's statement, leaning forward in his seat to stare at the blueprints on the tablet.

"The safe room is large, but if we get rid of it as an option, they'll have nowhere to go, they're outnumbered… it's just the matter of the safe room and if there's anything at all that we don't see."

"Hit the safe room first then," I answer without thinking twice, but then add, turning to face Jase, "Unless they take Aria there."

Her locked away in a room, refusing to let me in even though she knows I'll be waiting for her and only time is keeping her away from me, is exactly what our relationship has been. I can see it reversed though just as easily.

Tonight I take that option away. Tonight I change the course of our fate. I choose us. Forever. No more fighting; I've fought enough in this life already. I only want to love her.

"Is everyone in place?" I ask Jase and he nods solemnly. We left our home and every piece of property we own unguarded. Every single man is here. Every man ready for blood. The only exception is a small crew guarding Addison right now, far away from all of this.

"I've got the security feeds." As Declan speaks, my eyes open and I wait for the screen to flick to a new video stream, one that shows the hacked footage inside each and every one of Talvery's rooms until it lands on a picture of Aria.

The images flick by on the screen, moving as she moves, and focused on her expression.

My poor Aria. Fuck, I've never known pain like this before.

"You're good for something, Declan," Daniel tells him, with his hand on the loaded gun in his lap.

"Fuck you too," Declan replies with a smirk.

"Feels like old times," Jase says and I turn to look at him, looking at each of my brothers and Sebastian. It does.

"It's been a while, hasn't it?" I tell him, feeling each pulse in my veins. The tension, the buildup. But something else too.

"Since it's felt like everything is riding on this one moment?"

"Yeah," I answer him.

"Too long," Sebastian says lowly, checking his gun and then slamming the magazine into place with the butt of his hand.

"It used to be thrilling, though," Jase says quietly, glancing at the screen showing the men outside the door to where Aria's been taken. A few men wait outside, but Nikolai goes in with her. "This is different."

"There's too much riding on this one," I tell them all and their nods are instant.

"We'll get her and bring her home," Jase tells me and Sebastian looks between the two of us.

"When this is over," Sebastian says, "I'm not leaving. I'll bring Chloe home; she'll come with me." I don't have time to answer him.

"First Talvery, then Romano. Your ass isn't going anywhere." Jase's answer pulls Sebastian's lips into an asymmetric smirk.

It's hard to let the words go, but I tell my brothers something I often don't. "Thank you." I swallow thickly and then turn to each of them, the leather seats groaning as I do. "Thank you for being here. For helping me and for helping her."

"Of course," Jase says, his eyes searching mine and the sad smile showing. "We survived together. Fought together… Loved together."

"I wouldn't be anywhere else. You need me," Sebastian tells me and looks me in the eyes. "Mostly because I fucked up, but still, you need me."

His joke lightens the mood a touch, enough to let the other emotions in just slightly. The emotions that remind me she left me. The ones that prove to me it's because of me.

With his hand gripping my shoulder, Sebastian tells me, "We'll get her back."

"And I'll keep her," I tell them, meaning every word. I'll keep all of her every way I know how.

"All right, enough with this shit," Declan says, and Daniel huffs a short laugh. It's been a long time since I've had a conversation like this one. One that's real, and touches a piece of me that remains dormant. A piece Aria holds hostage.

"I've got it all covered now," Declan speaks up from the back of the SUV. "The safe room is empty, but it's not close enough to the outside rooms to be hit easily."

"Does Aden have vision anywhere near the safe room?"

"He can hit the west side through the hall window, send in the smoke bombs and ambush that side of the house. We'll be in and out with the bombs within a few minutes, but they'll react. The odds of coming out are not the best." Jase answers for Declan, and I can see the plan already formulating in his head.

Aden is already waiting on the other side. They're waiting for Jase's cue.

"We need to hit them all at once," I tell Jase. The adrenaline in my blood is nearly suffocating me. Only because I'm sitting here. I need to move, to get this shit over with and have her back. "Tell them all to hit on my command."

As I say the words, the vision on the screen changes and it turns back to Aria. Her arms are crossed tight, and she stands by herself awkwardly in the center room. Facing Nikolai, neither of them moving, but both of them the picture of regret.

There's no fucking way I won't do everything I can to hold on to her.

"Hit the towers, the front entrance, and the safe room all at once. We have more men than they do." The words leave me the second the screen changes again.

"What about Romano?" Declan asks.

"What about him?" The anger and hate in Daniel's tone reflects the same in every single one of us.

"He could try to make a move on us while our backs are turned," Declan says and then cuts to a feed showing his men lining the territory. They're ready to strike, waiting for Talvery to weaken. If we bring them down first, Romano will have us surrounded and if he desired, he could strike.

"He doesn't know we know, not yet," Jase answers him and then Sebastian states, "We'll keep the north side the strongest for Talvery, pushing his men toward the heaviest side Romano has armed. We don't have to kill them all, just enough to outnumber them. Enough to make them realize Talvery, the name, the empire, is no more."

"It's just like before, no one willingly dies for a dead man." Jase's eyes shine with the memories of all the challengers we've taken down in the past. The name Talvery may be old, it may hold power, but when the man is dead, the name will mean nothing.

"What's the plan?" Jase asks me and then adds, "Step by step."

"We need to get in close first," I tell him. "She's in the east wing, so we can cut the feeds, take out the east tower discreetly with no bombs, make our approach through that way and once we're in, hit the other towers and the safe room."

"They'll be looking everywhere but at us," Jase responds, nodding his head and breathing in deep. "You go in and get her, Bastian and I will come with and take out who-ever comes running."

"Kill the feeds as soon as we get close to the east tower. We'll walk along the tree line," I tell Declan and he's quick to answer, "The cameras rotate every ninety seconds. You're go-ing to need the feeds handled before you get past this road. Or else they'll see you coming."

"There are men on the ground," Jase pipes up. "Cut the feeds, we'll get in there, kill those two fuckers outside the east tower and use them to get in."

Sebastian looks at Declan and asks, "It's fingerprints right?" With a nod from Declan, Jase adds, "Dead fuckers still have prints. It'll work."

With my brother and my friend behind me, my men surrounding the enemy and ready to wage war, it's time. My heart pounds as I run through the forest and raise my gun, hearing the startled shouts from the towers regarding the security feeds going down. I can hear their fear; I can fucking feel it as I raise my gun in the shadows. The three of us shoot, the bullets muffled with the silencers, before the two men, men just like me, even see us. The first two men to die tonight. Their bodies are still warm, heavy and limp as we drag them to the security pad, wipe the blood from their fingers on our pants to gain entrance, and begin to end this war.

CHAPTER 19

Aria

"**I** CAN'T SEE YOU WITH HIM." NIKOLAI'S VOICE IS CALM, SOMEHOW SOUNDING forgiving as he watches me pace in my father's office.

I stare past him at the pictures on my father's wall. There's a picture of my mother and father, with my uncle between them. I never met him. In the photo he's holding them close, his arms wrapped around their shoulders. It's a black-and-white snapshot, taken just before my uncle was murdered. It's only one of nearly a dozen pictures on the wall to the right of my father's desk. But only that photo, and one other hold any of my attention.

I breathe in and out slowly as I stare at the second picture, trying to stand upright and not let on that anything's wrong.

It's Carter's house. The Cross brothers' home. The same photograph that's in Carter's foyer. An icy prick spreads over my skin and all I can hear are my shallow breaths.

I swear it's the same. I knew when I first saw it that the picture was familiar. I thought maybe I'd been there before, but this is why it was so familiar.

My father has a picture of Carter's old house, the house he destroyed, hung up in his office. Is it a fucking trophy? A reminder of something? My stomach roils as I cross my arms tighter, feeling more and more like a trapped animal. I wish my father were here so I could ask him. So I could face him after everything that's happened. If he were though… I can't even imagine where we'd begin. A lifetime has come and gone. I'm not the same person I was when I last stepped foot in this home.

It doesn't matter though. He's not here, and I doubt he'll come for me until he has the time. Business has always come first.

"What did he do to you, Ria?" Nik asks me and I turn to him. Seated in the whiskey-colored leather wingback chair in the corner of the room, I see Nikolai in a different light than I ever have before.

Not as my friend or former lover, not as the boy who needed me. But as a man in pain and on edge, reckless and wanting change, needing it and ready to take it.

I see him as a danger.

"Nikolai, you're scaring me," I whisper with a quietness that begs for them to stay silent, but somehow the words find him. The corner of his lips drag down as his eyes flick with a light of recognition.

"I don't mean to, I just don't think you realize what has to happen," he tells me and then swallows with a look of anguish in his features.

"What has to happen?" I ask him, feeling my hands go cold as I stand aimlessly in the room. Knowing I'm once again at the mercy of men who find me lacking.

"Today men will die."

"Men die every day," I'm quick to respond and he gives me a sad smirk with his huff, leaning forward with his elbows on his knees. He stares at the floor and not at me. His eyes close as I whip around to the door of the office, hearing shouts echo down the halls. The feeds are down. Nik's cell phone goes off, but only for a second before he silences it and his gaze moves from it to me.

"It's all right. You had to know he'd come for you," he tells me, his eyes begging me to deny it, but he already knows the truth.

The pounding in my chest intensifies, and a warmth spreads through me but not nearly enough to stop frigidness that clings to me.

"Will you hate me if I made it easier?" Nik asks me, shifting his weight and reaching behind him for the gun tucked in the back of his pants. "If I killed him, would you hate me?" he asks me but shakes his head before I can even answer. My lips are parted and the words are there, yes, *I'll hate you forever if you kill him.* The pleas not to are the same I've heard before, spoken from my own mouth.

"You know that I love you," he tells me and then he adds, "And you know he's no good for you." I watch the muscles in his neck tense as he swallows. He stands and pulls a drawer open in my father's desk, taking another gun, checking that it's loaded and placing it on the desk before closing the door.

"You ran from him… But still, you want him to live."

"I can't explain it," I tell Nikolai, watching every small movement.

He peeks up at me, hearing the trace of fear in my words and lowers his head. "I'd never hurt you, Ria. Stop looking at me like I would."

"There are different kinds of pain. And I've recently come to accept that some people, some men very close to me, can't help but to cause me the worst kinds of pain."

"Don't compare me to him," he retorts, and the menace in his voice is as chilling as the sharpness in his eyes when he looks at me.

The sarcastic and flat response comes from a place of pain deep inside of me. "How dare I do such a thing."

"You're just sick." Nikolai speaks more to himself than to me. "You'll see. When this is all over, you'll see."

"I've thought long and hard about that. About whether or not I was sick," I tell him as he rounds the desk and leans against the front of it. "I think maybe for a moment I was. Maybe when I wasn't well, and I know I wasn't well because of him. But I can see clearly now. And I'm thinking more about myself these days." My fingers itch to touch my lower belly, but I don't. I don't want him to know or anyone else. I'll bide my time and then I'll run far, far away. I'll be someone else. And leave all traces of Aria Talvery and this world behind.

"Don't you think if you were sick, you wouldn't know it?"

I nod once, feeling a strength rise inside of me. "You're not wrong, but the thing is, even if I am sick, I like who I am more now than I did before. I see the world for what it is, and I'm stronger for it." I don't tell Nikolai, but deep inside I know I can be whoever I choose. I can do whatever I choose to do.

At this moment, running is what I choose, because I want this child to live a life surrounded by love. And I don't know if it's possible to have that with Carter. No matter how much I love him or how much he thinks he loves me. He doesn't know how to love. And I won't allow that life for my child.

At that thought, it feels as if a jagged nail runs down the length of my chest from the inside. Tearing at me. It's not right and it's not fair, but nothing about this tale has been.

"You're strong, Aria, but I can give you a world where you don't have to be," Nikolai tells me. His voice caresses the pain that cascades over me. Three scenarios play in my mind, warring within.

One where Nikolai holds me like he used to. Where I look at him with the love and desire that used to be, and then I look down to a small child in my arms, one who doesn't belong to him. A baby who will forever remind me that I don't love Nikolai nearly as much as I once loved another. Nikolai would take care of me, he'd love me and provide for not just me, but also this baby. And I would use him; I know deep in my heart that's all it would ever be.

Another version of the fucked-up fairytale has me back on Carter's bed, cross-legged with an infant nestled and bundled in my lap while I peek up at the man I love, sitting across the room in a chair, watching me from a distance he chooses.

The father of my child.

The beast of a man.

If things were different, I'd never leave his side. But wishes and hopes do nothing. Things aren't different, and I won't raise a child with the venom and tension that comes with standing by Carter's side.

And in the third vision, the one I choose, I'm alone on a quiet porch, rocking an infant in my arms. I see the small home set back in the distance off a dirt road. Away from it all. Maybe a boy or maybe a girl, but either way, there will be no hate, no vengeance that lingers around us. The wind will whisper lullabies and although this baby won't have a father, I'll give him or her everything I have and protect them from what I once was and this vicious world I came from.

One day I'll tell him a story so raw and so true that he won't believe it. It will only be a fairytale gone wrong. More importantly, that child will be stronger and better than I ever will be. I can't choose a better life for myself. But I can give one to this little life.

"I love you, Nikolai," I whisper as I open my eyes and then I make sure he sees me, really sees me before I tell him, "but it's not the love you have for me. And I love another more than you."

"You left him," Nikolai reminds me and I nod my head, feeling the rawness scratch up my throat.

"If he would have shown me the love I needed, I would still be with him." I let my hand travel to my stomach, where I know Nikolai sees as I tell him, "Right now I can't risk anything."

The door to the office swings open without notice, bringing with it the sound of my father's voice. "Still be with who?" The words sound cautious. My heart races as he slowly closes the door behind him and the lights go out, darkness taking over until the backup power comes on.

My father stares behind me, sharing a look with Nikolai before looking back at me. My breaths come in quick pants.

"Father," I breathe out, and I don't know what to think. I don't know what to do. In many ways I feel like his enemy. Simply because I've fallen into bed, but also in love with the man who longs to see my father take his last breath.

"Still be with Carter?" my father questions, walking closer to me, each step feeling intimidating.

I can only swallow until he lets out a deep breath and looks down at me with sympathy. "I didn't hear everything," he says, his eyes flicking to Nikolai before finding my gaze again and continuing, "but child, this isn't your fault, and I'm sorry." A sudden wave of relief flows through me. My lungs are still and refuse to move, even with the reassurance. "It's all right, Aria." My father's voice is calm and gives nothing but comfort. I can't help but to move to him and as I do, he opens his arms.

To be loved unconditionally is something so rare. But from a parent to a child, there is forgiveness in every moment. The guarded walls crumble even though I'm so aware of Nikolai behind me and my father in front of me, coming forward to pull me in close. He whispers it isn't my fault. His words are apologetic.

He holds me close to him, he holds me like he has before, but back when I was a child. Back when I let him.

"I'm so sorry, Aria," he says and holds me tight, although his voice is tense.

"It's not your fault," I tell him, because it's true. This is the life we lead and breed. No one is to blame for the hate and havoc it brings. It simply exists.

"I'm scared," I confess against his chest. The smell of soft leather and spiced cologne wraps around me just as his arms do.

"You think you love him, and considering what he did, I understand." It's almost shocking to hear his words, but then he whispers, "I'm not sorry that I have to kill him."

My body stiffens in his embrace but if my father realizes that, he doesn't let on. A single breath leaves me and my eyes open, staring at the wall across from my father's desk where the pictures stare back at me. "I should have done it long ago," he says as I pull back slightly, wanting nothing more than to run once again. *Run far, far away*, I think as my fingers drift past my belly and I back away from my father. Pulling back from my father, I see his eyes are as cold and dark as they ever were.

One step, then two.

The second step comes with the shaking of the ground. A rumble at first, but then a movement so sharp, I nearly lose my step.

Bombs. One after another and seemingly all around us. Harsh intakes of air. A spike of fear and adrenaline.

We're under attack. And I don't know if it's Romano…. or if it's Carter coming for me.

Men scream, but not the two I'm with though. They're silent as I fall to the ground on my ass and move to the edge of the room. To hide in the corner and brace myself there. The explosions are close, but not close enough to hit us. Still, they keep coming. Each one sounding closer than the last.

Nikolai and my father don't seek cover like I do. They act like they expected it as they simply brace against the wall of the room, letting each rocking blow hit without a difference in their expression.

The ground shakes and the sounds of explosions reverberate through the room. The bombs must be close, because the shelves jostle and with it, books fall. I watch the gun as it rattles on the desk, the metal skimming along the edge as it finds its way closer to falling, but somehow manages to hang on, even as the monitor crashes to the floor, cracking the frame and forcing a scream from me with the next loud explosion.

That makes seven.

The lamp's shifted to the edge of the desk, where it topples in slow motion at the last blast. It hits the gun Nikolai left there on the corner, and my father's gaze lingers on the steel.

"Boss." Nik's voice is stern, direct, almost a statement rather than a question and the hard gaze between two men verifies my father recognizes that too.

"What can I do to help?" Nik's question is casual, at ease this time.

"Seven," I whisper the word, daring to go against the wishes of my frozen body. The only thing I can feel is the numbing tingle of fear. But I counted seven. "Seven explosions." My father's eyes stay on mine and only when he turns his attention to Nikolai am I able to breathe again. He doesn't answer me, he doesn't say a damn word to me as I stay where I am, hunkered down and counting each second from now until another bomb will hit. But the next one never comes.

The heavy footsteps carry through the room and in time with my quickened pulse as my father walks around his desk, kicking his fallen computer as he does. My shoulders hunch forward and my eyes slam shut at the cracking sound of the screen.

I shudder again when Nikolai lays a hand on my back, splayed and meant to comfort. I can't help but to let out a short cry and back away until I see it's him.

"Fuck," I gasp out and try to calm my racing heart. It's too much. This world is too much.

"You're all right here," Nik tells me and the moment he does, my father commands him away.

"Get down to the west wing. Get Connor and the rest of them. Block anyone who comes in." I've never seen my father look the way he does now. With both of his hands lightly placed on his desk as he stands at its head, everything on top of the sleek black surface is in disarray and even the paintings behind him are crooked.

The room reflects nothing of the controlled, powerful man who's ruled from that very spot for years. And neither does the look in his eyes. There's a sadness wrapped around the dark swirls of his gaze. And a sense of acceptance, plus a tiredness I've never seen.

"Dad?" I dare to speak up, and he dares to ignore me.

"Block off the hall and kill anyone who enters." He doesn't speak to me. Only to Nikolai.

A crease lines the center of Nik's forehead as he gestures to the phone in his hand, the screen of it brightening with notifications every few seconds. "There's no sign of anyone-"

"I know! You don't think I saw the messages?" my father screams at him with hurried words. Anger and fear lace his expression, but this time, Nik doesn't object. All I see is his back as his determined stride leads him away from me and out of the room.

Leaving me alone with my father.

I'm still on the ground, waiting for another sign of what's to come when my father tosses something across the room. It lands hard in front of me, maybe a foot away and again, I'm scared shitless. My stupid heart won't quit trying to escape my chest.

This is what war is, but I don't know how much more of it I can take.

"Your journal," my father says. "You should take it while you still can." I can hardly make out his words, let alone what the item is with the adrenaline and fear spiking through me. My sketch notebook I've long lost, the notebook that started all of this.

I'm still struck with betrayal at the knowledge that it was Nikolai. That all this shit started with him luring me out and letting me believe it was someone I loathed, someone who would have damaged it just to get a rise out of me, or worse, burned it or thrown it away, simply because he could. Knowing it wasn't Mika, and that it was Nikolai makes me hold the sketchbook tighter. I believe in fate and that everything happens for a reason.

The front cover is nothing special. Merely an array of wildflowers painted in watercolors. It came that way. But inside its pages are sketches of the world I used to live in. The one kept safe in the confines of my bedroom on the other side of the estate. Fantasies I dared to dream. And lives I've never lived.

As I stare at the journal, I realize how much has changed so quickly. But one thing never has. It will never change.

"I thought there would be clues as to where you'd gone," my father tells me, explaining why he has it. Nikolai stole it from me. As I crawl closer to it, clutching it close, I'm still reeling from his confession.

"Is Mom's picture still inside?" I somehow get the courage to ask him.

My father only stares at me, a hard gaze that I can't place. It's almost shame, almost hate that comes from him and I don't know why. He doesn't answer me, forcing me to swallow with a dry mouth and throat as I scoot closer to the notebook and let the pages flick by my fingers until they land on the same spot I'd last seen. The one where I drew her, but the picture isn't there.

Just as the sharp gouge in my chest seems to deepen, the edges of the pages fall from the pad of my thumb until they stop, revealing the picture tucked tightly just behind the front cover.

The kind eyes of my mother gaze at me, in black and white, and the memories of her dance in the back of my mind. When the days were not as long and filled with the terror they bear today.

Back when I knew I was safe and loved and nothing bad would happen, and yet it was all a lie.

With a small, sad smile, I swallow the dryness in my throat and pick up the picture to show my father, while whispering a ragged, "Thank you."

A cold prick sweeps over my shoulders, causing a shudder to run down my spine until I tuck the photo back away. It's an odd feeling. One that reminds me of how I felt in the bathroom this morning in Carter's room. A feeling like someone else is here.

"She was always so beautiful." My father's statement is hard. Not an ounce of emotion given to the words. Again my eyes find her photo on the wall, a younger version of my mother, hung beside the photo of Carter's home.

"She was," I speak without consent and then nod my chin toward the wall, and as I do, someone yells from down the hall. It sounds more like a command than anything else, somewhere off in the distance, but it's all I've heard since the ground stopped shaking.

I wait a moment, my body still, wanting to know more of what's going on, but my father doesn't hesitate. He doesn't seem to react at all to what's going on outside of this room, and I don't understand why.

"That's not the photo you keep looking at," he says and the chill comes back to me, like the edge of an ice cube running down the back of my neck. "Did he show you a picture too? The picture of his house?"

My stomach churns as I nod once, forcing my gaze to meet my father's. "Yes," I breathe the word, drawing strength from the truth and feeling an edge of defiance I didn't know I had. "Why do you have it?" I ask him evenly, slowly standing, and gripping the notebook tightly in my right hand.

"The same reason I've hung all these photos here. They're the failures that led to my demise," he tells me, turning to look at the pictures and ignoring me. "Each one of them, my mistakes."

I can feel the agony rip through me as I look back to my mother. To the picture of her with my uncle and my father. Swallowing thickly, I try to speak but I can't.

His finger taps on the glass of the picture frame, the one of Carter's house that was destroyed. "I should have made sure they'd all died that night. When I hung this, I thought they'd be the ones to kill me. They still may be. Maybe tonight even."

A part of me wishes to console my father, to assure him that it's going to be all right. But it would only be lies, and he knows better than that.

"Are they the ones who are here?" I manage to ask him, hiding my desperation to know and why I want to know. Anxiety whispers along every inch of my skin.

My father's smirk makes his eyes wrinkle and the rough chuckle is accompanied with the telltale cough that comes from a smoker's lungs. While I was away, praying he'd come save me, I forgot how old my father's become in the past few years.

"Yes, of course they are." His answer is what I'd hoped, although I know I shouldn't. My heart hammers and my pulse quickens, but I don't show my father anything. I give him no indication of how that knowledge makes me feel.

At my lack of shock, my lack of emotion, not knowing how to react as thoughts race through my mind, my father offers me a small smile and then points to the photo of my mother, tapping his finger once again, but this time on the very edge of it. Almost like he's afraid to touch it.

"You know that I love you," my father says and it's then that his voice cracks and his expression crumples. "I was never a good father, but I chose you and I thought it counted for something."

"You are a good father," I say, pushing out the words in a shallow breath, trying to contain the guilt and fear of what's to come. I could drown in my emotions as I take a shaky step closer to him, needing to hold him as he's held me before. "I know you were hard on me, but this life is hard and I needed it." I get it now, why he always made me stand on my own. Maybe he knew this day would come sooner than I did. The day someone would take it all away from him.

"No, no, Aria," my father says as he shakes his head. His eyes search mine, not giving away any secrets but hiding every one of them.

Another yell is heard, this time farther away and it takes my attention but only for a split second until I hear my father say, "Your mother didn't belong to me. She was supposed to marry my brother."

One beat of my heart, ragged and jagged.

"She loved him and his money… his power. He was supposed to inherit everything. He was the one meant to rule."

Another beat of my heart and my father takes down the photo, the frame making an awful cracking noise as he does, the frame splintering, from being so old perhaps. I know my uncle was supposed to be the don, the head of the family. He was older than my father, but he was killed before he could take charge.

What I didn't know, is that my mother was involved with my uncle. I've never been told such a thing.

"She fell in love with you after he died?" I assume out loud.

"She was pregnant and afraid," my father says, not looking at me at all, or the slow realization that comes to form on my face. "She needed someone to protect her after her quick affair with him, and I loved her. I wanted her."

I can't breathe, I swear to it. An unseen hand seems to strangle me as my father slowly raises his gaze to mine.

"What?" The disbelief cloaks the whisper.

"They were only together for a short time and most people had no idea. But when he was murdered, she was pregnant, alone, and with a price on her head."

"Mom?" I don't know how her name escapes me, my breath strangling me as it refuses to leave.

"I told her no one would ever know, and she accepted." The thumb of his left hand runs along the place a wedding ring would hug his ring finger. "I always wanted you. I always loved you as my own."

My head shakes on its own and my eyes go wide. Wide with shock, wide with fear in the way my father's speaking.

"I tried to love you and show you how much you were loved. Yes, I was hard on you. I was hard on you because this life is hard, but also … you look just like your mother."

I reach behind me for something to steady me, but there's nothing.

"She never loved me." As he speaks, the soft reminiscence is instantly replaced by hate. "Until she decided she wanted more. She wanted someone else and would do anything to get away from me. She was a rat. I'm not sure how many mistakes I truly made because of your mother. Taking her in, not killing her sooner, or having her murdered."

Everything in my body is cold, the numbing kind that makes me feel like I can't be here. Like this can't be real. He didn't. He didn't have Mom killed.

"No." The word comes unbidden as fear settles deep into my bones.

"You were never a mistake, Aria. Even when I'm gone, I want you to know that. I know I was hard and cold, but it wasn't because of you. I loved you."

I can see it in his eyes, he's telling me the truth. Every bit of it. Dark and callous.

"You couldn't have," I say, but my words are weak and desperate.

The sad smile carved into his expression is riddled with agony. "She was going to have me killed, Ria. It was either her or me."

"No." My memory is warped and twisted. My reality even more so.

"I do know she was a mistake, your mother was. One that's stayed with me and still lingers in this house."

I almost call him Dad; I almost beg him to stop. To tell me everything he just said was a lie. But I can't speak a damn word. I can't even move.

"I always had to see you, though. You were a constant reminder."

CHAPTER 20

Carter

"OﾠNE MORE HALL," I HEAR DECLAN TELL ME SOFTLY FROM MY EARPIECE. "Two men on the right at the corner."

The eerie calmness that comes at times like these surrounds me. With four large steps I make it to the end of the hall, stop right at the corner and wait. Listening to every sound.

Sebastian and Jase are quiet behind me, but they're there, both armed and ready with the silencers. Only Jase is marked with a splatter of blood, but each of us has killed since we slipped in through a window, shattering it during an explosion and sneaking into the dark halls of this forbidden castle.

We're moving too slow. The thought keeps my pace fast. Every second away from her is another moment something could happen to her. A moment someone could take her away from me.

It doesn't escape my attention that I almost died here nearly a decade ago. Every quiet step reminds me of what may have been had my life been cut short.

Turning back to my brother, I nod and all at once, the three of us step out into the hall. Holding my breath and then letting it out, my grip on the gun tightens, the metal kicks back, and the bullet whips through the air, hitting the back of some fucker's skull. There's a sharp crack, a mist of blood sprayed against the pristine wall to my right. The bang of another bullet and then another are followed by the thumps of limp, heavy bodies falling to the ground.

"Four men coming, from behind you and another to your left. They know something's wrong," Declan says in the earpiece as the adrenaline spikes and Jase and I share a glance.

"Get her, we'll take care of them," Jase tells me, reaching up and squeezing my shoulder with his left hand. Sebastian nods, holding his gun with both hands and keeping his back against the wall as the sound of footsteps and a yell for someone to answer echoes up the long corridor.

"I'll have her soon," I tell them both, "and then I'll come back here." I don't know why, but it feels like a lie. Like I'm not coming back.

Jase gives me a smirk and quickly turns around, the faint sounds of him reloading his weapon carrying over to me.

Sebastian looks over his shoulder one last time to look at me before he follows Jase back down the way we came.

Without them it feels different. It's not about revenge or murder. It's not about a war or a power play for territory. It's only about *her*. About Aria.

I won't fail her. I won't let her die.

Fueled by the memory of my nightmare, I move forward. Each step feels heavier, louder than before, even though I'm still silently moving through.

I'm vaguely aware of Declan telling me something, but I ignore him. He doesn't need to say a damn thing as I come up to the corner and hear voices.

Two voices.

Light filters under the closed door in the dark hall. And with it are the sounds of Aria pleading with her father. Begging him for something.

My heart twists into a wretched knot. That sound shouldn't exist. The pain in her cadence. It shouldn't be allowed.

My vision tricks me, giving me flashes of weeks ago. Of Aria on her knees and at my mercy. I wish I could take it back. As my hand settles on the cold steel knob of the door that mutes her cries, I wish I could take everything back.

Every piece of it. Even the moment I clung to life at the sound of her voice carrying through a closed door.

It only takes a half second for me to push the door open, the gun raised and ready to fire, but it's useless. The barrel of one already stares back at me.

"Did you really think I wouldn't be ready for you?" Talvery hisses as Aria sucks in a breath, wide eyed and backed in a corner. Tears stream down her face and I could kill the fucker now.

"Dad, please," she begs him and I can't stop looking at her, even as the sweat in my hand makes me hold the gun tighter.

"Drop your gun," he demands and the gun slips slightly in my grasp as I hear Aria whisper my name. Not in fear, not in anger. I can hear how she needs me. It won't be denied from her voice.

In my periphery, she takes a step toward me and her father cocks his gun in response. The click is resounding and foreboding. Aria stills instantly.

It's only now, in the face of actually having to make the decision, that I question if I can kill him in front of her. If I could steal her father from her.

"Don't," she begs him in a breathless whisper. She still loves me. I can feel it in the way she speaks. A piece of her still cares for me.

I tighten my grip on the gun, not knowing if she'll still love me after.

If she weren't here, he'd be dead. I could do it if she weren't here. But with her watching, still begging and hoping for the inevitable fate to change before her eyes… I'm hesitating. I've spent a decade waiting to kill this man. Waiting to make him suffer for what he did to me.

But if she hates me after… then I may as well be the one that died.

In any other situation, I wouldn't have hesitated. Talvery would be dead simply because he took time to speak. I need Aria to love me though. A life without love is no life at all.

I don't want to die, either. I don't want her to see me die.

For the first time in years, I don't want to die. I need to protect her. I need to make it right.

"Aria." I say her name simply because I need to see her one more time. I need to know she loves me still. I need her to know it's okay. But as she looks at me, her father speaks.

"Did you think I couldn't see you?" Talvery sneers, but I don't listen to him.

"Please, Dad," Aria begs, her chest rising higher and falling deeper.

"That I didn't have backup cameras?"

All I can think, is that I need to save her. In the back of my mind, although I'm looking between Aria and Talvery, all I can see is her on the floor of my office. On her knees between my legs, cold and not breathing.

I won't let it happen.

"I'm tired and growing old. But I'm not done fighting yet. And I'm not that fucking stupid," he says lowly and I know he's going to pull the trigger. "I won't lie down and die."

"No!" Aria's scream rings through the air at the same time that he speaks his last word.

Talvery's statement again means nothing, but Aria hurling herself forward, reaching for the gun tempting her on the corner of the desk, is everything.

Her lunge distracts both of us. But when he turns to her, I can't do anything but throw myself between the gun he points at her and the woman I need to protect. The only reason I've ever had to live.

My gun fires at him the same time his goes off, barely skimming the arm he holds the gun with as he cusses.

I don't feel the first shot. I don't even feel the second, but I see it. I see the barrel of the gun and even as the bullet flies toward me, I swear I see it. The sound of the shot is like white noise and it means nothing compared to the sound of Aria screaming. Her voice fills the room and it seems to drag across time as my heart beats slowly. Only a single beat to her long scream as she wraps her arms around me.

Her voice turns to a song, a lowly sung hum of words; I can't make out what she's saying as I stare at my chest, the bright red soaking through the crisp white shirt as I fall to the floor.

My arm doesn't brace me, it merely hits the ground hard, followed by my back and it's then that I feel the sharp twinges of pain.

I try to swallow, but blood comes up instead. A mouth full of it that spills from me as I try to say her name.

Somewhere in the back of my mind I think that I should have shot him when I first came in. I shouldn't have concerned myself with Aria. I should have killed him without thinking twice.

A dizzy sensation comes over me as my head drops back but I force my neck up, I force myself to look at Aria, to command her to get behind me, but she's not looking at me and I can't speak. Every time I try, hot blood fills my mouth. It's all I can taste; it's all I can smell. I struggle to breathe, to move even and it's not the pain. The pain is nothing. Something else is holding me down.

"No!" I hear Aria scream, but it sounds so far away.

"I'm sorry," I try to tell her, but the words are muffled as I choke on my own blood. Hate fuels me to keep my eyes open as Aria yells something I can't hear to her father. She's right here, so close to me, but I can't move my arms to hold her anymore. My body's so numb, so heavy.

I'm sorry I put her in the middle of this. I'm sorry I put her in danger. I'm sorry I made her want to run again. I'm sorry I can't protect her. That's my worst sin.

As I see the darkness settle in, the sounds fade to nothing, and her touch wanes, I'm most sorry that I can't protect her.

Fuck, no. I need to protect her still.

I don't want to leave her. I don't want to die.

"Aria," I try to say her name, but I can't.

I try to fight the heavy weight that's holding me down. "I love you," I say, but the words fail to be heard. Did I say them?

She must know them. She must.

"You can't die, Carter," I hear Aria whisper and she sounds so close but I can't see her, I can't feel her.

For the first time in so long, I'm scared. I'm terrified.

I couldn't care less about life and death. But I don't want to be without her. I need Aria. I need to protect her. And as the darkness takes over, I'm truly terrified that I'll never see her again.

The last thought I have, is that if I die, she can't die for me. Suddenly, the cold feels peaceful.

She didn't die for me. If the price to change the course of fate was that I must die for her… so be it.

CHAPTER 21

Aria

THE BLOOD IS EVERYWHERE. MY HANDS ARE STAINED WITH IT AS I APPLY pressure to the bullet wound and scream at Carter to answer me.

"Look at you." My father hasn't stopped talking, hasn't stopped shaming me for staying at Carter's side. Hasn't stopped shaming me for reaching for the gun.

I had to try. With a man on either side of me, both wanting to kill the other, I couldn't stand by helplessly, doing nothing.

The blood isn't nearly as hot as the tears that won't stop. He's not answering me; he isn't responding to me no matter how loud I scream. His name tears up my throat as I scream his name. As I do, the pressure lifts just slightly on the wound nearly in the center of his chest and more blood pools around him.

Hold him tight, or else he'll die.

Words from a man I've never met come back to me, and I shove my body down, clutching Carter and putting all of my weight on both of my hands, still compressing the wounds. "Don't leave me," I cry as my hair sticks to my wet face and the hot tears mix with his blood as I lay my cheek in the crook of his neck.

I can feel his heart.

It beats as the door to the office creaks open and my father yells at me to get up. To be a Talvery and to prove he made the right choice all those years ago. That I'm truly his daughter. His words mean nothing to me. They hang in the air. All I listen to is the faint beat of Carter's heart and how slow it is. It's slowing.

I only turn my head to look at my father when I hear him cock the gun again.

My throat is tight with emotion as I look from the barrel of the gun up to him. The pressure I have on Carter's gunshot wounds doesn't waver though.

"I love him," I plead with my father and as I do, I belatedly notice a gun laying only a foot from where I am, so close I could reach it. What a useless thing to come to me now. If I let go, Carter will die. I know it deep in my soul.

If I were to reach it, to manage to grab it and kill my father to end all of this, what point would there be in living?

I'd rather die like this, doing everything I can to save the one I love, than live knowing I let him die.

My eyes move from the gun to the portrait of his family home and I close my eyes, pressing my cheek to Carter's chest as I hold him tighter. I can't feel his chest moving anymore though. I don't hear him breathing either.

"Choose your family, Aria. Step aside and let me finish him. I forgive you," my father stresses the last sentence. Slowly, I look to him. His eyes glass over as he grips the gun tighter. "It doesn't matter what happened before, but now you need to listen to me. You need to act like the woman you were raised to be," my father tells me and instead of hearing him I only hear Tyler's words.

I can't look at my father, or the gun.

"I'm sorry," I whisper. Not to my father, but to the version of me that could have done better. To the hopes of what could have been and then I remember, I remember the small life inside of me and I cry harder. I mourn all of us and what we may have been had fate treated us better.

"Forgive me," I cry into the crook of Carter's neck and then I hear that voice again, the one I've only heard in my terrors. *Hold him tight, or else he'll die.*

"I am," I whisper to no one.

And with that I hear my father whisper how his own daughter betrayed him and then he tells me goodbye with a gunshot following close behind. The bullet is loud and it makes my shoulders jump, but I stay close to Carter, clinging to him with everything I have.

I know I heard it. I swear I did, but I felt nothing. Nothing at all.

My eyes open slowly, and I'm too afraid to breathe. I know I heard him shoot, but it didn't hit me. A long moment passes before I hear a body fall. First a thud and then a louder thump. I have to turn around, to face the desk to see my father, laying on his belly on the floor, his eyes staring ahead of him but looking at nothing as blood pools around him, spilling from the hole in his cheek.

A second passes, *tick*.

I can't do anything. The scream is silent.

Another second passes, *tock*.

And that's when I notice movement from behind the desk.

My eyes travel up the suit pants, to the fitted shirt covered in blood.

Nikolai's expression isn't cold, it isn't angry. He's heartbroken as he lowers his gun and I watch him swallow.

"Do you want to tell them it was you? Or should we tell them I did it?" he asks me and his last word is strangled. He looks between Carter and myself and I can't even answer him. I can't think about anything but how long it's been since I've felt Carter's heartbeat.

A weak pulse is the only response I get at that thought.

"Help me," I plead with him.

CHAPTER 22

They took him away. They took him away from me. Jase pried my fingers back and Sebastian pulled me away as I screamed. The memory loops over and over again, but it's not me. I'm merely watching it happen like the scenes of a movie.

"It hurts so much," I struggle to say out loud and I don't know who can hear me because I don't even know who's around me.

"You need to change, Aria." I hear Jase's voice, and the tremors rocking through my body only pick up.

"Is he okay?" I cry the words and he lets me fall into his embrace. When I look forward, Nikolai is watching. He saved me. He saved Carter.

"They're doing what they can," is all Jase tells me in hushed words, as if we shouldn't be talking and the tears fall, but I don't cry any longer. Instead I take in the room. I take in everyone. How did I even get down the stairs? How did I get here, and why are Nikolai and my father's men in the same room with Jase and Sebastian? There are other men here too. Men from both sides.

My face is hot; my pulse runs fast. Before I can beg him to take me to Carter, and bring him back to see me, I hear another voice.

"This truce isn't going to last long." Brett's voice carries through the room along with the sound of several guns.

The sound of guns raised quickly behind me, and seeing guns on all sides, heats my blood.

"Put them down." The words are torn from me and I'm quick to push Jase away. I'm walking on shaky legs, but with purpose until I rip the gun from his hand.

This war is over.

The bloodshed is over.

I'm fucking done with it.

A look of shock is written on Brett's face, but I have no mercy for him. There is no mercy for anyone, not anymore.

"There's been more than enough death today."

Carter. My heart rips in half at the thought of him dying. He's barely hanging on and I'm not by his side. I can't stop seeing his face. Or hearing the way he said my name.

The gun is hot in my hands and I turn to my left. Standing in front of the staircase, I slam the gun down on the table, shaking the precious vase my mother used to fill with flowers when I was a child. I declare, "I won't allow any more to happen." The darkly spoken words leave me even though I turn to no one.

In my periphery, I barely see the men lower their guns. Their eyes burn into me, wondering if I have any authority, and I wonder the same.

This needs to end, and I need to go to Carter. It's all I can think as the emotions well up in my throat.

"We want Romano dead," Jase speaks and his voice carries through the large space and all the way up to the tall ceilings.

"Fight with me," I tell him, hardening my words and feeling the anxiety stretch in every limb I have. Every inch of my body is hot. Every pulse seems loud and hard.

"Someone needs to pay for all this. And that man is Romano," I whisper to Jase, although it's loud enough for all in this room to hear.

"My father is dead, but I won't let anyone else die, not on your side," my voice tightens as I tell him, looking Jase in the eyes, "and not on mine. Is that understood?"

Jase's lip quirks. "It is," he says, and then turns to Nikolai.

"What about your father?" Brett asks me.

"He betrayed my mother and his loyalty," I speak up although my words are choked. I don't know what to think or believe; all I know is that he's dead and my mother is never coming back. I don't have any answers, I'll never have a way to acquire them. "My father's reign is over, and that's all that matters."

"Who reigns now?" someone to my right asks and the room resonates with the sound of shifting feet.

"We reign together." I don't hesitate to speak up. My voice is clear and carries strong conviction. "Until Romano is ten feet under, that's the top priority for all of us." I feel lightheaded with the tense air and the lack of a clear answer. "Right?" I push out the word, daring either Nikolai or Jase to disagree.

"Cross." The word is practically spit from Nik's mouth and the air thickens and practically suffocates me as I watch the men meet face to face.

"What's the status of your war, Hale?" It's been a while since I've heard anyone call Nikolai by his last name.

"My war?" he asks with a crease in his forehead, stepping up to Jase.

"I don't want to fight," Jase tells him easily, letting his tense shoulders fall and moving his hand away from his gun. My heart pitter-patters and Nik steps back slightly. "I agree with Aria," Jase says and swallows thickly, looking Nikolai in the eyes. "I side with her on this. We all fight together."

"You were on his side before," Nikolai comments as whispers spread through the room like wildfire. The hissing of the words doesn't stop when Jase speaks up along with Sebastian, explaining that Romano is now an enemy and they would rather side with me and my family than with Romano any longer.

"I have to admit, I'm surprised to still see you here," Brett says after a moment of quiet to Sebastian. "It's been a long time since you've come around." The air between the two of them is easy. They must know each other. Maybe from a time before this, I'm not sure.

"I chose my side."

"And what side is that?"

"The one with Aria."

My cousin's lips kick up into a half smirk. "I like that side," he tells Sebastian.

"You need men?" Jase asks and Nikolai answers, "We need guns."

"We have guns," Sebastian says easily as he leans against the wall.

"We can come to an agreement," I say to break up the conversation, ready for it to end. "There will be no more death between us." My voice carries a note of finality with it and no one disagrees as I walk to the end of the staircase, staring up its vacant space as I grip the railing.

The side of the house it leads to gives me an eerie feeling. A sickness in my gut. A fear that doesn't come from logic or truth.

The type of fear that lingers and creeps up on you. A fear of what has passed and is no longer. Death is stained in these halls. And with death, darkness.

"Where is Carter?" I ask and turn quickly, facing each man who was in that room, each man who pried me away from Carter as he lay on the floor, bleeding out with no sign of stopping.

Nikolai doesn't answer, and neither does Sebastian. The men on my father's side are quiet, but they watch me. I don't care if they do.

They should all know. I love him. I chose him.

"We didn't have time for the doctor to come to us. He's in the hospital," Jase answers me.

"And?" I ask, the word barely spoken.

"And we're waiting."

I won't cry in front of these men. I won't cry with an army watching my every move, an army who need strength and decisiveness. So I only nod.

"Aria, I'll handle this," Sebastian tells me and my cousin nods at him.

"What do we do with the house?" Connor asks. I've just learned he's Nik's second-in-command. "The cops may stay back, but reporters are going to come soon."

The men start to talk. A few at once, and I cut them all off.

"Burn it down." The words come from a place of hurt. A place of pain. "Burn this house to the ground," I give each word the hate they've earned before turning calmly to the men, still gripping the railing and telling them, "It was a house fire… and nothing more."

Silence and shock greet me. The house is eerily quiet, and from this day on, that's all it will ever be.

I don't know if these men will stick to the quick truce we've made or what will happen once I leave, but I'm done with all of it. The useless killing and the constant threats especially.

Before a single man can respond, I hold Jase's gaze and demand, "Take me to him." Finally releasing the railing, I step forward, my pace confident even as I fall apart, and head to the door. My stride doesn't slow and it doesn't wait for anyone.

I need Carter.

The war has changed; the players have transitioned, and pawns have been taken.

None of it matters if he dies though.

I need Carter.

⸺·❦·⸺

Are you okay?

I stare at the message on my phone for the longest time. The hospital's waiting room is vacant with the only exceptions being Addison and myself. I only left Carter's side because the nurse said I had to. Only four people are allowed to be in the room at one time. Sebastian and Carter's three brothers wanted to see him and I'd been in there since the moment we got here. It's been ten hours now.

I slept by his side, my hand in his and my cheek on the edge of his bed. I was only in and out of sleep though and each time I fell to the depths of a dream, he was there, waiting for me.

He holds me in my dream and tells me it's okay. But it's not. It's not okay. And I tell him that over and over again. He needs to come back to me. I need him here. I can't live without him.

With tears clouding my vision, I look at the message again and instead of answering Nikolai, I ask him the same.

Are you?

It took me a while to message him back, but his reply is immediate: *My answer depends on yours.*

"You okay?" Addison asks, breaking the silence in the room. The only sound is a clock at the far end of the waiting room clicking each time the numbers change. It mocks us.

Swallowing down the ragged lump in my throat, I grab her hand when she reaches for mine and I squeeze tight, but then I let her go, moving it back to my phone. "Just a message," I answer her weakly. Everyone asks if I'm okay, as if that's even a possibility right now.

Wiping under my eyes gently with the sleeve of the baggy black hoodie Sebastian gave me, I shake my head.

"I'm right here," Addison says with a weak smile that doesn't last. It merely flickers on her face.

"And I'm here for you," I tell her back and she leans into me, resting her head on my shoulder for just a moment before bringing her knees into her chest and wrapping herself in the blanket Daniel gave her. The waiting room is so cold. But I suppose it's better that way.

I didn't expect for this to happen. I finally answer Nik.

For what? he asks.

I want to tell him—all of it. To be taken, to fall in love, to learn who I am and what I want. I haven't told Addison or anyone about the baby. Only a nurse, who I confided in because I was scared with everything that had happened. I was scared the baby would be gone. She said she wouldn't be able to tell me unless I was at least six weeks pregnant. So now, it's a matter of waiting.

It's all a matter of waiting.

Talk to me. Where are you? Nik messages me.

Hospital. He's not okay. As I write the last word and press send, that sick feeling of loss weighs me down.

You really love him? Nik answers me with the question and I don't wait to tell him that I do. To admit it.

I want to stay with him, Nikolai. I need him to be okay.

I wait and wait this time as he types but doesn't send anything. All I'm given is a bubble of dots, letting me know he's there, but the words don't come.

I don't want to lose you, I write to him before he can answer. I can feel him slipping away in my heart. As if him realizing I truly love Carter and Carter loves me, is the last string breaking that once held us together.

He'll never let us be friends. If I was him, I wouldn't.

I know he's right, but it hurts. Saying goodbye is never easy.

I won't work under him, Aria. I have to leave.

I don't even know if he'll be all right, I message him back. It's selfish of me to want for him to be there for me, even knowing this is goodbye, but Nikolai has always let me be selfish. He's always loved me. And I'll forever love him. Just not the way I love Carter, and he deserves for someone to love him that way. Everyone needs someone to love like this. With your whole body and soul. To be consumed by it.

He'll be okay. Carter knows how to fight. And there's no way he'd let me have you. He'll come back just to keep me from you.

Nik's words break me. I know this will be the end of us and whatever we had. All he'll ever be anymore is a memory.

I'll always be here for you, but you have to reach out to me. I won't be something that comes between the two of you. I'm here for you, but when he comes back to you, you know I can't be there anymore.

I love you, is all I can tell him. My last words to him.

Always, he messages back. His last words to me.

He's right. I already know Nikolai is right. Whether he's just a friend or more, doesn't matter. It's either Nikolai or Carter and between the two, there's no decision to be made. It was always Carter.

But he needs to come back to me.

"I need you," I whisper the words, gripping my phone in both of my hands as I lean forward, praying to anyone who will listen.

The last time the doctor came out, they said the surgery was done. It's only a matter of whether or not he'll wake up. And they don't know that he will.

He can't leave me like this. It's all I keep thinking. How selfish am I in this moment, but I am. I need him. Carter can't leave me. He can't leave me alone. Not when it's finally over. My hand slips to my belly. Not when I didn't even tell him he has another life to care for.

My bottom lip wobbles as I let my head fall back against the hard wall and stare up at the stark white ceiling of the waiting area outside Carter's room.

"I need you," I whimper the words and I don't know if I'm speaking to Carter, the man I love who can do nothing but try to survive, or my mother. Praying to her to do something. To save him and to keep me from being left alone in this cold world.

"I need you," the whispered plea that comes from me is ragged as I close my eyes.

The last time I spoke these words like this was when I held my mother's dead body as she lay on the floor. In the room above where my father used to work.

My eyes slowly open as Carter's story comes back to me.

He said I knocked on the door.

He said I told my father I needed him.

He claims it was my voice.

And all the while I thought he was wrong because I never went to that side of the house. Not since I last spoke those very words and my mother died. All because I swear I used to feel her there. I never roamed to that side; it scared me to even think of going, because I felt her and I know she was angry. Bitter and waiting for something I couldn't give her.

Slowly the twine unravels in my mind. The truth pricks chills down my spine.

I don't know who knocked on the door. I don't know if that's why my father stopped and let Carter go or not.

But I know where those words came from.

How could my words, spoken on the floor above Carter when my father nearly beat him to death, be echoed years later? How could he have heard my pleas and think they were meant for him?

I never knocked on the door, that wasn't me, but I did cry out, "I need you." Only it was years before Carter would ever be brought into the room beneath the bedroom where my mother was murdered.

Those words were given to my mother. I spoke them, I know I did.

But they weren't for Carter. They were never meant for him or my father.

Years later, I think my mother gave them to him. She gave them to a vulnerable boy on the brink of death, so close to the edge of a place she lingered. She gave them to him, a helpless boy caught in a horrid place, who would turn into a ruthless, merciless man. And he would one day, give her revenge in return.

The story is there, tickling the edge of my mind, and it keeps me frozen in my seat, gripping the edge of the chair.

The last few months play out in my head, slow motion for some moments, and only glimpses for other scenes.

The only reason I fell into Romano's trap was because Nikolai took my drawing pad… the one that had my mother's picture in it.

I only fought for it because of the picture.

Swallowing is futile; my pulse quickens and an anxiety I haven't felt since I ventured into the east wing of my father's house returns. The wing where my mother died.

I remember the way I felt when I stabbed Stephan. My skin felt like ice. And there was a hand, a hand over mine that wouldn't stop. I couldn't stop stabbing him. The thought is sobering to my tired mind. The exhaustion that weighs my eyelids down seems to vanish as I try to swallow, each of the events that have led me to this point falling into place in my mind like puzzle pieces.

A chill spreads over my skin as I hold on to the armrest of the chair with a white-knuckled grip. My blood runs even colder, and I can't shake it. I can't shake the freezing fear that flows through me. It's something unnatural and my thoughts make no sense. It's not truth. It's not real. It's only a coincidence.

Still, I turn slowly, ever so slowly to Addison and ask her, barely breathing the words, "Do you think the ones we lost stay with us forever in some way?"

"Ria," Addison breathes out as she takes my hand in both of hers, freeing it from gripping the armrest and pats the top of it soothingly. "He's going to make it," she says and her voice is hoarse with emotion.

I shake my head, rubbing under my eyes with the hand she doesn't have and telling her, "No, not him. Not Carter." A second passes, one painful beat in my chest before I look into her soft gaze and ask, "Do you think others, others we loved but who have passed stay with us?"

She searches my gaze for only a moment before nodding her head.

"They must." Her answer is final with no room for doubt.

At the same time as the doctor walks through the doorway, heading straight to us, Addison adds, "Even death can't sever love."

CHAPTER 23

Carter

SHE WAS HERE. I KNOW IT. I CAN STILL SMELL THE SOFT CITRUS SCENT OF HER shampoo. As death threatened to drag me to hell where I belong, I swear I heard her sing for me. The cadence of her sweet, feminine voice, carried past the damnation I knew was sure to come and I clung to it.

I will forever cling to her.

I could hear her, even feel her, but I couldn't open my eyes. I couldn't speak either. All I wanted to do was to tell her I love her. But I couldn't.

I would rather her pull a gun out on me any day than to lose her.

Knock, knock. The door creaks open as the knocks filter into the room.

A trot in my chest proves I'm still waiting on Aria, but it's not her. My brothers come in, but Aria's not here. For a split second, I think maybe it was all in my mind. That she wasn't here at all.

Maybe it was only a dream.

Fear consumes every piece of me. She didn't die in my place. Aria can't die. No!

"Aria," I breathe her name and Sebastian tells me she's okay. She's in the hall waiting.

A sharp pain shoots through my chest, a pain I've never felt before and I can hear the beeping of a machine over and over as I grimace.

"You don't have to sit up," Daniel tells me, moving to my side and trying to keep me from moving. I want to go to her. To see her. "Don't overdo it," I hear Jase tell me. As my head starts to feel lighter, I focus only on breathing.

"Fuck off," I say and shove him away, ignoring the heat of an agonizing pain rip up my right side. I seethe inwardly and in that moment, at this weak moment in my life, the door opens and Aria's there.

It's all like a dream. My body slumps back, my focus entirely on her and the way her eyes lift to mine, brightening at the sight of me looking at her.

"Just relax," Jase tells me as he drags a chair across the room, cutting off my path to Aria for a split second and again I try to get up and go to her, but it fucking hurts.

Daniel tries to push me back down, a gentle push, but he can fuck off.

He doesn't need to do a damn thing anyway; the pain is enough to keep me from moving. It's such a sharp pain, I can feel it everywhere. It heightens the slight twinge from the needles in my arm. The pressure on my chest feels like too much.

All of this pain is negligible though. She's here. We survived.

"I'm fine," I grit through my teeth, refusing to take my eyes away from her.

"Have it your way," Daniel says then raises his hands and backs up to lean against the wall in front of me. His head rests against the cream walls, next to a painting of some church. Seeing it reminds me where I am. The doctor came in a moment ago. Saint Francis Hospital is small and off a back road. They're also now equipped with two dozen men outside this room, this hall, and this building.

The doctor said I need at least a week in bed. I'll give it two days.

I want to be home. With Aria.

I won't stay here for long.

"How are you doing?" Jase asks me and I give him a side-eye.

"Fucking peachy," I answer him. My heart tightens as I watch Aria take a half step closer. Her fingers wring around one another nervously. She's still quiet and hasn't said a word.

I remember those last moments, but I also remember that she ran away.

And the last time we were alone… I remember that too. How she cuffed herself to the bed at my command. At my arrogance.

Never again. I'll never let it happen again.

"What happened?" I hate that I have to ask and the knot in my throat nearly suffocates me knowing that regardless of what happened when I blacked out, my songbird went through it alone. I wasn't strong enough for her.

I failed her.

My throat constricts when Jase tells me Nikolai killed her father. He shot him and now we have a truce. One built on the condition that we join forces to eliminate Romano.

Nikolai was her knight in shining armor. I knew I'd owe him, but I never imagined I'd owe him for my own life.

"Romano is the new target then," I tell Jase with a tight voice, letting go of the jealousy and the hate I have for the first love Aria ever had. I force the semblance of a smirk to my lips as I shift on the bed. Every movement exacerbates the pain of the needles digging into my arms.

I needed a blood transfusion. Three ice cold bags of the shit. I may not have been able to speak or even open my eyes. But I felt it. I felt everything as I hovered the edge of death, fighting to get back to Aria, moving toward the sound of her mournful hums.

"It's the right move to go after Romano. We can let Talvery's men choose what position they take afterward, but for now, Romano is the only enemy," Jase says and Daniel agrees.

"I know." I swallow gravely and watch Aria in my periphery. My brothers may be in front of me, but I couldn't give two shits about them. I don't care about the war. The territories. I don't care about anything other than never putting Aria in the line of fire again.

"He knows we fucked him." Jase's voice is even as he slips his hands into his pockets. I can see through his jeans how he balls them into fists before releasing them and then does it all over again as he speaks.

My heartbeat is faint and the voices around me are nothing but muted white noise as I stare at him. The soft beeps of the monitor continue all the while I have to force myself to focus on what they're saying.

All I want to do is make sure we're all right. I need to know that Aria and I are all right and that she forgives me. For everything.

I'm so fucking weak for her.

She has me in every way she can. Forever more.

"With Aria being seen and involved, the Talvery men won't turn on us." He peeks over his shoulder and pauses, seemingly biting his tongue before adding, "For now."

I gauge Aria's response, but she gives away nothing. Nothing at all. Her small frame doesn't even sway as she keeps her focus on me. On the tubes that connect to the needle in my veins and the monitors on my chest. I wish I could rip the fuckers out right now. I don't want her to see me like this.

I may be weak for Aria, but I won't be like this, confined to this bed, for long.

"Nikolai won't betray us so long as he thinks Aria is safe," Jase says.

"Nikolai won't betray us," Aria speaks for the first time, her voice hard as she gives her full attention to Jase, daring him to deny what she's saying is true. "He'll keep his word."

"The war between our families is over. We'll act as one." Aria's strength and determination are barely offset by the raw emotion in her voice. The reluctance to accept anything else will be her downfall. But I'll catch her. And I will bend to her volition as best I can.

"For now," Daniel speaks up. "Someone from your ranks may want to go their own way, to take men and rally against you, Aria. But for now, Nikolai is on our side. And even if they split off, we can let them. We don't need to fight for their territory."

Aria assesses him, her chest not moving as she refuses to breathe. With a single nod, she gives way to what may happen. I've seen it before, small factions separating. Generally, it ends with bloodshed, but we'll handle that when the time comes.

Jase holds her stare for only a moment before nodding once. "Either way," he speaks to me, "Romano is a dead man. He can hide in his safe house all he wants. I'll find him. I'll kill him."

"Another day and the enemies change," Daniel comments.

"We can talk about it once you're feeling better," Jase says.

"You and Sebastian handle this, plan the attack, but keep me informed." The ease with which I give up control shocks Jase, if his raised eyebrow is any indication.

"I have other things to attend to." As I speak, my hand grips the edge of the bed and I wish it was Aria's hand. I need her close to me. I need to know every piece of us fits back together how it should, how it was meant to all along.

I need her to love me.

That's all I need.

"One more thing," Jase tells me, rocking on his heels just as Daniel kicks off the wall, ready to leave us alone. Jase can't get the fucking hint.

"What?" I don't hide my annoyance in the curt response. But it only makes both of my brothers smile.

"Do you remember that woman in the Red Room?" Jase asks me and I feel the pinch in my forehead as I shake my head no.

He lets out an exasperated sigh but says it doesn't matter. "Her sister is the girl we met in the Red Room. Jennifer something. She died and her sister is causing a scene. She's making threats and calling the cops."

"Who is she?" I ask him, wondering why the fuck we should care. Plenty of assholes call the cops on us when they don't know any better. We pay the cops to tell us exactly who and why. And we pay them well.

"The sister of the girl who wound up dead. The one we questioned about the SL stash bought in bulk."

I peek at Aria, who squirms where she stands, her gaze shifting from me to Jase.

"And?" My heart races, wondering what she's thinking.

"I figured I'd stop by and see what she knows."

"And how are you going to get that information?" Aria asks, again speaking up but only to make her presence known as well as her newfound authority.

"Don't worry, Miss Talvery," Jase rolls her name off her tongue, "I'll be a gentleman."

"I don't believe you," she tells him but the hint of a smile graces her lips.

"Do you need someone to come with you?" Daniel asks and it's only then that I realize how tired he is. How tired they all are.

"I can go on my own—I just wanted you to know," he tells Daniel and then looks back at me.

It's quiet in the room for a moment and every second that passes, I wonder if he's all right. Ever since Marcus told us the truth about Tyler's death, sadness and despair have clouded Jase's eyes.

"Are you okay?"

Agony ripples through his dark blue eyes, but he plays it off. He's always handled hardship that way. "You're asking me when you're the one strapped to a fucking bed?"

"I'll only be here for a day or two." I keep my voice low and warning. "Remember that."

Daniel's chuckle is genuine, but Jase's smile doesn't reach his eyes.

"Yeah, I'm fine. Why?"

Shaking my head, I say, "Nothing."

"Is that all?" Daniel asks Jase and he responds by holding up a finger. He goes on to tell me about the money coming in and how the last week's been fucked. How another shipment of sweets was stolen. I don't fucking care anymore. I just don't care. He can take on the problems now.

All the while Jase speaks, Aria's eyes don't leave me. I can feel her gaze burning into me. My flesh. My very soul.

"Could you guys give us a minute?" I ask my brother as a spike of pain ricochets up my right side, from my toes to my hip and up the back of my shoulder and down the front. My entire body is in agony.

But it's my chest that hurts the most. The pain that fills the vacant hollowness of my chest where there should be warmth. I finally look at Aria, letting my gaze roam down her small body. Her thin cotton shirt is wrinkled, presumably from waiting in the chairs all this time for me to wake up.

Please God, let her have waited for me. It must mean something for her to be here. I don't remember everything that happened, but I'm sure I told her I loved her. I'm certain if ever there were words I would utter as death came to take me away, they would be only those that spoke of what she meant to me. *Everything.*

"I need to speak with Aria."

CHAPTER 24

Aria

"**P**LEASE FORGIVE ME." I'VE ASKED HIM SO MANY TIMES TONIGHT. THIS TIME it's to his face while he's conscious, not while his eyes are closed and he's far away from me, close to death's door and never able to hold me again.

The second the door closed, I couldn't help but to plead once more for him to forgive me. "I shouldn't have left." I let the words fall from my lips as I make my way closer to him.

He has the darkest eyes I've ever seen, but the specks of silver pierce into me… always. The way he looks at me, as if I only exist to be consumed by him, will haunt me until the day I die. And I wouldn't have it any other way.

I'm dying inside being this far away from him. I need to touch him, to hold him and make sure he's really here. My heart doesn't believe he's all right. And it hurts inside of me like no other pain I've ever felt.

"As long as you forgive me, I'll forgive you of any and every sin you've ever dared commit. Just love me. All I want is you, Aria. I can't lose you." His last words are strained, the pain of his wounds showing even with the steady drip of the IV forcing painkillers into his veins.

I can't even think about forgiving him, knowing it didn't have to end like this. I didn't have to run. It seems childish now, standing in front of him, seeing the consequences of my fear and my rash decision to hide the truth from him and flee from it all.

"Carter," I say, and his name is a tortured word on my tongue. "I'm so sorry," I utter painfully as I reach for him, getting closer to the hospital bed and letting my hand fall onto his forearm. My legs are weak; I'm barely able to stand seeing him like this.

My beast, hooked up to a machine and riddled with pain. All because of me and my foolishness.

"Forgive me," I can barely get the words out, letting everything between us fall. Every pretense, every wall. There's no room for any of it between us. "I shouldn't have run from you."

"I forgive you." His deep voice is raw. "I already told you I have. All I want is you."

All the words I wanted to tell him are strangled in the back of my throat, refusing to come out at the sight of him.

"We aren't perfect. And if I could, I'd go back and change the way we came to be, but I'll be damned if I'd let you go."

He's saying everything I dreamed he'd say, but I still have to tell him and I can't

I can't bear to tell him why I left.

"It's okay, songbird," Carter tells me, soothing me and luring me to come even closer. "I love you," he whispers and that breaks me. Finally, and completely, I break for him. Every piece of me shatters.

And I've never felt more complete in my life. Thoroughly ruined for the man I love.

There's one secret left. One small truth that could change everything. And it won't be kept hidden any longer.

"Do you want to know something?" I ask him, feeling the tension in my body increased with anxiety. The secret I've been holding is going to swallow me whole unless I give it the freedom to be spoken.

With his gaze tired, the exhaustion of everything weighing down the strength Carter possesses, he brushes my cheek with his knuckles, and I take his hand in both of mine.

"Anything and everything," he tells me and lets out a deep exhalation.

With a small smile wavering on my lips, I let out the secret just beneath my breath, "I think I'm pregnant. That's why I ran." The secret punctures my chest, creating a crater so deep it will never be filled if Carter's reaction doesn't mend the wound. "I didn't know what to do."

He may forgive me for keeping it from him. But I never will. In this moment, seeing and feeling with every piece of me how much he loves me, I can't believe for a moment I ever dared to not tell him. To hide this from him.

A second passes and a thump in my chest feels raw and painful as pain and betrayal flash in his eyes.

"Pregnant?" he questions and I can only nod.

In the seconds that tick by without a response from him, without knowing what he's thinking, the pain trickles into my veins and I creep closer to Carter, needing him to give me something.

"I'm sorry," I whisper the words, feeling the remorse consume me. I was going to run away, and take his child with me. Tears fall freely down my cheeks. If he hated me, I would understand; there's no way I would ever forgive him had he dared to do the same to me.

There's a moment when someone looks directly into your soul, and you feel what they feel. The loss, the insignificance, the agony of being alone. I can feel it from him as he looks up at me and I can't stand seeing it. My hand finds his and I squeeze it with both of mine, needing him to know I'm here now. "I don't want to leave, and I regret it. I regret ever walking out that door," I plead with him. And he squeezes my hand back before bringing my wrist to his lips and leaving a slow, tender kiss there. A kiss that feels like goodbye.

Finally, he speaks and it's nothing that I ever expected. "I promise I'll be a good father. I swear to you I will."

I can't speak.

"Give me a chance. Just one chance," he begs me, as if I'd ever leave his side again. "I'll be good to you, I'll be a good father, I promise." He swallows thickly.

"I'm ashamed at what I did and who I was. Please, Aria, we don't have to tell him."

"What?" I question him as I struggle to keep up with whatever he's thinking. I know he's not well now, he's still in pain and on meds. He's only just woken up. "Tell who?" I ask him, my heart racing.

"Our baby," he says as he looks up at me and brings his hand to my cheek, his thumb running under my eye to brush away the tears gathered there. "We don't have to tell them what a monster I was," he whispers the strained words and I lose all composure, covering my mouth with my hand and falling into him. I'm mindful of my weight and make sure to keep it off of him, but my God do I need him to hold me. And I need to hold him.

In this moment and forever.

"I love you, Carter," is all I can manage when I finally look up to him.

My breath and words leave me as a heat flows over me, taking every bit of the bitter cold and banishing it from me. I crash my lips to Carter's and he's quick to cradle my head with his hand, pinning me to him and deepening the kiss. His tongue slips between my lips and I grant him entry. Our tongues mingle and he massages mine with swift, possessive strokes.

I don't breathe until he breaks away.

"I would do anything for you." He says the words as if they're a confession. "I swear, you are the only thing that matters to me. Nothing else matters. Only you and our baby." As he speaks, his hand slips to my waist. He gazes at my midsection as if he can already see me swollen with our child. The very vision is what caused me to run in the first place.

"I'm scared." The wretched confession makes me feel that much weaker.

"Don't be." Carter's words are simple, but impossible.

"I don't know what's going to happen," I tell him, feeling the raw truth of fear lingering in the statement.

Carter's eyes search mine as I climb into the small bed with him, needing to be closer to him and not giving a shit if there's barely any room. I need my body pressed to his. I need to feel him breathing. The second he embraces me, my worries slip away, lost in the haze of knowing I'm where I'm supposed to be. Beside Carter Cross. Our present and our future tied together.

"We will rule. That's what's going to happen, my songbird."

I can feel my heart twist in my chest, praying I'll be the woman he wants me to be. Praying our lives can't pull us apart anymore. And as my mind whirls with every possible outcome of what could be, I realize there's not a damn thing that could tear me away from him. Not one fucking thing.

"Marry me. You belong with me, Aria." Carter's dark eyes pin me in place, taking my breath and refusing to give it back. "Marry me," he repeats lowly, a barely spoken yet desperate whisper. His warm breath cradles my cheek as he lowers his lips to mine and gently kisses me before I can answer. With his forehead leaning against mine and his hand gripping my hip in place, he whispers his plea again. "Marry me."

I cling to him, burying my head in his chest and breathing in the scent of a man I'm madly in love with as I nod my head and let the ragged whisper leave me with the desperation for all of this to be real, "Yes." He's alive. He's with me. And he wants me as his partner, his wife, his love.

He lifts my head with both of his hands on my face and presses a soft kiss to my lips. It's only then that I taste the salt of tears I hadn't known I was shedding.

"You're everything to me," he whispers against my lips as he brushes away the tears with his thumb.

"Tell me everything is going to be all right," I beg him. My words beg him. My body caves to his in the way it's always willed me to. The moment I saw him, I knew deep in the marrow of my bones that I belonged to this man. The other half to my soul. Holding his life to mine is the worst thing I've ever felt in this world. Every second that passed, I was afraid to move, knowing he was bleeding out beneath me. He lost so much blood, he barely made it and I can't help but to think that if I'd made the wrong move, if I hadn't held him as tightly as I could for as long as I did, he wouldn't be here anymore. I would have lost him.

"I never want you to leave me again. Never," I whisper the last word, pushing myself closer to him; every inch of me that can be pressed against him is. And Carter does what he's best at. He keeps me close, holding me to him as if I'll fly away if only he loosened his grip. But I'll never do that again. Never.

"As long as you love me, it will." His words are whispered along my skin, sending a trail of goosebumps down my body as he plants a small kiss on my shoulder. "Because I love you." His rough stubble grazes my shoulder, and I hope it scars me. I hope I can feel him, see him, have evidence of his love forever.

"I love you, Carter." The truth is the easiest thing to speak in this moment. A raw confession that will save us from whatever is to come.

"I love you, songbird." His rough voice is deep, the depths of sincerity so true, it numbs every pain inside of me. Every pain that's ever existed.

⁕

Days have passed since we came home.

It's odd to think of this place as home, but that's all it is to me now. It's more of a home to me than my father's place ever was. Simply because of the people in it.

"You need to take it easy." I try to keep my voice from sounding like I'm nagging Carter, but every time he leans to his side on the bed to grab something from the bedside table, I see him grimace. "You're still healing."

I'm quick to reach over, careful not to put my weight on him and grab his phone for him. The vibrating of notifications is a constant, but even still, the moment I hand it to him, he silences it.

Jase and Sebastian have taken the lead while Carter's been on bedrest at home. It'll take time for the wounds to heal, even if my beast still thinks he's untouchable.

I still can't breathe around him. The fear of losing him won't leave me.

"You keep saying that," he remarks with the same evenness I give him, but the smile on his lips, the genuine happiness in his eyes, haven't left him since I told him about the baby. Every time I look into his eyes, I see it and it's so raw, so much so, that I can barely stand to hold his gaze.

"I'm serious, Carter," I reprimand him although my actions are anything but. Moving to straddle him on the bed, the sheet slips around me, puddling behind us as I settle gently in his lap and take his stubbled jaw in my hands. "I need you," I whisper.

The corners of his lips kick up, and his large hands wrap around my waist, gentle and comforting. I rest my forehead on his with my lips so close to his as he tells me, "I need you too."

He gives me a quick kiss. And then another.

"Did you take another test?" he asks me and I can hear the playfulness in his voice.

He thinks I'm odd for taking a pregnancy test every day, but I have my reasons. The line is supposed to stay strong and dark, because then it means the baby is still there and until the six-week mark is here, I need the tests for my sanity.

"Yes," I tell him. I almost mention how Addison's the one who told me. She said the line gets weaker if you lose the baby. She's waiting like I am.

Instead, I'm distracted by a kiss on my neck. A languid one that makes my nipples pebble. His rough stubble runs along my skin, instantly making me wanton.

"You need to heal." I practically hiss the words with longing as his lips move to the dip just below my collar and his right hand reaches up to my breast. Plucking my nipple between his fingers, he finally raises his gaze to my eyes and tells me, "All I need is you."

He's wrong though. There's so much more he needs. Much more than I could ever give him.

He's a wounded man, with scars so deep he can't help but to be weighed down by them.

I'm still waiting on edge for something to come between us, but Carter seems hellbent on keeping us together. And so am I. I won't allow for love not to be enough.

Carter's fingertips glide easily up my neck, leaving goosebumps in their wake until he wraps his hands around my throat. His thumb runs down the underside of my chin and then lower, down to the center of my throat. His lips are parted just slightly, his breathing ragged as he hardens under me, his thick length pressing against me.

"I will do anything for you." He utters the words with such an intensity before slowly raising his gaze to meet mine.

My damn heart belongs to him. It only starts beating when he looks at me like that. I swear it's true. Whatever else it does when he's not around isn't what it's doing now.

"You're so intense," I whisper, not knowing what else to say, but my words are lost in the haze of lust that lingers between us.

I don't know if it's the fact that I'm obviously hot for him or some other reason, but Carter gives me a lazy smirk before moving the back of his fingers up my silk shirt and gently pinching my nipple.

My natural instinct is to playfully smack him away, but he's too quick, grabbing my wrist and pinning it behind me.

Even while I straddle him, he commands me.

"You make me this way," he tells me with a deep voice and leans forward to kiss me at the same time as he pinches my hardened peak. I have to gasp as he does, breaking the kiss and arching my neck. He takes the moment to lightly run his teeth along my sensitized skin, and I know I'm done for. Any authority I had over him is gone.

Carter is an untamable beast. But I'll be damned if I'd have him any other way.

"It all feels better when I'm with you," he murmurs against my skin and his tone sounds raw and hints at the pain that will forever scar who we are. With both hands on his jaw, I stare deep into his eyes, bright with sincerity. "All of it," he tells me.

"It's going to be okay." I offer him words I pray are true. I'd do anything for this man and without anything between us, nothing will keep us apart.

"Better than okay," he says before kissing me sweetly, only breaking away to add, "I promise."

CHAPTER 25

Jase

IT WAS SUPPOSED TO BE ME.

The car moves over a speed bump a little too fast, and my hard body sways in the sedan. My grip tightens on the wheel, and I try to swallow the hard lump that's been suffocating me since I learned the truth about Tyler's death.

It was a hit… on me. A fucking hoodie is the reason Declan's ten feet in the ground and I'm still here, taking every day for granted.

Slowing at the stop sign, I let a deep breath calm the anxiety running through me. With a war raging and an unknown enemy taking pieces of us as he pleases, I don't have time to get lost in the unfortunate past. No matter how much I long to go back. If only we could go back.

The hum of the engine as I roll over another speed bump keeps me in the present.

I shouldn't have come out right now. Spending the afternoon in the burbs isn't exactly on my normal to-do list.

But I had to get out of the house and away from my brothers. The regret and guilt and mourning that lingers in their eyes haunts me day and night.

There's nothing I can do to change it. But I can pay Beth a visit and quiet her.

My keys jingle as the ignition turns off and the soft rumble of the engine is silenced.

Wiping a hand over my face, I get out of the car, not caring that the door slams as my shoes hit the pavement. The neighborhood is quiet and each row of streets is littered with picture-perfect homes, nothing like the home I grew up in. Little townhouses of raised ranches, complete with paved driveways and perfectly trimmed bushes. A few houses have fences, white picket of course, but not 34 Holley, the home of Bethany Fawn, also known as the woman who keeps raising hell at the Red Room. More recently she's been calling the cops and demanding answers. She's the woman who blames Carter for her sister's untimely death. Her sister Jennifer, a girl we met in the Red Room weeks ago. A girl in a mess she couldn't get out of, with a drug addiction she couldn't kick.

I know all about wanting someone to blame and looking for answers to questions that don't make any difference once you have them. Bethany's hurt and angry, but she won't find any answers from us. A simple warning should scare her off.

The skin over my knuckles tightens and the cuts from a few nights before crack open, sending a pain shooting up my arm. I welcome the seething reminder that I'm alive.

Knock, knock, knock. She's in there, I can hear her. Time passes without anything but the sound of scuttling behind the door, but just as I'm about to knock again, the door opens a few inches. Only enough to reveal a peek of her.

Her chestnut hair falls in wavy locks around her face. She brushes the fallen strands out of her face to peek up at me.

"Yes?" she questions and my lips threaten to twitch into a smirk.

"Bethany?" Her weight shifts behind the door as her gaze travels down the length of my body and then back up to meet mine before she answers me.

The amber in her hazel eyes swirls with distrust as she tells me, "My friends call me Beth."

"We haven't met before… but I'll happily call you Beth." The flirtatious words slip from me easily, and slowly her guard falls although what's left behind is a mix of worry and agony. She doesn't answer or respond in any way other than to tighten her grip on the door.

"Mind if I have a minute?"

She purses her her full lips slightly as the cracked door opens an inch more to cautiously reply, "Depends on what you're here for."

My heartbeat gallops, trotting faster in my chest as the anxiety rises. I'm here to give her a warning. To stay the hell away from the Red Room and to get over whatever ill wishes she has for my brothers and me.

It's a shame really; she's fucking gorgeous. There's an innocence, yet a fight in her that's just as evident and even more alluring. Had I met her on other terms, I would do just about anything to get her under me and screaming my name.

The swirling colors in her eyes darken as her gaze dances over mine. As if she can read my thoughts and knows the wicked things I'd do to her that no one else ever could. But that's not why I'm here, and my sick perversions will have to wait for someone else.

I lean my shoulder against her hard walnut front door and slip my shoe between the gap in the doorway, making sure she can't slam it shut. Instead of the slight fear I thought may flash in her eyes as my expression hardens, her eyes narrow with hate and I see the beautiful hue of pink in her pale skin brighten to red, but it's not with a blush, it's with anger.

"You need to stay out of the Cross business, Beth." I lean in closer, my voice low and even. My hard gaze meets her narrowed one, but she doesn't flinch. Instead she clenches her teeth so hard I think they'll crack.

With the palm of my hand carefully placed on the doorjamb and the other splayed against her door, I lean in to tell her that there are no answers for her in the Red Room. I want to tell her my brother isn't the man she's after, but before I can say a word she hisses at me, "I know all about Marcus and the drug and why you assholes had her killed."

My pulse hammers in my ears but even over it, I hear the strained pain etched in her voice. Her breathing shudders as she adds, "You will all pay for what you did to my sister." Her voice cracks as her eyes gloss over and tears gather in the corners of her eyes.

"You don't know what you're talking about," I tell her as the anger rises inside of me. Marcus. Just the name makes every muscle inside of my body tighten and coil.

The drug.

Marcus.

Before I can even tie what she's said together, I hear the click of a gun and she lets the door swing open, throwing me off-balance.

Shock makes my stomach churn as the barrel of a gun flashes in front of my eyes. She leans back, moving to hold the heavy metal piece with both hands. Lunging forward, still off-balance as fear stirs in my blood, I grip the barrel and raise it above her head, shoving her small body back until it hits the wall in her foyer.

Bang!

The gun goes off and the flash of heat makes the skin of my hand holding the barrel burn and singe with a raw pain. Her lower back crashes into a narrow table, a row of books toppling over and mail falls onto the floor as I stumble into her and finally pin her to the wall.

Her small shriek of fear is muted when I bring my right hand to her delicate throat. My left still grips the gun. She struggles beneath me but with a foot on her height and muscle she couldn't match no matter how hard she tried, it's pointless. Her heart pounds so hard, I feel it matching mine.

She yelps as I lift the gun higher, ripping it from her grasp. Both of her hands fly to the one I have tightening on her throat.

She tried to kill me. I can't fucking believe it.

Barely catching my breath, I don't let anything show except for the absolute control I have over her. The door is wide open and I'm certain someone would have heard. A faint breeze carries in from behind me and I take a step back, pulling her with me just enough so I can kick the door shut and then press her back to it. Her pulse slows beneath my grip and her eyes beg me for mercy as her sharp nails dig into my fingers. A second passes before I loosen my grip just enough so she can breathe freely.

Through her frantic intake, I lean forward, crushing my body against hers until she's still. Until her eyes are wide and staring straight into mine. The sight of her, the fear, the desperation, the eagerness to live … it thrills a dark side of me that's been begging to be brought to the surface.

"You're going to tell me everything you know about Marcus." I lower my lips to the shell of her ear, letting my rough stubble rub along her cheek. "And everything you know about the drug."

With a steadying breath, my lungs fill with the sweet smell of her soft hair that brushes against my nose.

I comb my fingers through her hair and let my thumb run along her slender neck before I lean into her, letting her feel how hard I am just to be alive. Just to have her at my mercy.

"But first, you're coming with me."

This is volume 1 of 3

ABOUT THE AUTHOR

Thank you so much for reading my romances. I'm just a stay at home mom and avid reader turned author and I couldn't be happier.

I hope you love my books as much as I do!

More by Willow Winters
www.willowwinterswrites.com/books